SO-BZH-367

THESE HAUNTED SEAS

PROPERTY OF
NationalCollege
Library

:00858

GuiBF 3/10 $4.00
$18.00/

THE NEW ADVENTURES OF STAR TREK: DEEP SPACE NINE®

The Lives of Dax (by various authors)

A Stitch In Time by Andrew J. Robinson

Avatar, Book One by S. D. Perry

Avatar, Book Two by S. D. Perry

Section 31: Abyss by David Weddle and Jeffrey Lang

Gateways: Demons of Air and Darkness by Keith R.A. DeCandido

"Horn and Ivory" by Keith R.A. DeCandido (from *Gateways: What Lay Beyond*)

Mission: Gamma, Book One—Twilight by David R. George III

Mission: Gamma, Book Two—This Gray Spirit by Heather Jarman

Mission: Gamma, Book Three—Cathedral by Michael A. Martin and Andy Mangels

Mission: Gamma, Book Four—Lesser Evil by Robert Simpson

Rising Son by S. D. Perry

The Left Hand Of Destiny, Book One by J. G. Hertzler and Jeffrey Lang

The Left Hand Of Destiny, Book Two by J. G. Hertzler and Jeffrey Lang

Unity by S. D. Perry

Worlds of Star Trek: Deep Space Nine, Volume One by Una McCormack; Heather Jarman

Worlds of Star Trek: Deep Space Nine, Volume Two by Andy Mangels and Michael A. Martin; J. Noah Kym

Worlds of Star Trek: Deep Space Nine, Volume Three by Keith R.A. DeCandido; David R. George III

Warpath by David Mack

Fearful Symmetry by Olivia Woods

COLLECTIONS:

Twist of Faith by S. D. Perry; David Weddle and Jeffrey Lang; Keith R.A. DeCandido

These Haunted Seas by David R. George III; Heather Jarman

FROM POCKET BOOKS
AVAILABLE WHEREVER BOOKS ARE SOLD
ALSO AVAILABLE AS EBOOKS

www.startrekbooks.com

STAR TREK
DEEP SPACE NINE®

THESE
HAUNTED
SEAS

David R. George III
Heather Jarman

Based upon STAR TREK® created by Gene Roddenberry,
and STAR TREK: DEEP SPACE NINE created by Rick Berman & Michael Piller

POCKET BOOKS

New York   London   Toronto   Sydney   Vanimel

Pocket Books
A Division of Simon & Schuster, Inc.
1230 Avenue of the Americas
New York, NY 10020

This book is a work of fiction. Names, characters, places, and incidents
either are products of the authors' imaginations or are used fictitiously.
Any resemblance to actual events or locales or persons, living or dead,
is entirely coincidental.

Mission Gamma Book One: Twilight ™, ® and © 2002 by CBS Studios Inc.
All Rights Reserved.

Mission Gamma Book Two: This Gray Spirit ™, ® and © 2002 by
CBS Studios Inc. All Rights Reserved.

STAR TREK and related marks are trademarks of CBS Studios Inc.

These titles were previously published individually by Pocket Books.

⊙**CBS** CONSUMER PRODUCTS *000858*

CBS, the CBS EYE logo, and related marks are trademarks of CBS Broadcasting Inc.
™ & © CBS Broadcasting Inc. All Rights Reserved.

This book is published by Pocket Books, a division of Simon & Schuster, Inc.,
under exclusive license from CBS Studios Inc.

All rights reserved, including the right to reproduce this book or portions
thereof in any form whatsoever. For information address Pocket Books
Subsidiary Rights Department, 1230 Avenue of the Americas,
New York, NY 10020

First Pocket Books trade paperback edition June 2008

POCKET and colophon are registered trademarks of Simon & Schuster, Inc.

For information about special discounts for bulk purchases, please contact
Simon & Schuster Special Sales at 1-800-456-6798 or
business@simonandschuster.com.

Cover art by Cliff Nielsen
Cover design by Alan Dingman

Manufactured in the United States of America

10 9 8 7 6 5 4 3 2 1

ISBN-13: 978-1-4165-5639-8
ISBN-10:   1-4165-5639-7

Contents

Historian's Note

These stories unfold from roughly from late May to mid July in the year 2376 (Old Calendar), beginning approximately three weeks after the events of "Horn and Ivory."

TWILIGHT
David R. George III

To Patricia Ann Walenista, one of the brightest stars in my sky, whose glow bestows warmth, whose light provides guidance, and whose every rise brings love and support

Acknowledgments

I wish to thank several people for their generous assistance and incomparable support during the writing of this novel. I must first express my gratitude to Marco Palmieri, not only for offering me this opportunity, but also for providing expert guidance, vivid creativity, and an awful lot of fun along the way. Marco's vision, enthusiasm, and drive for the *Star Trek: Deep Space Nine* novel "relaunch" keeps me coming back to the series as a reader and fan, and I am delighted to have been asked to contribute to the unfolding saga. Not only is Marco terrific to work with, but he's also a good guy.

I would also like to thank the other writers of the *Mission: Gamma* series, but in particular, Michael A. Martin and Andy Mangels. Both cheerfully and expertly provided answers to innumerable questions, and Mike's incredible volume of research for the relaunch made the difficult task of maintaining continuity much less arduous. Thanks, too, to Keith R.A. DeCandido, who also answered several questions about the *Trek* universe.

Because I did not get the opportunity to do so in the acknowledgments to *The 34th Rule*—since he and I wrote them together—I want to thank Armin Shimerman, who suggested that we write a *Star Trek* novel in the first place, and with whom it was an absolute pleasure to work. Armin is an incredibly talented artist—actor, writer, teacher—and I am fortunate to be able to call him a friend. I'm looking forward to his next novel, *Outrageous Fortune,* a follow-up to his marvelous *The Merchant Prince*.

On an even more personal level, thanks to Richie Hertz, whose big-picture mentality, keen wit, and razor-sharp intellect are surpassed only by his ability to turn on an inside fastball. He remains one of the very few people I know who appreciates a good physics joke. I value his friendship beyond measure.

Thanks also to the Ragan family, who have always welcomed me into their midst. I especially want to send my love and gratitude to Elizabeth, the loving and amazing matriarch; to Lillian, the sweet and caring aunt; and to the wonderful Audrey and Walter, who have truly made me feel like their son.

I also want to thank Jennifer "CJ" George and Anita Smith, two magnificent women whose constant love and encouragement never fail to bolster me. I am privileged to have them in my life.

And finally, thank you to Karen Ann Ragan-George. Each and every day, Karen does the impossible, by transforming the woman of my dreams into the woman of my reality. She not only made this book possible, she makes everything possible. To say that I could not have written this book without her love and nurturing does not begin to describe her contribution to everything I do and everything I am. Karen is my universe—and what a fabulous place to live!

PART ONE

VEXED THE DIM SEA

... All times I have enjoyed
Greatly, have suffered greatly, both with those
That loved me, and alone; on shore, and when
Through scudding drifts the rainy Hyades
Vexed the dim sea. . . .

—ALFRED, LORD TENNYSON, "ULYSSES"

1

He watched her die, and in that terrible instant, he relived the moment of their separation, felt the weight of the years since, and regretted everything.

Prynn's body landed in a heap beside the captain's chair, the foul smell of singed flesh already rising from her. Elias Vaughn looked down at her as he leaped from the chair, and saw the midsection of her uniform burned away. Past the seared edges of the fabric that remained, her skin was charred black. Blood seeped from her mangled body and pooled in her wounds like crimson floodwaters across a ruined landscape.

Vaughn pulled his gaze away and, with an emotional effort, moved past the remains of his daughter, toward the console she had a moment ago been operating. He suppressed the ache growing within him and focused on reaching the conn, on keeping *Defiant* intact and headed away from its attackers. Prynn was dead, but the rest of the crew were not.

With each step, Vaughn felt the labored vibrations of the impulse drive translating through the deck plates. Dark gray eddies of smoke swirled about the bridge, carrying with them the electric scent of overheated circuitry. Flashes of scarlet, the visual call to battle stations, shined here and there through the haze. He reached the conn and bent to assay the readouts, waving away the smoke with an open hand. The low moan of the straining engines deepened as Vaughn eyed the display, and he was not surprised to find the ship no longer holding course. He reached down to work the controls, but flames surged up from beneath the console. Vaughn threw an arm up in front of his face as he staggered back a step, the intense heat blistering his arm even through his uniform sleeve. The air pressure decreased a moment, the hungry fire gathering fuel for itself. The flames sounded like a banner whipping in the wind, loud enough for Vaughn to hear over the inconsistent thrum of the overburdened drive and the many alarms screaming for the crew's attention.

A voice called out above the din—"Weapons power to the shields?"— only to be followed by another shouting that *Defiant*'s weapons were offline. Lieutenant Bowers at tactical, Lieutenant Nog at engineering, Vaughn thought, startled for a moment to realize that he was not alone. Even as his instincts to save the crew had driven him to action, their presence had vanished from his mind; for long seconds, his entire universe had been smoke and flame, vibration and sound, and the image of his daughter's mutilated corpse.

Ensign ch'Thane worked the sciences station, Vaughn thought, forcing himself wholly back into the moment. And somewhere behind him, Lieutenant Dax and Dr. Bashir filled out the roster of bridge personnel. If any of them were saying anything, he could not hear them.

Vaughn looked past his upraised arm and squinted at the fire engulfing the conn. Streaks of brilliant indigo snaked up through the otherwise orange-yellow flames. *Chromium,* Vaughn thought, even as he began to move again, the recollection or misrecollection of which elements burned which colors incongruously percolating up from memory. He moved around the console and dropped to his knees. From this vantage, he could see the jagged margin of a hole in the decking beneath the conn, the flames erupting from it in great sheets. The explosion that had claimed Prynn had obviously occurred just below.

Defiant rocked suddenly and violently, inertial dampers failing for a second. Another Jarada disruptor bolt, Vaughn guessed as he felt the ship pitch forward. Too close to his goal to give it up, and knowing time was running out for the crew, he grabbed for the console support as he was thrown off balance. Somehow, his fingers found their mark and took hold. Pain flared through his right hand, his flesh binding itself to the hot metal in a horrible embrace. But he held on, pulling himself back to his knees and closer to the underside of the console.

A disembodied voice yelled something Vaughn could not make out, the fire bellowing in his ears like the roar of some mammoth molten beast. He listened for other words, but heard only the flames. A murky cloud seemed to pass through his mind, like the smoke churning through the bridge. He realized he was on the verge of losing consciousness.

With a bellow of his own, Vaughn thrust his free hand up under the conn and felt for the fire-suppression canister. His uniform sleeve caught fire, and beneath it, so too did his skin. His fingertips brushed the canister, amazingly still cool to the touch. Vaughn quickly pulled the cylinder free with one hand, then pulled his other hand from the console support, the pain of his skin tearing away an afterthought in the wake of his determination. He aimed and activated the canister, and a fog of chemical retardant spouted out in a billowy white cone, extinguishing his flaming sleeve. Parts of his arm felt the cold of the chemicals, but where his flesh had been scorched, it burned as though still afire.

Vaughn tilted the canister away from himself and attacked the flames where they emerged from the hole in the decking. The fire retreated briefly, then resumed, and Vaughn feared it might win his battle with it. He pushed himself forward beneath the conn and thrust the canister directly over the hole. The sound of the flames drowned beneath the onslaught of the pressurized chemicals, and finally, so did the fire.

Vaughn continued spraying, emptying the canister into the hole. With the fire extinguished, the force of the explosion that had caused it became clear—as though Prynn's maimed body were not proof enough. The roughly circular hole beneath the conn stretched nearly a meter in diameter, Vaughn saw. The deck plating twisted upward and outward, the metal blackened and bent as though it had offered the blast only minimal resistance.

"Aft shields failing," somebody shouted, the identity of the voice swallowed up by the discordant and increasingly loud pulse of the impulse engines, the speaker hidden by the veil of smoke. *Probably Bowers,* Vaughn thought as he rose to his feet. He dropped the canister to one side, but did not hear it strike the deck above the cacophony permeating the bridge. Warning signals punctuated the clamor, and though he could not make out their words, Vaughn heard other officers barking out information.

Vaughn bent over the conn, now between it and the forward viewer. He wanted to find the helm controls and bring *Defiant* back on course. If they were far enough away from Torona IV, then he could engage the warp drive—provided it was still intact—and possibly outrun the Jarada before they had time to mount a larger attack force.

The console was dark. The glassy surface of the display reflected the diffused overhead lighting, but no controls and no readouts shined within. A jolt shook Vaughn as though he had been stunned with a phaser. If they couldn't regain control of the ship, they had no chance of escaping the Jarada.

Vaughn looked up at the rest of the bridge, trying to see the crew through the haze. The ship shuddered again beneath another assault, but it must have been a glancing blow, effectively dissipated by the ablative armor, because nothing exploded and Vaughn was able to keep his feet. He waved at the smoke swimming around him, the gray miasma thinning now that the fire was out and the ventilation system could catch up.

He strained to see through the cloudy atmosphere. As the smoke swirled, he caught a glimpse of one of the crew in profile at the rear of the bridge. Distinctive dark markings spilled from a temple down the side of a fair face and neck, making the Trill unmistakable. "Dax," he called, "reroute flight control."

He watched her operate an aft console, and then she yelled, "I've got it."

Vaughn started toward the lieutenant, but stopped when he saw movement at the center of the bridge. On the floor beside the command chair, Bashir leaned over Prynn's unmoving body. The doctor held a tricorder in one hand and an instrument Vaughn did not recognize in the other.

Vaughn looked at the inert face of his daughter. Her porcelain features, normally tense and expressive despite their delicacy, were now slack, even peaceful, contradicting the awful mass of injuries her body had sustained. For a moment, he saw Prynn's mother, her own mien passive—at peace somehow, despite her obvious understanding of what was soon to come—in that instant he last saw her. He felt the familiar rage and anguish building within him, the enormous guilt not far behind, and he wondered how this could have happened again.

You have a mission, he told himself, and allowed the simple statement—his old mantra—to carry him away from his private darkness. He raced past Nog and Bowers, both intent on their consoles.

When he arrived beside Dax, her fingers were sprinting back and forth across the display—"Resequencing the reactors," she said, raising her voice amid the tumult—and after a few seconds, the vibrations of the impulse drive steadied. Several alarms quieted too, lessening the commotion considerably; now only a couple of staccato tones persisted in their warnings. Vaughn could have ordered them silenced, but they were a source of information, and in any dangerous situation, he sought information. "Taking evasive action," Dax continued. Better than the sound of the stabilized engines and fewer alarms was no sound at all: the absence of Jarada weaponry landing on *Defiant* as the lieutenant maneuvered the ship.

"How far from the planet?" Vaughn wanted to know. Dax told him. They were still too close to go to warp safely.

"Two more Jarada heavies emerging from the far side of the second moon," Bowers called from his station. Those were in addition to the pair of battleships Vaughn knew were already pursuing *Defiant*.

"If we can stay at full impulse," Dax reported, checking her readouts, "they won't be able to catch us. We only have to worry about the ones already firing on us."

If only we could stand our ground and defend ourselves, Vaughn thought. This was not a fair fight, though, and would not be even if *Defiant*'s weapons could be brought back online. Not because the bantam starship could not best a top-of-the-line Jarada vessel—or even bear up against several of them—but because this was a battle *Defiant*'s crew could not join. The Jarada were a strange and reclusive species, punctilious in the extreme, and often very difficult to deal with; they had once terminated contact with the Federation for two decades after a UFP representative had mispronounced a single one of their words during an introduction ceremony. But while temperamental in many regards, the Jarada were also in some ways predictable: they employed well-defined rules of engagement, and it was that fact about them that constrained Vaughn's actions right now.

"Sir," Nog yelled, a second after another alarm began bleating. "The impulse engines are losing power." Vaughn looked to Dax, wanting the information to prove false, but the alarm and her expression told him otherwise. And he had known better anyway: in his experience, only good news ever turned out to be suspect.

As if to underscore his thought, the tone of the impulse drive changed once more, flattening and slowing, and then *Defiant* rattled again beneath the force of a disruptor bolt slamming into the ship. Sparks flew from a port-side console, but despite the failure of the aft shields, the hull armor again withstood the attack. Bowers confirmed this a moment later, but the continued existence of *Defiant* had already told Vaughn what he needed to know. Effective as the ablative armor was at dissipating the effects of the Jarada weaponry, though, it would not hold up indefinitely; each attack thinned the hull plating, Vaughn knew, its layers vaporizing at the point of impact and dispersing the destructive energy out into space.

He stepped up to the tactical station, beside Bowers. Vaughn had actually anticipated the possibility of something like this turn of events during the past couple of days, but there had been no apparent solution other than for the crew to speed their way through it. And as bad as the situation now was, it would deteriorate even further if Vaughn gave in to temptation and defended *Defiant* by means other than retreat.

Less than three days ago, the Jarada had grudgingly helped the Federation save the lives of a half-million people in the evacuation of the human civilization from Europa Nova. During an extended incident in which previously unknown Iconian gateways—essentially, open doorways linking noncontiguous and often distant locations—had suddenly become operational, masses of lethally irradiated material had spilled out of an orbital gateway and threatened the population of the planet. A convoy led by the Bajoran Militia had managed to evacuate almost all of the Europani to safety, but five hundred thousand had been forced to flee through a second gateway, this one on the surface of their world and linking to Torona IV, one of the home planets of the Jarada.

"Status," Vaughn said to Bowers.

"Aft shields are gone. Aft armor down to sixty-seven percent." That measure would not need to diminish to zero, Vaughn knew, before the hull ruptured beneath a disruptor hit. And when that happened, explosive decompression would be just the beginning of a chain of rapid and catastrophic failures that would leave only debris and a bright energy signature where *Defiant* had been.

"What happened to those evasive maneuvers?" Vaughn called back to Dax, though the answer was clear: as quickly and as well as the lieutenant had taken to the demands of command, she was a good pilot, but not the career pilot that Prynn was.

That Prynn had been.

An unsettling mixture of pride and sorrow rose within Vaughn, quickly threatening to overwhelm him. Pressure built behind his eyes, and it struck him that, for the first time in years, it would be an easy thing to allow himself to break down, to give in to his pain and abdicate his responsibilities. But that was not really an option. He willed himself—as he had so many times before—to disconnect from his emotions. *You have a mission,* he told himself again. If he survived this encounter with the Jarada, there would be time later to mourn.

Dax announced an automated evasion sequence, and the impulse drive whined as it struggled to support the new instructions. Vaughn felt a shift in the pit of his stomach, the gravity generators and inertial dampers adjusting as *Defiant* sheared from its course. Tremors rumbled through the ship's superstructure, but at least for the moment, no weapons landed.

Vaughn peered at the main viewer. In his mind, he saw what was not visible on the screen: the near pair of Jarada ships dancing in lethal patterns about *Defiant,* the far pair charging toward the scene. He searched his vast experience for similar predicaments and recalled several, but none in which his actions had been so tightly restricted.

Vaughn had secured safe harbor on Torona IV for the evacuees by providing technical data about the gateways to the Jarada. In the few days since, Europa Nova had been completely evacuated, and Vaughn and his crew had then led a convoy to the Torona system. There, they had overseen the relocation of the half-million Europani to Bajor, where the rest of their population awaited eventual return to their world once it had been decontaminated. The last group of transports had broken orbit less than an hour ago, and in that time, the Jarada had apparently discovered that the gateways had been shut down, possibly for good, and certainly for the foreseeable future. Considering their xenophobic nature, the Jarada might have welcomed this, but instead, with the technical information they had been given now valueless to them, they had chosen to believe themselves duped by Vaughn.

"The near ships are splitting up," Bowers said. Vaughn turned from the main viewer—the starfield swooped and dashed, seemingly at random, he saw, as Dax tried to evade their attackers—and looked at the tactical officer. The alert lighting tinted the young man's dark skin on and off with a rich, rosy glow. "They're moving to flank us," the lieutenant said, his tone a blend of resignation and anger, Vaughn thought. "The far ships are closing the gap. They'll be in weapons range soon."

The initial attack on *Defiant* had come as the crew had prepared to leave orbit about Torona IV and begin the return journey to DS9. Vaughn had been speaking via subspace with a representative of the planetary regime, thanking him for the forbearance of his people in allowing the Europani on their soil. The official had responded with accusations of duplicity, the harsh, insectile clattering of his voice breaking into the smooth speech of the universal translator when his words could not adequately be interpreted. Before Vaughn could explain or apologize or offer some sort of recompense, the Jarada vessel assigned to escort *Defiant* within the Torona system had attacked. An instant later, planetary defenses had launched their own massive barrage, and a second Jarada vessel had charged into battle.

Defiant had withstood the initial assaults, the substantially fortified ship among the toughest in Starfleet, but it had also suffered significant damage. Vaughn had taken the only action he could: he had ordered retreat. If *Defiant* defended itself by employing any of its weaponry, he knew, the military protocols of the Jarada would send them in pursuit of the convoy. Almost the entire evacuation force consisted of freighters and personnel transports, civilian vessels incapable of outrunning Jarada warships, and with virtually no weapons or defense systems. The convoy carried a hundred thousand Europani, not to mention thousands of crew; the loss of life would be enormous.

"How long?" Vaughn asked Bowers, wanting to know how much time they had before they were besieged by all four Jarada ships.

"Six minutes."

Vaughn raised his hand to his forehead and wiped it clear of sweat. The air on the bridge, though steadily clearing of smoke, was stifling.

"Do we have warp drive?" Vaughn asked.

"The warp engines are intact," Nog told him, "but there's a microfracture in the port nacelle."

"How bad?"

"Bad enough: we wouldn't be able to maintain warp for more than a few seconds." Nog peered over his shoulder, and Vaughn noticed a gloss of perspiration coating the lieutenant's face, his huge, ribbed ears, and his large, bald head.

"How many?" Vaughn asked. He peered over at the main viewer again. He saw only stars, but pictured the two trailing Jarada warships descending toward *Defiant*, ready to join with their sister ships to put an explosive end to this one-sided battle.

"How many what?" Nog sounded confused, as though Vaughn had asked the question in another language.

"How many seconds would we be able to maintain warp?"

Nog's eyes narrowed, the fleshy ridge that ran from the top of each ear and across his brow descending in perplexity. Still, he turned to consult his console. "Forty seconds at most," he said at last. "But maybe no more than twenty-five."

"Lieutenant," Vaughn said to Dax. "How much time before we're at a safe distance to go to warp?"

"Seven minutes on a linear course," Dax answered immediately. "Almost a minute and a half after the third and fourth Jarada ships get here."

Vaughn turned in place, surveying the bridge, his mind working over the facts of the situation. They had to remain out of weapons range of the second pair of Jarada vessels; once those two ships entered the battle, it would end quickly. Vaughn could risk going to warp as close as *Defiant* was to Torona IV, and the ship would likely be safe. Employing warp drive this deep in a planetary gravity well carried a risk, to be sure, but incidents rarely occurred. The real problem would be that the Jarada would view such an action as depraved disregard for their world and their people, which would drive them to pursue the convoy.

Vaughn's gaze fell to the center of the bridge, to the captain's chair. To his surprise, Prynn's corpse no longer lay beside it, nor was Dr. Bashir still there. With all the commotion, Vaughn had not even heard the sound of the transporter.

Fury swam up from the depths of Vaughn's submerged emotions. His body involuntarily tensed, his wrath driving him toward physical action. His jaw set, his teeth clenched, his hands drew into fists. The Jarada had attacked *Defiant* and killed his only child—were still attacking, attempting to kill all the crew—and for what? Because they had been asked to assist in the rescue of a half-million people, and the price they had been paid had not satisfied them? Vaughn's lips pressed together, his eyes slammed shut, and in his intensity he wanted to return fire, wanted to vent the destructive power of this ship that had been designed to repel a Borg incursion. He visualized the remnants of the Jarada ships scattered harmlessly across the expanse of space.

The orders he knew he would not give floated through his mind. *Lock pulse phaser cannons. Arm quantum torpedoes. Fire at will.* Vaughn craved to avenge his daughter, and to guarantee the safety of the crew, but he understood well the repercussions of launching any assault against the Jarada under these circumstances. He thought briefly of the only other military vessel besides *Defiant* to accompany the convoy. The Cardassian cruiser *Trager* had remained well outside the Torona system during the evacuation, so that its presence would not incite the Jarada. But even if *Trager* were not still damaged from its many battles during the Dominion War, it would not be able to defend dozens of civilian vessels against an attack by a squadron of Jarada warships—an attack that would surely come should *Defiant* open fire.

Vaughn opened his eyes, again settling his emotions through a conscious effort. He slowed his breathing and tried to let go the tension in his body. His fingers unfurled, and he realized that his right hand hurt badly, the enveloping throb of his heartbeat a clockwork agony pressing in on his wounds.

Vaughn dismissed the pain as best he could, then turned toward Bowers. "Status of the cloaking device?" he asked, still searching for the tactics that would see the crew safely back to DS9.

"Operational," Bowers said.

"I thought we were not supposed—" started Ensign ch'Thane, but then he abruptly stopped speaking. Vaughn looked toward the sciences console, over on the port side of the bridge. Even though ch'Thane had already returned his attention to his readouts, Vaughn still perceived embarrassment in the science officer's tense back and hunched shoulders, the slightly curled posture of his antennae. Amid the turmoil, Vaughn unexpectedly felt one side of his mouth curl upward in a half-smile. He did not find the questioning of his prospective orders amusing, but the ensign's discomfiture was curious. From what Charivretha had related to him, young Shar stood well accustomed to challenging authority.

"What about the shields?" Vaughn asked Bowers. The air on the bridge, he noticed, was almost entirely clear of smoke now, though the ashen taste of the fire's residue still remained.

"Aft shields are gone," Bowers said. "Remaining shields down to thirty-seven percent port, fifty-one percent fore and starboard." He pressed a couple of touchpads and consulted a readout before continuing. "Ablative armor buckled on the port impulse casing. We've got a small hull rupture."

"We're leaking deuterium there," Nog added. "That's the source of the power drain."

"Does the leak affect all the impulse engines?" Vaughn asked.

"No," Nog said. "Just the port engine."

"Can we shut it down and reroute power to the other two?" Vaughn suggested. "And flush the deuterium so we're not leaving a trail for our friends?" He gestured vaguely in the direction of *Defiant*'s stern.

Nog operated his console. "We can stop the leak by shutting down the port engine," he confirmed. "But we've got nowhere to take power from for the other two. Weapons systems are down, shields are failing—"

"Get ready to do it," Vaughn ordered, cutting the engineer off. To Dax, he said, "Prepare to give me a linear course."

"Yes, sir."

Vaughn paced over to the engineering station and leaned in over Nog's shoulder to peer at the displays. "On my mark, take the port engine offline and vent the deuterium. Then reroute all available power to the other impulse engines, everything but for gravity, the cloaking device, and whatever you need for the warp drive."

Nog's eyes remained focused on his console, his hands working to set up the reconfiguration of the ship's systems, even as he sought clarification of Vaughn's orders. "Everything?"

"Everything," Vaughn said. Then, to be sure there was no mistake, he added, "Shields, any reserves left in the weapons, transporters, communications, sensors, life support." To the crew, Vaughn supposed, the orders must have sounded desperate, but he did not have time to explain why this course would provide them the best chance for survival. The Jarada were nothing if not intensely territorial; if they couldn't destroy *Defiant,* they'd be satisfied to drive her out of their domain, and the incident would end here. Escape meant the hundred thousand Europani still in transit to Bajor would be safe.

"Ensign ch'Thane," Vaughn said, stepping away from the engineering console. "Apprise the medical bay." If any casualties were being treated, the medical staff would need to know about the interruption of power.

"Sir," Nog said. "If we're at warp and the fracture in the nacelle widens, we could go up in a fireball."

"And if we stay here and allow four Jarada battleships to attack us in tandem, we *will* go up in a fireball." Vaughn made sure his tone left no doubt that his orders would stand. He had planned enough operations in his career, developed enough strategies, solved enough problems, that hesitation had long ago been banished from his decision-making process. "Time until the trailing ships are in weapons range?" Vaughn asked.

"Three minutes, twenty seconds," Dax said.

"That's how much time we've got to get far enough away from Torona IV to go to warp. Can we do it?"

"Depending on how much power we draw," Nog began, "how much power there is. . . ." His voice trailed off.

"You don't know?"

"I'd have to run an analysis, and that'd take a couple of minutes."

"No time," Vaughn agreed. "Lieutenant," he said to Dax, "shortest route, now." Then, touching the fingers of his right hand to Nog's shoulder, he said, "Go."

Nog responded by working his console, his hands moving with expert precision across the controls. His demeanor seemed to change slightly, Vaughn noticed, almost as though the engineer found relief in having something specific to do. In the short time Vaughn had been aboard Deep Space 9—not much more than a month—he had been impressed by Nog, and even seen the station's recently promoted operations officer grow in confidence. There was still something innocent and even wide-eyed about him, perhaps a healthy fear of the unknown and of death, but there was, Vaughn thought, a great deal of potential in the young man. And Nog's engineering skills only slightly overshadowed his remarkable ability to improvise.

As Nog discharged his orders, *Defiant* transformed. The atonal groan of the port impulse engine disappeared, leaving the smoother, softer hum of the pair that remained online. The shuddering of the deck also smoothed out.

"Port engine is offline," Nog said. "Deuterium conduits are clear. I'm rerouting power."

"Sensors and shields last," Bowers said.

The insistent, blaring alarms cut off abruptly. Even with the sound of the impulse drive, the bridge suddenly seemed almost quiet to Vaughn. He looked around in time to see most of the stations go dark: environmental control, transporter operations, communications. When the sciences console lost power, Ensign ch'Thane rotated his chair around to face the rest of the bridge. His antennae no longer bent downward, Vaughn saw, but seemed tense, as did the expression on his face. *He's trying to control his fear,* Vaughn thought, and then, recalling the Andorian response to danger, corrected himself: *Not fear; anger.* Something flickered off to the right, and Vaughn looked to see that the main viewer had gone blank.

"Power levels are coming up," Nog reported as he continued to redirect the ship's systems to funnel into the impulse engines.

The lights went next, plunging the bridge into momentary darkness before the emergency lighting came on. The few wisps of smoke still hovering about looked to Vaughn like phantoms haunting the scene. He found the pall menacing, and it occurred to him that he had spent a great deal of his career—a great deal of his life—bathed in the gloomy twilight of impending danger.

And then the emergency lighting went out. A claustrophobic blackness surrounded Vaughn. Only the engineering and tactical stations, and Dax's rerouted flight-control display, remained operational, their lonely glow like beacons in the night. The bulkheads felt closer now, and Vaughn was acutely aware of the smallness of *Defiant* about him, and of his own insignificance in the vastness of space.

The resonant drone of the impulse engines grew louder again, but remained steady this time. "We're approaching ninety percent of full impulse," Dax said, her face barely visible in the reflected light of her console.

"The near ships are closing in again," Bowers said, his words coming quickly and loudly.

"They don't—" Vaughn started, but then a thunderous jolt pounded *Defiant,* and another. Vaughn reached for the back of Nog's chair, but missed, and he went sprawling backward onto the deck. No alarms sounded, but something hissed loudly in the darkness. Vaughn rolled to his feet and looked toward tactical, where Bowers's shadowy figure hovered over his station.

"Starboard shields are down," Bowers called out. "Aft armor down to—" The tactical officer stopped speaking as his own console went dark. Vaughn could no longer see even a dim outline of the man. "Aft armor down to twenty-three percent," Bowers continued, obviously reporting the last reading he had seen.

"Sensors and shields rerouted," Nog reported, finding the last bits of power for the impulse engines.

"They weren't prepared for that burst of impulse power," Dax said. "We may have time before they can swing around for another pass." Another pass, another disruptor strike like the last one, Vaughn knew, and *Defiant*'s armor might not hold.

"Time," Vaughn said. The hissing stopped, but again the sound of the impulse drive wavered.

"Estimating ninety seconds before the third and fourth ships get here," Dax said. "Eighty seconds before we can go to warp. If the impulse engines hold up."

Good, Vaughn thought. They had made up time. He hoped it would be enough. Moving through the darkened bridge from memory, he found the center seat and settled into it.

"One minute until we can go to warp." Dax said. "With sensors offline, I can't tell where the Jarada ships are." Vaughn thought he heard the confidence present in the lieutenant's voice up to this point begin to drain away.

Another blast rocked the ship, though not as violently as the previous strikes. Had it, Vaughn realized, *Defiant* would likely not still be here. He stopped himself from asking Bowers for a status update; with the tactical station down, there was no way to know how much more the aft armor had degraded. But Vaughn did not need that data to know that *Defiant* would not survive another assault.

"Fifty seconds," Dax said. Then: "We're not going to make it."

Vaughn turned in his chair toward Dax. She was staring intently at her console, her face shining orange in its light. He could not make out the spots on the side of her face, but he could see her inexperience in her expression.

So young, he thought, and then about Shar and Nog, and even about Bowers and Bashir: *They're all so young.* Still, Dax's eyes never left her display. She was good, this one, and strong; command had been the right choice for her. Vaughn had no idea how good a counselor she might have become had she continued in that profession, but he was confident that, given the chance, she would make a fine commander, and sooner rather than later. And so he chose to trust her instincts now.

"Evasive maneuvers, Lieutenant," he said, "but give me no more than another seven seconds on our course."

Dax's hands moved in swift response to the order even before her acknowledgment passed her lips. *She anticipated me,* Vaughn realized, and wondered just how far a career in command might take her.

Vaughn faced forward in his chair, staring through the darkness toward the main viewer, which he could not see, and which was offline anyway. His right hand was a knot of pain, but it paled beside the ache in his heart. Just ahead of him, the indistinct shape of the conn rose from the deck, a mute marker of his daughter's violent death. He looked down to the side of the captain's chair, to where Prynn had been thrown by the explosion that had taken her away from him for good. In his mind's eye, he saw her lying there, the spark of life gone from her visage. He remembered that spark, that flash in her eyes, from the moment they had succeeded in evacuating the last of the Europani from their poisoned world, when she had smiled at him for the first time in years. And he remembered it from her childhood, and even before, from the time she had been an infant. Her dark, almond eyes had always seemed amazingly vivid to him, as though they contained the passion of her will. They were Ruriko's eyes.

"Forty seconds," Dax said. "Back on a linear course."

A chill gripped Vaughn as he sat in the darkness. The air on the bridge was still oppressively warm—the environmental systems had not been offline that long yet—but he envisioned the absolute cold of space bleeding away the kernel of heat generated on *Defiant* to sustain the crew. The image recalled the dreadful tableau Vaughn and an *Enterprise* away team had found not long ago aboard *Kamal,* a derelict Cardassian freighter adrift in the Badlands. Bodies everywhere, Bajorans and Cardassians frozen in death.

That had been a part of the incident that had driven Vaughn to Deep Space 9, away from the career he had worked—the life he had lived—for the past eighty years. Decisions of life and death, killing some so that others might live, battling alongside evil in order to conquer even greater evils. He had seen and experienced as much of that—more, much more, he amended—than he had ever wanted to. And so he had made the decision to live a life not laced with sorrow and regret, and to seek not ugliness and horror to be vanquished, but beauty and wonder to be explored. Yet here he was again, faced with risking *Defiant's* crew of forty to save a hundred thousand.

"Thirty seconds."

Vaughn braced himself, waiting for the final salvo that would boil away and penetrate the only protection *Defiant* had astern. Seconds ticked away in agonizing slowness.

When Dax reached *ten,* Vaughn told Nog to bring all systems back online. One step at a time, the ship limped back to life: lights rescued the bridge from darkness, consoles blinked back on, alarms cried out once more.

"At zero," Vaughn said, raising his voice to be heard above the alerts, "shut down the impulse drive."

"Aye, sir," Nog said.

Dax counted out the last five seconds with an expectant tone, and Vaughn thought he heard the return of her determination with each word. After "One," Dax said, "We're clear for warp."

At once, the thrum of the impulse engines faded, the tone deepening as the volume decreased. Vaughn said nothing, instead counting out another three seconds to himself.

"Sir?" It was Bowers, an edge clearly audible in his voice. He had expected the order to go to warp as soon as they were able, Vaughn surmised. But with all those civilian lives dependent upon what they did here, Vaughn could not afford to act without a margin of error.

Ignoring Bowers, he told Dax, "Go to maximum warp for ten seconds, then throttle down to warp three-point-seven and take evasive action." The lieutenant did not bother to acknowledge the orders as she set about implementing them. Vaughn imagined he could feel *Defiant* leap to warp.

"Monitor the fracture," Vaughn said to Nog.

"Aye, sir."

"The Jarada have gone to warp," Bowers said. "All four ships. They're in pursuit."

"Engage cloak," Vaughn said.

Bowers's fingers played across the control surfaces of the tactical station, but he hesitated before completing the command. "Sir, the Jarada will be able to read us cloaking." The lieutenant's hand hovered a few centimeters above his console.

"Do it," Vaughn ordered. Bowers complied, immediately bringing his hand down on a blinking touchpad. The bridge lighting dimmed in the telltale way that signaled the ship's stealth mode to the crew.

Come on, Vaughn thought, exhorting the Jarada to keep up their pursuit. He expected them to read *Defiant* cloaking, just as he expected that they had already read the microfracture in the warp nacelle. It never paid, Vaughn knew, to underestimate the enemy.

"Warp three-point-seven," Dax said. "Starting evasive maneuvers."

"Status of the fracture?" Vaughn asked.

"Stressed," Nog said. "But stable."

Vaughn ticked off another ten seconds in his head, then told Dax to bring the ship out of warp. "Take us to station-keeping."

"Dropping out of warp," Dax responded. Then, a few seconds later, she added, "Engines answering full stop."

"The Jarada are approaching the area," Bowers said.

"Of course they are," Vaughn offered. They had read *Defiant*'s course and velocity once it had gone to warp, seen where it had cloaked, and if they had detected the fracture on the nacelle, they would have calculated just how far the Starfleet ship could possibly travel before having to drop back to sublight speed. Now, if they utilized all of that information to determine a starting point and locus for a search—

"They're passing our position," Bowers said, and Vaughn could hear the smile on the tactical officer's face even without looking.

"No celebrations yet, Lieutenant," Vaughn said, though he tried to inject a sense of lightness into his tone. "Keep your eyes on them."

Seconds passed, then minutes, Bowers intermittently describing the movements of the four battleships. The Jarada vessels stopped not far beyond the most distant point to which *Defiant* could have traveled at maximum warp, given the damaged nacelle. Then they retreated, split up, regrouped.

"They're moving again," Bowers said finally. "Heading off on different vectors at warp one . . . describing helical trajectories—" Bowers suddenly looked up from his console. "They've set up a search grid." He did not need to add what they all already knew: the Jarada were looking for *Defiant* far from its current location.

"Excellent," Vaughn said. After they hunted fruitlessly for a while, he thought, the Jarada would guess that *Defiant* had taken evasive action and modified its speed after it had cloaked. Vaughn thought they would likely change their search strategy, call in reinforcements to assist. But space was big and *Defiant* small—and essentially invisible—and they already had an advantage over their pursuers; Vaughn had chosen the odd velocity—warp three-point-seven, not warp one or three or five—to hide their position that much more. This game of hide-and-seek was one Vaughn knew he would win.

"Lieutenant Nog," he said, "I believe you have a fractured warp nacelle to repair."

"Aye, sir," Nog said, bounding out of his chair and heading for the starboard exit. "Right away."

"Lieutenant," Vaughn called as the door opened before the engineer. "Everyone," he continued, still having to raise his voice above the alarms. He gazed around to include all of the bridge crew. "Well done." Nog smiled widely, his small, sharp teeth showing prominently. He nodded, then turned and left.

Vaughn sat back in the captain's chair. Exhaustion washed over him like a warm wave, trying to coax him into the deeper water of sleep—or perhaps unconsciousness. But there was much yet to do. There were still Jarada ships to avoid, and light-years to travel before *Defiant* arrived safely back at Deep Space 9. He would have to check to see if any other of the crew had been injured. His own left arm had been burned in the fire at the conn, his right hand even more so, and he would have to have Dr. Bashir patch him up.

And he would have to say goodbye to Prynn.

But not right now.

"Normal lighting," Vaughn said. "And get rid of those alarms." Around him, the bridge brightened and quieted, Bowers making the necessary adjustments. Vaughn looked up and said, "Ensign Roness, Ensign Senkowski, report to the bridge." Relief at the conn and engineering stations for Dax and Nog.

After the acknowledgments came back, Vaughn rested his elbow on the arm of the chair and let his head fall into his uninjured hand. He wanted very much not to think about anything, not to feel anything.

Vaughn closed his eyes. For now—for right now—he was content to pretend that he was at peace, in a life that continued to know no such thing.

2

Kira Nerys slid her thumb down the cracked, ruby-colored spine of the over-sized book. She felt the raised hubs and the textured surface of the aged tome, both smoothed from wear, and smelled the faint, musky scent of its binding. Flecks of gold passed beneath her touch, remnants of inlaid letters long ago eroded away by the attentions of many readers through many years.

"When the Prophets Cried," she said aloud, pronouncing the title in a voice not quite soft enough to be a whisper. Her hand descended to the base of the book, and she let her fingertips hang on the edge of the glass shelf. She stood like that for a few moments, her arm outstretched, alone in her office.

The old volume beckoned to Kira, like the open invitation of a longtime and trusted friend. Often throughout her life she had turned to the venerable work for spiritual and emotional guidance. Penned hundreds of years ago by Synta Kayanil, a vedek revered even in her own time for her insight, the collection of religious exegeses, historical recountals, and prophetic writings had provided Kira with a solid foundation on which to build and rebuild her faith—both in her gods and in herself. One of the few possessions she esteemed, and the only one she retained from her early childhood, the book had occupied a significant place in her life for almost as long as she could remember.

But now *When the Prophets Cried* had been denied her. With the Attainder imposed upon her by the Vedek Assembly, Kira was forbidden to study any of the Bajoran canon. Of course, she mused, she could simply pull the book from the shelf and read it anyway, and nobody would ever know.

Nobody but Kira herself.

She leaned in toward the book, her hand still dangling by two fingers from the shelf, the glass pleasantly cool to her touch. She breathed in deeply. Com-mingled with the musk of the cover was the slightly acid odor of the pages within. Kira had never really liked that smell, exactly, but it had always afforded her a sense of familiarity, even a sense of being . . . well, home, though the con-cept of *home* was necessarily a broad one for her. Before the end of the Occu-pation, less than eight years ago, she had lived her entire life either on the run or in a refugee camp, and so home had been wherever she had rested her head at night. To a great extent, she thought, that continued to be the case. Even having spent the years since the liberation of Bajor residing on DS9, she did not now think of the station as the only place she belonged. All of the Bajoran system—Bajor and the other planets, their moons, the wormhole, even the Denorios Belt, and yes, Deep Space 9 too—the entire system formed her home.

Kira stood away from the shelf and let her hand drop to her side. To her right, just within the limits of her hearing, voices and the workaday sounds of ops drifted through her closed office doors. She looked in that direction and, through the glass, saw personnel arriving for the start of the day shift, relieving the crew that had worked through the night. Kira had come to her office early today, ahead of the morning shift change, a consequence, she supposed, of the events surrounding the Iconian gateways and her days spent thirty thousand years in the past. Her experiences back in time—whether real or imagined—during a formative and long-forgotten era in Bajoran history had brought her to a deeper appreciation of her people, and to a greater sense of her own responsibilities in the present day. Her abiding trust in the Prophets, and in her own ability to walk the path They had laid out for her, had been reinforced in a way she had not known she had needed. She had returned to DS9 with a strengthened resolve to help her people through these turbulent times—despite the Attainder.

Because of her faith and her belief in the precepts of her religion, Kira would never challenge the edict set down by the Vedek Assembly. Ironically, a transgression of that very nature—acting in contravention of the wishes of Vedek Yevir Linjarin—had led to the Attainder in the first place. Allowing that the ancient Ohalu text unearthed at the B'hala archeological site might not be apocryphal, and convinced that the people had the right to decide the issue for themselves, Kira had posted a complete translation of the book to the Bajoran communications network. She had taken the extreme and irrevocable action, clearly opposed to Yevir's intention of keeping even the existence of the old work hidden, because she had believed it the right thing to do for her people. But the only reasons to violate the Attainder would be for her own benefit, insufficient cause in her mind to defy the vedeks.

Kira walked over to the replicator set into the wall to the side of her desk. *"Raktajino,"* she said. "Extra hot, with two measures of *kava."* The machinery hummed to life and, amid the striated shimmer of materialization, deposited a mug of the scalding Klingon beverage onto the replicator pad. Kira curled her fingers around the handle of the mug and brought it up to her lips. Wisps of steam carried the stout aroma of the black liquid wafting up to her nose. She sipped, and the hot, sweet *raktajino* felt strong and vitalizing as it flowed down her throat.

A smile crossed her face as she was reminded of Etana Kol, a sergeant in the station's security detail. Kol often remarked that the colonel's internal organs must be composed of rodinium in order for her to be able to drink such hot beverages, and Kira usually responded by claiming to have a taste for warp plasma or phaser fire or the like. The banter had become an ongoing ritual for the two women whenever they shared a meal at the Replimat after attending temple services.

Temple services.

For more than a month now, Kira had not prayed—had not been permitted to pray—among her fellow Bajorans. Even with her determination to face this time with dignity and fortitude, she could not deny that she missed visiting the temple and being surrounded by people who believed what she believed, who knew what she knew. And there were other things she missed as a result of the Attainder: experiencing the effects of an Orb encounter, speaking about matters of faith with vedeks and prylars . . . even simply wearing her earring.

Kira absently lifted a hand to her right ear as she crossed to her desk. She set the *raktajino* beside the desktop computer interface and sat down, brushing the tips of her fingers along her lobe as she did so. It still seemed strange to her, that sensation of a bare ear; she felt exposed somehow, almost as though she had left her quarters without fully dressing.

Recognizing the tenor of her thoughts, Kira pulled her hand away and let it fall onto the desk with a rap. She did not wish to think about those things that were missing from her life. Instead, she wanted to concentrate on all that she did have, and on the direction her life was headed—on the direction she would take it.

Dismissing thoughts of the Attainder with a shake of her head and a short, backward wave of her hand, Kira activated the computer interface and retrieved her agenda for the day. By design, she had no appointments scheduled during the morning—she had pushed the daily staff meeting back a few hours—but the afternoon would be full. After convening with her senior staff, she had the weekly meeting open to all station personnel, which typically lasted an hour or so, and after that, who knew how long it would take to listen to Quark itemize whatever requests or grievances the Promenade Merchants' Association had this month.

And speaking of Quark, she anxiously awaited the opportunity to talk with Ro about her foray with him to Farius Prime. Kira had already read the lieutenant's preliminary report on their disruption of the negotiations for the gateways between the Orion Syndicate and the Petraw—whoever they turned out to be—but she still had numerous questions about Ro's time undercover as Quark's escort. *That,* she thought, grinning, *ought to make quite a story.*

Kira picked up the mug and sipped again at the *raktajino.* Her final appointment for the day, she saw, would also be the most important: a subspace conference with the Starfleet Corps of Engineers that would provide her with an update on their efforts to decontaminate Europa Nova. While First Minister Shakaar and Minister Asarem and the rest of the Bajoran government had immediately responded to the Europani crisis by offering their planet as a temporary harbor, the sudden influx of two and a half million people—with another half-million on the way—taxed Bajor's resources. The sooner the refugees could be returned to their world, the better for everybody.

Kira keyed in her access code with her free hand and found that she had several messages waiting for her, as was often the case when she started her shift. She scanned down the list and saw that most appeared to be routine, but two caught her eye: one from Lieutenant Ro, and one, very surprisingly, from Taran'atar. Kira supposed that she was becoming accustomed to the Jem'Hadar's presence on the station, and her confidence in him had grown well beyond the simple fact of his assignment to DS9 by Odo. He had certainly proven himself as a soldier under her command. But she could also see that, for all his strength and military abilities, he still felt awkward and unsure here, often seeming to grope for understanding in this setting—and on this mission—that was clearly so alien to him.

The readout indicated that Taran'atar's message was audio only. Kira put down the mug of *raktajino,* now half empty, and touched the interface controls, which warbled in response. *"Colonel Kira,"* Taran'atar began. His usually resonant voice still sounded thin to her, as it had when she had visited him in the infirmary upon her return to the station. She recalled the image of him lying on the diagnostic pallet, looking as though he had been battered for hours, the green-gray skin of his face unnaturally colored blue and purple and black.

Difficult as it was to credit, Dr. Tarses claimed that those hideous bruises were indications of the superior capacity of Jem'Hadar to heal. When Taran'atar had been recovered by Lieutenant Bowers and Ensign Roness after he had returned from the Delta Quadrant through one of the gateways, his face had been a mass of open wounds. Bowers had transported him aboard *Rio Grande* and had managed to stem the bleeding, and by the time they had gotten back to DS9, the damage had already begun to mend.

Unfortunately, Taran'atar's facial wounds had been the very least of his injuries. One of his arms had suffered multiple fractures, and two of his ribs had been splintered. A bladed weapon not only had penetrated one of his biceps, but had traveled within, chewing up muscle tissue and then sawing its way back out. Another, more jagged blade had been plunged into his chest, leaving a gaping hole and slicing through one of his hearts. Two other of his organs had been damaged as well. It had been worse even than when the Jem'Hadar hatched by that genetically engineered renegade—Locken—had tortured Taran'atar; they had hurt him, but in trying to extract information from their prisoner, their attentions had been designed to keep him alive. The Hirogen in the Delta Quadrant had clearly had no such constraints; he had wanted to hunt down and destroy Taran'atar. When Kira had visited the infirmary and learned the extent of his injuries, she had wondered—and she wondered again now—what the combat between the two warriors must have been like; after all, as badly wounded as he was, Taran'atar had *won* the battle.

Kira listened to the rest of the message. Like all of Taran'atar's communications, it was succinct: he wanted to be liberated from the infirmary. *Liberated,* Kira thought, unable to suppress a smile, *as though he were a prisoner.* When she had first seen him after their ordeals, he had expressed his satisfaction that they had both reclaimed their lives. Now, she supposed, he wished to reclaim his life once more, this time from the clutches of Dr. Tarses.

Kira sympathized. She had never been much of a patient herself, had never wanted to lie about for long, even to expedite her own convalescence. She would see to it that Simon released Taran'atar as soon as medically appropriate—which, knowing the rapid recuperative powers of Jem'Hadar, would be soon, anyway.

She called up Ro's message, a text memorandum requesting the authority to regulate the pedestrian traffic on the Promenade. Ro had listed several justifications for the request, but Kira thought that she should have foreseen this herself. As busy a place as Deep Space 9 had always been, it had never been as close to capacity as right now. Almost five months after the war with the Dominion, businesses were finally returning to normal, and the trade routes were once again being plied—although not yet through the wormhole. The station also continued to function as a staging area for relief efforts to Cardassia, and now played a similar role in the evacuation of Europa Nova. And while a substantial majority of the refugees had been taken to Bajor, several thousand remained on DS9, along with the crews of scores of ships waiting to begin resettlement of the Europani once their world had been returned to habitability.

Kira turned in her chair and gazed out the large, oval window behind her desk. She could see at least a dozen ships, no two alike, a couple of them Bajoran, but most from out of the system. With so many crews aboard the station, Ro had already posted more security officers than usual along the Promenade, a move Kira supported.

She's been doing a good job, Kira thought as she turned back to her desk. She had not been that sure of Ro at first, but the new security chief had performed her duties seriously and well. And despite a rocky beginning, the two seemed to have developed a professional relationship of mutual respect.

Another aspect of the congestion on the Promenade, according to Ro, concerned the Bajoran temple and the Orb of Memory. As word of the Orb's rediscovery spread, many Bajorans were apparently undertaking a pilgrimage to the station to experience it for themselves. The Orb would eventually be moved to Bajor, once a suitable location for it had been selected and prepared by the Vedek Assembly, but in recent days the number of passenger transports arriving fully loaded from Bajor had increased dramatically.

Kira glanced back across the room, over at *When the Prophets Cried*. She had felt the urge to consult the old book this morning, not because she sought direction for herself, but because she hoped to gain some insight into the current, tumultuous times. Dramatic events had unfolded for Bajor during the past few months—the Ascension of the Emissary, the death of the kai, the banishment of the Pahwraiths, the unearthing of the Ohalu text—and Kira had begun to wonder if a new era might be dawning for her people. Allusions to a restoration of all the highest accomplishments the Bajoran people had ever achieved appeared in several canon sources, though conventional interpretations held that such a time, if it ever came, would be far in the future. But with the return of the Orb of Memory, Kira had started considering the possibility that the future had arrived.

She lifted the mug to her lips, then rose from her chair and went over to the replicator. She deposited the *raktajino,* no longer hot enough for her liking, on the pad, then touched a control to recycle it. Hazy, whirring strands of light swallowed the mug and converted it back into energy and raw materials. "*Raktajino,*" she said, once the mug had disappeared. "Extra hot, two measures of *kava.*" As the replicator hummed back into action, she turned and looked again at *When the Prophets Cried*.

The title referred to the Orbs, which, at the time Vedek Synta had written the tome, had been known only as the Tears of the Prophets. Bajoran faith represented the Orbs as indirect physical links to the Prophets themselves. During Vedek Synta's time, seven Tears had been known, and since then, three more had been found. When the Cardassians had withdrawn after the Occupation, they had taken all but the Orb of Prophecy with them, and the Orb of the Emissary, which had yet to be discovered. But over the last few years, the Orbs had begun returning to Bajor, a prophecy foretold by Vedek Synta, and which she hinted might be a preamble to the restoration and Bajor's greatest age.

Almost four years ago, Kira remembered, the Orb of Wisdom had made a circuitous route home, acquired by the Grand Nagus of the Ferengi from the Cardassian black market and eventually sold to the Bajorans when Ferenginar and Bajor had come to the brink of war. And then the Cardassians had given back the Orbs of Time and Contemplation. And now, after Commander Vaughn had found the Orb of Memory aboard a derelict Cardassian freighter, five of the original nine Tears of the Prophets were in the possession of the Bajoran people for the first time in Kira's lifetime.

Kira turned and picked up the new mug of *raktajino* from the replicator pad, but she remained standing there a moment, still considering Vedek Synta's old work. Kira could picture herself sitting on the ground, her legs up, with the book set open against her thighs, the pages, fragile with age, crackling as she turned them. As a child, as a teen, in the Singha refugee camp or on the run with the resistance, she had most often read the book that way, her back against a fence or a tree or a cave wall, wherever she happened to be. And prior to the Attainder, that was how she still read the book, very often, on the floor of her quarters or in a hidden corner of her office.

A short laugh escaped her lips when she remembered the day—*How long ago was it? Three years? Four?*—when Captain Sisko had paid an unexpected early-morning visit to her quarters and caught her reading on the floor, leaning against an outer bulkhead. She had been embarrassed, but the captain had quickly made her feel at ease, revealing his own predilection for lying out in the middle of a baseball diamond he re-created in a holosuite. That image of the captain sprawled out in a grassy field had amused her back then, and it amused her now.

She missed Benjamin Sisko. Not the Emissary or the commanding officer of Deep Space 9—though she missed those aspects of the man as well—but just her friend. He was an unusual man, not only because he had been touched by the Prophets, but because he was worthy of being touched by Them. A man of robust principles, quick to action, loyal, and strong. Kira believed that he would return one day from the Celestial Temple, as Kasidy had been promised in a vision, and she hoped that day occurred during her lifetime. She missed her friend.

A signal chirped in the quiet office, followed by the voice of Ensign Ling. *"Ops to Colonel Kira,"* she said.

"This is Kira. Go ahead, Ensign."

"Colonel, the U.S.S. Mjolnir *is hailing the station,*" Ling said. "*They're request-ing an approach vector and permission to dock.*" A note of hesitation played in the ensign's voice, echoing Kira's own confusion.

"*Mjolnir?*" she repeated. Captain Hoku and her crew were not due at the station for another three weeks. Kira put the *raktajino* back down on the repli-cator pad and moved back behind her desk. She sat down and quickly skimmed her overnight correspondence again, the computer interface beeping as she scrolled through the list. She saw nothing from Starfleet. "Ensign," Kira asked, "did they say why they were arriving so far ahead of schedule?"

"*No, sir,*" Ling answered right away. "*Should I inquire?*"

Kira's initial inclination was to say, "Yes, inquire," a remnant, no doubt, of her days in the resistance, when even a single, small piece of information might prove vital to the cause. Even as first officer and now commander of DS9, she frequently sought as much data as she could about any particular situation. But if Captain Hoku had wanted to provide that information right now, Kira real-ized, she already would have done so.

"No," she finally said. "Send my greetings and bring them in."

"*Aye, sir.*" The channel closed with a short tone.

Kira sat back in her chair, her arms sliding back along the glossy surface of the desktop until her wrists rested atop its rounded edge. *Mjolnir* had been slated to arrive three weeks from now, she knew, and a week after that, to begin a three-month tour of duty at Deep Space 9 while *Defiant* explored the Gamma Quadrant. Kira wondered if those plans had been changed.

A sudden, wild thought occurred to Kira: perhaps *Mjolnir* was carrying yet another Orb back to Bajor. The notion was an idle one, she knew, but it brought her back again to Vedek Synta's book. "Bajor Rising" was the title of one prophetic tale in the collection, a tale from which some inferred that the return of the Orbs would usher in a resplendent new age for the Bajoran people.

When the children have wept all, Kira quoted to herself, *anew will shine the twilight of their destiny,* and she realized that *When the Prophets Cried* had not been taken from her; as often as she had read it, as well as she knew it, that could never happen. *When the children have wept all,* she thought again, *anew will shine the twilight of their destiny.* This single sentence had sparked more controversy and disagreement than any entire section of Vedek Synta's book. Did *children* refer to the people of Bajor? Did the mention of weeping allude to the Tears of the Prophets? Did the word *destiny* only mean *fate,* or did it also connote the Orb of Destiny? And was *twilight* a reference to dawn—a beginning—or to dusk—an end? Even the very language itself evoked debate, with numerous translations generating wildly divergent versions of the passage.

Kira sat back up in her chair and spoke toward the center of her office. "Kira to Ensign Ling," she said.

"*Ling here, Colonel,*" came the response.

"What's the ETA of the *Mjolnir?*"

"*Checking,*" Ling said, and then, "*Ninety-four minutes.*"

"Thank you, Ensign. Kira out." She knew there was no merit to the idea that *Mjolnir* might be carrying an Orb. Her intuition had served her well over the years, especially with respect to tactics and warfare, but this was not intuition; this was fantasy, and she knew it. Still, she could not shake the feeling that something was coming. So much had happened during the past half-year, so many extraordinary events had come to pass, that she somehow felt that it could not be less than the auguring of things to come.

And she remembered too what the Iconian—if, indeed, it had been an Iconian—had warned: do not forsake the journey for the destination. Whatever was going to come to pass, and despite the Attainder, Kira had a role to play in the scheme of future events, a path the Prophets had paved for her, one she was not only willing to walk, but eager to walk. She had endured much anguish in her life, but so many of her people had endured so much more. The time had come to move past that. One day, she hoped, Bajor would become a beacon to the rest of the quadrant—even to the rest of the galaxy—that shined the way to freedom and faith and love. And Kira would do whatever she could to help make that happen.

The airlock warning signal pulsed in the small room atop the docking pylon, and Kira looked through the hatch window to see a giant standing in the inner compartment. A moment later, the alert ceased, and the circular hatch rolled open, its toothed circumference meshing along its matching track. A rush of air hissed briefly as the atmospheres in the airlock and the receiving bay equalized. Then the hatch retracted into the bulkhead, fully revealing the largest human being Kira had ever encountered.

She assumed he was human, anyway. He wore a Starfleet uniform with an admiral's insignia—five pips framed in gold, she saw, a fleet admiral—and stood at least two and a quarter meters. *Even taller than the Hirogen,* Kira thought. *Not as tall as the Iconian, but larger.* The man's physique rivaled his height, with a broad chest and shoulders, and a torso that did not taper as it fell to his waist. His legs looked as wide as tree trunks, easily three times as big around as her own. He appeared fit, neither overweight nor overly muscular.

"You are Colonel Kira?" the man asked, the timbre of his voice rich and deep. A vague accent she could not place tinged his speech.

Kira raised her eyes to look at the man's face, and only then realized that she had been peering at the rest of his body, struck by his considerable presence. She felt discomfited, but if the man noticed the accidental indiscretion, he gave no indication. He had no doubt elicited such reactions before, she concluded.

"Yes," she answered. "I'm Colonel Kira Nerys. Welcome to Deep Space 9." She moved forward toward the hatch, her right hand extended in the traditional human greeting.

The man stepped over the threshold separating the airlock from the receiving bay, and then down the steps, ducking as he did so. Kira could not tell if his head would have connected with the upper bulkhead, but she supposed the movement had been a practiced one, born out of necessity. "How do you do," he said, his measured words sounding formal. "I am Admiral Akaar." He pronounced it *Aka-ar,* and rather than shaking Kira's hand, the admiral raised his right fist to the upper left portion of his chest, then opened his hand and held it out away from his body, palm up. "I come with an open heart and hand."

Kira withdrew her hand, caught off guard by the greeting. She felt clumsy for having breached this protocol, despite being unfamiliar with it. Akaar must have perceived this. "A traditional salutation among my people," he explained.

Perhaps not human, then, Kira thought, although she recognized that not all Earth customs were uniformly practiced by all humans. "Well, welcome to Deep Space 9," she said.

Akaar inclined his head in acknowledgment. He met her gaze confidently, almost forcefully, with brown eyes so dark that they verged on being black. His face was pale and soft, Kira saw, almost doughy, with lines etched deeply into his features. His hairline began high up on his forehead, his hair steely gray and long, pulled backward into a knot behind his head. It put Kira in mind of Lieutenant Commander Worf—*Ambassador Worf,* she reminded herself, though she still had trouble envisioning the fiery Klingon as a diplomat—but Akaar's hair was not nearly as long, ending just a few centimeters below his neck.

"Do you have time to speak with me, Colonel?" the admiral asked. Though phrased as a question, the request sounded very much like an order. "It will require perhaps thirty minutes."

"Of course," Kira said. "May I ask what this is about, Admiral?" She wondered about the early arrival of *Mjolnir,* and about the presence on board of an admiral.

"I am headed to Bajor," Akaar said, "to assist with the resettlement of the Europani, and to observe the labors to send aid to Cardassia."

"I see," Kira said, curious about the need for a Starfleet admiral in either endeavor. She also realized that he had not actually answered her question. "Excuse me, Admiral, but I wasn't asking why you've come to Bajor; I was asking why you've come to DS9."

Akaar seemed to consider the question before answering, though his eyes remained on Kira. "Councillor zh'Thane will be accompanying me to Bajor," he told her. Charivretha zh'Thane, the Andorian representative on the Federation Council, had been visiting Europa Nova prior to the gateways crisis, and she had subsequently been evacuated to the station. "And I wanted to speak with you," he added.

"All right," Kira said, taking a step toward the turbolift. "The wardroom is closest, or we can go to my office—"

"If you don't mind," the admiral said, not allowing her to list all of their options, "we can use a conference room aboard *Mjolnir.*" Akaar moved aside and motioned back toward where the starship sat docked at the end of the airlock.

"All right," Kira said. Again, she felt uncomfortable, as though she had somehow tripped up with the admiral. She tapped her combadge, a quick burst of electronic tones signaling its activation. "Kira to ops."

"Ops, Nguyen here," came the immediate response. The words carried the slightly hollow quality of a transmitted voice.

"Chief, I'm going to be in a meeting on board the *Mjolnir* for the next half-hour," Kira informed him.

"Acknowledged," Nguyen said. *"Should I consider you unreachable, Colonel?"*

Kira looked to Akaar for an answer, but while he returned her gaze, he offered no suggestion as to his wishes. "Yes," she finally answered, slightly frustrated at her seeming difficulty in communicating with the admiral. "I'll check in when I'm back on the station. Kira out." She deactivated her combadge with a touch. She did not have to tell Nguyen that she should be contacted if an emergency arose.

Akaar turned and stepped back into the airlock. As Kira followed, she realized that she still had no idea why the admiral wanted to see her.

The conference room sat far forward in *Mjolnir*'s primary hull. The outer bulkhead angled dramatically inward toward the bow of the ship, giving the room an essentially triangular shape. A third as big as DS9's wardroom, it held a table that could accommodate eight people—*Fewer,* Kira thought, *if they were Akaar's size.* Great floor-to-ceiling windows lined the entirety of the outer bulkhead, and a large viewscreen was set into the long inner wall.

Akaar sat down at the conference table, his back to the windows. The chair actually creaked beneath him as he settled his enormous bulk. Kira felt a moment of embarrassment for the admiral, but he gave no sign that he felt similarly.

"Will Captain Hoku be joining us?" Kira asked as she sat down opposite the admiral. Past Akaar, she saw the tips of two of DS9's docking pylons reaching upward into view like great metallic fingers clawing at the heavens. In the distance, a Bajoran transport drifted lazily outside their grasp.

"No, she will not," Akaar said. He rested his forearms flat on the reflective black surface of the table. "I must inform you, Colonel," he said, "that *Mjolnir* will not be standing in for *Defiant* while it explores the Gamma Quadrant." He did not have an accent after all, Kira decided, but a tendency to overpronounce his words, enunciating with a slow, cautious clarity. "*Gryphon* will instead substitute for *Defiant.*"

"I see," Kira said, not pleased to have been left unaware until now of the change in Starfleet's plans. "I typically get some notice of these things."

"I am giving you notice now," Akaar said. Although his voice remained level, Kira detected a note of antipathy toward her that she did not understand. In the past, she had experienced few difficulties with members of Starfleet Command, who had always shown confidence in her abilities to command DS9—

Except for one person, she suddenly remembered. It must have been six weeks ago, back when the first minister had been returning from a monthlong trip to various Federation worlds. Shakaar had warned her of an admiral who had been championing a reversion to the station's former hierarchy, with a Starfleet captain installed in the top spot. The possibility that the unnamed admiral had been Akaar occurred now to Kira. If that turned out to be the case, she would not allow his presence here to threaten her. Although she had been in command of Deep Space 9 for only four months, she had served in the position well, and she had every intention of continuing to do so.

"Thank you, Admiral. I'll note the change for my crew," Kira said, determined to maintain an even bearing. During her tenure as the station's first officer, she had learned to better control her impulses, to think twice before acting. Now, as DS9's commanding officer, she had been further pressed to hone her diplomatic skills.

"Colonel," Akaar said, "I would like you to detail for me the evacuation of the Europani to Bajor."

"Almost three million people have been brought here from Europa Nova," Kira said, "and *Defiant* is scheduled back in a few days, accompanying the last of the convoys from Torona IV."

"Yes," Akaar said, but the word seemed less an agreement than merely a placeholder, a word to fill the time and segue to the next subject. "How are the Europani being housed on Bajor?"

The question surprised Kira. The information Akaar was seeking had nothing to do with either Deep Space 9 or Starfleet. "I'm not sure what you're asking, Admiral, but I received a report just yesterday that the refugees have been divided up into groups—large groups—and taken to several dozen cities."

"Where are the Europani staying?" Akaar persisted.

"In hospitals, some of them, obviously," Kira said, not really knowing the precise answer to the question, but making logical assumptions. "In schools, government facilities, inns. Perhaps even in private residences."

"And the Europani on the station," the admiral asked, "why have they not gone on to Bajor?" Akaar's voice held a neutral intonation, but his words seemed to carry an implicit criticism.

"Some of the smaller vessels in the evacuation came directly to the station . . . Bajor's orbit got a bit crowded for a while. It was faster for some of the refugees to disembark here. And for those who'd suffered radiation poisoning, we were able to treat them. Since we have the facilities, I saw no problem with that." Kira realized that her last statement might have sounded defensive, as though she were attempting to support her decision to allow thousands of the refugees to remain on DS9. She brushed the characterization aside. "We're functioning close to capacity right now," she went on, "but the station is in good shape."

"Do you know how the Europani on Bajor are being fed?"

Again, the admiral seemed to be asking for information well outside Kira's purview. She turned her chair away from the table and toward the inner wall of the conference room. "I can have one of my officers in ops upload whatever data we have about the Europani operations on Bajor." She pointed to the viewscreen set into the wall, then tapped her combadge. "Kira to Ensign Ling."

"Ling here. Go ahead, Colonel."

"Ensign," Kira said, "I'd like you to aggregate all of the information—"

"Colonel." Akaar raised his hand, the flat of his palm toward her, a clear signal that he wanted her to stop what she was doing.

"Stand by, Ling," Kira said, then closed the channel with another touch to her combadge. "Admiral?"

"Colonel, I have already seen the data you have available on the Europani situation. I do not need to see it again."

An angry response rose in Kira's mind—*Then why are you wasting my time?*—but she controlled her impulse to shout it across the table at Akaar. Instead, she stood from the chair and activated her combadge once more. "Kira to Ling."

"Ling here, Colonel."

"Belay my last order. Out." Kira ended the communication without waiting for a response. She looked over at Akaar, who remained seated and very still. "If you don't mind, Admiral," she said, barely able to contain her annoyance, "I have duties to tend to." She started for the door.

"Colonel." Kira stopped, the double doors sliding open before her with a soft whoosh. She turned back to face Akaar. "Colonel," he went on, "I am interested in what you have to say about the Europani rescue and resettlement operations. Raw data and reports have their places, but I wish to hear from *you*."

The words bordered on flattery, intimating that he held Kira's opinions in some regard, but she put no trust in them. Nevertheless, she chose to honor Akaar's request. She walked back over to the table, the doors to the conference room sliding shut behind her with a whisper. "What would you like me to tell you, Admiral?" she asked as she sat back down.

For forty-five minutes, Kira responded to Akaar's questions about the rescue and resettlement of the Europani as best she could. She doubted that her perspective added anything new to the admiral's understanding of the situation; some of the questions involved the station, but many concerned Bajor, which she was not always able to answer. They paused only once, so that Kira could check in with the station, letting them know that she would be aboard *Mjolnir* longer than anticipated. When she thought the admiral had finished speaking with her, she rose to leave.

"I have one more question," Akaar said. "Have the efforts to help the Europani had an impact on Bajor's aid to Cardassia?"

"Deep Space 9 is continuing to function as a staging platform for Cardassian aid," Kira said, placing her hands on the back of the chair she had been sitting in. "The situation has become more complicated with the Europani on the station, and all the ships and crews waiting to take them back to Europa Nova, but we're managing."

"Yes," Akaar said, seeming to acknowledge and dismiss Kira's reply at the same time. "What I am asking about is the aid going to Cardassia *directly* from Bajor ... directly from the Bajoran people."

"Oh," Kira said. This was not an issue that she particularly wanted to address. Following the war with the Dominion, Bajor, by virtue of its close proximity to Cardassia, had been the natural place from which to coordinate and launch relief efforts. DS9, with its docking and cargo facilities, and its status as the nearest Federation starbase, had been a further logical choice to assist. Kira had been comfortable with those decisions, though her tolerance for Cardassians had developed by degrees over the years. She had not come to such acceptance easily, nor even always willingly, but her experiences with men like Aamin Marritza, who had sought to force Cardassia to accept responsibility for the atrocities perpetrated by Gul Darhe'el and others during the Occupation, and like Tekeny Ghemor, who had fought the military dominance of his own government, had helped her understand that not all Cardassians were evil. And she had also come to believe that Bajorans could find both peace and strength in forgiveness and charity for their enemies.

Now the Cardassians required both. The choking stench of the fires consuming the Cardassian capital at the end of the war recurred to Kira, bringing her back to that horrible time. She remembered battling beside Damar to free his people from Dominion control, to help them escape the perfidy that would ultimately see eight hundred million Cardassian dead, including Damar himself. Kira had grown to respect Damar as a rebel and as a man, and she had to admit now that she had seen more than a little of herself in him.

She stepped back away from the conference table and gathered her thoughts. She paced the length of the room, searching for an appropriate way to respond to Akaar's question. "Yes," she said at last. "There's understandably been an impact." Understandable, because there was only so much food and medicine on Bajor, only so many resources.

But there's more to it than that, Kira thought. Her experiences with the Cardassians after the Occupation were very different from those of most Bajorans. For most of her people, their last contact with the Cardassians had been during the Occupation itself. And while the people of Bajor could be merciful, and while their government had agreed not only to help organize relief efforts but to contribute their own food and medicine and other necessities to Cardassia, many seemed to support the measures with great reluctance. And there were even those Bajorans who opposed the humanitarian efforts.

"Colonel?"

Kira turned at the far end of the room. "Yes, there's been an impact," she repeated. "There've been fewer ships, fewer supplies, going to Cardassia from Bajor since we've been dealing with the Europani crisis. But we're still continuing to coordinate the Cardassian relief effort, with supplies being provided by other worlds." The admiral said nothing in response, and Kira suspected that he wanted her to say more. But there was nothing more she wanted to say about it.

Looking toward Akaar from where she now stood, with the conference table no longer between herself and the windows, Kira saw a large portion of Deep Space 9 laid out below *Mjolnir.* She allowed her gaze to sweep along the arc of the station's outer ring, from which the docking pylons emerged like the impossibly tall towers of a great city. Her eyes traced the shape of the station around the outer ring to a crossover bridge, and from there, into the habitat ring and the central core. Light shined from ports throughout the structure, testament to the thousands who worked and lived here. The oval windows encircling the Promenade glowed brightly, and she could even discern movement within.

Atop the upper core sat the operations module, and visible to one side was a window in Kira's office. She recalled looking out this morning at the ships arrayed around the station, and then she thought about *When the Prophets Cried.* Her fanciful notion that *Mjolnir* might be bringing another Orb back to Bajor returned to her, and as quickly as that daydream had occurred to her earlier, it now abandoned her completely. She knew that none of the sacred artifacts were aboard. And still, she could not escape the feeling that something significant was coming to Bajor—something more than a taciturn Starfleet admiral.

And then suddenly Kira knew. *Mjolnir* *was* bringing something to Bajor. She regarded Akaar, who sat mutely observing her. She said nothing, and after a moment, the admiral interrupted the silence.

"Colonel Kira," he said, using her name for the first time since asking her identity in the receiving bay. "How do you like commanding Deep Space 9?"

Kira smiled. She could not be certain, but she thought Akaar might have seen her come to the realization. She walked back to her chair and sat down again at the conference table. The admiral wanted to know about her running the station, and so she told him. She spoke for an hour about the challenges of command, about the responsibilities of leadership, about the gratification of striding confidently into the future, all the while thinking about just what that future would hold for her people.

It was not an Orb of the Prophets that was headed to Bajor, she had realized. It was the Federation.

3

The springball struck the front wall high in the white oval. A short, high-pitched bell confirmed the score as the ball rebounded toward the left rear corner of the court. Asarem Wadeen sprinted across the floor, the rubber soles of her sports shoes squeaking on the black hardwood as she changed direction. She instinctively gauged the path and speed of the ball, and realized she would not reach it with a normal effort. At the last moment, she lunged, just managing to backhand the ball before it bounced on the floor a second time. She twisted as her momentum carried her hard into the side wall, her left shoulder absorbing the brunt of the impact with a thump that reverberated in the enclosed court. Recovering quickly, she pushed away from the wall and back toward the center of the floor. She crouched on the balls of her feet, her weight forward, her racquet swung back to a forehand position, primed to keep her solitaire volley going. But two deep rings told her that her return shot had gone wide, hitting the front wall beyond the outer foul line.

Asarem straightened and caught the ball in her gloved left hand as it bounced back to her. She could easily have backhanded the ball again and continued playing, but even warming up by herself, she liked to follow the rules the same way as when pitted against an opponent. It better prepared her for games, she felt, both physically and mentally.

Slipping her fingers from the glovelike grip of her racquet, Asarem let it dangle from the cord circling her wrist. She tugged the scarlet gloves from her hands, then unfastened the chin strap of her helmet. Beads of perspiration ran from her hairline down the sides of her face. Despite the coolness of the weather outside—the winter months had just begun, though the temperature never dipped too low here in Ashalla—the air in the court had grown close and warm. Her padded springball uniform, also scarlet, covered her from neck to ankles and offered no relief from the heat, although she would never play the full-contact sport without it. She believed herself a tough competitor, toned and fast, but at just a dozen centimeters past a meter and a half, many of her opponents stood a head taller—or more—than she did. She would never reject a challenge, but neither would she play unprepared or unprotected.

Asarem removed her helmet and cradled it upside down in the crook of her arm, then dropped her gloves and the springball inside it. She wiped the perspiration from her face and forehead with the back of her hand, and headed to the back of the court. Suspended from the cord around her wrist, her racquet swayed back and forth, tapping against her leg as she walked. At the rear of the court, beside the closed entryway, a storage compartment sat recessed into the wall. Asarem poked a finger through the hole in the transparent door of the compartment and pulled it open, its hinges creaking as she did so. She set the helmet down inside and retrieved a small gold locket strung on a delicate, matching chain. Holding the locket flat on her fingers, the chain hanging down, she slid the front panel aside with her thumb to reveal a timepiece within.

It was nearly half past the hour. *He's late,* she thought. *Again.* She shook her head slowly from side to side, her feelings a mixture of exasperation and disbelief. In the five and a half years she had served with Shakaar Edon in the Bajoran government, she had never known him to be late—had never even heard of him being late—for a single appointment. And yet this was the third time in a month that he had kept her waiting.

Asarem closed the locket, then reached into the compartment and placed it in her helmet. She slipped the cord of the racquet from her wrist, wondering what might have caused Shakaar to neglect their meeting. Though she had been looking forward to playing springball—the first minister usually gave her a good contest—she did not mind missing a game. But this meeting was to have been far more than that. In particular, they had planned to discuss Bajor's renewed petition for membership in the United Federation of Planets; Starfleet's Admiral Akaar was due to arrive soon, and—

There was a knock at the door, the sound of bare knuckles on wood. The rapping echoed in the court. Asarem tossed the racquet into the compartment—it rattled between the wall of the compartment and the helmet, sending the helmet teetering back and forth—then took a step over to the entryway and pulled open the door. She expected to see the tall figure of Shakaar, but instead she found herself eye-to-eye with Enkar Sirsy, his assistant.

"Minister," Sirsy said, looking in from the corridor that joined to the changing room and the other two springball courts in the building. Cooler, fresher air drifted in through the entry, a noticeable counterpoint to the heavy, faintly sour atmosphere around Asarem. "First Minister Shakaar asked me to come by."

"To play in his stead?" Asarem teased. "That doesn't appear to be a springball uniform." Sirsy wore a conservative but elegant dark blue sheath, belted at the waist, beneath a charcoal cloak. The outfit contrasted dramatically with Asarem's formfitting scarlet habiliments.

Sirsy glanced down at her clothes and smiled, several strands of her long, straight red hair falling forward over her face. She looked back up, brushing her hair back into place with one hand. "I suppose not," she said, then became serious again as she returned to the reason for her visit. "The first minister sends his apologies for missing your meeting. He wanted to know if you'd like to reschedule it."

Surprised in the first place by Shakaar's tardiness, Asarem was now disappointed at the suggestion of having to postpone their appointment. Had some of the other ministers done this—almost *any* of the other ministers, she amended—she would have ascribed political motives to them, but that did not follow with Shakaar. Since he had been elected first minister, carried into office on the strength of his renowned assaults against the Cardassians during the Occupation, he had certainly been a political force, but that force had always operated in the open, without resorting to deceit or covert manipulation.

But if he was not motivated by politics, then what was happening with Shakaar? For a man who had conducted his incumbency with the punctuality of a general executing precisely coordinated tactics, this third incidence of his lateness was noteworthy. Asarem wondered if he might finally be losing tolerance for his position.

She had become convinced through the years that Shakaar actually loathed holding elective office, that he would rather have withdrawn from public attention to a quiet, secluded life of farming back in his native Dahkur Province. She had come to believe that when the mantle of governmental leadership had been thrust upon him during the uncertain period following the death of the previous first minister, he had accepted it only because he felt an obligation to the Bajoran population to do so. Perhaps now, Asarem speculated, he had finally tired of living his life for other people.

"Sirsy," she said, "what's going on here?" She rested her hands on her hips, elbows out. "Is there something I need to know?" The muted sounds of another springball game—the slap of the ball against walls and racquets, the various rings of the scoring bells—floated through the corridor.

"No, Minister Asarem," Sirsy answered. "The first minister is just running behind today." Asarem wanted to believe that. Although she differed politically with Shakaar on numerous issues—opponents liked to characterize her as a hardliner, severe and immovable, a description she declined to refute—she also respected him and thought that he had served Bajor admirably.

As certain as she was that Shakaar detested being first minister, it was not as the result of anything he had ever made apparent to anybody; he had carried his burden close to him, far from the perceptions of others. But Asarem had served as second minister for as long as Shakaar had been in office, and while they had experienced difficulties working with each other during the first couple of years of his tenure, they had since developed a strong and fruitful professional relationship. He had never complained about the onerous weight of his position, but there had been times when circumstances and demands for action had combined to allow her to see through the cracks in his armor.

And yet, for all of that, Asarem remained convinced that when Shakaar's six-year term ended next year, he would seek reelection. Such was his sense of responsibility to the people of Bajor. And as much as she disagreed with some of his views, she would still support him. He was a vigorous, forthright man, dedicated and practical, open to the positions of others, and who had done much to push Bajor away from the painful past of the Occupation and into the promise of the future.

No, Asarem decided. *Shakaar is not surrendering. Just late.* She smiled, both at Sirsy and at herself. The first minister might not like his job, but she certainly loved hers. She had a talent for detecting the political maneuvering of others, but she also sometimes found herself chasing specters instead of substance. Like now.

"All right," she told Sirsy. Feeling suddenly matronly, standing with her hands on her hips like a mother questioning a child, she dropped her arms to her sides. "I'll check my schedule and see when we can set up a new meeting."

"Thank you, Minister." The young woman turned to go, but Asarem stopped her.

"Just a moment, Sirsy." She moved around the door and collected her helmet and racquet from the storage area. She closed the compartment—the hinges creaked again—then left the court, pulling the door shut behind her. Sirsy stepped back to let her out. "Does the first minister have any other commitments this morning?" Asarem asked. She did not want to have to postpone this meeting. She began walking down the corridor, and Sirsy fell in step beside her.

"Um, not this morning," Sirsy answered, looking up toward the ceiling, as though she might see Shakaar's schedule printed there. "He has two appointments early this afternoon." Sirsy's heels clacked along the stone tiles of the corridor; Asarem's rubber-soled shoes made barely any noise at all. "But I know that the first minister has several tasks he wanted to complete this morning."

"What about at the top of the hour?" Asarem asked. "After our springball game would have ended? Is he available then?"

"I'm not sure," Sirsy said. "I'd have to check with the first minister."

They reached the far end of the corridor, and Asarem stopped beside the door to the changing room. "Please do," she said. "I'll be at his office in three-quarters of an hour. I'm hopeful that he will be able to see me then."

"Yes, Minister."

"Thank you, Sirsy," she said, and headed into the changing room.

Asarem made it to the first minister's office in half the time she had estimated it would take her. She rushed through a shower, tied her shoulder-length, dark brown hair back behind her head, and changed into a simple brown shift and a rust-colored macramé overshirt, rather than the more formal suit she had intended to wear. With the situation with the Federation approaching a resolution of some kind, she was eager for an update from the first minister, and anxious to review their preparations for the imminent arrival of the Starfleet admiral.

Sirsy greeted her with a smile in the anteroom to Shakaar's office. The room, narrow but long, divided itself by function into two areas. Near the outer door, half a dozen chairs sat arrayed around a low, round table, interspersed with a couple of end tables equipped with companels. Further into the room, beyond the waiting area, Sirsy's large desk stretched in a wide arc beside the entrance to the first minister's office. Behind the desk, in the left-hand wall, stood a closed door that Asarem had always assumed led to a storage and supply area.

Though not brightly lighted, the entire place was warmly decorated, a reflection, Asarem thought, more of the assistant than of the first minister. Colorful impressionist paintings adorned the walls at comfortable intervals, complemented by the muted hues of various flowers sprinkled in vases throughout the room. A neutral carpet tied all the furnishings together, and a light fragrance, distinctly floral but not cloying, dressed the air.

Sirsy emerged from behind her desk, clearly pleased to be able to report to Asarem that the first minister could indeed meet with her. The young woman—

Sirsy must be nearing thirty, Asarem thought, at least a dozen years her junior—ushered her to the entrance to the inner office. Sirsy tapped on the door with her knuckles, then opened it and leaned in. "Minister Asarem is here, sir." She stepped aside to allow Asarem to pass.

Shakaar's austere office sprawled in marked contrast to the anteroom. The bare walls spread in arcs away from the doorway, curving outward until they met the back wall. The bare stone floor, though beautiful, lent the room a hard appearance, and the few pieces of furniture—a sofa and a couple of matching chairs around a low, circular table, and another small table and companel off to one side—did nothing to dispel that impression.

In the wall across from the door, several tall, wide windows marched from one end to the other, interrupted only by another doorway on the left side, this one leading to a balcony hanging from the back of the building. Usually, the windows and doorway provided the room's only vibrancy, Asarem thought, allowing the lush green landscape stretching beyond the city to adorn the room, like natural artwork borrowed from the countryside. In the springtime, she knew, a few months from now, an explosion of floral growth would dapple the vista with color, further enhancing the otherwise pallid room. Today, though, the windows and doors were shuttered against the cool, murky weather, further contributing to the room's severity.

Shakaar rose from the far chair, in the same motion deactivating a personal-access display device and sliding it onto the table before him. "Wadeen," he said, not with the amiability of friendship, but the familiarity of their professional relationship. He crossed toward her, and she moved into the room to meet him. Behind Asarem, the door to the anteroom clicked closed.

"Edon," she said. He took her left hand in both of his, his left thumb wrapping around hers. He smiled, but the expression seemed flat to her, forced onto his face by courtesy, she thought.

"Thank you for coming," he said. "I'm sorry for missing our game." Asarem bowed her head, closing her eyes briefly, to indicate her acceptance of his apology. He released her hand and motioned toward the sitting area. "Please." She passed him and sat down in the near chair; he returned to the chair in which he had been sitting, across the table from her.

"Thank you for seeing me," she said. "Have you heard from the admiral?"

"Yes, I have," Shakaar said. The smile had gone from his face now, she saw, and he seemed distracted. The inconstant glow of an oil lamp wavered over his features. Two large skylights, along with the windows and door to the balcony, usually afforded the room ample illumination, Asarem knew, but with the shutters in place and the cloud cover overhead, several lamps had been lighted instead. One stood in the center of the table between them, its flame flickering within its translucent chimney. "Admiral Akaar contacted me earlier," Shakaar continued. "He's arrived at Deep Space 9, and he'll be coming to Bajor to-morrow."

Asarem felt a surge of excitement. "That's wonderful news," she said. "The Federation must be closer than we thought to making a decision."

"Even closer than that," Shakaar offered. "Federation Councillor zh'Thane will be joining the admiral on his visit."

Asarem frowned. For a moment, she had the sense that they—the Bajoran government in general, and she and the first minister in particular—had all at once lost any control of the situation, that events were suddenly proceeding faster than they would be able to effectively deal with them. But then her self-confidence and her knowledge of their careful preparations for this entire process asserted themselves, and she recognized the impending sojourn on Bajor of the admiral and the councillor for what it was: an opportunity. "I had wanted to review our arrangements for the admiral's visit," she said, "but I guess we need to discuss more than that now."

"Yes," Shakaar agreed in an offhand way, his preoccupation evident. He stood and paced across the room, from light to shadow to light again, moving from the reach of one oil lamp to another. That side of the room was virtually empty. Asarem had wondered during her earliest trips here how the first minister could possibly function in his position without a desk in his office, but here was the answer. Shakaar had spent most of his lifetime living under Cardassian rule, and a lot of that time leading a guerrilla war against Bajor's oppressors. For decades, he had been ever on the move, running from place to place, his eyes steadfastly on the ultimate prize: the unshackling of his people. And this office reflected all of that, she had long ago realized: the almost hostile feel of a room with few places to work or rest; the lack of any explicit indication that this space belonged to Shakaar, and he to it; and, when the windows stood open, the distant view of Bajor's freedom and beauty, beyond immediate reach.

The first minister walked back over to the sitting area. "Yes," he said, "we have much to discuss." For the first time, Asarem noticed his casual dress, a basic gray tunic atop workman's pants, a look very different from the professional one he had cultivated in recent years. He bent and scooped the padd from the table.

"What is it, Minister?" Asarem asked. A flow of air from a heat register in the floor circulated past her.

Shakaar punched a control on the padd and it activated with a tone. He worked its controls and examined the display. Without taking his eyes from it, he said, "The Chamber of Ministers received a message this morning from the Cardassians."

Cardassians. The word brought Asarem up short, and she thought she understood Shakaar's remoteness, and even his missing their springball game. Almost eight years after their withdrawal from Bajor, the Cardassians remained a troublesome topic with which to deal. "Which Cardassians?" she asked. "What did they want? More aid, I presume."

Shakaar looked up at Asarem. "Their provisional government has—"

Asarem made a noise, not exactly a laugh, but a quick exhalation of breath, loud enough to stop the first minister in mid-sentence. "Forgive me, Minister," she said. "The irony of the Cardassians having a 'provisional' government is still . . . I'm sorry. After all that's happened, the Occupation, the Dominion

War ... Bajor sending medicine and foodstuffs to the Cardassians, coordinating additional aid to them ... after all this time, it's still hard to grasp it all."

"I know," he agreed. He looked back down at the padd. Asarem thought to say more, but there was too much—too many feelings, too many words. Her own emotions ranged from hatred to pity, from fear and anger to compassion and forgiveness. And her political stands ... well, they had changed through the years, and were perhaps still changing. "The communication came directly from Alon Ghemor, the legate heading their government." Shakaar paused, and Asarem could not tell whether the first minister hesitated because he thought the information he wanted to impart would be difficult for him to say, or for her to hear. She considered urging him on, but chose instead to wait. He stepped around the table and sat back down in the chair, reaching forward and letting go of the padd. The device clattered onto the tabletop. "Ghemor's message talked about Bajoran aid to Cardassia, and about the relationship between our two worlds," he finally continued. "Essentially, he's making noises, signaling his intent. Ghemor hasn't done so yet, but I think soon he's going to ask for normalized diplomatic relations between Bajor and Cardassia."

Asarem felt her jaw drop. For this possibility to arise now, during what she hoped would be the final negotiations with the Federation, would no doubt complicate matters. But whether now or later, when the Cardassians eventually did request normalized relations ... differing opinions would divide Bajorans, in the Chamber of Ministers, in the Vedek Assembly, and in everyday society. Shakaar would have to define his stance, as would she, and then lead the people down the proper path.

"I'm going to call the Chamber of Ministers into session this afternoon," Shakaar said, "just to feel everybody out." He leaned forward, his face aglow with the light from the oil lamp on the table. She could see the flame fluttering in his eyes. "Wadeen," he said, "what do you think?"

Asarem wanted to know that herself. It required no effort to recall the brutality with which the Cardassians had occupied Bajor for more than four decades, to conjure the horrors routinely visited upon those innocents interned at places such as Gallitep, and then to deny even the possibility that there could ever be normal relations between the two peoples. But it was also easy to recall that the Cardassians had risen up against the powerful Dominion at the end of the war, and to dwell on the incomprehensible fact that eight hundred million of them had then been put to death—executed, *murdered*. Asarem thought of all the Bajoran children orphaned during the Occupation—she had lost both parents herself, as well as her only sister—and then of all the Cardassian children orphaned during the war. Somehow, every opinion about relations between Bajor and Cardassia seemed right and wrong at the same time.

"I think," she said, and stopped, still struggling to organize her many disparate thoughts and emotions, still searching for the words with which to express them. "I think," she finally went on, "that this is an opportunity for the people of Bajor to demonstrate their strength."

4

Vaughn leaned against the wall just inside the doorway, peering through the dimness. In the corner nearest him, light emanated from a display panel, though it did not penetrate very far into *Defiant*'s simulated night. It illuminated the figure on the biobed, and spilled in patches onto the decking on either side. The quiet, almost haunting sounds of diagnostic tools trickled through the room and failed to fill it, like the distant strains of a musical instrument.

A shape passed between Vaughn and the display, briefly obscuring its light. Vaughn's gaze followed the form: Dr. Bashir walked slowly along the length of the bed, checking the readouts, measuring his patient's condition, making notations on a padd. After a few moments, the doctor reached up and touched a control, and the display above the bed went dark. The bed and its occupant vanished like the finale of a magic trick. The only light in the room now came from off to Vaughn's left, where the only other person in the room, a nurse, sat working at a console; she had evidently muted the controls she worked, because all he could hear were the dull taps of her fingertips on the touchpads.

Vaughn straightened, pulling his shoulder away from the bulkhead, knowing the doctor would approach him now. That was the way of doctors, following their training not only to treat their patients, but to manage their patients' family members and friends. Bashir would tell him to return to his quarters, to get some sleep, that there was nothing he could do for Prynn here. And Vaughn would make the noises expected of him, would resist the suggestions and then relent, promising to leave in just a few minutes; he would say just enough to placate the doctor and send him on his way.

"Sir," Bashir said, speaking in a hushed manner that matched the still, dark medical bay.

"Doctor."

"She's resting comfortably," Bashir said, not waiting to be asked. "I've given her a mild sedative to help her sleep, but she won't even need that in a couple of days." The doctor turned his head and looked in Prynn's direction. "The skin grafts are doing very well, and her internal organs . . ." His voice trailed off, and he turned back to Vaughn before continuing. "Well, she was very lucky."

Vaughn knew that. The blast that had sent Prynn flying unconscious across the bridge—that he thought had killed her—had done damage within and without her abdominal cavity, but the injuries to her viscera had been such that the doctor had been able to repair them with relative ease. The greatest danger to her had been in the first moments after the explosion, when she had come perilously close to losing so much blood that the extent of her other injuries would not have mattered. Had Dr. Bashir not been on the bridge, had he not so quickly transported Prynn to the medical bay . . .

Vaughn allowed the thought to die before completing it. He had already lived through the experience of believing his daughter dead; he did not need to revisit those emotions. "What's the prognosis for her recovery?"

"Oh, she'll be up and about in a few days," Bashir said. "Perhaps even by the time we get back to Deep Space 9." The repaired *Defiant,* having eluded the Jarada yesterday, had rejoined the convoy and resumed escorting it to Bajor. Still employing the cloak in the unlikely event that they encountered the Jarada again, the ship traveled at low warp, matching velocities with the slowest vessels in the procession. Consequently, it would be several days before *Defiant* arrived back at the station. "She'll probably be able to return to light duty in about two weeks, maybe sooner," the doctor went on. "Full duty about a week after that." Vaughn looked toward the corner of the room where Prynn lay sleeping. "And what about you?" Bashir asked. "How are you feeling?"

Though the doctor's voice carried no particular inflection, Vaughn interpreted the question as a reference to his emotional state: *How are you feeling about having watched your daughter almost die? How are you coping with having issued the orders that mangled her body and nearly took her life?* When he turned back to Bashir, though, he saw the doctor looking down at the gauzelike coverings wrapping Vaughn's wounded limbs. One soft casing protected his left arm from elbow to fingertips, and the other, his right hand. His burns had not been as severe as Prynn's, nor had they required grafts, but the dermal regenerations would take another day or two to complete.

"I'm tired," Vaughn said. "But I'm all right. I assume I'm healing under here." He raised his arms to indicate the dressings.

"That's what Nurse Richter tells me," Bashir said, tilting his head toward the woman working off to Vaughn's left. Earlier, the zaftig ensign, newly assigned to *Defiant* from the station's infirmary, had examined Vaughn and proclaimed his recovery proceeding as expected.

"Thank you, Julian," he said.

"It's my job," Bashir said, and then seemed to reconsider his response, because he added, "You're welcome, sir." Then, apparently out of things to say, he added, "Well. Have a good night, then."

"Rest well, Doctor," Vaughn said.

He watched Bashir walk over to the nurse and, when she looked up from her console, hand her the padd he had been using. The doctor asked her to monitor certain readings of their lone patient, and she took more than a cursory glance at the data she had been given. After a few moments, evidently satisfied, she said, "Yes, sir."

Bashir departed through the door opposite Vaughn, leaving him mildly surprised at not having been encouraged to vacate the medical bay himself. Delighted to have been wrong, he felt one side of his mouth curl upward slightly. He found people whose behavior he could not always predict interesting, primarily because he encountered so few of them. To this point in his tenure aboard DS9, Vaughn had not been particularly intrigued by Bashir— the man's actions had so far been eminently foreseeable, no matter his genetic enhancements—though he did like the doctor, whose keen intellect seemed matched by an intense sense of compassion.

With Bashir gone and the nurse busy, Vaughn paced over and stood beside Prynn's bed. Her form, her features, remained indistinct in the darkened room, but he didn't need light and eyesight to see his daughter. As he peered down at where he knew she lay, her image rose easily in his mind. Small sounds spread from around her like audible shadows, hints of the objects that cast them. The tiny electronic hum of a medical device buzzed near the center of the bed, knitting together flesh. Farther up, above her, the low, almost inaudible beat of the diagnostic display marched in time with a small blinking indicator, both signaling the panel's quiet mode. And at the head of the bed, Prynn's breathing, hard but even, confirmed her continuing life.

Vaughn closed his eyes and issued a long sigh, an expression of exhaustion and relief, he knew, but only *some* relief. From the moment he had seen—had thought he had seen—Prynn die, tension and fear, anguish and guilt, had cleaved to him, even through the revelation of her survival. His daughter had endured, yes, but if nothing else, the century of his life had brought him the sure knowledge that all existence fades, fragile as a leaf in winter. Whether Prynn eventually fell to earth first or he did, he felt he could no longer cling to a life that did not include her.

And yet he also knew that it might be beyond his ability—perhaps now more than ever—to change their circumstances. His previous efforts to reconcile with his daughter—he had made several attempts through the years—had all been vigorously rebuffed. Just a few weeks ago, after the surprise of finding himself assigned to the same post as Prynn had waned, he had asked her to have dinner with him; she had told him to go to hell. Now, with his orders not to return fire against the Jarada having contributed substantially to her injuries, his chances with her had likely worsened.

Strange, he thought, *the way things sometimes work out.* After living a turbulent life for so many years, Vaughn had recently dispatched many of the burdens of his decades of work, had seen into himself and then chosen to look back out in a new direction. He had wrestled a lifetime of difficult, sometimes painful duty, and won himself a reprieve. He had arrived at Deep Space 9 almost a new man, intent on finding his way to a life lived for simple joys, and not just for professional obligation. And when he had done that, he had found Prynn again. But she had still not found him.

If only it had been the work, he thought. If he had neglected his daughter in favor of his career, he could, even at this late date, atone for it. But his work had not been the problem; the problem had been what he had done.

The enormity of what Vaughn had brought down on Prynn seven years ago had never left him—and never could—and now he had compounded her pain and, consequently, his own. He leaned forward in the darkened medical bay, straining to see her face, but he could only discern the vague shape of its outline. He reached up, his wrapped right hand extending to where her arm would be. He wanted—he needed—some contact with his daughter, but before his hand reached her, he stopped and pulled back. For what seemed like a long time, Vaughn stood there, both maintaining a vigil and struggling for hope.

At last, he stepped away from the bed and walked over to where the nurse had continued working. She looked up at his approach, and as he had when she had examined him earlier, he noticed her eyes; a distinctive blue-green, they stood out, complementing her pale complexion and her reddish blond hair, which she wore in plaits that joined behind her head.

"Nurse," he asked, "do you know what Ensign Tenmei will be able to remember?"

"About the accident, you mean?" Richter asked, and Vaughn nodded. "Probably nothing at all. When she was awake earlier, she didn't know why she was in the medical bay. It's possible she might eventually recall being on the bridge, but the accident . . ." The nurse shook her head from side to side.

Prynn had spent most of yesterday unconscious, initially as a result of her injuries, and later, owing to the anesthesia administered prior to surgery. She had awoken a few times today, and though extremely tired, she had been coherent. Vaughn had been visiting the medical bay during one of her periods of wakefulness, and he had gone to her bedside. When their eyes had met, she had offered a wan smile, but Vaughn had known better than to take such an event to heart. He had simply been happy that Prynn was alive and would recover without any problems—at least, without any *physical* problems. He hoped that the most significant damage she had suffered had been to her body, because flesh often healed more quickly than the heart or the mind.

"Thank you," Vaughn told the nurse. He walked to one of the room's two exits, the doors sliding open before him. He stopped and looked once more toward Prynn, then continued out into the corridor. The shadowy ship seemed empty. Most of the crew would be asleep, he knew, with only a skeleton staff on the bridge and in engineering.

As Vaughn headed for his cabin, he knew that he would have to determine a new course of action, that he would have to figure out what to do, for himself and for Prynn. He understood that it would not be easy, and on top of that, that despite whatever efforts he ended up making, he might not be able to bring about the resolution he so desperately sought with his daughter.

Only one mission in his life had been more important. And more difficult.

5

The rain fell cold and hard. Kira reached the boulder at a dead run and threw herself down behind it. Her hands pushed into the sodden ground as she landed, mud oozing up wetly between her fingers and engulfing them. She rolled quickly onto her side and pulled her hands free, then regained her feet and crouched behind the great rock.

Why did I agree to this? she asked herself, not for the first time. She hated the holosuites. Seeking a setting in which to meditate was one thing, but this was another. Simulation or no, she was miserable. The temperature must have dropped fifteen degrees during her descent from the top of the ravine, low enough now that her breath emerged into the air in a white plume. Her uniform, soaked through two hours ago, added at least ten kilos to her frame. And the rain, misty and relatively warm at first, now plummeted down as though it had been hurled at the ground, as though the fat drops were themselves weapons in this battle.

Kira paused, catching her breath after her last dash. Around her, the unrelenting rain struck the saturated earth with a sound strangely reminiscent of applause. *I ought to take a bow and end this right now,* she thought. The holosuite safety protocols ensured that she would not suffer serious injury during the course of the program, she knew, but nothing prevented her from being wretchedly uncomfortable.

Lightning flashed overhead, illuminating the scene with an uncanny clarity, and lending everything an eerie, bluish white cast. Kira waited for the darkness to reassert itself, then bent low and peered out from around the boulder. It could almost have been night, so dense was the cloud cover. Thunder boomed, closer now than it had been, reminding her of the ever-encroaching sounds of warfare during the Occupation: grenades, mortar fire, bombs. Fresh and vibrant even eight years after the Cardassians had been driven from Bajor, the memories felt more unpleasant than the weather.

The ridge where Kira squatted clung to the side of the ravine five meters above its floor. Across from her and down, she could make out the shapes that marked her destination: a copse surrounding a small structure of some sort. "They hide within the canyon," Taran'atar had told her before the simulation had begun. "And they watch for pursuers."

Kira waited for the lightning to aid her reconnaissance. With each series of flashes, she focused on a different section of the ravine floor. Up and down the canyon, she saw nothing: no beings, no vehicles, no animals, and no visible traps. *Or maybe the whole area is a trap,* she thought. As inhospitable as the weather had been, the geography had proven even more difficult: the canyon walls fell steeply; the mud, as well as loose stone and shale, made footing precarious; and no obvious routes—either naturally formed or created by wear— had revealed themselves beneath Kira's scrutiny. She considered herself fortunate to have made it this far without incident.

She flexed her fingers, washing the mud from them in the rain. Lightning once more brought the scene into stark view. The stand of trees might be concealing something or someone, Kira thought, but the structure seemed the more likely hiding place, especially given the conditions. She wished she had a tricorder or a phaser with her—either would have allowed her to gather more information, and provided her with additional options—but she had agreed to Taran'atar's suggestion that she equip herself with only a knife.

"You are dead," the Jem'Hadar had intoned as they had entered the holosuite, his manner even more solemn than usual. "Go into battle to reclaim your life." It had always seemed such an alien philosophy to Kira. Even though she had often fought to save lives—her own and others'—it felt qualitatively different for her to act on the assertion that her life had already been lost. The simple shift of perspective required more of a commitment to the possibility of dying in battle than she believed healthy. For the right reasons, and there were many of them, Kira would willingly risk her life—and had done so on numerous occasions. But her instincts would always be to keep herself alive, not to recapture her existence from the clutches of death.

"Victory is life," she said aloud now, echoing the Jem'Hadar mantra. Her breath puffed out before her, and she thought, *Right now, I'd settle for "Victory is warmth."* Her joints had begun to ache, an effect of the chill and the damp.

Kira studied the structure as best she could from her present vantage. Small and constructed of stone, with a relatively flat, empty roof, the building projected an odd quality. No more than three meters tall, and just as wide and long, it featured neither doors nor windows, though a meter-square opening stood in the center of the wall facing her.

Easily defended from within, Kira thought. Anybody inside would be able to guard the entrance with a single weapon. Despite that particular advantage, such a design might still be characterized as strange. It was something else, though, that tugged at Kira's sensibilities: the roof. If it was actually made of stone, how could a flat roof support itself? And if the structure contained materials other than stone, then all was not as it appeared, and that meant there might be subterfuge at work here.

Kira wiped the rain from her face and shielded her eyes with her hand. She needed to find a course down to the structure, one that would allow her a rapid approach. As she scanned the ravine, though, another sound gradually distinguished itself from that of the rainfall. A great rushing sound, like the rain but more intense, identified the source of the noise even before Kira located it. Crawling forward and leaning out past the edge of the ridge, she spotted an overflowing stream coursing below, between herself and the structure. The ridge must have blocked it from view during her descent.

Lying flat on the ground, Kira waited for the lightning to detail the stream for her. At its narrowest, she saw, the water looked to be only five meters across, but it flowed swiftly. Depending on its depth, she might not be able to ford the stream without being dragged from her feet, possibly even swept away. She considered traveling upstream or down in search of a narrower place to cross, but even had finding one seemed likely, she had no desire to prolong this experience. For Taran'atar's sake, Kira did not wish to quit the simulation, but neither did she feel compelled to treat the success of this virtual mission as she would have a real one.

And even if she had wanted to invest as much effort as she could in this endeavor, she simply did not possess enough information to be able to do so. Taran'atar had presented her with a vague goal—capture a Rintannan, whoever that was—amid a few sketchy parameters: the need for stealth while descending into the canyon, his desire that she arm herself with nothing more than a knife. Kira would never have undertaken an actual mission like this without more data, including, most important, the *reason* for it. But when she had begun to ask questions, Taran'atar had either not wanted or not been able to supply her with answers. Instead, he had recommended that she treat the task as he always treated his: as duties divinely charged to him. Kira had not protested that the Prophets did not hand out assignments like military leaders, nor did she mention how unbefitting gods she found such behavior. Since she would be doing this for Taran'atar anyway, she had agreed to his conditions.

Seeing no ready path down to the ravine floor from her current viewpoint, Kira withdrew on her belly from the edge of the ridge, propelling herself backward with her forearms. Once back behind the boulder, she rose to her haunches again. She glanced down at herself and saw only a few small patches of orange where her uniform had not been covered or discolored by the dark mud of this place. Her boots were caked.

Kira waited for the lightning, then shifted her position to the other side of the boulder. Again, she peered out in search of a route from her location down to the structure. As she did so, she wondered what planet this was—*Rintanna, perhaps?*—and who lived here, and how and why Taran'atar knew of it. Had the Founders instructed him and his fellow soldiers to conquer this world, or had he come here as part of his own training? Was it a place in the Gamma Quadrant, or an environment entirely of Taran'atar's own creation? *No,* she thought then. *Not something he invented.* While he had clearly demonstrated a remarkable capacity to encode holoprograms from memory—she remembered watching him battle the eight-legged monstrosity he had called the Comes-in-the-night-kills-many—Taran'atar had shown no indication at all of having an imagination.

It took another twenty minutes, but Kira finally identified a path for the final leg of her descent. The additional time actually benefited her, because the rain eased, the lightning became less frequent, and the already dark afternoon began transforming into night. With a bit of luck, she would be able to approach the structure in stages, moving in the darkness from one point of concealment to another. She waited again for the lightning, taking a last opportunity to imprint her planned route into memory.

Then she moved.

Seven strides back along the ridge, she raced with one hand out in front of herself and the other to her side, using the feel of the foliage as an additional guide to her recall. Her hand raked through small, wet leaves, sending a spray of water up along her arm, and sounding, she hoped, like wind among the plants.

With her seventh step, just where she expected, there came a break in the bushes. Kira turned abruptly and felt for the slope with her foot. Finding purchase, she followed with her other foot and stepped sideways down the incline. Twice, she had to jog around larger bushes, and her footing continually threatened to give way, but she managed to reach the ravine floor before the lightning flared again.

Kira could hear the stream speeding loudly past her now, just a few paces away. She turned to her right, perpendicular to the source of the sound, and walked forward until her hands found an outcropping she had spied from above. She dropped to her knees behind the rock, removing herself once more from the potential view of anybody who might be looking out from the structure, or even from the copse, for intruders.

It took almost three minutes before lightning struck again, but Kira was prepared for it. As soon as the flash faded, she dashed out from behind the outcropping, turned toward the stream, and ran forward. At the point she judged to be at the edge of the rushing water, she leaped. As cold as the weather had been, the water seemed colder still. Iciness clutched at Kira's flesh through her already drenched uniform, but fortunately the stream came up only as high as the tops of her calves, allowing her to maintain a long stride. On the fourth step, though, her foot plunged into a depression, the water reaching up to her waist. She attempted to pull her other leg forward, to sustain her pace, and she might have made it had the current not been as strong. As she fell, she threw her weight forward as best she could. The frigidity of the stream shocked Kira physically. Her breath was forced from her lungs, and she gasped in a mouthful of dirty, gritty water.

Kira jerked her head backward, bringing her face clear of the stream. She felt the force of the current driving against the length of her body. Her feet came up off the streambed, and she began to be pushed along. Trying to breathe around gulps of water, she flailed with her arms, desperately searching for a handhold on something, anything, to prevent herself from being carried away. Her fingers closed familiarly around a fistful of watery earth, but the mud squeezed out from her hand and left her holding nothing. Kira reached with her other hand and felt the bristly texture of grass. She seized the stalks and pulled. The grass came free, but she moved forward enough to grab again, and this time, both hands found the grass. With all of her might, Kira hauled herself forward, her upper torso landing over her hands on the ground. She stopped for a moment, trying to bring a spate of coughing under control. Finally, she swung her legs up onto the bank and rolled away from the surging water.

Kira lay on her stomach for long minutes, her arms folded up beneath her chest, her forehead resting on the wet grass. The roar of the stream resounded as her breathing gradually returned to normal. A delicate mist tickled the back of her neck, but she couldn't tell whether it was the lighter rainfall or spray from the stream.

Kira pushed herself up onto her knees. She knew she had to find cover before the next stroke of lightning revealed her to whoever might be watching. She looked around, trying to establish her bearings. The location of the stream was obvious, and she had a rough idea of the direction of the structure, but it was no longer clear to her where she might conceal herself. She had seen several such places from atop the ridge, but she was no longer sure exactly where they were.

Gathering her strength, Kira rose and raced along the level ground. Lightning flared suddenly, revealing a large, tangled shape not far in front of her. She stumbled immediately to a halt, then groped in the ensuing darkness until she reached the gnarled form of the upended tree. She ducked behind the knotted, petrified roots, swinging her back to rest against them.

Next time, Kira thought, and then, *There won't be a next time.* Again, she considered putting an end to the simulation. She had seen it through this far, though, and so she might as well finish it.

This is what I get, she jokingly reproved herself, *for thinking about the feelings of a Jem'Hadar.*

Five days ago, Taran'atar had been discharged from the infirmary by Dr. Tarses, and he had come immediately to Kira's office. She looked across her desk at him and saw that, remarkably, the massive bruising on his face had already faded completely. Sustained by a Bajoran, such damage would have taken weeks to heal—if a Bajoran could have survived at all. According to Simon, Taran'atar's other, more serious injuries had mended, or continued to mend, at a similarly accelerated rate. *The Founders sure know how to build their soldiers,* she thought.

Standing before her desk in his usual black coverall, Taran'atar thanked her for expediting his release from "medical captivity," and informed her that he would be returning to "duty." Of course, beyond the few times he had participated in specific missions—the trip to Sindorin to apprehend Locken, the operation to evacuate Europa Nova—his self-determined duty of late consisted primarily of standing, unmoving and silent, beside the sensor maintenance station in ops. *To experience living among different lifeforms,* she supposed, as Odo had bade him, though she also guessed that Taran'atar standing at attention and observing people move about him had not been exactly what Odo had intended.

For their part, the crew had not yet grown entirely accustomed to the Jem'Hadar's presence, but they had at least become less suspicious of him, perhaps because he did little more than set himself in their midst, without generating any threat. Even now, as he talked with Kira, he simply stood across the desk from her, rigid and still. Kira had to admit, though, that even if she did not find him threatening, she did perceive that he was never distracted; he existed like an exposed nerve, she thought, ever prepared to react to the slightest stimulus. She would have offered him a chair, but she knew that he preferred to remain on his feet.

When Taran'atar finished speaking, which did not take long—the Founders had clearly not provided the Jem'Hadar with a prerogative for small talk—Kira inquired about any plans he might have beyond his return to duty. A precondition of the doctor releasing Taran'atar had been Kira's agreement that he would see no physically strenuous activity for another ten days. She hadn't expected any problem in fulfilling that promise, but besides his time in ops, Taran'atar also made occasional visits to the holosuites for the purpose of honing his already formidable combat skills. And after being bedridden for the longest period in his life, he wanted to do precisely that; he told Kira that he felt listless and unfit, and angry as well.

"Angry?" she asked.

"This isn't our way," he said. He gave no indication of what he meant by *this*, but it was obvious to her that he was speaking of the medical attention he had been paid during the past few days.

Kira pushed back in her chair and rose, her fingertips resting on the edge of her desk. "Surely the Jem'Hadar care for their own health," she said, actually curious about whether or not that happened to be true.

"We do," Taran'atar said, "but our health doesn't come from lying in a bed." His voice had declined to a deeper, harsher tone.

"Sometimes—" Kira started, and then stopped. She looked down, and the reflection of the computer display in the polished surface of her desk caught her eye. She stared at a green ellipse tracing its way through bright pinpoints—Commander Vaughn's proposed course for *Defiant*'s exploration of the Gamma Quadrant—and grasped her way through her thoughts. Her first reaction had been to argue Taran'atar's point, but she also wanted to understand his perspective. During the past few months, since she had taken charge of the station, Kira had attempted to be more receptive to points of view contrary to her own—first with the people under her command, and then with just about everybody with whom she came into contact. She still failed as often as she succeeded, she knew, but with Taran'atar, understanding sometimes came easily. He had been sent to Deep Space 9—exiled here was how she suspected he thought of it—and forced to live among people he did not comprehend, for a purpose he did not comprehend; for Kira, such circumstances were not entirely unrecognizable. And yet, if Taran'atar was going to live here, Kira hoped he would come to some greater understanding of the Bajoran people and the other inhabitants of the Alpha Quadrant; that had been Odo's hope as well.

"Sometimes," she finally said, looking back up at Taran'atar, "bed rest does bring health." She clamped her hands together in front of her in something of an apologetic gesture.

"Not for us," Taran'atar said. "Once our fitness for combat is sufficiently restored, a return to duty is required."

"Required by who?" Kira asked, but she already knew the answer: by the

Founders, and by the Vorta acting as their agents. But Taran'atar offered a different response.

"It is our nature," he said. Kira could not argue that; the Jem'Hadar had been genetically engineered, and were specifically bred, for warfare. "If necessary," he continued, "there can be an appropriate reduction in rank."

Kira glanced back down at her console as a notion occurred to her. She jabbed at the deactivation touchpad. The panel beeped and the screen went blank. Then she walked out from behind her desk. "Well, then," she said, smiling wryly, "I guess I'll just have to demote you to second." The Jem'Hadar used simple ordinal designations to signify position, she knew. Although she had never spoken about it with Taran'atar, she had always assumed that he had carried the rank of first, by virtue of his long life and his status as an Honored Elder among his people; he was twenty-two, ancient by Jem'Hadar standards.

Her remark about reducing his position had been intended as a joke, but Taran'atar did not smile, and Kira realized that she had never seen him do so. She wondered if he even possessed the capability; perhaps Jem'Hadar lacked the requisite musculature. She studied his features as she stood before him. The rough, pebbled texture of his hide, the bones protruding like horns from the center of his forehead and around the top of his head, and the smaller bones, almost like teeth, encircling his face, all composed a visage on which Kira could not even picture a smile. The thought saddened her in a profound way; even during the horrors of the Occupation, there had been sporadic laughter and humor and joy, slight victories in life, love, and friendship. For anybody, even a Jem'Hadar soldier, not to experience any of that during their lifetime . . .

When Taran'atar said nothing, Kira chose to return to the initial subject of their conversation: she would not permit him to engage in a holosuite combat program for the next ten days.

"I am sufficiently healed," he protested.

"Sufficiently, perhaps," she said. "But Dr. Tarses thinks there's a greater chance of you getting injured now than there would be if you waited another week." Kira decided as she spoke to trim the ten days down to seven, a compromise between the doctor and the soldier.

"I am a Jem'Hadar," Taran'atar said. "I am meant to battle. When there is no battle, I must prepare for the next one."

As Kira looked at Taran'atar, she experienced something that surprised her: she felt sorry for him. Although he had been on the station for a while now, it seemed clear that he was still out of place here. Kira wondered how she would feel if she were forced to live in an environment so alien to her, and further, how she would feel if she were not permitted to do the things that helped fulfill her needs. And then she realized that, because of the Attainder, she did know something about the latter.

At the same time, she would not jeopardize Taran'atar's health by allowing him to do battle—even simulated battle—before it was safe for him to do so. "You can run your holosuite programs as long as you only observe and don't participate," she said, attempting to find some middle ground. "Would that help you prepare for combat?" She moved back behind her desk and sat down.

"Mental preparation is vital," Taran'atar said, "but I have programs for that purpose."

"I'm sorry, then," Kira said. She tapped the resumption touchpad on her computer interface, intending the action as a signal that she considered the conversation at an end. The panel beeped, and the image of the green elliptic course, originating and terminating at the Gamma Quadrant terminus of the wormhole, blinked back onto the display.

Taran'atar did not move. Kira peered up at him. "Something else?" she asked.

"I would be interested in observing you in combat," he said.

"You mean Bajorans?"

"I mean you, specifically, Colonel," Taran'atar said. "I can create a new simulation for you."

Kira did not typically use the holosuites, preferring to engage not in virtual activities, but in real ones. In the past, she had occasionally been persuaded to accompany Jadzia, and she had gone to Vic's several times with Odo, but as a rule she stayed away. To Taran'atar, she said, "I don't think so."

He nodded, acknowledging her rejection, then turned and headed for the door.

"Wait," she called after him. Taran'atar stopped and turned back to face her. As she regarded him, she found that she really did empathize with him, since he was being denied the ability to practice some of the daily activities of his life. And she also realized something else: that Odo had sent Taran'atar here not just so that he could gain an understanding of life in the Alpha Quadrant, but also so that the people of Deep Space 9 could come to know him. Perhaps, Kira thought, she should make more of an effort to get to know this visitor to the station.

"What did you have in mind?" she asked.

Kira looked out between the twisted roots of the old tree. The rain had finally stopped, too late to make much difference to her, but the absence of lightning would allow her to approach her destination with less chance of being seen. Her eyes had attuned to the constant darkness now, and as she recovered from her experience in the stream, she scrutinized both the copse and the structure. As best she could tell, nothing moved in the trees, but she thought she saw a flicker of motion past the opening in the structure.

Kira turned and dropped onto the wet ground, leaning back against the contorted root system of the dead tree. She pored over her options. Given the paucity of information she had, her inclination would normally have been for further reconnaissance. In this instance, though, time played a role—she had already spent several hours here after her shift, and she had yet to have dinner—as did her preparation and equipment for the operation, both of which were noticeably lacking. As night arrived—or continued; the darkness of the storm effectively masked the time of day here—the temperature would drop even further. With no attractive alternatives, Kira decided that she needed to act sooner rather than later.

She reached down to her hip and unfastened the top of the sheath attached there. She grasped the haft of the knife Taran'atar had provided her and pulled the blade free. It fit her hand well, she noticed, something she had not bothered to test when she had strapped it on prior to the simulation. She made several different movements with it now—jabbing, slicing, throwing—then reversed it in her fist and drove it downward in a plunging motion. The contours of the handle rested snugly in her grip either way it was turned, and the balance of the blade made it feel less like something she was holding and more like an extension of her arm. Taran'atar had not merely provided her with a knife for this mission, she realized; he had designed and fashioned a personal weapon especially for her.

Kira pushed away from the roots of the tree and rose back up into a crouch. She turned and peered again at the structure. She put it at forty to fifty meters away, over even ground, though there looked to be a slight rise leading up to it. Several bushes and large rocks and another dead tree lay strewn about the landscape, but Kira mapped out a relatively direct route to the structure.

"Victory is life," she whispered again, and jumped up. She ran into the open and forward, taking long strides in an effort to reduce her number of steps, and thus diminish the possibility of tripping on something unseen on the ground. She maneuvered around a couple of bushes and a cluster of large rocks, then leaped over the other fallen tree. The cold air inflamed her throat, each breath feeling as though she had inhaled a mouthful of gravel.

Kira skirted another bush, and her foot came down hard on the edge of a rock. Her ankle twisted beneath her, and she allowed her body to fall in that direction. She bent at the knees and threw her arms wide, instinctively shifting her weight to avoid sprawling. Somehow, she managed to retain her equilibrium. She looked up to regain her bearings and saw that the structure sat only fifteen meters away.

A few steps farther along, Kira strode upward as well as forward, anticipating the slope she had spied earlier. Her foot came down solidly on the incline, allowing her to maintain her gait. She raced ahead, her eyes squinting to make out the opening in the wall of the structure.

The ground leveled off again, and Kira changed her course slightly, adjusting her heading for the center of the opening. Two steps from the structure, she lunged downward, her hands coming up in front of her like those of a diver about to enter the water. With her final step, she drove her foot hard into the ground and thrust her body through the opening, spinning around onto her back as she did so.

Kira recognized the feel of damp earth below her as she landed inside the structure and skidded toward the far wall. Even before she stopped sliding along, her hand came up with the knife, prepared to defend herself at close range or to throw it. Her head turned to the left as she scanned that side of the structure, then to the right as she searched the other side. The darkness made it difficult to see much, but Kira perceived no forms and no movement inside.

Whirling around on her backside, she pumped her legs into the ground and pushed herself into one of the corners adjacent to the opening. If anybody attempted to follow her inside, she would be able to defend the entrance from there. Her arm remained poised above her shoulder, ready to strike with the knife as necessary.

Nothing happened.

Kira regulated her breathing, bringing it under control after her sprint into the structure. She continued scanning her surroundings, squinting in the darkness and listening for any sound, trying to be sure she did not miss anything. She kept her arm raised and the knife at the ready.

Still nothing.

She considered the trees outside once more, and the potential for somebody to conceal themselves within the copse. She breathed in deeply and let out a long sigh. She was cold and achy and hungry, and maybe it was about time that she—

Something shifted behind her. Kira felt it at her elbow, the slightest movement, but she was certain she had not imagined it. She leaned forward, away from the walls, preparing to spring ahead, turn, and deal with whatever she found. Kira tensed, about to move, when something above seized her attention. She looked up to see a patch of clouds scudding across the night sky overhead, and her mind had just enough time to process the incongruity before the shadows descended on her.

All at once, Kira was surrounded and covered, dozens of amorphous shapes pushing in on her. Something slid painfully around the fingers of her hand, and she felt the knife slip from her grasp. She tried to bring her hands down to her sides so that she could push herself up off the ground and toward the opening, but something blocked her arms. Suddenly, something cylindrical slithered around her neck and began to tighten, like a large snake constricting its prey. Kira flailed wildly. Two or three of the shapes fell away, but too many remained. She forced her arms down enough so that she could claw at the slimy shape around her neck, but the pressure on her windpipe increased. Quickly, it became difficult to breathe.

"Computer," came a voice, "freeze program." Around Kira, all motion stopped, and the shape around her neck eased its grip. "Increase light to daytime level," the voice said. Kira closed her eyes as the light came up, letting her dilated pupils contract. After a few moments, she opened her eyes. Taran'atar stood just beyond her feet, gazing down at her. "You have failed to reclaim your life," he said.

With a measure of frustration, Kira reached up and pulled the shape from around her neck. The structure no longer existed around her, she saw; the trees were visible behind Taran'atar, and above, the sky. She looked down and saw a mass of nebulous forms she could not immediately distinguish, because their coloring so perfectly matched the dark brown of the earthen floor. As she studied the scene, though, she picked out the individual figures of at least a score of creatures, and she could see that there were many times that number all around. They resembled jellyfish, but with more substance to them; long, thick tendrils extended from flattened spheroid bodies. Kira pushed and pulled the creatures from atop her and rose to her feet. "I assume these are the Rintanna," she said.

"Yes," Taran'atar confirmed. "They are communal chameleons, often working together to capture or ward off foes."

"There was no structure," Kira said, chagrined. She had been correct about the oddity of the flat roof; it must have been composed of numerous Rintanna clinging to each other. To Taran'atar's credit, his expression remained neutral and he said nothing more, neither gloating at Kira's defeat nor patronizing her with any suggestion that she had done well. "They must be very strong," she said.

"Yes."

Kira looked down at the creatures, then bent and lifted one from the ground. It weighed less than she had expected—with several of them on top of her, they had seemed heavier—and its flesh had an elastic quality about it. She handed the creature to Taran'atar, who did not reach out to take it from her. "Here," she said, shaking the Rintannan. Taran'atar plucked the creature from Kira's hands, a quizzical look appearing on his features. "I captured a Rintannan for you." She turned and stepped over the creatures, finding small patches of ground where she could place her feet, finally clearing the area back into open ground.

"No," Taran'atar said. "You did not."

Kira peered out over the landscape, back over the area she had traveled. Even in daylight, the terrain looked difficult to navigate. Her gaze followed from where she stood—she could see the tracks her boots had left in the wet ground as she had run up to the "structure"—back to the downed tree she had hidden behind, and then to the overflowing stream; even frozen in the holosuite matrix, the foamy, choppy water appeared treacherous. Above the stream perched the ridge, and towering up behind it, the steep canyon wall down which she had descended.

"I'm reclaiming my life right now," she called back over her shoulder. When Taran'atar did not respond, she turned to face him. He no longer held the Rintannan. "Not bad," she said, pointing with her thumb back the way she had come. "Just a few hours to reach here, with no tools, and no data about the area or the aliens."

"You failed to attain your objective," Taran'atar said quietly. "Your life would not have been reclaimed."

Kira stepped forward. "Maybe if I'd had more information—or *any* information—about where I was going, or what I'd be facing, or if I'd had even a tricorder with me—"

"Not all missions are carried out under optimal conditions," he said.

"Optimal——?" Kira said, incredulous. She was not angry, but she felt that she had been given a goal virtually impossible to achieve, hamstrung by having neither enough information nor the necessary tools to accomplish the imprecise task set her. "Who would go on a mission without knowing something about what they were doing, or where they were going, or why they were doing it?" As quickly as the words had left her mouth, though, she knew the answer: Jem'Hadar would go into any battle, under any circumstances, if the Founders told them to do so. *And what would I do,* Kira wondered, *if the Prophets appeared and wanted me to embark on some unexplained mission?* She knew the answer to that too.

"I'm just frustrated; it's been an uncomfortable couple of hours," Kira explained, grateful that Taran'atar had not responded to her outburst. "You know, there's more to see on Deep Space 9 than ops and the holosuites. Maybe you should visit some other——"

A voice emerged from the comm system, interrupting her. *"Ops to Colonel Kira."* She recognized the voice as that of Ensign Selzner.

"This is Kira," she said, looking up out of habit. "Go ahead."

"Colonel, we just received word from Commander Vaughn," Selzner announced. *"The convoy has returned from Torona IV."*

"Is the commander back aboard DS9 yet?" Kira asked. *Defiant* had been gone for a week on its mission to retrieve the Europani refugees from Torona IV, during which time Vaughn and his crew had run into difficulties with the Jarada. The commander had sent an encoded message to Kira briefly describing the trouble, and now she wanted a detailed report. The crew had suffered three casualties, she knew, one of them serious, though fortunately none had died.

"No, sir," Selzner replied. *"Commander Vaughn reports that the* Defiant *and the* Trager *will be back at the station in about an hour."*

"The *Trager?*" Kira repeated, looking over at Taran'atar. He met her gaze with an expression of suspicion, which she knew must have matched the look on her own face. She was unsure why the Cardassian warship would be accompanying *Defiant* to Deep Space 9, though it seemed clear that it must have aided in the mission to Torona IV. The commander of *Trager,* Gul Macet, had offered and then provided similar assistance during the evacuation of Europa Nova. Afterward, during the period Kira had been thought lost in the Delta Quadrant, Commander Vaughn had invited Macet to the station, and *Trager* had indeed been docked at DS9 when Kira had returned. At no time, though, had Macet or any of his crew come aboard; Vaughn had authorized some repairs to the battle-scarred vessel, and it had departed shortly after Kira's arrival back on the station. Apparently, Macet had taken *Trager* to join *Defiant.*

"Yes, sir," Selzner confirmed. Kira considered contacting Vaughn before *Defiant* got back to DS9 and asking him for an explanation, but she opted to trust his judgment. He had served as her executive officer for only a short time, but he had already demonstrated intelligence and perceptiveness, as well as a level head.

"All right," Kira said. "I'll be up to ops shortly. Kira out." The comm channel closed, leaving her peering at Taran'atar, the distrustful aspect still decorating his face. She had seen that same look on the Jem'Hadar when Macet had first contacted her aboard *Euphrates,* back at Europa Nova.

"You are right not to trust him, Colonel," Taran'atar offered.

"Maybe," Kira said. "Macet helped us at Europa Nova, and he's apparently helped out at Torona IV too, but . . . his continued presence around DS9 and Bajoran operations . . . it makes me nervous."

"He is an admitted traitor," Taran'atar said simply. And that was part of Kira's problem. Macet had told her that he had fought in Damar's resistance against the Dominion, and if that was true, it validated Taran'atar's characterization of him; he had been a traitor to the Cardassian-Dominion alliance. But if Macet had been a turncoat, then it also meant that he had swung his loyalties to those Kira herself had supported. To complicate matters further, Macet was also a member of Dukat's family. All of which combined to make it difficult to determine either Macet's true intentions or his true nature.

"I know," Kira told Taran'atar. "I know." She glanced down at herself, at her muck-covered uniform and hands, and decided that she had indulged Taran'atar long enough. "Computer," she said, "end program."

Around her and Taran'atar, the world of the Rintanna faded out of existence, and with it, the holographic mud that had been clinging to her uniform. She started for the door, but then something occurred to her. She turned and immediately saw what she was looking for, sitting a couple of meters away on the floor of the holosuite. She quickly retrieved it. "Thank you for this," she said, holding up the knife for Taran'atar to see. He inclined his head in response.

Kira slipped the knife into the sheath at her hip and headed for ops. Somehow, it seemed appropriate that she had armed herself before going to deal with the arrival of Macet.

6

Prynn Tenmei watched as the garnet tide rose in a massive wave. The surfer, a Bolian in a black wet suit, dropped in late, catching the steepest part of the wall of water. He rode down to the midpoint of the wave, then executed a slick series of gouges—sharp, fast turns—that threw fans of spray up from the tail of his yellow board. He straightened his course momentarily, then cut back and went vertical, climbing up toward the crest. The board sliced through the water swiftly and smoothly. He boosted, redirected the board in midair, and came down as the wave started to roll over. The lip pitched far and clean as he descended, the falls crashing down and forming a tube. The surfer shot the tube, carving up the wave with a level of skill Prynn had not often witnessed.

"Wow," she said, expressing aloud her appreciation for the surfer's exceptional abilities, even though she was alone in her quarters. She watched him ride the wave out, then reached up and operated the controls of the companel to replay the sequence. The entire recording, a collection of different surfers in different locales, lasted almost an hour, but this particular run impressed Prynn more than any other. Not only was the Bolian's technique remarkable, but so too was the setting. The distinctive color of the water unmistakably established the location as the Canopus Planet, a place Prynn had never been. She had heard only superlative appraisals of the surfing there, though, and she intended to experience it for herself one day.

Although grateful that Captain Hoku had left the recording for her when *Mjolnir* had docked at the station last week, Prynn was also disappointed that she had missed a chance to visit with her former commanding officer. Prynn's first posting out of the Academy had been aboard *Mjolnir,* where she had learned a great deal . . . including the art of surfing. The captain hailed from Hawai'i, an archipelago in the middle of Earth's Pacific Ocean, where surfing—or *he'enalu,* "wave sliding," as the natives called it—had been practiced for more than a millennium. Prynn, unable to resist almost any activity that involved high velocity and any sort of piloting, had quickly taken to the sport, spending many of her off-hours aboard *Mjolnir* in the holodeck with one or another of the captain's many simulations.

Prynn took hold of the arm of her chair and adjusted herself as the Bolian surfer began maneuvering again along the wave. A dull ache had suffused her midsection for days, and now her flesh had begun to itch. She lowered her hands to her sides, feeling through her shirt the specially treated dressing wrapping her lower torso. She had thought that once she was no longer confined to bed, it would be much easier to make herself comfortable, but that had turned out not to be the case. Part of the problem, she knew, lay in her own temperament; she enjoyed physical activities, and eschewed pursuits that required only sedentary involvement. Injured or not, she would have had a difficult time simply sitting around her quarters.

Prynn leaned her forearm heavily on the smooth surface of the companel and repositioned herself once more in the chair. Today was the first day since the accident that she had been allowed on her feet; she had spent the entire voyage back to the station in *Defiant*'s medical bay, and all of yesterday in DS9's infirmary. Dr. Bashir claimed that her recovery was proceeding apace, but it already seemed as though her mobility had been limited, not for days, but for weeks. And though she felt better now than she had at any time since the explosion, she still tired easily.

The Bolian surfer completed his run for the second time, and Prynn deactivated the recording with a touch to the companel controls. "Computer," she said. "Record a subspace message to Captain Kalena Hoku of the *U.S.S. Mjolnir*."

"Proceed," responded the computer.

"Captain Hoku, this is Prynn Tenmei," she said, squarely facing the companel so that her image could be recorded. She smiled, happy to be in touch again with this woman she liked and respected so much. "When I returned to Deep Space 9 after your visit here, I was given the surfing—"

The door chime sounded, and a knot immediately formed in Prynn's stomach. The smile left her face in an instant, as though it had fallen off. Only a handful of people on the station would be calling on her right now, and she did not wish to speak with any of them. "Computer," she said, "stop recording and erase."

"Recording terminated."

Prynn swiveled her chair toward the door. She did not say anything right away, and she briefly considered not answering at all. She had not served for very long aboard DS9—less than half a year—and she had not yet made many friends. Although rather gregarious as a rule, she had spent most of her free time during her first few months on the station with Monyodin—

Her breath caught as she thought of him, the image of his face so clear in her mind's eye, as though she had just seen him. *Wishful thinking,* she told herself. During the Jem'Hadar assault on the station almost two months ago, Monyodin had been fatally wounded by a chemical gas leak. He had died several hours later in the infirmary, with Prynn sitting by his side.

Since then, she had begun socializing again, but she had also kept her new crewmates at arm's length. She had grown friendly, to some extent, with Nog and Sam Bowers, but they had already visited her earlier this morning, as had Colonel Kira. No, Prynn suspected that she was being looked in on by Dr. Bashir or Nurse Richter—both of whom she had seen quite enough of during the past week, even as nicely as they had treated her—or possibly by Counselor Matthias. Prynn actually liked the station's new counselor—she appreciated Phillipa's straightforward manner—but she had no desire to discuss the accident. Her body had been traumatized, but not her mind or her emotions; Prynn not only could not remember the explosion, she could not even recall the events leading up to it.

She thought about what she could do or say to cut short any visit by Bashir or Richter or Matthias.

Or worse, by her father.

The chime signaled again. Prynn took a deliberate breath, trying to calm herself, then realized that the fingers of her right hand were wrapped tightly around the arm of the chair. She relaxed her grip, took one more deep breath, and said, "Come in."

The door slid open to reveal the tall, cool figure of Vaughn. She watched as he peered inside, his steely blue eyes scanning the room for her. When he spotted her off to the side of the room, at the companel, he smiled—a small, unsure sort of a smile, she thought, that barely moved the silver hair of his beard.

"May I come in?" he asked when she said nothing.

The word *no* screamed in her mind like a red-alert klaxon, and the urge to give it voice almost overwhelmed her. She had weathered the couple of visits Vaughn had paid her in *Defiant*'s medical bay during the trip back to the station, but there had always been other people present, and he had neither stayed long nor said much. She worried now that, with just the two of them, such would not be the case. If she told him to leave, though, she feared that might itself provoke a conversation that she did not want to have with him. Finally, she said, "Yes."

Vaughn lifted his foot over the high Cardassian sill and took one step into the room. As the door closed, he clasped his hands behind his back, a bit of body language Prynn recognized at once: he was nervous, a rarity for him. Vaughn smiled again—that same, unsure smile—and gazed around the room. Before now, he had never been to her quarters.

Prynn sat quietly as Vaughn surveyed the room. Her discomfort grew as she saw him look from one place to another, taking in her personal belongings. On the wall to his right, a pair of prints hung in pewter frames, one of *Mjolnir*, and the other of the *U.S.S. Sentinel*, Prynn's second posting. On the same wall, on the other side of the replicator, a large free-form sculpture, composed of metal rods and sheets, kept Bajoran time in a complex series of movements; she had acquired the clock not long ago, at an art show on the Promenade.

Vaughn turned his head and examined the other side of the room, where she sat, and Prynn followed the direction of his eyes. He regarded the abstract mobile that depended in blacks and grays and whites from the ceiling in the corner nearest him, then looked over the narrow tables lining the wall on either side of the companel station. Several other pieces of kinetic art were displayed on the tables, including silver and gold orreries of both the Terran and Bajoran planetary systems. Then his gaze found her.

"How are you feeling?" he asked.

"I'm fine," Prynn said, and knew that she would have to say more. "I've been in better shape," she added, "but I'm improving."

"Good, good," Vaughn said, and he took another step into the room. He seemed to struggle to find something to say. He looked away from her and over to the seating area in the center of the room, where a chair and ottoman, along with a sofa, sat around a low, oval table. Prynn felt a jolt of panic when she looked over there herself and spied a framed picture of her mother. Without thinking, she rose, one hand on the arm of the chair as she pushed herself upright. She made her way toward the sofa, too quickly. What had been a dull ache flared into a stronger pain now, a throbbing line across her midsection where her muscles cautioned against her sudden movements.

"Are you all right?" Vaughn asked, the concern in his voice plain. She also heard him take a step closer to her.

"Yes, yes," she said, waving him away without looking around at him. As she reached the sofa, a twinge in her abdomen made her wince and bend over. She brought one arm up to her belly as the other leaned on the edge of the sofa.

"Here, let me—" Vaughn started, moving in close now and taking her elbow in his hand.

"No," Prynn said sharply, snapping her head toward him and freezing him in place. "No," she said again, this time with a softer tone. "I'm all right." She extricated her elbow from his grasp, moved around, and lowered herself onto the sofa. "Dr. Bashir said it's all right for me to walk around, just not to do too much."

"How bad is it?" Vaughn asked. "I mean, I've spoken with the doctor, and I know you're going to recover completely, but how bad is the pain?"

"Not bad," she lied, forcing herself to quiet her breathing. Her skin felt clammy beneath her clothes. Given the choice, she thought, she could live with the pain, but it infuriated her that even walking just a few steps required such an effort from her recuperating body. And the last thing she wanted was help from Vaughn. "Dr. Bashir told me that he could block the pain, but that if I was going to be on my feet, he'd rather not," she explained. "He wanted me to be able to feel what I was doing to my body so that I wouldn't overexert myself."

"I guess he's gotten to know you already, then," Vaughn said lightly, and when she looked up at him, he smiled at her, not quite so tentatively as before. She said nothing. All she wanted was for this conversation to end and to be left alone. "Really," he went on, more serious, "you shouldn't push yourself."

"I should be able to return to part-time duty within the next week, according to the doctor," she said, ignoring Vaughn's admonition. "I'd like to do that."

"I know," Vaughn said. "Whatever the doctor's recommendation, I'll abide by it."

Prynn nodded and looked down. Silence seeped into the room, and she tried to think of something to say to prevent it from surrounding them. She could only summon the most innocuous of words, words she could not utter because they would only demonstrate how she craved to avoid talking about anything substantial with Vaughn. Nothing she could think of to say would keep her afloat as the quiet rose around them.

"Prynn."

It was only the second time since he had transferred to Deep Space 9 that he had called her by her given name—by the name that *he* had given her. She knew that it meant he wanted to say something to her, not as her senior officer, but as her father. It made her skin crawl. She refused to look up at him, instead keeping her eyes focused down toward the floor. Beside her, Vaughn moved, walking around the table toward the chair opposite her. As he did so, she quickly reached forward, grabbed the picture of her mother, and lowered it facedown onto the table.

When he reached the chair, Vaughn turned to her. He did not sit, nor did he say anything right away. She cast about for something that would stop him from attempting to talk with her on a personal level, but again she failed.

"I'm sorry," he said at last. And she knew that he was, and why. For her injury, of course, though that was absurd; he could not be held responsible for the actions of the Jarada, or for the explosion on *Defiant*'s bridge. But she knew that he intended his apology to encompass much more than that anyway; he meant to apologize for what he had done to her mother.

Now she raised her head and looked at him. Though he appeared fit, his faced seemed drawn, his eyes old. This was not the first time he had told her he was sorry, but as in those other times, it did not matter. They were merely words to Prynn, and they meant nothing.

"It was an accident," she told him, her tolerance for Vaughn's visit rapidly diminishing. Then, wanting to be clear, she added, "The blast aboard the *Defiant* was an accident. There's no need to apologize for that, Commander." The last word slipped from her lips before she could stop it. She desperately wanted him to leave, but antagonizing him would not serve that purpose.

Again, silence filled the room like rising water, threatening to drown her. In her mind, she heard herself yelling at him to get out—out of her quarters, off of the station, out of her life—but she would not do that. But she could do nothing else, either. She closed her eyes, simply wishing that he would just go.

Instead, Vaughn sat down in the chair. Prynn opened her eyes to find him staring at her. He sat unmoving, his arms resting along the arms of the chair. No trace of emotion showed on his face now. "Are you still planning to be aboard *Defiant* for the mission to the Gamma Quadrant?" he asked, seemingly apropos of nothing. And then he added, "Ensign," and she understood that he was drawing a line.

"Yes, I am," she said, aware that Vaughn already knew this, and knew how much she loved piloting, especially starships. Her advancement from *Mjolnir* to *Sentinel* to *Defiant* had brought her to the point where she would be alpha-shift conn on the coming mission—which posed its own problems, of course, since Vaughn would also be on the bridge for the alpha shift. But during the evacuation of Europa Nova, she had demonstrated—to herself and, she had thought, to Vaughn—that she could work with him at a high, professional level. The mission to the Gamma Quadrant would be a wonderful opportunity for her.

"Then I think you need to establish a better relationship with me," he said.

She felt another jolt, this time not of panic, but of rage. *Is he threatening me?* she asked herself. He could not force her to love him or like him or forgive him, she knew, but he could see her transferred, or reassigned to other duties, or kept away from the missions that would allow her to succeed and advance. She could not allow that. She had worked hard to attain her station; she would not go backward, and she would not stand still.

"Commander," she said, careful to control her tone, to keep it civil and professional, and not accusatory. Past Vaughn's shoulder, the avant-garde metal clock ticked off the seconds. "I've earned that position. I want to—"

"You're an excellent pilot, yes," he agreed, "but there's more to functioning well as a Starfleet officer than the ability to perform a job. There are interpersonal skills, and they include getting along with your commanding officer, no matter how much you blame—" He stopped, apparently checking his choice of words. "—no matter how much you dislike him," he finished.

"Commander," she said, her anger dissipating somewhat as her need to defend her record asserted itself. "Commander, I have not allowed our personal differences to interfere with the performance of my duties."

"No?" he asked. Prynn blinked, astounded. As much as she despised Vaughn, she had striven to follow his orders diligently and to the letter, and in professional situations to treat him accordingly. She found it unbelievable that he now suggested otherwise. "Ensign," he went on, "wasn't it you who said you had to pretend you could stomach just being in the same room with me, and then told me to go to hell?" She began to protest, but he held up his hand, stopping her. "We were alone, and I had given you permission to speak freely. And it's not as though I don't know how you feel about me. The problem is, it's not just me who knows that; it's clear to a lot of people on this station that our relationship is . . . *strained*. It provides for a tense working atmosphere, and it undermines my authority, particularly since I've been permitting it to go unaddressed."

Prynn glanced away, and she saw the overturned picture of her mother on the table. She knew that she would have to tread lightly here. She wanted to tell him that, no matter his maneuverings, he could not make her love him, that whatever they once had between them had long ago perished. But she also understood that there was some measure of truth to what he was saying. She had seen the expressions—first of confusion, and later of recognition and sadness—on the faces of Nog and Shar, of Lieutenant Ro and Colonel Kira. Still looking away, she admitted it. "You're right."

"I might be able to deal with your attitude toward me indefinitely aboard the station," Vaughn told her, "but if you're going to serve on *Defiant* for three months while we explore the Gamma Quadrant, then you'd better learn to get along with me." He stood up.

"Yes, sir," she said. She continued looking at the picture frame lying flat on the table, facedown.

"Look at me, Ensign." His voice carried the tone of command, and she knew that she not only had to look up at him, but that she had to do so with nothing on her face: not anger or animosity, and not a mask covering those emotions. All at once, it came to her that this could be a defining moment in her Starfleet career. Resentment started to build within her, but she quelled it immediately. She would put herself beyond caring what kind of a father Vaughn was to her. From a professional standpoint, that was the appropriate action to take, but on a personal level, wasn't that the right thing to do too? Wouldn't her life—and his—be easier if they didn't have a contentious personal relationship, but rather no personal relationship at all?

Prynn lifted her eyes and met Vaughn's gaze, letting the tension and ire drain from her. "Yes, sir," she said, her tone even, responding to him as though he had just ordered her to take the ship to warp.

"Do you understand me?"

"I do, sir, yes," she said, and then risked adding, "and you're right."

Vaughn's eyes held hers for a long time. *He can go either way,* she thought. He could believe what she had said, or he could think she was only telling him what he wanted to hear. She pushed the thoughts away, for fear that they would appear on her face. She piloted herself now, and her emotions, and she had never confronted a more difficult test of her flight skills. She fought the controls to keep her course straight and true.

Vaughn relented. "Good," he told her. "I'm glad." He turned and headed for the door. She did not turn her head, but allowed herself to slump slightly. She felt completely drained of energy. She heard the door slide open, but Vaughn's footfalls stopped before they reached the corridor. "Prynn?" he said, and the command in his voice had gone. Regardless, she stood up and turned, facing him across the room.

"Sir?"

"I *am* sorry," he said. "For everything."

"I know," she told him. He regarded her for a moment more, and she hoped he would not say anything else. Finally, he turned on his heel and left. The door slid closed after him.

He's sorry, she thought, staring at the closed door. *For everything.* And she found that she believed it, believed that Vaughn was indeed sorry for all that had happened. *But it's not enough,* she thought. *It will never be enough.*

PART TWO

TO SAIL BEYOND

THE SUNSET

Push off, and sitting well in order smite
The sounding furrows; for my purpose holds
To sail beyond the sunset, and the baths
Of all the western stars, until I die.

—ALFRED, LORD TENNYSON, "ULYSSES"

7

The universe is filled with unimagined wonders.

Elias Vaughn stood in the aft section of *Defiant's* bridge, thinking this as the clatter of refit and repair work surrounded him. Several of his alpha-shift command crew—Bowers, ch'Thane, and Prynn—worked at their respective stations, confirming the modifications and repairs to their equipment. Half a dozen other technicians from Nog's engineering team sat, stood, and lay all around the bridge, their hands buried inside the ship's infrastructure. Nog himself was not present, though Vaughn occasionally heard his voice over the comm system as he called up from engineering, coordinating efforts with his personnel on the bridge. The electronic squeals and quavers of diagnostic sequences filled the room like an atonal symphony, with the thuds and clanks of equipment being moved, along with the many voices, providing accompaniment.

Vaughn studied a monitor in the aft bulkhead of the bridge. He watched as a bright green line drew a rough ellipse on the black screen, weaving through white pinpoints that represented stars, and beginning and ending at a blue disk designated BAJORAN WORMHOLE/GAMMA QUADRANT TERMINUS. This marked the course *Defiant* would take on its three-month mission. Vaughn had spent hours plotting various routes through unexplored sectors, attempting to maximize the number of civilizations and interesting celestial objects the crew might encounter, while keeping the ship as far from Dominion space as possible. He had solicited feedback from Colonel Kira, as well as from Science Officer ch'Thane. He had even spoken with Quark—in general terms, and without providing any of the proposed courses to him—about what he had heard regarding the various sectors under consideration. Quark had professed to being delighted to help the station's new executive officer, but had also managed to elicit a promise from Vaughn to bring him back something "worthy" in return.

All told, little was known about the areas *Defiant* would be traveling. Before contact with the Dominion had made such voyages impossible, explorers from the Alpha Quadrant had managed to chart only a relatively small volume of the Gamma Quadrant. Federation astronomers had carried out some rudimentary star charting, of course, and several reports and rumors about various trading factions had come to light, but not much more than that. In the end, Vaughn had decided on a course that would take *Defiant* through areas with both a large number of main-sequence stars and some identified celestial rarities—a dual binary system here, a cluster of brown dwarf stars there.

The port door to the bridge whispered open, and Vaughn looked over to see Ensign Roness enter. The tall, svelte blonde carried a padd in one hand and a spanner—a blue, two-pronged tool with an elongated handle—in the other. She paced over to the flight-control console, where she conferred with Prynn. Roness would function as the beta-shift conn officer during the voyage. Right now, Vaughn had assigned her the task of collating the refit and repair data for *Defiant*.

Vaughn tapped a control below the display, and a series of red arcs appeared at intervals along *Defiant*'s course. The arcs, looping away in both directions from the green ellipse at various points, symbolized the paths of the probes the crew would launch throughout the mission, a supplement to the readings taken from the ship. As best he could, Vaughn would see to it that he and his crew learned as much as possible during their expedition. With luck, they would discover marvels.

From the time he had been a boy, gazing up at the night sky on Berengaria VII, Vaughn had apprehended the vastness of space. And with the enthusiasm and credulousness of youth, he had readily envisioned himself traveling the great expanses in search of wondrous beings and places. He had learned all he could about Earth's eminent explorers—Leif Eriksson, Ferdinand Magellan, Meriwether Lewis and William Clark, Neil Armstrong, Jonathan Archer, and so many others—and dreamed about the days when he would join their ranks. Back then, he could not have known that circumstance and a talent for intelligence would long deny him the opportunity to explore.

Now, a year past his centenary birthday, Vaughn recalled the aspirations of his childhood. It amazed and gratified him that they had somehow endured, despite his casual disregard of them through the decades. He looked at the representation of the path *Defiant* would take beginning six days from now—at the path *he* would take—and renewed his belief that the universe would never exhaust its treasures.

"Sir?" a woman's voice said behind him. Vaughn turned to Ensign Roness. She no longer carried the spanner, but she still held the padd in one hand.

"Yes, Ensign?" Vaughn said. He tried to remember the officer's first name—he was still getting to know the crew—and thought *Tilda* and *Greta* before recalling that it was *Gerda*.

"You wanted the latest status reports on the ship, sir," Roness said, offering the padd to Vaughn. From the tone of her voice, it did not sound as though she particularly enjoyed making this delivery.

"Something wrong, Ensign?" he asked. He reached out and took the padd from her, but did not look at it.

"It's just, well, I don't think you'll be completely pleased about the progress the crew has made," she explained.

"So far," Vaughn told her, glancing down at the padd but not actually reading it, "I am delighted by the progress we've made. Not to worry."

"Thank you, sir," she said. "Where should I report next?"

Vaughn took a half-step to the side and looked past Roness to the conn. "Ensign Tenmei," he said, raising his voice just enough to be heard above the noise of the work being done.

Prynn turned immediately in her seat to face him across *Defiant*'s bridge. "Yes, sir?" she said.

Vaughn hesitated an instant, the sight of his daughter at the conn still evoking the painful memory of the moment he thought her life had been lost. On the heels of that emotion, though, came hope: Prynn had addressed him without the slightest trace of animus, either in her voice or on her face. He had to give her credit; since their discussion two weeks ago, she had been the model officer, giving him no reason to have to revisit the issue. It pleased him tremendously that she had something in her life—her work—that allowed her to face down her troubles, even if he was one of them. At the same time, he knew that while thought and emotion drove behavior, so too could behavior influence thought and emotion; if Prynn's professional relationship with him continued in a positive way, it could potentially impact her personal feelings about him.

"Can Ensign Roness assist you at the conn?" he asked her.

"No, sir," Prynn told him. "I'll be done in here in just a few minutes, but I'll be going down to help Lieutenant Candlewood with the computer core. He said he could use some extra bodies for some of the work."

"Thank you, Ensign," Vaughn said, and looked back at Roness. "Report to Lieutenant Candlewood and give him whatever assistance he needs."

"Aye, sir." Roness turned and left the bridge.

Vaughn examined the padd. The words DEFIANT REFIT/REPAIR STATUS marched across the display. Vaughn touched a control and brought up a list of categories into which the work on the ship had been divided. Color-coded progress bars beneath each category indicated how much work had been completed, ranging from red—zero percent—through orange and yellow to green—one hundred percent. Most of the tasks that would augment *Defiant* for exploration—Shuttlepod Removal and Pod Bay Reconfiguration, Biochem Lab Installation, Stellar Cartography Lab Installation, Sensor Recalibration, and the like—had been finished a month ago, though final diagnostic testing and any required adjustments had yet to be concluded. The only major refit modification left partially done was the expansion of the library computer system from a purely military mission profile to a military/sciences hybrid. The bulk of the work that remained involved repairs to the ship—hull breaches, damage to the port thruster package, ablative-armor replacement—a result of clashes *Defiant* had been engaged in during the past three weeks, including the one at Torona IV.

One by one, Vaughn toggled between the list of categories and detailed descriptions of the work completed and the work remaining. Considering the major modifications to *Defiant,* as well as the unanticipated repairs and the narrow time frame, the crew had done an extraordinary job. Still, not everything added up quite the way Vaughn had hoped. He thumbed through the list a second time, searching for any time that could be made up within the next week. Then he looked a third time.

We're behind schedule, he finally allowed himself to think. And no matter how many times he studied the status reports, he chided himself, that was not going to change. Which meant that he could either try to push the crew harder, try to obtain additional resources, or push the launch back. Uncomfortable as it was for him to recognize the problem, it was actually easy for him to arrive at a solution. The crew had already pushed themselves, and Vaughn had no intention of using crew downtime to make up the deficit in the schedule; time away from duty, he well knew, played a vital role in productivity, and beyond that, the crew had earned it. And the addition of more personnel—in short supply in Starfleet these days anyway—would be mitigated by travel time to the station. Clearly, Vaughn would have to set the beginning of the mission back by at least a day.

A heavy thump to Vaughn's right pulled his attention away from the padd. He turned to see Lieutenant Bowers and Ensign Merimark struggling with one of the library computer interface modules. The two had it perched on the side of a console, and Vaughn could not tell whether they had dropped it there after removing it or during an attempt to install it.

"Mr. Bowers," Vaughn said, selecting the senior of the two officers to address. "Get an antigrav up here for that."

"Yes, sir," Bowers said, the expression on his face showing his obvious annoyance with himself that he had not used an antigrav in the first place. He left Merimark holding the module in place on the edge of the console—it did not appear to be a strain for her—and then headed out through the starboard door.

Under normal conditions, a decision to delay the mission would hardly cause any concerns for Starfleet Command, simply by virtue of its necessity. In this case, though, it might be problematic. Not all of the admiralty agreed that the time had come for renewed exploration of the Gamma Quadrant. Any attempt to delay the launch date would allow those opposed to the mission another occasion to voice their disapproval. And whenever that happened, minds could be changed.

Vaughn personally knew several admirals who believed the end of the war was still too close for the Federation to be intruding anywhere near Dominion territory, even despite Odo's invitation for the resumption of peaceful exploration. Odo, they argued, composed but one small piece of the Great Link, and it remained to be seen whether his influence could forge a lasting peace between the Dominion and the civilizations of the Alpha Quadrant. Because a lot had been lost during the war, Vaughn understood and respected that position, even as he disagreed with it.

He blanked the display of the padd, then made a note to himself to confer with Colonel Kira about the needed delay to the start of the mission. After that, he would inform Starfleet Command of the necessary change in plan, and he considered which admiral would be best to contact first. *Not Nechayev, and not Jellico,* he concluded immediately. *Admiral Walter,* he decided. Walter was a proponent of exploration, considered a reasonable man, and a strong figure within the admiralty. He would, Vaughn thought, help preserve the prevailing sentiment that venturing into the Gamma Quadrant need not wait. And if some of the admirals did consider withdrawing their support for the mission, well, then Vaughn would just have to bring his particular brand of persuasion to bear. Despite being "only" a commander—his rank had always served his aims—Vaughn's tenure in Starfleet had lasted longer than the careers of most of the Command admirals, and his influence had a corresponding reach.

Vaughn checked the time on the padd. His next meeting, he saw, was only a minute away. As though caused by his realization, the bridge's port door slid open to admit Taran'atar. It did not surprise Vaughn to find Jem'Hadar—or at least this one—as punctual as Tholians.

"Taran'atar," he said. The Jem'Hadar stepped over to Vaughn.

"Colonel Kira told me to meet you here, at this time," Taran'atar said.

"Yes," Vaughn acknowledged. "Thank you for coming. Let's go to my ready room. There are some things I'd like to discuss with you."

"Very well," Taran'atar said.

Vaughn led the way off the bridge, anxious to consult with somebody who had already traveled the Gamma Quadrant.

"Please, sit." Vaughn stood behind his desk, gesturing across to a chair there. Taran'atar regarded it with a look that bordered on contempt, and then sat down stiffly. Vaughn sat too, and then operated the computer interface on his desk. He brought up a chart, then swiveled the display around so that both he and Taran'atar could see it. "I wanted to confer with you about this region of space." The wormhole's Gamma terminus sat squarely in the middle of the diagram. Dominion space spread above it, the blur of the Omarion Nebula, the former home of the Founders, distinctively contained within its borders. *Defiant's* course emerged and returned to the wormhole, stretching down and to the left on the plot. Vaughn tapped on the screen, pointing to the area through which *Defiant* would be traveling. "We intend to explore this region. Are you familiar with it?"

As Taran'atar examined the display, Vaughn was struck by a sense of déjà vu. Or perhaps what he experienced owed less to a feeling that he had lived this exact scene before, and more to his long memory of the planning of uncounted missions. Vaughn had never sought assistance from a Jem'Hadar soldier like this, nor had he ever plotted a course for exploration, but this was how he had always operated: seeking as much information as possible, from different sources and different viewpoints, allowing him to paint as complete a picture as he could of whatever situation he would be entering, and to plan his actions accordingly. Vaughn did not like to be surprised.

"I am familiar in part with this area of space," Taran'atar said. "Can you provide a more detailed view?"

Vaughn worked the controls again, and the chart he had been studying earlier returned to the screen. The green path marking *Defiant's* course looped out from the blue disk of the wormhole. Taran'atar looked at the display, then reached up and cut an arc across it with his fingertip. "Here," he said. "I know something within this area." Vaughn keyed in a command, and the neighborhood of space immediately bordering the wormhole, including the area Taran'atar had indicated, grew to fill the screen.

"Would you be more specific?" Vaughn asked.

"I have visited these systems," Taran'atar said, pointing to the two stars closest to the wormhole along *Defiant*'s course. "And I have knowledge about these," he went on, running a finger around the next three stars.

"Nothing beyond that?" Vaughn asked.

"To my knowledge," Taran'atar explained, "the Dominion has never traveled beyond these systems."

"I see," Vaughn said. He should have been disappointed—the five stars Taran'atar had identified had already been mapped and surveyed by Federation vessels—but he found that he was not. "Do you know of any life in these systems?" he asked. "Or of any unusual or rare phenomena?"

"The systems are lifeless," Taran'atar pronounced, "and entirely ordinary." That matched the information that the Federation had collected.

Vaughn touched a control and blanked the display. "I'd like to ask you something else," he told Taran'atar. "Do you think that the Dominion will try to thwart our attempt to explore the Gamma Quadrant?" Vaughn himself felt sure that the Dominion would pose no threat, believing—and with solid intelligence to back up his belief—that the Founders and their minions would remain in their own territory for some time to come. What interested him right now, though, was how Taran'atar viewed the situation.

"You watched the message I delivered from the Founder," Taran'atar said. "He told you that the Dominion would not interfere with your peaceful exploration of the Gamma Quadrant, as long as you leave them alone."

"Yes," Vaughn said, "I did see that message. But I wasn't asking you to repeat it for me; I was asking what your opinion was."

"My *opinion?*" Taran'atar said, as though the concept did not extend to Jem'Hadar. "My opinion is not necessary. *No* opinion is necessary. The Founder said it, therefore it is so."

"I see," Vaughn said. "Well, thank you for your time and assistance." He stood up, and Taran'atar stood up as well, quickly, almost as though preparing to fend off an attack. "That's all I needed."

Taran'atar did not acknowledge the end of the meeting with a word or even a nod, but immediately headed for the door. But before he exited, he turned back toward Vaughn. "Why are you doing this?" he asked.

"You mean exploring the Gamma Quadrant?"

"Yes." Taran'atar took a step back toward the desk. "You apparently know nothing about where you are going, and you worry about being attacked by the Dominion."

"The point of exploration is the unknown," Vaughn said. "We wouldn't really be exploring if we traveled to a familiar place." He smiled, but the humor seemed to make no impact on Taran'atar. "And I'm not worried about the Dominion."

"There are other dangers," Taran'atar said, his words and tone almost threatening. "So why do this?"

"Because it is our nature," Vaughn said. "Humans and many other races find meaning for their lives in extending the knowledge of themselves and their people. The yearning to explore drives us."

Taran'atar appeared to consider this, and then said, "It is a weakness."

Vaughn smiled and sat back down. "What isn't?" he said. "Thank you again." Taran'atar looked at him for a moment, then turned and left.

Vaughn swung the display back toward his side of the desk, then brought up the display of *Defiant*'s full course once more. A small, yellow rectangle now enclosed the stars Taran'atar had referenced. The area was small, and *Defiant* would sail beyond it in a day or two, traveling into the unknown. Vaughn realized that, for the first time in a very long time—perhaps for the first time in his career—he would be heading out on a mission with virtually no idea of what he would encounter.

Strangely enough, that suited him.

8

Kira stood back from the outer bulkhead in her office and took in the painting she had just had hung. A plain, gilded frame bordered the large canvas, a meter tall and half again as wide. In the lower right foreground, the greenish white form of Bajor sat nestled in the blackness of space, the land and oceans discernible beneath the wisps of cloud circling the globe. A sliver of Endalla, the first and largest of the five moons, peeked out from the middle left of the painting. Derna and Jeraddo and the other moons, smaller but still recognizable, danced with Endalla about Bajor.

Though Kira had an appreciation for art, never had any work captured her attention as this one had. Prior to the evacuation of Europa Nova, the Promenade Merchants' Association had held an art festival, and Kira, ambling through the show as a sign of support, but with no intention of purchasing anything, had been taken with this piece. Done in short, narrow strokes, the painting— entitled *Bajor at Peace*—had been done by a woman named Acto Viri, from the province of Wyntara Mas. Kira had not found the rest of Acto's displayed work very impressive, but she had returned again and again to *Bajor at Peace*.

On one of her later visits during the show, Kira had been stunned to discover something in the painting she had not noticed in her previous viewings: in the upper left corner, a hint of blue, slightly larger than the white lights of the stars, looked out on Bajor and her children. It almost seemed like a mistake, like an accidental brushstroke, but Kira knew that it was not. Though not visible to the unaided eye from Bajor, this was the Celestial Temple.

Kira had not purchased *Bajor at Peace* then, but sometime after she had returned to the station through the Iconian gateway, she had contacted Acto Viri and asked if the painting was still available. It had arrived on a transport this morning. Now Kira stood back and appreciated anew this wonderful depiction of Bajor in its place in the universe.

Even the stars are right, Kira thought, automatically clustering them into the constellations she had known since childhood. She spotted the Forest, the Runners, and her favorite, the Temple. She looked for others and found the Flames—

Kira's eyes locked on the triangular formation of stars. One of the lower stars in the configuration, she knew, was Sol. *Earth's star. Benjamin's star.* The thought of the Emissary usually brought a smile to her face, but now she also thought about Captain Sisko's son. No one had seen or heard from Jake in two months, not since he had left DS9 to visit his grandfather on Earth. His disappearance had not been established until two weeks after that, when Kasidy Yates had spoken with Joseph Sisko and learned that, not only had he not heard from Jake, but he knew nothing at all about an impending visit from his grandson.

While Federation authorities had looked for Jake on and around Earth, the DS9 crew had actively searched for him throughout the Bajoran sector.

Kira had also questioned Quark at length; the unscrupulous Ferengi had sold Jake the shuttle in which the young man had intended to travel to Earth. She had been ready to tear off Quark's ears if she had found out that he had given Jake a defective ship, but Nog had told her that he had checked it himself, and that it had indeed been spaceworthy. And the crew had never discovered any debris or other indications of a destroyed shuttle anywhere in the sector.

The search for Jake had been suspended during the Iconian gateways crisis, with so many ships needed to evacuate Europa Nova. During the past three weeks, Kira had reinstituted the hunt for the younger Sisko, but as the crew's responsibilities shifted to other tasks, and no sign of Jake appeared, those efforts had necessarily waned.

Kira tried to shake off her melancholy. She took one last appreciative look at the painting, then returned to her desk, and to the work she had not yet completed tonight. On her desktop computer interface, she brought up the list of ships still circling the station, which had begun to thin this afternoon. In the next four or five days, she knew, they would all be gone, leaving Deep Space 9 alone at the threshold of the Celestial Temple once more.

Well, not alone, she corrected herself. *Defiant* would not be departing to the Gamma Quadrant for another six days—*Seven,* she amended, taking into account the one-day delay—and Captain Mello would be arriving shortly with *Gryphon.* Kira recalled that *Mjolnir* had originally been slated for the three-month tour at DS9, and a swell of annoyance grew within her. She liked Captain Mello, but she had not seen Captain Hoku in quite some time—not since before the war with the Dominion—and she had been looking forward to spending some time with her old friend.

It's more than that, Kira thought as she studied the departure schedule for the next week. She knew that she would catch up with Kalena soon enough, and that as a stand-in for *Defiant,* the *Akira*-class *Gryphon* was better suited to the task than the *Norway*-class *Mjolnir.* What bothered her was the way Starfleet had informed her of the change in plan—*Mjolnir's* early arrival three weeks ago had been a surprise—and more than that, the demeanor of Admiral Akaar. She had not cared for him much, and she was pleased that he had remained at the station only long enough to speak with her and collect Councillor zh'Thane. Now he was the first minister's problem.

On the display, Kira saw that many of the vessels at the station would be voyaging to Bajor tomorrow. As the Europani resettlement got under way, they would transport the refugees aboard and then ferry them back to their world. Whatever few difficulties Kira had with Starfleet—mostly the administrative matters they burdened her with, as well as the occasional troublesome admiral—she thought highly of their Corps of Engineers. She had received word earlier that day that the specialized technical arm of Starfleet had managed to completely decontaminate the radiation-scarred world of Europa Nova; remarkably, they had taken less than a month to do so. Concerns that the population of three million Europani might overburden Bajor's available resources had now been rendered moot, though Kira was happy that, despite the risk, her people had immediately offered refuge when the crisis had arisen. She still remembered with bitterness and guilt the incident, six years ago, when she and her people had turned away the Skrreea in their time of need.

"Ops to Colonel Kira." The voice belonged to Ensign Selzner. Kira tapped her combadge, which chirped to life.

"This is Kira," she said. "Go ahead."

"Colonel, we're being hailed by a ship requesting clearance to dock," Selzner explained. *"I thought you would want to know: it's the* Trager.*"*

Macet, Kira thought. *What's he up to?* This marked the third time that he and his warship had been to Deep Space 9 within the last month. On the previous two occasions, the ship had docked after assisting with the Europani. After the gul had helped evacuate Europa Nova—and before Kira had returned to the station—Commander Vaughn had authorized repairs to *Trager* at DS9. And after Macet's aid at Torona IV, Vaughn had convinced Kira to allow additional repair work to the ship.

Could that be why he's been assisting us? She thought. Somehow, Macet trading his help for free starship maintenance didn't seem quite right. That sounded more like Ferengi behavior.

"Put Gul Macet through to me, Ensign," Kira said.

"Aye, sir," Selzner replied.

A faint electronic signal accompanied the appearance on the display of Gul Macet.

"Colonel Kira," he said, smiling. *"How nice to see you."*

"Gul Macet," Kira said. She returned the smile, wondering if it looked as false as it felt. She had learned since the Occupation not to judge Cardassians as a species, but to see them for who they were as individuals. But what confronted her now consisted of more than simply a Cardassian face; this was the face of the unholy Dukat, a likeness to which she had still not grown accustomed. "I'd like to know the purpose of your visit to Deep Space 9 before I authorize you to dock."

"Ah ... of course, Colonel," he said, hesitating a bit as he spoke, as though he had not expected to have to justify his arrival in Bajoran space.

The arrogance, Kira thought. Perhaps Macet was not, after all, quite as different from his cousin as he professed to be. "Is there a problem, Macet?" she said. "Don't you have a good reason for visiting the station?"

"Yes, of course, Colonel, of course," he said, and though the tone of his voice differed from Dukat's, his selection of words seemed very recognizable. *"It's simply that . . . well, I thought you would already have been apprised of our arrival. We're here to help transport the Europani back to Europa Nova."*

Kira reached a hand up and tugged idly at her right earlobe for a moment. She suddenly felt foolish, distrustful as she had been in view of this offer— *another* offer—of assistance from Macet. Still—

"How do *you* know about the Europani returning to their planet?" Kira had only been informed this afternoon by the SCE that the decontamination had been completed.

"I was contacted by Admiral Akaar."

"Admiral—" Kira started. "I see." Suddenly, her caution with Macet seemed entirely misdirected. She regarded the gul, concentrating on the tufts of hair fanning out from the corners of his mouth down to his jaw, the most distinctive variance between his appearance and that of Dukat. Another question occurred to her—why was *Trager* coming to the station rather than to Bajor, where the majority of the refugees were located?—but the answer came to her right away: the thousands of Europani on DS9 could be taken back to their world in one trip, together, aboard what would be, by far, the largest vessel in the task force. And sending all of the Europani on the station onto one ship would significantly ease coordination of boarding procedures for Kira's crew. "I'm sorry, Gul Macet," she said, realizing that she could not deny the value of his aid or the apparent quality of his intentions. "You have my authorization to dock." Then, trying to spare them both an awkward moment, she added, "I'm just a little tired this evening."

"Not at all, Colonel," Macet said, graciously not making an issue of Kira's initially adversarial manner. *"My crew and I are at your disposal. We'll wait until your people are prepared for the Europani to board* Trager.*"*

"Thank you," she said. "It's night here, so it'll probably be eight to ten hours before we can begin."

"I look forward to hearing from you," Macet said. *"And Colonel . . . my crew will remain aboard ship while we're at Deep Space 9."*

Neither of the times that *Trager* had docked here before had Macet or any of his crew come aboard the station, and considering how much the gul resembled his infamous cousin, Kira realized what a wise decision that had been. She wanted to tell Macet now that such a restriction was not necessary, that he and his crew were welcome on DS9. But even if Kira welcomed these Cardassians aboard, would the same be true of the Bajoran civilians on the station? In particular, what would be the reaction to a Cardassian gul who so resembled the justifiably reviled Skrain Dukat?

"Acknowledged," Kira said. Macet nodded, and then his image vanished from the screen. Kira thumbed the channel off, then contacted ops.

"Selzner here, Colonel," came the reply.

"Ensign, give Gul Macet clearance to dock when the *Trager* arrives," she said.

"Yes, sir."

Kira slumped back in her chair. She hoped Macet's willingness to assist in Bajoran operations was genuine, and that his motivations were of a charitable—or at least diplomatic—nature. She remained skeptical, and criticized herself for the feeling. She had fought her entire life to free her people from the tyranny of the Cardassians and, thank the Prophets, they had been freed. But how full, how rich, would that freedom be if the people of Bajor could not escape the tyranny of their own fear and hatred and racism?

Kira peered across her office at the bookshelf where *When the Prophets Cried* stood, and recalled the passage in which Vedek Synta counseled her people to embrace their enemies as they would their friends. Such noble sentiments pervaded Bajoran canon, but had been little espoused during or since the Occupation. How can you wrap your arms around somebody who is torturing or raping you, or working you to death, or simply killing you?

Memories and anger threatened, and Kira pushed them away. She knew she was destined always to be a soldier, but she commanded Deep Space 9 now, and that made her a leader, and even a diplomat. Even after everything that had happened in the last decade, from the end of the Occupation to the Ascension of the Emissary, Kira could not help thinking that Bajorans faced a critical juncture in their history right now.

She considered Admiral Akaar, his question to her about Bajoran aid to Cardassia, and his informing the Cardassians that the Europani would be returning to their world from Bajor. *And all that,* she thought, *after the first minister had asked the Federation to reconsider Bajor for membership.* She wondered if Akaar had come here to make the final determination about that, perhaps along with Councillor zh'Thane. And if so, would Bajor's relationship with Cardassia be a factor?

Kira suddenly felt very tired. She stood up and headed out of her office. The doors slid open, and as she descended the stairs into ops, the eyes of the few crewpeople—and of Taran'atar—turned toward her. "Good night," she said, and the crew—but not the Jem'Hadar—returned her farewell. She walked around the upper level and into the turbolift, then turned, facing back into ops. "Habitat ring," she said, and then specified the section where her quarters were.

As the lift started down, Kira saw a young Bajoran man—Corporal Aleco Vel—working at a console on the far side of ops. Kira realized that, like her, the young man had never known anything but contempt for the Cardassians. She remembered her father telling her of a time, back when he had been a boy, when Bajorans and Cardassians had coexisted in a peaceful relationship. And the generations older than that of her father surely could recall such times as well. Because of that, she thought it might be easier for them to see a future in which Bajor and Cardassia could once again live together in peace. But for people like Kira, and like that young man in ops, the Cardassians had only ever been the enemy.

The turbolift finished the vertical part of its journey and moved laterally, out toward the habitat ring. In a way, Kira supposed, the Cardassians presented a more difficult problem for Bajor now than they ever had. *Fighting's easy,* she thought. *Acceptance and accord are hard.*

All the way out to the habitat ring, and then around to her section, the sight of Corporal Aleco stayed in the front of her mind. When the turbolift reached its destination, Kira still wondered if her generation would ever be able to reach into the future, away from the Occupation and toward embracing the Cardassians. She thought that now, finally, she was ready to do that, but as for her Bajoran sisters and brothers, she was not so sure.

9

The main square in Brintall sat at the city's edge, tucked beneath the tallest mountain in a range that stretched to the horizon in either direction. Councillor Charivretha zh'Thane stood on a balcony perched above the square, one story up in one of the many low buildings that bordered three sides of the public meeting place. The fourth side lay open to the mountain, a vast, verdant wall towering above the city. Charivretha's eyes rose with the land, past the timberline and along cold, gray rock, up into the azure Bajoran sky. Wisps of cloud flirted with the mountaintop, their bright whiteness almost indistinguishable from the snows decorating the summit.

Charivretha, not easily impressed, appreciated the vista before her. A balmy breeze, no doubt born above the ocean only a hundred kilometers away, floated through her floral hairstyle, ruffling her white, petaloid locks and caressing her antennae. The day had been hotter earlier—too warm even for an Andorian—and, knowing that the summer months had arrived here in the southern hemisphere, Charivretha had anticipated an uncomfortable stay in Brintall. Despite the lightweight fabric of her floor-length dress—a lustrous gray that set off her cerulean skin and matched her eyes—she had expected the temperature and the thousands of people who would pass through the square to make this a long and difficult day. But as morning had faded into afternoon, the Bajoran sun had hidden behind the great mountain, releasing the city from its potentially torrid clutches. Now, what could have been the hottest time of the day had transformed into a soothing, prolonged dusk.

"I love the summer afternoons here," said the person to Charivretha's right, as though commenting on the councillor's thoughts. The woman had to raise her voice a bit to be heard above the susurrations of the crowd that filled the square below. "It's one of my favorite places."

Charivretha looked away from the mountain and over at Asarem Wadeen. The Bajoran second minister stared out over the landscape like a young *chei* regarding his *zhavey*. Charivretha recognized that expression. *Though not from Thirishar, at least not in a very long time,* she thought, not without some acrimony. "You're from here, aren't you?" she asked, also speaking up a touch so that she could be heard.

Asarem looked up—she stood a dozen or so centimeters shorter than the councillor—and smiled. Over tan slacks and a white blouse, the minister wore a tailored maroon jacket that fell to the tops of her knees and demonstrated her familiarity with the area's temperate summer weather. "Yes, I am," she confirmed. "Well, actually, I'm from a little town farther north—" She pointed to the right. "—called Lecelon. But I think of this whole area as my home."

"And yet you reside in the capital?" Again, Charivretha thought of her *chei*, so far from Andor—and from his bondmates—for so long now.

"I do," Asarem said. "With the Chamber of Ministers convening there, and the Vedek Assembly, and all the work I do with the first minister, it just made more sense to live in Ashalla than here," she explained. "But I visit when I can."

Even that—an occasional trip home by Thirishar—was something with which Charivretha could have coped. For so long now, her *chei* had obstinately refused to face his obligations, to her, to his bondmates and, most distressingly, to his people. Since she had last seen him on Deep Space 9 a few weeks ago, she had seriously contemplated the possibility of employing her considerable influence to see him reassigned within Starfleet, specifically to a posting on Andor. Europani and Bajoran matters had kept her occupied since she had accompanied Admiral Akaar here, but even one or two well-placed subspace communications could have begun the process. She probably would not have approached Akaar—she was unsure how he would have reacted to her request, in light of the complex relationship he had with his own people—but she knew many other admirals in Starfleet Command. Perhaps an even more effective resource, though, would have been Commander Vaughn; Elias had always proven himself to be somebody who could get things accomplished, swiftly and thoroughly. And only six days remained before Thirishar departed aboard a Starfleet vessel, bound on a dangerous mission that would, under the best of conditions, keep him away for months.

None of that would have been effective, though. Charivretha had realized after contemplating such a plan that it would not have resulted in Thirishar returning to Andor. Her young *chei* was stubborn and willful, and when she had reflected on their last conversation, she had concluded that he would sooner resign from Starfleet than go back home. That was why it had been necessary for her to set another course of action in motion.

"You have a lovely planet, a lovely city," Charivretha said, her diplomatic instincts continuing the dialogue, even as her mind traveled other paths.

"Thank you. I think so," Asarem said. "I've never been to Andor, though I have heard some interesting things about it. What's it like?"

I'm not the only politician here, Charivretha reminded herself, and her thoughts moved automatically down the avenues she would have to send the conversation to deflect Asarem's inquiry. But before she spoke again, the glass doors leading out to the balcony parted in the middle. Green, patterned curtains covering the glass on the inside swayed as the doors folded inward. First Minister Shakaar and Admiral Akaar stepped outside, an improvised communications center visible in the room behind them—behind Shakaar, anyway; because of his size, it was difficult to see anything past the admiral.

Like Asarem and Charivretha herself, Shakaar had dressed today in a more formal manner—in an olive jacket and matching slacks, with a russet shirt—than he had during the meetings the three of them, along with Akaar, had conducted these past weeks. When Charivretha and the admiral had first arrived, pomp and custom had seen each of the quartet in ceremonial attire, but as the days of their informal summit—held without their staffs—had grown longer and more complicated, they had all resorted to casual togs. Well, all of them but Akaar. *Starfleeters,* Charivretha thought. *They never want to give up their uniforms.* But the admiral had at least forgone his dress wear during their meetings, in favor of what he wore for regular, everyday duty. Today, though, he was back in full dress.

"They've begun," Shakaar pronounced, and Charivretha and Asarem both turned to peer out at the square. Since receiving notification yesterday that Europa Nova had been rendered habitable again by the Starfleet Corps of Engineers, Bajoran officials had organized the efforts necessary to return the Europani to their world. That coordination, led by the first minister's industrious assistant, had begun here in Brintall, where one of the smaller refugee groups, numbering only in the thousands, would be the first sent home; this group consisted of core personnel, including government leaders, physicians, disaster workers, and law enforcement. Later, and in the days ahead, the remainder of the three million refugees, currently housed all over Bajor and on Deep Space 9, would follow.

Charivretha looked to the four corners of the square, and then to four other areas surrounding a beautiful fountain in the square's center. Eight triangular zones had been roped off in the corners and around the fountain, set aside, she knew, as the places from which the refugees would be transported onto the ships waiting in orbit. The crowd milled about somewhat anxiously—Charivretha's antennae detected the heat output of the humans and conveyed their anticipation to her—but everybody seemed to respond dutifully to the members of the Bajoran Militia controlling the operation. Not only did the crowd seem particularly well behaved, Charivretha noted, but they were also relatively quiet, their combined voices a mere hum. She supposed that their excitement at going back to Europa Nova must have been tempered by their knowledge that, although decontaminated, their world would still bear the scars of the crisis they had endured. The civilization of the Europani had been saved, but now they would have to tackle years of rebuilding.

As Charivretha watched, Bajoran Militia personnel directed refugees into the designated areas. Silver, cylindrical devices—the councillor recognized them as pattern enhancers—stood atop tripodal bases at the three corners of each zone. Lights at the upper tips of the devices indicated their operational status. The enhancers, she knew, would facilitate transport from such a congested area.

After Charivretha saw a group of Europani dematerialize in a coruscation of white light, she turned to Shakaar. Behind him, voices emerged from within the building, some with the tinny character that distinguished them as emanating from communications equipment. The ad hoc comm setup provided a means of harmonizing the efforts of the ground-based personnel with those of the crews on the ships above. "Congratulations," Charivretha said, offering her compliments. "The completion of this operation will be a notable achievement for the Bajoran people."

"Thank you, Councillor," Shakaar said. "We're pleased that we've been able to help the Europani."

"Bajorans know something about losing their homes," Asarem noted. "It's been a pleasure and a privilege to help prevent that from happening to these people." She swung her arm out over the edge of the balcony, taking in the throng below.

"And we are very grateful for that." The voice came from just beyond the first minister and the admiral; from their reactions, it seemed that neither of them had heard anybody come up behind them. The two men moved aside, revealing the speaker, whom Charivretha knew at once. The woman, an older human with lines etched deeply into her face around her eyes and mouth, smiled broadly. "*I* am grateful," she added. With short, curly hair as white as Charivretha's, the woman looked almost like an albino Andorian, though few Andorians lived long enough to develop loose folds of flesh hanging from their neck, as this human had.

The woman reached her right hand out to the first minister, who took it in his own. "President Silverio," Shakaar greeted her warmly, but she raised the index finger of her left hand to stop him. "Grazia," he corrected himself, honoring the woman's preference to be addressed by her given name, something Charivretha was aware of from the time she had spent with the Europani leader prior to the crisis.

When Silverio's hand parted from Shakaar's, she took a stride past him and reached out to the second minister. "Grazia," said Asarem, stepping up and clasping the offered hand. Charivretha did not require her antennae to identify the genuinely cordial relationship between the Europani president and the two Bajoran ministers.

"And of course," Silverio went on, turning toward Charivretha and Akaar, "we're thankful to the Federation for all they've done for us." As Charivretha shook the Europani president's hand, the admiral made the traditional Capellan gesture of salutation. Silverio dipped her head to acknowledge Akaar, then asked, "Would you mind if I addressed the crowd from up here?" She looked around to apparently include all of them in her request. In turn, Charivretha, Akaar, and Asarem all looked toward Shakaar.

"Please," the first minister said. He walked forward, slipped his hand around Silverio's elbow, and escorted her to the solid wooden railing surrounding the balcony. Both Charivretha and Asarem retreated to make way for the Europani president. As she backed up, Charivretha noticed the design carved into the wood of the railing, a series of mountains, one much higher than the rest, clearly meant to evoke the surrounding geography.

Silverio raised her arms and her voice, motioning and calling to her fellow Europani. Charivretha heard Shakaar duck back inside and speak to the technicians in the communications center, asking them to tell the members of the Bajoran Militia in the square to halt operations while the president spoke. Silverio's voice, which Charivretha found relatively loud for such a small, old woman, could nevertheless not carry enough to drown out the sounds of the crowd. But as the people nearest the balcony heard her asking for their attention, they turned toward her and quieted, and like a ripple in a pond, the silence washed out from the balcony in an expanding semicircle, until all eyes were on Silverio.

"My fellow citizens," she began, "while we head today for home, we must stop to thank the United Federation of Planets and Starfleet for their steadfast help in evacuating our people to safety." Applause welled up within the square, a sound like a breeze rustling through leaves. When it diminished, Silverio continued. "We must also thank our Bajoran hosts for their help and for their gracious hospitality." Again, applause rose up. The Europani president smiled at the crowd, and Charivretha expected that she would step back after a moment, the political gratitude of her people—gratitude no less genuine for being political—appropriately expressed. Instead, she resumed speaking. "But we must thank the Bajorans for more than that. First Minister Shakaar tells me that their katterpod harvest this past year was a particularly strong one, so strong that the Bajoran government has agreed to send several shipments to Europa Nova to help us—" Applause swelled once more, but now raucous cheers joined it. Charivretha heard the rest of Silverio's words—"as we recover from the effects of radiation on our crops"—only because she was standing so close to her.

The announcement was a revelation to Charivretha. Not only had she been unaware of the development, she had not even suspected it. Considering the amount of time she and Admiral Akaar had spent with the first and second ministers since arriving on Bajor, she wondered when such an arrangement could have been negotiated. *Perhaps Kaval put the deal together,* she speculated, thinking about the Bajoran minister of state. *But no,* she thought. For all of the conventional wisdom that held to Shakaar's distaste for politics and public life, it seemed to Charivretha that the first minister involved himself in virtually all Bajoran matters of government, particularly those concerning off-world issues. Despite intelligence passed to the Federation Council—including excerpts from Captain Sisko's reports to Starfleet—that purported to make plain Shakaar's dislike of his job and his preference for an easier, more isolated life, Charivretha simply could not countenance such a notion. In her experience, it required more than mere commitment to successfully discharge the duties of high office; it demanded desire.

The applause and cheers continued for a few moments, and then Silverio went on. "The first minister has also agreed to provide us generous shipments of *kava* nuts and *pooncheen* fruit," she said, mentioning two more Bajoran staples. Again, the crowd erupted.

Charivretha felt a tingling in her antennae, a by-product of her surprise. She turned and gazed up at Akaar. He made eye contact with her immediately, but for a long moment it seemed as though he would not react to President Silverio's announcements. Finally, though, the edges of his mouth curled up in a smile so slight that she would likely have missed it had she not known him so well.

These past few months, as the subject of Bajor's entrance into the Federation had been revisited, one of the issues that had arisen had concerned the readiness of the Bajorans to join a larger community. Their remote location at the edge of explored space had not only left them vulnerable throughout their history—at least, throughout their *recent* history—but had also contributed to a practical isolationism, even if they had never set out to segregate themselves from the greater interstellar population. The Bajorans certainly had a deserved reputation as a spiritual, artistic, and gentle people—at least when not dealing with their longtime oppressors, the Cardassians—but their capacity to readily establish cooperative relationships with the people of other worlds had been questioned by some in the council, including Charivretha herself.

She turned back toward Silverio just as the woman concluded her short address. "We owe the Bajorans our fervent gratitude," Silverio said, "and we humbly offer them our heartfelt friendship." This time, Shakaar and Asarem applauded with the crowd, moving to the balcony on either side of the Europani president. The three political leaders stood there for a few moments, basking, it seemed, both in the positive feelings of the assemblage below and in each other's company.

When Silverio, Shakaar, and Asarem finally turned and stepped away from the railing, Charivretha wondered if the foodstuffs going to Europa Nova were examples of largesse or trade. In either case, she knew that the reduction in Bajor's available stockpile of food would have an effect on the aid they were sending to Cardassia. Assistance would continue to come from Federation and other worlds, of course, and she assumed the effort would still be managed by personnel on Deep Space 9, but she would have to examine the impact this would have on the Cardassians. *Probably negligible,* she guessed, since the use of Bajoran personnel and territory to stage the humanitarian efforts outweighed the importance of the relatively small amounts of food Bajor was contributing. Still, she would have to look into it.

The two ministers flanked the Europani president as they walked past Charivretha and Akaar. "I'm happy that Bajor could play a role in rescuing your people from disaster," Shakaar said to Silverio, "but I'm even happier that those efforts have resulted in a new partnership between our worlds."

"I am too." Charivretha watched as Silverio—*Grazia,* the councillor joked to herself—reached up and slid her arm into Shakaar's.

Charivretha and Akaar followed as the group went back into the communications room. The first minister told the Bajoran Militia personnel stationed there that the transport of the Europani could resume. "We'll be in the conference room," Shakaar added, and he and Asarem escorted the Europani president out.

Behind them, Charivretha stopped, appreciating the diplomacy she had just witnessed. Akaar halted beside her, and she looked up at him. He said nothing, but smiled again in that almost imperceptible way. She considered saying something about the implications, about the meaning, of what they had just seen, but then realized that they did not need to discuss it right now. She started walking again, and the admiral fell in step beside her, both of them, she was sure, having taken appropriate note of Bajor's continued growth within the Alpha Quadrant community.

10

The door glided open, and Nog stepped off the bridge and into the corridor. Voices and the electronic cheeps of diagnostic testing followed him out, then cut off abruptly as the door closed behind him. He walked quickly forward, paying little attention to anything but the padd he held in his raised hand. He studied the tabulated readout, analyzing the data. Words and numbers, colored green and yellow and red, and arranged in rows and columns, spelled out the results of the level-one diagnostic he had just completed on *Defiant*'s modified library-computer interfaces.

We're almost there, Nog thought, encouraged. Only a handful of the readings on the padd appeared in yellow, signifying marginally functional equipment, and only one—a measure of the data flow rate to a secondary interface in the stellar cartography lab—appeared in red, indicating an actual failure. He glanced up as he reached a junction, where the corridor curved back around to the left, and another stretched off to the right. Nog jogged to the right and headed toward the main corridor on the port side of the ship. *Stellar cartography,* he thought, shaking his head as he turned right again at the next intersection. The new lab had proven the most troublesome—

Nog barreled into somebody. The hand in which he held the padd slammed back into his own body. His other hand reached out and groped for the wall as he tried to maintain his balance, but his feet became entangled and he tumbled sideways onto the deck. Twisting his body around at the last moment, he rolled with the impact as he had been taught to do at the Academy. The other person landed next to him with a thud, and he heard the rattle of several small objects striking the deck.

"I'm sorry, I'm sorry," Nog said hurriedly, knowing that the collision had been his fault. He had been looking at his padd and not where he had been going, so intent on his work that he had not even heard the other person approaching the intersection. *And when a Ferengi doesn't hear something,* he thought, *it's their mistake.*

"No, no, I'm sorry, sir." Nog recognized the pitch and tone of the woman's voice immediately, as well as the slight but distinct cadence of her strange accent. Nog lifted himself onto his elbows and looked over at Ensign Roness. She reached over to him, putting her hands around his left biceps, apparently attempting to help him up even as she moved to rise herself.

"Gerda, it's all right," he said, tapping one of her hands lightly as a signal to her to let go of his arm. She did, and they both got to their knees and then to their feet.

"Are you hurt, sir?" Roness asked. She stood considerably taller than Nog did, and she peered down at him with an expression of obvious concern, and perhaps even of fear. She had, after all, just sent a senior officer sprawling onto the deck. "I didn't see you, I—"

"It's all right," Nog repeated. "I wasn't looking where I was going." He patted at his uniform, mechanically brushing away the dirt and dust he imagined to be there but did not actually see. He looked past Roness and down at the decking behind her, leaning first to his right and then to his left, until he finally spotted his padd. Nog stepped by her, bent, and retrieved it. "I was too busy checking diagnostic results," he said, holding up the padd to illustrate his point.

Roness smiled at him then, displaying a mouthful of perfectly aligned, perfectly white teeth, which looked to Nog far too squarish and blunt to be of any real use. As he had so many times before, he wondered just how *hew-mons* managed to chew their way through their food. As he considered her dentition, Roness walked past him, stooped down on one side of the corridor, and picked something up. Then she moved to the bulkhead opposite and grabbed something else. She stood and turned toward him, lifting both of her hands to show him the two padds she was holding. Her wide smile had transformed into a sheepish grin, and she shrugged comically. Nog laughed, a short, loud explosion of breath.

"I guess we're all pretty busy checking diagnostics these days," Roness said.

"I guess so," Nog agreed. Then, remembering that the ensign had also been knocked down, he asked, "Are you all right?"

"I am, I'm fine," she said. "Just a little bit surprised, that's all."

"Me too," Nog said with a smile. "So how's the work going?" he asked, pointing to the two padds she still held raised before her.

"Really well," she told him, lowering her arms. "Ensign Senkowski and his team just finished repairing the last of the hull breaches, and they're nearly done replating the ship's armor."

"That's great," Nog said enthusiastically. "I guess we won't need to push the launch back again."

"No, thank goodness for that," Roness said. Her eyes widened as she spoke, revealing the obvious importance to her of meeting the new schedule. Several of the crew, including Nog, had felt embarrassment at having to delay the start of their mission, although Commander Vaughn had lauded their efforts to refit and repair *Defiant* over such a short span of time.

"Well, I need to get down to the computer core," Nog said. Then, remembering that he carried the rank of lieutenant—something that still surprised him sometimes when he thought about it—he added, "Carry on, Ensign."

"Yes, sir," she said. "Thank you, sir." She started down the corridor and disappeared around the corner, apparently headed to the bridge. Nog turned and resumed his own course. This time, he only peeked occasionally at the padd, keeping his head up and his eyes primarily on his surroundings.

When he reached the port turbolift at the bow of the ship, he reached up with his empty hand and touched the control plate. The door slid open and he entered the lift. "Deck three," he said. "Port computer core." As the car descended, he raised the padd and began studying its contents again. *I'm not going to run into anybody just standing in a turbolift,* he thought, smiling to himself.

Nog was pleased by what the readouts on the padd indicated, and by the other reports he had received within the last couple of hours—including what Ensign Roness had just told him. Repairs to the ship were proceeding as expected, and the last major refit work to be completed was the conversion of the library computer. That involved both a modification to the existing interfaces, and a restructuring and reloading of scientific data to the dual computer cores. In the last few days, Lieutenant Candlewood and his team had made considerable progress, finishing almost all of the interface upgrades and loading more than half of the necessary data. Only the secondary systems in the stellar cartography lab continued to give them any significant trouble, as almost all of the systems in that lab had since they had begun its installation. If he could, Nog would have locked on to the entire lab and transported it out into space—except of course that, on an exploratory mission like the one *Defiant* would be embarking on, stellar cartography would see more use than just about any other system on the ship.

Nog felt the lift slow and complete its vertical descent, then felt it move horizontally toward his destination amidship. *At least we'll be able to leave the station in five days,* Nog thought, as pleased as Ensign Roness had been that Commander Vaughn would not have to delay the start of the mission a second time. Of course, they could probably gain an entire day back on the timetable. Nog was scheduled to be off duty three days from now, but if he worked instead—

No, Nog thought as the turbolift eased to a stop. Commander Vaughn had been clear and firm when he had announced the one-day postponement in the launch of the mission: he had required all crewmembers to take their regular time away from their duties. *That's probably the smart thing to do,* Nog conceded as the turbolift door slid open. Although he would have been content to work every day until they departed for the Gamma Quadrant, he recalled how miserable Uncle Quark's employees had been before they had formed a union and demanded, among other things, fixed time off.

Nog strode out of the lift, turned right down the corridor—and barreled into somebody, although it felt more like he had run into some*thing* this time. Whoever or whatever he had struck, it sent him reeling backward. He lost his balance and fell onto his back. He let go of the padd and slapped the decking with his open hands as he landed, trying to absorb some of the impact—again, as he had been instructed to do at the Academy. He yelped as the air was knocked out of him, a high-pitched squeal that reminded him of Uncle Quark. He labored for breath, then recalled his training and tried to control his breathing. He closed his eyes and concentrated, realizing then that his head must have struck the deck, because he felt suddenly dizzy.

Slowly, air returned to Nog's lungs, and his head stopped spinning. He struggled up onto one elbow, took a deep breath, and shook his head to clear it. Only when he had opened his eyes did it occur to him that, unlike when he and Ensign Roness had run into each other, nobody had tried to come to his aid this time. The reason became immediately apparent: Nog recognized the black boots of the figure standing in front of him even before he looked up and saw their owner.

Nog gasped. He rolled his eyes up, but did not lift his head, as he took in the boots, the black coverall, and then the hideous face of the Jem'Hadar. Instinctively, Nog listened, hoping to hear the footsteps or the voice of an approaching crewperson. But he heard nothing but the machinery of *Defiant,* his own shallow breathing, and the breathing of the Jem'Hadar. Nog was alone with him, he realized . . . alone with *it.*

"Don't hurt me," Nog whispered, and he could hear the tremors in his own voice. Fear gripped him, and all of the rationalizations he had made to himself—and that other people had made to him—about trusting this Jem'Hadar, about allowing this murderous being to remain on the station, fled from him in an instant. All at once, it was of no consequence that Odo had vouched for this thing; Odo was not here, was not on the station or even in the Alpha Quadrant, and this creature had been designed and hatched to be a killing machine. Nothing changed that, not Odo's intentions, not the Jem'Hadar's independence from ketracel-white, and not all of the people on DS9 who wanted to believe that peace with the Dominion meant that nonviolent coexistence with the Jem'Hadar was possible. Colonel Kira, Admiral Ross, Captain Picard, Commander Vaughn—they had all been fools, and now Nog would pay the ultimate price, as though he had not paid enough already.

The Jem'Hadar towered over him, like one of the docking pylons rising high above the rings of Deep Space 9. Living on the station for as long as he had, and then attending Starfleet Academy, Nog had grown accustomed to having to look up at almost all of the people he met, but not like this. From his position on the deck, he felt as though he were staring a kilometer up into the sky. The 53rd and 235th Rules of Acquisition occurred to him—"Never trust anybody taller than you," and "Duck; death is tall"—and he understood them as he never had before. His father had first recited the rules—

Father. Nog pictured him, thinking about how he would react to the news of his son's death: he would be devastated. Anger joined with Nog's fear as he imagined the terrible sadness his father would feel. Quickly, vowing to battle both his fear and this monster, Nog moved, reaching his left hand up to his chest and slapping at his combadge to activate it. "Nog to security." The words had left his mouth before he realized that his combadge was no longer pinned to his uniform. It must have fallen off, either when he had collided with Ensign Roness, or when he had collided with . . . this.

Nog lifted his head and looked up at the Jem'Hadar. It squinted down at him, clearly sizing up its prey. Nog hurriedly looked around, searching for something, anything, that would help him. *The padd,* he thought, trying to find it. He could throw it at the Jem'Hadar's face, maybe buy himself enough time to get back into the turbolift—

Nog whirled his head around as he caught movement in his peripheral vision. The Jem'Hadar had stepped forward and now reached down to grab him. Nog thrust his feet hard against the deck, his legs acting like pistons as he scurried backward away from the monster. With one impact, pain shot through his left knee. He rolled onto his side and tried to push himself to his feet. For a moment, he thought he would make it, and then the Jem'Hadar's hands closed around his chest and side like vises. Nog's feet came clear of the deck as he was lifted. His anger and resolve slipped away, leaving him alone once more with his fear. He opened his mouth to scream—Starfleet officer or not, he did not want to die—but only air emerged. His ears went cold.

"We are not at war with each other," the Jem'Hadar said as he settled Nog back onto his feet.

Nog stopped trying to scream, but he remained agape. The monster's voice, which he had not heard in quite some time, and never at such close range, came out not as a growl, but full and rich. The sound startled Nog, and he stared up at the Jem'Hadar's face. For long seconds, the creature's powerful hands remained locked around his upper torso, and Nog thought that if the Jem'Hadar squeezed, it would crush the life out of him. Nog closed his eyes, waiting for the inevitable.

But the creature released him. His body now unsupported, Nog's leg started to give way beneath him. He staggered to the left a step, his knee buckling. He reached down and wrapped his hands around it, forcing it straight and keeping himself on his feet.

"Did you hurt your leg?" the Jem'Hadar asked.

Nog stood back up and stared into the face of the enemy. Not much more than a year ago, the lower part of his leg had been destroyed by a blast from a Jem'Hadar weapon. The memory—still clear, still haunting—surrounded Nog like a toxic fog, choking him as it closed in around him. In his mind, he hunted for something to give himself air, to protect him from the suffocating closeness of his memories and his terror. What he found was hatred.

"You blew my leg off," Nog said, his voice hissing through his clenched teeth.

The creature's brow knotted. It cocked its head at an angle, obviously not understanding Nog's words.

"A Jem'Hadar shot my leg off," Nog said, his voice louder now. *Why am I standing here?* he asked himself. *Why am I talking to this creature?* He should leave, he knew, turn and escape as swiftly as he could. But he did not move. Instead, he watched as the Jem'Hadar peered down at his leg. "It's biosynthetic," Nog said.

The Jem'Hadar nodded. "You are fortunate to have reclaimed your life," it told him, its voice lacking any detectable inflection, as though simply reciting a cold fact.

It is a cold fact, Nog told himself, and then pushed the thought away. "I don't feel 'fortunate,'" he spat, and an image rose in his mind, vivid and real: he saw himself holding a phaser trained on this monster before him. In the fantasy, Nog did not hesitate; he depressed the trigger and fired a beam of white-hot energy into the Jem'Hadar's chest, vaporizing it into nothingness. "Would you feel 'fortunate' to trade your leg for a hunk of rock in the Chin'toka system." It was not a question. Nog knew he should leave while he could, but somehow the depth of his loathing kept him there; he wanted—he *needed*—this creature to express remorse for what the other Jem'Hadar had done to him.

"The Chin'toka system," it said. "I am aware of it. The Dominion housed a primary communications relay there during the war." For the first time, Nog thought he detected emotion in the creature's voice: resentment, maybe even anger.

Good, Nog thought. *Let it feel what I feel.*

"Seventy-two Jem'Hadar were killed in that action," the creature continued, and now Nog was certain that he heard anger in its voice.

"You were trying to kill us," Nog said, struck by the incongruity of offering up a defense for Starfleet's attempts to save the people of the Alpha Quadrant from the invading hordes of the Dominion.

"It was the Founders' will," the Jem'Hadar said.

"That doesn't make it right," Nog said, the volume of his voice climbing.

"Of course it does," the Jem'Hadar avowed. "Everything done in the name of the Founders is right."

"Shooting my leg off?" Nog's voice had risen almost to the point of screaming.

"The Jem'Hadar soldiers you fought were trying to kill you, I'm sure," the creature said. "Their mission was to defend the communications station. They were carrying out their duty. You fought them. Shooting you was the appropriate thing to do."

Nog seethed, and he suddenly felt the urge to lunge forward at this monstrosity, regardless of the consequences.

"Everything done in the name of the Founders is right," the Jem'Hadar repeated. "If that was not true, then I would not be standing here." It leaned forward, bringing its face to within centimeters of Nog's. "Or *you* would not be standing here." The threat carried in the words only reinforced the menace on the Jem'Hadar's face.

Nog staggered backward, unable to stand his ground. This creature, this Dominion *soldier,* would one day reclaim its birthright, Nog knew; it would kill again, and it would do so soon.

Nog turned and looked at the bulkhead beside the turbolift, then reached over and touched the control plate. The door opened, and Nog backed into the car. "I'm *not* standing here," he said, mustering what little defiance he could. As he moved to the rear of the lift, he spotted his padd near the bulkhead on the far side of the corridor. His eyes were still on it as the door slid closed.

"Port airlock," he said, and the lift started its horizontal journey to the bow of the ship. Nog would go back to the station and report to Colonel Kira what had happened, and make her understand how dangerous the Jem'Hadar was . . . except that he knew that she would not understand. She believed Odo—they all did—and she would ascribe Nog's warnings to fear, and to the terrible injury he had suffered in the Chin'toka system.

Nog would still go back to the station, though. He would go to ops, work one of the sensor consoles, and return to *Defiant* only once the Jem'Hadar had left it.

They were carrying out their duty, Nog thought. Which was true, he supposed, except that their duty was to kill and to conquer. These creatures, these *things,* had been created specifically for that purpose. They were no better than charged phaser banks, chambered quantum torpedoes, and with no more conscience or morality than those weapons. And worse than that: they *liked* what they did, every one of them.

Nog's hands began to tremble.

"I hate them," he said aloud, and knew that he was right to do so.

PROPERTY OF
National College
Library

11

"I'm ruined," Quark said. He threw an elbow up onto the bar, dropped his chin into it, and peered out at empty chairs, empty tables, and worst of all, an unmoving dabo wheel. Treir, his newest dabo girl—an Orion, tall, gorgeous, and majestically green—stood by the gaming table with her arms folded across her chest, looking painfully bored. Two of his waiters, Frool and Grimp, stood quietly in a corner, leaning against a wall and looking equally uninterested in being there. Business had been so slow tonight that Quark had sent the rest of his staff home.

The virtual night of Deep Space 9 encroached on Quark's as it rarely had recently, sending shadows and silences into the lightly populated establishment. The festive colors reflected by the dabo wheel, and usually sent spinning around the room, instead rested statically on the walls. A dreary dimness hung between the orange and yellow stained-glass artwork on one side of the room, and the many hues of the bottles sitting behind the bar on the other. The absence of the whoops and cries of dabo players and the overlapping conversations of a large crowd left the place bereft of meaty sound, with the occasional, reedy ring of glassware a lonely underscore to the relative quiet.

"'Ruined,' Quark?" Skepticism filled the voice of Ro Laren, who sat across the bar from him. Quark looked over to see her eyebrows raised on her forehead, and a closed-mouth smile that he thought just might be hinting at mischief. The two were by themselves at the bar, at the end farthest from the entrance.

"Ruined," Quark maintained. "Just look at this place." He brought his elbow up off the bar and motioned with both hands at his establishment. Ro swiveled on her stool and gazed around. "It's not even twenty-six hundred and there are only—" Quark hurriedly scanned the room from side to side, then glanced up at the tables on the second level, aggregating the clientele with practiced precision, though tonight that did not take much of an effort. "—seven customers here." He raised an arm and pointed across at the dabo table, where a Tellarite freighter captain sat bent over the gaming surface, her head resting on the wager board between her splayed arms. "And one of them's not even conscious."

Ro laughed at that, just a short chuckle, but it affected Quark as though it were music. *And not that Klingon opera tripe,* he thought; thanks to Jadzia and Worf, Quark had heard more than enough of that overdramatic bellowing during the last eight years. No, Ro's laughter sounded light and lyrical, like a Betazoid dance suite.

"Well, I'm not saying you're not having a bad night," Ro amended, spinning back toward the bar. "But ruined?"

"I'm telling you," Quark said, "this is the start of a downturn. I can feel it in my lobes."

"Your lobes, huh?" Still, the impish smile remained on her face.

Quark grasped the edge of the bar and bent forward, as though about to offer Ro something in confidence. "Never," he began, his voice conspiratorially hushed, "underestimate the lobes of a Ferengi."

Ro leaned on her forearms over the bar and dropped the volume of her own voice, obviously playing along. "I'll remember that," she said.

Quark pushed back from the bar and smiled himself. "You do have to admit, we've got some pretty nice, pretty large ears." He waved in the general direction of the side of his head.

Ro sat back on her stool and threw up her hands in what Quark took to be mock frustration. "What is it with men and size?" she said. "Not everything worthwhile is big."

"Or tall," Quark said without missing a beat. To his delight, Ro smiled widely.

"Or tall," she agreed. They regarded each other across the bar for a moment, and Quark felt that they had made a connection beyond his flirting with her. "Still, I don't think you're ruined," Ro finally said, turning her head and looking around. The moment passed.

"Listen," Quark told her, "closing time is hours away, nobody's gambling, nobody's using the holosuites, and Morn's not even here." He peered toward the other end of the bar, where his best customer for more than a decade typically sat. The usually reliable Morn, Quark knew, had forgone the bar tonight in favor of his own quarters, where he was giving a poetry reading for anybody on DS9 who wanted to attend; Morn had sent invitations to every personal companel on the station. "Plus, I've got only six conscious customers, and one of those," he said, teasingly referring to Ro, "is only drinking *pooncheenee*." He reached forward and picked up the short, translucent blue glass sitting on the bar in front of Ro. "Another, Lieutenant?" he asked. Quark had no taste himself for the sweet, fruity beverage—he kept it in the bar primarily for use as a mixer—but a lot of Bajorans liked it.

Ro made a show of considering the question, the ridges at the top of her nose wrinkling together. Then she asked, "What else have you got?"

Quark turned and set the empty glass down in an area he reserved for discards, of which there were pathetically few right now; later, one of his employees would recycle the used bottles and glasses, utilizing the replicator. Then he examined the shelves at the back of the bar, and the bottles that lined them in various shapes, sizes, and colors. *What can I give Laren?* he asked himself, searching for something with a bit of flavor and character. Not finding anything to his liking, he checked the stock below the bar, finally pulling out an amber bottle with a distinctively curved, tapered neck. "Saurian brandy?" he asked, offering the label for Ro to inspect.

"Sure," she said. "Why not?"

Quark bent behind the bar again and retrieved a crystal snifter. He set it down in front of Ro and removed the leather hood from the top of the bottle, letting it dangle from the cord that was attached to a strip surrounding the base of the neck. "Captain Sisko never used to come in here much," he said as he poured out two fingers of the brandy, "but this was his favorite drink, so I used to keep it around for functions."

"Functions?" Ro asked. She slid her upturned palm beneath the bowl of the glass, her middle and fourth fingers on either side of the stem, and lifted the brandy to her lips.

"Starfleet conferences, political meetings, the occasional party," Quark explained. "I'll say this for the man: for a Starfleet type, he sure knew the value of quality catering."

"Hmmm, this is excellent," Ro said after she had taken a sip of the brandy.

"Have you ever had it before?" Quark asked.

"I have, just not in a very long time," Ro told him before raising the snifter to her lips again. She took a second sip, then lowered the glass to the bar. "So, you're not all that fond of 'Starfleet types,' huh?"

"Well, you have to admit, they're not always all that much fun." He grabbed the hood and replaced it atop the brandy bottle.

"No," Ro agreed. "But they do keep the peace."

"Sometimes," Quark said, the tone of his voice falling to convey his cynicism. He recalled the incident a few years ago when the Bajorans had barred all Ferengi from their system and from the wormhole, and how the Federation had refused to involve itself. He refused to dwell on the memory—some of what had happened back then remained too painful for him to think about, even now—but his estimation of the Federation and Starfleet still lingered. "When it's in their own interests to do so," he added.

"You know, Quark," Ro said, her mischievous smile returning, "I was a Starfleet type."

"Oh, you may have been in Starfleet," Quark said, discounting the idea with a wave of his hand, "but I'm sure you were never the Starfleet *type*." He bent and placed the Saurian brandy bottle back below the bar.

Ro took another sip of her drink. "What makes you say that?"

"Well, for one thing, that's a Bajoran Militia uniform you're wearing, not a Starfleet one, which means you didn't stay in Starfleet. And for another, just look around." Quark gestured to include the rest of the bar. "You're here, but I don't see any Starfleet types. And the *Gryphon*'s been docked at the station off and on for three days now, in between trips to Europa Nova, so we've got another few hundred of them wandering about." Quark shook his head and rolled his eyes. "They're probably all down in Morn's quarters listening to him spout poetry."

Ro laughed so hard that she nearly choked on her drink. A lilt Quark had not heard before emerged at the upper reaches of her chortles. The sound delighted him.

"What's so amusing?" somebody asked. Quark looked away from Ro to see that Commander Vaughn—still clad in his uniform despite the lateness of the hour—had entered the bar. Quark's attention had been so focused on Ro that he had not even heard the commander approach. Normally, Quark would have been concerned by the lapse—*Ears open, eyes wide,* went an old Ferengi saying to which he had always subscribed—but the truth was that his ears had been open and his eyes had been wide; they had simply been filled with the intoxicating sound and sight of Ro Laren.

"Good evening, Commander," Quark said. "Just the old joke about a *hew-mon,* a Klingon, and a Romulan walking into a Vulcan embassy."

"I know that one," Vaughn said, and Quark recognized the commander's graciousness in allowing him to avoid honestly answering the question. "It's not that funny."

"Ah, well, I guess humor is in the ear of the beholder," Quark said, intentionally paraphrasing an old *hew-mon* expression.

"I guess it is," Vaughn said. "Lieutenant, how are you this evening?" he asked, addressing Ro.

"I'm fine, Commander, thank you," she said, and Quark noticed a sudden stiffness in her manner.

"You know, we never did get a chance to talk about your experiences in Advanced Tactical training," Vaughn said. "I'd still like to do that." For a horrible moment, Quark thought that the commander would sit down. He actually liked the old man—Vaughn had so far treated him with respect, even asking for his opinions about the Gamma Quadrant—but Quark did not want any intrusions into this unexpected time with Ro. Fortunately, Vaughn did not take a seat, nor did he even burden Ro with having to answer his question. "Of course," he told her, "it'll probably have to wait a few months until I return from *Defiant's* mission."

"I'll look forward to it," Ro said, and while her voice and the expression on her face seemed genuine, Quark thought he detected an aspect of discomfort in her response. She raised her glass and drank more of the brandy.

"Very good," Vaughn said. "So, Quark, did you procure that item I ordered?"

"Oh, yes," Quark said, suddenly remembering that he had received the item earlier today. He had been paying such close attention to Ro that it had not occurred to him when Vaughn had come in. "Just a second," he said, moving down the bar in search of the bottle. He found it quickly and hoisted it up by its neck onto the bar. "Here you are, Commander."

Vaughn reached forward and slid his hand around the bulbous bottom of the dark-green bottle, then spun it around so that he could read the label. Apparently satisfied, he said, "That's the stuff."

"Glad to be of service," Quark said. "Now, how will you be paying for that?"

Vaughn smiled, and Quark smiled back, knowing what the old man would say. "Obviously it's slipped your mind that you asked for payment in full when I ordered it."

"Oh, that's right," Quark said, putting on his expression of sudden remembrance, though he knew it would not fool Vaughn. "My mistake, Commander."

"Thank you, Quark," Vaughn said, hefting the bottle into the crook of his arm. "By the way, you wouldn't happen to have an old holosuite program set on Earth, would you?"

"Actually, I do, Commander," Quark said, pleased that this intrusion might at least lead to more business. He reached below the bar and pulled out a small metal box, flipping open its lid to reveal the orange tips of several dozen isolinear rods.

"I'm actually looking for something specific," Vaughn said. "Do you have anything from North America in the twentieth or twenty-first centuries relating to space travel?"

"Earth space travel in the twentieth century?" Quark said, mulling over the request. "Had *hewmons* even left their planet back then?" Quark had not intended the question as an insult, but he realized as soon as he had said it that it might have sounded that way. Before he could rephrase it, though, Vaughn answered.

"Just barely," the commander said with a smile, clearly not offended.

Quark considered the request, knowing he had nothing exactly like what Vaughn had asked for, but trying to think of any other holosuite programs that might satisfy the commander's needs. "I'm afraid I don't have that," Quark said hurriedly, "but I do have several other twentieth-century Earth programs: Paris, New York, Las Vegas—that's an amazing program—"

"Thank you, no," Vaughn said, interrupting Quark's list. "I didn't think you'd have what I was looking for, but I thought I would ask, just to be sure."

"I'm sorry, Commander," Quark said. "I could look for something like that for you, though . . . special-order it."

"Perhaps when I get back from the Gamma Quadrant."

"Believe me," Quark told him, "I could use the business."

"So I see," Vaughn said, turning and surveying the empty bar.

Quark took the moment to look over at Ro. Her eyes were cast downward, at the surface of the bar. She seemed uncomfortable.

When Vaughn turned around toward the bar again, Quark looked back up at him. "The station has quieted down considerably since the Europani departed," Vaughn offered.

"The Europani," Quark agreed, "and the crews of the ships taking them back to their planet."

"Of course," Vaughn said. "Well, I hope business improves for you. Thank you for this." He indicated the bottle, then looked to Ro. "Good night, Lieutenant."

"Commander," Ro said, looking up and smiling, though it appeared to Quark like a professional smile and not a personal one.

Quark watched as Vaughn exited the bar. When the commander had gone, Quark turned his attention back to Ro. "You were awfully quiet," he said, trying to achieve a tone of nonchalance. He flipped the lid closed on the box of isolinear rods.

"Yeah," she said. "Actually, I like Commander Vaughn. It's just that . . . well, I guess you were right: I'm not really the Starfleet type."

"Take it from me," Quark told her, "that's not the worst thing in the universe." He bent and returned the box of holosuite programs to its place beneath the bar.

"Maybe not," she said, seeming suddenly pensive. She was quiet for a few seconds, and then said, "May I ask you a question, Quark?"

"The answer is *yes*," he told her immediately. In a heartbeat, another smile blossomed on her face.

"You haven't even heard the question yet," she said.

Quark leaned on the bar and looked into Ro's eyes. "I trust you," he said.

Ro chuckled warmly, and Quark felt a chill run through his lobes. No sound had affected him like that in a long time, not even the delicious chink of latinum. Ro held his gaze a moment longer, then asked, "Are you really ruined?" He could not tell whether that was the question she had initially intended to ask him.

"Well, *ruined* might be putting it a little strongly," he admitted, pushing away from the bar. "But business has been mostly slow since the end of the war. Having the Europani and the convoy crews on the station helped, but profits dipped while I was away at Farius Prime."

"Sorry about that," Ro said. She had been the one who had secured his cooperation in the whole Iconian gateways mess, through a mixture of cajolery and coercion, though he liked to think that he would have gone along anyway, simply as a favor to her. "Well, maybe not that sorry," she said, her tone light. "There *was* that nasty bit of business on Cardassia."

"Yes, well, if you want to include my financial reversals there," he said, playing along with her teasing, "then business is really in decline." All of which was both true and troubling, Quark knew, but somehow it did not seem like such a bad thing to joke about it right now. "And that doesn't even take into account the generous contract I gave Treir."

" 'Generous'?" Ro asked. She lifted the snifter and sipped once more at the brandy.

"You wouldn't believe it if I told you."

"Maybe not," she said. "Actually, I thought she was working out." Ro looked over her shoulder at the dabo table, and Quark followed her gaze. The Tellarite captain had not moved, but Treir had sat down and was now leaning her head against her hand, her elbow propped up on the table.

"Well, I have to admit that her presence in the bar has turned some heads and brought in some customers," Quark said. "The freighter crews *loved* her. Of course, that was up until two days ago, when there were still people other than Starfleet types on the station."

"Personally, I like the lull," Ro said. "It's allowed me the first real free time I've had since I've been here."

Quark grunted his disagreement. "When it's quiet, business suffers. And when business suffers, I'm not happy."

"Oh, I don't know about that, Quark," Ro said. "If not for the quiet, I might not have come in here."

Quark could not be certain—he had never been terribly good at judging these things—but he thought he might not be the only one flirting now. He started to respond, but then he heard something. He turned from Ro and looked off into the middle distance, concentrating and trying to identify the sound.

"What's wrong?" Ro asked.

"Nothing," Quark said. "I hear a group of people . . . a *large* group of people . . . heading this way."

"I don't hear anything," she said. "Are you sure?" By way of an answer, Quark looked back at her and tugged at one of his ears. They waited for a few seconds, and then Quark saw that Ro could hear it too. The voices increased in volume as they drew closer, with laughter and yelling mixed in. A moment later, Morn wandered into the bar at the head of a boisterous throng. The bald Lurian strode directly over to his usual seat, plopped himself down, and looked around for somebody to serve him. Several of Morn's companions joined him at the bar, while the bulk of the crowd scattered to various locations—including, Quark was pleased to see, the dabo table. Treir had risen from her seat, he saw, and now stood in a sultry pose next to the dabo wheel. Remarkably, the Tellarite captain had been removed to a nearby table, where she sat groggily back in a chair, apparently trying to shake off her night of hard drinking. The noise level in the bar had, in a matter of a few seconds, escalated dramatically. Quark and Ro looked at each other in amazement.

"That must have been some poetry reading," Quark finally said, raising his voice to be heard.

"I guess so," Ro said, also raising her voice.

Quark scanned the room for Frool and Grimp, got their attention, and pointed where he wanted them to go. "I should never have let Broik leave for the night," he said to himself. Then, to Ro, he said, "Excuse me for a minute." He started toward the other end of the bar to serve Morn, but stopped when Ro called after him.

"Good night, Quark," she said, standing from her barstool.

"No, you're not leaving," he said, hoping that he could wait on his customers and then return to his conversation with her.

"Like I said," she told him, "I liked the lull."

Quark thought about what he could possibly say to convince her to stay, but he could see her discomfort with the raucous crowd, so he simply said, "Good night, Laren."

"Thanks for the brandy," she said, gesturing back at the nearly empty snifter as she began walking toward the door. "Put it—" She stopped, came back to the bar, and leaned across it, obviously wanting to say something to Quark without anybody else hearing it. He leaned over the bar, putting his ear up close to her lips. "Put it on my tab," she whispered.

Quark turned and smiled at her. *Beautiful* and *considerate,* he thought; she must have realized that he extended lines of credit to very few of his customers, and that he wanted as few people as possible to know that he did so at all.

"Thanks again," she said.

"Anytime." He stood motionless behind the bar and watched her leave. When she had gone, he said it again: "Anytime." Then he turned and paced down to the other end of the bar.

"Okay, Morn," he said, "which one of your usuals will it be?" But even amid the call of profits, he was still thinking about Ro Laren.

12

Akaar exited the turbolift—ducking his head out of long-standing habit—and stepped into the dimly lighted corridor. Capellans as a rule possessed keen eyesight, slightly sharper than that of humans, but he found it did him little good aboard this station. With such a low level of afternoon illumination, he wondered how much darker it became here at night. He imagined wandering around in complete blackness, tripping over raised doorsills, banging his head on low transoms, and ending up hopelessly lost in this dreadful Cardassian labyrinth.

Akaar peered both ways down the corridor. He had consulted a station directory and diagram prior to heading down here, but now he could not recall which way he needed to go. He spied what seemed to be a companel in the bulkhead opposite the turbolift, and he walked over and tapped its reflective surface. The panel came to life, a Cardassian "shatterframe" display appearing on it, accompanied by a short series of electronic tones. Akaar studied the unbalanced, asymmetric polygons arranged around the central, circular viewing area, and decided that the station's crew—Starfleet and Bajoran personnel alike—rated commendations simply for serving in this inhospitable setting.

"Computer," he said, "direct me to Commander Vaughn's quarters." His voice echoed faintly in the empty corridor. The panel hummed briefly, but did nothing more. Akaar waited for a moment, then reached up and tentatively touched the screen again. Another series of tones sounded, and then the computer addressed him.

"State request." It surprised Akaar that the voice was not male, and even more so that it was not entirely unfriendly.

"Computer," he repeated, his fingers still pressed against the panel, "direct me to Commander Vaughn's quarters."

"Restate request."

Akaar sighed. Attempting a different approach, he said, "Computer, locate Commander Vaughn."

"Commander Vaughn is in his quarters."

"Computer, where are Commander Vaughn's quarters?" he asked, and the computer dutifully recited the level, section, and cabin numbers that Akaar had already ascertained from the station directory. "Computer, how do I get there from my present location?"

"Restate request."

Akaar dropped his head, then sighed a second time. Clearly, his assessment of the computer as "not unfriendly" had been premature. He dropped his hand from the companel, which blinked off after a couple of seconds. He looked both ways down the corridor again, then arbitrarily set off to the left. He passed two doors on one side of the corridor and two on the other, determining from the increasing numbers on the accompanying wall plates that he was headed in the right direction. At the next door, though, the number unpredictably decreased. He stopped in his tracks, thinking that perhaps abandoning Deep Space 9, né Terok Nor, to the Bajorans, and thus to the Federation, had actually been part of an insidious Cardassian plot to sow madness through the galaxy.

He decided to walk as far as the next turbolift. If he had not located Vaughn's quarters by that point, then he would contact ops and ask for assistance, embarrassing as that would be. *A fleet admiral, decades in space, with tens of thousands of light-years behind me,* he thought, *and I can't even locate a cabin on a space station.* He laughed quietly to himself, and then thought that perhaps this had not been the Cardassians' doing after all, but Vaughn's; it would have been just like Elias to find some means of concealing the location of his quarters.

Akaar started down the corridor again, fully prepared to admit defeat. The next door he came to was Vaughn's. He laughed again, although this time with less humor; he realized that he had been entertaining a hope that he would not find Vaughn, and that he would not have to tell his old friend what he had done. *A fool's daydream,* Akaar told himself, and then he touched the access panel. A moment later, the door glided open. He lifted his feet over the sill and bowed his head beneath the upper doorframe, feeling as though he had to fold himself up in order to move around this station. *Not that* Gryphon *or* Defiant *or any other Starfleet vessels are much better,* he thought. He looked forward to the day when Capella would construct its own space stations and its own starships, with doorways and chairs and beds that would comfortably accommodate larger people.

Akaar glanced around as he entered the room. The layout and furnishings seemed standard: a sitting area, a dining table and chairs, replicator, companel, a closed door on the far side of the room that doubtless led into a bedroom. Nothing appeared out of the ordinary or even noteworthy; anybody could have lived here. *These could even be guest quarters,* Akaar thought, except that even lodging for a guest typically contained some sort of adornments. Here, there was nothing, though he supposed the absence did not stand out unless you looked for it. The walls featured no paintings or other artwork, and no books or pictures or other personal items sat on any of the tables. Akaar knew that Vaughn had been on the station for only a couple of months so far, and that he always traveled with few belongings, meaning that he had probably arrived here with very little. And perhaps he had not even decided whether he would remain on Deep Space 9 for the long term. *Or perhaps,* Akaar thought, *these quarters are just the way Elias wants them.*

Vaughn himself stood on the opposite side of the room, in front of a wide, eye-shaped window. Dressed in his uniform, he looked no different from the way he had the last time Akaar had seen him. Of course, through all the years Akaar had known him, Vaughn's appearance had never seemed to change much.

"Did you travel halfway across the quadrant to inspect my quarters, Admiral," Vaughn said from the window, "or are you going to greet me with an open heart and hand?"

"Elias," Akaar said, striding farther into the room. Vaughn walked over from the window, and when they met, Akaar extended a hand to him. Vaughn did the same, and they wrapped their hands around each other's forearms.

"L.J., it's good to see you," Vaughn said.

"And you," Akaar responded. "Although I am never certain where I will find you next." Throughout their careers in Starfleet, Akaar had unexpectedly encountered Vaughn on a number of occasions, in a number of locales. Before coming to Bajor, though, Akaar had been aware of Vaughn's presence on DS9; *all* of the admiralty knew of his transfer here, though not all of them supported the move.

"I do make my way around," Vaughn agreed. He released his grip on Akaar's arm, and Akaar did the same. Vaughn then walked past him and over to the sofa. "Please, have a seat."

"I have been seated for days," Akaar told him. He followed Vaughn over to the sitting area, but the two remained standing.

"The Bajorans?" Vaughn asked.

"During the weeks of meetings we had with them, yes," Akaar said, "but during the past few days, it has been the Europani. When you have hundreds of crew and thousands of passengers aboard an *Akira*-class starship, there is not much you can do but stay in your quarters." Over the past four days, Akaar had made numerous trips between Bajor and Europa Nova aboard *Gryphon,* part of a sizable convoy ferrying the Europani back to their newly decontaminated world.

"Just be grateful Europani aren't the size of Capellans," Vaughn joked. "You would've had to sleep on the outside of the hull." Akaar laughed as Vaughn walked over toward the dining area. "If you won't sit, L.J., can I at least get you something to drink or eat?"

"Considering the friendly nature of this station," Akaar said with measured sarcasm, "I am afraid to see what may emerge from a Cardassian replicator." Again he followed Vaughn across the room.

Vaughn circled around the dining table and stepped up to the replicator. "Deep Space 9's not unfriendly," he said. "It's got character."

"As does a black hole," Akaar said, "but I would not want to spend any time in one." .

Vaughn gestured at the replicator. "So what would you like? It's only seventeen-thirty, but are you in the mood for an early dinner?"

"I have not had a meal since early this morning, so I am hungry," Akaar said. "I do not suppose any Capellan foods are programmed into the replicators here. I have been craving some *koltari* stew lately."

"Let's see," Vaughn said, and ordered the dish. Akaar was not surprised when the computer asked him to furnish parameters for it. Vaughn shrugged, then inquired about any Capellan foods at all; none were available. "Sorry," Vaughn said. "I've done a bit of tinkering since I've been here, though, and I've managed to introduce a few new meals, and improve some others. There's a better-than-fair approximation of that dinner we had on Earth, in Rome, back during the last Tholian visit." Akaar did not recall the meal to which Vaughn referred—though he certainly remembered the calamity with the Tholians—but he trusted his old friend's memory and intentions. Vaughn ordered a family-style serving of *"pasta fagioli,"* which did not sound familiar to Akaar, although he thought he recognized the preparation of "extra garlic."

The food materialized on the replicator pad in a wide, deep bowl, quickly filling the room with a delicious redolence. All at once, the memory of the dinner Akaar had shared with Vaughn in Rome rushed vividly back to him. "For this," Akaar said, "I will sit down." His mouth already watering, he took a seat at the table, thinking that the full aroma of the food was reminiscent of the pungent meals traditionally prepared on Capella. Knowing Vaughn as he did, Akaar was sure that the selection had not been coincidental.

Vaughn set the bowl in the center of the dining table, and then from a compartment beside the replicator, he retrieved bowls, utensils, and linens, which he laid out for the two of them. Then he pulled out a squat, dark-green bottle from a second compartment. "Something to drink?" he asked, holding the bottle out for Akaar to see. He recognized it at once as *grosz,* a Capellan liquor.

"Where did you manage to find this?" Akaar asked, reaching out and taking the offered bottle. Thinking that he had not partaken of *grosz* in quite some time, he examined the label, then had to look at it a second time to be sure of what he had seen. "This is from my home territory," he said, hearing a mixture of astonishment and delight in his own voice.

"When I learned you'd be spending some time on the station," Vaughn explained, "I asked the barkeeper on the Promenade to try to track some down for me. Turns out that he's got some interesting connections and is quite resourceful."

"Evidently," Akaar said, mindful of the fact that Vaughn had just revealed the existence of his own interesting connections and his own resourcefulness. Vaughn had not been on the station three and a half weeks ago, when Akaar had visited briefly with Colonel Kira, but the colonel had surely informed Vaughn of it when he had come back. Few people outside Starfleet Command and the Federation Council were aware, though, that Akaar would be returning to Deep Space 9 and staying for an extended period. Akaar chose not to inquire about the source of Vaughn's information, both respecting his friend's privacy and understanding the futility of asking such questions of him.

Vaughn produced two glasses while Akaar removed the wire cage around the mouth of the bottle. He pulled the cork free and then poured out the clear liquid, tinged lightly purple. He waited until Vaughn sat, then held up his glass in a salute. Vaughn raised his own glass. "To old friends," Akaar offered.

"And getting older all the time," Vaughn added.

Akaar nodded, aware that Vaughn, eight years his junior, had passed the century mark himself more than a year ago. He pushed his glass forward, tapped it against Vaughn's, and drank. The *grosz* flowed down his throat with a heady warmth, and a sharp, challenging taste even better than he remembered. He let out an appreciative sigh. "Thank you, my friend," he said.

"My pleasure," Vaughn told him. "Welcome to Deep Space 9."

Akaar picked up a ladle and served himself from the bowl of hearty soup. "You make me feel welcome, but the rest of the station ..." As his voice trailed off, he recalled the difficulties he had encountered on the way here. "Can you explain the numbering scheme of the quarters on this level?"

"I'm not sure that I understand it myself," Vaughn said. "But I think it may have had something to do with Gul Dukat's twisted notion of security."

"Make it impossible for his crew to find their own quarters?" Akaar asked rhetorically. He finished serving himself and passed the ladle over to Vaughn. "Very clever," he added derisively. The mention of Dukat reminded Akaar of another Cardassian: Dukat's cousin, Macet. He asked Vaughn his opinion of the gul.

Vaughn did not answer immediately, but appeared to consider the question as he put food in his bowl. Finally, after setting the ladle down, he said, "Macet's intentions seem genuine to me, but regardless of his intentions, his assistance has been invaluable. Without the use of his vessel during the evacuation of Europa Nova, we would have lost a lot of people."

"I am sure you are aware that he also helped return the Europani to their planet during the past few days," Akaar said, and Vaughn nodded his agreement. "Without *Trager,* we would still be shuttling between Bajor and Europa Nova." Akaar took his first spoonful of the soup and found that it tasted as good as it smelled. "This is excellent, Elias."

"One of my favorites," Vaughn said, starting on his own meal.

"I invited Macet to Deep Space 9 after we finished the resettlement," Akaar said, "but he declined."

"We've performed repairs on his ship at DS9 twice now," Vaughn said, "and on both occasions, I asked him to come aboard the station. Neither time did he or any of his crew leave *Trager.*"

"I suppose that is understandable," Akaar said, knowing that Gul Dukat had caused the people of the station—all of Bajor, in fact—a great deal of horror and suffering. "I wonder what sort of a reception Macet would receive on Deep Space 9."

"Mixed at best," Vaughn said between mouthfuls of food. "I'm sure not everybody shares my opinion of his aims."

"What about Kira?" Akaar possessed a great curiosity about the colonel, one not sated by his single conversation with her. Knowing what she might soon be faced with, he hoped to learn what he could expect from her.

"I can't speak for Colonel Kira, of course," Vaughn said, "but I believe she is cautious about Macet."

"Cautious," Akaar asked, "or suspicious?"

"Probably both," Vaughn allowed. "But I think it's worth noting that when the Europani required assistance, she put aside any negative feelings for the greater good."

Akaar said nothing for a moment, considering this information as he ate. Then he asked, "What do you think of her, Elias?"

"I like her," Vaughn said simply.

"That is not what I am asking, and you know it."

"She's strong, decisive, loyal, solid under pressure," Vaughn expounded, not hesitating to provide his opinions. "Not always as diplomatic as a commanding officer might reasonably be expected to be, but I actually find that refreshing." Vaughn paused, apparently thinking about how else he could characterize the colonel. "Passionate," he finally said. "Quick to temper sometimes, but she also seems to be committed to enjoying her life. I haven't known her long obviously, but . . . you read her report of the time she spent—or *thought* she spent—in Bajor's past?"

"Yes," Akaar said.

"I think that experience has had a profound affect on her," Vaughn said. "She's young to be in such a position of authority, particularly for somebody with no formal military or command training. Even so, I feel privileged to be serving under her. There are things Starfleet could stand to learn from Colonel Kira."

Akaar found himself surprised at Vaughn's strong assessment of Kira, considering how short a time he had served with her. "What about her feelings about the Cardassians?"

"Passionate," Vaughn repeated.

"What exactly does that mean?" Akaar wanted to know.

Vaughn reached out, picked up his glass of *grosz,* and took a healthy swallow. "I don't know her well enough to know what goes on inside of her. But I do know that she's led a complicated and difficult life. You know what the Cardassians did not only to her people and their way of life, but to Kira personally, and to her family. She lived the first twenty-six years of her life not knowing a day of freedom from oppression, and she's spent a good part of the past eight years fighting to prevent that from happening again." Vaughn drank again, then lowered his glass back onto the table. "All of that, and yet she fought beside the Cardassian resistance during the war, and her first action when faced with Macet was to accept his help. And since the war, she's been generally supportive of the relief efforts to Cardassia."

Akaar listened to Vaughn's comments attentively. He would still make his own judgments about Kira, but he appreciated the benefit of knowing Vaughn's mind about the colonel. Even when Vaughn was wrong, Akaar knew, his evaluations still often managed to provide valuable insights.

Over dinner, the conversation crossed many subjects. Vaughn asked about Councillor zh'Thane, a mutual acquaintance, who had accompanied Akaar first to Bajor, then to Europa Nova, and finally, today, back here to Deep Space 9. And Akaar wanted to hear Vaughn's account of what had gone wrong at Torona IV. Since *Defiant*'s nearly disastrous encounter there, diplomatic relations between the Federation and the Jarada had completely broken down. Vaughn seemed pleased to learn from Akaar that the Federation Council was content, at least for now, to let the relationship between the two governments founder; the council considered it simply too difficult right now to deal with the xenophobic, isolationist Jarada, an opinion also shared by Starfleet Command. And although the admiralty continued to consider Torona IV strategically important, Akaar explained, they were also confident that no other Alpha Quadrant power would be able to cultivate an alliance with the troublesome Jarada.

As the afternoon blended into the evening, and as the dinner and their conversation progressed, a feeling of discomfort began to overtake Akaar. In any circumstances, his presence on Deep Space 9 would have seen him visit with his old friend, but knowing that he had come to Vaughn's quarters with an additional purpose made him uneasy. Although Akaar had been careful to maintain his usual phlegmatic manner, he thought that Vaughn might have picked up on his anxiety once or twice.

After the meal, Akaar and Vaughn repaired to the sitting area, where they sat across from each other and emptied the bottle of *grosz*. "No phaser practice for us tonight," Vaughn said with a smile.

"I believe you have already stunned me," Akaar said, holding up his glass. Then, knowing that he could put it off no longer, he asked, "How is Prynn?"

Vaughn's expression did not change, nor did he delay in responding, which Akaar interpreted as indications that he had indeed been expecting the subject of his daughter to arise. "She's well," he said.

"I've followed her service record," Akaar said. "Her evaluations aboard *Mjolnir* and *Sentinel* were quite good. She is considered an exceptional conn officer."

" 'A bit intense,' " Vaughn quoted one of Prynn's previous captains, a judgment of which Akaar was aware. "But she's young," Vaughn explained with a shrug.

"She was not always that way," Akaar said as gently as he could. Vaughn leaned forward and placed his glass on the low table at the center of the sitting area. Only a few sips of *grosz* remained, Akaar saw. Vaughn rested his elbows on his knees and stared over at him, and Akaar suspected that his old friend knew where the conversation was headed.

"Do you have something to say, L.J.?" Vaughn asked.

"Elias, do you think it wise to have Prynn on *Defiant* for your mission to the Gamma Quadrant?" Akaar asked. He attempted to avoid being either overly nonchalant or too intense with the question. If any chance existed of leading Vaughn to the proper course of action here, it would require a careful effort.

Vaughn continued peering at Akaar. "You said it yourself: she's an excellent conn officer."

"And you said, 'a bit intense,' " Akaar countered.

"She deserves an opportunity at alpha shift," Vaughn said, ignoring Akaar's comment. "And right now, *Defiant* can use her."

Akaar finished his *grosz* and deposited his glass on the table beside Vaughn's. A purple-tinted drop slid down the inside of the glass. "There are reasons that Starfleet discourages family members from serving together," he said.

"We send entire families out on starships these days," Vaughn argued.

"Not the captain's family, and certainly not when some of them are officers in the crew," Akaar said, his voice rising as he struggled to make Vaughn see the folly and the danger of having his daughter serving aboard his ship. "You should know that better than most."

Vaughn flew up onto his feet as though he had been launched from the sofa. He strode away from the sitting area and across the room, over to the window. He stood there for a moment, then leaned on the sill and looked out into space. He said nothing.

"Having Prynn on your bridge is irresponsible and dangerous," Akaar said, refusing to back down, although it pained him to have to deal with Vaughn about this. "Especially if her intensity . . . especially if she still blames you for what happened to her mother."

"L.J.," Vaughn said, still gazing out the window.

"I'm sorry, Elias, but I've taken steps to have Prynn reassigned."

Vaughn whirled around. "What?"

Akaar rose and regarded Vaughn across the room. He hated having to do this, but he knew that it was the right thing. He only hoped that Vaughn would be able to see that too.

"Don't do this," Vaughn said, seething, his words wrapped in a concentration of anger Akaar had rarely, if ever, seen in his old friend.

"Captain Mello has agreed to take Prynn aboard *Gryphon,*" Akaar said, "and she will reassign her alpha-shift conn officer to Deep Space 9 so that you can have him for the mission to the Gamma Quadrant."

"Don't do this," Vaughn said again. "Please."

Akaar walked over to Vaughn, hoping to close more than just the physical distance between them. He looked into Vaughn's eyes, expecting to see anger, but instead saw only anguish. *No,* Akaar thought. *Not just anguish.* There was also something he had never before seen in Vaughn: fear. "This is the right thing," Akaar went on. "I think you know that."

"I know what you're saying," Vaughn admitted. "Do you believe I haven't thought through all of this? I have." He turned away again and peered out the window. "I've fought with myself over and over, made the same arguments that you're making. I've thought about reassigning her . . . I've thought about transferring myself."

"But you transferred here to try to mend things with Prynn in the first place," Akaar said.

Vaughn turned from the window. "No, that's not the case. I mean, I knew she was here, but . . . something else motivated me to stop what I was doing, to change my direction . . ."

" 'Something else'?"

Slowly, Vaughn divulged a strange and unsettling tale about an encounter he had experienced with one of the Bajorans' Orbs of the Prophets. From anybody else, Akaar would have considered the story either a fabrication or a delusion. But not from Vaughn. Still—

"I have never known you to trust in mysticism," Akaar said.

"No, you're right," Vaughn said. "And I don't know if that's what this was. Maybe, maybe not. I've been thinking of it as a personal epiphany. But not about Prynn; about me. I want to explore."

"Then explore," Akaar told him. "But do not bring Prynn with you."

Vaughn paused and looked down. He seemed to be gathering his thoughts—gathering *himself*—and Akaar could not recall ever having seen Vaughn in such a desperate state. When he looked back up and spoke, his voice grew low and beseeching. "This may be my last opportunity to reconnect with my daughter. Things have been improving; we've been working well together the last few weeks. L.J., you know what it was like to grow up without your father. Imagine if you had also not had your mother."

The personal nature of Vaughn's appeal startled Akaar. A spill of emotion washed over him suddenly, bringing with it his long-simmering melancholy about never having known his father, and the fear he always felt when he thought about how close his mother had come—more than once—to losing her life during his infancy and childhood.

"Why would Prynn still be on DS9, and ready to pilot *Defiant*," Vaughn asked, "if some part of her didn't want to reconcile with me?"

"She loves her job," Akaar said, recognizing the weakness of his argument, and that the direction of the conversation had changed.

"She loves her job more than she hates her father," Vaughn agreed. "And that's a start."

Akaar gazed at Vaughn, and he felt his resolve slipping away. Finally, Akaar dropped his head. "All right," he said, and hoped he would not regret the decision.

"Thank you," Vaughn said, his voice thick with gratitude and relief.

"I have to inform Captain Mello," Akaar said. He turned away from Vaughn and headed for the door. "Thank you for dinner, and for the *grosz*."

"L.J.," Vaughn called, and Akaar stopped and turned back to his friend. "If you're concerned that I'll somehow jeopardize the crew because Prynn is on the ship, I can promise you, that won't happen."

"I know that," Akaar said. "But sometimes it becomes necessary for a commanding officer to make difficult decisions . . . even to make sacrifices. And I know that you will do what is best for your crew."

"Thank you for that," Vaughn said.

"Do not thank me," Akaar told him. "*That* is what concerns me: that you will do the right thing for your crew, even if it is the wrong thing for you and Prynn. I am not worried about your crew, Elias; I am worried about you and your daughter."

Vaughn said nothing. Akaar held his gaze for a moment, then turned toward the door, which opened before him. He left Vaughn's quarters, not knowing whether he had just done his old friend a favor, or consigned him to a terrible fate.

13

The sun shined down on the mountains and glinted off the distant ribbon of the river. The vibrant colors of the autumn—the green of the grass, the reds and oranges of the leaves falling from the trees—had deserted the landscape now, overtaken by the muted hues of winter—the yellow of the dead grass, the brown of the barren trees. Kasidy Yates gazed out from the porch at the vista before her and knew that another change was coming; snow had been forecast here for later in the month, and soon all would be dusted white. Already, in the past week, some of the higher peaks had been frosted.

Kasidy reached up and grabbed the edging of the deep-blue shawl draped across her shoulders, pulling it closed about her. The weather had grown warmer today than it had in weeks, in part because the winds had died down, but a chill continued to blanket the land. Kasidy breathed in deeply, enjoying the crisp freshness of the air, though she missed the rich, sweet scent of the *moba* fruit that grew on this land in summer.

Now, come on, she told herself. *You've only been living here a couple of months.* But she had visited here in the summer, when the *moba* fruit had ripened and hung down from the trees in succulent, violet globes. The aroma had captured her senses back then, and now she looked forward to next summer, when she would live in the midst of that splendid bouquet with—

Kasidy stopped the thought before completing it, not ready to think again about who would be with her in the future, because that also meant thinking about who was not here now. Instead, she opened the shawl and peeked down at the swell of her belly beneath her sweater. A smile came instantly to her lips as she ran a hand over the bulge in her flesh, in her body, that still seemed so strange to her, but that by next summer would be her son or daughter.

Kasidy walked the length of the porch to its western end, where sunlight streaked past the overhang and illuminated a patch of the wooden planking. She reached out from beneath the shawl to grab the arm of one of the two rockers, and pulled it over into the sun. She sat down without too much effort, although such maneuvering became more troublesome for her each day; she could only imagine the level of difficulty her final trimester would bring.

A cloud scudded by overhead, sending a shadow sweeping across the land toward the house. Kasidy wrapped the shawl tightly around herself, and when the cloud had passed, she tilted her face up and let the comforting rays of the Bajoran sun warm her. She closed her eyes, and this time she could not keep herself from thinking about Ben; she never could, not for long. He had loved this place, had looked forward to witnessing the change of seasons, and now she lived here, wishing every time she closed her eyes that, when she opened them, he would be here too. One day, she believed, that would be true. One day, she would open her eyes, or come around a corner of the house, or look out past one of the *moba* trees, and there he would be, smiling so wide, with the love he felt for her reflected in his eyes. And he would come to her, and then this house, this land, would truly be theirs.

She lowered her head and opened her eyes. Ben was not there. That was hard, but somehow, it was also all right, at least for now. There might come a time, she knew, when she would not be able to hold on to her hope, and on to that last, evanescent connection she had experienced—or thought she had experienced—with Ben almost half a year ago. For now, though, she remained content, even amid the despondency and the emptiness, to believe that she had communicated with him in whatever realm he had ascended to, and that what he had told her—what he had *promised* her—would eventually come to pass.

In all the time she had been together with Ben, Kasidy had never really understood the Bajoran religion, not in any deep and emotional way. She supposed the conceit of her own beliefs—the conceit of almost anybody with religious beliefs—prevented such understanding. Well-defined theological convictions did not admit contrary viewpoints, for even the consideration of alternate possibilities ran contrary to the notion of faith. Lately, she had begun to wonder if she should—or even could—find her way out of such a self-limiting perspective.

As for Ben, she had never understood how he had done what he had done. He had never been an impractical man, and yet somehow, over time, he had allowed himself to be made an icon of an alien spirituality. She knew that he had come to have a deep and abiding love for the Bajoran people, and that he had actually conversed with their "gods," but she could not imagine taking on such an enormous responsibility. It was one of her concerns about being here on Bajor, where her relationship with Ben threatened to make her something of a minor figure in their religion herself.

A low sound drew Kasidy's attention away from her thoughts. She looked around and listened for it again, but heard only the lyrical trickle of the creek that ran through the property. She peered into the distance, where the sun bathed the Kendra Mountains golden and sent shimmers along the winding form of the Yolja River. Farther north, though, she saw thunderheads moving down the valley, darkening the ground beneath as they sailed in this direction. A jagged streak of lightning flashed from the sky to the ground, out beyond the nearby town of Adarak, and the thick, cottony rumble of faraway thunder threatened again.

In a few minutes, the wind picked up, pushing its way through the skeletal *moba* trees, and carrying with it the electric smell of the oncoming storm. Kasidy huddled tighter beneath her shawl, knowing she would have to head inside soon. *It's just as well,* she thought. *I have to finish that letter to Joseph*—

Movement caught Kasidy's eye, past the trees, and she looked off to the right, down the unpaved road that led from Adarak. A lone figure was walking in this direction, she saw. Her heart seemed to jump in her chest, the thought of Ben still fresh in her mind. She tsked at her silliness; she could not yet tell the identity of the figure, but the light complexion eliminated Ben as even a remote possibility.

Or Jake, she thought, sadness buffeting her like the cold wind. It had been weeks—*months,* she amended—since anybody had seen Jake; she had not heard from him since she had moved to Bajor. She missed that bright young man for so many reasons. She had known and liked Jake longer even than she had known Ben, and the two had been friends from the day they had met. And after Ben had vanished, she had found solace in sharing her grief with Jake, and in being able to see so much of his father in him. When she had learned that Jake was missing, sorrow had overwhelmed her and taken her to the brink of despair; only the life forming within her had brought her back and allowed her to look forward again.

Kasidy stood from the chair and walked to the other side of the porch, nearest the road. *Who can this be?* she wondered. When she had first relocated to Bajor, she had received scores of visitors, well-meaning locals—and others too, from all over the planet—wanting to do whatever they could to help the wife of the Emissary. Kasidy had not wanted to insult anybody, out of her own sense of politeness, but also because of Ben's love for these earnest people. As the days had passed, though, Kasidy had begun to speak privately with some of her visitors from Adarak, and she had let them know that while she appreciated the assistance and the good wishes, she also sought a measure of solitude. To her surprise, the people of the town had understood, and now they not only left her to herself—for the most part, anyway—but also exercised a protectiveness of her, keeping uninvited guests away as best they could. They monitored the local transporter, and kept the roads and skies clear of unauthorized traffic. Kasidy still received messages on her companel, as well as an occasional visitor, but the person she saw most these days was Itamis Nath, the local postmaster; while mail almost always arrived in her delivery box via transporter, he sometimes would come out himself—just to check on her, she was sure.

The figure coming down the road waved, and Kasidy pulled a hand from beneath her shawl and waved back, though she still could not identify the person. *Not Nath,* she could see that, and not anybody she knew from town. *Maybe a stranger,* she thought, absently biting her lower lip. She hoped she would not be faced with another of the Bajoran faithful; she suddenly found herself not in the mood for a guest, particularly not for one wanting to worship her missing husband or her unborn child. Whoever the caller, they wore a wide hat, she saw now, and did not seem to be that tall—

Nog, Kasidy finally recognized. She smiled, realizing that what she had mistaken for a hat was actually his ears. She wondered why he had come all the way to Bajor unannounced, and why he had walked out to the house rather than using the transporter in Adarak. She had known Nog for as long as she had known Jake—the two young men still considered themselves best friends—and she had actually gotten to know him well in the weeks and months after Ben's disappearance; Ben had helped Nog become the first Ferengi in Starfleet, and Nog had regarded Ben with appreciation and respect. After Jake had also gone missing, Nog had contacted her at least once a day, ostensibly to update her on the hunt for Jake, but the two had continued talking daily even after the search efforts had slowed. They had subsequently become good friends. Like the locals here, he had also become protective of her.

He had even modified one of the escape pods from *Xhosa* for her, so that she could keep it behind the house in case of emergencies; with her being pregnant, he had not wanted her to have to walk half an hour into town if the local transporter went down for maintenance or for some other reason.

She watched Nog as he walked up the dirt road toward the house, and she revised her earlier feeling about not wanting guests; she was pleased to see him. She had intended to contact him on Deep Space 9 this afternoon, after she had finished her letter to Joseph. She wondered again why he had come all this way without letting her know first—

And suddenly Kasidy understood the reason for Nog's visit. *They found Jake's body,* she thought, something Nog would have wanted to tell her, not by subspace, but in person. *No,* she thought. *No, not again.* She stepped off the porch, intending to run to meet Nog.

But what about Nerys? Kasidy had also become good friends with Kira Nerys in the last few months, and she could not imagine the colonel not shouldering the burden of delivering such terrible news. *Maybe . . .*

"Maybe you should just wait till he gets here," she said, chiding herself for leaping to such an awful conclusion. Still, as she waited, she could not shake off the feeling of dread that had descended upon her.

Even before Nog reached the house, though, she felt herself relax. The Ferengi wore a wide, toothy smile as he approached, an indication that he was not delivering bad news to her—although he might be delivering something; she saw that a small box dangled from one of his hands, his fingers tucked beneath a string wrapped around it. When he got within earshot—actually, with his ears, he had probably been within earshot for quite some time, she thought, amused at herself—she called to him. "Hi, Nog."

He waved again with his free hand, and when he finally turned off the road and up the path to the house, he said, "Hi." He was not in uniform, but clad in comfortable-looking blue pants and a green sweatshirt, underneath a light jacket. He lifted the box as he walked up, offering it to her. "Here, I brought you some Argelian teacakes. I know how much you like them."

"Why, thank you, Nog," she said, touched by his thoughtfulness. As she reached out and took the box from him, she asked, "Where did you get them? I usually couldn't get any on the station."

"They're from Uncle Quark," he said.

"Really?" Kasidy asked, slightly embarrassed by the obvious skepticism in her voice. Quark had always treated her well enough, particularly after she had become involved with Ben, but such a considerate act was hardly characteristic of Quark's dealings with her—or of his dealings with anybody else, as far as she could tell.

"He doesn't know," Nog admitted. "He wasn't in the bar when I left the station. Treir's running the morning hours."

"Treir?" Kasidy asked. The name did not sound familiar to her.

"Uncle's new dabo girl," Nog explained. "Although I get the feeling she thinks she's his business partner. Anyway, she let me take them."

"So you stole them?" Kasidy teased. "That's not very Starfleet of you."

"Don't worry. When I tell Uncle they were for the Emissary's wife," Nog said, "he'll thank me for cultivating good relations with the Bajorans."

"And then post an account of his good deed to the Bajoran comnet," she said with a laugh. "Come on in the house." She stepped back up onto the porch and started toward the door.

"I forgot what time of year it was down here," Nog said. His shoes clocked along the porch behind her. "My lobes are freezing."

Kasidy opened the door and went inside, Nog coming in after her. The front room, the largest in the house, spread away from the door in all directions. Kasidy spent most of her time these days here, either huddled around the fireplace or sitting at the picture windows that looked out on the scenic landscape. She liked the openness of the room, the great windows and the vaulted ceiling an inoculation against potential feelings of claustrophobia. She enjoyed reading books or recording letters in this space, often composing missives to Ben—and lately, to Jake—so that, when they returned, she could easily share with them what they had missed, as well as how much she had missed them.

"I'm sorry about your ears," Kasidy told Nog, "but you should be all right in here." She had burned a fire earlier this morning, and the room still retained much of the warmth that had been generated. "Why didn't you transport over?" Kasidy asked, curious. "For that matter, why didn't you let me know you were coming?" She walked across the room, pulling the shawl from her shoulders and dropping it onto an easy chair. She stopped with the box of teacakes at the kitchen doorway, and turned back toward Nog.

"I guess because I didn't even really know I was coming," he said. "Not until I was on my way." He strolled over to his left, skirting around a sitting area and moving toward the stone hearth. "I had the day off, and I realized that if I stayed around Deep Space 9, I'd end up working on the *Defiant*. I knew Commander Vaughn wouldn't like that, so I decided to get off the station." As he spoke, Nog looked at Ben's collection of African art from Earth that adorned the walls, and then along the mantel, at the framed photographs there: Ben and Kasidy at their wedding, a portrait of Ben in his dress uniform, a montage of Jake at different ages, and others. His gaze did not linger on the photographs, Kasidy noticed—she could not look at them herself without becoming wistful—but quickly traveled upward. Above the mantelpiece hung a reproduction on parchment of a painting Ben had loved, and that Kasidy had come to appreciate herself, *City of B'hala*. "Before I knew it," Nog went on, "I was on a transport headed to Bajor. So then I thought I would come visit you." He turned and looked over at her from across the room. "I hope it's all right."

"Yes, of course," Kasidy said. "But why didn't you transport out from Adarak?"

"I don't know," Nog said, looking nervously down at his feet. "I guess I just felt like taking a walk." For the first time, Kasidy detected a note in Nog's voice that something might be wrong.

"Well, I'm glad you came by," she said, opting not to question him about it, but to let him tell her in his own time, in his own way. She held up the box and said, "I'm just going to put these on a plate. Can I get you something to drink? Maybe something warm?"

"That would be great," Nog said.

Kasidy thought about what she could serve Nog; her replicator had not been programmed with any Ferengi selections. "You don't care for tea, do you?" she asked him.

"Not really," he said.

"How about some hot chocolate?" she tried.

"If you have salt to go in it," Nog said. The notion of combining chocolate and salt did not appeal to Kasidy, but after leading a freighter crew comprising people from several different species, she had long ago ceased to be surprised by the various things people chose to eat.

"I certainly do," she said. "I'll be right back." She headed into the kitchen. While she removed the string from around the box and set some of the teacakes out on a plate, Nog spoke to her from the front room.

"This place looks just like the model," he said.

"The" model, Kasidy noted, *and not "Captain Sisko's" model.* She wondered if Nog had intentionally avoided using Ben's name for her sake.

"That's right, you haven't been here since we finished," she said, and felt momentarily awkward herself for having referred even indirectly to Jake, who had helped her during the early stages of the house's construction. "I'll take you on a tour later." She pulled a tray out of the cupboard and placed the plate of teacakes on it. She got out two smaller plates and some linens, and then tracked down a saltshaker. *Good thing I stocked the kitchen,* she thought. She had done so because to do otherwise would have meant that this was not Ben's house; he loved to cook.

"I remember these windows from the model," Nog said. "They're great."

"Yes, that's one of the things about the place that I like best," she said. She activated the replicator—Ben might have been a cook, but she was not—and ordered a mug of hot chocolate for Nog and a cup of apple-cinnamon herbal tea for herself. She loaded the two drinks onto the tray and then carried the light repast out of the kitchen. Nog had crossed to the side of the room opposite the fireplace, she saw, and stood now at the windows, looking out at the view. He had taken his jacket off, which she saw hanging on the coatrack beside the front door. "Here we go," she said. She set the tray down on a small table, between two chairs that faced the windows. Kasidy sat down, and Nog walked over and sat in the other chair.

"So how are you feeling?" he asked.

"Good," she said. "It's getting harder every day to move around normally, but overall, things are good." She took one of the small plates and put two of the teacakes on it.

"I'm glad to hear that," Nog said.

"So what's this about Commander Vaughn not wanting you on the *Defiant?*" she asked, recalling what Nog had said a few minutes ago.

"No, it's not that," he explained. He picked up the mug of hot chocolate in one hand and the saltshaker in the other. "The crew's been working so hard to get the ship ready to explore the Gamma Quadrant that he just wants to make sure we're all well rested."

"Sounds reasonable to me," she said.

"Me too," Nog agreed, "though none of the crew were too happy when we had to push the start of the mission back a day."

"So when are you leaving?" she asked, and suddenly felt an unexpected pang of loss, knowing that she would not see Nog again for another three months.

"The day after tomorrow," he said.

She took a bite of a teacake, trying to distract herself from her emotions. "Hmmm, these are terrific, Nog. Thank you for bringing them."

"You're welcome," he said, and sprinkled a liberal measure of salt into his mug. He drank deeply, licking his lips afterward. "This is good too."

"So are you looking forward to the mission?" Kasidy asked.

"Yeah," Nog said. "It'll be nice to be on the *Defiant* without having to head into battle." He paused and looked down, his eyes focusing on the mug in his hands. He seemed distant all of a sudden, and Kasidy wondered if the thought of going into battle had been the cause. Nog had been traumatized by the loss of his leg during the war, she knew, and though he had been fitted with a perfectly functional biosynthetic replacement, it would not have surprised her to learn that he still sometimes suffered from the memory of the ordeal. She chose not to intrude into his silence, and finally, he looked up and said, "Anything to get off the station right now."

"Is there something wrong on DS9, Nog?" she asked, concerned about the young man.

"It's just . . . the other day . . ." Again he looked away, clearly struggling to deal with something. "No, not really," he said at last. "I just want to get away."

"Okay," she said, not wanting to add to his troubles by pressuring him to discuss them. If he wanted to talk with her about it, then she would let him find the way to do so.

"I guess I wanted to say goodbye to you before I left," he said then, seeming to recover from whatever had occupied him. He shook more salt into his mug and took another hearty drink. "We'll be gone for three months."

"I know," she said. "You just make sure that you come back." She immediately regretted her words, knowing that it evoked the disappearances of Ben and Jake.

"I'll be back," Nog promised, and Kasidy wondered how many such assurances she would hear in her life, and whether any of them would ever turn out to be justified. Nog set his mug back down on the tray—rather deliberately, she thought—and then locked his eyes with hers. "I also wanted to tell you that Jake's coming back too."

"What?" The assertion shocked her, too much for her even to be happy about the claim. She put her own cup back down on the tray, a little too quickly, and tea spilled over the rim and onto her fingers. She ignored it. "Nog, what do you mean?"

"I mean that I know Jake is all right," he said confidently. "That he's alive and not hurt or anything."

"*How* do you know that?"

"I don't know how I know," he admitted. "I just do."

"So you don't *know*," she said, trying to control the annoyance she felt and prevent it from growing into anger. She raised her hand to her lips and mechanically licked the drips of tea from them. "You just *believe* he's okay."

"Listen," Nog insisted, leaning toward her in his chair, "people keep talking about Jake being missing or in trouble because he would never just leave the station and not tell anybody where he was going."

"He did tell us," Kasidy pointed out. "He said he was going to visit his grandfather on Earth."

"Right," Nog said. "But I don't think he was ever going there."

"Why not?" she asked. "Did Jake say something to you?"

"No, no," he said. "I would have told you—I would have told *everybody*—if he did. But before he left, I kind of got the feeling that maybe he wasn't going to Earth after all."

"But why did you get that feeling?" she wanted to know.

"I don't remember, exactly," Nog said. "But I do remember the feeling. It was the last time Jake and I talked before he left, and it seemed to me like he wasn't going to Earth, and that he was specifically trying *not* to tell me that."

"But why wouldn't Jake tell you where he was going or what he was doing?" she asked, of both Nog and herself. "Why wouldn't he tell me?"

"I don't know," Nog said. "But you know Jake. If he thought there was any chance he wasn't coming back, he would've said goodbye."

"Yes," Kasidy agreed hesitantly. She looked away from Nog and toward the window, trying to make sense of what he was saying, *wanting* to make sense of it.

"I don't know why Jake didn't want us to know where he was going," Nog said, "but he's smart and strong—"

"Like his father," Kasidy said without thinking.

"Exactly," Nog said. "I'm telling you, I *know* he's coming back." It was preposterous, of course. Nog had not presented any new facts, other than his recollection of having a feeling that Jake might not have been headed to Earth. But even if that turned out to have been an accurate feeling, it still remained that Jake had not been seen or heard from in two months.

And yet, Kasidy thought. Nog's assertion that Jake would return, unsupported though it might be, for some reason bolstered her. In the vigor of Nog's certainty, she found comfort, and even a renewed hope.

"You know," he said, "Jake really likes you." Kasidy looked back over at Nog. "I mean, he loves you, but he also *likes* you. He thinks you're great." The words touched Kasidy deeply. "I'm telling you, he wouldn't leave without saying goodbye." She nodded her agreement to him. Whether true or not, Nog's conviction filled her with a feeling of strength she had been lacking for some time. She committed to herself that she would consciously hold on to that feeling for as long as she could.

They sat for a while in a comfortable silence. When she heard light taps at the window, Kasidy looked up. Small, clear droplets had started to collect on the glass. "It's raining," she said.

"Yeah," Nog said. *"Choritzing."*

"What?" The word meant nothing to her.

"Choritzing," Nog repeated. "The Ferengi have a hundred seventy-eight words for rain. This—" He pointed toward the window. "—is *choritzing*."

"Oh," Kasidy said. "Okay." They sat and watched as some of the drops grew heavy enough that gravity pulled them sliding down the window. "I like the rain," she said.

"Me too," Nog said. "It reminds me of home. Back on Ferenginar." Kasidy looked over at him, and he suddenly smiled broadly at her. "So what are you going to name the baby?" he asked. Kassidy smiled back at him. This was a question Nog asked her with some regularity, the joke between them being that almost every time he asked, she gave him a different answer.

"Well," she said, "if it's a girl, Octavia Lynn."

"Okay. Maybe a little too *hewmon,* but okay," he said, pleasantly teasing her. "And what if it's Jake's brother?"

"Half-brother," she corrected.

"How can you have half a brother?" Nog asked.

"Ben is Jake's father," Kasidy explained, "and he'll be the baby's father—"

"Right," Nog interrupted. "So they'll be brothers."

"But Jake and the baby will have different mothers," she forged ahead, "so they'll be *half*-brothers."

"How can you have *half* a brother?" Nog repeated, but she thought from the expression on his face that he was kidding her. *"Hew-mons,"* he said again, rolling his eyes, and they both laughed. When she finally told him her current choice for a boy's name—Marcus Dax—he playfully suggested that Marcus Nog might be a better option.

They talked for a long time after that, about her solitary life on Bajor, and about his work on *Defiant,* and about Colonel Kira and Dr. Bashir and Quark and other people. They even spoke more about Jake, and also about Ben, in a way that she thought neither one of them had in a long time: without frustration or sadness, but with the simple joys of love and remembrance. They sipped at their tea and hot chocolate—Kasidy refilled their cups twice—and nibbled on the teacakes, which Nog also salted. When they finally rose from their chairs so that Kasidy could show Nog around the house, she thought that she felt stronger and more positive than she had in a very long time. And for his part, whatever had been troubling Nog when he had arrived seemed to have left him as well, as least for the time being.

As they were leaving the front room, Kasidy stopped and looked down at Nog. "Thank you for coming," she said to him. He smiled up at her, and then she showed him the rest of the house that she and Ben and Jake had built.

14

Thirishar ch'Thane snapped the panel back into place and stood up. He bent over the console, touched a sequence of controls, and watched as the level-five diagnostic ran through its automated functions. Words and numbers flew across the display too rapidly to be read, and the testing sequence signaled its completion with a beep a moment later. A readout appeared on the screen, and Shar tapped a touchpad with a long, slender finger, scrolling through the list of system checks and verifying their outcomes. As with the previous four diagnostics he had executed today on the stellar cartography lab's secondary interfaces, the results all showed green. But the information he most sought, the time required to run the diagnostic, appeared at the bottom of the list: two point three seconds.

Success, Shar thought. He quickly downloaded the testing data to a padd, packed the engineering tools away into their compartment, and left the lab, headed for *Defiant*'s airlock. For whatever reasons, the installation of the new stellar cartography lab had given the refit crews more difficulties than any other system during the past few months. The primary systems had passed their final checks only a week ago, and the secondaries just within the last three days. Shar had not been satisfied with the data flow rate, though, and when all of the other refit and repair work had been finished, earlier today, he had decided to make one more attempt to improve performance. Now, at the end of his shift, he had finally achieved his goal.

As he walked through the main port corridor toward the airlocks at *Defiant*'s bow, he found the ship not only eerily quiet, but unusually still. In dock, neither the impulse engines nor the warp drive were engaged, of course, but gone too were the sounds and disturbances produced by a ship filled with engineering and maintenance staffs. Most of the crew had left *Defiant* about midafternoon, he knew, encouraged by Commander Vaughn to spend their last night before the mission relaxing.

Nearly empty as the ship was, the lighting in the corridors had been dimmed, and although Shar knew it not to be true, the air felt colder and drier to him than it usually did. He experienced such reactions sometimes when he had been in the ship's or the station's environment for an extended period. It caused him no real trouble, but simply made him uncomfortable. The temperature and humidity maintained aboard the ship matched those on the station, which in turn matched those considered optimal on Bajor. He could always tolerate the conditions—he had certainly become more accustomed to them during his years at Starfleet Academy and on the *U.S.S. Tamberlaine*—but sometimes he looked forward anxiously to returning to his quarters, where he could regulate the environment according to his own preferences.

For more reasons than that, though, he wished he could go to his quarters right now. Tonight, he would be having dinner with *Zhavey,* at her request. He did not want to, really, because he knew what she hoped to accomplish by such a meeting: to convince him to return to Andor and take part in his *shelthreth*. Under other circumstances, he might have summoned the will to decline her invitation, but in just fifteen hours, he knew, he would be heading to the Gamma Quadrant for three months, where he would easily be able to avoid her attempts at coercion.

As he neared *Defiant*'s airlocks, he recalled the relief he had felt weeks ago when he had learned that *Zhavey* had left the station, bound for Bajor aboard *Mjolnir*. And when he had found out that *Kree-thai,* the Andorian vessel assigned to her for diplomatic missions, had departed the station a few days after that, he had assumed that she would not be coming back to DS9. But two days ago, she had returned here aboard *Gryphon,* and earlier today, *Kree-thai* had returned as well. He assumed that meant that she would soon be leaving aboard her ship, either back to Andor or to the Federation Council chambers on Earth. He had not been surprised when she had asked him to dinner, realizing that, no matter her agenda, she would want to say goodbye to him. And as much as he disagreed with her on some issues, Shar loved *Zhavey,* and he hoped that they could part on pleasant terms.

As he started into the airlock, Lieutenant Candlewood strode in his direction from *Defiant*'s main starboard corridor. "Calling it a day, Ensign?" the computer specialist asked. He wore his dark brown hair in tight ringlets about his head, his aquiline nose his most distinguishing feature.

"Yes, sir," Shar said, stopping and waiting for the lieutenant to reach him. When he did, they walked side by side through *Defiant*'s open airlock.

"Do you think she's ready?" Candlewood asked, patting the ship's bulkhead just before they stepped across the threshold separating the ship and the station. Even after all his years among humans, their proclivity for referring to space vessels with a feminine pronoun perplexed him.

"Yes, sir, I do," Shar told him.

They reached the end of the station's airlock, and Candlewood worked the control panel to open the hatch. They stepped down into the docking ring, the hatch rolling back into place behind them. A Starfleet security guard, whom Shar recognized but whose name he did not know, nodded as they passed. Shar and Candlewood entered the nearest turbolift together, and Shar waited until the lieutenant had specified his destination in the habitat ring before stating his own.

"So, are you going to relax tonight, Ensign," Candlewood asked, smiling, "or have a last wild night before we ship out for a quarter of a year?" Shar understood that the question must have been intended as a joke, although the point of the humor eluded him. He answered in the only way he knew how to: seriously.

"I'll be having a . . . busy . . . night, sir," he said, thinking of the possibly difficult hours with *Zhavey* that lay ahead. The turbolift stopped and the door opened. The lieutenant looked over and smiled, apparently believing that Shar had meant something other than he actually had.

"Well, just be ready tomorrow morning," Candlewood said as he exited the lift. "It's going to be a long mission."

"Yes, sir," Shar told him. "I'm looking forward to it."

Shar stood at the door to *Zhavey*'s quarters and tried to think of a good reason not to enter. Several occurred to him, but none compelling enough to act upon. He knew what the next few hours would likely bring—if he could last that long—but considering that he would not be seeing *Zhavey* for a long time after tonight, he felt that he owed her the show of respect and love that he truly had for her. He promised himself to be attentive to her in their time together, to try not only to listen to her arguments but to avoid patronizing her with simple acknowledgments, as he had during their last couple of encounters. He had thought through the choices he had made in his life many times—and still continued to do so—but he would try tonight to listen to *Zhavey* with a new ear. He had committed to the course of his life right now, and he did not see himself returning to Andor any time soon, but he wanted to demonstrate for her the regard she deserved not only as his *zhavey* but as the wise, strong woman she was.

Shar took a deep breath, and then coughed, the cool, stale air catching in his throat. If nothing else, at least he would get to spend the evening in a physical atmosphere more to his liking. He lifted a hand to the signal panel beside the door and hesitated. He looked down and realized that he still carried the padd he had brought from *Defiant*. He thought briefly about taking it to his quarters, but recognized the thought as a poor excuse to delay the inevitable. One of his antennae tingled as he stood there, and he reached up and scratched at its base through his thick mop of hair. He suddenly thought of Thriss—her willowy form, her lovely face, her long, straight hair—and decided he had been thinking too much about this. He should go inside before he ended up doing *Zhavey*'s work for her.

Shar stabbed at the signal panel. Almost immediately, the door glided open. Charivretha stood at the far end of the room, between the window and the doorway to the bedroom.

"Come in, Thirishar," she said, a smile decorating her features as he had not seen in a long time. He stepped inside, at once aware of the satisfying increase in the temperature and moisture content of the air.

"Good evening, *Zhavey*," Shar said. He moved farther into the room, toward a nearby table, where he intended to put down his padd. "Thank you for inviting—"

Somebody's behind me. Shar sensed the presence via his antennae, back and to his left. He whirled, and in that moment before he saw the person, he realized that the electromagnetic signature he had detected belonged not just to anybody, but to an Andorian—and not to just any Andorian. Standing in the shadows in the front corner of the room stood a tall figure with a rugged appearance, his hair in long, tight locks like Shar's, but pulled back tightly against his head and tied together.

At first, Shar did not recognize his bondmate, encountering him in this context. And then he did. Stunned, he said, "Anichent."

"Hello, Shar," Anichent said, smiling. He walked out of the corner and embraced Shar. For a moment, Shar stood there, his arms at his sides, not knowing what to think, what to feel. And then his hands came up around Anichent's back, and he hugged his bondmate close. He had not seen him in person in—

How long? Shar asked himself. He did not know. He had also not known until that instant how much he had missed Anichent. The surge of emotion surprised Shar, and he held on tightly to his bondmate for long moments. Finally, they pulled back and regarded each other. Shar put his hands on Anichent's upper arms, looking at his handsome features. "What are you doing here?" he wanted to know. Anichent said nothing, instead shifting his gaze past Shar.

That was when Shar sensed the other presence behind him. As he had just done, he spun around, knowing the identity of the person even before he saw her. Dizhei—shorter, a bit stout, but in a pleasing way—stood in the other corner at the front of the room.

And suddenly, Shar understood. As Dizhei moved toward him, he stepped back and turned again, this time toward *Zhavey.* The many thoughts intertwining in his mind drained away, leaving behind a dangerous emptiness. His muscles tensed, rage coursing through his body as though his blood were afire. The padd he still held shattered as his hands clenched into fists. He dropped the pieces where he stood, and before he could stop himself, he charged across the room. A sofa sat between the front of the room and *Zhavey,* and Shar took it in an easy bound. As he landed, his knees bent and his elbows pulled back, his body ready to leap and strike at—

Zhavey.

In the last moment before his family would have been torn irrevocably apart, Shar regained enough control to stop. He pushed the anger back down, unfulfilled. He stood up fully from his crouch, trying to marry his body to his mind once more. He looked at *Zhavey* and saw an expression on her face, not of fear or resentment, but of sadness. Even with Charivretha in front of him, and two of his bondmates behind him, he felt utterly alone.

"What are you going to do, my young *chei?*" she asked quietly, and he knew that the question encompassed more than whatever actions he would take in the next few minutes. But Shar realized that he could not even have told her what those next few minutes would bring from him, let alone the coming days and months and years.

"How could you do this?" he hissed at her. The quality of his voice scared him, directed as it was at his *zhavey,* and when he spoke again, he did his best to moderate his tone. "*Why* would you do this? Do you think—"

Thriss walked through the doorway from the bedroom and stopped next to *Zhavey.* "We all did this, Shar," Thriss said gently. "We miss you."

"Thriss," he said, her name barely audible as it passed his lips. He loved all of his bondmates, but Thriss . . .

He raced to her and swept her up in his arms, spinning her around. He squeezed her tightly, thinking nothing but her name, feeling nothing but her warm body clutched against his. "Thriss," he said. "Thriss."

"We love you," Dizhei said behind him.

With difficulty, Shar released Thriss. Keeping a hand on her shoulder, he looked over at Dizhei and Anichent, who had both walked across the room to them. "I know," he said. He gazed again at Thriss and said, "I love you," and then looked at his other two bondmates, including them in his declaration.

"Then come back with us," Anichent said. "Come home."

Shar sighed and looked away, dropping his hand from Thriss's shoulder, his energy sapped. "We've talked about this," he said.

"No," Thriss implored him, "*we* haven't; *you* have. You've made the decision for all of us."

"I'm not responsible for your lives," he snapped, and he saw tears forming in Thriss's eyes. "What am I supposed to do?" he asked her, and then he walked through the little group, looking at each of them, asking the question of them all, even *Zhavey*. "Am I supposed to let you—or let our biology or our culture—decide for me what my life will be?" He walked past the window, away from all of them.

An uncomfortable silence filled the room. He heard somebody sniffle, and he knew that Thriss was crying. He fought the urge to go to her, knowing such an action would only aggravate the problem. He tried to think what he could say to them that he had not said before, tried to think how he could make them see why he had to continue on the course that he had chosen, and why that course mattered not just for him, but for them as well, and maybe for all of Andor.

"Nobody wishes to decide your life for you, Thirishar," *Zhavey* said into the silence. He could tell by the way she delivered her words that she had measured them carefully before speaking. He turned to her. "Your life is your own," she continued. "Once you have completed the *shelthreth,* you may return to Starfleet, or do anything else you wish. You would never have to set foot on Andor again." Thriss sobbed, and Dizhei went to her, putting her arm around her shoulder and gently wiping away her tears.

"I—" he started, and he wanted to say *will,* and he wanted to say *can't,* and he did not know what to say. "Maybe," he said at last, and somebody gasped, though he could not tell which of his bondmates it had been. "After I return from the mission—"

"No," *Zhavey* stopped him. "What would happen if you did not return?"

"I have a commitment," he said, knowing the moment that the words had left his mouth that they had been the wrong ones to say.

"Commitment," echoed *Zhavey,* and he could see that anger had also risen in her, anger that seemed barely contained. "And what of your commitment to your bondmates? That has existed longer than your Starfleet career. And it is a *personal* commitment. More, it is an obligation to your kind."

"I did not make that commitment," Shar said, regretting the difficult truth, but having no choice but to counter *Zhavey*'s argument. "It was made *for* me." He and his bondmates had been pledged to each other as children, the result of circumstance and DNA matching. Still, he had not left Andor prior to their *shelthreth* because he did not love them; he had grown to love each of them, and he had no desire to see them hurt. But he also could not—*would not*—take part in the self-destructive patterns that Andorian culture imposed on its members in the name of saving the whole. As much as *Zhavey* and his bondmates—and almost all other Andorians—considered their social practices the salvation of their species, Shar viewed those same practices as their demise. And he had committed himself to finding a different solution to their biological dilemma.

Zhavey walked across the back of the room to him, until they stood face-to-face. "You have an obligation to your family, to these people—" She pointed behind her toward the others. "—and to your society." She paused, and when she spoke again, she softened her tone. "You have *romantic* responsibilities," she said. "Go look into Thriss's eyes and see if you can still tell her that you won't come home."

Shar saw the beseeching expression on *Zhavey*'s face, and he would have done almost anything to prevent her from continuing to feel the way she must be feeling. He searched for the words to say, and more than that, he searched for some measure of coherence in all of the emotions churning within him. *I love my bondmates,* he thought. *I love my* zhavey *and I love my people. And I hate what they're all doing to themselves.*

Before he could find what to say next, *Zhavey* spoke. "You *will* do this," she said. It was enough to get him moving.

"I can't," he said, and he strode quickly across the room. He had to stop to wait for the door to the corridor to open fully, and in that second he heard Thriss call his name: "Thirishar."

He left without looking back.

PROPERTY OF
National College
Library

15

Not only had Kira never seen Commander Vaughn this way, she could never even have *imagined* him this way. As they ran down a list of station matters they had decided to review prior to *Defiant*'s departure this morning, the normally reserved Vaughn moved haphazardly about, like an escape pod being tossed about in the Badlands.

"Commander," she said, looking up from the computer interface on her desk, "do you intend to *walk* to the Gamma Quadrant?"

"Excuse me?" Vaughn said. He paced from one side of her office to the other, crossing in front of her desk. When she did not respond to him, he stopped and peered over at her. "I'm sorry. What did you say, Colonel?"

"I just wanted to know if you were going to need the *Defiant* on your mission," she told him, straight-faced. "Because if not, then you can leave the ship here." He stared blankly at her, apparently oblivious of either her humor or the reason for it. What she had taken for mere distraction now began to concern her. "Commander, are you all right?"

"Oh," he said, almost as though coming out of a trance. He looked down at himself and seemed to realize the cause for her question. "Forgive me, Colonel," he said, and he walked over to her desk and sat in one of the chairs in front of it. "I'm a little . . . anxious."

"So I noticed," she said. "It's all right. It's just that I've never seen you like this."

"To tell you the truth," Vaughn said, "I don't know if I've ever *been* like this." He smiled, a slight, nervous expression that lent a youthful quality to his features.

"Like what?" she asked him. "Have you got reservations about taking the *Defiant* into the Gamma Quadrant? Because Odo promised that the Dominion wouldn't interfere with peaceful exploration."

"No, no, I've got no reservations," Vaughn told her. "And I'm not concerned about the Dominion." He paused and looked off to the side, absently brushing his hand over his beard. He appeared pensive, as though making a decision about something. The expression on his face looked familiar to Kira, and she realized that she had seen it once before: in the Bajoran temple on the Promenade, just before he had revealed the reasons he wanted to take the position as her first officer—reasons that had included his Orb experience. She said nothing now while he remained silent, and then finally he turned back to her. "I've wanted to do this for a very long time," he said. "Since I was a boy."

"A boy?" Kira asked, surprised at the revelation. In the time Vaughn had served on Deep Space 9, she had come to think of him as a man who could get things done, and who could do anything he chose to do. But she inferred from his words now that he had essentially had a yearning to explore all his life, a yearning that had gone unfulfilled, and that registered to her as uncharacteristic of him.

"Yes," Vaughn said, leaning his forearms on the front of her desk. "When I was very young, my mother used to take me out into the wilderness occasionally. She'd make a fire and we'd sit around and talk and keep warm."

Images came to Kira's mind as Vaughn spoke: sitting with her two brothers and her father around a fire, either at the Singha refugee camp, or out in the rough country, on the run from the Cardassians. Despite the horrors they had all suffered during the Occupation, she recalled those times with her family fondly.

"And I remember," Vaughn continued, "that when the fire would start to sputter, I'd crawl into my sleeping bag. As the fire continued to diminish, and my eyes became accustomed to the darkness, I would be able to see more and more stars." Although Vaughn still faced her across her desk, Kira had the impression that his eyes did not see her, but gazed back into the past. "And I remember thinking that if the universe was truly infinite, then that must mean that everything you could possibly conceive of must be out there somewhere."

"I remember thinking that same thing when I was a girl," Kira said, although she did not add that what she had most wished for back then had been a Bajor where her mother had not been killed, and where her brothers and her father were not always hungry . . . and where there were no Cardassians.

Vaughn smiled at her, his eyes twinkling, obviously unaware of the cloud that had passed through her heart. As he went on, Kira let go the dark aspect of her recollection, focusing instead on the marvels of an infinite universe. As though putting voice to her thoughts, Vaughn said, "I also thought that there must be wondrous things out there of which I couldn't possibly conceive. Anyway, that mystery, that promise of not only the unexpected, but the *unimagined* . . . that was what filled my childhood with the desire to explore."

"What happened?" Kira asked.

Vaughn did not answer right away, and Kira could not tell whether he was trying to pinpoint in his mind just what had happened to take him away from those dreams, or whether he was deciding if he could talk about it. "A lot of things happened, Colonel," he finally said. "As I'm sure you know, a lot of things happen to all of us." She could only nod her head slowly in agreement.

They sat quietly for a moment, and then Kira glanced down at the time on her desktop display. "Well, Commander," she said, "you've only got ninety more minutes before you officially become an explorer."

Vaughn lifted his arms from her desk and sat back in his chair. "If we can get through this list," he said, pointing at the display. "Sorry for the digression. What was the next issue?"

Kira reached forward and operated the console, paging to the next item. "Personnel rotation while the *Defiant* is away," she said. She scanned the duty and shift changes Vaughn had proposed and that she had approved, and she made a decision. "You know what, Commander?" She swiveled the display around so that Vaughn could see it. Then she worked the controls again and the screen went dark. "We've already been over these issues; there's really no need to go over them again."

"Are you sure, Colonel?" he asked. "I'm happy to review the list with you."

"I trust your work on all of this," she said. "And even if there's a problem," she added with a smile, "I think we can handle it."

Vaughn smiled back. "I think so too."

"So," she said, rising from her chair, "why don't you go explore the universe?" When Vaughn stood, she extended her hand to him across the desk. He took it with a strong, solid grip. "Walk with the Prophets, Elias," she said.

He bowed his head to her. "Thank you, Colonel."

As she released Vaughn's hand, the door chime sounded. Vaughn turned toward the door, and Kira peered around him to see who it was: Admiral Akaar. It had surprised Kira somewhat when the admiral had returned to DS9 a few days ago. It remained unclear to her how long he would be on the station or what his exact purpose here was—he had been vague when she had contacted him in his quarters aboard *Gryphon* and asked him about it—though his presence here, and that of Councillor zh'Thane, supported her belief that the Federation might soon take action regarding Bajor's admittance. "Come in," she said, and the doors parted and slid open. The admiral entered, and Kira could not help but make note once more of his enormous size.

"Colonel," he said.

"Admiral," she acknowledged him.

"I wanted a moment with Commander Vaughn before he left," Akaar said. Kira motioned toward Vaughn, an invitation to the admiral to proceed. "I wish to bid you a safe and prosperous journey, Commander," he said.

"Thank you, Admiral," Vaughn said, and he raised his right fist to the left side of his chest, making the same gesture to Akaar that the admiral had made to Kira when she had first met him. Akaar returned the gesture. "I was just on my way to *Defiant* right now." Vaughn looked to Kira. "Permission to disembark, Colonel," he said in a rather official manner, but Kira thought she saw a gleam in his eyes.

"Permission granted," she said.

"Colonel," the admiral said simply.

"Admiral."

The two men turned and left her office. When the doors had closed, she walked out from behind her desk and over to the right, where she peered through a window into ops. She watched Vaughn and Akaar enter the turbolift and then descend out of sight. She continued to stand there for a moment, hoping that Vaughn would find the substance of his boyhood dreams where he was going. She also thought that he would be missed on the station while *Defiant* was away. And more than that, she realized that she considered him a friend, and that she would miss him too.

16

Shar hoped the first day in the Gamma Quadrant would be an easy one. He had not slept at all during the night, unable to prevent his thoughts from traveling again and again to Thriss—and to Anichent and Dizhei, too, and even to *Zhavey*, but mostly to Thriss. He felt so physically and emotionally exhausted that he had even considered asking Commander Vaughn to replace him on duty today, but he thought that the commander would have been displeased that one of his crew had not heeded his instructions to get enough rest prior to their mission.

Shar specified *Defiant*'s dock as his destination, and felt the lift begin its journey. He set down his duffel, but resisted the temptation to put a hand or a shoulder against the wall for support. He rubbed his face with his hands and tried to shake off his fatigue. Perhaps he would be able to sleep for a little while aboard the ship. It was still early, and *Defiant* would not depart the station for almost ninety minutes; he typically only slept three or four hours a night, anyway, so an hour's rest now would be helpful. He had decided to embark now partly because he had been unable to sleep anyway, but also because he had wanted to avoid the possibility of another confrontation with *Zhavey* and his bondmates. He had checked his companel this morning before leaving his quarters—he had enabled a security protocol to prevent anybody but station personnel from contacting him over the comm system—and he had seen that *Zhavey* and Anichent had left several messages for him through the night. They might even have come to his quarters, for all he knew, but he had placed a security lockout on his door as well.

The lift slowed to a stop, and Shar reached down and retrieved his duffel. He exited the turbolift and approached the airlock that led to *Defiant*. Lieutenant Costello stood guard this morning, he saw. "Good morning, Lieutenant."

"Good morning," Costello said.

Shar walked up to the security scanner and operated its controls, activating it. "*Please identify for access to* U.S.S. Defiant," a computer voice instructed him. Shar placed his hand in the center of the scanner, which lighted up at his touch.

"Ensign Thirishar ch'Thane," he said. "Science officer."

"*Identity confirmed,*" the computer said.

Costello turned at her post and worked a control panel beside the airlock entrance. The hatch spun open and retracted into the bulkhead. Shar started to climb the steps.

"Thirishar."

He stopped and turned toward the turbolift. Thriss stood there, her lovely face slightly swollen, her eyes bloodshot. She must have been crying this morning, he thought, and then realized that she had probably been crying most of the night. Of all of them, Thriss had always been the most emotional; that had bothered him at first, but over time he had come to appreciate her passions as an integral part of her great beauty. To see her like this . . . it broke his heart.

Shar stepped back onto the deck, and Thriss raced over and threw her arms around him. Embarrassed, he told Costello, "I'll . . . I'll be just a moment." He dropped his duffel on the deck and led Thriss down the corridor a dozen paces. He heard the airlock door close behind them.

"What are you doing here?" he asked, facing her and putting his hands on her hips, and then he realized the absurdity of the question. "I mean . . ." He let his voice trail off; he did not know what he meant.

"Thirishar, please," Thriss said, staring into his eyes and clutching at his arms, her sadness palpable. Tears pooled in her eyes and slipped down her cheeks, leaving silvery trails along her beautiful blue skin. Shar reached up and wiped them away, then put the palm of his hand gently against her face.

"Oh, Thriss," he said, and there was no denying how much he loved her. If this had been only about his feelings for her, the decisions he had been forced to make would have been different, and they would have been easier, for all of them.

"Don't go," she pleaded. "We love you. *I* love you. I need you." He could not bear her sorrow, and to know that he had been the cause of it . . .

"Thriss," he said, pleading himself. He took his hand from her face. "What am I supposed to do?"

"Come back to Andor with us," she said, but the inflection in her voice told him that she knew he would not go back to Andor. And that—her terrible, desperate sense of resignation—pierced him to the core, and he knew that he could not continue to disappoint her.

"I will," he said, and her eyes opened as wide and bright as full moons. For a moment, his heart felt full, and nobody in the universe existed but the two of them.

"You will?" she asked hesitantly, as though even her question might make him rescind his words.

"I will," he repeated. "I'll visit Andor as soon as I return." Thriss's face darkened, like somebody turning off a light.

"No," she said. "Please. Now."

"Thriss," he told her, "this is what I can do right now. But it's a promise. I will go to Andor." He searched for something more to say to her, something that would convince her of the truth of what he was saying. He reached up and tapped his combadge. "Ch'Thane to Lieutenant Ro," he said. He kept his eyes on Thriss.

There was a delay, and then he heard Ro's sleepy voice. *"This is Ro,"* she said.

"Lieutenant, I'm sorry to wake you," he said, "but I need to ask you for a favor."

"What is it, Shar?" she asked, and he was surprised to hear the level of concern in her voice. *"What do you need?"*

"My, uh, my bondmates are here on the station," he said, "and they're going to be here until I return from the Gamma Quadrant." The darkness had left Thriss's face, he saw, but now he could not tell what she was feeling. Had his promise made her happy—or at least happier—or did she think that he would not live up to his word? "Uh, at least, one of them will be staying," he told Ro. "Perhaps all three. I'd like for them to be able to stay together in my quarters. Will you arrange that? I know it's an unusual request."

Ro did not respond immediately, and Shar feared that he might have irritated her by waking her for something that probably seemed trivial. But then she said, *"I'd be happy to give them access to your quarters, Shar. Where are they now?"*

"They're staying with my *zhavey*—with Councillor zh'Thane. Their names are Shathrissía zh'Cheen, Thavanichent th'Dani, and Vindizhei sh'Rraazh."

Again, Ro did not respond right away, and then she said, *"I'm glad I'm recording this conversation. Trying to spell those names would probably be a waste of time."*

"Thank you, Laren," Shar said.

"You're welcome," she said. *"Safe journey, Shar. Ro out."*

Shar deactivated his combadge. He looked into Thriss's eyes and still could not tell where her mind, where her heart, was. "I love you," he said. He leaned in and kissed her. She did not respond right away, but then she reached her arms around his neck and opened her lips, and they kissed deeply. For a long, exquisite moment, they stood together as one, a joyous union of love. *Yes,* he thought. *I'll go to Andor.*

Their lips parted and he stepped back from her. "Wait for me," he said, looking into her eyes. She walked back with him to the airlock, which Lieutenant Costello opened after Shar had gone through the security check again. Shar squeezed Thriss's hand, then picked up his duffel and mounted the steps to the airlock. The hatch rolled back into place behind him.

This time, he did look back, turning and gazing through the window in the hatch, but Thriss had already gone.

17

Vaughn settled into the captain's chair on the bridge of *Defiant*. A hum—no, not a hum, a vibration, something felt and not heard—played beneath the sounds of the ship and crew at readiness. A sense of anticipation imbued the tableau, even beyond Vaughn's own excitement. He peered around at the alpha-shift command crew and watched as they prepared the ship for departure. Consoles emitted electronic tones all around the bridge.

Soon, Vaughn thought. Soon the ship would spring completely to life, and they would be on their way. And after all these years, *he* would finally be on *his* way.

Directly ahead of him, Prynn reviewed a display showing the first leg of *Defiant's* course. Vaughn experienced a pang of remorse and anguish for what had happened at that console a month ago, but he quickly dealt with it, replacing the useless emotions with the happiness in his heart that Prynn had survived her ordeal, and that she would now share with him this journey into uncharted territory.

Vaughn looked to his left, where Ensign ch'Thane sat at the sciences console, which now possessed a great deal more functionality than it had when *Defiant* had been only a battleship. Now, though the vessel still had teeth, it had also been provided with enough scientific equipment and capabilities to carry them through their extended mission of exploration. Ensign ch'Thane and the rest of the crew would engage in more investigative science in the next three months, Vaughn was sure, than all that had been done aboard *Defiant* since the original ship had been commissioned five years ago.

Next to ch'Thane, stationed at the environmental-control console since he had no responsibilities right now in the empty medical bay, Dr. Bashir sat quietly, gazing around the bridge himself. Vaughn made eye contact with Bashir, and the doctor offered him a smile. Vaughn nodded.

On the starboard side of the bridge, Lieutenant Nog occupied the engineering station, and aft, Lieutenant Bowers stood at the tactical console. Lieutenant Dax, whom Vaughn had chosen to serve as his executive officer for the mission, stood at his right hand. *A fine crew,* Vaughn thought. *All of them.*

He tapped the controls in the console to his right and opened a shipwide comm channel. "This is Commander Vaughn," he said. He had known for a few days now that he wanted to speak to the crew before they embarked on their voyage, but he had not planned on exactly what he would say. With the moment upon him, though, he found that ideas and words came easily. "On Earth," he said, "more than five centuries ago, a small band of people set out across the vast, unexplored continent of North America. They traveled on foot, by raft, and with pack animals, for almost two and a half years and covering more than six thousand kilometers." A recollection occurred to Vaughn as he spoke, of sitting as a boy and reading about, and being enraptured by, the accomplishments of these and so many other explorers.

"On inhabited worlds all over the galaxy, similar courageous expeditions have taken place," he continued, wanting to include all of the crew in his vision, and not just the humans. "The great Jalia, who discovered the Outer Islands on Ferenginar." Vaughn peeked over at Nog, who returned his gaze with a smile, the lieutenant clearly pleased and probably surprised. Vaughn winked at him. "The intrepid Andorians, Shetthius, Shintral, and Chorna, who first circumnavigated their globe." Vaughn glanced toward the sciences console to see ch'Thane looking back over at him, a smile now on his face. Vaughn went on to list valiant explorers from each of the civilizations represented aboard *Defiant,* and as he did so, he was gratified to see the rest of the bridge crew turn toward him as they listened.

"The two men who led the expedition across the North American continent on Earth, Meriwether Lewis and William Clark, were set a mission to explore an expanse of unknown wilderness, to chart the lands they traveled, to seek out what new life there might be, to befriend the peoples they might encounter, to keep a record of their journey, and to bring that knowledge home." He paused, thrilled that this moment had come at last. "They called themselves the Corps of Discovery. Let us therefore, on this stardate, rededicate ourselves to that ideal." To Vaughn's surprise and delight, the bridge crew—led by Prynn, he saw—applauded.

He closed the comm channel with a touch to the console, and then his gaze went to Dax.

She did not hesitate. In a voice that filled the bridge, she said, "All stations, report status." The beeps and chirps of their equipment sang through the bridge, and in turn, each of the crew joined the chorus.

"Tactical and communications, ready," Bowers said.

"Navigation and flight operations, ready," Prynn said.

"Science and sensors, ready." Ch'Thane.

"Impulse engines are online, warp power available on your command." Nog.

"Life support at optimum. Medical bay standing by." Bashir.

"The ship is ready, Captain," Dax said. "Your orders?"

Captain, Vaughn thought. *A fellow could get used to that.* "Seal the airlock and signal DS9 that we are ready to depart."

"The airlock is sealed," Nog reported a moment later.

"Deep Space 9 signals that we are cleared for departure," Bowers said.

"Release the docking clamps," Vaughn ordered. "Aft thrusters at one-quarter, port and starboard thrusters at station-keeping."

"Docking clamps have been released," Prynn said. "Aft thrusters, one-quarter." Around them, the ship seemed to change, like a great beast waking from its slumber, though Vaughn suspected that the feeling might have been attributable more to his imagination than to reality.

"Ensign ch'Thane," Vaughn said, "let's see where we're going. Activate the main viewer."

"Main viewer, aye." At the bow end of the bridge, the large, primary viewscreen blinked to life. Ahead of them loomed the great, exotic form of Deep Space 9, the station receding gradually before them.

"We have cleared the station," Prynn said.

"Ensign Tenmei," Vaughn told her, "set course for the wormhole."

"Course laid in," she responded immediately.

"Ahead one-half impulse," Vaughn said. "Take us in."

The thrum of the impulse engines pulsed through the ship. On the viewscreen, the stars slipped from port to starboard as *Defiant* yawed onto its new heading. Seconds passed, and then the wormhole blossomed before them, a spinning maelstrom of blue light and circular shape, glowing purplish white at its center. The ship dove into the light, and then the light vanished, replaced by a bizarre kaleidoscope of luminous colors and alien contours. Vaughn watched in fascination until they emerged from the wormhole into the Gamma Quadrant, ninety thousand light-years away from where they had entered it.

"Ensign Tenmei," Vaughn said, "set us on our planned course."

Prynn deftly operated her console. "Course laid in, sir."

"Ahead warp factor six," Vaughn said.

Vaughn felt *Defiant* leap forward beneath him, charging toward the unknown. Their mission to explore the Gamma Quadrant had begun.

PART THREE

GLOOM THE DARK SEAS

There lies the port; the vessel puffs her sail;
There gloom the dark, broad seas. My mariners,
Souls that have toiled, and wrought, and thought with me—
That ever with a frolic welcome took
The thunder and the sunshine, and opposed
Free hearts, free foreheads—you and I are old;
Old age hath yet his honour and his toil.
Death closes all; but something ere the end,
Some work of noble note, may yet be done,
Not unbecoming men that strove with Gods.

—ALFRED, LORD TENNYSON, "ULYSSES"

18

Kasidy sat in a chair in front of the hearth. The warm breath of the crackling fire washed over her, chasing away the chill from the front room. Outside, the wind whistled through the eaves and lifted snow against the house, the frozen granules striking the window with a sound almost like rain.

"The excavation is advancing faster than any of us expected it to," Prylar Eivos Calan said, seated in a chair to Kasidy's left. "We may even be able to begin a new dig in the northwest section of the city by springtime."

Kasidy listened without much interest as the Bajoran monk spoke about the archeological efforts proceeding at B'hala. She understood the historical and religious significance of the ancient city, especially considering that it had been lost for twenty millennia. She supposed she could have been proud that Ben had been the one to discover the ruins, or maybe she could have even attempted to deal with his loss by involving herself in something that had been so special to him. Jake had done that, working at the site for three months after his father had vanished. But in truth, B'hala scared her.

"There is some fragmentary anecdotal evidence to suggest that we may find the city's main shrine in the northwest section," Eivos continued.

When Kasidy thought of B'hala, she remembered how Ben had been hurt while researching its location, in an accident that had come dangerously close to killing him. And she also could not help recalling that, just a couple of months ago, a text had been unearthed there that some Bajorans believed identified the child she would give birth to as an important figure—the Infant Avatar—in their religion. B'hala held fascination and spiritual meaning for many, she knew, but for her it remained a source of anxiety.

"Of course, the timetable and order in which we'll move into the other sections of the ruins haven't been completely determined yet," Eivos went on.

"Of course," Kasidy said, interjecting in the hope that she might be able to move the conversation to another topic. "Can I get you some more tea, Prylar?" she asked.

"Oh," he said, looking down at the empty cup he held perched on his thigh. "Uh, no, thank you," he said. He peered over at her cup, which she rested on the arm of her chair. She reminded herself that she needed to get a little table for this area. "But may I get you some more?"

"No, no," she told the prylar, "I can get it myself." She started to brace herself to stand, but before she could, Eivos stood up himself and plucked the empty cup from her hand.

"Nonsense," he said. "If my wife ever found out that I allowed a pregnant woman to wait on me, she would refuse to allow me back in the house." Kasidy returned his smile. "Herbal tea, were you having?" he asked. As Eivos walked between her and the fire, headed for the kitchen, she felt a momentary drop in temperature, like swimming through cold water in a warm pond.

"Yes, apple-cinnamon," she said, actually grateful that she would not have to get up. She thought about when Nog had visited her almost two weeks ago, just before he had left for the Gamma Quadrant. She found it difficult to believe that she had so much less energy and mobility now than she had then. She peeked back over her shoulder at the picture windows on the other side of the room, remembering when Nog had called on her. Thinking of him made her a little sad; she missed their daily conversations, and she hoped that, wherever he was right now, he was safe.

Kasidy heard Eivos say something in the kitchen, followed a moment later by the warble of the replicator. Back when Jake had been working at the dig, he had told her stories about Prylar Eivos, about how dry he was, and how his monotone could put an android to sleep. But she actually liked Eivos—and really, so did Jake—and she enjoyed his occasional visits. He had been one of the many who had contacted her when she had first moved to Bajor, but unlike with most of the others, she had perceived his offers of neighborly assistance to be completely unmotivated by her status as the wife of the Emissary.

Eivos emerged from the kitchen and delivered her cup of tea. She took it from him and sipped at the warm, sweet liquid. "While I'm up," he said, "may I make you something to eat?"

"Oh, no, thank you," she said. "You didn't come over here to spend the afternoon serving me."

"Maybe, maybe not," he said as he stood beside her. "My wife tells me that there are few acts more virtuous than serving an expectant mother."

"Well, you tell Audj I like the way she thinks," Kasidy said. "And make sure you bring her with you the next time you come out."

"I will," he said. "In the meantime, even if I didn't come out here to wait on you, I did come out for a reason." Eivos crossed behind her to the front door, where he had hung his coat on the rack. "Actually, I brought you something," he said. Kasidy watched as he dug first through one pocket, and then another, eventually pulling out a small package of some sort. He walked back over toward the fire and offered it to her.

Kasidy reached out with her free hand and took it. The package was slender, ten or twelve centimeters in length, she guessed, wrapped in plain, white paper, and tied in the middle with a red ribbon. "Is this a gift?"

"It is," Eivos said. "It is a gift for a very specific purpose."

Kasidy moved to put her teacup down so that she could open the package, and Eivos graciously took the cup from her. She pulled one end of the ribbon, and it came free. She dropped the ribbon in her lap and unfolded the paper. Inside lay an exquisite crystalline figurine made of an amber-colored stone . . . a Bajoran, she saw, just able to make out the ridges at the top of the miniature's nose. The neck, though, sloped out toward the shoulders, like a Cardassian's. *How odd.* As she raised the artifact to her eyes to look at it more closely, it caught the reflection of the fire and burned with an inner, golden light. And the eyes, she saw, seemed almost to gleam with a light of their own. "This is beautiful," she said.

"I'm glad you think so," Eivos said, sitting back down.

"What is it made of?" Kasidy wanted to know.

"A material called jevonite. The piece was discovered at B'hala, and we—"

"B'hala?" Kasidy asked.

"Yes," Eivos said. She could see that he detected her uneasiness. "Actually, that's one of the reasons I brought it. I originally was going to ask the Bajoran Archeological Authority and the Vedek Assembly if we might make a gift of the figurine to Jake, as a token of the work he did himself at B'hala, but primarily as a keepsake of his father." The generosity of spirit embodied by such a gift touched Kasidy, and she knew it would have touched Jake. "But with Jake still missing," Eivos continued, "and knowing how close the two of you are . . . well, I just thought this might be a nice keepsake of Jake for you."

Kasidy gazed down at the figurine. "I . . . I'm . . ." she stammered, unsure how to express her gratitude, unsure how to convey how much Eivos's kind gesture stirred her. She wished that it had not been found at B'hala, but—

"This piece was one of the last things I discussed with Jake when he was working at the site," Eivos said.

Kasidy looked over at the prylar. "Thank you," she said. "This means a great deal to me."

"I'm so glad," Eivos said, and she could hear the joy in his voice at having given her something like this.

"Prylar, I have to tell you, you're the only member of the Bajoran religious order who doesn't make me feel uncomfortable."

"How kind of you to say," Eivos told her. "I certainly understand, though. With the unrest these days in the Vedek Assembly, I sometimes find it difficult myself not to feel ill at ease among my peers."

"Unrest?" Kasidy asked. She picked up the paper the figurine had come wrapped in, along with the ribbon, and dropped them on the floor beside her chair. She held the figurine in one hand in her lap.

"Yes, I'm afraid so," Eivos said. He leaned over from his chair and offered Kasidy her cup of tea back. She took it from him with a smile. "When the translation of the ancient—and some believe apocryphal—Ohalu text was posted to the Bajoran communications net, it initiated a major division within the Assembly." Kasidy knew that Kira had been the one who had posted the translation to the comnet, an act for which she had been Attainted by the vedeks.

"How bad is it?" Kasidy asked, concerned that the greater the impact of Kira's act, the less likely it would be for her Attainder to be withdrawn.

Eivos sighed heavily. "It's not good, I'm afraid. The divide seems to grow wider each day. It is very disturbing. I'm worried that the very unity of the Bajoran religion may be at risk." He sounded troubled, and Kasidy understood why. While political differences had always existed within the Bajorans' government—particularly in the first days of the provisional government that had been established after the end of the Occupation—their religion had stood as very nearly a monolithic source of harmony for them for a long time, even *through* the Occupation. There had always been issues regarding who would be the next kai, or what actions the Vedek Assembly should take in various situations, but overall the Bajoran religion had remained united. There was the Pah-wraith cult, of course, but that had never threatened overall religious accord. A true schism within the faith could, Kasidy suspected, bring tremendous turmoil to Bajor.

"I'm very sorry to hear that," she said. "Is there anything you can do to address the situation?"

"I do what I can," Eivos said. He sat quietly for a moment, his expression one of pained contemplation. Then he shrugged and seemed to throw off his worries; Kasidy suspected that he simply did not wish to burden her with his troubles. "Who knows?" he said. "Maybe we'll find another text at B'hala that will repair the damage caused by the first one."

"Maybe," Kasidy said, but although the Bajoran religion had certainly been full of surprises in the last few years, she somehow doubted that Eivos or anybody else would find anything in the ruins to offset what had happened—what was continuing to happen—in the Vedek Assembly. That would have to be accomplished by the vedeks themselves, and after what that august body had done to Kira, Kasidy had no confidence that they would be able to find a solution. Following Eivos's lead to change the subject, though, Kasidy said, "You were telling me about possible plans to excavate in the northwest area of B'hala."

"Yes," he said, and he immediately launched back into a discussion of the archeological site. Kasidy listened, smiling and nodding as appropriate, but her mind drifted to Deep Space 9. Later, once Prylar Eivos had left, she would contact Kira on the station to make sure that she knew what was happening on Bajor.

19

Beneath a clear daylight sky and a high moon, Vaughn stood at the top of the low mortar-and-stone tower and looked out over the city. Modern buildings flowed in circles away from his location, the metal and glass of their construction tinted in delicate shades that coalesced into a magnificent tapestry of color. Numerous greenswards sat interspersed throughout, perfectly placed as natural counterpoints to the artificial hues all around. Busy pedestrian thoroughfares roamed between the buildings, both the spokes and the rims of the concentric wheels in which the stunning metropolis had been laid out.

Even as Vaughn appreciated the breathtaking beauty of the city, though, he found the dull, formless quality of the sounds that rose from it disturbing. The brown noise of movement and machinery reached him, an almost random agglomeration of acoustic elements that seemed as empty as the bountiful colors here seemed full. Conspicuously absent were the sounds of voices, music, and anything utilized as an aural communication or signal.

And still, the city was a masterwork. Walking through it during the past few days had been like walking through a painting. The colors and contours of the buildings impressed the eye in the same way that art did, as though the perfect shade or shape had been chosen at every point. The buildings, though no taller than one or two stories, gave the suggestion of slender height. Flowers and foliage accented both structures and streets, and public meeting places stood set off from the flow of pedestrian traffic by statuary and sculpture. Belowground, a complex transportation grid, using capsules about the size of a Starfleet shuttle, allowed individuals easy, fast access to both local and distant points.

Vaughn turned and offered his admiration of the vista—"Your world is truly beautiful"—then lowered his chin and peered down at the optic net spread across the chest of his uniform. A wave of hues and forms splashed across the fine mesh, a translation of his words into the visual language of the Vahni Vahltupali.

The being with Vaughn—whose name the translator approximated as "Ventu," but whom Vaughn had come to think of as "Red-Blue-One"—shimmied slightly in response, sending a complicated series of orange-yellow ripples across his flesh. Vaughn's own modified translator decoded the communication as "Life is a beauteous thing."

And that, Vaughn thought, *sums up the Vahni.* Four billion beings with a benevolent, global government, at peace among themselves, with their world, and with what they knew of the rest of the universe. And they had a technological sophistication that matched their social achievement. Accomplished astronomers and physicists, they had traveled throughout their solar system, discovered subspace, and now stood on the brink of developing both warp drive and transporter technologies. All in all, Vaughn was pleased that the Vahni had found *Defiant.*

The crew had been on the sixth day of their journey in the Gamma Quadrant, charting and studying the Vahni system via long-range sensors, when they had received a subspace transmission. The message had lacked an audio component, but its visual portion had shown two strange beings, essentially humanoid in shape and size, but wildly different in most other respects. The beings—two of the Vahni Vahltupali—had two legs below a long, narrow torso, two tentacles that approximated arms, and a bulbous, headlike projection atop their frame. Tall and slender, they each possessed a firm but malleable and many-jointed skeleton, allowing them to contort their bodies dramatically. They had neither vocal nor auditory organs, but a complex ocular organ ringed their heads. Most intriguing of all had been their flesh, over which they could exercise remarkable control, changing its color and texture in whole or in part.

The two beings sending the message had been different colors, one a reddish blue and the other a greenish yellow, but the shapes and hues flickering across their skins had been identical and had repeated. The crew had concluded that the Vahni communicated via the epidermal patterns, and they had set out to decode the transmission. Ensign ch'Thane had succeeded fairly quickly in determining the rudimentary meaning of the message, which had been an invitation to the Vahni world. Vaughn had considered the matter carefully, since the Prime Directive generally barred Starfleet contact with prewarp civilizations, but a gray area existed in the regulation when the civilization itself initiated first contact.

For a day and a half, Lieutenant Nog and his engineering staff, along with Lieutenant Candlewood and Ensign ch'Thane, had worked with Vahni technicians to develop a translation system. The Vahni had previously made contact with two other spacefaring—and verbal—species, and so they had already created equipment for the task; it had therefore only been a matter of adapting it to the *Defiant* crew's universal translators. The completed device included an optic patch of fine mesh spread across the chest of each Starfleet uniform, with the interface between the patch and the universal translator mounted in a small casing worn on the hip. The system worked amazingly well, given the diverse natures of the two methods of communication, though occasional lapses did occur.

"We've enjoyed our stay here," Vaughn told Ventu, who had been one of those who had first contacted *Defiant*. Ventu served within the government here, on one of the many councils given over to affairs of state; the jurisdiction of his council included establishing relations with off-worlders, and he had acted as Vaughn's guide during the crew's time here. "We thank you for your hospitality," Vaughn continued, and then he waited while the translator interpreted his words and sent them shimmering across his chest. Ventu shifted, and a burst of colors bloomed on his flesh, twisting and spinning into complex forms and then vanishing.

"Our people like you being here," came the interpretation of Ventu's response. The neutral tone of the voice produced by the translator seemed to

Vaughn a poor analogue for the vibrancy of the original communication. "We are [*untranslatable*]." A low tone signaled the words that could not adequately be deciphered. "Your people are friendly and we welcome you to our world always."

"Commander," someone called out, the sound of a raised voice in this environment oddly intrusive. Vaughn looked out over the wall surrounding the top of the tower and saw Lieutenant Bowers and Ensign Roness approaching along with a bright-blue Vahni. Bowers and Roness both waved, and the bounces in their gaits and the smiles on their faces told Vaughn that they had been enjoying their time in the city—as had all the crew. Over the last couple of days, the entire complement of *Defiant* had cycled down to the planet at one time or another, all of them enchanted by the unique inhabitants of this world. "We're coming up," Bowers called, pointing to the tower while colors flickered across the front of his uniform. Vaughn held his hand up, not waving, but indicating that he had seen and heard the lieutenant.

Vaughn turned back to Ventu. "When we return to our own people," he said, "they will send others here to establish formal relations with you." Vaughn's translator drew his words.

"We will look forward to that time," Ventu flashed. The Vahni then bent at his midsection, just above the tops of his legs, his head coming down to within centimeters of the floor. He reached out a tentacle, and the four smaller, opposable tentacles at its end wrapped themselves around the handle of a cloth bag he had carried here. Ventu opened the bag, then reached in with his other tentacle and withdrew what appeared to be a fist-sized ball composed of an iridescent, silvery material. He stood back up and held it out toward Vaughn.

"What is this?" Vaughn asked, taking the object.

"It is a remembrance for you of the Vahni Vahltupali." Vaughn turned the ball around in his hands and examined it. The structure of the object was not solid, he saw, but resembled a crumpled piece of paper. As he manipulated it, the surfaces seemed to move, as though covered with a thin layer of liquid.

Apparently sensing Vaughn's confusion, Ventu extended a tentacle and slipped one of his digits beneath a thin strip of the silvery material, which Vaughn had not seen. Ventu pulled the strip loose with a quick snap, and the ball began to unfurl. In seconds, the object had straightened into a flat sheet, about the size of a companel display. On its surface was a hologram of the city from its tallest point: the tower in which they stood. Vaughn understood now why the Vahni had wanted to bring him to this location before he transported back up to *Defiant*.

"This is wonderful," Vaughn said. He peeked at the other side of the object and saw the shimmering, silvery material. "Thank you."

"To have a new friend is wonderful," Ventu flashed. "You are welcome."

Vaughn heard footsteps echoing to his left, through the archway at the top of the stairs. He compressed the picture Ventu had given him back into a ball—it collapsed with almost no effort—found the strip, and fastened it back in place. A moment later, Bowers and Roness emerged from the archway, followed by their Vahni guide. "Commander," Bowers said, his breathing slightly labored after having climbed the four flights to the roof of the tower. "Brestol just took us on a tour of their natural-history museum. Have you seen it?" Vaughn watched the patch on the lieutenant's chest as he spoke, fruitlessly trying to correlate his words with the forms and colors into which they were coded.

"No, I'm afraid I haven't," Vaughn said. He bowed his head toward Brestol, a greeting he was sure required no translation, and indeed, Brestol made a similar motion in response.

"It's truly amazing, sir," Bowers enthused. "The evolutionary chain on this planet . . . I'm no biologist, but I've never seen anything like it."

"I think we're going have to perform an emergency transport to get Ensign T'rb out of there," Roness said with a chuckle, referring to one of the ship's science officers. Then, evidently realizing that she was speaking to her commanding officer, she straightened, dropped her smile, and added a hasty, "Sir."

"At ease, Ensign," Vaughn said.

"Yes, sir," she said. "Thank you, sir."

Vaughn suppressed his own smile. *So young,* he thought. Roness had shown herself to be an able crewperson, with a good attitude and solid piloting skills, but she could stand to lose some of her earnestness. *In time,* he thought, although he suspected that continued exposure to Lieutenant Bowers might speed that process for her. "I assume you two are headed back to the ship?" Vaughn asked.

While Roness issued a sober and immediate "Yes, sir," Bowers had something else in mind. "Actually, sir, we were hoping we might stay on the surface a bit longer." *Smart,* Vaughn thought, for Bowers to ask in person rather than over a comm channel; let the commanding officer know that you are prepared to perform your duties as needed, show him the respect of a face-to-face request, but also let him see how much you want something.

Vaughn looked to Ventu and asked whether he had any objections to some of the crew spending more time on the planet. "We welcome your people at any time," came his interpreted response. Vaughn turned back to Bowers and Roness.

"Check the duty roster with Lieutenant Dax. If she can spare you, then you can stay," Vaughn told them, and then added lightly, "whichever of you two actually want to stay, that is." Clearly, both Bowers and Roness had come seeking permission to remain on the planet longer, but the young ensign had lost her nerve. "No matter what, though, I want everybody back aboard ship in two hours." He had scheduled *Defiant* to depart the Vahni world and resume their exploration of the Gamma Quadrant four hours from now.

According to Dax, quite a few of the crew had expressed a desire to stay with the Vahni, not just a few more hours, but a few more *days.* Vaughn could certainly understand that; the Vahni Vahltupali were a lovely people, inquisitive and friendly, with an impressive civilization. And *Defiant's* itinerary did allow for some flexibility in the amount of time the crew spent at whatever stops they made along the way. For Vaughn, though, the encounter with the Vahni had merely whetted his appetite for exploration, and he was anxious to resume their mission. More time spent here, he thought, might not leave them enough time to make some other discovery farther along their course.

"Thank you, sir," Bowers said, his translated words careering brightly across the front of his uniform. "We'll contact Lieutenant Dax right away."

"Thank you, sir," Roness echoed. Vaughn nodded, and the two officers headed back through the archway and down the stairs, accompanied by their Vahni companion.

Vaughn regarded Ventu once more. He held up the compressed picture. "Thank you again for this," he said. "I hope to see you again someday."

"Again, you are welcome," came the slightly stilted response. Vaughn wondered about the degree of accuracy to which the translators functioned. They were obviously sufficient to their task, but he also suspected that the awkward sentences they produced might imply room for improvement. Perhaps when the Federation established formal contact with the Vahni, even better translators could be developed.

"Farewell," Vaughn said, and he tapped his combadge. "Vaughn to—"

Suddenly, the floor heaved to the right, throwing Vaughn and Ventu off their feet in the other direction. The compressed picture flew from Vaughn's grasp as he thrust his hands out to break his fall. He caught himself in time to cushion his impact, but his head struck the stone floor just above his left eye. A tremendous boom split the air, as though thunder had rumbled from a cloud directly above them. Vaughn had enough time to recall that the sky had been clear, before his instincts told him that the city was being rocked by seismic activity. The violent shaking of the tower went on and on, as did the almost deafening roar—and now Vaughn thought he could hear those roars not just here at the tower, but in the distance as well. *Yes,* he thought again, *a quake.*

Vaughn lifted his head and pushed his upper body up off the floor. He searched for Ventu, and saw him lying on his back a couple of meters away. Empty, white whorls erupted on his flesh, the Vahni equivalent, Vaughn guessed, of screaming in terror.

Vaughn struggled to his knees and then to his feet, the tower still shuddering dramatically beneath him. He staggered his way across to Ventu and reached down to try to help him up, but the Vahni would not move, his tentacles wrapped tightly about his body. Vaughn reached up and slapped at his combadge, but found that it was no longer there. He looked back toward where he had fallen, but the shaking made it impossible to focus his eyes on one spot.

The floor thrust to the side again, sending Vaughn off balance. As his feet shifted, he spread his legs and lowered his center of gravity, preventing himself from going down. He moved back to Ventu and stood over him, making sure the translator patch on his chest faced the Vahni. "You have to get up," Vaughn shouted, barely able to hear his own voice above the cacophony. Ventu did not move, though his flesh continued to flash brilliant white eddies. Vaughn felt at his hip to make sure the translator hardware was still there; it was. "We have to get out of here," he yelled, and he moved around to Ventu's head, crouched, and shoved his hands beneath his tentacles. He hoisted the Vahni onto his feet, surprised to find the alien heavier than he had expected. Ventu looked at Vaughn—at least Vaughn thought he did, because the pale swirls diminished—and Vaughn pointed to the archway. "Come on," he yelled. "We have to get down." Ventu wrapped his tentacle around Vaughn's arm. The two leaned on each other in order to keep their balance in the still-moving tower, and they took two steps toward the archway.

That was when the tower collapsed.

Vaughn had no idea whether or not he had lost consciousness, but in his next moment of awareness, the shaking and booming had ceased. He opened his eyes and found his vision blocked by something just centimeters from his head, a brownish gray object he could not identify. The stale smell of dust clogged his nose, and small sounds—pops and cracks, almost like wood burning—reached his ears.

Slowly, he began flexing his arms and legs, testing his spine, attempting to take stock of his body. He lay facedown atop a hard, irregular surface, and every part of him ached, though everything at least seemed intact. Cautiously he began to push himself up. Something moved beneath him and he stopped, waiting to see what would happen. When nothing did, he raised up all the way and looked around.

Below him sat only rubble, he saw, the obvious remnants of the tower. Vaughn had landed on top of the pile of crushed mortar and stones; one of the stones had been in front of his face when he had opened his eyes. The four-story edifice had disintegrated into a mound maybe four meters high. He got to his knees, perching precariously on the loose stones, and looked around for Ventu, but he did not see him.

"Bowers," he called. "Roness." He waited a few seconds, then called the names again. Neither officer responded. He hoped that they and their Vahni companion had made it out of the tower before it had crumbled.

Vaughn looked beyond the rubble beneath him and out at the city. Vahni packed the pedestrian thoroughfares now, some running, but most just milling about. He saw a lot of bone-white flesh among the crowds, the residue, he assumed, of fear. Smoke rose from the city in three or four places, though the ebon plumes were narrow, suggesting that they had not spread and might be brought under control quickly. He also saw several laserlike beacons, their light dazzlingly purple, shooting up into the sky from separate locations, a Vahni method, Vaughn surmised, of signaling an emergency.

Vaughn scanned the buildings nearest him. While some had suffered damage—broken glass lay everywhere, and some external structuring had bent and twisted—he saw that none of the buildings had collapsed. Whatever had occurred—*a quake,* Vaughn still speculated—had clearly taken a toll on the city, but it appeared that only the old tower had been destroyed.

The pops and cracks of debris settling continued beneath Vaughn, and the jumbled hum of many footsteps blew innocuously through the air. Past the small sounds, though, a heavy, unnatural silence draped the scene in a way he found haunting. *Because I've heard silence like that before,* he thought; it had been the sound of death among the living.

Vaughn examined the heap of rubble and began easing himself down from it. He moved along carefully, taking his time not to dislodge any of the loose masonry. A few times, stones fell from the pile as he began to put his weight on them, but he moved slowly and avoided tumbling down after them.

When he reached the ground, Vaughn examined himself. Dirt coated his uniform, which had been slashed open in several places; the right thigh of his trousers hung down from the top of his knee, and his exposed skin had been badly abraded. His hands were cut and bleeding. Half the translator patch had been torn away, and the interface no longer hung at his hip.

Vaughn walked the perimeter of the wreckage, searching for his crew-people and the two Vahni. A thick dust hung suspended in the still air; Vaughn felt it in his eyes and throat, and he waved a hand before his face as he walked, trying to ward it off. A third of the way around, he spotted the bright-blue Vahni—Brestol, he remembered—leaning over two bodies in Starfleet uniforms. Ashen patches infested Brestol's body, as though the pigment had been drained from sections of his flesh. He extended his tentacles out to the fallen officers, apparently trying to help them.

Vaughn raced over and crouched on the other side of Roness's body from Brestol. "Are you all right?" he asked, peering over at the Vahni, then recalled that the translator patch on his chest had been damaged. Brestol looked at him for a moment and did nothing, and then a yellow ring swirled around his midsection. Vaughn gestured, attempting to indicate all of the Vahni's body. In response, Brestol reached out a tentacle to Vaughn's head, touching him gingerly above his left eye. A rainbow of colors streamed back along his tentacle. Vaughn lifted his hand and felt his head where Brestol had touched it; his skin was tacky, and his fingers came away reddened by blood. Vaughn shrugged, not expecting the Vahni to understand, and turned his attention to Roness.

The ensign lay on her right side, her arms in tight against her body, her blond hair falling across her face, a purplish bruise on her forehead. Vaughn placed two fingers against her neck. He felt a strong pulse, and he exhaled loudly, unaware until that moment that he had been holding his breath. He moved on his hands and knees a meter or so past Roness to where Bowers lay on his back. Again, Vaughn felt for a pulse and found one, though not as strong as Roness's. He inspected Bowers's body for injuries, and found a gash on his left arm bleeding badly.

Seeing that Bowers had lost his combadge, Vaughn turned back to the ensign. He gently moved her arm from across her chest. She stirred as he did so. A spark of sunlight glinted off her chest, and Vaughn reached in and picked her combadge from her uniform. He squeezed the device, and its familiar electronic tones were like music in the horrible quiet.

"Vaughn to *Defiant*." He waited a moment, and then tried again. Nothing. He started to consider what alternatives he had if could not contact the ship. If there had been an attack on the planet—

"Commander, this is Dax." The lieutenant's voice seemed rushed and serious. *"Are you all right?"*

"Is the ship?" he asked.

"We were hit by something," Dax said. *"Hard. We don't know what. Systems are just coming back online."*

"What about the transporter?" Vaughn asked. He heard Dax say something to somebody on the ship before she responded.

"The transporter is up," she said.

"All right," Vaughn told her. "I have two injured, one possibly badly. Only I have a combadge, so you'll have to lock on to the three human lifesigns at these coordinates."

"Aye, sir."

Vaughn looked to Brestol and described a circle with his finger to include the three *Defiant* crew, then pointed to the sky, trying to indicate that they would be returning to the ship. The Vahni tilted his head back and looked at where Vaughn was pointing. Suddenly, a stark, white whorl spun across Brestol's torso, and then the terrible pallor seemed to crawl across his flesh. Vaughn lifted his head and followed Brestol's gaze. He could not believe what he saw.

"Commander, we're locked on to you," Dax said through the combadge.

"Energize," Vaughn said. And as the transporter effect surrounded him, sending bright motes of light across his vision, the last thing he saw was the sky falling.

20

Kira saw the concern on Kasidy's face: the creases at the top of her nose, the slight downward tilt of her eyebrows, her forceful gaze.

"Is there anything you can do?" Kasidy wanted to know.

"Like what?" Kira asked, more sharply than she had intended. She looked away from the companel to compose herself. Through the glass doors of her office, she saw the crew working in ops. She shifted in her chair and addressed Kasidy again. "I'm sorry, I didn't mean to snap. It's just . . ." She hesitated, seeing the difficult truth of the situation. "I've tried pretty hard these past few months to live with the Attainder, and most of the time, I do pretty well. But sometimes—" And here lived the truth she hated. "—sometimes it's still difficult."

"You don't have to apologize, Nerys." Kira saw that Kasidy's face had become a little rounder since the last time they had spoken. "It sickens me what Yevir and the rest of them did to you. That's why I wanted to tell you about this. If there's a problem in the Vedek Assembly, like Prylar Eivos said, they may try to blame you for that too."

"And they might be right," Kira said. Kasidy looked shocked at the notion. "I'm not saying that I'm responsible for their actions, but I *did* post the Ohalu text on the Bajoran comnet, and I defied a vedek to do it. I did it because I believed it was the right thing to do, and despite being Attainted because of it, I'd do it again." For the first time, though, Kira wondered if she would; after what Kasidy had told her, the repercussions of her actions might end up being far larger—and far worse—than she had ever anticipated.

"But if they hold you responsible for the division in the Vedek Assembly . . ." Kasidy's voice trailed off, and she looked down, obviously troubled. Behind her, Kira could see a window, and beyond it, snow blowing past.

"It's snowing there," she said.

Kasidy looked up again. "Yeah, for a couple days now. We've gotten a dozen centimeters."

"A dozen?" Kira said, cheerfully surprised. "Have you been outside?"

"Yes, a few times," Kasidy said, her mood seeming to lighten a bit. "When the wind dies down, I like to go out for walks. It's very peaceful and quiet when there's so much snow on the ground."

"And very cold," Kira added with a smile.

"I wear layers," Kasidy said, and then, pointing to her growing belly, she added, "whether I want to or not." They both chuckled at that. "You ought to come for a visit."

"I know, I know," Kira said. Kasidy had asked her several times in the past few months to go see the new house. Kira had always said that she would, but so far that had not happened, and she really did not know why. The station and all the duties required of her certainly filled much of her time, particularly with Commander Vaughn now off in the Gamma Quadrant, but she realized that it also must be something other than that. To Kasidy, she said, "It's been a long time since I played in the snow."

"You really should visit, Nerys," Kasidy said again. She seemed tired to Kira. "I'd love to see you."

"I know, I will," Kira said. "When I can. In the meantime, though, don't worry about me; I'm fine."

"I know you're not fine," Kasidy said.

"I am," Kira insisted. "I won't tell you I'm happy or even indifferent about the Attainder," she explained, "but I'm dealing with it. And there's really nothing more they can do to me, no matter what happens in the Vedek Assembly. I still have faith, Kas. Don't underestimate the power of that." She found it awkward to have this conversation with Kasidy; after all, Kira's gods had apparently taken Kas's husband from her, at least for now. And maybe, it occurred to her, that was one of the other reasons Kira had not visited Bajor.

"All right," Kasidy said. "But this still worries me."

It worries me too, Kira thought, though not for the same reasons it worried Kas. Kira could handle the personal consequences of having uploaded the Ohalu text, but the possibility that there might be a division within the Vedek Assembly troubled her. Kira remembered the infighting that had occurred in the provisional government after the Occupation, and how it had weakened her people and stymied their progress. A spiritual rift, though, would be worse than that. The Bajoran faith had seen the people through the worst period in their history, had made them strong and seen them come through the fire united. A religious schism could fracture that unity.

"Kas, please, don't worry about me," Kira implored. "I really am fine. The only thing I want you concentrating on is that little baby you're going to have in a couple of months."

"Well, there's not much chance of me forgetting that," Kasidy said in a funny, exaggerated way. "I'll talk to you again soon, Nerys."

"Okay," Kira said. "Bye, Kas." The companel screen went blank for an instant, and then the symbol of Bajor appeared on it. Kira reached forward and deactivated the panel with a touch; it chirped and winked off. She sat and thought for a moment, then stood up and walked to the doors of her office, but stopped before they opened. She had been headed to speak with Admiral Akaar, but just what would she say to him? That she had concerns that some of her people might take actions that threatened Bajor's admittance to the Federation? Kira did not even know for sure that the presence of Akaar and Councillor zh'Thane on the station had anything to do with that—except that Kira had been around Starfleet long enough to know that they did not leave their admirals sitting around somewhere for no reason, and she was sure the same was true of the Federation Council and their members. What she needed to do—what she would do—would be to meet with the admiral and finally determine what he was doing here.

And what if he is here to address Bajoran membership in the Federation? she thought as she returned to her desk. Not for the first time, she wondered what the near future would bring for her people. Three years ago, when Bajor had been on the brink of entering the Federation, Kira had not only come to accept the inevitability of the event, but to embrace it as the positive step forward it would be for Bajorans. Now, she found herself worried that it would not happen.

As Kira understood it, no restrictions existed with regard to the spiritual beliefs of Federation worlds. Certainly, member planets were not required to practice only a single religion. But if a schism had developed in the Vedek Assembly, and if it widened enough to threaten the peace and unity of the Bajoran people, what then? Would a population splintered by religious strife be permitted to join the Federation? And even apart from that, what would it mean for her people?

Kira did not know, and she hoped she never would.

21

Ezri Dax sat in the command chair on *Defiant*'s bridge and stared in amazement at the main viewscreen. She had never witnessed anything like this. The lone moon circling the planet of the Vahni Vahltupali had suddenly and inexplicably shattered.

Silence gripped the crew. Just moments before, the bridge had been full of sound and motion, the ship struck by something and propelled from its orbit. The crew had been thrown about, systems had fallen offline, and *Defiant* had careened toward the planet below. Only Nog's ability to bring flight control back up quickly, and Prynn's superior piloting skills, had saved the ship. Now, though, they all sat numb, transfixed by the sight of tens of thousands, maybe hundreds of thousands, of fragments hurtling through space, the remnants of what had just been a dense, inert lunar body.

Ezri gaped at the scene, her mind working to make sense of what she saw, trying to find a context that would make it seem real. Instead, it felt as though she were trapped in some horrible holosuite program. And then a memory—an *echo* of a memory—reverberated in her thoughts. *Praxis,* it came to her, and she knew the recollection spilled from another lifetime. *Curzon,* she thought, though which host it had been mattered less than the content of the old thought: the Klingon moon, half of it blown out into space by an industrial accident. The massive Klingon energy-production facility on the moon had failed disastrously, the result of a tragic miscalculation. But the Vahni moon had been desolate, an empty, lifeless body.

On the viewscreen, masses of debris tore through space, and a voice, another echo—*Audrid, maybe, or Jadzia*—resonated in her mind: *Do something.* She stood up and went over to the sciences station, pulling her eyes from the viewer. Shar looked up at her as she approached, an expression of appalled disbelief on his face. His antennae appeared to recede a bit, as though retreating from the image before him. "Shar," she said, "I need you to chart the courses of the biggest pieces." *Pieces,* she thought. *Of a moon.* The words did not fit together. "Anything that could cause damage on the planet." On the main viewer, it appeared as though most of the moon had been pulverized, leaving only dust and small fragments that would burn up in the planet's atmosphere, but there also looked to be a number of sizable pieces left.

"Yes, sir," Shar said, and he turned to his console.

Ezri moved across the bridge to the tactical station. Ensign Merimark worked her controls, a silver earpiece protruding from her left ear. Ezri put her hand on the young ensign's shoulder. After a moment, she removed the earpiece and said, "We've heard from eighteen of our people on the surface, counting Commander Vaughn."

"Is anybody hurt?" Ezri asked.

"Some of them are reporting injuries, but nothing serious," Merimark said. "They all want to stay on the planet to assist the Vahni." The ensign consulted her panel again, then said, "Three of the crew are still unaccounted for—Bowers, T'rb, and Roness—but two of them may have been the ones with Commander Vaughn."

"Try to keep reaching them, Kaitlin," Ezri told her. "Inform the others that they can stay on the planet for now."

"Aye, sir," Merimark said, and worked her console.

Ezri moved over to where Nog sat at the engineering station. "What's the ship's status?" she asked.

"Whatever hit us carried a massive amount of energy," Nog said, glancing up. "It overloaded the shields and created a feedback surge that knocked just about everything else offline. The backups and secondary backups tried to engage, but they also overloaded."

"Then how do we have any systems at all?" Ezri asked.

"Most of them shut down automatically before they suffered any damage," Nog said. "The majority of the damage was done to the EPS power couplings and some of the ODN manifolds."

"So you were able to bypass the downed junctions," Ezri concluded.

"Yes," Nog said. "We're actually not in bad shape." Nog looked back up. "It shouldn't take more than a day or so to replace the failed junctions."

"Good," Ezri told him. "Start putting together a repair plan."

"Yes, sir," Nog said.

The starboard door opened with a whisper, and Commander Vaughn entered the bridge. He looked hurt. Blood had caked in an irregular patch above his left eye, two dried, red trails snaking from it down the side of his face. His uniform, covered in a brown-gray layer of dirt, had been torn open in a dozen places, his bruised and bloodied flesh showing through them. "Report, Lieutenant," he said, stepping up to Ezri. She told him what they knew and gave him the ship's status. Vaughn confirmed that Bowers and Roness had been with him and were now in the medical bay, neither one of them hurt badly, though Bowers might be out of commission for a couple of hours.

"Lieutenant," Shar said from his station, addressing Ezri, then adding, "Captain," when he saw Vaughn. "I've charted the debris field. I've identified any fragments of the moon that will strike the planet, and that are large enough and traveling at such an angle that they'll produce an impact yield greater than ten megatons."

Ten megatons, Ezri thought, and wondered exactly what that meant, and then knew almost immediately—probably from Jadzia's experiences, she guessed—that such a strike would be capable of wiping out a small city. Any fragments significantly larger than that would threaten the entire planet.

"How many, Ensign?" Vaughn asked.

Shar hesitated for just an instant, as though not wanting to deliver bad news, Ezri thought, and then he did just that: "Two hundred thirty-one. And they'll begin hitting the planet in less than six hours."

• • •

Ezri raced into the two-tiered shuttlebay where *Chaffee* and *Sagan* were berthed. Both of the shuttles had already been powered up, and a low whine buzzed through the bay, like the sound of bees in a hive. The small compartment, barely larger than the craft it housed, felt cold to Ezri, though she suspected that the sight of open space below the shuttles, just beyond the force field, spurred her imagination. Lieutenant Candlewood stood beside *Chaffee* on the lower tier, she saw.

"Lieutenant," he said, "Tenmei and Roness are already on board the shuttles and ready to go."

"All right," Ezri said, pleased that Gerda had been in and out of the medical bay as quickly as she had. "Let's go, then. I'll take the *Sagan*."

"Aye, sir," Candlewood responded, and he immediately boarded *Chaffee*.

Ezri sprinted to the bulkhead and began climbing the yellow rungs built into it. With so many lives at risk, she was eager to board *Sagan*. The Vahni interplanetary ships carried no weapons, leaving *Defiant* and its two shuttles as the only line of defense.

Ezri reached the second tier and hurried aboard *Sagan*. She quickly closed the hatch and took a seat in the cockpit beside Gerda. The plan was simple: *Defiant, Chaffee,* and *Sagan* would attempt to destroy the lunar fragments threatening the planet. *Defiant,* with its superior weaponry, would focus on the half-dozen largest bodies, which measured hundreds—and, in two cases, thousands—of meters across. If any of those bodies struck the planet, Ezri knew, it would have not just consequences local to the point of impact, but global implications, maybe even to the point of generating a nuclear winter. The exacting process of destroying the massive fragments would take some time, so that they would not end up just broken apart; fracturing the biggest lunar pieces would only increase the amount of work that had to be done, without significantly decreasing the danger to the Vahni. In the meantime, *Chaffee* and *Sagan* would demolish the smaller, but still potentially lethal, fragments.

"Let's go," Ezri said, working her controls, configuring them for the weapons and sensors they would need. Within moments, *Chaffee* and then *Sagan* had dropped from *Defiant* and into space. The debris field spread before them. The number of objects seemed vast, the task ahead impossible. Lunar fragments stretched from one side of their visibility to the other, from the top to the bottom, and reached away from them for kilometers.

Ezri sensed movement beside her, and she turned to find Gerda looking at her, the realization of the enormousness and difficulty of their job clearly showing on her face. "We can do this," Ezri told her with a certainty she did not feel. But she had learned from Commander Vaughn that confidence served as an important tool of command—of leadership. "We're lucky there aren't even more large fragments than there are." Whatever destructive force had torn apart the moon, at least it had reduced it mostly to rubble that would not threaten the planet.

"Aye, sir," Gerda said, and Ezri could see the young woman collect herself, a sense of resolve settling on her features. It was a noteworthy moment for such a junior officer. Gerda operated her console, and *Sagan* sprang toward the debris field. The shuttles would begin in the middle of the pack, destroying the most dangerous fragments first, those with the steepest angle of entry, then work their way outward along spiral courses.

Ahead of *Sagan,* a cluster of nine fragments rolled end over end toward the planet below. Ezri checked her instruments and saw that only two of them were large enough to threaten the Vahni; the others would either burn up as they encountered the planet's atmosphere, or be deflected back out into space. And there, Ezri knew, lay the primary danger of this mission. They did not have enough time or power to destroy every fragment headed toward the planet, only those that posed a threat; that meant that they would need to maneuver through the debris field to specific targets, and while the smaller fragments might not have been a danger to the planet, they absolutely would be to the shuttles.

Ezri watched the readouts for optimal weapons proximity, even as she keyed in a phaser lock on one of the tumbling rocks. When *Sagan* flew into range, she hit a touchpad, unleashing the shuttle's fire. *Sagan* jarred slightly as the phasers sprang into action, the drone of their activation seeping into the cabin. Streams of phased energy raced into the eternal night of space. The phaser lock was true: the largest fragment in the cluster vanished in a burst of light and energy. In her mind, Dax supplied the explosive sound that would never be borne in space.

"Only two hundred twenty-four to go," she said to Roness, subtracting one from the number of fragments the shuttles had been charged with handling. Then she worked to retarget the phaser lock.

Ezri slumped back in her chair, exhausted. Her arms, extended over her console as she had worked the targeting locks and the phasers, felt leaden. For nearly six hours, the crews aboard *Defiant, Chaffee,* and *Sagan* had battled the debris field, winnowing the number of potentially deadly lunar fragments down one by one. Now, finally, only one remained, and it had already been reduced by *Defiant*'s phasers from seven hundred meters across to two hundred meters.

"You did a terrific job," Ezri told Gerda. The ensign had also fallen back in her chair, looking as tired as Ezri felt. They had parked the shuttle above the planet, a comfortable distance off *Defiant*'s port bow as the ship completed the destruction of the last fragment. *Chaffee* had similarly settled into station-keeping on the starboard side of the ship.

"Thank you," Gerda said, smiling. "You too."

Ezri smiled back, and then exhaled a long, loud breath. Though successful, the mission had not gone flawlessly. Twice, *Chaffee* and *Sagan* had been called in to assist *Defiant* when larger fragments had broken up under the ship's assault. *Chaffee* had also been clipped by one of the smaller rock masses, which had caused a plasma leak in one of its subscale warp engines. Since they had not been using the warp drive, it had not been a problem; Candlewood and

Prynn had isolated the leak and thereby stopped it, but it would have to be patched later.

Ezri felt not only pleasure and relief that the threat to the planet had been neutralized, but also a sense of satisfaction and accomplishment for the role she had played in making that happen. She had directed the coordinated operations of the shuttles with a surety and skill she had not been fully aware that she possessed. Some of her thoughts and actions had been driven by the ingrained experiences of Dax's former hosts, she knew, but she also felt that she had brought some of her own qualities to bear. Commander Vaughn had so far been an excellent mentor to her, schooling her not so much in the details of command as in the attitude and mind-set required to lead effectively. She felt fortunate to have so adept and willing an instructor.

Ezri glanced over at Gerda and noticed the bruise on her forehead. "By the way," she said, "I'm so glad that you weren't hurt down on the planet."

Gerda peered over at her with a devilish grin. "Oh, you're just saying that since I successfully navigated us through all those space rocks."

"Well," Ezri said playfully, "that didn't hurt." The two chuckled, a welcome moment of relief after the last, tense hours. "Really, though, how are you feeling?"

"Actually, I've got a bit of a headache," Gerda said. "Dr. Bashir told me I had a mild concussion, and that I shouldn't go to sleep for a few hours." She laughed again. "I guess that wasn't much of a problem, was it?"

"I guess not," Ezri agreed, laughing herself. Gerda's sense of humor was one of the things she really enjoyed about the young woman.

"You know what I'm going to do when we get back to the ship?" Gerda asked.

"Sleep for two days?" Ezri suggested. The constant, low-level hum of the shuttle seemed restful now, uninterrupted by the sounds of the engines and the phasers. Ezri thought that if she closed her eyes, she would not wake up again until somebody pulled her bodily out of the shuttle back aboard *Defiant*.

"That too," Gerda said. "But right now, I've got a taste for a big, fat *jumja* stick."

"Really?" Ezri said. "How can you eat those things? They're so sweet."

"They're good," Gerda protested. "It's a natural sweetness."

Ezri wrinkled her nose and shook her head, lightheartedly exaggerating her dislike of the Bajoran confection. Before Gerda could respond, a flash of light caught Ezri's attention. She sat back up and gazed out the forward windows.

"What is it?" Gerda asked, also sitting back up in her chair.

"I think that the—" Another spark flickered above the planet. "The light show's just beginning for the Vahni." The leading edge of the debris field had reached the planet, the remaining, smaller fragments burning up as they plunged through the middle atmosphere. Ezri felt tremendously gratified that the Vahni would be able to look up to the sky right now in wonder rather than in fear. Even in the daylight, they would be able to see the meteors as they blazed out of existence, the rock masses done in by friction with the atmosphere as they fell from space.

They watched for long, silent minutes as the lunar fragments disintegrated in magnificent, fiery bursts scores of kilometers above the planet's surface. Then something flared off to starboard. Ezri looked in that direction and saw only *Defiant* off in the distance. She reached up to her console and started to work the sensors. "Did you see that?" she asked Gerda.

"I thought I saw something," she answered. "I'm not sure—"

"*Defiant* to *Sagan*," came Commander Vaughn's voice over a com channel.

Ezri touched a control on her panel. "Dax here. Go ahead, Captain," she said. She continued operating the sensors.

"*Lieutenant, the fragment we were trying to destroy just broke into three pieces,*" Vaughn said. "*The phasers may have ignited some volatile material inside it.*" Ezri found two of the pieces with the sensors, then finally located the third, farther away from *Defiant* than she had expected. She scanned the masses of rock, and saw that the readings did indicate the residue of an explosion. "*Defiant can still handle the two pieces nearest us,*" Vaughn continued, "*but we're not going to have time to destroy the third.*" Ezri saw the problem detailed on her readouts: the third fragment had been accelerated by the explosion ahead of the other two— and, she noted, into a dense area of the debris field. Even though the remaining fragments were small, it would be a tricky journey for the shuttle to maneuver through them.

"We've got it, Captain," Ezri said. Considering the damage *Chaffee* had sustained from its collision with one of the fragments, *Sagan* was obviously the better choice for this task. "Dax out."

Gerda worked at her controls, and *Sagan* began to pulse with energy as the engines came back up to full readiness from standby mode. "What about a tractor beam?" she asked.

"It's traveling too fast," Ezri said. She quickly plotted a course through the debris field and laid it into the navigational computer. "Do you have the course?" she asked.

"Laid in," Gerda said. "Bringing us about."

The shuttle surged forward and then to port, toward the planet. Ezri looked up, through the forward viewport, and saw sparks of light below, the lunar fragments dying in flames as they rushed down. Suddenly, a rock mass soared past the shuttle off to starboard. Ezri consulted the sensors and saw that they had entered the debris field, hundreds of fragments ahead of them, and thousands approaching rapidly from behind. She picked out the one they were after.

"Targeting," Ezri said, waiting for the computer to acquire a lock. The indicator on her panel flashed green. "Phasers locked." She reached to fire, but *Sagan* lurched to starboard as Gerda screamed a warning, but too late. Ezri flew from her chair and slammed into the bulkhead. Pain seared through her right shoulder as she felt it give way. She cried out, the sounds of her pain swallowed by the increased thrum of the engines.

"Are you all right?" Gerda yelled, not taking her eyes from her console.

"Yes," Ezri yelled back, not caring about the truth of her response. She tasted blood, and thought that she must have bitten her tongue or the inside of her cheek. She struggled back up and into her chair as Gerda righted the shuttle, the pulse of the engines quieting.

"We were about to get hit by one of the fragments," Gerda explained. Knowing what had been coming, she had obviously been able to brace herself as she had maneuvered the shuttle out of danger.

Ezri found that she could not raise her right arm up to her console, so she grabbed her arm with her left hand and lifted it there. Still able to move all her fingers, she worked the sensors, searching again for their target. She found it as it entered the planet's upper atmosphere, but their evasive maneuvering had taken them away from it. "We need to get back on course," she said.

"I know," Gerda said. "We also have to avoid being knocked out of the sky." She paused, then said, "Brace yourself."

Sagan rolled to port, dipped, then rolled to starboard before righting itself again. Ezri held on to her console with her left hand and kept herself seated. She studied the sensor display, her eyes on the readings of the fragment as they neared it once more. "Targeting," she said as she worked the phaser controls. She waited. Finally, the indicator blinked green, but almost immediately it reverted to red. The shuttle began to shake as it shot through the upper atmosphere. The targeting indicator changed from red to green and back, two more times.

"I can't get a lock," she said, which meant that she would have to target the fragment manually. She could do that, but she could not risk missing and sending a volley of deadly phaser fire into the planet below. "We're going to have to come up from underneath."

"We can't do that," Gerda said. "We'd be flying head-on into the debris field."

Ezri understood Gerda's warning—it was one thing to fly amid the lunar fragments traveling in their direction, and another to fly into them going in the opposite direction—but she had no time to explain why they had to do this. "Do it," Ezri said. To her credit, Gerda hesitated for only a fraction of a second, but in that instant, Ezri knew that the ensign wanted her to take the shot now and get the shuttle out of there. But she could not—would not—take that chance. They had not worked this long, this hard, to save the Vahni, just to end up killing some of them themselves with errant phaser fire.

Around them, the shuttle grew louder as it raced downward. The huge mass of the planet filled the forward windows, green and brown land visible through white clouds. The flashes of the burning lunar fragments continued to wink on and off in front of them like guttering candles. The vibrations in the cabin increased as *Sagan* broached the middle atmosphere.

And then they were turning, pulling up and around in an arc. The planet slipped out of sight—*too slow*, Ezri thought, but she knew that such a maneuver at greater speeds would have torn the shuttle apart. At last, the stars filled the windows, *Sagan* heading back away from the planet. Ezri reacquired the fragment on the scanners and tried another phaser lock, which again failed. She enabled manual firing and concentrated as the shuttle and the fragment rushed headlong at each other. She fired, the phaser blast barely audible in the noisy cabin.

The fragment did not disappear from the sensors. The distance between *Sagan* and the rock mass diminished rapidly. *One more shot,* she thought, *maybe two,* but her hands were already working her panel. Another phaser strike surged from the shuttle.

Ahead of them, the fragment exploded in an intense blaze of yellow-red light.

"Yes," Ezri hissed through clenched teeth, knowing that, while they might have saved the people below, she and Gerda were still in danger. On her sensor readout, she saw two more fragments approaching the shuttle fast. "Come about," she ordered, looking up in time to see a mass of burning rock charge past *Sagan*. "There's another one," she shouted, following it with the sensors. With no time to establish a phaser lock, she fired a spread directly in front of the shuttle. Ahead, another fragment flashed as it disintegrated.

She checked the sensors again, and saw a huge swarm ahead, too dense to travel through, too wide to escape, too many to destroy. "Land," she yelled. "We've got to land." If they could even get low enough, below an altitude of about fifty kilometers, the fragments would never reach them, burning up in the atmosphere above them. She thought about transporting to safety, but she could not allow the shuttle to crash and possibly kill any of the Vahni.

Gerda brought *Sagan* around in a tight arc, the starfield slewing away. Ezri waited to see the horizon of the planet, wanting to know that they were no longer headed upward. Sensors showed that another fragment had just missed them, and she knew this was going to be close. Maybe if she could rig the warp drive to overload and vaporize the shuttle, then they could transport—

A mass of rock slammed into the rear of the shuttle. Power destabilized for a second as the shields went down. The interior went dark, and then emergency lighting flashed on, bathing the cabin in a dull red glow. The noise inside the shuttle increased dramatically, deafeningly, and Ezri realized that the noise-suppression plating must have been breached.

"We've lost attitude control," Roness yelled.

Another fragment crashed into *Sagan*. The sickening sound of rending metal filled the cabin. The shuttle moaned like a wounded animal, and then it began to tumble. Ezri flew out of her chair, just able to bring her left arm up as she struck the ceiling. *Now,* she thought with maddening clarity, *the shuttle will head back down to the planet.* She was thrown into the side bulkhead, and then backward. She had just enough time to be amazed that she did not feel any pain.

And then darkness took her.

Ezri awoke slowly. At first, she became aware of sounds around her, soft, syrupy rhythms she could neither place nor understand. Her first coherent thoughts were of Trill, and of the Caves of Mak'ala. For a time, she drifted in her mind through the interconnecting pools, communicating with the other symbionts, and waiting an almost painfully long time to move out into the world, and then from there to the rest of the universe. And then, finally, she was Lela Dax, and more than the sum of the two of them. Lela, and then Tobin, and then all the rest, through to Ezri. Ezri Dax, aboard *Destiny,* Deep Space 9, and *Defiant.*

Aboard *Sagan.*

Ezri opened her eyes and did not know where she was. She peered at the ceiling and recognized *Defiant.* She tried to lift her head, but found herself too weak.

"Doctor," a woman's voice said, "she's awake."

Ezri heard footsteps, and then a face entered her field of vision, a woman with blue-green eyes, and reddish blond hair braided and pulled back against her head. Ezri knew this woman, she was sure. She remembered having a drink with her in Quark's the night before the mission ... yes, when the woman and Sergeant Etana had been saying goodbye ... the woman's first extended mission, her first extended time away from Etana. "Krissten," she said.

"Yes," the nurse said.

"Ezri," came another voice, and it took Ezri only a second to recognize Julian's mellifluous tones. His dark, handsome face appeared above her, beside the nurse's. "How are you feeling?"

She opened her mouth to speak, but only an unintelligible sound emerged.

"That's all right," Julian told her, reaching up and running a hand tenderly across her forehead. "You've been thrown around quite a bit. The good news is that you're going to be all right." He smiled at her, a smile that she had already taken into her heart.

"The shuttle," she finally managed to say. "We were on board the shuttle."

"Yes," Julian said, and his face changed slightly, she saw, the smile maybe no longer as wide.

"What—" she started, and again she tried to raise her head. Julian put a hand on her shoulder and restrained her, gently pushing her back down. "What happened? The Vahni?"

"You saved the Vahni," Julian said.

The fog seemed to begin lifting from around Ezri, and she became more aware of her surroundings. She turned her head to the right and saw a biobed and medical displays. "How did I get here?" she asked.

"Later, Ezri," Julian told her, and he looked up at the nurse. She nodded and moved away.

"What happened?" Ezri asked, raising her voice.

"Your shuttle lost power," Julian told her. "As it started to fall back toward the planet, we were able to grab it with a tractor beam and transport you off."

The nurse reappeared, and it looked as though she handed something to Julian.

"What about Gerda?" Ezri wanted to know. "How is she?"

"You need to rest," Julian said, and he reached up toward her neck.

"No, now," she said, her voice loud and insistent. "How is Gerda?" Instead of an answer, she heard the sibilant puff of a hypospray, like somebody whispering into her neck.

"Rest, now, Ezri," Julian said, not responding to her question. But as she closed her eyes and let sleep pull her back into its velvety folds, she could not help but think that Julian had already given her an answer.

22

Taran'atar stood alone inside the turbolift, watching the walls of the shaft rush horizontally past the open front end of the car. He reviewed the details of his current operation, as few and as simple as they were, and thought about delaying his plan. He could even abandon it completely.

You taste fear, he told himself, disgusted with his vacillation. He had been charged with a campaign by the Founder, and he would see it through, however long it required, however many operations he had to prepare and execute. No matter the vagueness of the Founder's directive, or its apparent pointlessness. A god had spoken, sent him a mission, and he would see it through.

Or die.

The turbolift slowed, then stopped in front of a set of doors. They parted and slid into the bulkhead, revealing a corridor within the habitat ring. Taran'atar waited. When nobody entered the lift or passed by, he shrouded and moved out. The muted sounds of voices drifted to him, some coming from farther down the corridor, others from behind the closed doors of the quarters on this deck. The smells of food and of the beings who lived here permeated the air. He detected no threats to him, and so he set out purposefully toward his objective.

As he walked, Taran'atar thought about the Founder, who had instructed him to immerse himself in the various cultures he would encounter on Deep Space 9, and in the various aspects of life in those cultures. After spending as much time as Taran'atar had on the space station, doing little besides standing in the operations center and going into battle when he could—even if that meant utilizing the holosuites—he knew that he must do something more. He had observed Colonel Kira in combat, both in the Delta Quadrant and once in the holosuite, and he had spent a few days in the week prior to *Defiant's* departure roaming the ship, but still, he knew that had not been enough. Even the colonel had suggested to him that there was more to see here than just the operations center and the holosuites. And so he had begun to travel to various locales throughout the station.

Two people came walking down the corridor together toward Taran'atar. One was a human male in a Starfleet uniform, he saw, the other a Bajoran female in a Militia uniform. He wondered if they might be coming from the place to which he was headed. As they drew nearer, talking with each other, Taran'atar gauged their movements, waited as long as he could to commit, and then flattened himself against the bulkhead. They passed him, never even having suspected his presence. Contempt welled up within him for these Alpha Quadrant beings and their pathetic observational abilities, but then more of the Founder's words echoed in his mind: *Don't judge them. Experience and try to understand, only. Judgment will come later.* He put the beings out of his mind and continued on down the corridor.

The first place Taran'atar had gone to "experience" Alpha Quadrant life, other than the operations center, had been *Defiant*. After Commander Vaughn had asked him to come aboard the ship to answer questions about the Gamma Quadrant, Taran'atar had decided to remain aboard, and he had returned daily, roaming through the ship and watching the crew as they prepared for their mission. But then the little being, the Ferengi, had run into him. And the Ferengi had feared him.

Correctly so, Taran'atar thought now. Jem'Hadar soldiers had maimed the little being, destroyed one of his legs. The Ferengi had experienced the superiority of the Jem'Hadar, and his subsequent fear was justified. Taran'atar understood, though, that his encounter with the Ferengi had not served the goals the Founder had laid out for him. He had inspired fear, and had himself felt disdain for the pitiful little being, and neither of those things furthered his mission. He had failed, and that was unacceptable.

After that, Taran'atar had selected other locations and activities with which he was not familiar. He had already visited several of these—shrouded, to avoid incidents like the one with the Ferengi—and now he was about to visit another. He arrived at a set of closed doors, beyond which lay his destination. He stood across the corridor and waited for somebody to enter or exit.

Thirteen minutes and thirty-five seconds later, the doors opened, and a human woman in a Starfleet uniform walked out. "Okay, bye," she said, looking back into the room. Out of habit, Taran'atar measured her at a glance—medium height and weight for her species and gender, blond hair, green eyes, the blue collar that designated her as working in the sciences. When she had cleared the way, he moved quickly, turning sidelong to steal through the closing doors. Once inside, Taran'atar peered to his right, then took two silent steps to an empty space along the bulkhead.

The room was fairly large. Three oval windows in the back wall looked out into space, the trio flanked on either side by a pair of wide, tall cabinets. The cabinet on the right stood closed, but the one on the left was open; inside were several empty shelves, but others were filled with colorful artifacts that Taran'atar could not identify. A table sat in front of the leftmost window, with two long, but much lower, tables lining the left and right bulkheads. In the center of the room, mats and pillows and blankets were strewn about, and amid these meandered nineteen small beings.

Children, Taran'atar thought, grasping the concept, if not the reality, of what he saw. Two other beings—fully formed males—stood near the windows. All of the beings appeared to be either Bajoran or human, though two of the children may have been descended from both species.

The children were even smaller than Taran'atar had anticipated. He found himself unable even to speculate about their ages. Had they been Jem'Hadar, he would have put them at just a few days old, but he knew that most humanoids developed far more slowly than that. It was a sign of weakness.

Taran'atar stopped himself. *Withhold judgment,* the Founder had told him. Taran'atar stood against the wall, watched, and listened.

In an unsystematic, even a chaotic, manner, the children gathered up the mats, blankets, and pillows, and carried them over to the open cabinet. There, they dumped their cargo into a pile. One of the adults—the human; the other was Bajoran—thanked them, picking up the material and placing it onto the empty shelves in the cabinet. Despite the lack of ceremony, the actions seemed ritualistic to Taran'atar, though he could not fathom their meaning.

After the children had completed their task, they returned to the center of the room, where they sat down on the floor. Near the middle of the three windows, the adult Bajoran thanked the children for cleaning up, then asked them if they wanted to look at some animals. The children sent up a clamor, some of their words indecipherable, but they identified the Bajoran man as Gavi. From the table by the window, Gavi picked up a group of placards, each a third of a meter by half a meter in dimension. Then he crouched down, setting the placards on his thighs.

"Okay," he said, "what animal is—" He raised the top placard and displayed it for the children. "—this?" Taran'atar at once recognized the pictured beast, a brown-haired, four-legged pack animal native to Bajor called a *pylchyk*. The children all yelled their own responses, most of which were correct. Gavi said, "That's right. This is a *pylchyk,*" apparently ignoring the children who had called out the wrong answer, or given no answer at all. "This animal lives on Bajor, and the people there use it to carry supplies and to tend their fields." Gavi's tone of voice, and the manner in which he pronounced his words, seemed very strange, almost as though he believed the children incapable of hearing or understanding him. Taran'atar wondered if these might be defective children. He knew that defective Jem'Hadar were occasionally bred; when that happened, they were simply destroyed.

Gavi looked over at one of the children, a small human girl, and said, "Can you tell me the name of this animal, Claudia?" The girl, who had not properly identified the animal the first time, stared back at him without saying anything. "This is a . . ." He waited for the girl to say the name of the animal, but she said nothing. "Come on, Claudia, I know you can do it. This is a *pyl* . . . a *pyl* . . ."

"*Pylchyk,*" the girl erupted, and all of the children cheered.

Taran'atar watched as Gavi went through all of the placards, showing them to the children and then asking questions and talking about the animals on them. Taran'atar found himself fascinated by the process, despite—or perhaps because of—his lack of understanding about the purpose of the exercise. And Gavi even presented pictures of a few animals—including *treni* cats and cotton-tailed *jebrets*, both supposedly native to Ferenginar—of which Taran'atar had absolutely no knowledge.

After Gavi had shown all of the placards, he asked the children who among them wanted to draw. The group made loud noises in response, several of the children putting their arms up in the air as though attempting to call attention to themselves. Gavi then asked what they should draw today, and again the children responded, although Taran'atar could not tell if all of the responses actually answered the question. Gavi held up his hands, palms out, and quieted the children by saying, "Wait, wait, one at a time." Then he pointed to the child closest to him, a young girl who looked essentially human, but with some vague Bajoran characteristics. "What would you like to draw today, Mireh?" he asked her.

"I want to draw the wormhose," she said.

Gavi smiled at the girl, leaned in, and poked her in her midsection. "Okay, Mireh. We can do that. But it's not called a 'wormhose.'"

The girl laughed—at least, Taran'atar thought it was laughter, though it could have been some other sort of spasm. "It's not?" she said.

"No," Gavi told her, and then he addressed all the children. "Who knows what it's called?" he asked. A number of the children pushed their arms straight up into the air again, and two of them yelled, "The wormhole!"

"That's right," Gavi said. "The wormhole." He leaned back in to the girl. "Can you say that, Mireh? Can you say *wormhole?*"

The girl looked at him, crossed her arms in front of her, and said, very definitively, "Yes."

"Well, okay," Gavi said, laughing. He stood up and said, "So let's draw." The children stood up and headed for the little chairs around the tables at the sides of the room. Gavi joined the human man, and the two moved across the room to the other cabinet, from which they extracted large pieces of white paper and what appeared to be colorful drawing implements.

Something bumped into Taran'atar's leg. He looked down, just in time to see himself finish shimmering back into visibility. A human boy stood beside him, apparently having wandered while making his way to one of the tables. A sense of shock filled Taran'atar at even having been approached without realizing it. And for this boy, this little human, to have penetrated his concentration and concealment . . . he felt humiliated.

"Look at the alligator," the boy said, staring up into Taran'atar's face. Unlike the Ferengi aboard *Defiant,* this being displayed no fear of him. He gazed up at Taran'atar with a smile, then raised his arms. "Up," the boy said.

The human man yelled—*"Hey, get away from him!"*—and then Gavi gasped. Taran'atar looked up to see the two men glaring at him. Gavi walked slowly forward, his arms outstretched, palms out, as though trying somehow to ward off Taran'atar. "Don't do anything," he said, and Taran'atar wondered what he thought Taran'atar might do. "They're only children," he added.

As Gavi neared, Taran'atar looked past him at the other man, and saw an expression of fear and anger on his face. It occurred to him that perhaps these men had also encountered Jem'Hadar in the past, as the Ferengi had, and perhaps they had been wounded by them as well. The children, though— Taran'atar saw that most of the children were peering at him and smiling; some looked surprised, and some looked curious, but none of them appeared scared. *Interesting,* Taran'atar thought, though he was unsure of the import of what he had noticed.

Gavi stopped two paces from Taran'atar. Still moving slowly, he bent down and reached out for the boy. His fingers closed around a sleeve of the boy's shirt, but the boy pulled his arm away, his eyes never leaving Taran'atar. Gavi, with an obvious sense of desperation, lunged forward, snatched the boy by the shoulder, and reeled him into his arms. The boy said, "No," loudly, but Gavi told him to be quiet in a very stern tone of voice, and the boy quieted.

"Take him, Joshua," Gavi said, staring at Taran'atar's face, but clearly not speaking to him. The other man stepped forward and gathered the boy up, then moved back toward the windows again. Gavi asked, "What do you want?"

Taran'atar held Gavi's gaze for several seconds before he said anything. The Bajoran stood slightly crouched, his muscles tensed, his attention focused, and Taran'atar perceived that he would stand his ground if Taran'atar charged. After three months on the space station, this was perhaps the most interesting thing Taran'atar had learned.

"Only to observe," he said at last.

Gavi's expression did not change, although Taran'atar sensed an alteration in his stance. A moment ago, he had been poised to fight, but now he had relaxed somewhat, evidently trusting Taran'atar's words.

A fool, Taran'atar thought. He could be on the man before he had a chance to scream, snapping his neck where he stood. This time, Taran'atar did not correct himself about judging the beings here; this was simple truth.

"I think," Gavi said, "I think you should leave."

Taran'atar nodded. "Yes." He took two quick paces to the doors, which opened before him. He stopped for a moment, still curious about all that had gone on here, not so much with respect to the two men, but with the children. Taran'atar turned and looked back into the room, at the boy who had bumped into him.

The boy looked back at him for a moment, then held out his arms in Taran'atar's direction, and said, "Alligator."

Taran'atar whirled and left, more confused now than ever about life in the Alpha Quadrant.

23

Vaughn was angry.

Clad in full dress uniform, he stood in an area that the Vahni called the Remembrance Garden. The word *remembrance* induced just that for Vaughn right now, bringing to mind the lovely picture of the city that Ventu had thoughtfully presented to him. Both the gift and the giver had been lost in the collapse of the tower, and as Vaughn stood amid the enormous congregation of Vahni assembled in the garden, he craved vengeance: for Ventu, for the more than three thousand Vahni who had died in the quakes and aboard their interplanetary ships, and for Ensign Roness. But vengeance, Vaughn knew, always carried with it a steep price, and in the end it paid for nothing. Short of that, the need for justice beckoned, though like so many things—beauty, truth, duty—the notion of what constituted just actions varied with perspective.

At one end of the garden—an area in the city's largest park that could easily have accommodated *Defiant* for landing—a group of Vahni marched solemnly up onto a proscenium. The lack of ordered sounds, disturbing to Vaughn even before the tragedy, he now found almost unbearable. The shifting mass of bodies in the garden made a noise like a collective death rattle. For comfort, he clung to the sounds of the crew, sad though they were; more than half of the ship's complement had accompanied him to the ceremony, and all had wanted to attend. The memorial had lasted nearly two hours now, and as the crew had listened via their translators to the sentiments of the several Vahni officiating, tears had flowed. Sam Bowers had been particularly hard hit by the loss of Gerda Roness, though Nog, T'rb, Kaitlin Merimark, and Jeanette Chao had also been close friends of the young ensign. Dr. Bashir had also seemed very moved during the Vahni tributes, though Vaughn suspected that the doctor's emotions were further beset by his concern for Dax; besides her own harrowing experience in the shuttle, she now faced dealing for the first time with losing a person under her command.

The Vahni on the stage had arranged themselves in rows atop a tiered platform, and one of them stepped forward from the center of the lowest row. Two large displays, one on either side of the stage, ensured that all in the crowd could view the proceedings. "My [*untranslatable*] Vahni Vahltupali, and our honored friends from the United Group of Planets," the woman conveyed, "as we conclude our observance, we would like to share our grief through a rite of [*untranslatable*]." Low tones stood in for the missing words.

Around the garden, the Vahni all bowed, and Vaughn saw the ocular organs ringing the heads of those nearest him squint closed. Then a change passed through the many-hued assemblage, the flesh of all the Vahni drifting from their natural colors to an indigo so dark that it was almost black. No sounds came through the translators. Vaughn bowed his head and closed his eyes, wondering what human analogue there might be for this communal experience. Were the Vahni crying? Chanting? Was this a moment of silence—a moment of *darkness*?

Right now, darkness suited Vaughn. The irony of what had happened here, with respect to his own life, had not eluded him. He had recently climbed from a life of secrecy, struggle, and death, into one of openness, cooperation, and exploration. And here, less than two weeks into his first mission of discovery, the darkness had risen up behind and overtaken him. But Vaughn would not lament his own fate at a time when the futures of so many had been ripped away, and the futures of those left behind had been irrevocably damaged. What he would do was what he had done for decades: he would fight.

Already, the easiest battle had been won. In the three days since the destruction of the Vahni moon and the quakes on their world, the crew of *Defiant* had obliterated the potentially deadly fragments of a planet in the Vahni system that had also been destroyed. While *Sagan*'s extensive damages would require a week to ten days more to repair, *Chaffee*'s plasma leak had quickly been patched. The mended shuttle and *Defiant* had tracked down those planetary fragments that might have, in time, headed toward the Vahni world and caused great devastation.

The tougher battle, though, still needed to be fought.

This time, the enemy would likely not be as easy to detect or vanquish as rocks floating through space. Since the Vahni moon had shattered, Ensign ch'Thane and his team of scientists had been able to determine that a strange, unidentifiable energy pulse had passed through the system at warp speed. The velocity implied an artificial cause, but although the crew had been unable to ascertain the exact nature of the pulse, all observable indications actually indicated a natural source.

Vaughn heard a rustling sound, and he raised his head and opened his eyes to find that all of the Vahni had reverted back to their regular colors. The Vahni at the front of the stage stood up fully and again addressed the crowd. "Now, please join us as we [*untranslatable*]." Without turning—what need did they have to turn, Vaughn realized, when their eyes encircled their heads?—she raised her tentacles high, paused, and then brought them down dramatically. The flesh of the group on the stage erupted in a panoply of colors and forms, the individuals synchronized for the first few seconds, and then diverging in an amazing visual display. The translators captured the initial seconds—"We look to the sky and see"—and then delivered only the low tone that signaled uninterpretable communication. All around the crew, Vaughn saw, the Vahni in the crowd began changing the colors and shapes on their flesh in time with the changes occurring on the Vahni onstage.

They're singing, Vaughn thought in wonder. His sense of appreciation for this extraordinary species only served to redouble his resolve to prevent the destructive force of the pulse from ever being visited upon them again. According to the Vahni, such events had been taking place on their world for more than two centuries. They had always occurred without warning and in no discernible pattern, except that the length of the intervals between them had decreased each time, while the level of destructive power had increased. Two hundred years ago, the quakes had happened decades apart, causing little damage; the latest event had followed the previous one by less than a year, and obviously had been the most powerful they had ever experienced. Worse than that, Ensign ch'Thane's simulations revealed that, had the Vahni moon not been in the path of the pulse, effectively eclipsing it and preventing most of it from ever reaching the planet—and *Defiant*—the surface of the Vahni world would have been devastated, and many of its inhabitants lost. Vaughn knew that if another pulse passed through the system, with no moon to provide even the possibility of escaping its full force, the Vahni civilization would likely be wiped out.

And Vaughn would not allow that to happen.

24

The door chime signaled, and Kira looked up from a padd to see Admiral Akaar outside her office. "Come in," she said flatly. Although pleased that the meeting she had requested three days ago would at last take place, she did not feel particularly happy about having to deal again with the laconic and disobliging admiral. This time, though, she vowed that she would wrest some answers from him.

The doors parted, momentarily allowing the bustle of ops to enter along with Akaar, then shut behind him with a click, isolating her office once more. She put the padd down and opened a hand in the direction of the chairs in front of her desk. "Please, Admiral," she said. "Have a seat." She walked out from behind her desk and over to the replicator. "Can I get you something to eat or drink?"

As he sat, Kira noticed a padd in his left hand, its display dark. "No, thank you," he said, and she thought she detected a tinge of annoyance in his voice.

Of course, Kira thought. *This is my office, my territory, and I'm in control.* Even something as simple as offering food demonstrated that, she knew. It had not escaped her notice that for her first meeting with Akaar, he had insisted that they use a conference room aboard *Mjolnir.* Since then, he had been to her office one other time, to bid farewell to Commander Vaughn. Her only other contact with him had been via companel, when she had attempted to learn more about his—and Councillor zh'Thane's—continued presence on the station, which was when she had requested this meeting.

Kira had not intended to get anything for herself from the replicator, but now she decided otherwise, wanting to maintain every small measure of control over this meeting that she could. She turned away from the admiral and ordered a *raktajino.* The replicator brightened and hummed, a mug materializing on the shelf in a haze of illumination. The hearty scent of the steaming liquid immediately floated through the room. Kira wrapped an index finger through the handle of the mug and lifted it to her lips. She imagined Akaar seething behind her at her deliberate movements, but when she turned and walked back to her desk, his face remained impassive. He had put his padd on the edge of her desk, she saw.

"So—" Kira said as she set the mug down and sat in her chair, but the admiral interrupted almost before the word had even left her mouth.

"Colonel," he said, "it has come to my attention that, in the past two years, the Federation has provided Bajor with a number of large- and mid-scale industrial replicators. Would you please detail for me the uses to which they have been put?" As had happened during their first meeting, Kira found the admiral's inquiry more like an order.

"Well," she finally said, "I'm aware that two of the large replicators are in use at the Bajoran shipyards." And as quickly as that, she realized, Akaar had seized control of the meeting. She peered down at the cool, reflective surface of her desk, at the inverted image of the admiral between her padd and the mug of *raktajino,* and she thought it fortunate that no weapon happened to be lying within arm's reach at the moment, or she might not have been able to resist the temptation to use it.

"Two?" he asked. "Do you believe that is a sufficient number to support military readiness for Bajor?"

Kira felt as though a warning shot had been fired across her bow. These questions followed in the same vein as those Akaar had asked when he had first arrived at the station, implicitly impugning the Bajoran government, and perhaps even the Bajoran people. "Forgive me, Admiral," she said, striving to retain some measure of diplomacy, "but isn't this information available to you from sources other than me?" She resisted her inclination to further suggest that Akaar had already acquired the data he now purported to seek from her.

"Regardless, Colonel," Akaar said, "does that mean that you cannot—or will not—answer my questions?"

A surge of energy coursed through Kira's body along with the anger rising in her. She felt the need to get up and move about her office as a means of dispersing her frustration. Such an action, though, would likely cede even more control over the meeting to Akaar. Instead, she reached up and rested her arms atop her desk.

"I can answer your question, Admiral, and I will," she told him. "But I'm the one who asked you here." *Three days ago,* she added to herself, and then it occurred to her that his meeting had nothing at all to do with her request to see Akaar; it was taking place now only because *he* wanted to see *her.*

"Of course, if you are not comfortable discussing your people . . ." the admiral said, as though Kira had not spoken at all. He allowed his thought to remain unfinished.

"Not at all," Kira responded, with what she took to be just a little too much detachment to be completely convincing. She worked the console on her desk, accessing the latest reports she had regarding Bajoran shipbuilding. "There is a third large-scale IR in use at the shipyards, as well as two mid-scale units," she said.

The admiral nodded almost imperceptibly. "Do you think Bajor is committed to its own defense right now?"

"Of course it is," Kira said, her voice rising. "The common defense is one of the central foundations of our government. But I don't care how many replicators the Federation has provided, they're still spread pretty thinly across Bajor. If you're implying that there is some other—"

"I am implying nothing," Akaar said calmly. "I only wish to know if you believe that Bajor is prepared to stand on its own."

"I believe that's what I said, Admiral," she told him, and she could hear her anger slipping into her voice.

"And what are your reasons for believing that?" he asked.

Kira brought her hands down flat on the surface of her desk, spread wide, fighting the urge to push herself up out of her chair and stalk through the office. "You know what, Admiral?" she said. "I think maybe this is a conversation you'd be better off having with First Minister Shakaar or Minister of Defense Reydau."

"I am having this conversation with you," Akaar said, and for an instant, his eyes smoldered. Kira thought she saw anger there, but not just anger—something else that she somehow perceived had nothing at all to do with either her or Bajor. "Your people are widely regarded as spiritual, Colonel," he went on, the look on his face gone so quickly that Kira wondered if she had imagined it. "Is it possible that your collective spirituality defines your society so much that it precludes developing a strong military infrastructure?"

"Admiral," Kira said, taking her hands from atop the desk and dropping them onto the arms of her chair. "The number of replicators we choose to use in the shipyards can't be used to characterize our dedication to defending Bajor. There are other needs: housing, roads, dams, power plants . . ." Kira did not appreciate having to defend her people. But she also believed in her people, and she took strength from that belief. "As a society, we must defend ourselves, but we're also accountable for other responsibilities. And yes, our spirituality guides us along our collective path."

"What about those not on the path?" Akaar asked.

Kira erupted, the oblique reference to the Attainder the final disrespect she was willing to take from this man. She slapped her hands onto the desktop and shot up out of her chair. "That's it," she said. "This meeting is over."

Akaar looked at her, his eyes almost on a level with hers even though he remained seated. He wore his face like an empty mask. He did not move. "Colonel," he said. "I am simply asking about your people, trying to learn about their ways of life, about who they are."

"There's been nothing simple about any of your questions, Admiral," she said. "In the few times you've talked to me since your arrival, you've managed to question Bajor's commitment to providing aid to Cardassia, our willingness to defend ourselves, our spirituality, the way I run this station, and now the Attainder."

Akaar gradually stood up to his full and imposing height. Kira, at half a meter shorter, never took her gaze from his. She refused to be intimidated—not by his size, not by his rank, not by anything. "I was not making reference to your Attainder," Akaar said, and Kira thought that maybe—*maybe*—his demeanor had melted a bit; had he perhaps perceived that he had crossed the line? "I am not here to pry into your personal life."

"Why *are* you here?" she demanded. Kira did not expect an answer, since none had been provided by the admiral during his time on the station, but this time, she actually received several.

"I am in the Bajoran system to meet with Councillor zh'Thane and Minister Shakaar," Akaar said. "I am on Deep Space 9 to help preside over a summit. And I am in your office to inform you that, three days from now, a delegation from Bajor, and two from the United Federation of Planets, will be arriving on this station."

"A summit?" Kira echoed. "Delegations." Her mind spun back to her first meeting with Akaar, when she had guessed at the reason for his visit. "Does this have to do with Bajor being admitted to the Federation?" she asked. Again she did not expect the admiral to be forthcoming with information, and again he surprised her.

"It does," he told her.

Although Kira had suspected that this event sat poised on the horizon, the confirmation still knocked the wind out of her. She thought she had been prepared for this, but was she? And were her people? She slowly sat back down, feeling a bit dazed. Across from her, Akaar took his seat again as well. Questions formed in rapid-fire fashion in Kira's mind, each leading directly to the next. Before she could decide which to ask first, though, the admiral answered the most important of them all.

"Several months ago," he said, "Minister Shakaar officially requested the renewal of Bajor's petition for membership." Kira knew that had been the purpose of Shakaar's visit to the Federation not long ago. "Pending this summit," Akaar continued, "the renewed petition will either be approved or denied."

"What happens if it's denied?" Kira wanted to know.

"Bajor will be ineligible to reapply for membership for a period of no less than five years," Akaar said. He picked up the padd he had brought with him and activated it. The device, almost hidden by his massive hands, blinked to life with a quiet sequence of quick, electronic tones. "In addition to Councillor zh'Thane and me, First Minister Shakaar will be attending, as well as the Trill and Alonis ambassadors to the Federation." He worked the controls on the padd, then handed it across the desk to Kira. "This is a list of the staff members accompanying the two ambassadors and the minister," he said. Kira took the padd and scanned its contents, reading through the list of names, orange letters displayed on a black background. "The summit will begin the day after the delegations arrive."

Kira looked up from the padd. As the practical considerations of hosting such an event on the station occurred to her, the shock of learning what lay ahead in the next few days began to fade. "Obviously you'll want to step up security while the ambassadors are on the station," she said.

"Yes," Akaar agreed. "Given the nature of the negotiations, though, I would like it to be handled in as low-profile a manner as possible."

"Of course," Kira said, finding it odd to suddenly be working *with* the admiral, rather than feeling as though they were operating at cross-purposes. "Diplomats want to be safe, but they also don't like to be smothered."

"That is my experience as well," the admiral said. "I do have a concern about the security arrangements, though." So did Kira; she always did. Deep Space 9 was a big place that saw a lot of visitors, sitting as it did at the most important junction in the quadrant. Still, they had managed to keep the station secure for more than eight years, through far more difficult circumstances than they would be facing now. "Colonel," Akaar went on, "do you think your chief of security will be capable of performing the tasks that will be required of her?"

"Of course," Kira said at once. Her own reservations about Ro had been allayed both by the fine job she had been doing and by a general improvement in her attitude since being assigned here. "If I didn't think Lieutenant Ro capable of *doing* the job, then she wouldn't still *have* the job."

"Of course," Akaar said. "But do you have any doubts at all about her willingness to follow orders? Because I am inclined to replace her for this duty with Lieutenant Spillane, the security chief aboard *Gryphon.*"

"Are you asking me if I *trust* Lieutenant Ro?" Kira asked, bewildered. She knew that Ro had experienced some troubles when she had served in Starfleet, and that she had eventually walked away from it completely, but Kira nevertheless found it stunning that a Starfleet admiral would question the woman's integrity. "I don't doubt Ro," she said. "She's been a valuable addition to my staff." Kira considered whether or not to say more, to say the thought that had come to mind, and then decided that she would. "I'm sure she would even make a fine Starfleet officer."

Akaar rose from his chair, apparently ready to end the meeting. "If Bajor is admitted to the Federation, Colonel," he said, "then which members of the Bajoran Militia are offered positions in Starfleet will be decided on an individual basis." For once, the admiral's antagonistic implication did not seem directed toward Kira. "But you run this station, and so the personnel decisions are yours to make." He started for the doors. "Good day, Colonel."

Something occurred to Kira, though, and she stopped him with a word. "Admiral?" He turned back to her as the doors opened. The sounds of consoles and voices drifted into the office from ops. "Are matters of Bajoran faith, and our relief efforts to Cardassia, and our military capabilities—are those things relevant to Bajor's admission to the Federation?"

"Everything Bajor does, everything Bajor *is,*" he proclaimed, "is relevant." They regarded each other across the room, and then Kira stood, choosing to end the meeting by once again assuming a small measure of control.

"Thank you, Admiral," she said, clearly dismissing him. Akaar turned and exited. She watched him go, thinking about her dealings with him, which she now viewed in a somewhat different light than she had for the past six weeks. His many questions now seemed understandable—though not necessarily reasonable—given the circumstances. To Kira, it now appeared that the admiral had been attempting to take Bajor's pulse through her, a prospect she did not especially like, considering the Attainder and the recent tension in her professional relationship with the first minister. Still, as Kira reviewed all of Akaar's pointed questions, she did not feel threatened, either for herself or for her people. Bajorans could stand up to any scrutiny. In the end, she felt certain that their renewed petition to join the Federation would be approved.

Kira sat back down. And as she thought about Bajor joining the Federation, she wondered, if he were here, what Captain Sisko would think.

25

Bashir approached the cabin he shared with Ezri, anxious to see her before she returned to duty later today. He always looked forward to the two of them spending time together, of course, but he was motivated now more by his concern for her. After the incident aboard *Sagan*, Ezri had stayed overnight in the medical bay, and then at Vaughn's orders, had remained off-duty for the next two days—owing not to her physical injuries, but to allow her some time to cope with the death of Ensign Roness. Bashir had privately concurred with that decision, but Ezri had asked to take a shift today, and the commander had agreed—prematurely, Bashir feared. Ezri had been understandably despondent since the incident, and he worried about her adding to her own burden by resuming her duties too soon.

The door to the cabin opened with a low breath of air. As Bashir stepped across the threshold, he felt the tension in his body: the rigidity of his arms, the stiffness of his back, his hands clutched into fists. He willed himself to relax, not wanting to anticipate—and thus contribute to—any negative emotions that Ezri might be experiencing. When he had left for the medical bay this morning, she had still been asleep, and so he did not yet know how she was feeling today.

Inside their small quarters, Bashir was immediately pleased to see Ezri in her uniform, working at the companel, as though she had begun to move past the terrible sorrows of the past few days. Perhaps it would not be too early for her to return to duty, after all, he thought. "Hi," he said, any remaining anxiety quickly draining from his body. "Are you ready for lunch?" But when Ezri turned toward him, he saw her eyes rimmed in red. Tension flooded through him once more, though he strived not to show it.

"Hi," Ezri said, attempting to inject a lightness into her tone and manner that she very obviously did not feel. "Actually, I'm not really very hungry."

Neither Ezri's appearance nor her admission surprised Bashir; this was what he had expected. The loss of Roness had been difficult for Ezri, he knew, not least of all because her orders had led directly to the ensign's death. "That's all right," he said, trying to deflect attention from her lack of appetite. "I'm not all that hungry myself." As he looked at Ezri, he noted her pale complexion, as well as a slight puffiness below her eyes, both indications of her recent sleeplessness. She had awoken abruptly several times during the past two nights, and although she had not spoken of nightmares, Bashir felt certain that she had been visited by them. "What're you doing?" he asked, pointing to a series of numbers and several blocks of text on the companel. He hoped to ease Ezri's grief, at least for the moment, simply by behaving as though nothing were amiss.

"I'm just looking at the readings of the pulse," she said, glancing around at the display. Bashir did not quite know what to make of that. Ezri was no scientist, and although several of Dax's previous hosts had been, he doubted that she would be able to add anything to the crew's research. "I'm not having much luck," she added, confirming his thoughts. To this point, Bashir knew, Ensign ch'Thane and his staff had been unable to identify the precise nature of the pulse, although the direction from which it had traveled had been evident. *Defiant* now journeyed back along that path, Commander Vaughn hoping that the crew could find a means of ending the threat to the Vahni. Bashir felt the vibrations of the engines through the decking as the ship flew at warp.

He moved farther into the room, walking over to the lower of the room's two beds and sitting down on the edge of the mattress. "How are you feeling?" he asked, tapping at his shoulder. When *Sagan* had been struck by the lunar fragments, Ezri had suffered a hairline fracture of her left radius, and an anterior dislocation of her right sternoclavicular joint. Bashir had repaired and treated both injuries, and by now, any discomfort should have faded completely. But Ezri answered his question in a different way than he had asked it.

"Actually," she said, "I'm feeling pretty down." She switched off the companel, but continued sitting before it.

Bashir nodded, his heart heavy. "That's completely understandable after what you've been through," he said. He wanted to go to her and take her in his arms, but by remaining seated, Ezri seemed to indicate that she wanted something else from him right now besides comforting. "Maybe it would be a good idea to take another few days before you go back on duty," he suggested to her.

"No," Ezri said at once. "I have to go back to the bridge."

"I know you feel that way," Bashir said, "but you've been affected so deeply by what happened that—"

"I'm supposed to be affected," she interrupted. "We're all affected. I'm sure even Commander Vaughn has been having difficult moments since—" She hesitated only an instant before saying the words. "—since Gerda died."

"Yes, of course," Bashir said, supposing that she must be right: their small crew of forty—thirty-nine now—had all been hurt by the loss of one of their own. Vaughn had held a memorial yesterday, and there had been few dry eyes. Oddly enough, Ezri had managed not to cry at the service, even though she had wept back in their cabin both before and afterward. "We're all affected," Bashir went on, "but it's obviously different for you; you were there."

"I'm the first officer," Ezri declared. "I have to return to duty."

"Ezri," he said, and now he did stand up. "The crew can get along without you for a few more days."

"Without *me,* yes," she agreed. "But not without their first officer. The position is my responsibility. I can't let my personal situation, my emotions, paralyze me. I have professional obligations. The ship needs a first officer, and not somebody substituting in the position, but the person chosen for that duty."

"I understand," Bashir said. He took the few steps over to her and put a hand tenderly on her shoulder. "You need to take your mind off of what happened, and maybe even to prove to yourself that you can do the job."

"No, that's not it," Ezri said, her voice rising. She stood, and Bashir let his hand fall from her shoulder. She paced past him, then turned to face him from the corner of the room. "This isn't about my needs. It's about my responsibilities." She paused, looking down at the floor, and when she spoke again, her voice had quieted. "I feel horrible about Gerda. I wish she hadn't died, and I suppose that if I could, I'd give up my life for hers. But I know that I did the right thing. The actions Gerda and I took, the orders I gave, saved so many lives down on the planet . . . I feel survivor's guilt, but I don't feel guilty for the command decisions I made."

Bashir heard the words of a counselor in what Ezri was saying, and he wondered if she was helping herself with the truth, or hiding behind it. He worried that she might be overcompensating for her part in the loss of Roness. In fact, ever since Tiris Jast had been killed, Ezri had taken on more and more responsibilities, and Bashir could not help thinking now that so many of her actions in the last few months had been *re*actions to tragedy—as though, by assuming a position of leadership, she would be able to avert such disasters in the future.

"Even if you don't feel responsible for Roness's death," he told her, "you still have emotions. You said yourself that you feel down, that you feel horrible."

"Yes, I do feel that way," Ezri said. "But I told you how I was feeling because I need to talk about it, not so that you can protect me."

"It's my job to protect you," he said, taking a step toward her.

"As my lover," Ezri asked, "or as the ship's chief medical officer?"

"Both, I suppose." As *Defiant*'s CMO, he had the authority to relieve Ezri—or anybody else—of their position, even over the objections of the captain. He had not considered invoking his power to keep Ezri from returning to duty, but if that became necessary . . .

"You don't have to worry about me professionally," Ezri said. "I have resources available to me to deal with the responsibilities of my position, resources that nobody else aboard has."

Bashir understood the reality of that: eight other lifetimes of experiences, collected within the Dax symbiont. But Ezri was not any of the other of Dax's hosts, and he believed that she had not even fully integrated all of their memories. Because of Jadzia's presence and experiences while aboard DS9, Bashir had studied a great deal about Trill physiology, and he realized how difficult joining must have been—must still be—for Ezri, who had never trained for it. During the last eighteen months, he had witnessed firsthand the problems that she had experienced as she learned to exist as a joined being.

So yes, Ezri had resources, but Bashir was not convinced that she would be able to avail herself of them in a way that would help her right now. Dax's previous hosts had memories of coping with loss, but they also had memories of *feeling* loss, and those might be recalled to Ezri now, perhaps even deepening her sorrow. Joining, Bashir knew, required a delicate balance even under the best circumstances, and he was not convinced that Ezri had yet achieved the equilibrium she would need to live out a healthy, joined life.

He said none of this to her, though, wanting neither to add to her troubles, nor to deny her the support she sought from him right now. Instead, he said, "All right," agreeing not to address his concerns about her resuming her position as the ship's first officer. He opened his arms, and she went to him. As he held her, she told him how she felt, about the tremendous emptiness and sadness she carried inside her, and about her guilt at having survived when Roness had not. Bashir listened, trying to provide her the support she needed.

But he also knew that he could not surrender his other concerns about Ezri. He would continue to be there for her, to give her guidance when she asked for it, and to help and love her through it all. But when she returned to duty, he would also watch her.

Watch, and worry.

26

Quark listened to the sounds of the bar—a fair number of voices, but neither enough rings of glassware nor enough groans of loss at the dabo wheel—and he realized that he actually missed Dr. Bashir and Chief O'Brien. Of course, the 57th Rule of Acquisition—"Good customers are as rare as latinum; treasure them"—never proved more true than when good customers abandoned you. Even though they were Starfleet types, Bashir and O'Brien had at least known how to drink and spend money. They might not have gambled enough to satisfy Quark's appetites, but darts had been a thirsty game for them.

Quark glanced from behind the bar over to the corner where the dartboard still hung. Dr. Bashir still played occasionally, but things had certainly not been the same since the chief had gone back to Earth. "Earth," Quark muttered. *"Hew-mons."* He shook his head in disgust.

Grabbing a rag, he began to wipe down the bar, lamenting his middling fortunes as he did so. Since the Europani and the convoy crews had departed the station, business had sunk to a steady but unspectacular level. As he had expected, the presence of the *Gryphon* crew on the station had done little to improve profits, and the absence of *Defiant* had actually hurt them. Quark still hoped that commercial traffic through the wormhole would eventually resume, but he did not, as a rule, put much stock in hope. The 109th Rule of Acquisition said about dignity what might just as well have been said about hope: that "and an empty sack is worth the sack." At this rate, Quark would wither and die in the bar decades from now, having earned just enough profit to pay for his Certificate of Dismemberment and maybe, just maybe, a little memorial plaque for the corner. "It can replace the *frinx*ing dartboard," he mumbled to himself.

"Dabo," came the cry of several voices from across the room, and Quark peered over to see only a handful of gamblers around the wheel. Treir, long, slender, and deliciously green, stood over the dabo table, her scant outfit clinging alluringly to her body, its iridescent fabric titillating the eye by allowing just enough jade skin to show through without causing a riot. But only just. She had been one of the few bright spots in the bar recently—though he paid her dearly for that brightness—usually generating a good turnout around the dabo wheel.

As Quark continued to swab the bar, he saw Grimp approach carrying a tray with several glasses of varying shape, size, and color. One of them, an orange-tinted flute, stood almost completely full. Grimp came around the bar and started to unload the empties onto the recycle shelf. Quark wiped his hands with the rag and tossed it beneath the bar, then walked over to Grimp and pointed at the full glass. "What's this?" he wanted to know.

"Argelian sparkling wine," Grimp said. "Lieutenant McEntee wanted to try it."

"She wanted to *try it?*" Quark asked, already jumping ahead and knowing what he would hear.

"Ah, she, ah, she didn't like it," Grimp stammered. He had loaded all of the empty glasses onto the shelf, and now he lifted the flute and reached to put it there as well. Quark seized his wrist and stopped him, the sparkling wine splashing over the rim of the glass and onto both their hands.

"She did pay for it, though," Quark demanded. "Right?"

"Well, ah, since she didn't drink it—"

"Grimp, you fool," Quark said, raising his voice. "I'm running a bar here, not a charitable taste-testing facility." The waiter flinched at the loud words, his eyes squinting and his shoulders hunching. Grimp's cowering reminded Quark of his own brother, back in the good old days when Rom had worked in the bar, before he had become station engineer, before he had become—

But that was a subject Quark did not need to think about right now; his mood was sour enough without having to think about how Rom was currently working to destroy Ferengi culture. He released Grimp's wrist, and said, "Go back and charge her for the drink." The waiter hesitated, obviously not wanting to confront the *Gryphon* officer. "Charge her," Quark insisted, "or it's coming out of your salary." Maybe he would dock Grimp's pay anyway, he thought, for either impertinence or incompetence—or maybe for both. Grimp put the flute down on the recycle shelf, the glass clinking against another, then slunk with his tray back out onto the floor.

A movement drew Quark's attention, and he looked down to the end of the bar near the entrance. Seated there, Morn held up a tall, blue, and empty glass, wiggling it in Quark's direction. *Thank the Blessed Exchequer that there are some constants in the universe,* he thought. He quickly retrieved the rag and wiped the sparkling wine from his hand, then ducked beneath the bar and pulled out a short, bulbous bottle. An emblem of the First Federation adorned the import hologram around its squat neck. Quark removed the stopper from the clear bottle as he strode over to Morn, who had deposited his glass in front of him. Quark poured out a healthy serving of the bright orange *tranya*. "Well, my friend," Quark said as he sealed the bottle back up, "I hope you're having a better evening than I am."

Morn offered a sideways glance—very nearly a leer—at a lithe Mathenite woman sitting beside him. He winked at Quark, then raised his replenished glass, obviously about to make a toast. Before he could, though, a loud crash and the clatter of breaking glass filled the bar.

The bottle of *tranya* still in hand, Quark raced out to find Frool sprawled on the floor. The waiter still held a tray in his outstretched hands, pieces of broken glass scattered out in front of him in many colors. Quark lowered himself to his knees beside Frool to be sure he was all right. The waiter had somehow hurt his leg last week, and he had been limping around ever since. Quark had warned him to be careful, but he clearly had not listened.

Frool rose to his feet—Quark rose with him, a hand steadying the waiter's back—and brushed himself off. "I'm all right," he said. He pointed to the shattered glass on the floor. "Sorry about that."

"Frool, you gimp," Quark said, and his words filled the bar, which had quieted at the sound of the crash. Quark turned and raised his arms out in front of him, gesturing with his fingers to his customers. "Everything's all right, folks. Nothing to see here. Just go back to your drinking and gambling." He looked over at Treir and saw again the empty seats around her. "Plenty of room at the dabo wheel," he added. Slowly, the noise level began to increase as people returned to what they had been doing—mostly talking, Quark assumed, since none of them were drinking, gambling, or spending enough.

"I'll clean that up," Frool said, indicating the bits of glass on the floor.

"You do that," Quark said. "And it's coming out of your wages." Frool nodded resignedly and moved off. Quark looked to the customer nearest him—Ensign Ling from ops, seated at the bar—shrugged, and said, "You just can't get good help these days." He started to head back behind the bar, but then another eruption of sound accosted him.

"Dabo," came the yell of mingled voices. Quark reached past Ensign Ling and put the bottle of *tranya* down on the bar, then hurried toward the dabo table. As he walked, the heavy clink of latinum drifted to him. Normally a beautiful sound, in this context—Treir counting out somebody's winnings—it made him sick.

At the table, Quark took hold of Treir's elbow and leaned in beside her. "What's going on?" he asked.

Treir shifted and bent, reducing her height of nearly two meters, and then draped a long, perfectly toned arm across his shoulders, the side of her body rubbing up temptingly alongside his. "We're paying off another lucky winner here at Quark's," she said with an appealing lilt in her tone. "Just like we always do." Quark knew she had said this as an enticement to the people at the table, and to anybody else within earshot, but there were not nearly enough customers around the dabo wheel to suit Quark. More than that, her words carried a little too much truth for him right now; he shuddered to count how many times she had paid out on a spin of dabo this evening.

"Well, stop doing it," he groused. "And get some more people gambling," he added, louder.

In an instant, Treir had extricated herself from around him. She faced Quark, peering down from her full height. "Get 'em yourself," she said, the singsong quality of her voice now gone. "I can't force people to come into this—" She hesitated, and Quark dreaded whatever descriptive noun she would choose to finish her sentence. "—place," she finally said, apparently realizing—and wisely so—that it would not benefit her to insult the establishment that paid her salary.

Quark stared up at her. "It's your *job* to get customers to come in here and gamble," he told her. At the table, two people stood up and moved away. Quark pointed after them. "Look," he said. "See what you're doing. Now you're chasing customers out of here."

"You're about two milliseconds away from chasing me out of here, Quark," she said. Then, lowering her voice to an ominous pitch, she said through gritted teeth, "You'd better watch it."

Quark had just about had enough. He thought that perhaps he should chase Treir and her steep salary out of here. This did not mark the first time since he had hired her that she had argued with him. Worse than that, she often behaved as though she were his business associate, rather than merely his employee.

"Listen," Quark told her, "if you want to leave—" He stopped. He had just heard something unexpected to his left, but when he looked in that direction, he saw nobody there. *Odo,* he thought immediately. The constable always used to attempt to insinuate himself into the bar to spy on him, but Quark had learned to distinguish the nearly subaudible sound of shifting fluid that Odo made, no matter his form. But Quark dismissed the notion as quickly as it had come to him. Not only was Odo off on some planet in the Gamma Quadrant oozing around with the Founders, but the only similarity between the sound Quark had just heard and the sound Odo made was that there appeared to be no source for it.

And then something occurred to Quark. He reached out to the dabo table and swiped an empty glass from atop it. He lowered it to his side, then whipped his arm upward, tossing the glass in the direction of the sound. The glass tumbled in a swift, flat arc, reflecting the orange and yellow light produced by the artwork on the wall.

And then the glass froze in midair.

The air beyond the unmoving glass shimmered, and a Jem'Hadar soldier flickered into existence. Quark heard several people gasp around the bar. He could not really tell from the face—they all looked alike to him—but from the black coverall the Jem'Hadar wore, he assumed this was the one Odo had sent here. The idea that the former constable might try to reach through the wormhole to disrupt Quark's business seemed a natural one.

The Jem'Hadar did not move, but stood staring directly at Quark. Other sounds rose in the bar now: glasses being put down on tables, chairs being pushed back, footsteps. Quark looked quickly around and saw that many of his customers had gotten up, and still others had already started toward the exit.

"Quark to security," he yelped, and the sounds of people rushing toward the door grew in number and volume. Still, the Jem'Hadar did not move, and Quark supposed that was a good thing. The last time a Jem'Hadar had appeared in the bar, he had later killed numerous people and attempted to destroy the station. This one often used the holosuites, causing Quark only the trouble of frequent repairs, but that was a much different thing than suddenly appearing in the middle of the bar out of nowhere. When he received no response to his call for help, he said again, "Quark to sec—"

"This is Ro," came the lovely voice of the lovely lieutenant. *"What can I do for you, Quark?"*

"Lieutenant," Quark said, purposely not using Laren's given name, wanting to impress upon her the need for her professional assistance. "We've got a serious disturbance in the bar. We need help."

"I'll be right there," Ro said, and Quark was pleased to hear a sense of urgency in her voice. He heard the comlink close.

Quark stood motionless, continuing to stare at the Jem'Hadar. He wanted to turn and run, or at least back slowly away, but he feared that might incite the soldier to violence. He remembered vividly how a Jem'Hadar had maimed his nephew, destroying one of Nog's legs. So he remained still. Directly behind him, he heard Treir's careful, measured breathing, and he could tell that she was scared too. That troubled Quark even more; Treir was a tough female.

"Well? What do you want?" Quark finally blurted, unable to control his fear. The Jem'Hadar said nothing and continued to stare at him. The eyes reminded Quark of somebody else, he realized: Garak, with that cold, intense glare that could seemingly penetrate neutronium. Quark had heard a rumor a while ago that Garak, when he had served with the Obsidian Order, had once stared at a man for ten hours straight, ultimately forcing the man into submission, and though Quark had never been able to substantiate the claim, he had never for a moment doubted its veracity.

The sound of footsteps rapidly approaching out on the Promenade reached Quark. When he heard them enter the bar, he took a chance and turned. Ro stood just inside the entrance now, phaser drawn and held out ahead of her. Sergeant Etana and Sergeant Shul flanked her, their weapons also in their hands. People streamed past them, headed out onto the Promenade.

Quark watched as Ro scanned the room, her eyes quickly finding him. "Quark," she said, "what is it? What's the trouble?" Before he could answer her, though, he saw that her gaze had moved past him and had evidently taken in the Jem'Hadar. "Taran'atar," she said. "Is there a problem?"

"Not with me," the Jem'Hadar said.

Ro approached the dabo table, her phaser now held at her side and pointing down toward the floor. As she reached Quark and Treir, she nodded to Treir and made a quick motion with her head, obviously indicating that she should leave. Treir apparently did not need any more invitation than that; she backed away toward the door.

Ro stepped directly up to Quark. "What did he do?" she asked him, clearly referring to the Jem'Hadar.

"Do?" Quark said. "He chased away what few customers I had."

Ro nodded, then looked over Quark's shoulder for a second. "How did he do that?" she asked. "The broken glass by the bar?"

"What?" Quark asked, and then remembered the tray his waiter had dropped. "No, no, that was Frool. But this Jem'Hadar was slinking around here, invisible." His voice rose and his words began coming faster. "And then he appeared out of nowhere and terrified everybody—me included. You saw them pouring out of here." He pointed past Ro toward the door.

A sympathetic expression played across Ro's face, and Quark thought that she could see how angry and frightened he felt. Then she looked back over toward the Jem'Hadar. "He looks like he's been drinking," she said, any sense of exigency suddenly leaving her voice.

"What?" Quark said, perplexed. He moved to Ro's side so that he could see both her and the Jem'Hadar, and then he saw the glass in the Jem'Hadar's hand. "No, no," Quark protested. "I threw that in his direction when I heard a strange noise. That's how I got him to uncloak."

"I see," she said, nodding her head. To Quark's dismay, she holstered her weapon.

"Wait, what are you doing?" he said, his words emerging in a rush.

"Taran'atar," Ro said, stepping toward the Jem'Hadar, "what are you do-ing in here?"

"I am observing," he said. "Nothing more."

"I see," she said. She turned back toward Quark, and she still looked as though she felt sorry for him. "So you're not here to hurt anybody?" she asked, obviously of the Jem'Hadar.

"No."

"All right," she said. She motioned to her deputies, and said, "Etana, Shul, you can go." Then she walked back over to Quark.

"You're not letting him go?" Quark said.

"He hasn't done anything criminal," Ro explained.

"Can't you at least get him out of my bar?" Quark wanted to know.

Ro sat down at the dabo table. "Quark," she said, lowering her voice, ap-parently so that only he could hear her. "You can't deny admittance to some-body just because of his species. You know that. I'm sure you've been the victim of that sort of attitude."

"But . . ."

"I know how you feel," she said. "Believe me, there've been plenty of people I'd have liked to have kept out of plenty of places." A lightness dressed her words, and Quark thought that she was trying to ease his tension. He was grateful—more than grateful; happy—for her concern, but it did not change the situation in the bar.

"He's wrecking my business," he said. "When you arrived, you saw those people—those *customers*—leaving."

"I'm sorry, Quark," she said, and he believed her. "I really am. But simply being a Jem'Hadar isn't a crime."

"But disturbing the peace is," he said. "And incitement to riot."

"All I see right now is incitement not to play dabo," she said. "And that's not a crime," she repeated.

"It ought to be," Quark persisted. "I'm not joking."

"I know you're not," Ro said. She leaned forward on her chair so that her face drew very close to his. He could smell a delicate scent on her, and it sur-prised him; he had never noticed her wearing perfume before. The bouquet was somewhat mild, but still very pleasant—and the idea of it, of her dabbing it onto her body, was much more than merely pleasant. "When I get off duty," she said, "maybe I'll come back here and play a little dabo myself."

Quark felt a tingle in his lobes. "You will?" he asked, his voice now a whisper.

"It might be fun," she said. "I've been thinking these past few days about taking a few risks."

"Well, if you're up for some risks," Quark started, but then he heard a footstep. He jerked his head up to see Taran'atar moving toward the bar. Quark backed away from Ro a step. "You have to do something about him," he said, pointing.

Ro sat back up and watched the Jem'Hadar as he crossed the room. Quark saw the few customers who remained allow him a wide berth as he passed. Fortunately, the Jem'Hadar did not stop at the bar, but continued walking and headed out the door. "He's scaring my customers, Lieutenant," Quark said, again employing Ro's title in an attempt to impress upon her the seriousness of the situation.

She looked back at him. "All right," she said. "I'll speak with Colonel Kira about it."

"Make sure you tell her what you saw," Quark insisted. "This isn't just about me; it's about the people on the station being able to enjoy the vital services I provide."

Ro smiled at him. "Of course," she said. She stood up, then walked around the dabo table and out the door.

Quark sighed heavily. He tried to think of what he could say to the few customers still there to encourage them to spend their money, but nothing came to mind. *What a night,* he thought. He straightened his jacket with a tug at the waist, then went back to the bar. Frool had come back, he saw, and was preparing to clean up the broken glass. Grimp had also returned to the bar, and Quark considered asking him whether or not he had succeeded in getting Lieutenant McEntee to pay for the drink she had sent back, but he found that he did not have the energy. *I'll just dock his pay, anyway,* he thought. *Just in case.*

Then he wondered if Laren would actually come back to the bar later. She had probably been joking, but he thought he would put on some cologne himself. *Just in case.*

27

The planetary system had been obliterated.

Vaughn leaned forward in the command chair and peered at the main viewscreen as *Defiant* approached the devastation. A vast field of debris—most fragments no larger than a human fist—stretched across billions of billions of cubic kilometers. These were not planetesimals; this was not a solar system in the early stages of being born, but one that had lived and died. Every planet, every moon, every comet and asteroid, had been pulverized here—everything but the star, which they assumed had endured by virtue of its considerable mass, density, and energy. Vaughn had many times witnessed the cruelty of an indifferent universe, and he could only hope now that the system had not been inhabited—and that this would not be the fate that would ultimately befall the Vahni Vahltupali.

"I'm seeing the same strange energy readings we recorded in the Vahni system," Lieutenant Bowers reported from tactical. As he and the rest of the bridge crew worked, the sounds of programmed tones, the audio cues of the various panels, played through the air like an electronic concert.

Vaughn lifted his chin from his hands. "This didn't just happen, though?" he asked. The debris seemed too widely dispersed for this to have occurred recently.

"No, sir," Ensign ch'Thane confirmed at the sciences console. Nog and Prynn worked the other primary bridge stations. "The pulse did pass through the system, but the residual energy readings, and the granularity and distribution of the rubble, indicate that this happened over time, probably the result of multiple events."

"All of which supports what the Vahni told us," Vaughn said, nodding slowly. "That this has been afflicting their planet for centuries." And if all of the Vahni information proved accurate—and Vaughn had no reason to believe otherwise—then they could expect another, more powerful pulse to sweep through their system in less than a year—possibly even in just a few months. Vaughn leaned back in his chair and sighed heavily. "Is there anything to suggest how much farther away the source of the pulse might be?"

"No, sir," Bowers said. He paused, operating his controls, and then said, "Captain, I'm reading a concentration of energy about a hundred fifty million kilometers from the star . . . and there's a mass there . . ."

"It's a planet," ch'Thane announced.

"Intact?" Vaughn asked, and thought, *How can that be?* He stood up and walked over to the sciences station.

"Yes, sir," ch'Thane answered. He consulted his display, and then quoted readings for the planet's mass, diameter, and distance from its star, all of which fell within the normal range for class-M worlds.

Vaughn leaned toward the console, bringing a hand up on the back of ch'Thane's chair. "Are there life signs?" he asked, searching the panel himself for an answer. "Or any indications of a habitable ecosphere?"

The ensign worked his controls before responding. "I can't tell," he finally said. "The energy readings are interfering with sensors."

Vaughn straightened and turned toward the main viewscreen, as though he would be able to see the unexpected planet across the cold kilometers. He looked at the rock fragments tumbling silently through space, barely visible in the darkness as they caught the negligible light of the distant sun, and he thought he suddenly understood something. "Ensign," he told ch'Thane, "transfer the coordinates of the planet to the conn." Vaughn paced back over to the command chair. "Shields," he said.

"Shields up," Bowers confirmed a moment later.

"Ensign Tenmei," Vaughn said, "take us in over the ecliptic." The debris of the system had spread out more or less along the plane of the solar equator. "Best speed."

"Aye, sir," Prynn said. Her hands moved deftly across the flight-control console, summoning *Defiant*'s wings. The bass hum of the engines sent deep vibrations through the ship's structure.

Vaughn sat down and gazed toward the viewscreen again. The stars shifted and the wreckage of the system fell away as *Defiant* changed its heading. Vaughn imagined the energy pulse repeating across decades, across centuries, growing ever stronger, battering planets and moons into nothing but shards, and he wondered how a lone world could have survived when nothing else had. And as *Defiant* brought the crew closer to the mystery, he could conjure up only one explanation: the planet had to be the source of the pulse.

The atmosphere roiled, a cauldron of churning shadows. Currents and eddies seethed through the dark, gray sea of clouds, imparting to it an inhospitable, even violent, appearance. The cover ensphered the planet, an inexplicable mixture of aeriform elements and energy surges—energy reminiscent of the pulse itself, though on a much smaller scale.

Vaughn sat in the command chair and watched the turbulent scene on the viewscreen. Ensign ch'Thane had calculated the orbits of the Vahni world and the one below, as well as the sidereal motions of their respective stars, and verified that the pulse had come from here. Further, the science officer had utilized stable cloud masses at the poles to determine the rotational period of the planet, allowing him to pinpoint the area on the surface where the pulse had originated. *Defiant* circled above that location now in a geosynchronous orbit.

"Anything?" Vaughn asked, his eyes still on the viewer, still on the heaving, twisting mass of clouds obscuring the planet. The sight put him in mind of another world, from across the galaxy and long ago, beset by the throes of a nuclear winter. In this case, he thought, the comparison might turn out to be apt.

"Negative," ch'Thane responded, checking his readouts. "I'm still not receiving any telemetry from the probe."

"It should emerge from the atmosphere in just under four minutes," Lieutenant Bowers offered.

"Thank, you," Vaughn said. When sensors, communications, and transporters had failed to penetrate the sea of clouds, Vaughn had ordered a probe launched, in the hope that it could reach the surface and gather useful data about whatever was down there. Contact with the probe had been lost as soon as it had descended into the atmospheric cover, but it had been programmed to return to the ship at a specified time.

The bridge grew quiet as the crew waited, only the gentle rumble of the thrusters intruding into the stillness. Vaughn glanced around and saw Nog and Prynn staring at the viewscreen, while Bowers and ch'Thane studied their panels. The crew seemed bound by a sense of tension, Vaughn thought, which he recognized as an amalgam of anticipation and anxiety; they wanted very much to help the Vahni, and at the same time, had doubts about whether they would be able to do so. Whatever data the probe provided would likely determine the nature and extent of the action they could take.

Vaughn recalled the terrible threat to Europa Nova not long ago, and he understood that if the *Defiant* crew could not put an end to the pulses, then the Vahni would have to be evacuated from their world, just as the Europani had. Considering that first contact had only just been made, and that the Vahni did not possess warp drive, suggesting a rescue effort to Starfleet would be a delicate matter. The notion of sending a squadron of evacuation vessels into the Gamma Quadrant, and the massive logistics involved in transporting more than a thousand times as many individuals as had been moved from Europa Nova, would also not be welcomed easily. Vaughn felt certain, though, that he could convince the right admirals—and the right Federation councillors—to see the Vahni civilization saved. But unlike the Europani, the Vahni would never be able to return to their home, which would doubtless be destroyed by the next pulse.

"One minute," Bowers announced into the silence. And then, "Thirty seconds," and after that, "Ten." Vaughn watched the viewscreen, though he knew the ship's sensors would pick up the probe well before his eyes did. "Zero," Bowers said at last.

Vaughn waited. Ten seconds. Twenty. Half a minute. The low buzzes of failure—indications of unsuccessful attempts to communicate with the probe, and to scan for it—reached Vaughn from the tactical and sciences stations. "Ensign ch'Thane?"

"There's no contact from the probe," he answered, a hint of disappointment rising in the science officer's usually even voice.

"I can't read it on sensors either," Bowers added.

"All right," Vaughn said, running a hand through the silver hair of his beard. "Let's give it a little longer." He reached over to the console to the left of the command chair. He tapped at the controls, walking his way through a couple of menus until he accessed a chronometer. He noted the ship's time, and then allowed fifteen minutes to pass. The bridge crew said nothing, alternately checking their instruments and gazing up at the viewscreen at the convulsing atmosphere displayed there. "Report," Vaughn finally said.

"Still no contact with the probe," ch'Thane responded at once. Bowers simply looked up from his console and shook his head when Vaughn looked his way.

"All right," Vaughn said. "Either the probe failed on its own, or something caused it to fail. Opinions?"

"The energy surges within the atmosphere might have affected it," Nog suggested. "They could have shorted out or overloaded some of its systems. If guidance or propulsion were damaged, then the probe might have crashed."

"Sir," Prynn said, turning her chair around to face Vaughn, "even if the probe withstood the energy surges, it may not have survived its flight through the clouds." She peered over her shoulder toward the viewscreen, at the writhing atmosphere, then looked back at him. "It looks like a rough ride."

Vaughn nodded and stood up from the command chair. "Is it possible," he asked the bridge crew, "that the clouds themselves are the source of the pulse?"

"I don't think so, sir," ch'Thane said. "There doesn't appear to be any means within the atmosphere to generate that amount of energy. I think it more likely that the clouds have retained the energy within them as a result of the pulse passing through them from below."

"I concur, sir," Nog said. "The elemental composition of the clouds wouldn't support the production of energy." Bowers also added his concurrence.

"So we clearly need to find out what's down there," Vaughn said. Prynn turned back to her console as he walked toward the sciences station. He stopped to the left of the conn. "Ensign ch'Thane," he said, "is it possible that some sections of the atmosphere are less dense than others? Or contain fewer or weaker surges?"

The science officer looked up from his panel. The soft lights of his display lent a slight, orange cast to one side of his blue face and white hair. "Yes, sir," he said. "It may even be likely; the atmosphere is clearly in flux, which would probably leave some areas not as deep as others. But I'm not sure if the sensors will be able to penetrate the clouds at any depth."

"Let's find out," Vaughn said. He looked down at Prynn. "Ensign Tenmei, break geosynchronous orbit and take us down. Keep us—" He turned to ch'Thane. "Five kilometers, Ensign?" he asked. With the possibility that the probe had been damaged by its passage through the clouds, Vaughn would not want to risk a similar fate for *Defiant*.

"That should be a safe distance," ch'Thane said.

"Keep us five kilometers above the clouds," Vaughn told Prynn.

"Aye, sir," she said. Vaughn watched as her hands danced expertly across her console. "Viewer ahead," he ordered, and one of the crew—probably Bowers—made the adjustment. Vaughn saw the image change to a flickering starfield, the flickering the result of the rubble in the system moving between the ship and the backdrop of distant stars. On the left stretched the gray arc of the planet. As Vaughn watched, the planet began to fill more of the screen, Prynn guiding *Defiant* downward. The image imparted a sense of movement, though the inertial dampers prevented an accompanying sensation. The dark horizon loomed as the ship grew closer to the planet.

Prynn counted out the distance to the top of the cloud cover. The beeps and tones of the conn were joined by those of the tactical and sciences consoles as Lieutenant Bowers and Ensign ch'Thane operated the ship's sensors. Prynn reached five kilometers, and the ship leveled off, the arc of the planet stabilizing on the viewscreen.

"I'm not reading past the clouds," ch'Thane reported, "but scans indicate that they do vary in density and depth."

"Very good," Vaughn said. "Let's find the—"

The ship was rocked. Vaughn felt himself pitch forward, and he instinctively reached for the flight-control console. His hand found it as his body twisted around, leaving him facing aft. He managed to keep from losing his footing. The ship shuddered, a roar filling the bridge, as though *Defiant* had been pounded by weapons fire. "Prynn," he yelled over the noise. He saw her hands moving across her panel even before he issued the command. "Take us up." He wondered how she could even see her controls, let alone work them, with the ship shaking as much as it was. But then *Defiant*'s flight smoothed out, the sound returning to its earlier level. *No,* Vaughn realized. *The sound's not the same.*

"Something hit us from below," Bowers reported without having to be asked. "Shields are down to seventy-one percent."

"Thrusters are offline," Nog said. "The impulse engines . . ." A note of confusion laced the engineer's voice.

"I brought them online when the thrusters went down," Prynn explained. That accounted for the change in the sound of the ship, Vaughn knew. He dropped his hand from the side of the conn and made his way back to the command chair, where he sat down heavily.

"Any other damage to the ship?" Vaughn asked. "Casualties?"

"Reports are coming in," Bowers said. "Nothing more major than the thrusters. And only a few bumps and bruises for the crew."

"We were hit by a discharge of energy from the clouds," ch'Thane said.

"Were we attacked?" Vaughn wanted to know.

"I don't think so," ch'Thane said, working his console. "It was more like lightning striking a lightning rod." That, at least, was reassuring.

"Sir," Nog said, "I need to get below to help Ensign Permenter with the thrusters."

"Go," Vaughn said. "Ensign Tenmei, will you be able to maintain a standard orbit using the impulse engines?"

"Yes, sir."

"Ensign ch'Thane," Vaughn said, hearing the starboard door open and close behind him as Nog left the bridge, "determine the safest minimum distance for the ship above the clouds. We still need to find out what's down there."

"Yes, sir," the science officer said.

As the crew set about their tasks, Vaughn thought back to when he had stood on the Vahni world, looked up to the sky, and seen the awful sight of their splintered moon. He peered at the viewscreen, at the forbidding environment below, and thought, *And somewhere down there is the cause.*

Vaughn looked at the desktop computer interface in his ready room and studied the records provided by the Vahni Vahltupali. A translation in Federation Standard marched across the bottom half of the display below the ideogrammic Vahni text. The written language of the unique alien species reflected their physical characteristics; their complex symbols echoed the shapes and colors Vaughn had seen dashing across their flesh.

Vaughn squeezed his eyes shut and rubbed a thumb and forefinger over his closed lids. He was tired and frustrated, having found nothing in the Vahni data to assist the crew in penetrating the sea of clouds surrounding the planet below. For the last fifteen minutes, Vaughn realized, his attention had wandered from his research to the content of the message he would soon have to transmit to Starfleet Command. He would need to detail the plight of the Vahni, and impart a sense of urgency to—

"*Bridge to Captain,*" came Lieutenant Dax's voice over the comm system. She had taken some shifts off after the accident aboard *Sagan* and the loss of Ensign Roness, but she had then insisted on returning to duty. So far, she seemed to be recovering well from her ordeal.

"Vaughn," he responded, still rubbing his eyes. "Go ahead."

"*Sir,*" Dax said, "*we've found something.*"

Vaughn dropped his hand from his face and opened his eyes. The twisting, multihued Vahni text greeted him, but in his mind, he saw the crew on the bridge. "I'm on my way," he said. He pushed a control and blanked the display, then rose and left the ready room. He crossed the main port corridor into one of the side halls behind the bridge, and a moment later he entered *Defiant's* command center.

"Report," he said.

Dax looked over her shoulder at the sound of his voice, then stood from the command chair. "We've been scanning the cloud cover for places the sensors can see through," she said, "and we found a complete break."

Vaughn stopped beside Dax and peered at the viewscreen. In several places, the atmosphere had shifted, allowing a small but unobstructed view through the clouds. Vaughn spied a nondescript patch of brown that he took to be land. "What do you make of it, Ensign ch'Thane?"

"I believe it's simply a result of the constant movement of the clouds," he said. "We're on the side of the planet almost diametrically opposite the source of the pulse, so if that's what's causing the atmospheric effects, they may be less pronounced here."

"There's no guarantee how long the break will remain open," Dax told him. "Sensors and transporters and communications still can't scan past the clouds because of the energy surges, but we may be able to get a probe through."

Vaughn looked at Dax and nodded. "Do it," he said.

Five minutes later, another probe was launched. As it flew toward the break in the clouds and then started down, Vaughn ordered it to be tracked on the viewscreen. He and the rest of the crew watched the probe descend, the magnification on the viewer increasing as it did. Several times, the shifting clouds obscured the view, but they were able to follow the probe until, finally, it leveled off and began its trip around the planet. With luck, it would be back on the ship by morning, providing data about whatever was down there.

As Vaughn peered at the viewscreen, though, he had a sudden intuition that he would not like what the probe would find.

28

The heavy doors to the security office opened with a whir. Kira strode inside and up to the desk, a padd clutched at her side. Even half a year after his departure, she felt a moment of loss whenever she entered here and did not see Odo at the post he had held for so long. Behind her, the doors closed with a solid click.

"Colonel," Ro said, sounding startled as she looked up from the display on her desk.

"You sound surprised to see me," Kira said.

"Oh, well, yes," Ro admitted, "but only because I was just sending you a message to see if I could meet with you tomorrow." She glanced back down at her desk and touched a control. "But I guess I don't need to do that now."

"What did you want to see me about?" Kira asked. She noticed the security monitors behind Ro, and was pleased to see that all of the holding cells stood empty.

"Well," Ro started, sitting back in her chair, "about Quark." Kira smiled, although she felt no humor. The answer hardly came as a shock to her. With Odo gone, it had been only a matter of time before the unscrupulous Ferengi had begun to extend the limits of his attempts to bend, if not break, the law. Kira had certainly expected him to grow bolder with the changes in station security personnel over the past months.

"What's he done now?" Kira asked. "He and Morn aren't staging vole fights again, are they?" Before the Europani refugees had left the station, two of them had complained of seeing the over-sized Cardassian rodents, though at the time, Kira had ascribed the reports to overactive imaginations.

"No, no," Ro said. "Actually, it's not Quark that's the problem; it's Taran'atar."

Kira blinked. "Taran'atar?" she said, a sudden sense of dread washing over her about what Ro might say. Part of the feeling, she knew, was personal—she had begun to like the Jem'Hadar—but part of it stemmed from persistent concerns about the Dominion. Kira had noticed Taran'atar spending less time in ops during the last few days, and she had intended to ask him about it. She had assumed that he had been using the holosuites, engaging in his combat programs. Now, she hoped that had been the case, and that the trouble that had arisen was no more serious than a complaint from Quark about the holosuites' being damaged. She stepped forward and took one of the chairs in front of the desk. "What happened?" she asked Ro.

The security chief related a story about Taran'atar unshrouding in the bar a short time ago and frightening Quark's customers. That might not have been so bad by itself, Kira thought, but then Ro talked about a report she had only just received. Yesterday, apparently, Taran'atar had unexpectedly appeared in one of the child-care facilities on the station, scaring everybody there—so much so that they had even been fearful of informing security about it. It was one sort of misdeed to bother patrons in a bar, Kira thought, and something else entirely to terrorize children.

Kira stood up and paced the security office, her arms folded, still holding the padd. She turned back toward the desk and started to ask questions about what had occurred in the child-care facility, but Ro told her that she had not yet begun to investigate the episode. She had witnessed the aftermath of Taran'atar's appearance in Quark's, though. "I don't think he meant to unshroud," Ro said, "and I really don't think he meant to scare anybody, but he certainly did."

"Not just Quark?" Kira asked, walking back toward the desk.

"No," Ro said. "I saw a lot of people racing out of the bar, and it seemed pretty clear who they were racing away from."

"All right," Kira said. "I'll speak to Taran'atar about it tomorrow." Today had been a long enough day without adding any additional responsibilities to it. After she left here, she intended to head straight for her quarters.

"Thank you, Colonel," Ro said.

Kira sighed and sat back down. This was not a problem she wanted to have right now, just days ahead of the summit between Bajor and the Federation—which was the subject she had actually come here to discuss. She informed Ro about the impending arrivals of the Bajoran, Trill, and Alonis delegations on Deep Space 9, and about the need for heightened, but discreet, security.

Ro moved forward in her chair, leaning her elbows on her desk. "Aren't the Alonis water-breathers?" she asked.

"They are," Kira said. "But they won't be expecting us to modify any of our accommodations for them. They'll be using aquatic rebreathing devices while they're on the station, and they'll return to their ship every night." She looked down and activated the padd she had brought with her. It came to life with a chirp, and she handed it across the desk to Ro. "This is a list of the members of all the delegations," Kira said. "Councillor zh'Thane and Admiral Akaar will be attending the talks as well."

Ro took the padd and glanced at its contents, then looked back up at Kira. "What's this about?" she asked.

Kira hesitated briefly, recalling how secretive Akaar had been about the summit, but then she decided that the security chief would need as much information as possible in order to properly discharge her duty. Kira told Ro about Bajor's renewed petition for membership in the Federation, and that the coming talks would produce an outcome, one way or the other.

Ro's mouth opened as Kira spoke, and the color drained from her face. Kira saw but did not understand the reaction. Ro looked off to the side, as though in thought. "I knew there was a reason he was at the station," she said, almost too quietly to hear.

"You mean Admiral Akaar?" Kira asked.

Ro turned back to Kira as though waking from a daydream. "Oh, uh, yes," she said. Ro's expression went blank. "I'd just been wondering why he's been here at DS9," she said, but Kira could see that there was more to Ro's reaction than simply casual curiosity. She remembered Akaar's concerns about Ro's abilities and her dedication to duty.

"Do you know the admiral?" Kira asked. "I mean, did you know him prior to him coming to the station?"

"Yes," Ro said. "When I was in Starfleet. We had a . . . professional disagreement." The admission was clearly uncomfortable for her to make.

"What sort of 'professional disagreement'?" Kira asked.

"I'd . . . prefer not to discuss it, Colonel," Ro said.

Kira quickly grew angry at the uncommunicative response—she had about had enough of those lately—but she just as quickly squelched the feeling. As commander of the station, she continued trying to prevent herself from reacting too hastily in any circumstances. Now, instead, she attempted to put herself in Ro's place, imagining a disagreement between herself and a superior—and the Prophets only knew how many times that had happened during her life. She only had to think of the Attainder for evidence of that. "I understand, Lieutenant," Kira said. "But I have to ask you if this disagreement with the admiral will have any effect on the performance of your duties."

"No, sir," Ro said definitively. "Not from my end."

"Are you sure there's nothing I need to know about this," Kira asked. "Because if there is, I want to know about it now."

Ro did not answer right away, but paused and seemed to consider the question, which Kira appreciated. Still, Kira did not expect Ro to divulge what she had already chosen to keep to herself.

"Colonel," Ro said at last, "the admiral doesn't like me, and I don't like him either. He probably doesn't think I'm capable of doing this job, or any other job, for that matter. Frankly, I don't care. I'm going to do my job the way I'm supposed to, the way you expect me to, no matter what the admiral thinks."

"That's good enough for me," Kira said, satisfied with both Ro's honesty and her attitude. She stood up. "Develop a security plan for the period that the delegations will be on the station, and let's meet in my office tomorrow morning to discuss it. Ten hundred hours."

"Yes, sir," Ro said. "Thank you."

Kira nodded, then turned and left, the doors opening at her approach. She felt positive about the meeting she had just had with Ro, but as she walked along the Promenade, she realized that she also felt uneasy—not about Ro, but once more about Admiral Akaar.

29

The complex of buildings slumped across the landscape in disrepair, but still remained standing—everywhere but at its center. There, in a circle roughly a hundred meters in diameter, no hint of a structure existed. Instead, only a gray darkness endured—darkness, and energy.

Nog looked away from the aerial view of the complex on one monitor and over to the accompanying sensor data on another. He reviewed the limited information for the *I don't know how many times,* he thought, and realized that he was not going to reach a conclusion different from the one he had already drawn. He peered over at Shar, who stood beside him in the aft section of the bridge, and saw a somber expression on his friend's face. Although Nog would certainly characterize Shar as a serious individual, the Andorian often wore a smile—as a means of both blending in and warding off unwanted attention, Nog suspected. But serious or not, smiling or not, Shar usually maintained a steady manner, neither upbeat nor down. Since they had departed Deep Space 9, though, Nog had noticed his friend keeping almost completely to himself—not an easy feat, considering that the two shared their cramped quarters. Shar had brightened during the contact with the Vahni Vahltupali, but right now, though Nog doubted anybody else on board would be able to tell, Shar seemed terribly low. And with what the sensor readings from the probe had revealed, Nog could not really blame him.

Shar did not look up at Nog, but continued to study the contents of a padd in his hands. Nog looked to his right, at the rest of the bridge. The sounds of voices and consoles filled the air, an aural mixture not unlike that in Uncle Quark's bar, he thought—except that the voices in the bar did not often talk about sensor readings, and the beeps and tones of consoles substituted here for the clatter of the dabo wheel. Around the bridge, Nog saw several pairs of crewpeople in conversation: Merimark and Rahim at the tactical console, Cassini and T'rb at sciences, and Vaughn and Dax near the main viewscreen. Nog was sure that, like himself and Shar, they were all discussing or analyzing the data they had finally collected from the planet.

The second probe had successfully negotiated the break in the clouds, and then circled the planet at relatively low altitude, flying as far below the atmospheric cover as reasonable. While the probe had been scanning the surface, the breaks in the clouds had been swept closed, but others had appeared this morning, allowing it to find its way back into space. During its ascent, it had been impacted by an energy surge, but it had survived the incident and returned to *Defiant.*

Nog turned back to the monitors set into the aft bulkhead. The sensor scans of the planet showed an industrial civilization, but in ruins. There were no life signs beyond those of flora; enough sunlight apparently penetrated the gray sea of clouds to allow plants to survive on the surface. The most important information the probe had gathered, though, concerned the site that Shar had identified as the source of the pulse. Scans had failed to discern anything about the building complex there due to the energy readings at its center, but the energy readings themselves had proven critical in Nog's analysis. In the hour that the probe had spent circling above the complex and harvesting data, the energy level had increased at a consistent rate—and that had brought Nog to his conclusion.

He peered over at Shar again. "What do you think?" he asked. Shar looked up from the padd. His antennae had a particular crook to them, a certain . . . attitude. Over time, Nog had learned to read Shar's mood, at least sometimes, by the position of his antennae. And what he saw now told him that Shar had reached the same troubling conclusion that he had. A moment later, Shar answered Nog's question and confirmed that suspicion.

"I'll go get the captain," Nog said. He walked along the starboard side of the bridge—past Merimark and Rahim at tactical, and Senkowski at the engineering station—and up to Commander Vaughn and Lieutenant Dax standing near the starboard side of the viewscreen. Beyond them, the dead planet hung in space, shrouded in its gray pall. Vaughn and Dax both looked over at him as he walked up.

"Yes, Lieutenant?" Vaughn said.

"Captain," Nog said, "Ensign ch'Thane and I would like to speak with you; we've completed our analyses." Vaughn gave a short, quick nod, and gestured toward the aft section of the bridge. Nog turned and led the way back, with Vaughn and Dax following. Shar looked up from the padd again as the group approached.

Nog pointed to the monitor displaying the building complex. "As you know," he said, addressing Vaughn and Dax, "this is where we believe the pulse originated. Specifically, here." He tapped the center of the screen, indicating the great, shadowy circle at the heart of the buildings. "Because of the energy readings in this area—" Nog worked the controls below the second monitor, searching for the data that would illustrate his words. He found it and pointed it out to Commander Vaughn. "You can see from these scans," Nog said, "that interference from the energy prevented the sensors from picking up anything for kilometers around the complex." Vaughn and Dax both nodded.

"Can you tell if the energy is a natural phenomenon," Vaughn asked, "or artificial?"

Nog looked over to Shar, who said, "No, we can't." The science officer reached up to the monitor and traced a circle along the boundary between the complex and the gray patch. "Sections of the buildings here appear to have collapsed, which could indicate a natural phenomenon that the builders of the complex were not expecting. But it may be that this is some sort of energy-production facility, and the builders somehow lost control of it."

"Either way," Dax said, "whether the energy occurs naturally or artificially, this must be what destroyed the civilization on the planet."

"Actually, we're not certain about that," Nog said. "Scans around the rest of the planet show it to be perfectly habitable—" Shar passed his padd to him, and he passed it to Vaughn. "—and the pulse appears to have emanated outward and upward from the complex, not along the surface."

"But the planet is devoid of life," Dax noted.

"That's true," Nog agreed, "but we're just not sure why."

"Any idea how we might be able to stop the pulses?" Vaughn asked.

"Not yet," Nog said. "But from the level of the interference with the sensors, we were able to determine the current magnitude of the energy at the site. And the rate at which it's changing."

"Changing?" Dax said.

"Yes," Nog said. "The amount of energy there is increasing considerably."

"Why?" Vaughn asked.

"We don't know," Nog said. "But we can tell that it is increasing at a combinatorial rate."

"Combinatorial?" Dax said. She sounded shocked, and Nog thought that she clearly understood that such a rate of change was far greater than either a geometric or exponential progression.

"Yes," Nog said. "And if it continues increasing like that, then the amount of energy there will soon match the amount in the pulse we encountered in the Vahni system."

"Meaning that another pulse will launch into space," Vaughn concluded solemnly.

"We think so," Nog said.

"How long?" Vaughn wanted to know.

Nog glanced over at Shar again, not for scientific support this time, but for moral support. Nog did not want to answer Vaughn's question, because he did not want the information he had to be true. But he knew that it was.

Nog turned back to face Vaughn and Dax. "Three and a half days," he said.

Before Vaughn issued his final order, he glanced down at the padd on his desk. In the upper right corner of the display, a flashing icon denoted the active link to the ship's library computer, and in the middle of the screen, a blue progress indicator had almost reached the three-quarters mark. The download of the Vahni data, together with the translation algorithms for their written language, was taking some time.

Vaughn looked back up at the figure of Lieutenant Dax standing across from him. Her soft, round features had drawn into a tense expression, but she wore it well, he thought; the situation warranted concern, and she seemed neither panicked nor unsure, despite the tremendous responsibility being thrust upon her. "If something should happen on the planet," Vaughn told her, continuing their conversation, "if we're not back in eighty hours, I want you to take *Defiant* out of here."

"Yes, sir," she said. To her credit, she spoke without hesitation, although Vaughn knew that even the idea of abandoning three of the crew must have troubled her, particularly after the loss of Ensign Roness. It would have bothered any officer. Vaughn had certainly left enough people behind in his career to know that it never got any easier. *And sometimes,* he thought, *you end up leaving yourself behind . . . or pieces of yourself.*

Vaughn stood up and walked around the desk. "Lieutenant," he said, locking eyes with his first officer, "I want to be very clear about this." As much as he could, he would ease this burden for her by making this decision now, and not requiring her to make it later. "I don't want *Defiant* here even a minute past the deadline I've given you. Even if we can't save the Vahni, we're at least going to save the crew."

Dax straightened, her bearing changing subtly. She nodded slowly and seriously, her hands slipping out of sight behind her back. The expression on her face appeared to belong momentarily to somebody else. "I understand," she said in a voice that also seemed only partially her own. "I won't wait."

"Good," Vaughn said, and he circled back behind his desk again. "Believe me, though," he went on, "if we can't stop the next pulse from launching into space, I don't intend to be on the planet for it. There are buildings still standing down on the surface, but there certainly aren't any people."

He leaned to his right and checked the padd again, his fingertips brushing the smooth, glassine desktop. The progress indicator had edged up toward the eighty percent mark, he saw.

"Sir?" Dax said, and now her voice sounded exclusively like her own again. "What about the Vahni Vahltupali? If you can't stop the pulse on the planet, and we can't stop it in space, then should we contact them? Should we contact them now and tell them about the situation?"

Vaughn sighed. He had thought about this himself during the past few hours. "My decision would be not to," he said, sitting back down. "If the next pulse is even as powerful as the last one—and the Vahni records tell us that it will be more powerful—then they have virtually no chance of surviving. At the very least, the quakes that will wrack their planet will decimate their civilization. They don't have starships, and none could arrive from the Alpha Quadrant in time to evacuate them."

"So what good would it do to tell them that their society was facing annihilation?" Dax asked rhetorically, answering her original question. She brought her hands out from behind her back and clasped them together in front of her waist. "There would be panic."

"Panic," Vaughn agreed, "and fear and sorrow and pain. I see no reason to visit that upon them." What he did see, though, was an opportunity to further demonstrate his confidence in Dax's leadership. She had learned a great deal and performed well in the few months since she had chosen to pursue the command path, and his belief in her was tacit in his having assigned her as *Defiant*'s first officer for this mission to the Gamma Quadrant. At the same time, the Starfleet crew on DS9 were not exactly overburdened with command personnel, a circumstance that had obviously contributed to Dax's rapid rise to a position of such authority. Vaughn certainly felt her capable, but because of the fast and dramatic increase in her responsibilities, he endeavored to demonstrate his faith in her whenever the chance arose. "If I'm not on *Defiant* when it departs, though," he told her, "then whether or not to contact the Vahni will be your decision. If we don't make it back to the ship, the only order I'm binding you to at that time is to get the crew to safety."

"Yes, sir," she said.

"In the meantime, keep Lieutenant Nog and Ensign T'rb focused on finding a means of defeating the pulse in space," he said. "Maybe if we can't shut it down at the source, they'll be able to find some way of dealing with it up here."

"Both the engineering and science staffs are already working on the problem," Dax said.

"I know," Vaughn said. "*Defiant* has a fine crew."

Dax nodded her agreement. "One last thing, Captain," she said. "What about the *Sagan*? Should I keep a team working on it?" The necessary repairs to the shuttle would still take another five to eight days to complete.

"Yes," he said after a moment's thought. "Unless those personnel are specifically needed for the effort to stop the pulse. We're not that sure of our facts; maybe the energy buildup will start to diminish, or the rate of increase will, and we'll end up here for more than three days. In that case, the second shuttle might be of some use to us." Vaughn did not need to dwell on the fact that, once he took *Chaffee* down to the planet's surface, he and the shuttle crew would be isolated from *Defiant*—and from any assistance, should they require it. Neither communications, sensors, nor the transporter could penetrate the energy in the cloud cover. Lieutenant Dax and Dr. Bashir had already raised concerns about that issue, but Vaughn had quickly decided that whatever potential risk there would be to the shuttle crew was easily offset by the almost certain danger to the Vahni.

"Understood," Dax acknowledged.

"Is there anything else, Lieutenant?" Vaughn asked.

"No, sir," she said. "Except . . . good luck, Captain."

"And to you, Lieutenant," Vaughn said. "I know I'm leaving the ship in good hands."

"Thank you, sir."

"Dismissed."

Dax started for the door, but she stopped when a voice sounded over the comm system. *"Ensign ch'Thane to Captain Vaughn."*

Vaughn tapped his combadge. "Go ahead, Ensign," Vaughn said.

"The shuttle is ready to go," he reported.

"Very good," Vaughn said. He glanced down once more at the padd. The progress bar had now passed the eighty-five-percent point. "I'll be there in about twenty minutes," he said. "Vaughn out."

Dax nodded and continued out of the ready room. Vaughn watched her go, the deck's main port corridor briefly visible beyond her as the door opened and closed. He turned in his chair to the computer interface on his desk. With practiced movements, he quickly accessed the file of sensor readings the probe had recorded at the source of the pulse. Vaughn really had no idea what they would be able to do once they got down there, even if they were able to learn more from a closer examination. The best hope, of course, lay in the notion that the pulse might be the product of a mechanism that could be shut down, or that they could destroy with the shuttle's phasers. Somehow, Vaughn doubted any solution would turn out to be that simple.

Not for the first time, the prospect of unleashing the phaser cannons and firing a salvo of quantum torpedoes occurred to him. In his mind, he saw the powerful weaponry pounding the planet, the surface collapsing and eventually liquefying amid a hail of light and explosions. But for all they knew, the energy of the phasers and torpedoes—if they could even penetrate the cloud cover and be delivered accurately to their target—might hasten or even strengthen the next pulse.

Vaughn again reviewed both the raw numbers of the sensor data and the analyses the crew had so far done. To this point, they had learned very little. He could only hope that going down to the planet would provide them with more information.

A few minutes later, a tiny chime signaled the completion of the download. Vaughn switched off the computer interface, then reached over and picked up the padd. He sequenced through a quick diagnostic to verify the success of the data transfer. He then opened one of the Vahni files to ensure that the translation algorithms functioned properly. As the colorful and complex shapes of the written Vahni language marched across the display, the plain letters of Federation Standard crawling along beneath them, Vaughn vividly recalled the scene of the crowd singing at the memorial service, their "voices" a prismatic flow of forms and contours.

Vaughn switched the padd off and stood up. He reached over past the computer interface, to where he had earlier tossed his old Starfleet field coat. Surface temperatures around the source of the pulse had read mild during the day, but would likely drop during the night. Vaughn put on the coat—which he had managed to hold on to since his days as a cadet—and tucked the padd into an inside pocket. Then he headed for the shuttlebay.

The door to the shuttlebay opened to a jet of fire. Along the starboard side of the battered *Sagan,* Ensign Permenter guided a laser torch across a section of twisted hull plating; where the ruby beam contacted the metal, sparks flew in a bright fountain. The starboard warp nacelle, which had nearly been torn from the shuttle during its ascent through the Vahni atmosphere, lay on the deck behind *Sagan,* still in obvious need of repair. Beside Permenter, Ensign Gordimer used a tricorder to monitor the work being done. Both officers wore protective eyewear. Gordimer, Vaughn knew, was a security officer, but on a ship with a crew of only forty during an extended mission, people often had to labor outside their specialty.

As Vaughn started into the shuttlebay, he heard somebody call to him from behind, barely audible above the hissing drone of the metalworking. "Captain." Vaughn turned in the doorway to see Dr. Bashir rushing to catch up to him.

"Yes, Doctor?" Vaughn said, raising his voice to be heard.

"I need to talk with you, sir," Bashir said as he reached the doorway. Vaughn looked at the doctor, saw the serious expression on his face, and stepped back out into the corridor. The door glided shut, cutting off the noise of the laser torch.

"What is it, Doctor?" Vaughn asked. "I assume this can't wait."

"I'm sorry," Bashir said. "I've been struggling with whether or not to approach you about this, and, well, I've decided I really don't have much choice."

"Make it quick," Vaughn said, his voice registering the annoyance he felt at being delayed. "Time is a factor here. I need to get on the shuttle."

"That's just it, sir," Bashir said. "I'm wondering whether you're the right person to be going on this mission."

"Excuse me?" Vaughn said, nonplussed that the ship's chief medical officer seemed to be taking exception to personnel assignments.

"You're the senior officer on the ship, Captain," Bashir explained, "and for you to take part in a potentially dangerous away mission—"

"Just a minute," Vaughn said, interrupting. "Who would you have replace me on the shuttle?"

Bashir had a ready answer. "Lieutenant Bowers, I think, would be a good selection."

"Lieutenant Bowers," Vaughn echoed, and he suddenly thought he understood the doctor's motivation. He took a couple of steps past Bashir, then turned back to face him. "Not Lieutenant Dax?"

"Bowers, I believe, has more experience on away missions," Bashir said, although he did not sound entirely convinced of his own words.

"I see," Vaughn said. He considered several ways of dealing with the doctor on this issue, but quickly opted for expediency. "Are you worried about me going down to the planet," he asked, "or about Lieutenant Dax being left in command of *Defiant?*"

"I'm concerned about Lieutenant Dax," Bashir admitted. "I won't deny that. After what she's been through, I'd also say that's a legitimate concern."

"You're right, it is," Vaughn said. "Which is why I took it into account when I made my decision. I believe Lieutenant Dax is up to the task I set her."

"With all due respect, sir," Bashir said, "that may not be the case. She may seem to be all right when she's on duty, but off duty, she's—"

"Don't tell me," Vaughn said.

"But, sir—" Bashir began to protest.

"I don't want to know," Vaughn reiterated. He looked down a cross-corridor and away from the doctor for a moment, attempting to rein in his displeasure at having to deal with this now. At the same time, he realized that Bashir's apprehensions about Dax were not without reason. "I like Lieutenant Dax," Vaughn said, looking back over at the doctor. "I suppose that we've even become friends in a way that Curzon and I never managed to. But I'm also her commanding officer, and in the middle of a mission. And what I see from her professionally right now is that she has worked out the loss of Ensign Roness."

Bashir nodded. "What I'm suggesting," he said, "is that perhaps she hasn't actually worked it out as well you think she has."

"But that's my point," Vaughn said. "In her job as a Starfleet lieutenant, as first officer of this ship, she's behaved perfectly well. Whatever her private feelings are, she's not allowed them to interfere with the performance of her duties." Vaughn paused, then said, "I have confidence in her abilities."

"As do I," Bashir returned at once.

"But what is this about," Vaughn asked, "if not her ability to command under stress?" When Bashir did not respond right away, Vaughn stepped back over to him. "Is it maybe about the *difficulty* of command, about the substantial burden of its responsibilities, especially under stress, and you wanting to shield her from that?"

"I suppose it might be," Bashir said, looking down briefly.

"Don't be so troubled by that, Julian," Vaughn said. "It's not a wrong or bad point of view. I understand it, and even appreciate it. But I can't permit it to influence my command decisions."

"Of course, sir," Bashir said in a tone that seemed to indicate his understanding.

Vaughn moved away from Bashir and said, "Carry on, Doctor," dismissing him.

"Yes, sir," Bashir said.

Vaughn walked forward and the door to the shuttlebay opened. He expected to be greeted with the screech of the laser torch slicing through metal, but instead, only the voices of Permenter and Gordimer reached him. As Vaughn started through the doorway, Bashir called after him again.

"Good luck, Captain," he said.

Vaughn glanced back over his shoulder. "And to you, Doctor," he said. Then he continued into the shuttlebay, and the figure of Bashir disappeared behind the closing door.

The shuttlecraft *Chaffee* hied to port and down. The great, veiled mass of the planet swung into view in the forward windows, implying the movement that the inertial dampers denied. Vaughn scanned the clouds for breaks and saw none. Already, the shuttle had descended toward the planet twice, only to have to pull back when the transitory routes through the cover had been swept closed.

"The depression is increasing," Ensign ch'Thane reported. He sat at the front starboard console, working the shuttle's sensors; Vaughn sat directly behind him. Their scans could not penetrate the clouds and the energy surges contained within, but they could visually detect where the cover had parted in an area; ch'Thane tracked such an area right now. "It seems to be stretching far down."

"If it opens all the way through, I'm ready for it," Prynn said at the flight-control console. "I've put us into a tight spiral course around the central point of the hollow." Vaughn watched as her hands moved fluidly across the panel, operating her controls like a conductor leading an orchestra.

Minutes passed, and Vaughn sat quietly, allowing the two ensigns to do their jobs. The deep, solid hum of the engines pervaded the hull of the small vessel, enclosing the cabin in a cushion of steady vibration and sound. The stars swam sideways past the windows as *Chaffee* circled above the potential breach in the clouds. Monitors to either side of the two main consoles displayed the images of the constantly stirring atmosphere directly beneath the shuttle.

Vaughn gazed at the monitors, but he could see nothing but the agitated expanse of gray. Still, a quarter of an hour later, Ensign ch'Thane announced that a route completely through the cover had opened. "It's the same point we've been focused on," he said.

"Acknowledged," Prynn said. "Bringing us in." She worked her controls, and the nose of the shuttle dipped toward the planet. Ahead, the horizon rose in the windows until it was lost from sight, the planet filling the view.

"Twenty seconds until we reach the top of the cover," ch'Thane said. Vaughn peered through the windows and still could not discern the passage through the clouds. As they descended, though, details of the atmosphere became visible, evanescent structures of air, billows and wisps and swirls. "Ten seconds." A helical formation curled away to port. With nothing to provide perspective, Vaughn found it impossible to gauge scale. What seemed like a small coalescence of vapor could easily have been kilometers long.

And then the grayness swallowed the shuttle. *Chaffee* bucked and began to shake as the colorless walls of air shot upward past the windows. Vaughn recalled the mythical tale of Jonah, as well as his own past experiences when he had felt, either figuratively or literally, as though he had been in the belly of the beast.

"I'm getting intermittent energy readings," ch'Thane said. "No discernible source." The shuttle began to rattle more strongly, as though the vibrations had reached a point of resonance. Vaughn clasped the arms of his chair, trying to steady himself. The cockpit became a shuddering blur, and the hum of the engines fluctuated, rising and falling as the shuttle made its way downward.

Vaughn looked at the monitor to Prynn's left, but had difficulty focusing on the image. "Energy readings are climbing around us," ch'Thane said, raising his voice to be heard above the increasing sound in the cabin. "The clouds are moving . . . the break is shifting below us."

"I see it," Prynn said calmly. Her gaze had left her panel, Vaughn saw, and had shifted to the monitor displaying the path below *Chaffee*. She held her arms tensely over the conn, her fingers moving sporadically as she adjusted the shuttle's course. *Chaffee* veered to port, and Vaughn felt his momentum shift as the gravity of the planet asserted itself over the inertial dampers.

The shuttle trembled as though something had struck it, and a loud boom filled the cabin. Vaughn imagined the fragments of the Vahni moon as they had battered *Sagan,* incapacitating Dax and robbing Ensign Roness of her life. "That was an energy surge," ch'Thane called over the rising noise. "I can't tell where it came from."

Vaughn looked to his right, to the system status monitor set into the bulkhead there. "Power's down three percent," he read, struggling to keep his eyes steady. "The shields are holding."

"As long as the shields stay intact," Prynn said, "we can get through anything." Vaughn looked over at her and saw tremendous concentration reflected in her features. He would not have been surprised if he learned that she had no idea that she had even spoken. "Hold on," she said a moment later, and Vaughn did so, clutching tightly at the arms of his chair. The shuttle rolled to port, the clouds spinning in the opposite direction in front of the windows. Prynn righted *Chaffee* for a moment, then maneuvered back the other way.

Then something slammed broadside into the shuttle and sent it plowing through the air. It could have been a current of air shearing into *Chaffee,* Vaughn supposed, but he suspected that they had been rammed again by a surge of the mysterious energy. He tried to read the status monitor, but found it impossible with the shuttle shaking so violently now. Vaughn saw the clouds now up against the windows; *Chaffee* had been pushed from the break in the atmospheric cover and into the cover itself.

Prynn rolled the shuttle to starboard, and then did it a second and third time in rapid succession, the circular acceleration keeping everybody in their seats. Vaughn felt a momentary sense of vertigo, and then the shuttle straightened. At the windows, the gray air had moved away again; Prynn had pulled the shuttle back into the breach. The shaking lessened, and Vaughn read from the status monitor. "Power is surging in the port engine," he said.

Vaughn saw Prynn glance down at her console, then back up at the monitor. "Cut power to it for ten seconds," Prynn said. Ensign Ch'Thane looked in her direction and did nothing. "Do it," Prynn said again, yelling now, "or the engine will shut down automatically." Ch'Thane moved then, calling out his actions as he followed Prynn's directions. Vaughn watched the power level of the port engine drop to zero on the status monitor. After ten seconds, ch'Thane reengaged power, and the readouts returned to normal.

"One more time," Prynn called. "Hold on." She pulled the shuttle over to port, and then plunged the nose down. Vaughn lost all sense of orientation, but felt an increasing acceleration, as though he were falling from a great height. He looked through the windows again and saw tendrils of gray air buffeting them. *Chaffee* began to quiver again—

And then stopped. The flight of the shuttle stabilized and quieted, and the view before the windows cleared. Prynn pulled *Chaffee* up, leveling it out, and only then did Vaughn realize that they had been shooting nose-first toward the ground. He consulted the status panel. "Engine power is down nine percent," he read.

"That's not bad for the pounding we took," Prynn said. Verifying that, ch'Thane calculated the enormous amount of energy that had struck the shuttle. "I don't think all of those were surges," Prynn said. "I think anytime the

clouds came into contact with the shuttle, there was a discharge of energy."
Ch'Thane concurred with that conclusion.

Vaughn stood up and stepped between Prynn and ch'Thane. He raised his
hands up and rested them on the backs of their chairs. "Well done," he told
them.

Vaughn leaned forward and peered out the windows. Above, an unbroken
sea of clouds stretched to the horizon in every direction, diffuse sunlight penetrating through them. Below, a nearly lifeless terrain spread out before the
shuttle, dark patches dotting the rugged topography, the colors washed out in
the gloom.

"Look there," Ensign ch'Thane said, bringing his hand up and pointing
just to the right of their flight path. Vaughn gazed in that direction and saw a
series of shapes rising up in the distance from the otherwise barren landscape.
As the shuttle drew closer, the shapes resolved into buildings.

"It's a city," Vaughn said.

"Captain," Prynn said, "I've calculated our course, based on the coordinates collected by the probe." She looked up at him. "We're traveling in the
wrong direction."

Vaughn took a last look at the city, then said, "Bring us around."

"Aye, sir." She operated her console, and the shuttle tilted to port. Within a
few seconds, the city had slipped from view.

"How are sensors functioning?" Vaughn asked.

"There's some interference from the energy in the clouds," ch'Thane said,
"but we're getting solid readings."

"Good," Vaughn said. "Scan astern for the city, and get what you can. I
want to learn as much as possible while we're down here."

"Yes, sir," ch'Thane said, and he worked his controls.

The shuttle began to straighten, pulling out of its wide turn to port.
"Coming onto our new course," Prynn reported. Vaughn watched as she
headed the shuttle toward the source of the pulse, half a world away.

30

Kira walked down the dimly lighted hall, tired after a long shift. She had accomplished a great deal today, but the one item that had eluded her had been a conversation with Taran'atar. Now, on her way to her quarters for a light dinner and a period of meditation, she had decided to track him down and deal with the matter before another incident occurred. She had contacted him via the comm system and found him in a holosuite; he had offered no objections to her stopping by to speak with him.

Kira stepped up to the door of the holosuite, wondering what spectacle she would witness this evening, what sort of hideous, unimaginable beast she would find Taran'atar fighting. *Or will it be something simple,* she thought, *like a Borg?* She had observed him taking part in his combat training programs several times now, and it had been both horrible and fascinating to watch him in battle. She found the precision and callousness with which he killed troubling, even in a simulated environment, but at the same time, his tactics and physical abilities impressed her. Certainly, for a humanoid his size, his strength, dexterity, and stamina were unparalleled. So far, she had watched him defeat a huge, insectile beast with claws that could have snapped him in two; an incredibly fast, flying creature with twenty-centimeter fangs and razor-sharp wings; a horde of *mugato;* and a small army of Breen soldiers.

Now, as she touched the control pad beside the door, she found herself more than a little curious about what she was about to see. The door opened with a mechanical hum, and for a moment Kira could not make sense of the scene that lay before her. The walls, floor, and ceiling of the holosuite appeared black, but matched the actual surfaces of the room in dimension. Taran'atar stood near the center of the space, peering straight ahead. A series of blue filaments hung in the air before him, some straight, some curved, some vertically oriented, some horizontally. Much smaller than the lines and figures, a series of red markings marched through the air all about them.

Kira moved inside and around to her left, along the line of the wall, attempting to get a better view of the scene. She circled around toward Taran'atar, to see from his angle the images suspended in the air before him. Only when she had drawn close to him did she get an idea of what she was looking at: mathematical equations and their graphical representations.

The symbols in red were unrecognizable to her, but the manner in which they had been laid out suggested mathematics, as did the lines and figures. There seemed to be x-, y-, and z-axes hanging in the air, as well as several other forms, including curves, cones, parabolas, and several irregular polyhedrons. This looked essentially like a trigonometry lesson.

"What is this?" Kira asked.

Taran'atar must have heard her enter and approach him, of course—few things escaped a Jem'Hadar's notice—and so he did not start when she spoke.

When he answered her, he continued to stare at the mathematical tableau. "You know it as 'calculus,'" he told her, "or 'differential equations.'"

"Well, some people know it as that," Kira said.

Now, Taran'atar turned and looked at her. "I do not understand."

"Mathematics and I never got along very well with each other," she said.

Taran'atar stared at her and said nothing. She was about to explain her remark when he finally said, "Let me render the statements in your own language." He ordered the computer to translate the symbols into Bajoran. The red characters vanished, replaced a second later by others.

Kira shrugged. "I recognize the numbers and letters now," she said, "and even some of the symbols, but it's all still Romulan to me."

Taran'atar studied the statements for a moment. "This is not Romulan," he said.

"It's just an expression," Kira explained. "It means that I don't understand it."

Taran'atar regarded her silently, his eyes staring into hers. "How can that be?" he asked. "You operate spacecraft, you utilize weaponry."

"Yes, I do," Kira agreed. "But that doesn't mean I understand the numbers behind them."

"But . . ." Taran'atar seemed at a loss for words, and despite his continued and evident discomfort with being on Deep Space 9, as well as his curt nature, Kira had never before seen him speechless.

"I learned by doing," she told him. "And the more experience I gained, the easier it became to acquire new skills and sharpen the old ones. But as for the theory behind piloting a runabout or aiming a phaser . . . I guess a lot of the technology helps with that."

"What if you lacked the technology?" Taran'atar asked her. "What if your survival depended upon this?" He gestured toward the red figures and blue shapes, his hand passing through one of the equations and—Kira assumed—the curve it defined.

"If I had to rely on mathematics to live," Kira said, a smile on her lips, "then I suppose I'd die." Taran'atar said nothing. "Well, maybe I wouldn't die," she amended, "but I'd have to act intuitively, not by calculation. Like I did in your simulation with the Rintanna."

"Do you understand none of this?" Taran'atar wanted to know, looking again at the mathematical layout. For all of the unfamiliar experiences Kira had seen him endure since arriving aboard the station, he seemed more puzzled now than ever.

Kira turned her full attention to the graph and the statements. A memory of her father and her brother, Pohl, attempting to tutor her rose vividly in her mind. The scent of the parchments on which she had tried to do her exercises filled her nostrils, and she could almost hear her brother's frustrated voice endlessly repeating the intricate concepts to her. She peered at the mathematics hanging before her and looked for anything more than just familiar. She walked around Taran'atar and indicated a pair of equations. "This is a derivative of that," she said, pointing first to the lower equation, and then to the upper.

She then found the two-dimensional curve that went along with it, a tangent connecting to it at one point. It was probably the simplest set of equations and figures in the room. "It's the instantaneous rate of change at the intersection of the curve and the slope." To her surprise, Taran'atar nodded.

"Yes," he said.

She tried to find something else she understood, but could not. "These are more derivative symbols," she said, waving her hand through several other statements, the red light flashing over her skin like momentary tattoos, "but I don't understand them."

"They are partial differential equations," he said.

Kira suddenly realized that Taran'atar obviously read Bajoran. The Jem'Hadar really were amazing creatures—*beings,* she corrected herself; *people*—and she wondered what they might evolve into once unshackled from the Founders' demands that they live only as soldiers. She remembered when a Jem'Hadar infant had been found and brought to the station more than five years ago. Odo had believed that the Jem'Hadar, which had developed into an adult in only a few days, could be freed by the proper care from his genetically engineered predisposition to violence. Kira had disagreed with him, and she had ultimately been proven right in that instance, but now, here was Odo making the argument to her all over again, and this time, she was beginning to see that he might be right after all.

"Partial differential equations," Kira said, echoing Taran'atar. "I guess I'll have to take your word for it."

"For the limitations you possess," Taran'atar said, "your combat skills are truly amazing."

The comment surprised Kira. "I'm not sure whether that's a compliment or an insult," she said.

"It is simply a fact."

"All right," Kira said. "So what is it you're doing here?" she asked, suspecting that she already knew the answer.

"I am training," Taran'atar said.

"Of course," she said. "Which is what I expected, except that I thought you'd be in here fighting some powerful, deadly creature."

"The mind must be trained as well as the body," he said, "otherwise neither will survive long."

"That's true," Kira agreed, thinking about the mental and emotional discipline it took to struggle against the Cardassians during the Occupation. She also recalled that Taran'atar had told her that he had programs to train his mind; she just had not expected any of them to be a mathematics lesson. "Anyway," she went on, getting to the purpose of her visit here, "I'd like to talk with you about what happened in Quark's last night, and in the child-care facility the other day."

"Very well," Taran'atar said.

"What were you doing in those places?" Kira asked.

"I was doing as the Founder instructed me to do," Taran'atar said.

"I've noticed that you haven't been spending as much time in ops recently," Kira said.

"As the Jem'Hadar have seen in battle, humanoids are given to developing patterns," Taran'atar said. "When a high percentage of what I saw and heard in the operations center began to repeat my earlier observations, I decided I should go elsewhere."

"You got bored?" Kira said, feeling herself start to smile. Taran'atar looked at her and said nothing. Kira put her head down and walked forward into the center of the room, thinking about how best to proceed here. When a blue line and several red symbols crawled up her arm, she stopped, turned, and stepped back out of the mathematical display. "So you decided to observe other aspects of life on the station," she said. "Where did you go?"

"The first place I went was *Defiant*," Taran'atar said.

Given the long conflict between the Dominion and the civilizations in the Alpha Quadrant, Kira felt herself grow concerned at this revelation. A moment's reflection, though, convinced her of the futility of such a concern. Taran'atar already had essentially unlimited access on the station, something even more obvious from a practical standpoint when considering his ability to shroud; he could go just about anywhere on the station without anybody knowing about it. More than that, though, Dominion personnel had already spent time on both DS9 and *Defiant*, and whatever military secrets Starfleet held had doubtless been fleeting. And besides, Kira actually trusted Taran'atar, at least to a point, both because of his behavior since he had come aboard, and because of his ties to Odo.

"Why the *Defiant?*" Kira asked.

"As I walked through the ship after my meeting there with Commander Vaughn," Taran'atar explained, "I decided it would be a good place to continue my observations. So I spent several days there."

"All right," Kira said, satisfied with his answer. She could see the blue lines of the display reflected in his eyes. "Where else did you go?"

"The gem merchant's establishment," he said, and Kira wondered how the proprietors would greet that news. Of course, even had Taran'atar been an enemy, she doubted he would have posed a threat to their merchandise; she could not picture a Jem'Hadar wearing an earring or a necklace. "The security office," he continued. "The child-care facility, the flower merchant's establishment, the bar and gaming establishment."

"I see," Kira said, thinking she might have to mention something to Ro, in light of the increased security that would be needed for the upcoming summit. Even though she trusted Taran'atar, she did not believe the delegates—or Admiral Akaar—would enjoy learning that a Jem'Hadar soldier had access to secured areas. "But why did you shroud yourself?"

"At first, I did not," Taran'atar said. "But on board *Defiant*, I encountered a Starfleet officer who reacted to me with great fear." Kira resisted the temptation to ask who it had been, not wanting to change the focus of the conversation. She supposed it might have been Permenter or Richter, or maybe—

Nog, Kira thought, and realized that he had better reason than most to fear the Jem'Hadar.

"Because such a reaction to my presence interfered with my mission," Taran'atar continued, "it seemed a reasonable course to shroud myself, particularly when I chose to enter areas beyond direct control of Starfleet and the Bajoran Militia."

"But why did you unshroud last night then?" Kira asked.

"Because the Ferengi heard me," he said.

Kira was stunned. "Quark *heard* you?"

"Yes," Taran'atar said, and he seemed abashed by the admission. "I underestimated the sensitivity of Ferengi hearing."

Me too, Kira thought but did not say. She had always known that the ears of the Ferengi were not just for show, but she had never known they were that good. "What about in the child-care center?"

"I was paying attention to many things," Taran'atar said in a rush, his tone almost defensive. "Somehow, I allowed a . . . a child . . . to run into me."

"I see," Kira said, having to stifle a laugh. She tried to imagine a little girl or boy unmasking the imposing Jem'Hadar, and could not. "Well, there have been complaints from the child-care center and from Quark. Now, I'm not inclined to agree with just about anything Quark has to say, but Lieutenant Ro told me she witnessed a number of customers fleeing the bar when you appeared."

"That is correct."

"I think a lot of people still aren't used to a Jem'Hadar soldier being on the station," Kira said, "especially since we were attacked by some not that long ago. On top of that, though, I think maybe when you unshroud in front of them, it makes them feel as though you're spying on them."

"I am," Taran'atar pointed out.

"Yes, but I mean they think that you're going to hurt them," Kira explained, "that you shrouded in order to sneak up on them and attack them."

"I would not do that now," Taran'atar said. Kira chose not to think about the implications of the word *now* in his statement.

"I believe you," Kira said. "But until the people of the station get used to you, I think maybe it'd be a good idea not to shroud when you're observing them."

"But it's clear my presence can be disruptive," Taran'atar said.

"At first, sure," Kira agreed. "But that's the point. You need to give these people the chance to grow accustomed to you, so your presence *won't* be disruptive."

Taran'atar seemed to think about Kira's words for a moment, and then he said, "Very well."

"Thank you," Kira said. "I'll let you get back to your—" She glanced again at the mathematics filling the center of the room. "—training," she finished. She headed for the door, the mathematical symbols dancing confusingly through her mind. Maybe before she went to her quarters, she thought, she would stop in the bar and get a drink.

31

Ezri watched the pulse leave the planet. The energy radiated outward from a point on the surface in a golden wave, an ephemeral trail fading behind it. As the planet rotated, the pulse swept across surrounding space in all directions. Eventually, it reached the world of the Vahni.

Ezri felt her heart pounding in her temples, louder in her head than the throbbing of the warp core behind her. After experiencing the effects of the pulse firsthand, she found it difficult to view the simulation and not revisit all that had happened—both on the Vahni world and on the shuttle. *But I have to push those thoughts away,* she told herself. It was one thing to indulge her feelings off-duty, but right now she had work to do.

"So here's what we've come up with," Nog said. He stood next to Ezri at the primary console. His demeanor, typically rushed and animated when he discussed a potential solution for a problem, now seemed flat. Ezri had come down to engineering after Nog had informed her that he and his staff might have developed a defense against the pulse, but now she understood that, whatever they had developed, it did not satisfy the chief engineer. She reached up and rubbed the side of her forehead, tired after a long day; she had not been sleeping all that well recently.

Nog tapped at the controls on the console, and the display above it reset. At the center of the screen, near the blue circle that represented the planet below—and which should have been gray, Ezri thought—two green segments appeared, wedged together in a shallow V pointing toward the planet. Nog pressed another touchpad, and the simulation reran. Again, the energy wave spread from a point on the surface of the planet, but this time the segments deflected a portion of it in other directions. Beyond the segments, a region devoid of the destructive energy extended all the way to the other blue circle, the one representing the world of the Vahni.

Ezri took her hand from the side of her head and pointed to the segments. "All right," she said. "What is that?"

"It's a pair of amplified, finely focused deflector fields," Nog said. The concept did not seem to excite him.

"Amplified by what?" Ezri asked. "And focused by what?"

Nog worked the console again, and two schematics of *Defiant,* one lateral and one overhead, replaced the simulation on the screen. "We think we can tie warp power into the deflector grid," Nog explained, still lacking the enthusiasm he usually demonstrated when discussing engineering matters. He indicated several points along what Ezri recognized as the warp-power backbone, presumably at points of intersection with the deflector grid, although her knowledge of the ship's systems did not extend that far. "Then, if we defeat the surge protection, we can use the navigational deflector to project the strengthened fields."

"Nog," Ezri said, looking away from the display and over at the engineer, "you don't sound particularly happy about this plan."

"I'm not," he admitted. The light from the display shined on his face, lending it a pale tint. "If we can even make these modifications work, then in the best case, the navigational deflector will be completely destroyed, and the warp drive might overload."

"And if the warp drive overloads . . ." Ezri said, leaving the sentence dangling for Nog to finish.

"Then we'll either be adrift," he said, "or a fireball."

Ezri looked again at the skeletal cutaways of the ship, trying to put Nog's words into perspective. "Let me get this straight," she said. "What you just told me is the *best*-case scenario?"

"Yes," Nog said. He operated the controls once more, bringing the simulation back up on the display. "The modified deflector fields," he said, resting the tip of his index finger on the green segments, "have to be generated from somewhere. Obviously, the safest place for *Defiant* to do that would be behind the fields." He slid his finger off the segments, over to the area the pulse failed to penetrate.

"And if the fields don't work, if they don't redirect that portion of the pulse, then the pulse will strike *Defiant*," she said, not needing to add that the ship could not survive such an event.

"Right," Nog said.

"So what are the chances of this working?" she wanted to know.

He shrugged. "Three percent," he said. "Maybe five. The problem is the enormous amount of energy in the pulse. And the fact that we don't understand how it's being generated."

Ezri bit anxiously at her lower lip. Movement caught her attention, and she peered to her right to see another engineer, Tariq Rahim, working at a console. Looking back at Nog, she asked, "How long would you need to set this up?"

"Ten hours," he said.

"So if we decided to try this," Ezri said, thinking aloud, "you'd have to begin the modifications about two days from now." And if Commander Vaughn had not returned to the ship by that time, then Ezri would have to measure a three-percent chance of saving four billion Vahni against a ninety-seven-percent chance of losing the *Defiant* crew. "All right," she said. "See if you can get us something with better odds."

"Aye, sir," Nog said, and she could hear weariness in his voice. He had been working to find a means of stopping the pulse almost since the moment it had destroyed the Vahni moon.

"And make sure you get to bed before too long," Ezri told him. "You're not going to solve anything if you're falling asleep on the job."

"Aye, sir," Nog said again, offering her a weak, but seemingly genuine, smile. "I just want to try one more thing with this simulation," he said, pointing to the display. Ezri looked in that direction just in time to see the entire console go dark.

"What—" she started, looking back up, but she stopped when she saw two other stations wink out across the room. Nog stabbed at the controls, but nothing happened. Ezri saw Rahim making the same attempts at the other dead consoles.

Nog dropped to his knees and pulled an access panel free. Ezri squatted down beside him. Nog set the panel aside, leaning it against the bulkhead, then peered in and examined a complex clutch of optic fibers, isolinear chips, and other equipment. Ezri wanted to ask questions, but she knew that Nog would tell her what had happened once he had figured it out himself. He reached inside and checked several connections. When he withdrew his hand, he said, "We've lost an engineering circuit."

"Shouldn't the backup take over?" Ezri asked.

"It should," Nog said. He looked over at Rahim, who was still trying the controls on one of the other dead consoles. "Tariq," Nog said, "I need a spanner."

"Yes, sir," Rahim said. The crewman reached over to an open case on an adjoining console, pulled out a tool, then brought it over to Nog. "Here you go," he said, handing the spanner to Nog.

"Thanks," Nog said. He switched the tool on, then inserted it carefully into the access port. In almost no time at all, the console sparked back to life. Ezri peered across the room and saw the other consoles still dark. "The main circuit shut down," Nog said, "but for some reason, the power didn't shunt to the secondary."

"Why not?" Ezri asked. "And why did the main circuit shut down?"

"I don't know," Nog said. He grabbed the access plate and set it back in place, the magnetic locks sealing with a clank. "All I did," he said as he stood up, "was to manually switch over to the backup circuit." He handed the spanner back to Rahim, and said, "See if you can do the same for the other consoles."

"Yes, sir," Rahim said. He took the tool and started back across the room.

"It's probably just a bad monitor or a bad switch," Nog said. "I'll get somebody to track the main circuit and see what happened."

"All right. Let me know what they find," Ezri said. She headed for the door, which slid open before her. Before she left engineering, though, she turned back toward Nog. "Just make sure it's not you crawling around the Jefferies tubes all night," she said. "Get some sleep."

"I will," Nog said, and this time his smile was wider.

Ezri stepped out into the corridor and made her way to the nearest turbolift. As the car rose on its short journey from deck two to deck one, she rubbed at her eyes, exhaustion setting in. Still, tired as she felt, she hoped to find Julian awake. She needed to sleep, but she needed—and wanted—his company first.

She turned out of the lift into the main starboard corridor, walking toward the bow of the ship and the cabin she shared with Julian. The dim, night lighting here, a vivid contrast to the bright lights of engineering, reinforced her fatigue. As she passed the short corridor on her left that led to the bridge, she briefly considered and then quickly rejected the idea of stopping in to get a status from Lieutenant Bowers; the ship's second officer knew his job.

Then, as though her thought had summoned him, the voice of Bowers came over the comm system. *"Bowers to Dax."*

She tapped her combadge. "Go ahead." She stopped walking, waiting to hear what the lieutenant wanted before continuing to her cabin.

"I thought you should know that we just detected a hull breach," he said.

"How bad is it?" she asked, feeling immediately and fully awake, as though a glass of cold water had been thrown in her face. She turned back toward the hall leading to the bridge.

"It's just a few square centimeters," Bowers said, *"and the force fields are having no problem containing it."* He seemed serious, but not hurried or upset, which she took as a positive sign.

"Do you know what caused it?" Ezri asked.

"Not for sure," Bowers said, *"but it's on the bottom of the ship, aft, so we think it might have started when* Defiant *was struck by the discharge from the atmosphere. There is an energy reading at that spot on the hull."*

That made sense, Ezri thought. "Have you scanned the exterior of the ship for any other energy readings?" she asked.

"A cursory scan showed nothing," Bowers said. *"We're now conducting a more rigorous search. I've also sent a team down to repair the breach."*

"Good," Ezri said. "Check with engineering too. They just had a main circuit shut down. The backup's online now, but see if that problem's related to the breach."

"I'll do that," Bowers said.

Ezri took a beat, thinking about the writhing cloud cover below them, suffused with energy, and the possibility that it had somehow reached out and punched a hole through the hull of *Defiant*. "And take the ship to a higher orbit," she told Bowers. "Let's not stay any closer to the planet than we need to."

"Yes, sir."

"Is there anything else, Lieutenant?" she asked.

"No, sir."

"All right. Thanks for the update," she said. "Dax out." She pressed her combadge, deactivating it. She again contemplated going to the bridge, but the ship was in good hands. More than that, part of being an effective command officer meant knowing her own limitations, and though she no longer felt tired, she knew she nevertheless needed to rest. She only hoped that she would not dream again of her time on the shuttle.

32

Ro Laren ambled up to the security office doors. Surrounded by the quiet shadows of the early morning, she stopped and peered into the dark, empty office. After a few moments, she stepped back and eyed the access panel, but despite the sizable number of security measures remaining to be implemented between now and tomorrow—when the Bajoran and Federation delegations would arrive on the station—she realized that she had not come down to the Promenade for that purpose. With the morning shift change and the start of her day still more than an hour away, work was the furthest thing from her mind.

Except that's not true, she thought. Almost all she had been able to think about during the last day and a half had been her position as Deep Space 9's chief of security.

Ro turned away from the office and began strolling along the Promenade. She considered bringing the lights up—after all, she knew the security codes that would allow her to do so—but she decided against it. She found right now that she liked the dim illumination and the silence; they allowed her to feel a sense of tranquillity.

Except that's not true either, she scolded herself. The thoughts that had troubled her for much of last night—and for yesterday and the night before that—had not brought her anything even resembling peace. When Kira had informed her the night before last of the upcoming summit, and of the realistic possibility that Bajor might soon join the Federation, Ro had essentially tried not to think about it. She had instead attempted to concentrate on her duties, even during her off-hours, busily preparing the station, her staff, and herself for the enhanced security requirements. Still, her own personal concerns had continued to intrude into her thoughts.

Ro yawned as she passed the Replimat and the florist to her left, and the assay office and an empty storefront—formerly Garak's tailor shop, she had been told—to her right. She had gotten little sleep last night, probably no more than a couple of hours, and it had been her restlessness that had sent her out of her quarters so early this morning. Even as she had tried to push it away, the prospect of Bajor entering the Federation had unsettled her. If it happened, she knew, then the Bajoran Militia would no doubt be rolled up into Starfleet. She had absolutely no idea whether or not she would be offered a position—although if Akaar's presence on the station indicated anything, then she supposed she would be fortunate not to end up reinstated and then tossed in the brig. Even if she was invited to rejoin Starfleet, though, she did not know if signing up for another tour would be such a good idea—either for her or for Starfleet. If nothing else, her stints aboard *Wellington* and *Enterprise* had demonstrated her difficulties fitting in to a command hierarchy and following orders.

Which is why you're in the Bajoran Militia now, right? Ro thought, chuckling aloud. She rolled her eyes and shook her head at the inanity of it all. She had moved around a great deal during her adult life—even within Starfleet—and yet she had never managed to find a place where she felt that she belonged.

Except maybe here, she allowed. Unexpectedly, she had grown to like this place. And she did not want to have to leave it.

As Ro walked by the hair salon, she reminded herself that she needed to make an appointment soon; her straight black hair had grown uncomfortably long, reaching past the tops of her shoulders. The ordinary nature of the thought provided an odd counterpoint to her anxieties about Bajor joining the Federation, and about the uncertainty of her near future. If she had been asked several months ago, back when the Bajoran Militia had assigned her to DS9, if she thought that she would ever feel comfortable on the station—a facility with a significant Starfleet presence—let alone want to stay here, she probably would have laughed. At that time, her expectations had been that, before long, she would end up either resigning from the Militia or being expelled from it.

And yet, despite her negative outlook back then, the situation had begun to work out here. After a tentative beginning, Ro had settled into her job, and what had started as a rocky relationship with the station's commander had mellowed into something far less problematic. She had also made friends here, spending time with Nog and Shar—two young and distinctly unusual Starfleet officers—as well as with Hatram Nabir, a seamstress who had opened up a shop on the Promenade not long after Ro had arrived here. For that matter, she had even developed some sort of a positive rapport with Taran'atar. She still shied away from socializing in large groups, but she found that the geography of the station, as well as its immense size, allowed her the opportunity to be as social or as private as she wished—far more so than did living aboard a starship. She even seemed to feel a sense of home here, although her lack of familiarity with the sentiment made such a characterization suspect.

In reality, Ro thought, she had lived an almost hermitic existence, at least in terms of relationships. She had not isolated herself from people, but she had completely contained her positive emotions for a very long time. As a result, people had come and gone from her adult life with dizzying rapidity—a pattern that echoed the events of her childhood, she knew, although she never liked to explore such thoughts or memories for too long. She had tried a few times to come to terms with what she had experienced in her youth, even once seeking out a counselor when she had been in Starfleet, but she had found herself not yet ready to deal with such matters.

I'm probably still not ready, she thought, though without bitterness.

Ro passed Hatram's shop, and up ahead, the security office slipped back into view along the circumference of the Promenade. She supposed she would begin her workday now after all. As much thinking as she had done during the past day and a half, she really did not like to analyze things too closely or for too long. All she needed to know right now was that, given a choice—something she believed unlikely—she would opt not to leave this place or these people just yet. It seemed somehow cruel to her that she would finally find a place where she felt like she fit in, and then be forced from that place; it also seemed perfectly in keeping with her tumultuous life.

During Ro's trip around the Promenade, the level of light had risen, on its way toward full illumination for the simulated daytime hours on the station. As she neared her office, she tried to blank her mind, and when that failed, she started running down the list of security measures she and her staff would need to address today. Before she reached her office, though, she stopped. To her left sat the entrance to Quark's.

Feeling a pang of disappointment that the bar was closed—even though all of the establishments on the Promenade were closed at this time of day— she realized that she had come down here so early for the opportunity to see and talk with Quark. Of course, she could not reasonably have expected him to be here at this time of the morning; the bar would not open for a few hours, and he would likely not even be there at that time. Recently, she had noticed that he had assigned Treir to manage the morning and afternoon shifts, and Quark, as far as she knew, was not an early riser. Still, even given all that, she had felt the desire to talk with him—not specifically about what she might face in the coming days, since neither the upcoming summit nor the reason for it were public knowledge yet, but just to share his company. She had certainly enjoyed their many conversations over the past few months. He had hinted at wanting a romance with her, but she suspected that those hints amounted to little more than Quark's roguishness. And yet he had been kind, even sweet, to her. Yes, he had some strange values—Ro had never really understood the desire to acquire material objects—but he had so far been a good friend to her. And he certainly knew how to listen.

With those ears, she joked to herself, *how could he not be a good listener?* She laughed aloud, the sound a lonely one on the empty Promenade. She would have to remember to mention her observation to Quark; she thought he would enjoy the humor.

Ro walked up to the doors of the bar and peeked inside, raising her hand to shield her eyes from the lighting overhead. The bar was empty. She shrugged, then stepped back and continued on down the Promenade to her office. Inside, she sat down at her desk and accessed her itinerary for the day. For the most part, her schedule consisted of various tasks related to the increased security for the summit. She also had another meeting with the colonel later this morning so that they could discuss all of the preparations. The day would be full, and by the time Ro finished working, she knew, Quark would be busy running the bar. She could visit him there, of course, but even though business had been slow lately, the bar was hardly conducive to having private conversations; Quark's were not the only ears on the station.

Maybe I'll try to see him after he shuts down the bar tonight, she thought. *Or maybe not.*

33

Sunrise did not exist here. The constant ceiling of clouds blinded the planet to its star. Night fell as black as eternity, and the days existed in a perpetual dusk. Vaughn looked up through the forward windows and saw that the dark had been replaced, not by the reds and oranges and yellows normally associated with dawn, but by the diurnal gray of this shrouded world. Shortly after penetrating the clouds, *Chaffee* had passed the terminator and flown into the night, and the shuttle had now emerged once more into the dim daylight of the planet.

"What's our status?" Vaughn asked in the quiet cabin. Nobody had spoken for a while. Ch'Thane looked up, but Prynn did not, instead keeping her gaze on the flight-control console.

"We estimate that we're less than an hour from the site," Prynn said, answering first, even though she had not looked up from her panel.

"'Estimate'?" Vaughn asked.

"As we get nearer the source of the pulse," ch'Thane explained, "the energy readings are increasing. It's inhibiting full sensor contact, making our scans erratic."

"I see," Vaughn said. He peered through the windows at the relentlessly monochromatic sky above. Below, a mountainous region spread before the shuttle. Their path around the planet had so far taken them only over land.

"We're getting pretty good reads within about a hundred kilometers of the shuttle," Prynn added, "but little beyond that range."

Vaughn felt his weight shift as *Chaffee* veered to port. Ahead, one of the taller mountains in the range slipped away to starboard. Vaughn waited until Prynn had leveled the shuttle, and then he dropped a hand heavily on the back of ch'Thane's chair. "Ensign, since we're so close, I'd like you to prepare our equipment." They had brought scientific equipment with them with which to better examine the source of pulse, some of which would require Shar's expertise to set up.

"Yes, sir," ch'Thane said, rising from his chair.

Vaughn stepped aside, allowing the ensign to pass on his way to the rear compartment. Then Vaughn moved forward and settled into the seat at the starboard console. This was, he realized, the first time that he and Prynn had been essentially alone since he had visited her quarters back on the station. He glanced over at Prynn, who remained intent on her own console. Vaughn felt a strong urge to say something to her, to attempt to draw her out. He wanted to engage her in a dialogue that would, even for a short time, pull them out of their positions as commander and ensign, and push them into their roles as father and daughter. With so much at stake right now, Vaughn understood the comparative insignificance of his failed relationship with Prynn, but he also knew that they would have little to do until they reached the source of the pulse.

The shuttle angled again, this time to starboard. Vaughn looked out the windows and saw another large, rocky peak sliding away from their path. Beyond it, another chain of mountains reached upward, some seeming almost to touch the dark sky above. It reminded him of a murky landscape painting he had once seen a long time ago, though he could not immediately recall when or where that had been.

"Sir," Prynn said, momentarily startling Vaughn out of his thoughts. "Those two mountains ahead of us?"

"Yes?" Vaughn said, looking first at Prynn, and then back out the windows.

"I can keep us low and take the shuttle between them at our current altitude," Prynn said, "or I can ascend and split them higher up."

"Why would we fly higher if we didn't have to?" Vaughn wanted to know.

"Because if we go in low," Prynn explained, "we'll have to pass through a divide between the mountains that's about two hundred meters wide."

Vaughn slowly nodded his head. Traveling at speed through such a narrow channel, he knew, would leave very little margin for error. "Can you do it?" he asked, peering over at Prynn to judge her response. For the first time, she returned his gaze, a confident expression on her face.

"Yes," she said seriously. Then, as though remembering that she wished to conduct all contact with him in an exclusively official manner, she added, "Sir." No animosity or anger entered her mien, only a sense of simple professionalism.

"Then do it, Ensign," he told her, careful to keep the pain he felt from sounding in his voice, instead treating her as she obviously wanted to be treated. *I can't fault her for that,* Vaughn realized; Prynn was giving him precisely what he had demanded from her. The rest, he could only hope, would come in time.

"Yes, sir," she said, and she turned her attention back to her panel. She tapped at various touchpads on her console, her movements fluid and unrushed, as though she were playing a delicate instrument. The beeps and chirps from her console sounded almost like a melody. Vaughn could feel no changes in the shuttle's flight, but when he consulted his panel, he could see them on the sensor displays.

As *Chaffee* neared the two mountains, Vaughn looked up through the windows. The two peaks seemed to rise above the shuttle like twin giants. The sharp, severe appearances of crags and tors loomed above the shuttle like unspoken threats, promising an unforgiving reception in the event of a piloting mistake. *Chaffee* raced toward the area where the two mountains came together, and for just a moment, Vaughn reconsidered his decision and thought about ordering Prynn to take the shuttle higher.

But then it was too late. *Chaffee* roared into the chasm between the two huge masses. The sheer rock walls on either side of the shuttle rocketed past, their surfaces a blur. Vaughn heard more electronic tones as Prynn continued to adjust their course. He waited for *Chaffee* to emerge from its difficult route, and as the seconds passed, the flight between the mountains seemed to take too long. The image of the chasm dead-ending flew through Vaughn's mind, the shuttle slamming into the cold rock face at such speed that there would not even be time to realize that death was at hand.

But Prynn would have consulted the scans of the chasm, and if the sensors had not provided a clear picture, if their erratic functioning had not allowed her to see all that she had needed to see, then she would not even have proposed their current course. Vaughn knew that, having great respect for Prynn's piloting abilities, including whatever judgments those skills required of her. By all accounts, including his own limited observations, she numbered among the best in Starfleet.

Gradually, the shuttle began to shimmy. As the trembling increased, Vaughn examined the sensor displays for the reason. Had an energy discharge from the clouds struck them, as one had struck *Defiant,* or had *Chaffee* suffered some system problem? Vaughn grabbed the edge of his console with both hands, steadying his gaze and allowing him to see the readouts. A strong wind funneled through the chasm, he saw, no doubt buffeting the shuttle and causing its shaking.

And then, in an instant, the shuttle steadied. On either side of *Chaffee,* the chasm walls fell away, and the shuttle flew out into open air. Below, several smaller peaks rose up, but they were set widely apart, allowing the shuttle to skim through them with ease.

Vaughn peered over at Prynn. Not for the first time, he saw her mother in her—in her delicate but intense features, but also in her temperament. Like Ruriko, Prynn would do what needed to be done, regardless of the personal consequences.

"You're an excellent pilot," he told her quietly.

She looked over at him, and for one brief moment, Vaughn felt a sense of connection—*personal* connection—with her. Her eyes seemed to clear, and her expression to soften, and he had the sense that she had let go of all that had come between them. He so regretted what he had done, and now might finally be the time to beg for her forgiveness.

But in the next instant, Prynn's walls had gone back up. "Thank you, sir," she said, and she looked back down at her console. Vaughn watched her a moment longer, thinking of what he could possibly say to reach her, but then he turned back to his own panel. With an effort, he let it all fade from his mind, concentrating on the sensor readings laid out before him. He and Prynn sat that way for long minutes, the silence keeping them apart.

As *Chaffee* eventually neared the end of the mountain range, scans indicated a city ahead. The shuttle had passed several already along its route, all of them devoid of life. Most of the cities had revealed the manner in which they and their inhabitants had fallen, if not the reasons for their demise. One city had consisted of nothing but the blackened husks of buildings, burned and left standing like some charred monument to death. Another had been filled from one end to the other, and beyond the metropolitan limits, with ground vehicles, all pointing away from the city as though the entire population had attempted to flee at once, and then been trapped together in their panic. Another had evidently been under siege, battlements raised along its outskirts in defense against a fleet of military-looking vehicles surrounding it; both the attackers and the attacked had been battered in apparent mutual annihilation. Strangely enough, there seemed to be no indication that the pulse had been the cause of any death or destruction.

The shuttle cleared the last of the mountains and flew in over foothills. The city spread out on the plain beyond, a large, modern collection of buildings that stretched for kilometers. Vaughn consulted the sensors and read no life signs. "Can you bring us in lower?" he asked Prynn.

"Yes, sir," she said. She nosed *Chaffee* downward, leveling off as the shuttle cleared the edge of the city.

Vaughn peered through the windows and saw only stillness. As with the other cities they had passed, scans put the age of this one at hundreds of years, but unlike the others, there were no indications of what had happened to the people who had dwelled there. The buildings looked worn by time and wind, but stood relatively intact. The city appeared untouched by any sort of destruction, and unaffected by any mass exodus. Vaughn could easily visualize entering any of the buildings below to find it looking as though somebody still lived there. Would there be any indications that the inhabitants had abandoned their homes, or that they had been driven out? Or would they appear to have been there one moment, and then unaccountably gone the next? *Or would we find the remnants of bodies?* Vaughn asked himself, his thoughts running, as they seldom did, to the morbid. He shook his head, trying to clear his mind, but instead, another thought bloomed: all the inhabitants who had lived in the city below were still there, dead by their own hand.

Vaughn gripped the side of his console and took a deep breath. He had to get hold of himself; such thoughts did not serve him or the mission. He looked over at Prynn as she calmly piloted the shuttle. "Take us back up," he said.

"Yes, sir," Prynn acknowledged, and she quickly pulled *Chaffee* back up to the altitude at which they had flown around the planet. Vaughn watched as the ground retreated below, and he felt unexpectedly pleased as the shuttle rose. Concentrating on his odd feelings, he was surprised when Prynn spoke again. "What happened on this planet?" she asked.

"I don't know," Vaughn said, continuing to look at the city as it passed beneath them. Discarding his peculiar thoughts, he tried to speculate about what could have caused such widespread but disparate destruction of the civilization here. *The pulse,* he told himself, although he did not understand how that could be. He could only hope that the answers lay ahead of them. And to Prynn, once more, he said, "I don't know."

The energy readings had increased dramatically as *Chaffee* neared the source of the pulse. Vaughn peered over ch'Thane's shoulder at the sensor displays; the ensign had returned to the cockpit after preparing the scientific equipment. Scans seemed to indicate at least one more city between *Chaffee*'s current position and the source of the pulse, although readings in that direction were more erratic now than ever. Directly below the shuttle, surface conditions read calm and cool, with temperatures hovering around ten degrees. Gravity pulled marginally weaker than on Earth, and the atmosphere held a slightly higher oxygen content, though it was certainly breathable. *Good,* Vaughn thought. Unless conditions at the site differed significantly, they would be able to disembark *Chaffee* without having to use environmental suits; as streamlined and sophisticated as the Starfleet issues had become over the years, Vaughn found that they still hindered natural movement.

"I'll get our gear," he told Prynn and ch'Thane. He turned from the forward console and headed for the rear of the shuttle. He stepped into the aft compartment, which doubled as a transporter pad. Moving past the scientific equipment, he reached for a section of the starboard bulkhead. He opened a small storage closet, in which hung outerwear for the crew. He gathered this up in one arm, then pulled out a small locker, about half a meter long and not quite as deep or as tall; the box contained phasers, tricorders, and beacons.

Vaughn carried the gear back out into the main cabin. He dumped the jackets and his old field coat onto a chair, and then set the locker down on the floor. He squatted before the box, unlatched it, and then flipped open its lid, revealing four phasers packed in the upper tray. He pulled one free and attached it to his hip.

A sudden movement in Vaughn's peripheral vision caught his attention. He turned and looked toward the bow of the shuttle in time to see a dark form move out of sight off to starboard. He stood up and started forward. "What—" he started to ask, concerned that he already knew the answer, and then the shuttle shuddered violently. Vaughn flew across the compartment into the port bulkhead.

"We've been struck by an energy surge from the clouds," ch'Thane called, confirming Vaughn's suspicions. "Engine power is down thirteen percent."

"I'm taking us down," Prynn said, not waiting for authorization. Vaughn felt *Chaffee* tilt down toward the ground. He looked through the forward windows and saw an empty plain below. Once they landed, they could assess the damage, make needed repairs as quickly as possible, and continue on their way.

Another blast thundered into *Chaffee*. Vaughn felt the shuttle drop precipitously, a wavering sensation filling his stomach. He thought they would fall from the sky, but then Prynn somehow reined *Chaffee* back under her control.

"There's another—" ch'Thane yelled, but too late. Another bolt of energy struck the shuttle. Vaughn hurtled toward the rear of the cabin. He slammed into the bulkhead and collapsed onto the deck. When he looked up, he was amazed to see Prynn still at her station. Ch'Thane, obviously knocked from his seat, now wrestled his way back to it.

Suddenly, a tremendous report shot through the cabin, followed by the horrible moan of tearing metal. Vaughn looked up at the ceiling and saw the dark, writhing sea of clouds above. For a moment, his mind could not process the image, and then he realized that a meter-square section of *Chaffee*'s roof had been torn open. He saw the blue tinge of an emergency force field and hoped it would hold. Ch'Thane called out, but Vaughn could not make out his words.

Vaughn felt the shuttle veer to port, then dip, and he wondered if Prynn was running evasive maneuvers. *Just get us to the ground in one piece,* he thought.

Holding on to a chair, Vaughn pulled himself back to his feet. He steadied himself with a hand to the bulkhead, then shuffled back into the aft compartment. He reached the transporter controls and punched at the touchpads, intending to establish a lock on *Chaffee*'s crew of three. If Prynn could not keep control of the shuttle, then he could beam them—

The transporter panel was dead.

Vaughn peered back through the doorway and out through the forward windows. The ground approached quickly, and he saw Prynn still working hard at the conn. Then another surge hammered into *Chaffee,* and air screamed through the breach as the shuttle decompressed, the force field obviously gone. The hull screeched as the compromised structure struggled against the forces of its flight. An acrid scent, like that of molten rock, filled the cabin.

Vaughn watched as a shadowy form pushed into the cabin through the hole in the ceiling. An amorphous, shifting mass of gray whirled through the compartment. Ch'Thane turned and saw it just as it reached him. A dark wisp seemed to graze the blue flesh of the ensign's face, and he screamed. The terrible, ugly wail rose loud enough to be heard over the wind, and over the sounds of *Chaffee* breaking up around them. Vaughn had rarely heard such a cry of agony, but something else about it struck him: it seemed less like a cry of pain than of anguish.

Chaffee swerved to port then. The gray tendril withdrew from the cabin as though the shuttle had jerked itself away from its clutches. Their forward momentum slowed, and the wind dropped significantly. For an instant, Vaughn thought that Prynn—amazingly still at her post—might actually be able to land them safely.

And then *Chaffee* crashed.

34

Bashir crawled through the Jefferies tube, a medical tricorder clutched in one hand. The metal grating that formed the base of the conduit rattled as his knees came down on the rigid surface. Voices echoed back to him from around a corner up ahead, the identities of those speaking impossible to distinguish above the din he made as he moved forward.

Bashir reached the intersection of three tubes and turned down the one to his right. Not too far in front of him, Ezri, Lieutenant Nog, and Ensign Gordimer sat one after the other in the enclosed space. Beside them, Bashir saw, several access panels had been removed from one of the bulkheads, revealing some of the ship's circuitry within. As he neared the trio of officers, he slowed, quieting his approach so that he would not interrupt their conversation.

"—*completed the scans,*" said a woman's voice that did not belong to Ezri, obviously being transmitted through a combadge. *"The readings only occur at your location. There's nothing on the exterior of the hull or anywhere inside the ship."* Bashir recognized the voice as that of Ensign Merimark.

"What about transporter signatures?" Ezri asked, glancing up at Bashir, but clearly still speaking with the ensign. Her words rang in the tube, echoing down the long metal conduit.

"We found none," Merimark said.

"All right. Thank you," Ezri said. "Dax out." She raised a hand to her combadge and closed the channel, then addressed Bashir. "Doctor," she said. He understood the need for such formality, but he also found it somewhat amusing, considering that she had come here directly from their cabin. For that matter, he had also just come from there, not long after she had left.

"Lieutenant," he responded, acknowledging Ezri. He nodded at Nog and Gordimer, who both responded in kind. Nog, he noticed, also held a tricorder, one doubtless configured for engineering use. Bashir lowered himself to a half-sitting, half-lying position in the cramped space. He peered across the conduit at the exposed circuitry—the middle of the three open sections was dark—and saw what appeared to be a bypass of some sort. A bundle of optical fibers emerged from one section, snaked along the floor of the Jefferies tube past the middle section, and connected back into the third. "What's going on?" he asked, the reason Ezri had called him here not immediately evident to him.

"Last night," she explained, "we experienced a minor power disruption in engineering." He recalled her mentioning that when she had returned to their quarters last night. "Ensign Leishman has circumvented the problem—" She swept her hand through the air above the obviously improvised bypass. "—but this appears to have been the source of the disruption." Ezri indicated the middle section.

Bashir looked, but beyond the circuitry being dark—and therefore without power, he assumed—he observed nothing out of the ordinary. He searched for something he could recognize as foreign, but saw only the expected assemblage of isolinear optical chips, fiber-optic cables, and routing and junction nodes . . . except—"Is this what you're referring to?" he asked, pointing to a gray substance pooled along the length of the middle section.

"Careful, Doctor; don't get too close," Ensign Gordimer said. "We're not sure what we're dealing with here."

Bashir had not intended to touch the amorphous mass without scanning it first, but he understood that Gordimer's position in security required him to practice caution. "Don't worry," Bashir said, withdrawing his hand, but continuing to try to get a good look at the substance in the poorly illuminated tube. The mass appeared inert and viscous, almost like a thick pool of grease, but dark gray rather than black. "I don't think it's going to leap out at me."

"I wouldn't be too sure about that, Doctor," Nog said.

"What?" Bashir asked, turning his head to look over at the engineer.

"We haven't seen it moving," Ezri clarified, "but the ship had an unexplained hull breach at about the same time as the power disruption in engineering." Bashir remembered her mentioning that last night as well.

"You think this entered the ship through the breach and traveled here?" Bashir asked, peering back down at the patch of gray. He opened his medical tricorder, and started scanning.

"Possibly," Ezri said. "Nothing has transported onto or off the ship, so we don't know how else this might have gotten here."

Bashir studied the display on the tricorder. "I am getting energy readings," he said.

"Which makes sense," Nog said. "Somehow, this thing interrupted the flow of power, causing the outage in engineering, but it also carried enough energy to prevent the secondary system from engaging."

"You say that as though it were planned," Bashir told him. "But stars have energy, and they're not alive. This substance may simply be holding an electrical charge." He continued examining the tricorder scan. "These energy readings, though . . ."

"They're nothing you're familiar with," Ezri finished for him.

"No," Bashir agreed.

"They match the readings we took of the pulse," Nog said. "And of the clouds surrounding the planet."

"Really?" Bashir said, looking up again. He reached up and wiped a hand across his forehead, his hand coming away wet with perspiration; the air in the Jefferies tube was still and close.

"We think that when *Defiant* was struck by the energy surge from the cloud cover, this may have been deposited on the ship," Nog said.

"And eaten through the shields and the hull, and then crawled here?" Bashir asked, his tone conveying his skepticism.

"We've seen stranger things," Ezri said.

"Yes, of course, but this—" He peered back down at the substance, and then consulted the tricorder once more. "I'm reading no organic compounds, nothing beyond a very rudimentary physical structure, no musculature . . .

nothing to suggest a morphogenic matrix . . . I think it's very unlikely that this object is alive."

"Is that conclusive?" Ezri wanted to know.

Bashir touched a control on the tricorder and ended the scan. As he folded the device back into its compact carrying form, he looked over at her. "No," he said. "I'll need to run a series of more complex tests."

"All right," Ezri said. "I'd like you to do that." She turned to Gordimer. "Ensign, I want you to go up to the transporter and beam the object directly to the medical bay."

"Yes, sir."

"Doctor," she went on, "establish a containment field about the object while you study it."

Bashir noted the seeming confidence with which Ezri practiced command; the set of her body, the certainty in her tone and words, the quick decisions, all painted her as a person completely in charge of both herself and the situation. And yet, knowing as he did the personal price she was still paying for the loss of Ensign Roness, he wondered just how well her professional calm and resolve, forced as they must be, actually served her. He hoped that the mask she wore while on duty would not blind her to . . . well, to anything. Commander Vaughn seemed to find such behavior constructive, but Bashir felt far less sanguine about it. He believed that Ezri should not be making decisions, either for the ship or for herself, either concentrating too much on the death of Roness, or completely ignoring it.

He mentioned none of this now. Nor did he know when he would be able to speak with her again about such matters; he hoped he would not have to. All he said now was "Aye, sir." Then he turned and crawled back down the Jefferies tube the way he had come, headed for the medical bay as he had been ordered, with Ensign Gordimer thumping along behind him.

Bashir wheeled the portable stand to the center of the empty medical bay and set its brake. The white apparatus stood as tall as a diagnostic bed, with upper and lower shelves about half that size. He felt along the side of the upper shelf until he located the small control pad there, and then he activated the unit's locator; the signal, like that of a combadge, would facilitate transport. He also set the parameters for a containment field, which he would establish about the substance once it had been beamed to the medical bay. He tapped his combadge. "Bashir to Gordimer."

"This is Gordimer," came the ensign's immediate response. *"I'm at the transporter, sir."*

"I'm ready here," Bashir told him. "I've initiated a transport locator."

After a momentary pause, Gordimer said, *"I've got it. I'm all set."*

Bashir told the security officer to stand by, then tapped his combadge again. "Bashir to Dax."

"Dax here," she said.

"We're ready to transport," he informed her.

"*All right,*" she said. "*Dax to Gordimer. Energize.*"

Bashir took a step back from the stand and waited for the bright white streaks and the high-pitched drone of the transporter. He waited, but nothing happened.

"*This is Gordimer,*" the security officer said. "*I can't get a transporter lock on the object. The transport sensors can read its energy, but they can't establish a lock for some reason.*"

"*Try using a positional transport,*" Nog suggested, his voice coming over the channels opened to Dax. "*Beam everything up to five centimeters above the bulkhead that the substance is sitting on.*"

"*Yes, sir,*" Gordimer said. "*Resetting the transporter . . . energizing.*"

This time, the light of the transporter shimmered above the stand in the medical bay, accompanied by a familiar hum. But when the light faded and the hum quieted, nothing had materialized there.

Nothing but air, Bashir thought, knowing that the positional transport would have attempted to beam everything within its target location. "This is Bashir," he said. "I've still got nothing here."

"*The substance is still here,*" Dax said. "*Ensign Gordimer, would y—*" She stopped speaking in mid-sentence, in mid-*word,* with a suddenness that told Bashir that something had happened. He heard a sound like one somebody would make when punched in the stomach, the air rushing from their lungs.

"Lieutenant Dax?" he said. He waited just long enough for a response, and when none came, he said, louder, "Ezri?" He took a step toward the door, but stopped when Nog spoke.

"*Doctor, the object moved, and Lieutenant Dax accidentally came into contact with it,*" he said, urgency sounding in his hurried words and raised voice. "*She's lost consciousness.*"

"Ensign Gordimer," Bashir said at once. "Lock on to Lieutenant Dax's combadge and transport her directly to biobed one in the medical bay." For emergency situations, Bashir knew, the coordinates of various locations in the medical bay had been preprogrammed into the ship's transporter.

"*Yes, sir,*" Gordimer said.

Bashir turned and sped over to the bed. "Bashir to Richter," he said, contacting his primary medical assistant.

There was a pause, and then the sleepy voice of the nurse sounded over the comm system. "*This is Richter,*" she said. It was still early in the day, and Bashir had apparently just woken her.

"Krissten, we have an emergency," he told her. "I need you in the medical bay."

"*I'm on my way,*" she said without hesitation, any drowsiness she felt now gone from her voice. "*Richter out.*"

An instant later, the effervescent white light of the transporter filled the space above the bed, accompanied by the telltale whine. Even before Ezri had fully materialized, Bashir reached up and switched on the medical sensors. When the transport had completed, he peered down at her only long enough to see that she lay facedown, with her eyes closed and her complexion grown terribly pallid. Then he looked back up at the diagnostic display above the head of the bed. Her respiration was shallow, her heart rate down and fluttering, her neural activity nearly nonexistent—almost all of her vital signs had plummeted.

Bashir raced across the medical bay, heading for a storage cabinet. As he passed the portable stand at the center of the room, he reached out and tried to push it away. He had set the brake on it, though, and instead of rolling away, it toppled over. The stand crashed onto the deck with a clang, the sound uncomfortably loud in the quiet medical bay.

Bashir opened the cabinet and quickly pulled out a hypospray and a vial of cordrazine. As he dashed back over to Ezri, he affixed the powerful stimulant to the hypo. At the bed, he reached his empty hand to Ezri's neck, pulling down the collar of her uniform with two fingers, her pale flesh clammy beneath his touch. He administered the hypo just below her ear, the small device hissing briefly as it worked.

On the medical display above the bed, the heart-rate monitor slowly changed, the number of beats per minute increasing, the rhythm of her heart smoothing out. Bashir waited, but few other readings improved. In particular, her neural activity remained dramatically low, a consequence almost unheard of with the use of cordrazine. Strangely, though, the neural energy of the Dax symbiont, though skewed, measured at a level not much different from normal.

Behind him, one of the doors to the medical bay opened. Footsteps approached, and he looked up from the tricorder to see Ensign Richter appear on the other side of the bed. She wore her reddish blond hair loosely about her head, he saw, with a curl to it that was not evident when she pulled it back in braids. Bashir felt a moment of surreal displacement, and of confused curiosity about himself, wondering why he even noticed such insignificant details right now.

"Oh no," Richter said as she peered down at Ezri. "How is she?" she asked, even as her gaze rose to check the readouts for herself.

"She's in a coma," Bashir said flatly. "She's dying."

35

Treir reached across the dabo table for the gaming rondure. As she did, the bare flesh of her shoulder brushed against Hetik's brawny triceps—equally bare—and she felt an instant of heat. In the morning quiet at Quark's—only a handful of customers sat scattered about, having their breakfasts—the fleeting touch seemed intense enough to be heard. The strength of her reaction surprised her. In the past few years, she had only pretended at such feelings—for which she had been kept warm in other ways. But not like this. She found the unexpected jolt more than a little liberating.

Treir had hesitated in that sultry moment, and now she began moving again. She swiped the rondure from its cup in the dabo wheel and held it up before Hetik. "So," she said, peering past the transparent orb with the starburst pattern at its center, "that would pay off on . . . ?"

"Pass five and half under," Hetik finished, and then he explained the structure of the payouts.

Beauty and *brains,* Treir thought, and then laughed at herself for such schoolgirlish notions. Still, a woman could look. And with Hetik, there was plenty at which to look. Right now, she satisfied herself with a gaze just a fraction too long into eyes she thought of as the color of night. "Right again, my *cheltol,*" she said, the appellative slipping out before she could stop it.

"*Cheltol?*" he asked.

"Uh, it's an Orion term for a . . . uh . . . *capable* . . . male student," she stammered, choosing discretion over description. It occurred to her that this must be how some of her own admirers felt. And she also considered what else she might be able to teach this sweet young man beside dabo.

Treir reached out and took Hetik's hand in hers, placed the rondure in his palm, and closed his fingers around it. His dark, delicious flesh complemented her green coloring, she noticed. "Now you give it a whirl," she said, nodding her head toward the wheel, and then scolding herself for the unintended double entendre. As interesting and even delightful as she found her unanticipated responses to Hetik this morning, that was not why she had brought him here. This was business.

Hetik grasped the side of the dabo wheel and spun it around. The twitter of the wheel filled the room, easily overtaking the intermittent ring of flatware on dishes. He dexterously rolled the rondure from his palm to the tips of his thumb and forefinger, then reached down and sent it swirling around the upper, outer rim of the wheel.

"Treir." The voice cut through the ambient sounds of the bar like a diamond through glass, sharply and without much effort. Both Treir and Hetik looked up from the dabo table to the entrance of the bar, where Quark had just arrived.

Treir muttered an Orion oath. *What's he doing here?* she thought in frustration. For the past few weeks, Quark had delegated the management of the bar during the morning hours to her. At first, he had still come to the bar himself at that time, keeping obviously watchful eyes—*and attentive ears,* she added—on her. Lately, though, he had stopped showing up in the morning. And despite her certainty that he still somehow managed to monitor her activities, through the use of surveillance devices or confederates or some other devious means, she had begun to feel some sense of autonomy during the times she was at least nominally in charge of the bar. Perhaps, she thought now, that had been naïve. As she decided what she should do, she absently clutched at her necklace, a collection of emerald green jewels set in a pattern of interlacing triangles.

As the chirrup of the dabo wheel slowed, Quark started for the table. "Stay here," Treir told Hetik, squeezing his upper arm to emphasize her words. She strode in Quark's direction, her long legs quickly eating up the short distance. She intercepted him about halfway to the table. "Quark," she said, modulating her tone so that she sounded very pleased to see him. "What are you doing here?" She let herself almost sing the words, an attempt to focus Quark's attention on her. Behind her, she heard the wheel come to a stop, and the staccato sound of the rondure bouncing into a cup.

"What are *you* doing?" he demanded, even gruffer than usual. She saw that he looked upset, and she wondered if his mood had anything to do with his increasing flirtations with the station's security chief. Two nights ago, after that Jem'Hadar had appeared as though from nowhere, she had watched Quark and Ro coquet with each other; she had also heard Ro suggest that she might return to the bar later that night, but Treir had not seen her in here since. Nor, she suspected, had Quark.

Now Quark leaned to his left and peered past Treir toward Hetik. "We don't allow gamblers to touch the dabo wheel," he complained to her in a lowered voice. "Let alone allow them to make the spins." He looked angrily up at her. "Wasn't that the first thing I taught you?"

Treir bent at her knees and slung herself around to Quark's side. As she slithered a bare arm across his shoulders, she said in a breathy voice, "But not the last thing you're going to teach me, I hope." Obvious, and Quark would see the words as a ploy, but he often responded to such advances regardless. She draped herself around him, her tall, lithe form folding up in such a way that she actually seemed to become the same size as the much smaller Ferengi.

"Really?" Quark asked, looking at her lasciviously. "And what else would you like to learn?" Treir liked predictable behavior; it had kept her in luxurious accommodations, elegant clothing, and a relative life of leisure for some time.

"Oh, I don't know," she said, gently kneading his shoulders. "I'm sure you'll think of something interesting for me." She started to ease him around toward the bar and away from Hetik.

"Wait a minute," Quark said, setting his shoulders and not allowing Treir to turn him. "The dabo wheel." He pointed in that direction.

Bad instincts, Treir railed at herself. She had moved too quickly to get Quark away. She knew better, but she had acted rashly. *Probably because I was flustered by Hetik,* she thought, but that was a poor reason. "Don't worry about it, Quark," she said, trying to segue now from a personal mode to a business mode. "There's no latinum on the table."

"Then what's he doing?" Quark wanted to know. He extricated himself from Treir's hold. She pulled away from him, and in the blink of an eye, she towered over him once more. Quark looked up at her accusingly. "Is he rigging the dabo wheel so you two can steal me deaf later?"

"Be careful what you say, Quark," she told him. "I know you were just in a bad mood the other night when you intimated you were going to fire me, and maybe you're in a bad mood now, but you don't want to drive away just about the only thing drawing customers in here."

Quark made a show of peering slowly around the bar at the few patrons present. "Yeah," he said. "I'm turning them away at the door."

"It's breakfast time," she said. "Don't be sarcastic." She added a smile to her admonishment, attempting to find the right attitude that would work with Quark today. Treir had initially believed that his supposed pursuit of Ro had been for the sole purpose of gaining some business advantage relating to her position aboard Deep Space 9. His continued sour mood, though, was beginning to convince her otherwise.

She held her hand out toward the dabo table. "That young man's name is Hetik," she said. "He made a pilgrimage here to see the Celestial Temple for the first time, and he—"

"I don't care what his name is or why he's here," Quark said. "I want him to stop touching my dabo wheel." He glared over at Hetik. "And tell him to put some clothes on."

Treir glanced over at Hetik. The meaty young man was paying no attention to them, instead studying the dabo table. He wore a pair of tight black shorts and a small matching top that barely covered the upper portion of his torso. He looked very good—very sexy—and he seemed remarkably at ease. Treir knew well how uncomfortable it could feel to wear so little in public. In fact—

"He's wearing more than I am," she said. Her outfit—provided to her by Quark, of course—consisted of little more than a pair of narrow bands of shimmering silk, one at her chest and one just below her waist.

"You have more parts people want to see," Quark said with a leer.

"Some people," Treir agreed. "But some would rather see Hetik's parts." She realized then how far this conversation had sunk, and that it would not likely improve, and although Quark's mood might, there was an immediacy to her need to discuss Hetik with him. She had intended to speak with him later, convinced that by the time he arrived at the bar this afternoon or this evening, she would have been able to prove to him the worth of what she had done.

"Anybody who wouldn't prefer your parts is a fool," Quark said.

"Perhaps," Treir said. "But fools spend their latinum as much as the wise do—maybe more so."

"That's true," Quark said, but then he looked up at her with a quizzical expression. "But what's your point?"

"My point is, maybe Hetik could bring in a new set of customers, and thereby improve profits."

A smirk played across Quark's face, his skepticism evident. "I don't think so," he said.

"Well, that's too bad," Treir told him, "because he's your new dabo boy."

Quark's eyes widened, and then his mouth dropped open, completely revealing his pointed, unaligned teeth. He closed and opened his mouth several more times. *Like a fish,* Treir thought, *gasping when removed from water.* Finally, Quark managed to form words. "He's my new *what?*"

"Your new dabo boy," she repeated. "I hired him."

Again, Quark's mouth oscillated between closed and open. "You *what?*" He brought a hand up to his chest, as though he were suffering a heart spasm.

She moved toe-to-toe with him and stared down directly into his eyes. "I hired Hetik," she said, enunciating each word slowly, "to be your new dabo boy."

Quark returned her gaze, still agape. "He's . . . he's . . . you . . . you . . ." he sputtered. It seemed to Treir as though he did not know what to be upset about first: a dabo *boy* in his establishment, or her—an employee—hiring a new worker.

"Listen to me, Quark," she said, dropping any pretense from her voice and manner. "If some people come in here to ogle me while they're drinking and gambling, then other people will come in to ogle him." She pointed a thumb back over her shoulder toward Hetik.

Quark shook his head, then closed his mouth and seemed to regain his composure. "Nobody's going to come into the bar to see either one of you," he snarled, "once I have the two of you thrown out an airlock."

Treir felt her features harden, and she leaned down until her face was only centimeters from Quark's. "Be careful with your threats, Quark," she said in a fierce whisper. "Hetik might hear you."

"What he's going to hear," Quark said, apparently unfazed by Treir's words, "is me firing him." He backed up a half-step, then started around her. Just before he would have passed her, she reached out and took hold of his upper arm. Quark stopped, and they regarded each other.

"Don't do it," Treir said. She knew that this would work, that Hetik's presence in the bar would bring in more customers, which would necessarily increase her own tips. And she liked Hetik and wanted to help him. She leaned in toward Quark. "Perhaps we can come to some sort of accord about this," she said, breathing warmly in his ear.

Quark pulled back and stared at her for a few moments, his eyes squinting into slits. He appeared to consider Treir's request. Then he said, "I'm a romantic, but I also know the 229th Rule of Acquisition: 'Latinum lasts longer than lust.'" He pulled his arm from her grasp, but before he could take another step, she grabbed him again. This time, she pulled him in close to her.

"Then at least let me do it," she said. "I hired him; let me fire him."

Quark jerked his arm free. "Fine," he said. "I just came in to get a bottle of *grosz* for Admiral Akaar." He looked over at Hetik, and then back at Treir. "Make sure he's gone when I come back in tonight," he told her.

"Fine," she said.

Quark started to head for the bar, presumably to retrieve the *grosz*, but then he stopped, came back, and leaned in to her. "Just be happy I'm not firing you too," he said. Then he made his way to the bar. She watched as he pulled out a stubby, dark green bottle and carried it out.

Once Quark had gone, Treir finally turned to Hetik. She saw that he was now looking at her. She started toward him, wondering what she would say.

36

The smell of smoke reached him first.

Vaughn regained consciousness as though a switch had been thrown. One moment, his mind did not exist, and the next, awareness deluged him. With his eyes closed, his other senses painted the canvas of his circumstances. As he breathed in the acrid smoke, it irritated the dry membranes of his nose. A bitter taste coated his mouth, and his throat burned as though he had swallowed broken glass. His body ached within and without, his muscles strained, his flesh battered, and the air felt unpleasantly cool about him. The crackle of live flames reached him from several directions, but not so close that he could feel their heat. And beneath it all, something else made itself known ... a noise that held more substance as a feeling than as a sound ... like a far-off wind whispering at the very limits of hearing, moving air with a force diminished by distance.

Vaughn opened his eyes. He lay on his back, propped up against a section of bulkhead in what had been the rear of *Chaffee*'s forward compartment. The front of the shuttle was gone. No, not gone. It sat on the open ground thirty or forty meters away, engulfed by fire. A pillar of thick black smoke rose up from it, reaching for the gray clouds above as though for a kindred spirit.

Between the two sections of the destroyed shuttle, wreckage littered the ground. Two smaller fires burned off to the right, and hills sat far off in the distance to the left, but otherwise, the landscape extended away desolate and un-variegated, a flat, brown plain. Vaughn glanced over his shoulder and saw the bulkhead separating the fore and aft compartments. Through the misshapen doorway, the aft portion of the shuttle appeared relatively intact, although the roof had been almost completely ripped away.

Something moved directly to Vaughn's right, just a meter or two away. The broken remnants of a chair tumbled from atop a heap of debris, and he saw a hand reach upward. "Prynn," he said, his voice rasping, the word barely understandable. He gulped, trying to clear his throat, then coughed forcefully. Mucus filled his mouth, and he spat to his left, not surprised to see streaks of red mixed in with the yellowish fluid. "Prynn," he called again, pronouncing her name clearly this time.

"I'm here," she said, and she waved her hand. "I'm stuck." She sounded remarkably calm in light of what they had just endured.

"Hold on," Vaughn said. He set one hand against what remained of the bulkhead to his left, and the other down on the decking beneath him. He pushed himself forward and upward, and managed to get to his feet. His body ached everywhere—in his joints, in his muscles, on his flesh, and he felt a throbbing pain on the inside of his cheek—but he seemed to have escaped any significant external injuries. "I'm coming," he told Prynn. He stepped carefully over and around masses of ruined machinery, leaning toward the aft compartment in order to compensate for the forward tilt of the decking.

When he got to the chair Prynn had pushed from atop herself, he reached down and lifted it out of his way. He swung the bent object back in the direction he had come, setting it down with a thud. Then he stepped forward and pulled away a snarl of mangled circuitry, revealing Prynn. She looked shaken and bruised. Her face and neck showed multiple cuts, and a long gash arced from her temple all the way down to her chin. A blood vessel must have ruptured in one of her eyes, because the sclera had turned a dark red. "Can you see out of both eyes?" he asked her.

Prynn glanced around, then back up at him. "Yes," she said. "But my arm." She pointed up toward her right shoulder, beyond which her arm disappeared beneath a fractured section of hull plating. She tried to push the plate away with her free hand, but it did not move at all beneath her efforts.

Vaughn studied the situation for a moment, then glanced around in the unlikely hope that he might spy a tricorder lurking somewhere nearby. Ideally, he would scan behind the metal slab before attempting to extricate Prynn. If some portion of her arm had been severed, the plating might actually be preventing her from bleeding to death; on the other hand, she might be losing blood right now.

Seeing no tricorder, Vaughn moved to his left and wrapped his fingers around the top of the hull plate. He had expected to find the metal warm to the touch, perhaps even hot, but it was actually cold. He pulled gingerly on the heavy slab, testing its weight; he did not want to manhandle it away from Prynn only to have it crash back down on her an instant later. Satisfied that he could move it, Vaughn repositioned himself so that he could brace his legs against an unbroken section of the starboard bulkhead. Setting his hands beneath the top of the slab, he pushed, using the combined strength of his arms and legs. The plate shifted forward a few centimeters and stopped, the loud screech of metal scraping against metal erupting from its lower edge.

From somewhere below him came the sound of movement. Vaughn felt sweat forming on his forehead as he struggled to prevent the plate from falling backward. He grunted as he tensed his arms and legs, pushing with as much force as he could manage, and still the plate began to slip back.

"I'm free," Prynn yelped suddenly. Vaughn looked over to see his daughter moving away from the metal slab. As quickly as he could, he jumped back out of the way, onto the dirt beyond the fallen shuttle. The broken section of the hull slammed back down. Vaughn turned and spat again, and again he saw blood. He wondered just how bad his internal injuries were.

Prynn tottered to her feet, and relief flooded over Vaughn when he saw her raise her right arm and flex her shoulder, elbow, and fingers. Her uniform had been torn open in a dozen places, he saw, and her combadge no longer hung on her tunic. Considering what they had just been through, though, she appeared more or less unscathed. "Are you all right?" he asked.

"I'm okay," she told him as she found her way out of the wreckage and onto open ground. She faced him across a few meters and raised a hand to the side of her face, feeling cautiously at the wound there. She pulled her hand away and examined her fingertips, which were now red with blood.

He walked up to her. "You've got a deep cut here," he said, drawing a finger through the air along the side of her face. He looked closely at the gash, then said, "It looks like the blood's clotted, so you should be all right."

"You've got quite a few cuts yourself," she said, pointing up at his face.

"And I can feel every one of them," he said with a halfhearted smile.

Prynn turned and peered back at the smashed aft section of the shuttle. "We need to find a medkit," she said.

"We need to find Ensign ch'Thane."

"Oh no," Prynn said, distress filling her voice. "Shar."

Vaughn glanced down and saw that, somehow, his combadge still hung on his uniform. He reached up and pressed it, and it warbled to life. "Vaughn to Ensign ch'Thane," he said. He waited a few seconds, then repeated the call a second time, and then a third.

There was no response.

Prynn turned and surveyed the area, and Vaughn did the same. They began searching the nearby ground around the wreckage of the aft section. As they looked, Vaughn's gaze alit on the distant pyre of the shuttle's bow.

"The front of the shuttle," he said, and he rushed by Prynn and back into the mass of debris from which they had just come. He heard her say something as he moved as quickly as he could through the twisted doorway and into the aft compartment. Everything lay in a shambles—he stepped on a phaser as he entered—but by simple fortuity, he saw what he needed immediately, lying in a corner and propped up against a dented metal locker. Vaughn took two long strides, bent, and picked up the fire-suppression canister.

He made his way back out of the wreckage. Prynn, he saw, had already started toward the fiery bow section. He ran to catch up with her. A million small aches nagged at him, but he counted himself fortunate that he could even stand up at this point.

Prynn stopped several meters from the burning cockpit, her arms thrown up in front of her face. As Vaughn reached her, he felt the heat of the fire coming at him in waves. The flames roared, the sound sending him back six weeks to the explosion on *Defiant's* bridge, to when he thought he had lost his daughter. But he had no time for that now. "Stay here," he yelled to Prynn. He walked forward a few steps, wanting to get close enough to be able to use the canister effectively, but the heat grew unbearable. He stumbled to the right, starting around the wreckage in search of a break in the fire that would allow him to move closer.

As Vaughn circled, he saw something through the blistering air, glimpsed as though through rippling water. He backed away from the fire to get a better view, and saw only a pile of metal and circuitry lying another twenty meters away. He continued around, though, looking not at the fire, but out at the surrounding land. Another heap came into view, and Vaughn recognized the gray of a Starfleet uniform and a trace of blue that could only be Andorian skin.

"Prynn," Vaughn called. "Shar." He dropped the canister and ran. As he drew closer to the fallen ensign, he saw that his body had landed in an awkward position, like a rag doll tossed carelessly aside. Ch'Thane lay facedown, his left arm bent back in a way that seemed impossible for a human or an Andorian; at best, the shoulder had been dislocated, and at worst, it had been torn apart.

Vaughn dropped to one knee beside ch'Thane's head and felt for a pulse at the side of his neck. Vaughn knew little about Andorian physiology, but he knew enough to ascertain that the young man was still alive. He got up and began working his way around ch'Thane's body, searching for any visible injuries. He heard Prynn's footsteps race up and stop.

"How is he?" she wanted to know.

"He's alive," Vaughn said, not looking up. He moved down along ch'Thane's body. As he reached the knee, he noticed a dark patch below ch'Thane's shin. Vaughn examined that area of the leg and found a tear in the uniform pants. He reached two fingers from each hand inside the hole and pulled in opposite directions, the sound of tearing cloth strangely out of place in this alien environment. Vaughn examined ch'Thane's leg, and what he saw made him want to turn away.

"What is it?" Prynn asked, her concern obvious. "Is he all right?" Vaughn heard her take a step closer, and he looked over at her and locked his eyes on her face.

"Stop," he commanded, and she did, looking up and meeting his gaze. The dried blood from the gash, coupled with the injury to her eye, made her appear as though she was wearing a mask on one side of her face. "Stay right there and listen to me. Ensign ch'Thane is all right, but I'm going to need your help to keep him that way." She nodded mutely, and Vaughn thought that shock might be setting in. "I want you to go back to the aft section and find a tricorder and a medkit." Prynn turned immediately and started back the way they had come. "Wait," he called, and she stopped and turned back toward him. "I think I saw the emergency survival cache in the aft compartment," he said. "See if you can open it. If you can't, or if you can't find it, then you'll have to search through the wreckage for loose equipment. I also need something I can use as a splint."

"A splint," Prynn echoed.

"Yes," he told her. "Now go." She headed away at a run.

Vaughn looked back down at ch'Thane's leg. Halfway between the ankle and the knee, the jagged end of a bone protruded through the young man's skin. The white of the bone sharply contrasted with the blue of Andorian flesh. Indigo blood spilled from the wound and darkened the dirt beneath.

Vaughn stood up and hastily pulled off his uniform tunic. He kneeled back down again and lifted ch'Thane's leg just enough to allow him to slide one sleeve under the thigh. Vaughn pulled the sleeve out the other side, then tied it together with the other one as tightly as he could. The blood flowing out of the leg wound ebbed at once.

"We're getting you help, Shar," Vaughn said quietly. He reached up and again felt for a pulse at ch'Thane's neck. "Don't die on me now," he said. "Don't die on me."

The day had moved on.

Vaughn pulled his coat closed against a breath of cold wind, grateful that the outerwear had survived the crash. He moved out of the wrecked aft section of the shuttle, carrying three handheld beacons, the last items that he thought they would need. As he and Prynn had ministered to Ensign ch'Thane's injuries—and to their own—and then as they had raided the emergency survival cache and set up a camp around the fallen officer, Vaughn had begun to decide how they would proceed. Now, as he made one last inspection of the downed shuttle, he settled on a plan. *Not necessarily a good plan,* he thought, but of the few options available to them right now, it had been a simple matter to identify the best course of action.

As Vaughn stepped from *Chaffee*'s splintered decking onto the hardpan, he peered around. The two smaller fires burning closest to here had sputtered out, leaving behind smoldering mounds of seared machinery. The larger fire enveloping the shuttle cockpit still blazed, though it had abated. Overhead, the incessant cloud cover continued to hold the planet's daytime hours in a continuous dusk. The gray conditions gave Vaughn the sense of an impending rainstorm.

Or of an impending attack, he thought.

He eyed the never-still sea of shadows above, remembering vividly the murky form that had penetrated the roof of the shuttle, and which had looked very much like an extension of the cloud cover. Vaughn had considered the idea that the clouds might actually be life-forms, but nothing the crew had learned so far, either aboard *Chaffee* or back on *Defiant,* supported such a possibility. The "attack" on the shuttle had likely been akin to a lightning strike, he thought, with the clouds discharging energy, and the shuttle acting as a ground and conducting it; back aboard *Defiant,* when the ship had been similarly struck by an energy surge, Ensign ch'Thane had offered the same analogy.

Before returning to the makeshift camp he and Prynn had set up, Vaughn decided to loop around the wreckage of the aft section, just to make certain that nothing else they might be able to use had been thrown clear. They had already been fortunate that the emergency survival cache had come through the crash dented, but intact. *Starfleet should make their shuttles out of the same material as their survival lockers,* Vaughn thought, a flippant notion that had occurred to him on several other occasions; this was not the first shuttle accident he had lived through.

As Vaughn reached the back of the smashed shuttle, he looked back along the line of *Chaffee*'s descent, expecting to see long gouges where it had skidded along the ground, perhaps even a small impact crater where it had first hit. Instead, he saw only a level, unbroken plain. Vaughn squatted and set the beacons down, then pulled a tricorder from an outside coat pocket. He opened the device and scanned the area; although interference from the energy in the clouds and at the source of the pulse hindered long-range scans, it remained possible to gather short-range readings. In this case, Vaughn's scans only confirmed what his eyes had already told him: *Chaffee* had come down hard, but at neither the vertical nor the horizontal speed he would have expected. However that had happened, it had probably saved their lives.

At least for now.

Vaughn closed up the tricorder and placed it back in a coat pocket, then bent and collected up the beacons. He wiped at the corner of his mouth with a knuckle, his saliva no longer streaked with red. What he had thought might be a symptom of an internal injury had turned out to be nothing more than the result of a chunk of flesh he had bitten from the inside of his cheek. He had mended the wound and stemmed the bleeding, although his cheek still ached.

Vaughn went back around the wreckage and headed toward the fire that was still consuming the shuttle's cockpit. As he walked, he noticed again the remote hum that he had first heard when he had regained consciousness after the accident. So far as he could tell, it had never stopped; it felt like *Defiant* traveling at warp, that constant background drone and throb of the engines that permeated the ship. *It's the voice of the clouds,* he thought, the audible effect of all the energy surrounding the planet.

Vaughn passed the flickering orange flames burning the forward section of the shuttle. Beyond, the small encampment came into view—although calling it an *encampment* seemed an overstatement to Vaughn. The area he and Prynn had staked out around Ensign ch'Thane consisted of little more than bedrolls, blankets, and the locker that had contained the survival cache. A second locker, which had held a small, portable shelter—a thin but insulative and weatherproof material and a collapsible framework over which it fit—had broken open during the crash, its contents ripped apart.

As Vaughn approached, he saw Prynn standing over ch'Thane, a tricorder in her hand, no doubt checking his condition. The ensign lay on his back now atop one of the bedrolls, wrapped in a thin metallic blanket that confined his body heat and kept him warm. Vaughn had treated ch'Thane's fractured leg—as well as his dislocated shoulder, three bruised ribs, and numerous cuts and contusions—as best he could, but damage to one of the young Andorian's less identifiable organs demanded more medical knowledge and ability than either he or Prynn had. They had stabilized the ensign enough to move him onto the bedding, though, and his vital signs had improved somewhat. He had even shown indications of reviving, but Vaughn had decided to administer an anesthetic, to keep him both unconscious and out of pain. Ch'Thane appeared to be out of immediate danger, but Vaughn knew that he would require a doctor's attention soon.

"How is he?" he asked Prynn. She looked much better now, after Vaughn had tended to her bumps and bruises, and after she had cleaned herself up. He had been able to heal almost all of her thankfully superficial injuries, with the exception of the one to her eye. The deep red surrounding her dark iris and black pupil made the eye appear opaque and therefore blind, but her vision actually remained unaffected.

"He's the same," she said, answering him across ch'Thane's body. A gust of wind blew past, and she pulled the collar of her jacket up higher.

Vaughn peered down at the young man, whose usually bright blue skin had grown dull. "He's lucky to be alive," he said. "We're all lucky to—" Vaughn stopped as he looked up at Prynn and saw tears in her eyes. She turned away from him and moved a few paces away.

"I'm sorry," she said. She raised her arm, and Vaughn assumed she was wiping away her tears. He heard her breathe in slowly and deeply, then she dropped her arm and turned back around. "It's just that . . . we were friends," she said. "Becoming friends, anyway."

Vaughn thought that there was probably even more to it than that; just before he had arrived at Deep Space 9, the station had been attacked, and Prynn had lost coworkers and friends, one of whom she had been very close to. Now he wanted to go to his daughter and wrap his arms around her, hold her and tell her that everything would be all right. But apart from all that had come between them over the years, he understood that she needed something other than that right now. "Ensign Tenmei," he said gently, "we weren't . . . lucky . . . were we?" He emphasized the word by isolating it.

"We *were* lucky," Prynn said, pushing the tricorder closed and slipping it into a jacket pocket. "But not *just* lucky."

Vaughn nodded. He told her what he had seen—what he had *failed* to see—in the downed shuttle's wake. "How did you do it?" he asked, genuinely curious, but also wanting her to focus on her involvement in their survival.

"It's an old shuttle pilot's trick," she said, and for the first time since the crash, she seemed to perk up. "There are certain maneuvers you can make with a crippled shuttle . . . at the end, the antigravs saved us."

"Antigravs don't work at speed," Vaughn noted.

"We decelerated as we broke apart, and I used the emergency thrusters to brake us even more at the right moment," she explained. "Then I overcharged the antigravs. It's a split-second timing thing. They call it the 'Sulu Shuttle Stunt.' " Vaughn nodded, impressed. He recognized what Prynn had described so matter-of-factly as a maneuver that even the best shuttle pilots would fail to perform successfully nine times out of ten. *She really is exceptional,* he thought, and he told her so, making sure to speak as her commanding officer, and not as a proud father.

"Thank you," she said, accepting the compliment graciously. Vaughn opted not to ask her for whom the "old shuttle pilot's trick" had been named, Hikaru or Demora. He had known them both, and neither answer would have surprised him. Instead, he handed her one of the beacons.

"Here," he said. "I thought these might be useful." Prynn took the beacon, found its activation switch, and turned it on. A powerful beam of white light emerged. She shined it at the ground around her feet, and then off into the distance; even in the dim daylight, it had a considerable range.

Vaughn walked around Ensign ch'Thane. He set the other two beacons down, then grabbed a bedroll and lowered himself into a sitting position on it. "We need to discuss what we're going to do," he told Prynn. She switched the beacon off and set it down with the others.

"I've actually had some thoughts about that," she said, pulling the tricorder back out of her jacket. She opened the device and worked its controls. "I scanned the rear section of the shuttle, and it just might be possible to scrounge enough salvageable components from different systems to repair the transporter." Transporter technology, Vaughn knew from Prynn's record, had been a secondary area of concentration for her during her Starfleet service. "We obviously wouldn't be able to beam back to the ship through the clouds, and with the levels of the energy at the source of the pulse, I'm not sure how close we could get to there, but we might be able to get closer."

As a commander, Vaughn listened to Prynn's proposal with satisfaction, pleased simply in terms of her professionalism. Here was an officer actively seeking a solution to their dilemma, and though her thoughts had turned to preservation of the away team, they had also included an attempt to find a means of completing their mission. "How long would that take, and how likely is it to work?" he asked.

"I don't know," she said, studying the tricorder. "Based on the readings of the wreckage, I'd guess about a day." She looked up. "But I can't really tell how close it would be able to get us to the pulse," she admitted.

Vaughn turned his head away from her and peered off into the distance, integrating her comments into the framework he had already developed for the continuation of their mission. His eyes found the still-burning husk of *Chaffee*'s cockpit, and he watched the bounding flames as they persisted in birthing the rising black smoke. Not far from there, he saw the fire-suppression canister still lying where he had dropped it earlier.

Finally, Vaughn looked back up at Prynn. "Yes, try to get the transporter working," he told her. "If the pulse can't be stopped, we have no idea what effect it will have on the surface of the planet, but it'd probably be a good idea to get as far away from it as possible."

Prynn's brow knitted in obvious puzzlement. "You don't want to use the transporter to try to get closer to the pulse?" she asked.

"If you can make it work in time to make a difference," Vaughn said, "then yes, you should try it."

"*I* should try it?" she asked.

"Yes," he said. "In the meantime, I'm going to try to get there on foot."

"You're going to walk there?" she asked, her voice rising in surprise. "Alone?"

"Somebody needs to tend to Ensign ch'Thane," he said, glancing over at the unconscious Andorian. "And you'll also be working on the transporter."

Prynn seemed to consider this, and then she asked, "How far is it?"

"Based on the levels of the interference," he said, "I think somewhere between fifty and two hundred fifty kilometers. But it's impossible to know for sure."

Prynn let out a long, heavy breath. "Two hundred fifty kilometers in two and a half days?" she said doubtfully. "You'll never make that, even under the best conditions."

"Which is why I'm hoping that the distance is closer to fifty kilometers," he said. He chose not to address the fact that, even if he made it to the location in time, he still had no idea how—or even if—he would be able to prevent the next occurrence of the pulse; all along, they had known that they would have to learn what they could when they got there, and hope that they could improvise a solution.

Vaughn stood up and faced Prynn. "If you succeed with the transporter, and if you can beam yourself close to the pulse, then do so," he said. "Otherwise, get yourself and Ensign ch'Thane as far away as possible. Whether or not we stop the pulse, the crew will finish repairing *Sagan* in a few more days, and they'll send it down to look for us." He did not bother to add that if they could not stop the pulse they would have to survive its effects in order to be rescued, something far from sure, considering that the planet was completely devoid of animal life.

"All right," Prynn said, accepting his orders. Her features fell still, her expression unreadable.

"If I can stop the pulse, or if I can't but I somehow survive it," he said, "then I'll come back here."

"All right," she said again, still stone-faced. Vaughn wished he knew what she was thinking. He understood the familiar and troubling echo she must be hearing from seven years ago. *It doesn't matter,* he told himself. *Not now.* They each would do what was required of them in order to try to save the Vahni Vahltupali. "When will you go?" she asked.

"Now," he said. "I just need to gather some provisions."

"I'll get the rations," she said. She went over to the survival cache, opened the lid of the locker, and reached inside. Vaughn watched her for a moment, then gathered the few items he had decided to take with him on his trek: a bedroll, a beacon, one of the metallic blankets; he already carried a tricorder and a phaser. He wrapped the beacon and the blanket inside the bedroll, then affixed the lightweight bundle to his back, fastening it with bands across his shoulders. Prynn returned with a dozen thin, metallic envelopes, along with two containers of water. Vaughn deposited the rations envelopes in various pockets of his coat, and slipped the carry straps of the water containers over his shoulders.

"I'll report approximately every hour," he said. Although Vaughn's combadge had been the only one not lost in the crash, they had found several others in the survival cache, and Prynn now wore one on her jacket. "With the interference from the energy, I'm not sure how long we'll be able to communicate."

"I understand," she said simply. A silence fell that Vaughn found awkward, and he found himself at a loss for something to say. Finally, Prynn said, "Good luck."

"You too, Prynn," he said. He looked in her eyes, her injured sclera changing her appearance dramatically. He pulled out his tricorder and began scanning. He studied the readout, then turned with the tricorder held out in front of him, searching for the highest level of interference. When he found it, he started walking in that direction, leaving Prynn behind him.

For the first time in a very long time, he did not look back.

37

Dax drifted through the pools in the Caves of Mak'ala.

No, not drifted. Floated. Swam. Pushed.

Dax pushed *through the murky waters, the usually gentle, welcoming pools now impeding progress. The cool, damp air above stagnated as well, resisting any movement through it. A difficult tranquillity reigned.*

Dax sent out a message, but the blue-white veins of energy died quickly, reaching nowhere, and nobody. The pools sat strangely still, absent not only of other symbionts, Dax realized, but seemingly of existence itself. Somehow, the life-carrying waters, and perhaps even the caves, had slipped beyond the universe.

A shadow fell, gray and mysterious. Dax felt it as it stole light and heat, an unexpected eclipse. The darkness descended on the pools, and Dax dived down—pushed down—suddenly desperate to escape the clutches of the unsettling pall. But the dim mantle pushed down too, roiling the waters. A distant siren sang, a lonely echo in the churning flow of this other existence. Dax tumbled, end over end, side over side, tossed about by the pulsing movements. The memory of the motion sickness that once afflicted Ezri rose and—

Ezri.

Ezri was here, Dax knew. Ezri Tigan. The next host. Or the previous one. Dax could not remember. The current host . . . the current host . . .

There was no current host. Dax was Dax, and only Dax.

But how could that be? There had been hosts, and if they had gone, then there could only be death. Pain, and then death.

Dax reeled, mentally, emotionally, physically. The beclouded pools spun, eddies and gyres pulling Dax down deep into the gray waters. Pulling Ezri down—

Ezri was drowning.

And Dax knew. Death enveloped Ezri, surrounded her, and yet Dax would go on. But that was not the compact Dax had made. Ezri would protect the symbiont, and Dax would protect the host.

The waters grew heavy with their motion, oppressing even as they promised release. A new life, a new existence called . . . a cherished *existence . . . but none of that mattered. Only Ezri mattered.*

Dax drifted upward. Floated. Swam. Pushed.

Dax struggled, understanding that the struggle would be the life or death of both of them. Accepted that. Cherished *that.*

Ezri, *Dax cried, and fought to find her in the growing shadows.*

Ezri Dax regained consciousness in the medical bay for the second time in a week. She recognized her surroundings immediately. The quality of the light shined differently here than in the rest of the ship, both a bit brighter and a bit harsher. The diagnostic scanner mounted in the bulkhead above her beat in time with her heart. And of the voices she heard, one belonged to Julian.

This time in the medical bay, his was the first face she saw. "Can you hear me?" he asked gently, his dark, handsome features drifting into sight above her.

"Yes," she tried to say, but her tongue felt thick and slow in her mouth, and the sound she produced only approximated the word. She tried to concentrate on speaking, on coordinating the muscles of her mouth, and realized that her mind seemed thick and slow as well.

"Slowly," Julian said, and a warm feeling filled Ezri as a smile bloomed on her face.

Slow, she thought ponderously, *is all I can do.* She sensed herself floating back down into the folds of unconsciousness, and she fought to remain awake. Her eyes closed, and she forced them open again. "Yes," she pronounced deliberately. "I can hear you."

"Good," Julian said. His eyes sparkled above a thin, tight-lipped smile she had seen many times before. He was pleased, she could tell, but also worried and unsure.

"What . . . what happened?" she wanted to know, still struggling to swim up to full consciousness.

"Later," Julian told her. He reached up and laid his strong hand atop hers, the warmth of his touch almost overwhelming her. Her vision blurred, and a tear spilled from each eye, down the sides of her face.

"Julian," she said. She pushed her body to move. She turned her hand over so that she could take hold of his. He glanced down for a moment, and then she felt him squeeze. He smiled again, but fully this time, with no reservations or concerns—only with love. "What happened?" she repeated.

"You need to rest now," he told her. "We can discuss it later."

"No," Ezri said with as much vigor as she could marshal. "Tell me now, Doctor."

"I'm afraid you're off duty, *Lieutenant,*" he said, a sternness and seriousness underscoring his words. She was in the medical bay, it occurred to her, with no memory of how she had gotten here, and so of course Julian must be upset about whatever had happened. But that only strengthened her resolve to learn what had taken place.

"Julian, I *need* to know what happened," she said, imploring him to talk to her.

He breathed in and out deeply through his nose, his nostrils flaring. "You've been in a coma for several hours," he finally told her. "I was barely able to keep you alive." He glanced up and over her head, probably at the diagnostic panel. When he looked back down, he said, "Frankly, I'm not even sure how I was able to bring you out of the coma."

"You didn't," she said without thinking. She lifted herself up off the bed, sliding her elbows back underneath her and propping herself up. Her head spun.

"Easy, easy," Julian entreated. He put a hand to her shoulder and tried to restrain her, and then to ease her back down. She resisted. "Lieutenant Dax,"

Julian said in his strong physician's voice, "you need to rest. Your body has been through an enormous trauma."

Ezri relented, allowing herself to be lowered back down onto the bed. "What happened?" she asked again, driven to talk about what she had been through. "I remember heading to a Jefferies tube . . . one of the engineers found something . . ."

"Later," Julian told her. "I want you to rest right now."

Ezri struggled up again onto her elbows. "Dr. Bashir," she said, injecting a tone of command into her voice, "there are four billion Vahni lives at risk right now. I don't have time to rest."

"Look," Julian said. "You're not going to be able to help anybody if you attempt to do too much too soon and simply end up collapsing." He stared directly into her eyes as he spoke, his expression hardened. She lowered herself back down onto the bed.

"I'll lie back down," she said, "and I'll rest. But first you have to tell me what happened. It's important that I know."

At last, Julian relented. "Ensign Leishman found an amorphous gray substance in one of the Jefferies tubes—"

"Yes," Ezri said, the recollection springing forth from somewhere in her clouded mind. "The substance. We were trying to transport it." She remembered that Nog had been with her in the tube.

"That's right," Julian said. "According to Nog, it somehow moved when we attempted transport. He said he didn't actually see it move, but that suddenly, it was elsewhere on the deck, and your hand was touching it. You collapsed immediately."

"Julian," she said, reaching up and grasping the sides of his shoulders. "The substance is alive."

"All right," he said, taking her hands in his own and lowering them back to her sides. "But you have to rest now." He looked back over his shoulder. "Nurse Juarez," he said, "would you prepare a hypo?"

"You have to listen to me," she said when he peered back down at her. She saw how tired he looked, saw the tension in his features, and she understood how hard this must have been on him. "I'll rest," she told him, "but first you have to listen to me. And tell Lieutenant Bowers." She heard footsteps, and then saw Juarez above her as he stepped up to the bed. He held a hypospray in his hands, she saw; Julian reached across Ezri's body, and Juarez handed it to him.

"All right," Julian said. "Tell me."

"The substance is alive," she said again. "I sensed it while I seemed to be unconscious."

"'Seemed to be'?" Julian asked with evident skepticism.

"I didn't fall into a coma," she forged ahead. "Or maybe part of me did, but I was . . . I was . . . it's an enormously powerful mind. And very alien. And I think it knows about the pulse."

Julian looked over at Juarez. The two men seemed to share a moment of nonverbal communication, and then they looked back down at her. "All right," Julian said. "I'll inform Lieutenant Bowers." He held the hypospray up in both hands and checked the setting. Ezri could see that he did not believe what she had told him. She had been in a coma, and whatever she told him she had experienced, he would ascribe to dreaming, or whatever you called the state your mind entered in such circumstances.

And maybe he's right, she admitted to herself. But she did not think so. And despite Julian's arrogance—born of his superior knowledge and abilities—she knew that he would pass on what she told him to Lieutenant Bowers.

Julian lowered his hands, preparing to administer the hypospray. "Wait," Ezri said. "I have to tell you one more thing." Julian withdrew the hypo. "The being . . . I think it took me to another universe." This time, the expression on Julian's face reflected not skepticism, but curiosity. It was almost as though she had furnished him an important piece of a puzzle.

"I'll inform Lieutenant Bowers of everything you've said," he told her. "But now it's time for you to rest." He reached forward again, and Ezri felt the slight pressure of the hypo against the side of her neck, its tip slightly cool.

She was very tired. She had used so much energy coming back here, she thought, and the sense of that suddenly became clear in her mind. She recalled a struggle against gray clouds, and the recollection came to her not like a memory, but like a dream of a memory, the way the lives of Dax's past hosts often came to her.

Ezri heard the brief whisper of the hypospray close by her ear. It occurred to her that Dax had heard or felt similar sounds—quiet, short, sibilant—so often back in the Caves of Mak'ala. And thinking of the symbiont's time in the pools back on Trill, she slid beneath the waves of sleep.

The next time Ezri opened her eyes, she woke naturally from sleep, rather than regaining consciousness. She still felt tired, but she also felt much better. Her mind had cleared, and her thoughts came easily now. She reached her arms out to each side and stretched, yawning heavily and, at the end, loudly.

"Well, hello," she heard Julian say from across the medical bay. She lifted her head and peered across the room. Julian handed something to Nurse Richter—Juarez appeared to have left—and then started toward her. His demeanor—the sound of his voice, the expression on his face, the ease of his gait—seemed light-years away from where it had been earlier. From his manner, she supposed that her condition had improved markedly. "How are you feeling?" Julian asked as he arrived beside her bed.

"I must be feeling much better for you to be smiling like that," Ezri joked. She offered a smile of her own, then shifted on the bed and sat up, swinging her legs over the side.

"Well, as a matter of fact, yes, you are," he agreed. He peeked up at the diagnostic panel. "All of your vital signs have returned more or less to normal, and—" He reached up and tapped at a control, which beeped twice in response. "—your isoboramine levels have increased significantly."

Ezri looked up at Julian, her smile vanishing instantly. "My isoboramine levels were low?" she asked. Isoboramine, she knew, was a neurotransmitter chemical essential for a joined Trill; it functioned as a medium for the transfer of synaptic processes between host and symbiont. If the amount of the chemical dropped below a certain level, the symbiont would have to be removed in order to keep it alive; in such a case, the host would die.

"Yes, they were," Julian said apologetically. "I'm sorry. I didn't mean to spring the information on you like that."

"I know," she said, reaching over and squeezing his hand as a sign of reassurance. "But tell me what happened."

"Actually, I'm not entirely certain," he said. "But I used the standard benzocyatizine treatment. It didn't work initially, but once your vital signs stabilized, it took hold."

"And all of this," Ezri asked, attempting to make sense of what had happened to her, "because I touched the creature we found in the Jefferies tube?"

"Well, I'd still hesitate to say that the substance is alive," Julian said, "but your contact with whatever it is seems to have been what injured you."

"If it's not alive, then what is it?" she asked. "And whether it's alive or not, how did it do what it did to me?" She brought her hands down on the bed on either side of her body and pushed herself off, hopping onto her feet. She held on to the bed for a moment, making sure that she could stand after what she had been through, and after having been on her back for hours. Julian took hold of her upper arm, steadying her.

"Are you all right?" he asked.

"Yes," she said, lightly brushing away his hand. "I'm okay." She walked unhurriedly across the medical bay. Ensign Richter turned from a console on the other side of the room, saw Ezri's slow progress, and started to rise out of her chair. Ezri waved her away, and the ensign hesitated, then returned to her seat. "What is it?" Ezri asked, turning to Julian and repeating her question about the substance.

"We don't know yet," Julian said, following her across the room. He passed her and went to the console where Ensign Richter sat, picking up a tricorder there. "But we did learn some things about it, thanks to you." He walked back over to her.

"Thanks to me?" she asked.

"Yes. Let me show you." Julian motioned to a companel in one wall, and the two of them strode over to it. He opened and worked the tricorder, then keyed a sequence of touchpads on the companel. On the larger display, an image appeared of the section of the Jefferies tube in which they had found they substance. The gray pool sat draped from the location Ezri had last seen it and out across the floor of the tube. Oddly, the seemingly liquid material did not drop through the metal grating.

"This is the substance as it appears right now," Julian said. He touched a control and a white line traced the edges of the free-form shape. "After you mentioned being in another universe, I thought about the incomplete sensor readings we've been getting, and it occurred to me that perhaps the substance exists in more than what we consider 'normal' space." He touched another control, and a second, red line appeared, drawing an amorphous shape that abutted the first.

"This is a part of the substance in another universe?" Ezri asked, pointing at the area on the display bounded by the red.

"Not in another universe, no," Julian said. "But in another stratum of our own. This portion of the object—" He indicated the same area Ezri had. "—exists in subspace. We've found other parts of the substance in other areas of space, which explains why we've had such trouble taking meaningful scans of it. It might also tell us similar things about the energy pulse."

"You think they're related?" Ezri asked.

"Well, we had the same sorts of difficulties taking sensor readings of the energy pulse and the energy in the planet's cloud cover," Julian said, "so it may be that the energy also extends into other domains within our universe. The engineering and sciences teams are now taking that into account as they try to find a means of stopping the next pulse."

Ezri nodded slowly, and thought, *What does this all mean?* "I have another question," she said, attempting to piece together all of the strange facts. "If my isoboramine levels were affected, then that means that the link between Ezri and Dax was compromised. Is it possible that happened because another connection was established, one between the symbiont and the substance?"

Julian wrinkled his brow. "That would presuppose that the substance is alive," he said, "and we really have no significant evidence of that."

"We have my experiences," she said. "I—that is, Dax—sensed a consciousness in another universe."

"Or maybe you or the symbiont dreamed that," Julian suggested.

"Maybe," Ezri said, and she had to allow for that possibility. "But I didn't dream the reduction in my isoboramine levels. Maybe that allowed Dax to communicate with, or at least sense, this other mind."

"It's possible, I suppose," Julian said. "But I'm not sure how we could ever prove that, or make use of it."

Ezri paced away from the companel and across the room, back over to the bed in which she had awoken. Something she felt she needed to know dwelled just beyond the horizon of her memory. *Maybe because it's not your memory,* she thought. She raised a fist and tapped her forehead, as though she could physically dislodge the missing recollection from its hiding place. Ezri wondered if Trill initiate training would have helped her integrate not just the memories of Dax's former hosts, but also those exclusively of Dax—because that seemed to be what she required here: access to the recall of the symbiont. Something important had happened when she had been in that coma, something Dax knew. Since being joined, she had experienced many confusing thoughts and emotions, but she had never felt like this, isolated from what had become the other half of her mind and heart.

Ezri touched her fist to her forehead and held it there. She closed her eyes, and at once, a gray wave seemed to wash over her. The soothing waters of the Caves of Mak'ala, she thought at first, but then another interpretation came to her: the dim, energy-filled clouds surrounding the planet below, and the substance spilling across the surfaces in the Jefferies tube. And finally, she had what she was looking for.

She turned around and faced Julian across the room. "I have an idea," she told him.

38

Quark strode out of the turbolift and onto the Promenade, his mood as dark as a Jem'Hadar's hearts. He listened and could tell immediately, even before he reached the bar, that his fortunes had not improved much. If the proverbial wise man could hear profit in the wind, Quark wondered what sort of a man that made him. *Besides poor,* he thought. As he walked toward the bar, his ears told him the approximate number of customers there—too few—and the number of those playing at the dabo table—several more than at any time during the past couple of weeks, but still not enough.

I should have stayed in my quarters, he thought. Except that even an afternoon spent foraging through the quadrant's financial and commodities exchanges had not held any fascination for him. It vexed Quark to see his idiot brother's so-called reforms being implemented on Ferenginar, crippling so many of the markets. But even Quark's anger at Rom could not keep his mind occupied for very long.

Quark only glanced at the floor as he slipped behind the bar; the last thing he needed to see right now was just how close his employees came to outnumbering his customers. He looked at the mess Frool and Grimp had managed to leave—remarkable, really, considering the dearth of business—and grabbed a rag. He began to swab the surface of the bar, wanting to occupy himself. But as he concentrated on the simple task, with his eyes cast down, his ears still remained open. And he did not hear her.

Again.

Quark had neither heard nor seen Ro Laren since she had chased the Jem'Hadar soldier from the bar two nights ago. She had talked about coming back later that night, but not only had she not returned since then, she had also been conspicuously absent from the Promenade. Quark had not even seen her in her office.

Females and finances don't mix, he reminded himself. He never seemed to remember that when he needed to. And he had been fool enough to believe that she had actually begun returning his flirtations.

Quark grumbled, lifting a V-shaped glass half-filled with a light-green liquid. He wiped the condensation from its base and from the place it had rested, then set it back down. The Boslic woman sitting on the other side of the bar, whose drink this seemed to be, was not even paying attention. She sat turned away, peering in the direction of the dabo table. Quark thought about suggesting to her that she go play, but then a voice reached his ears.

"Pass five, pass five," the voice said. "Sorry, no winners this time." Quark had no problem with the outcome—it was about time that the dabo wheel began spinning again according to the advantages of the house—but the voice should have belonged to Treir. It did not; it belonged to a man.

Quark shifted to his left and looked past the Boslic woman. Around the dabo table sat a couple of men and a half-dozen women. Treir, who should have been operating the game, was nowhere in sight. Instead, the young, scantily dressed Bajoran man she had brought in earlier today stood in her place. As Quark watched, the man—Hetik, was it?—held the rondure up before the gamblers, his hand dancing dramatically through the air, and then, with a flourish, he placed it in the wheel and sent it spinning around.

The edges of Quark's lobes warmed as anger rose within him. Not only had Treir—an *employee*—had the audacity to hire somebody, and not only had she concocted the position of dabo *boy,* but he had ordered her to get rid of Hetik by the time he returned to the bar. And yet there the man stood, with Quark's latinum spread out on the table before him.

Quark flung the rag down behind the bar, furious. He would fire Hetik, and then, when he found Treir, he would dispatch her as well. Sensuous or not, green or not, Treir had overstepped her bounds more than once, and by more than just a bit. Quark had had enough. He turned—

—and almost ran into Treir. Quark pulled up quickly, surprised not only to see her there, but that she had approached without him hearing her. *Am I that distracted,* he asked himself, *or is she that good?* He thought his ears had been open, but now he realized that he had only been listening for the sound of Laren's voice. As he looked up at Treir, though, he knew that none of that mattered at the moment; what mattered was him regaining control of his bar.

"I told you to get rid of him," Quark said without preamble, pointing over at Hetik. He spoke loudly, not caring who heard him. This was his business, and he would—

"I have a proposition for you," Treir said, interrupting his thoughts. She spoke in soft tones, but her eyes stared down hard at him. Her manner seemed to imply that there would be no subterfuge here, no use of wiles—feminine or otherwise—only business dealings.

"Why would you want to get rid of *him?*" somebody asked to Quark's right. He looked in that direction and saw that the Boslic woman had turned in her seat toward the bar. The triangular slope of her forehead, and her dark hair and eyes, reminded him of Rionoj, a freighter captain with whom he occasionally dealt. This woman was shorter and heavier than Rionoj, though, and clearly did not have the sense to tend to her own business; she had evidently heard Quark and seen him gesture toward Hetik. "He's beautiful," she said. "In fact, I may go play a little dabo myself."

Quark resisted the impulse to tell the woman to go. Instead, he simply smiled and nodded. Then he turned back to Treir, who had not moved a millimeter. "A proposition?" Quark said, sidling away from the bar and over toward the shelves behind it, putting a little distance between himself and the Boslic woman. Treir glided over with him.

"Yes, a proposition," she said. "Let Hetik work here for a week before you make a decision about whether to keep him on or not. If you decide to let him go at that point, then I'll pay his wages."

Quark felt the ridge of his brow rise, surprised at Treir's promise of actual latinum. She obviously wanted very much for Hetik to work here. Quark did not know why—although considering the amount of clothing these two wore in public, he thought he could guess easily enough—but he did see an opportunity for a small profit. "What sort of wages did you agree to pay him?" he asked. Treir told him, and actually, the amount was fairly low, only a fraction of what Quark currently paid her. "I'll tell you what," Quark said. "I'll keep him on for a week, and then I'll pay him. But if I decide to fire him, I won't pay *you* for the week."

Treir said, "No, that's not fair," but her shoulders slumped, and Quark knew that he would get what he had demanded. He took a step past Treir, heading toward Hetik, but she stopped him. "All right," she said.

Quark gazed up at her curiously. "Why are you doing this?" he asked.

"If I tell you," Treir said, shaking her head, "you won't believe me."

"Tell me anyway."

"Because I think it's good business," she said. "I mean, look." She nodded her head in the direction of the dabo table, and Quark looked over there. "I know it's only eight people," she went on, "but he's only been here a few hours, and that's the most people we've had playing dabo in weeks."

Quark shrugged and looked back at her. "Coincidence," he said. "And even if it's not, him drawing one or two more dabo players a night is not going to justify keeping him on the payroll."

Treir suddenly smiled broadly, which unnerved Quark. "Oh, he'll do better than that," she said. "And the two of us together will do *much* better than that." Quark wondered if Treir and Hetik might be planning something other than simply trying to draw more dabo players into the bar. He doubted it, but he also resolved to keep his ears open.

"Well, why don't you two drum up some business right now," he offered sarcastically. "We could use it."

"Sure," Treir said, nodding.

"Oh, and I'll draw up a contract for our little agreement," he told her.

"I'm sure you will," Treir said, and she headed for the dabo table.

Quark watched her go, confident that he had just made himself some easy latinum, Still, it brought him little joy. He peered down at the floor, then bent and retrieved the rag he had thrown down. He tossed it on the recycle shelf, beside a couple of short glasses and a tall, slender blue bottle. Then he found an unused rag beneath the bar and resumed his cleaning.

"Hey, Mr. Quark, long time no see." Vic Fontaine had finished singing for the night, and as the lights came up in the nightclub, he descended the steps at the right-hand side of the stage. Quark sat alone at a table in the space between there and the bar, one elbow up, the side of his face resting on his closed hand. "So what's doin'?" Vic asked as he passed by, no doubt headed to get a drink. Quark might not have visited this holosuite program in a while, but he had spent enough time in it to know that the singer liked to imbibe after his last set.

"You don't want to know," Quark intoned, answering—and not answering—

Vic's question. He watched as the musicians on the stage packed up their instruments. One of the men seemed to be having some difficulties getting his curved, gold-colored horn into its black case.

"Oh no?" Vic said. Quark glanced over and saw him perched on the edge of a stool, a quick nod of his head getting the attention of an older, gray-haired man tending bar. "Vodka and tonic, rocks," Vic ordered. Then, looking over at Quark, he asked, "Somethin' to drink?"

Quark shrugged. He was about to say no, but then decided otherwise. "I'll just have a snail juice," he said.

"Snail juice, right," Vic said, shaking his head as he motioned again to the bartender. Quark peered back at the stage and saw that the horn player had managed to wrestle his instrument into its case. All packed up, the musicians started to leave, most going backstage, but a couple descending onto the floor and heading out the front entrance. A moment later, Vic stepped up to the table and set a short, frosted glass down in front of Quark. "So, you mind?" he asked, gesturing to the chair on the other side of the table.

"Sure, why not?" Quark said. Vic put his own drink down with a thud softened by the white tablecloth. Then he sat himself down.

"So, I don't wanna know what's doin' with you?" he asked. "Or you don't wanna tell me?"

"Believe me," Quark said, "it's not very interesting, and it doesn't have a happy ending." He lifted his face from atop his hand, then dropped his arm onto the table and wrapped his fingers around his drink. The glass felt cooler than he usually liked his snail juice, but then, why should he ever expect to get what he wanted?

"Hey, you don't wanna sing, that's fine with me," Vic said. "I been doin' it all night."

"I heard. Well, at least the last few songs," Quark said. He had come up to the holosuite after he had closed the bar. He had been surprised to see so few holographic patrons in the club. *My business is so bad,* Quark had mused, *it extends all the way to Las Vegas in 1962.* Now, to Vic, he said, "You sounded good." Quark actually enjoyed the *hew-mon* music that Vic sang, though it really did not sound very *hew-mon;* the music seemed too . . . sophisticated to be of Earth origin. In fact, Quark would not have been surprised if he found out that *hew-mons* had appropriated the style from some other people on some other world that they had assimilated into the Federation. They were worse than the Borg.

"Thanks for sayin' so," Vic said. "With ears like those—" He pointed his chin in the direction of Quark's lobes "—that means a lot."

"Don't mention it." Quark picked up his drink and absently moved it around in a tight circle, swirling the snail juice around. He heard the shells ticking along the sides of the glass.

Vic lifted his own glass and took a healthy swallow. "So," he said, lowering the drink back to the table, "how's business?"

In an annoyed monotone, Quark said, "Don't mention that either." He plunked his glass down and slumped in his chair.

"Uh-oh. Trouble at the till?"

"Trouble everywhere," Quark lamented, and he complained about Treir.

"Treir," Vic mused. "She's the green one?"

"Yes," Quark said. "How did you know?" He was certain the Orion woman had never used this holoprogram.

"It's amazin' what you can learn cooped up in a memory buffer," Vic explained. "I'll tell you what, though. You twenty-fourth-century types are more colorful than the strip at night. It's fabulous."

"Yeah, well, I don't care what color she is," Quark moaned, "she's been causing me grief." He told Vic about what she had done today, and about how she continued to behave like his business partner rather than his employee.

"Hmmm. Seems to me that if a farmer puts a fox in charge of guardin' the henhouse," Vic said, "and then the fox eats the hens, well, it ain't the fox's fault."

It took a moment for Quark to decipher Vic's words. "You're saying it's my fault?" he asked.

"Hey, pallie, I don't know, I'm not there," Vic said. "I'm just sayin'."

"Well, stop saying," Quark told him. "Besides, I've got a lot more problems than just Treir. Things haven't been the same since the war, I've got monsters chasing away the few customers I do have, and romance is dead."

"Hey, I know somethin' about the effects of war, and all you can do is ride it out," Vic said. "Now, I don't know from monsters, but I can tell you that not only isn't romance dead, it ain't even sick."

"Maybe not in Las Vegas," Quark muttered. He lifted his glass again.

"Not in Vegas, and not on that floatin' bicycle wheel of yours. Not anywhere, at any time," Vic maintained. "Look, if a lonely, little-lobed lightbulb like me can get the girls, what does that say about a big-eared, smartly dressed guy like you?"

"These lobes aren't what they used to be," Quark said. He raised his glass and took a swig—and gagged, and then spit the mouthful of whatever it was out in a spray, just missing Vic. Quark managed to get the glass back onto the table, half its contents spilling out. Around his coughs, he managed to say, "That's . . . not . . . snail juice."

"Mr. Quark," Vic said, leaning one arm onto the table, "this is 1962. If there's somebody somewhere on Earth drinkin' liquefied snails, I don't know about it, and I don't wanna know about it."

"What is that?" Quark asked, wiping his mouth. The vile drink had combined an unbearable iciness with some harsh and unidentifiable taste.

Vic held up his glass. "Same as I'm drinkin'," he said. "Vodka and tonic."

"It's awful," Quark said, wiping his mouth with the flat of his hand. "The next time—"

The comm signal sounded, two short, low tones. *Incoming message for Quark,* the computer announced. Quark had set up the holosuite comm system tonight so that nobody could get directly through to him. He had thought that Treir might want to talk, might want to try to get him to change his mind about their agreement. But he had decided that he did not wish to be disturbed.

"Whoever it is, tell them I'm busy," Quark said. But then it occurred to him that maybe Ro was trying to contact him, and as unlikely as that seemed, he could not help finding out. "Wait," he told the computer. "Who is it?"

"The message is from Lieutenant Ro," the computer responded.

Quark felt his heart begin thudding wildly in his chest. His lobes tingled. "Computer, put the message through," he said, sitting up in his chair.

Laren's voice rang through the comm system. *"Lieutenant Ro to Quark,"* she said simply.

"This is Quark." He looked over at Vic, but the hologram was gazing off toward the bar.

"Quark, I'm sorry to bother you while you're in the holosuite," she said. *"I stopped by the bar, but you'd already closed up."* She paused, and then said, *"I hope I'm not interrupting anything."*

"Not at all," Quark said. "What can I do for you?"

"Well, I just got off duty—" That surprised Quark; it was late. *"—and I don't really feel like going to sleep, so . . . I guess I was just looking for some company."*

Quark could not believe it. He felt his mouth drop open, and he quickly closed it, folding his lips around his teeth. "Uh, all right," he said. "Where are you?"

"In my office."

"All right," he told her. "I'll be there in five minutes." That would give him enough time to stop in the bar and put on some cologne.

"Great," she said. *"Ro out."* The com channel closed.

Quark peered over at Vic again, who still pretended that his attention was elsewhere. "Well," Quark said, standing up, "nice talking to you."

Vic looked over at him. "Always a pleasure," he said. Quark headed for the door. Behind him, he heard Vic say, "I guess romance isn't dead on the ol' wheel after all." Quark did not bother to stop or look back. But he did smile.

Quark strolled with Ro in the dim, nighttime illumination of Deep Space 9. They walked through one of the crossover bridges and headed from the docking ring toward the habitat ring. It had been more than two hours since he had met Ro in her office, and they had been meandering about the station and talking ever since. They had both admitted to being tired and to having had a difficult couple of days—Quark had actually claimed more than merely a couple—but their time together had been comfortable and filled with laughter. Quark realized that their senses of humor—rooted in their similarly sarcastic sensibilities—meshed well.

"So then what happened?" Ro asked, carrying on their conversation.

"Well, then I signed aboard a freighter—" he began.

"Wait a minute," Ro said. "What about the apprenticeship with the district subnagus?"

"I decided to leave that," Quark said.

"All right," Ro said, stopping in the corridor and turning toward him. Quark stopped as well. As he faced her, he saw the arc of the docking ring through the windows, the stars shining brightly beyond the station. Ro playfully jabbed a finger in his direction, and said, "You're not telling me everything."

With a raffish tilt of his head and a lowering of his voice, Quark said, "What are you going to do, Security Chief? Interrogate me?"

Ro opened her mouth in a smile. "You'd like that, wouldn't you?"

Quark smiled back at her. "I believe I would," he said.

Ro shook her head and rolled her eyes, then started walking again. Quark followed along, catching up to her in a couple of steps. Just up ahead, he saw, stood the closed set of doors that separated the crossover bridge from the habitat ring. "So," Ro said, "are you going to tell me why you left the apprenticeship?"

"Ah ... the subnagus requested that I leave," Quark told her.

" 'Requested'?" she asked skeptically.

"Well, he suggested . . . he told me to leave," Quark offered. "Ordered me, really."

"Ordered, huh?" Ro asked, pronouncing her words slowly and melodramatically. Quark got the sense that she suspected what he was going to say, or at least the type of thing that he was going to say, and that she now played up her end of the dialogue for effect. "And why would the subnagus order you out of your apprenticeship if he regarded you so highly?"

"I was . . . well, I was also highly regarded by his sister," Quark admitted, pretending to be abashed.

They arrived at the doors to the habitat ring, which opened before them. They stepped through, and Ro stopped again. "Quark, you *rake,*" she said, a wide smile on her face. She reached out and pushed at the front of his shoulder with the tips of her fingers.

"Now, can I help it if females find me attractive?" he said.

"No, I guess you can't." They stood there for a moment, and then Quark held his hands out, one in each direction. "Which way do we go now?" he asked.

Ro looked both ways down the corridor, then moved up to a companel set into the bulkhead opposite the doors. She touched the panel, and said, "Computer, what time is it?"

"The time is zero-three-fifty-three hours."

Ro's eyes widened. "Is that right?" she asked Quark.

"I think so," he told her. "We've been walking for quite a while."

"I really need to get some sleep," she said. "It's been a long couple of days, and the next few aren't going to be any shorter or easier."

"Aren't you down this way?" Quark asked, pointing his thumb back over his shoulder.

"Yes," she said, "and I won't even ask how or why you know that."

"Are you kidding?" Quark said as they headed in that direction. "A new chief of security is appointed to the station, and I'm not going to know where they live? Please."

Ro chuckled. "What was I thinking?" she said.

When they reached her quarters a few minutes later, Ro opened the door and stepped inside. Quark discreetly remained in the corridor. "Thank you for the company," Ro said.

"Thank you," Quark said. "I enjoyed it."

"I did too."

There was a brief pause as they stood there, and the notion of moving forward and kissing Ro shot through Quark's mind at warp speed. Instead, he simply said, "Good night, Laren."

"Good night," she said, and then, before he could turn away, "May I ask you a question, Quark?"

"The answer is *yes,*" he said at once. Her lips formed into a smile again, as lovely a sight as Quark thought he had ever seen.

"You haven't even heard the question yet," she said.

"I trust you," he told her.

"Well, don't," she said. "You may not like this question."

Quark did not like the sound of that statement. "Go ahead," he said anyway.

"Do you think . . . do you think that women like the cologne you're wearing?"

Quark felt immediately embarrassed. "Not anymore," he said.

Ro must have sensed his humiliation, because she said, "I'm sorry. I didn't mean to hurt your feelings. I mean, you obviously like it, and I'm sure that Ferengi women must like it too."

"It's very popular on Ferenginar," Quark confirmed.

"I'm sorry," Ro went on. "It's just . . . I thought you'd want to know."

Quark was astounded. Why would he want to know that he smelled bad to a female he liked? Except that, if she had not told him, he realized, then he would have continued to smell bad to her. This way—

"It's all right," he told her, and meant it. By telling him that she did not like his cologne, she had actually shown him both respect and trust. "I appreciate you saying something to me. The last thing I want to do is repel you."

"Oh, well, even without the cologne," she said, her voice thick with sarcasm, "you still repel me."

Quark nodded. "You repel me too."

"Good night, Quark."

"Good night, Laren."

On the way back to his own quarters, Quark twice jumped up and clicked his heels.

39

Vaughn had walked for hours. Night had fallen now, and it had fallen hard. With no moons to reflect sunlight through the clouds, and the remote light of the stars unable to penetrate the atmospheric cover, darkness reigned. Vaughn hiked now toward his destination holding the beacon out before him, illuminating the ground a few meters ahead. He imagined peering down on himself from a height, a solitary mote in the empty ebon setting. So completely had the day vanished around him that Vaughn felt utterly alone, adrift on a virtually invisible sea, with the shore nothing more than a distant, impossible memory.

I am alone, he thought. As far as he knew, there were only two other people on this entire planet, and he had walked away from them. *A modern-day Michael Collins,* he romanticized. Four centuries ago, as humanity had first set foot on another world, Michael Collins had become the loneliest human being in history. He and two other astronauts, Neil Armstrong and Buzz Aldrin, had journeyed from the Earth to the moon in a two-vehicle tandem spacecraft, one of which had then descended to the lunar surface. Collins had remained in the orbiter, and when it had circled around the far side of the moon, he had been cut off from all communication. By himself aboard *Columbia,* he had been farther from Earth than any single human had ever been, and totally unable to contact anybody, anywhere. The sense of isolation, Vaughn had always thought, must have been profound.

" 'Here men from the planet Earth,' " he quoted aloud, " 'first set foot upon the moon.' " His words fled into the night, the sound of his voice small and insignificant in the vast, unseen emptiness about him. Vaughn recalled his first trip to the Sea of Tranquillity, and to the preserved remnants of man's first steps out into the cosmos—the base of *Eagle,* the landing craft; the camera that had transmitted images of the event back to the people of Earth; the flag of the old nation-state that had sent the astronauts. Vaughn's life had already changed by that time—he had been pulled away from his childhood dreams of exploration and into the world of special ops—but he had still been overcome by a sense of awe during that visit to the landing site.

Now he remembered the last sentence on the plaque that those early space travelers had left behind: *"We came in peace for all mankind."* For Vaughn, those words epitomized the spirit of discovery. They reflected his aspirations to explore the universe with amity for all, to gather and share whatever wondrous new knowledge he could. This mission to travel the Gamma Quadrant had been intended to serve those purposes, but it had instead transformed into a rescue mission, at least for now. *We came in desperation to save mankind,* he thought. *To save the Vahni.*

As Vaughn strode through the darkness, he felt the ground begin to ascend beneath him. For the last couple of hours, the gentle swells of grass-covered hills had risen and fallen in his path, reducing his pace, and worse, causing him to exert himself more. His legs and feet still felt good—the grass actually cushioned his footsteps somewhat—but a dull ache had developed at the top of his right leg, near his hip. The pain was mild, but what had at first been an occasional twinge now occurred with every step.

Vaughn stopped, tucked the beacon beneath his left arm, and pulled out his tricorder. He scanned along his right side and saw that he had strained his hip flexor. Nothing could be done about it, though, since he had left the medical supplies back with Prynn and ch'Thane. He would simply have to live with the pain.

Vaughn swung around and performed a sensor sweep back along his path. He searched for the downed shuttle and the life signs of Prynn and ch'Thane. He found nothing and tried again. As he had drawn closer to the source of the pulse, interference from the energy there had increasingly affected both sensors and communications. On his third attempt, he picked up the shuttle, and shortly after that, human and Andorian biological signatures. Vaughn had traveled more than fifty kilometers from there, he saw.

That seems right, Vaughn thought, considering how long he had been walking, and that he had been able to maintain a steady pace, at least until encountering the hills. He had rested for ten minutes every two hours, unfurling the bedroll and lying atop it in order to rest his body as completely as possible in that short interval. He had also eaten the contents of two of the rations packets, and sipped periodically at the containers of water. As the day had departed, the temperature had fallen, down into single digits, which at least had the benefit of lessening his need for water. Fortunately, cool as it had become, his old coat and his almost constant movement had kept him warm.

Fifty kilometers, Vaughn thought. That meant that the facility surrounding the place from which the pulse emanated could be anywhere from just beyond the next hill to two hundred more kilometers away. He turned back in the direction of his destination and scanned ahead. Energy again interfered with his readings, but then they cleared and revealed something just a few kilometers away. Sensors revealed buildings, machinery, thoroughfares—and no energy readings. What lay ahead was not the source of the pulse, but a city. A *dead* city; as with all those they had flown over in the shuttle, this one showed no indications of extant life.

Vaughn took the beacon in his hand again and began forward. As he climbed the hill in his path, he checked the time on the tricorder and saw that it had been fifty-seven minutes since he had last spoken with Prynn. During his march across the planet, he had contacted her once an hour, allowing them to update each other on their progress; while Vaughn had tried to reach the source of the pulse, Prynn had begun her attempts to configure a working transporter from the wreckage of *Chaffee.*

Vaughn thumbed off the signal that would sound on the hour, then closed the tricorder and returned it to a coat pocket. He reached up and slapped at his combadge, the electronic tones of its activation sounding hollow and slight in the open air. "Vaughn to Tenmei," he said. Seconds passed with no response.

"Vaughn to Tenmei," he said again. He waited longer this time, and was about to speak again when he finally heard Prynn's voice.

"This . . . Tenmei . . . can . . . me?" Bursts of static split her words apart. *"Repeat . . . Tenmei . . . hear me?"*

Vaughn stopped in his tracks and turned back in the direction of the crashed shuttle. "I can hear you, but just barely," he said, raising his voice. "I'm obviously too far from you now, too close to the pulse site. Are you all right?"

". . . fine . . . Shar's vitals are improv . . ." came Prynn's response, again punctuated by the white noise of the energy's interference. *". . . some success . . . porter . . . ther day . . ."* Vaughn waited to hear more, not wanting to miss anything she said by talking while she might still be transmitting. When he heard nothing more, he went on himself.

"I've covered more than fifty kilometers so far," he said. "I don't know how far I am from the pulse, but there's a city a short distance up ahead. I'll probably walk for another hour or so now, then stop and sleep for about six hours before continuing." In truth, Vaughn would have preferred to keep going until he collapsed, but he knew he would be more likely to reach the site of the pulse in time if he did not completely exhaust himself. He waited once more for a response, but none came. He tapped his combadge again. "Vaughn to Tenmei," he said. "Vaughn to Tenmei."

Nothing.

Vaughn turned and continued on his way. When he reached the top of the hill, he tried one final time to reach Prynn. But past the chirp of his combadge and the sound of his voice, he heard nothing but the insubstantial background whine of the clouds.

Somehow, it felt as though he had lost his daughter again.

40

Kira stood in her bedroom and slipped into the jacket of her dress uniform. She fastened it closed, then tugged at its hem, straightening it and trying to get it to sit comfortably on her body. She glanced briefly in the mirror, but she did not see her reflection; all she could see, all she could think about, were the locusts.

They had come in her dreams, billions of insects sweeping en masse across Bajor. They darkened the skies and eclipsed the sun, sending her world into an eerie darkness. Kira remembered running through a city—Ashalla, she thought—dashing down the pedestrian thoroughfares and yelling to people, warning them of the descending swarm.

She had woken up hours ago, sweating, the bedclothes torn from the mattress. She had been unable to fall back to sleep, instead replaying the fragmentary dream—the *nightmare*—over and over in her mind. Even now, as she prepared for the day, prepared to meet the officials as they arrived at the station, she could not let it go. The sinister images still haunted her.

Kira left her bedroom and walked into the living area of her quarters. She headed for the door, intending to go to her office for a few hours before the delegates began arriving. A feeling stopped her in the middle of the room, though, and she turned, her gaze coming to rest on a photograph she kept on a side table. Captain Sisko—Benjamin Sisko, the Emissary—peered out from within the frame, his sleek, handsome aspect a source of strength for her even today, more than half a year after she had last seen him.

Except that today, the likeness of Benjamin Sisko also reminded Kira of when Bajor had been on the verge of entering the Federation three years ago. After the Emissary had experienced a *pagh'tem'far*—a sacred vision—he had urged the Bajorans not to join at that time, and they had heeded the advice of their religious icon. And the Emissary's *pagh'tem'far*, Kira knew, had been one of locusts.

Kira breathed in and out quickly, her mind racing. She had no illusions that she had experienced any sort of a vision during the night, but she wanted to understand what her subconscious had been attempting to communicate to her. She need not be touched directly by the Prophets in order to trust her instincts. Her dream might not presage Bajor's future, but it surely indicated what Kira *thought* might happen, and how she felt about those possibilities.

Feeling a bit light-headed, Kira raised her arms to her waist and locked her hands together. She closed her eyes, then slowed and deepened her breathing, concentrating on one of her many meditation rituals. By degrees, a sensation of calmness spilled over her.

Kira opened her eyes and looked over again at the photograph of the Emissary, drawing hope from her memory of him. She started for the door, leaving thoughts of locusts behind. *That was the past,* she told herself, choosing to interpret her dream now not as an omen of things to come, but as a recollection only of things that had come before. *Within months, or even weeks, Bajor might be a member of the Federation.* Kira left her quarters, headed for her office and marching foursquare into the future.

As the airlock hatch rotated open, Kira tugged one last time at the front flap of her uniform, trying again to make it sit properly on her body. She actually liked the formal dress of the Militia—the soft, brushed fabric, the lavender coloring, the Bajoran style—but she just could never quite wear hers comfortably. She had fussed with the long wraparound jacket for half the morning, but nothing she did seemed to make any difference for more than a few seconds.

Get used it, she told herself. After all, she would be in the uniform for the rest of the day. She would greet the Alonis delegation when they arrived at the station in a few hours, and then Shakaar and his staff later in the day. This evening, she would host a reception for all of the guests.

Opposite Kira in the corridor, Lieutenant Alfonzo, who had opened the hatch, continued to work at a panel set into the bulkhead. The ring of heels on the metal decking of the airlock drowned out the beeps of the panel. Two figures emerged through the hatchway and stepped down into the corridor. The first stood a head taller than Kira, slender, and he moved with a natural grace. A second man accompanied him just behind and to his left, shorter, but solid and muscular. A narrow river of irregularly shaped spots flowed from each man's forehead and down the sides of their face and neck.

"Welcome to Deep Space 9," Kira said. "I'm Colonel Kira Nerys, commander of the station." She stepped forward, holding out her hand in salutation. For a moment, she flashed back to the first time she had met Akaar, and she wondered if she had once again made a diplomatic blunder. She thought back to her seven years as DS9's first officer, and she could not recall Captain Sisko ever having such problems receiving visitors to the station. But then the first man raised his own hand and clasped Kira's. His hand felt cold, and Kira remembered that the same had been true of Jadzia, and that it was true now of Ezri.

"I am Seljin Gandres," the man said, "Trill ambassador to the Federation." He had long brown hair, down past his shoulder blades, far longer than she had ever seen on a male Trill. His eyes were a rich brown, but Kira also thought that they lacked a depth that she had always perceived in Jadzia's eyes, and that she even saw now to some extent in Ezri's. Even had Kira not read the biographical synopsis Starfleet had provided on the ambassador, she thought she would have been able to tell that he had not been joined to a symbiont. "This is one of my aides," Gandres continued. "Hiziki Gard."

Gard eased his way past the ambassador with a poise Kira found unexpected, given the man's short stature and his muscled physique. He offered his hand, and Kira took it. "Welcome to the station," she said.

"Thank you, Colonel," he said. "A pleasure to meet you." As with Gandres, Gard possessed an icy grasp. Unlike the ambassador, though, his eyes gave the impression of great knowledge and experience, belied by the outward appearance of his age. Kira released his hand, and with an effortless bearing, he slid back into his subservient position behind and beside Gandres.

"Ambassador," Kira said, "the local time here is ten hundred hours, and we've planned a reception for all the delegations at twenty hundred, so you've got ten hours until then. In the meantime, I'd be happy to conduct you on a tour of the station, if you're interested, or I could have you escorted to the quarters we've arranged for you and your staff."

"Pardon me, Colonel," Gard said, "but would it be possible to inspect the quarters before occupying them?"

Gandres turned his head and peered down at his aide. "Forgive my aide's impertinence, Colonel," the ambassador said, "but he is in charge of security for our contingent, and he is . . . thorough."

"I intended no disrespect," Gard said, bowing his head. Kira recognized the truth of his words—he had intended no disrespect—but she also understood that he made no apology for wanting to see to the security needs of the ambassador.

"Not at all," Kira said. "Lieutenant Alfonzo can take Mr. Gard there now." She gestured with an open hand toward Alfonzo, who had completed his task at the panel, she saw. "Just so you know, though, we have tightened security on the station in anticipation of the summit." She spoke directly to Gandres, but she intended her words for Gard as well. "The arc of the habitat ring in which the delegations will be housed has been swept and closed to all but authorized personnel. We've also closed this section of the docking ring, as well as the crossover bridge connecting this location with your quarters."

Kira wondered if she should have asked Ro to join her in welcoming the delegation to the station. She had considered doing so, but had decided that such an action would have been antithetical to the low profile Akaar had requested. Kira had also opted not to burden her security chief with having to wear a dress uniform for the day; Ro struck her as someone not particularly comfortable in formal settings.

Over the past two and a half days, Kira had met with Ro several times in order to discuss security for the summit. In Kira's opinion, Ro had done an exceptional job of both planning and implementing the new procedures and mechanisms. Even simply coming out to the docking port just now, Kira had been impressed not only by the execution of the new protocols, but by their unobtrusiveness. Ro had posted security officers throughout the station at critical locations, of course, but she had also devised a means of keeping them at a distance from the delegations. Lieutenant Alfonzo, Kira knew, had just now collected the individual sensor signatures of the ambassador and his aide. As the two men moved throughout this section of the docking ring, their assigned section of the habitat ring, and the crossover bridge between, force fields would raise and lower along their paths, both before and after them, far enough away to occur without being noticed, but close enough to provide a genuine measure of protection. The same would be done for every member of the two Federation delegations and the Bajoran delegation. It was, Kira thought, an ingenious solution.

"We also haven't announced the summit to anybody on the station beyond the necessary personnel," Kira concluded, "and First Minister Shakaar has not made a public announcement of it yet on Bajor, so few people are even aware that it will be taking place."

"I appreciate your diligent efforts to ensure our safety," Gandres said. "Actually, before taking a tour of the station or settling into our quarters, there is somebody aboard I would like to meet." Kira had been expecting this. "We . . . that is, the Federation Council . . . understand that a Jem'Hadar soldier is now living aboard Deep Space 9."

"That's true," Kira said, "although we don't think of Taran'atar as a soldier." She took care to respond in a manner that would signal her intent not to contradict the ambassador, but simply to provide him with information.

"Is he a diplomat then?" Gard asked.

"More a student studying abroad," Kira found herself saying. "He was sent here by Odo to observe and try to understand life in the Alpha Quadrant," she went on, "and he's been doing that." She was pleased now that she had asked him not to shroud on the station.

"I understand," Gandres said.

Kira moved to her left and touched a companel set into the bulkhead there. The panel sprang to life with an electronic tone, a Cardassian "shatterframe" display appearing on it. "Computer," she said, "locate Taran'atar."

"Taran'atar is in ops," the computer replied. Kira lowered her hand, and the panel winked off.

"Ambassador, I'd like to accompany you to ops," Gard said. "I can verify the security arrangements for our quarters later."

Gandres listened to his aide, then said to Kira, "If you have no objection, Colonel."

"Right this way," Kira said, motioning toward the doors of the nearest turbolift, across from the airlock and a few paces down the corridor. Gandres and Gard turned in that direction, but before they reached the lift, the doors opened. Admiral Akaar appeared, his huge form expanding out of the car as though he had been stuffed within its confines.

"Colonel," the admiral said, looking at her before turning his attention to Gandres. "Ambassador," he said, bringing a closed fist up to his chest, and then opening it before him. "I welcome you with an open heart and hand." To Kira's surprise, Gandres returned the gesture.

"L.J.," the ambassador said, "how are you?"

"I'm well," Akaar said. "Colonel Kira has been most hospitable." Although she kept her expression neutral, Kira was shocked by the statement; as far as she was concerned, her relationship with the admiral had been nothing but adversarial. He need not have told the ambassador that, of course, but then, he need not have said anything at all. "And how are you?"

"I'm doing well," Gandres said. Then, turning, he introduced Gard. "One of my aides, Hiziki Gard. This is Fleet Admiral Akaar."

"A pleasure to meet you," Gard said, and he held out an open hand to the admiral. Kira felt both paralyzed and fascinated, unable to move or say anything as she watched the aide make the same mistake she had. Akaar seemed to appraise Gard for a moment, then reached out and took his hand. A phaser blast could not have stunned Kira more. She looked at the hands of the two men as they came together, Gard's engulfed within Akaar's, but the two held their stance solidly for a few seconds before letting go. Kira realized that she did not understand the admiral at all.

"Seljin," Akaar said, looking back at the ambassador, "I'd like some of your time today. There are some issues I wish to discuss before tomorrow."

"Of course," Gandres said. "We can talk right now. Is there somewhere we can go?"

"How about back aboard your vessel?" the admiral asked. At first, Kira thought that Akaar was again trying to gain control of a meeting, but then she realized that, while he had taken her aboard *Mjolnir*, a setting with which he had been familiar, in this case, he was consenting to a setting with which he was not familiar.

"I would recommend meeting aboard our ship as well," Gard offered. "At least until I can verify the security precautions on the station."

Gandres acknowledged Gard with a nod, then turned to Kira. "Thank you for welcoming us to Deep Space 9, Colonel," he said. "I'll be in touch with you later."

"You're welcome, Ambassador," she said. Gandres and Akaar disappeared into the airlock, and Kira pointed to Alfonzo. The lieutenant operated the airlock controls. The hatch rolled closed along its geared runway. "Have somebody relieve you here," she told Alfonzo, "and then escort Mr. Gard to the quarters for the Trill delegation."

"Aye, sir," Alfonzo said.

"Thank you, Colonel," Gard said.

Kira nodded, then turned and strode down the corridor, headed for her office. She started to attempt to decipher Akaar's behavior, but found herself at a loss to do so. She thought she understood him now less than she had before.

Forget it, she told herself. There were more important things that she needed to focus on right now. She did not know how long the summit would last, but she suspected that the next few weeks aboard the station would prove very interesting.

41

Prynn heard her father cry out in pain. She watched him writhe on the ground, the gray sky reaching down and wrapping its wisps about his body, torturing him in some incomprehensible way. He thrashed about, his agony plain. Dull brown dirt kicked up and coated his uniform as he struggled to free himself from the violent and mysterious shadows.

She tried to move toward him and could not, tried to scream and found herself mute. *Dad,* she thought, an appellation she had not used for him in years. Desperation knotted her stomach. He could not leave again. She had to go to him, had to help him, even after all that had come between them. She fought to get to her knees, pushing herself up, pushing against—

—the bedroll.

Prynn opened her eyes on a desolate world, beneath a sky just beginning to pale from black to the distressed color of cinders. Dawn had come to this empty place, as much as it could. *Or maybe this is dusk,* she thought. Maybe that was all this world knew anymore.

Prynn had risen to her hands and knees on the bedroll, she saw, and she remembered battling to move in her dreams. She sat back on her haunches, the soft, metallic blanket sliding from her shoulders with a sound like sand slipping through her fingers. Whatever images and sounds, whatever thoughts and emotions, had populated her dreams seemed to drain away now as she sought to recall them. Her father . . . her father . . .

A moan rose to her left. Prynn looked that way, still feeling bound by the fetters of sleep. But then she saw Shar. His blanket had fallen from him, and his upper body had come partially off his bedroll and onto the ground. His arms moved in small, irregular spasms. He seemed to be asleep, but also in pain.

Another moan escaped Shar's lips. The familiarity of it brought Prynn to the recognition that this sound had invaded her dreams, had masqueraded as the voice of her father's agony. *Why not Mom's?* she thought suddenly, not knowing why the question had come, but deciding at once that she did not want an answer to it.

As Prynn made her way over to Shar, the charred, skeletal remains of *Chaffee*'s bow caught her eye. The flames had stopped burning late yesterday, but even now, narrow strands of smoke escaped the wreckage and drifted upward. The calm of the scene contradicted the awful chaos of the crash.

Prynn reached down beside Shar and picked up the tricorder she had set to monitor his condition during the night; she had wanted to be alerted if he required medical attention while she slept. She had also left a second tricorder near the head of her own bedroll, configured to patrol a perimeter around their small camp. Nothing had triggered an alarm on either device.

Standing over Shar, Prynn reset the tricorder to an interactive scanning mode. Shar cried out again as she held the device over him near his head. She slowly moved it down the length of his body, and saw that he had mended some overnight. His vital signs had not improved much, but they had at least remained level. His dislocated shoulder and bruised ribs appeared better, obviously owing to Vaughn's treatment, but his horribly splintered leg would demand more than the splint and the simple first aid he had been given. Worst of all, the injury to one of his internal organs would continue to threaten his life if he did not see a doctor before long.

Prynn put down the tricorder, then retrieved the medkit from the survival cache and prepared to administer a painkiller. The hiss of the hypospray against Shar's neck seemed unusually loud against the backdrop of silence. She stood back up and stayed there for a few minutes, the spent hypo in her hand, watching and listening as Shar's movements calmed and his moaning ceased. Then, very gently, she eased his upper body back onto the bedroll, pulling the blanket over him and up to his chin.

As she returned the hypospray and the medkit to their places, a chill ran through Prynn's body. The temperature had dipped during the night, though not too much, and her blanket had kept her warm. Already this morning, the temperature had begun to rise back toward yesterday's level of low double digits—not exactly comfortable, but not terrible either.

Prynn retrieved a ration pack and a water container from the cache, then returned to her bedroll. She slipped on her jacket, then sat down and consumed what would have to pass for her breakfast. As she ate, she thought about the day ahead. She would continue to work on reconstructing the transporter from the salvageable components of the shuttle wreckage, and she would have to consider reviving Shar at some point. He had neither eaten nor drunk since before the crash, and she had no means of providing him sustenance intravenously.

When she finished eating, Prynn put the water container and the spent ration pack back in the cache, then took a combadge out of a jacket pocket. She set the combadge to maintain an open channel with her own, and placed it near Shar's head. She had done the same thing yesterday, wanting to keep a comlink open to him while she was away from the camp. She also set the tricorder back to an automated scanning mode to monitor his condition.

Then, gathering the few tools she had, she headed out to *Chaffee*'s aft section, where she would work on the transporter and an escape from this dead planet.

The bent metal panel seemed to pull free, but then it snapped back into place. A sharp edge caught the index finger of Prynn's left hand, slicing it open. Pain flared, and she sat back amid the debris of the downed shuttle and kicked out in frustration. Her boot impacted the panel, drawing a loud clang, and then one side of the panel slipped down a few centimeters. A second later, the entire metal piece fell away from the bulkhead.

Prynn looked at the newly revealed circuitry that she had been trying to access, then laughed. The sound was a lonely one in the empty wastes, made more so because she knew that it contained no humor. She peered up through where the roof of the shuttle should have been and regarded the forbidding sky. The clouds, despite their constant movement, stared back like the unchanging and impenetrable walls of a prison.

Her finger throbbed, and she lifted her hand and examined it. Blood flowed from a cut running lengthwise up the tip. She raised her finger to her lips and sucked at the wound, clearing it, then looked at it again. The cut reached deep into her flesh, she saw, and it filled quickly again with blood.

Prynn put her fingertip back in her mouth, applying pressure to the cut. She got to her feet and walked from the rear compartment of the shuttle, out through the path she had cleared through the wreckage. The soles of her boots scraped along the ground as she strode back toward the burned-out shell of *Chaffee*'s forward section and, beyond it, the camp.

As she walked, she thought of Vaughn, walking himself, trying to reach the source of the pulse. He was out there somewhere, alone, and she wondered what he was feeling right now. And she wondered what she herself was feeling. After he had departed yesterday, she had gone to work on the transporter and, even given the circumstances and the surroundings, that had somehow provided her a sense of normality. Prynn had been able to focus on the work, narrowing her vision and thoughts to the task at hand.

Today, though . . .

Today had been different. While she had continued to make progress with the transporter, her mind had begun to wander. She had found herself recalling the days after her mother had died, and the terrible sense of loss that, though experienced less often as the years had passed, had never really left her—and never would, she knew. Prynn supposed that such morose remembrances stemmed from facing her own mortality. With rescue from *Defiant* realistically impossible during the next day and a half, and Vaughn's ability to stop the pulse uncertain at best, she understood that the remainder of her life might now be measured in hours. She did not want to die, and she would do everything she could to prevent that from happening, but for all of that, her thoughts dwelled not on her own death, but on that of her mother. The days of despair Prynn had experienced after her mother's death continued to recur to her, no matter how much she attempted to concentrate on recovering the transporter.

The days after Mom's death, she thought, *are still going on.* Seven years later or seventy, each day Prynn lived would be a day lived after that dreadful event. And no matter what happened in the next day and a half, that would always be the case.

Prynn passed the blackened bow of the shuttle, the camp coming into view beyond it. Shar, she saw, had not moved from atop his bedroll. She headed directly for the survival cache, where she took a dermal regenerator out of the medkit. She cleared her wound once more, then raised the device and switched it on. A narrow blue beam emerged from the tip, accompanied by a high-pitched whine. As she ran the healing light across her fingertip, her flesh began to knit together, a pinpoint of heat sparking her nerve endings. Within a minute or so, she finished, and deactivated the regenerator.

Something moved at the periphery of her sight. Prynn turned quickly, and saw nothing. She gazed out at the open land beyond the camp and saw only a barren vista. She peered at the metallic blanket pooled on her bedroll, and then over at Shar—

Shar's eyes were open and looking at her. He resembled a corpse, with empty eyes staring without seeing from a face that had lost any trace of vibrancy, his blue skin ashen. Prynn's breath caught for an instant, but then Shar lifted a hand that had come out from beneath the blanket . . . slowly, tentatively, as though motioning to her with a great effort.

Prynn sprinted the few steps over to Shar. She kneeled down beside him, dropping the dermal regenerator and scooping up the tricorder beside his bedroll. She reset the device, then took Shar's hand as she scanned him. His condition, she saw, had not changed much from earlier, although she did detect a shift toward dehydration.

Shar squeezed her hand, and she set the tricorder aside. He tried to speak with her, but his mouth made only small, smacking sounds. Prynn got him some water, then helped him lift his head so that he could drink it. He coughed with the first sip, but then managed to get the water down. When he finished drinking, Prynn eased his head back down onto the bedroll.

"Your eye," Shar said, and she remembered the injury to her sclera.

"I'm fine," she said. "It looks worse than it is."

"What happened to you?" Shar wanted to know. "And to me?" Prynn told him about the crash, pointing out the demolished bow section twenty meters away. Shar looked in that direction, and then back at her. "What about Commander Vaughn?" he asked, his voice rising with concern.

"He's fine," she said flatly, anger welling within her. The emotion surprised her—not her negative feeling for Vaughn, but the suddenness and the unexpectedness with which it had come upon her at this moment. *Why?* she asked herself. *Why did that happen?* Because somebody had been worried about her father? Why should that make her angry?

Because he doesn't deserve anybody's concern, she concluded. Except that even she hoped for his continued well-being right now, since he was attempting to save four billion people. And even though she despised him, she did not wish him dead.

To Shar, Prynn conveyed Vaughn's intention to travel on foot to the source of the pulse. She also mentioned how communication with him had failed once he had traveled too far from the camp.

"Will he have time?" Shar wanted to know.

"I don't know," Prynn said. "And if he makes it there, will he be able to do anything? I don't know that either. But Vaughn . . ." She hesitated, wanting to reassure Shar, but hating the words she was about to use. "Vaughn is good at his job." *So good,* she could not prevent herself from thinking, *that he sent my mother to her death.* Prynn knew that the bitterness she felt would show on her face, and so she picked up the dermal regenerator and paced back over to the survival cache. She made a bit of a show of replacing the device in the locker, hoping she had successfully covered her emotions.

"If Commander Vaughn can't stop the pulse," Shar said behind her, "then we're going to die." His voice, it seemed to Prynn, carried fear and pain, but not the fear of death, and not the pain of his physical injuries. Something else occupied him, she thought.

"Shar," she said, turning back to face him, "I'm working on repairing the shuttle's transporter. Some of the primary circuits were destroyed in the crash, but both backups are relatively intact." She explained Vaughn's orders, that she should first try to fulfill the mission of stopping the pulse, and then one way or the other get Shar and herself as far away from the pulse as possible. "In a few days, *Sagan* will be repaired and Lieutenant Dax will send it down to rescue us."

"If we live through the pulse," Shar said.

"We'll make it," Prynn said with a sense of surety she did not feel. She noticed Shar's face tensing. His jaw set, his eyes narrowed, and his antennae moved in a manner she could not interpret. "Shar?" she asked, taking a step toward him. He said nothing, but his gaze had left her, and now he stared up at the sky. "Are you all right? Are you in pain? Can I get—"

Shar rolled his upper body onto his left elbow, and looked over at her in a way that stopped her in midsentence. Color rushed into his face, patches of deep blue blooming on his cheeks and forehead, a dramatic contrast to the stark whiteness of his hair. Prynn could not tell whether he was hurt or angry. He stared at her for a long moment. Finally, he said, *"Zhavey."*

"What?" She did not understand.

"My mother," he said, and she realized that he had interpreted the word for her. Prynn had heard about the complications of Andorian biology, that they wed in groups of four, and that they even reared their children in such family units. She knew that Councillor zh'Thane was one of Shar's parents, and she wondered if that was to whom he was now referring.

"Your mother?" Prynn asked.

"Some part of her . . ." he said, and trailed off. "She made this worse."

"I don't know what you mean," Prynn said. "Shar, I'm sorry, I don't understand."

"Just before we left Deep Space 9," he said, "she brought my bondmates to the station."

"Oh," Prynn said, startled by the revelation. She did not know what else to say.

"She was trying to manipulate me into returning to Andor." His right hand balled into a fist. "And she succeeded. I agreed to visit my bondmates on Andor when we get back from the Gamma Quadrant." Shar lifted his fist a few centimeters and then brought the meaty part of it down onto the ground.

"Shar, you don't have to think about that now," she told him. "Listen, you don't have to do anything you don't want to. Your mother—"

"I *promised* to go back," he said, yelling the word. "And when I don't . . ." He looked away from her, his gaze drifting toward the ground in front of him, but the vacant look in his eyes told Prynn that he was seeing something else, some image in his mind. "It will kill Thriss to lose me." Shar raised his right fist again, higher this time, and then he thrust it against the ground, knuckles first. Rage hardened his normally soft features.

"Shar," Prynn called, but already, he had brought his fist back up. He pounded the ground again, and then a third time, and he did not stop. His knuckles hammered the ground, faster and harder, and Prynn heard the awful sound of his bones breaking. "Shar," she called again, then turned and moved back to the survival cache. She quickly dug inside for what she needed, then raced around Shar, to his back. She dropped down behind him and pushed the hypospray against the side of his neck. Her fingers brushed his flesh, and she felt the tautness of the muscles beneath.

Shar punched once more, then stopped, his arm pausing as he raised it. Prynn put a hand against his back and lowered him down onto the bedroll. She reached across his unconscious form and grabbed the tricorder there, then scanned him. When she had determined that his condition remained stable, she examined his hand. Several layers of skin had been torn away from his knuckles, and blood seeped from the wound. Bones in all of his fingers had fractured.

"So this is what they mean by 'Andorian fury,'" she said, glad that the soporific she had given Shar would keep him asleep for at least several hours. She stood up and went once more to the medkit, to retrieve what she would need to treat Shar's new injury. It seemed almost impossible to credit the transformation she had just witnessed. Shar, normally quiet and reserved even in social situations, had changed in an instant into somebody she barely recognized. She had not felt threatened herself in any way, but the incident had still affected her.

This is Vaughn's fault, she thought. He had left them here. Had left *her* here. Again.

Again? she asked herself. *Now I don't even know what I'm thinking.* She attempted to clear her thoughts as she returned to Shar's side.

For twenty minutes, Prynn tried to concentrate on administering first aid, tried to focus on Shar's hand and on nothing more. When she finished doing what she could, she headed out to resume her work on the transporter. But even as she started for the aft section of *Chaffee,* she peered back over her shoulder—not at Shar, not at the camp, but off toward the horizon. She did not know why, but she could not shake the image of her father walking away from her.

42

Treir slid the plate onto the bar. "Here you go," she said, referring to the small, lightly browned cakes, covered in a thick, fruit-filled glaze. "Skorrian fritters in a Kaferian apple compote." Morn looked at his breakfast approvingly. Treir reached below the bar and pulled out a set of dining utensils wrapped in a linen napkin. She set the package beside Morn's plate, then reached down and patted his hand. "Now, don't eat too fast," she teased him. "I know one of your stomachs must still be filled with all that Maraltian *seev*-ale you had last night." Morn rolled his eyes, nodding his head in agreement.

Treir smiled and moved down the bar, away from Morn. She poured herself a glass of water, then peered over toward the dabo table. The late morning tended to be the slowest time of day in the bar, between breakfast and lunch for most of DS9's denizens, but that had changed today. Word of Hetik's presence in the bar must have spread through the station like the Symbalene blood burn. A dozen people—mostly women, but a few men, too—surrounded the dabo table now, a situation remarkable not only because of the time of day, but because in recent weeks, Quark's had not seen so many gamblers at one time even at night. And she felt certain that business would only continue to increase in the days ahead.

"Thirteen through, thirteen through," she heard Hetik say, announcing the outcome of the latest spin and play.

"Bastion?" somebody called raucously. When it was busy, the dabo table was by far the loudest spot in the bar—and maybe anywhere on the station.

"Sorry," Hetik said. "No bastion." A collective groan went up among the gamblers, but a groan that nevertheless held a note of enjoyment. Win or lose, these dabo players were having fun, another detail that boded well for future business. The thick clink of gold-pressed latinum rang through the room as Hetik collected the winnings of the house.

A distinctive-looking woman at the far end of the bar signaled to Treir with a wave. Treir walked over to the woman—tall, with a rough, grayish skin, a long, narrow neck, and strikingly luminous eyes—and took her order for a refill of her drink. She picked up the Melkotian woman's empty glass and moved back down the bar to find the bottle she needed. To her surprise, she saw Quark standing in the doorway, and to her delight, she saw him looking over at the dabo table with an expression of satisfaction on his face. Then he looked around, saw her, and smiled.

Treir quickly replenished the Melkotian woman's drink, went back to the end of the bar, and set it down before her. When Treir turned back around, Quark had come around the bar. "Is this all Hetik?" he said as he approached, inclining his head in the direction of the dabo table.

Treir smiled and shrugged. "What do you think?" she said. Quark glanced back over at the pack of gamblers, his astonishment seemingly surpassed only by his conspicuous glee. "So," she said, reaching out and playfully brushing a fingertip across the top of his bald head, "do you have the contract for our agreement about Hetik?"

"Contract?" Quark said, turning back to her. "Forget it." He waved a hand between them, as though physically dismissing the notion.

"Are you sure?" Treir asked, deciding that, at this point, she wanted more than simply Quark's easy acceptance of her new hire. "I mean, I already told Hetik that he would only be here for another six days." She had not really done that, but she wanted Quark to acknowledge her worth.

"You what?" Quark said, the sharp, toothy smile disappearing from his face.

Treir slid a hand languorously along the edge of the bar, dipping her body down until the entire length of her arm rested flatly on the smooth surface. She leaned her head against her biceps and peered innocently up at Quark. "Is that a problem?" she asked. "I realized after you left last night that you really didn't want Hetik here, so I told him this morning that we would be letting him go."

Quark stared at her for a moment, his mouth dropping open. He was obviously aghast. "Let's not be . . ." He paused, and then smiled. "Treir," he said, his voice dripping with as much charm as he could muster.

"Quark," she said in a low, throaty tone, flirting along with him. She lifted her head from her arm, and eased off the bar toward Quark. She glided a hand around his back, and brought her lips near his ear. "Is there something you want to tell me?" she asked in a whisper.

"Yes, of course," he said, his arm coming up around her waist. "Hetik can stay."

Treir purred in Quark's ear, and then said, "And what else?"

"Your idea to hire him was a good one," he admitted, with only the slightest hint of reluctance. Then he turned his head and looked up into her eyes. "You're an asset to the bar," he said seriously.

"Well, that's almost a declaration of love," somebody said. Treir looked over and saw the station's chief of security standing a short distance down the bar. Treir got the impression that she had been there for a few moments.

"Laren," Quark said anxiously, dropping his hand from around Treir's waist, though Treir left her arm around his back. "I mean, Lieutenant Ro."

"Good morning, Quark," Ro said, the corners of her mouth threatening a smile. She seemed entertained by the scene Treir and Quark had been playing out.

"Good morning, Lieutenant," Treir said. "What can I get for you?"

"Oh, don't let me interrupt," Ro said. "Finish your business first."

"Uh, we were done," Quark said.

"Actually, *I* wasn't done," Treir told him, running a finger slowly along the top of his ear.

"Oh no?" Quark said, gazing back up at her, his hand returning to her waist. His attention seemed far away, his euphoric moment an obvious by-product of her touch.

"If I'm such an asset to the bar," Treir suggested, "then perhaps I'm under-paid."

Quark grinned, and Treir suspected that he actually appreciated her audacity. "I don't think so."

She raised her free hand to the base of Quark's neck and straightened the silver bauble strung between his lapels. "Well, then," she said, "perhaps a position change."

Quark reached up and toyed with her necklace—a bold move, Treir thought at first, considering that Ro was still here. But then she realized that her initial assumption about Quark's interest in the lieutenant—that it had only to do with Ro being DS9's chief of security—must have been correct after all. "What sort of a . . . position . . . did you have in mind?" he asked, continuing his flirtation.

"Oh, I don't know," she told him. "Junior partner sounds interesting to me." She skimmed a finger down the edge of one of his lobes.

"I don't know about junior partner," Quark said, "but maybe we can discuss a merger." Treir winked, but before she could say anything more, Ro interjected.

"Quark," she said, her voice harder now, evidently no longer amused at the byplay. Treir looked over at the lieutenant and saw only seriousness on her face. "Colonel Kira wants to see you in her office as soon as possible."

"Colonel Kira?" Quark said, and all at once, his focus changed. He took his hand from Treir's waist and moved away from her. He took a few steps down the bar until he stood directly across from Ro. "What does she want?"

"You'll have to ask her," Ro said sternly.

"But I didn't do anything," Quark protested.

"No," Ro said. "Of course you didn't." She looked and sounded angry, but as she turned and marched out of the bar, something in the way Ro carried herself made Treir think that she was also hurt.

Treir peered down at Quark, who now looked worried after the news that the colonel wanted to see him. She smiled, realizing that she had not quite understood the situation between Quark and Ro after all. Quark's interest in the lieutenant might or might not have been genuine, might or might not have been motivated only by expediency, but Ro . . . wonder of wonders, Ro actually liked Quark.

Treir shook her head, thinking that the universe really was an amazing place.

43

Vaughn walked through the dead city. The heels of his boots pounded along the empty street, reverberating in the metal canyons formed by the tall buildings on either side of him. He moved quickly, steadily, the hard surface putting more strain on his back, legs, and feet than had the softer, undeveloped ground, but it also allowed him a faster pace. His hip still ached, but he ignored it.

Sleep had come easily to him last night, the result of a lifetime of "battlefield" service. Through the years, Vaughn had come to understand the value of rest in the fulfillment of missions, and he had trained himself to sleep under difficult circumstances. Last night had been different only in the dreams that had come. The nightmares.

Vaughn could not recall the images that had haunted his slumber, but he had woken with a start before dawn. Disoriented in the pitch blackness of this world's night, it had taken him a moment to recall his circumstances. He had consulted his tricorder and seen that he had slept for little more than four hours. He had considered attempting to get more rest, but quickly abandoned that idea, finding himself wide awake and anxious to continue on his way.

It had taken him only a couple of hours to reach flat land and, shortly after that, the city. The collection of structures had risen before him like a small range of hills, low in the foreground, climbing higher in the distance. He had entered the city and made his way through it for three hours, choosing not to rest until he had left it behind him. Other than the sizes of the buildings, he had found little variation marking one area from another.

Now, Vaughn walked on through the city, surrounded by neglect. The buildings, whether one story tall or ten, showed that they had long been deserted. Dirt adorned their sides like spatters and streaks of brown paint—but not just their sides. Every building in the city stood open to the outside, every window shattered, masses of glass shards lying alongside walls like crystalline moats. Land vehicles likewise sat exposed, their own windows reduced to fragments. A patina of dust lay over everything like an immovable veil. Nobody had lived here for a very long time.

But the former inhabitants of the city had not abandoned their homes for some other place; they had left it for death. Bones littered the urban landscape, some scattered about as though strewn by some inimical force, others together in intact or nearly intact skeletons. The remains appeared to be those of humanoids, with two arms and two legs. The skulls were larger than that of a human, and the thoracic cavities were bound by ribs oriented not horizontally, but vertically.

Curiosity drove Vaughn to stop and explore the macabre scene, but he could not take the time away from his journey. Still, as he passed the skeletal remnants of the people who had obviously once lived here, the tricorder and his own eyes told him many things. Beside one fractured set of bones after another sat a handheld weapon. He saw affixed to buildings and lampposts numerous nooses, below which the skeletons of the hanged had fallen in heaps. Other collections of bones lay smashed in the street, the clear result of people plummeting from tall buildings to their deaths.

Vaughn wondered what had driven these people to kill each other, but even as he did so, he understood that no civil war had occurred here. For whatever reason, the hundreds of thousands who had lived in this city had chosen to abandon their homes in the fastest way possible. The fatal wounds caused by the handheld weapons had all been self-inflicted, the nooses had been strung up by those intending to sling them around their own necks, and nobody had been thrown from atop a building—they had all jumped. The population here, Vaughn was suddenly convinced, had committed mass suicide.

As he walked past the dead, he used his tricorder to study the city they had left behind. Readings put its age on the order of centuries, with indications that it had last been inhabited two hundred years ago. Machinery, also long dead, permeated the buildings. Computers and communications equipment spread throughout the city, through every structure and down into subterranean conduits. Circuitry junctions sat on street corners every few blocks, encased in large cubes that stood twice as tall as Vaughn, and that had been dusted brown through the decades.

Vaughn speculated that perhaps technology, or its misuse, had somehow brought these people to their demise, although he could not see how. The other lifeless cities that *Chaffee* had flown over had been brought to their ends in different ways—by fire, by panic, by abandonment, by siege—and Vaughn could find no common element among them beyond the deaths of their citizenry. What little information he possessed failed to add up to any obvious conclusion.

At the next intersection sat one of the large circuitry junctions. Vaughn raised his tricorder and took sensor readings of the cube. Like the others he had scanned, this one housed a union of several citywide technologies. He recognized computer and communications relays, set in a sophisticated configuration, but he detected nothing that might send the entire population of the planet to its death, particularly in so many disparate ways.

Vaughn lowered the tricorder and glanced down the street. He was nearing the far border of the city, he knew, beyond which lay more open, undeveloped land. *And somewhere close,* he hoped, *the site of the pulse.* If he could put—

Something moved up ahead. Vaughn stopped immediately. He turned his head slowly, peering from one side of the street to the other. He saw nothing. His first inclination was to attribute it to the wind, but the air had been calm, not even disturbing the layer of dust coating everything here. *Perhaps just a shadow then,* Vaughn thought as he lifted his tricorder, intending to scan the street ahead of him. *The result of a random swirl of the unceasing cloud cover—*

Movement came again, and this time Vaughn saw its source. A half-block down, on the right-hand side, a figure peered out from around the side of a building. The face looked human. Vaughn watched the figure for a few seconds, and then it moved again, reaching a hand out and gesturing toward him.

No, Vaughn realized. Gesturing him forward.

Vaughn took a step toward the figure—toward the *man*—and stopped, waiting to see its—*his*—reaction. The man continued motioning Vaughn forward, and something about the way he did so seemed oddly familiar. Vaughn started ahead again, and as he did, he moved his thumb up onto the tricorder controls and activated a scan.

When Vaughn had closed to within twenty meters, the man held up his hand, palm out. Vaughn stopped. The man peered around, then gestured again, this time pointing across the corridor.

Corridor? Vaughn thought. The man pointed across the *street.* Vaughn looked there and saw nothing, but a sense of déjà vu overwhelmed him. It seemed ludicrous to even consider that he had lived a sequence of events like this before, but the feeling remained strong. Suddenly, without thinking, Vaughn lifted his empty hand and pointed past the man. The man nodded, as though acknowledging Vaughn, and then he came out from behind the building and into the corridor.

Street, Vaughn told himself, but already his thoughts had moved past that. The man was wearing a Starfleet uniform. An *old* Starfleet uniform.

And Vaughn recognized him.

The man turned and started running away, the clap of his boots on the pavement echoing in the empty street. "Wait," Vaughn called, and sprinted after him. Still running, the man waved back toward Vaughn, as though to quiet him down. "John, wait." The man reached the next intersection and rounded the corner, disappearing from sight.

Vaughn raced toward the cross street, already knowing what he would find when he got there. He would look where the man had run and see nothing. The man would have vanished, leaving no trace beyond Vaughn's doubting of his own mental state.

Vaughn reached the intersection, stopped, and peered down the cross street. Almost a block down, the man continued to run, his footsteps still resounding. Vaughn took a step, preparing to follow, but then stopped again. He did not have time for this. Unless and until he could demonstrate that chasing the man would provide a means of stopping the pulse, he had to go on. For all Vaughn knew, he was imagining this entire encounter. And maybe that, some form of mass delirium, had been what had carried the people of this world to their ends.

Vaughn raised his tricorder and scanned the receding figure. The readings indicated a human male, in good health, approximately fifty years of age. Vaughn looked up again and saw now that the man had gone—perhaps around a corner, perhaps back to wherever he had come from. Perhaps back into the recesses of Vaughn's mind.

In the dust coating the streets, Vaughn saw a set of footprints leading away from him, in the direction the man had taken. Vaughn followed them back down the street, tracing them to where the man had emerged from beside the building. The footprints ended there.

Transporter? Vaughn thought. But that would hardly explain everything. Time travel? Holograms? Illusions or *de*lusions? A sensor sweep revealed no residual energy readings, other than those present everywhere on the planet. No transporter signatures, no chroniton particles, no photonic emissions.

He replayed the scans that he had initiated when he had first started toward the man. He saw the same readings: a healthy, fifty-year-old human male. Then he played back the visual record the tricorder had captured. He worked the controls in order to display a magnified image of the man's face. Vaughn recognized it at once: the long, narrow countenance, the angular features, the graying hair above the ears. He remembered the day—*What? Sixty, sixty-five years ago?*—when he and the man had run down the corridor of a starship together, making the same gestures they had just made in the street of this dead city. And Vaughn remembered all that had been lost back then, so many years ago.

He doubted his perceptions, and even his sanity. But he also suspected the technology running through the city, despite that his tricorder registered nothing functioning within its confines. Regardless of the explanation for whatever had just happened, though, it was time for him to move on.

Vaughn turned back in the direction he had been traveling before he had seen the man, and started walking again. He would be out of the streets in another hour, back into open land. He had to focus on his journey now, on reaching his intended destination and stopping the pulse from launching into space.

And still, as his footfalls bounced between the wasted buildings of this wasted city, he could not banish from his mind the image of the man he had just seen: Captain John Harriman of the *U.S.S. Enterprise*.

44

Kira reviewed the list of food and drink for the reception. She sat at the desk in her office, tapping at the padd, which emitted tiny electronic tones as she paged through the entries. The Bajoran selections pleased her, and included *alva*, shrimp, *hasperat* soufflé, and *mapa* bread with *moba* jam, along with several bottles of spring wine and a variety of teas. One other item at the end of the list caught her attention. "How did you get *foraiga?*" she asked. The delicacy was very difficult to obtain, even on Bajor itself.

"Colonel, I've been doing business in this system for more than a decade," Quark said. "And I'm a Ferengi. I know how to get things." He stood across from her, waiting for her to authorize his catering menu.

"You know how to get things," Kira told him, "and you also know how to overcharge for them." His greed never slackened, she thought as she looked at his charge for the *foraiga*.

"Fine, take it off the list," Quark said, with what Kira took to be feigned nonchalance. "I thought Minister Shakaar would enjoy it, but if you think it's too expensive . . ." He left his statement dangling, obviously probing for information.

"I never said Shakaar would be at the gathering," Kira reminded him, offering a cold smile.

Quark patted his chest with one hand. "My mistake," he said. "I guess I just assumed that all of this fine Bajoran food wouldn't be for just you and Lieutenant Ro." His voice seemed to catch when he mentioned Ro, but the sound was so slight that Kira might have imagined it. Perhaps the security chief had been giving Quark a particularly difficult time lately—something she would have to laud Ro for, if true. "Besides, you don't usually wear your dress uniform."

"All right. The *foraiga* is fine," Kira said, choosing to ignore Quark's observation, and moving on to the rest of the menu. She could have—and probably should have—delegated this responsibility, but she liked Quark to know that she personally kept her eye on him. And with the importance of the summit, she wanted to ensure that the reception this evening would be a success. Of course, Kira knew virtually nothing about Alonis or Andorian or Capellan food, and Jadzia's tastes had ranged well beyond her homeworld of Trill. "What's this?" Kira asked, spying another item with a sizable price. *"Kagannerra?"* She highlighted the item on the padd, then leaned forward and held the device out to Quark so that he could see it.

"That's a type of kelp," he said, only glancing at the padd. "Very large fronds. Quite flavorful, I understand."

"Kelp?" Kira said. She pulled the padd back and looked again at the price beside the item. "This is what you want to charge for *kelp?*"

"Excuse me," Quark said, affronted—or pretending to be affronted, Kira assumed. "There's not a lot of call for food for water-breathers on this air-filled station." He held his arms out wide, as though to take in the whole of DS9. "I couldn't find any food native to Alonis anywhere in the sector. I did manage to locate a shipment out of Pacifica that contained the *kagannerra* and some other items known to be enjoyed by the Alonis."

"All right," Kira relented.

"And I was lucky to find that," Quark continued, as though Kira had not spoken. "The ship won't even arrive at the station until two hours before the gathering. The fees I had to pay just to have the ship diverted to Deep Space—"

"All right, Quark," Kira said, louder. She applied her thumb to the authorization control surface, then handed the padd back to Quark. He took it, and in the same motion, held out a Ferengi banking device, which had appeared in his hand as though from nowhere. She applied her thumb to the control surface on that device, sighing with exasperation. She found her dislike for Quark only exacerbated by having to do business with him.

"I'm sorry, Colonel," he said, unapologetically checking Kira's thumbprint on both the padd and the banking device, as though she might have attempted to cheat him in some manner. "Perhaps if I'd had more time—"

"Yes, you're right," she said, cutting him off again, but this time, she actually regretted doing it. She had to admit that she had asked a great deal of him, calling him to her office late this morning, and then requesting his catering services for this evening. Remarkably, it had taken him only an hour to prepare a menu that included food and drink for people of five different races. He might be overcharging for his services, but he really did know how to cater a function. "Thank you, Quark," she said. "Next time, I'll try to give you more notice."

Quark nodded. Their business at an end, Kira reached forward and activated the computer interface on her desk, intending to return to her work. When Quark did not move, though, she looked back up at him. "Something else?" she asked.

"Actually, I was just curious what the occasion was for a gathering of such an eclectic group of people," he said. This time, Quark's attempt at nonchalance was completely transparent. Given his avarice, it seemed clear that he thought there might be some sort of business prospect for him here—a supposition that actually worked to Kira's benefit in this case. She had waited as long as she had to approach Quark about catering the reception as part of her general intention to keep news of the summit quiet for as long as possible. After the war with the Dominion, numerous powers had expressed concerns about Starfleet maintaining an exclusive military presence at the wormhole. Both the Klingon and Romulan Empires had been particularly vehement in their opposition to such an arrangement, although nothing had yet come of that opposition. The Tholians and the Gorn had also voiced apprehension about perpetuation of the status quo at Bajor, as had several other governments. The longer Kira could keep word of the summit from spreading, she thought, the better.

To Quark's question about the reason for the gathering, Kira responded, "We're celebrating my naming day."

Quark tilted his head to one side, clearly annoyed. "If you don't want to tell me, Colonel, that's fine."

"I don't want to tell you."

"That's fine."

"Good," she said, standing up behind her desk. "Then I won't keep you from getting ready for the gathering."

"Of course," Quark said, and he finally turned and left. As soon as the doors closed behind him, the voice of Ensign Ling emerged from the comm system.

"Ops to Colonel Kira," she said.

"This is Kira. Go ahead."

"The Alonis ship, Arieto, *is on approach to the station,"* Ling reported. *"They should be docking within the hour."*

"Acknowledged," Kira said. "Let me know when the ship arrives."

"Aye, sir." The channel closed with a short tone.

Kira, still standing, idly tapped her desktop with her fingertips. She wondered what Quark's reaction would be when he found out about the summit. She knew that he had long professed an aversion to the Federation, and if Bajor actually joined—

Kira realized something she had not previously considered. If Bajor did join the Federation, with its essentially moneyless economy, then Quark's business would be . . . well, no longer a business, as far as he would be concerned. Deep Space 9 would officially become a part of the Federation, and there simply would no longer be an environment here in which to earn profit. Quark would doubtless have to leave the station.

A smile decorated Kira's face at the thought of that greedy troll being forced to relocate. At the same time, though, she remembered vividly what it had been like to be displaced from her own home, something that had occurred with regularity throughout her life. And Deep Space 9 was Quark's home; she was fairly certain that he had been a resident of the station for longer than anybody else. And right now, he had no idea that his life might soon be thrown into turmoil.

The smile faded from Kira's face. She sat slowly down in her chair, surprised at the genuine sympathy she suddenly felt for Quark.

45

"It's too dangerous," Julian said. He had paced around the ready room and now stood near a far corner, as though seeking refuge from what Ezri had been suggesting. His features had grown tense, and she could see him shifting from disagreement and resistance toward anger. She needed to defuse the situation, not only for Julian's sake, but for her own; in order to implement her proposal, she would require his support.

"Well," she said, shrugging, "we can't let Sam do it." She motioned toward Lieutenant Bowers, who sat across the desk from her. He looked at her with surprise, and she smiled. "Unless you want to, that is."

Bowers held up his hand and shook his head. "No, thanks," he said lightly, matching her tone.

"Look, this isn't a joke," Julian said, walking back over to the desk. He did not laugh or smile, but despite that, and despite his words, she could see that the anger welling within him had eased for the moment, replaced by frustration. "There just isn't enough evidence to justify what you're proposing," he told her, holding her gaze, as though he could convince her of the fact of his position through sheer force of will.

"You keep saying that," Ezri said, "but it's not really the case. Whatever that object in the Jefferies tube is, I sensed a mind when I came into contact with it."

"That can hardly be considered evidence," Julian said dismissively.

"You're wrong," Ezri challenged him. "It *is* evidence. Whether you find it convincing or not is another matter."

"Then let me state it plainly: I don't find it convincing," he said.

"You've made that clear, Doctor," she told him, her own anger rising. She took a beat to rein in her emotions. She would not persuade Julian to support her plan by fighting him. "There's also the simple fact of the object's appearance on the ship. It penetrated the hull and *traveled* to the Jefferies tube." She glanced over at the computer interface on the desk. A view of the Jefferies tube showed on the display, the mysterious dark gray mass still lying along the bulkhead and down on the grating. The object had not moved since yesterday, since they had attempted to transport it. Ensign Gordimer had established a containment field about the location, although because of the object's multidimensional nature, they could not be certain that such a measure would restrict its movement.

"We don't know for a fact that it entered the ship through the breach," Julian argued. "It might have emerged from subspace exactly where it is."

"Even so, that would seem to imply some sort of movement," Bowers observed, obviously seeing Ezri's point. "And we also know that it moved within the Jefferies tube."

"Movement isn't proof of life," Julian said, turning and walking across the room again. "Stars move, planets move, oceans move, but they're not alive."

"That's not quite the same thing," Ezri said after Julian had turned back toward her. "And no, the object's movement isn't proof that it's alive, but it does suggest the possibility."

"A 'possibility' isn't enough to justify the risk you want to take," Julian maintained.

"I think it's more than a possibility that this thing is alive; I think it's a probability," she said. "More than that. I believe it *is* alive. I sensed a mental contact with it."

"You were in a coma," Julian implored her. "You might have dreamed that."

"Yes," Ezri said immediately, which seemed to surprise him. "You're right. I might have dreamed it. But I didn't dream the drop in my isoboramine levels." Ezri had already voiced her opinion that the change in her body chemistry indicated that a connection had been made between Dax and the object.

"Your body and the body of the symbiont have a physical link, facilitated by the isoboramine," Julian said, walking back toward the desk. "Even though you touched the object, no physical link was made between it and the symbiont."

"Maybe a connection was made through subspace," Bowers suggested.

"Maybe," Dax agreed, looking over at the lieutenant. "But back in the pools on Trill, Dax communicated with other symbionts not by physical contact, but by energy surges. And there's certainly plenty of energy around here these days." She peered up at Julian. "You even said yourself that the object and the energy in the clouds and in the pulse might be related."

"I did," Julian admitted, "but that was only speculation. All of this is only speculation."

"I think it's more than that," Ezri said. "And if I'm right about the object being alive, and about Dax being in mental contact with it, then I might also be right about it having knowledge of the pulse." She took a breath and raised her hands up onto the desk, putting them there palms down. "Julian, Sam," she said. "I'm not sure that what I want to do will work. Maybe the object isn't alive, or maybe Dax won't be able to communicate with it, or maybe we won't learn anything that will help us stop the pulse. But I am sure—we're all sure—that if another pulse launches into space, the Vahni civilization will be destroyed."

"I know what's at stake," Julian said quietly. "But you can't quantify life. You can't say that risking one to save another, or even another four billion, is justified."

"You also can't *qualify* life, Julian," she told him. "You can't say that it's better to save Ezri Dax than it is to save even one Vahni Vahltupali."

Julian leaned forward, putting his hands on the desk, his fingers splayed. "I can say that. It's better for me."

Ezri saw the love and the pain in his eyes. She understood what she was asking him to face, but she also knew that it was the right thing to do. "It would be better for me too not to try this," she said. "I don't want to die. That's why I need you, to make sure that I don't."

Julian grunted and pushed himself away from the desk, again retreating across the room. "You don't want to die?" he asked, and Ezri was surprised to hear skepticism in his voice.

"No," she said, not knowing why Julian would even ask such a question. "Of course not."

He looked at her anxiously, then looked away. She could see him holding something back from her.

"What is it?" she asked. Julian looked over at Sam, and Ezri gathered that he did not want to reveal what was on his mind in front of the lieutenant. "It's all right, Doctor," she said, emphasizing to him that this conversation, this disagreement, was wholly professional, and that it would not divide them personally. "You can speak your mind."

"I am concerned, Lieutenant," Julian said haltingly, "that your fervor to put yourself in harm's way may be an overcompensation for the loss of Ensign Roness."

Ezri felt momentarily stunned at the statement—at what sounded very much to her like a betrayal. Since returning to duty after Gerda had died, Ezri had performed her duties skillfully and without agonizing over the loss of a crewperson under her command. Off duty, though, in her quarters—in the quarters she shared *with Julian*—she had suffered. Continued to suffer. And Julian knew that.

She opened her mouth to respond, but Bowers spoke first. "Pardon me, Doctor," he said, "but I don't see any 'fervor' here. I just think the lieutenant has an understandable desire to do what she can to try to save the Vahni."

"Thank you, Lieutenant," she said to Bowers. She studied Julian for a moment and saw the pain still in his eyes—pain at the trauma she had undergone yesterday. "I'm not eager to do this because of the risk involved," she said. "But you're right to question me about that, Doctor, because you know how much the death of Ensign Roness has affected me on a personal level." Ezri suffered the loss because Gerda had been a young officer with a long life and career ahead of her. And because Gerda had been her friend. And yes, because it had been Ezri's orders that had sent the young woman to her death. Ezri had cried in Julian's arms about it more than once, and he too had been emotionally affected by what had happened, perhaps even more so than she had. But even with all of that, Ezri had managed to find solace, and the strength to perform her duty, from her belief that she had made the right choices, given the right orders. Ezri would bring Gerda back to life in an instant if she could, but the two of them had saved tens of thousands of Vahni lives. Now Ezri wanted to save billions.

"I'm sorry," Julian said. "I'm not questioning your ability to command . . . I just . . ."

"You don't have to explain," Ezri told him. "I understand." She stood up. "But you're wrong about my motivations. I was a counselor, and I know what's going on inside of me. This has nothing to do with Gerda. This has to do with saving a lot of people, and me believing I may be able to help accomplish that."

"But the risk . . ." he said.

"There's risk in everything we do. But I believe that a direct, planned contact with the object—" She pointed to the display, to the image of the gray mass, without looking away from Julian. "—might allow Dax to communicate with whatever intelligence is behind it, and possibly find some means of stopping the pulse. And I believe that you'll be able to keep me alive while I try. In my judgment, it's a risk worth taking."

Julian gazed at her and said nothing.

"Sam," Ezri said, "what do you think?"

Bowers stood from his chair. He looked from Ezri to Julian. "I don't like it," he said. "It's dangerous, and I have no idea how to measure the chances of success." He turned back to Ezri. "But under the circumstances, I also think it's a risk we should take."

Ezri nodded to Bowers, then regarded Julian. He looked at her for a long time. Finally, he lifted his hands up at his sides, then let them clap back down against his body. "All right," he said.

46

Something's going on, Quark thought as he marched along the Promenade toward the bar. Kira in a dress uniform, Alonis and Trill coming to the station and attending an event with an Andorian and a Capellan—one of the only Andorians on DS9 being a Federation ambassador, and the only Capellan, a Starfleet admiral. This would be more than a "gathering," as Kira had called it. Something was definitely happening, and Quark wanted to know about it.

He strode along, darting left and right through the midday crowd, anxiously rapping the padd in his hand against the side of his leg. He dashed past the bar without even glancing inside, heading instead for the security office. Laren would know about whatever was going on, and she would tell him.

If she'll even talk to me now, he thought.

The doors to the office parted before Quark. He began speaking as soon as he stepped inside. "Laren, I just came from—" He stopped at the sight of the person standing behind the desk. She turned from peering at one of the security displays just as the office doors clicked closed.

"Can I help you, Quark?" Sergeant Etana asked.

"No," he said, drumming his fingers against the padd. "No, I . . . where's Lieutenant Ro?"

Etana looked left and right, then back at Quark. "Not here," she said. The expression on her face suggested that she thought Quark had asked an improper question.

"I can see that," he said, not bothering to hide his annoyance. "Can you tell me where she is?"

"She's working on a security issue," Etana said evasively.

I'm sure she is, Quark thought. He realized that this gathering tonight must be why Laren had been working such long hours the past few days. He spun on his heel and, without saying anything more to Etana, bolted out of the office.

Quark sped across the busy Promenade toward the bar. He had to find Laren as soon as possible. *And not just about the gathering,* he thought, recognizing the other cause for his sense of urgency: he had flirted with Treir in front of Laren. What had he been thinking? After he and Laren had spent such a wonderful few hours together last night, walking through the dark, quiet station, talking and laughing. "Idiocy must run in my family," he muttered as he entered Quark's.

He quickly slipped behind the bar, headed for the companel at the far end. He skirted by Treir, who was busy serving a customer. "Hey," she said, "how did it go with Colonel Kira?"

Quark ignored her, dropping his padd on a shelf with a clatter. He ducked down below the companel and worked to unlock a compartment there. As he did, Treir came over and bent down beside him. "Is everything all right?" she asked. "Didn't she approve the menu?"

"Yes, yes she did," Quark said hurriedly, not wanting to be distracted. He reached up to the shelf and pulled the padd from it. "Here," he said, handing it to Treir. "Can you take care of this?"

Treir took the padd and examined it. "Um, sure," she said, "but if I'm working on the catering, then who's going to run the bar?"

Quark looked at her, but he had to replay in his head what she had just said. "You stay in charge of the bar," he told her. "Find Broik and have him work on the catering." He turned back to the compartment.

"All right," she said. She stayed beside him for a moment more without saying anything. Finally, she stood up and moved away.

Quark finished unlocking the compartment, then slid its door open. He reached inside and withdrew a small, unexceptional box. Holding it on his knee, he flipped open the lid, revealing a cache of isolinear optical rods. Quark pulled out a particular rod, then closed the box and set it back inside the compartment. He rose, then instinctively glanced around to make sure that nobody was watching him too closely. Satisfied, he opened a hinged access plate in the companel, pushed the security-breaching rod into a receptacle, then flipped the plate closed. Not wanting anybody to hear what he was doing, Quark chose to key in his query: LOCATE LIEUTENANT RO.

The response came back at once, spelled out on the display: LIEUTENANT RO IS IN THE WARDROOM.

Of course, Quark thought. The gathering tonight would be held in the wardroom. Laren was no doubt securing the area. He entered another command: IDENTIFY PERSONNEL IN WARDROOM. A list of three names appeared, Laren's and those of two other security officers. Quark wanted to talk to Laren, but he would wait until she was alone.

He deactivated the companel, then removed the orange isolinear rod and slipped it inside a jacket pocket. He would return to his quarters and monitor Laren from there, then go see her when the opportunity arose. First, though, he dropped down to the compartment again, sliding the door closed and locking it.

As Quark stood up, the companel emitted a quaver that signaled an incoming audio message. He touched a control to receive the communication, foolishly hoping it might be from Laren. "Quark's," he said.

"I want to use a holosuite," a rich voice announced. Quark recognized both the words and the tone at once. It was the same message as always, delivered in the same manner—which, despite its lack of courtesy, still worked better than having the Jem'Hadar stalk into the bar before going to one of the holosuites. *"Program* Taran'atar Seven."

He quickly checked the availability of the holosuites on the companel. "This is Quark. I'll send somebody with your holoprogram up to holosuite one." The channel closed without even an acknowledgment from the Jem'Hadar. "Not only are they ugly and nasty," Quark mumbled to himself, "but they're also rude." He turned toward the bar, located the right box of programs on a shelf beneath, and picked out *Taran'atar Seven.*

Quark peered around, searching for Treir. His gaze found her at the dabo table, delivering drinks to a group even larger than this morning. He looked for Frool and Grimp, and saw them also busy with customers. Actually, now that Quark noticed, the bar had quite a few patrons, at least for this time of day. *For any time of day, lately,* he thought. And yet the increase in business failed to cheer him.

Deciding just to deliver the holoprogram himself, Quark hurried out from behind the bar and over to the nearer of the spiral staircases. He bounded up, one hand sliding up the outside railing, his footfalls ringing on the metal stairs. At the top, he headed for the holosuites. He found the Jem'Hadar waiting, rigid as a statue. *As a gargoyle,* Quark thought. He remembered when the soldier had unshrouded in the bar three nights ago, and how unnerving and frightening that had been. Now, though, seeing the Jem'Hadar in this context, wanting to enter a holosuite, Quark felt less threatened—not *un*threatened, but less threatened.

"Here," he said, holding up the isolinear rod. The Jem'Hadar reached forward, delicately plucked it from Quark's hand, and turned without a word toward the holosuite door. Quark started to go, but them an abrupt chill coursed through the outer ridges of his ears. Anxiety gripped him. He did not know the purpose of Kira's gathering this evening, but an image came to him of the Jem'Hadar tearing through the wardroom, leaving a slew of mangled bodies in his wake—one of them Laren's. He turned back to the Jem'Hadar, who was operating the panel in the bulkhead beside the holosuite door. "Why are you here?" Quark asked, startled to hear a note of challenge in his voice.

The Jem'Hadar took his hand off the panel, looked over, and regarded Quark for a moment. "I am here to train," he finally said. "This program simulates—"

"No," Quark interrupted, waving off the explanation. "Why are you *here*, on Deep Space 9?"

Again, the Jem'Hadar looked at him for a few seconds without saying anything, and Quark got the uncomfortable feeling that the soldier was deciding whether to answer his question or break his neck. Very quickly, the fear Quark had felt the other night in the bar returned. It suddenly seemed like a bad idea not only to have asked the question, but to have come up here in the first place. Quark contemplated running, but then the Jem'Hadar spoke. "I am on this station," he said, "in order to observe life in the Alpha Quadrant." Quark declined to point out that the Jem'Hadar could not do much observing in a holosuite—well, unless it was a certain type of program, but he chose not to mention that either. "And I am also here to keep an eye on you."

Quark's lobes went cold. But then he realized that what the Jem'Hadar had said made no sense. What possible interest could the Founders have in a Ferengi bartender? And then the answer occurred to him. "Odo sent you here," he said.

"The Founder sent me, yes," the Jem'Hadar said.

Two things immediately became clear to Quark. First, his concerns about the Jem'Hadar were baseless; Odo would not have allowed the soldier to come to the station if any real chance existed of something bad happening. And two, even ninety thousand light-years away, the constable still wanted to be a thorn in his side. "Odo told you to keep an eye on me," he said.

"Yes."

"And you believe the Founders are gods," Quark said.

"The Founders *are* gods," the Jem'Hadar insisted. He resumed operating the panel, and the door to the holosuite glided open. Quark could see the holographic emitter system in the walls beyond. The Jem'Hadar walked through the doorway.

"If the Founders are gods," Quark blurted, "then how could they have lost the war?"

The Jem'Hadar stopped just inside the holosuite and turned back toward Quark. "The Founders did not lose the war. The Jem'Hadar failed them. The Vorta, the Cardassians, and the Breen failed them."

"Of course, it's never the leaders' fault, only their minions'," Quark said, and he actually took a step forward. "You know, I knew Odo longer than anybody on the station. I knew him *better* than anybody. And I never once thought of him as a god." It rankled him, he realized, that anybody did.

"That demonstrates nothing about the Founder," the Jem'Hadar said. "It only demonstrates something about you."

"It demonstrates that I'm observant," Quark said.

"It demonstrates that you court death."

Quark stepped back now, unsure whether to accept the statement as a joke or a threat. Somehow, he did not believe that a genetically engineered soldier would have much of a sense of humor.

"You needn't worry. I won't hurt you," the Jem'Hadar said. He turned toward the panel just inside the door, raised his hand, and slipped the isolinear rod into a slot. "Because the Founder instructed me not to."

"How nice of him," Quark said. "What else did Odo say about me?"

"He said you were a lawbreaker, scurrilous, loutish, avaricious, deceitful, devious, and short." The Jem'Hadar touched a control, and the holosuite transformed from a dim, empty room on a space station into a bright, sprawling beach on the edge of an amethyst lake.

"There, you see?" Quark said. "He was wrong, so how can he be a god?"

"I am sure the Founder was not wrong," the Jem'Hadar avowed, still peering at the panel.

"Well, I am short," Quark allowed, "but a lawbreaker? Scurrilous and loutish? And those other things? Please."

"I've observed nothing to suggest the Founder's description of you is inaccurate."

"All right," Quark said, warming to the opportunity to prove Odo something less than a god. "Let's say that he was right, that I am all those things. You know that Odo was chief of security on the station when he was here, right?"

The Jem'Hadar looked over at Quark now, apparently curious. "Yes," he said.

"Well, if I'm a lawbreaker, then doesn't that mean that Odo should have arrested me and put me in prison?" Quark argued. "But here I am, free. Which means either Odo was wrong and I'm not a lawbreaker, or he was right, but he wasn't a good enough chief of security to catch me. Either way, I'd say that doesn't make him much of a god." *I should've been a Vulcan,* Quark thought, dazzled by his own display of logic.

The Jem'Hadar said nothing.

"Well," Quark said. "All right then." He started to leave.

"Wait." To Quark's surprise, the word sounded more like a request than a command. "The Founders created the Jem'Hadar. *Created* them. We exist by their providence. Is that not a characteristic of divinity?"

"I wouldn't exist if not for my mother," Quark said. "I don't lose sleep over it."

"But your mother did not create the entire Ferengi species," the Jem'Hadar said.

"Listen, with enough latinum and the right scientists, you can create just about anybody or anything," Quark said. "So what?"

The Jem'Hadar said nothing again. Then he turned and paced deeper into the holosuite, his boots kicking up puffs of white sand as he neared the edge of the bluish purple water. Quark, enjoying being able to confound this genetically engineered soldier, walked forward and through the doorway.

The Jem'Hadar stopped and turned back toward him. "What do you most want?" he asked.

"What?" Quark had not expected such a question.

The Jem'Hadar strode back across the beach until he reached Quark. "What is it that you most desire? Wealth?"

Quark laughed, a response combined of amusement and anxiety as he peered up into the Jem'Hadar's intense eyes. "Wealth," he confirmed. "Of course."

"If a Founder chose to, he could become a brick of gold-pressed latinum," the Jem'Hadar said. "Or ten bricks. Or a thousand."

"That's not exactly the same thing as having wealth," Quark contended. "A Founder couldn't spend himself."

The Jem'Hadar stepped around Quark and moved back to the panel inside the doorway. He touched a control, and the scene around them gained substance. The lake began to undulate, the gentle waves nipping at the shore. The crisp smells of vegetation floated through the air, carried along by a caress of breeze. The pacific nature of the holoprogram seemed at odds with the character of the Jem'Hadar. "And why do you spend?" he asked.

Quark shrugged. "To acquire things, of course."

"But the Founders do not need to acquire anything," the Jem'Hadar said, moving past Quark again and heading back across the beach toward the water. "The Founders can be anything they wish to be. They are free from the need for wealth, because they already have everything—they already *are* everything—in the universe."

"Yes, but . . ." *But what?* Quark wondered, his gaze drifting downward. He had never considered Odo's nature in quite the way the Jem'Hadar had just described it. Odo had never quite been like that, reveling in all that he could become, although Quark supposed that he could if he chose to. In a sense, the Jem'Hadar was right; Odo could have just about anything he wanted, because he could *be* just about anything he wanted. Of course, in all the time Quark had known him, the constable had only wanted three things: to serve the cause of justice, to have Kira love him, and to return to his people, all things that he could not have simply by shifting his form. But then, Odo had nevertheless managed to acquire all of those things. He had meted out justice for years, Kira had come to love him, and he had finally gone back to live with the Founders.

Odo has everything he ever wanted, he thought. The truth of that astounded Quark. Odo was no longer with Kira, of course, but that had been his choice.

"Computer," the Jem'Hadar said, "begin program." Quark looked up. He thought that the holoprogram had already been running, but obviously the Jem'Hadar had only activated the setting parameters up until now. At first, Quark detected no change in the holosuite, but then a deep vibration reached his ears. The sound increased in volume, originating somewhere behind the Jem'Hadar. Quark peered out at the surface of the lake and saw a mass of water being displaced, churning upward. As the rumble grew louder, the movement of the water grew more violent. Quark looked at the Jem'Hadar's face. The soldier was smiling.

The lake bubbled upward in a frenzy. With a crashing sound, the surface broke, and a huge shape burst out of the water. Quark saw a creature out of a nightmare, with a rugged, black hide, two golden, vertical slits for eyes, and a gaping maw that held enormous triangular teeth. The beast bellowed, an ugly, angry cry. The Jem'Hadar turned to face it. Quark turned and raced from the holosuite. Even though this was only a simulation, he had no desire to witness this sort of thing.

Quark headed out across the upper level of the Promenade toward the nearest turbolift. The image of the horrible creature in the holosuite stayed with him only an instant. Odo's face replaced it in his mind, along with the notion that the constable essentially had acquired everything he had ever wanted. *And I can't get almost anything I want,* Quark thought bitterly. Not the moon for which he had always longed, not great monetary wealth, not even much of a business. And he also might have thrown away whatever small chance he might have had with Ro Laren.

But now Quark decided he would do what he had to do to change that.

47

Vaughn took a last sip of water, then sealed the container and set it aside. He stood up, packed his bedroll—the blanket and beacon inside it—and strapped it to his back. He slung both water containers over his shoulder, then started up the side of the hollow in which he had chosen to rest.

At the top of the incline, a roadway stretched away to the left and right. Vaughn had found the road a few hours ago, on the way out of the city. It measured a dozen or so meters across, traveling through the rise and fall of the landscape in a predominantly straight line, directly toward the complex surrounding the source of the pulse. Walking on the even terrain beside the road allowed him to maintain a steady gait, while at the same time putting less strain on him than if he were to move along the harder surface of the road itself.

Vaughn turned left and resumed his journey. A long upgrade lay ahead, the summit about a kilometer away. He slipped his tricorder out of a coat pocket and performed a scan. As he had drawn nearer the site of the pulse, the range of the sensors had decreased dramatically, though the amount of interference from the energy still confirmed that the road continued in the right direction. He closed the tricorder and slid it back into his coat.

Above, the dark sea of clouds gloomed, matching Vaughn's mindset. Since his encounter in the city with Captain Harriman—or whoever or whatever it had been—he had spent considerable effort conceiving of possible explanations. Time and again, though, his mind would drift from asking questions and searching for answers, to recalling his days with Harriman. Over and over, he had to force his thoughts back to the situation at hand, a problem of focus that did not usually afflict him.

In the end, he figured that the problem broke down simply enough: either that had been Harriman back in the city, or it had not. If it had been Harriman, then how had he come to be here, and why? And why from so long ago? Had there been a reason he had not responded when Vaughn had called to him? Most important, how would this affect the mission to disable the pulse?

On the other hand, if it had not been Harriman—which seemed far more likely—then who or what had it been? Had it occurred only in Vaughn's mind, or had it been real? And if real, then how had it been accomplished, and why? Again, most important, what effect would it have on his mission?

What most troubled Vaughn was the agreement between what he had perceived and what his tricorder scans had shown. If it had not been Harriman, or at least a human male, then either both Vaughn and the tricorder had been fooled, or Vaughn's perception of the tricorder had been fooled. Either way, it left the accuracy of the two most valuable tools he had right now—the tricorder and his mind—in doubt.

As Vaughn hiked up the gradient, leaning into the slope, his thoughts wandered again from Harriman's apparent presence here to those dangerous days spent with him—*What? Sixty-five years ago?* He remembered with horror the catastrophe of *Ad Astra,* in which lives and hopes had been lost. He recalled the mission to remedy the damage done, to avert the unwinnable war . . . the success, but at a cost. Vaughn had still been a young man then, in his thirties, and naïve.

No, not naïve, he thought, a word that carried negative connotations with it. *Innocent.* Back then, he had believed in the virtue of fighting evil, without really understanding the toll that such fighting could take.

Now, alone on this planet, he shook his head and laughed, with not humor but curiosity. He had not thought about *Tomed*—*really* thought about it—in years, perhaps decades. And yet for the last few hours, he had come back to it again and again. All this time later, he found that those ancient emotions could still take hold of him, as though he were experiencing them for the first time. He knew now that he would always carry within him the simple hollowness of the tragedy, along with the complicated sorrows that came from fighting in the shadows.

Underneath the gray skies, Vaughn marched alongside the road, up the incline. Pebbles crunched in the dirt beneath his boots, a sharp contrast to the spectral hum still pervading the air like the aural equivalent of mist. As he approached the summit of the upgrade, a shape became visible in the distance, slowly climbing into view. Vaughn's hands balled into fists, a symptom of the adrenaline that began to course through his body. If he had reached the complex around the pulse already, then he would have an entire day to determine a course of action to save the Vahni.

But as Vaughn topped the rise, he saw only a single structure. A dark tower of some sort, it sat perhaps another kilometer away, reaching up from the center of the roadway itself. It appeared to be about as tall as the road was wide, its base measuring about half that size. Vaughn pulled out his tricorder and attempted a sensor scan, but the interference from the energy made it impossible.

Vaughn kept his gaze on the structure as he continued walking, looking in particular for movement. He saw none. He wondered about the purpose of the structure. Considering its placement, he speculated that it might have functioned as a checkpoint of some sort. He looked for openings in the side facing him, and saw a rectangular doorway at ground level, and several narrow slits in a vertical line above it. With its dark coloring and slightly irregular edges, it appeared to be constructed of stone and—

Vaughn stopped. He checked the tricorder again, but still could not take a reading. It didn't matter. He had drawn close enough now to recognize the structure. It was identical to the tower at the center of the Vahni city.

In less than a quarter of an hour, Vaughn had reached the tower. When he had come within half a kilometer, he had been able to scan the structure: stone and mortar, four stories tall, a single doorway, and a stairway that ascended up the inside walls to the roof. He did not have the readings of the actual Vahni tower—why would he?—so he could not compare the two structures, but his memory found them indistinguishable.

What's going on? Vaughn wanted to know. Was he in a holosuite somewhere, or was this all occurring in his mind? Maybe he still lay back in the wreckage of *Chaffee,* unconscious or even comatose, imagining all of this.

Except . . . this did not seem like a holosuite or an illusion or a dream. Of course, he understood that he might not be able to prove such a belief one way or another. It had been more than a day since the shuttle had gone down, though, and all of the events since then—finding Prynn alive, treating the badly wounded ch'Thane, walking for kilometers across the empty land, passing through the city—had all seemed real. But then, so too had Harriman.

Standing beside the doorway, Vaughn patted a hand against an outer wall of the tower. The stone felt cool to the touch, hard, rough. He closed his eyes for a moment, and the sensations remained.

Vaughn pushed one side of his coat back, allowing him to draw his phaser. He tapped at the control surface on the top of the weapon, configuring it to a powerful but nonlethal setting. He turned around to face back the way he had come, leveled the phaser, and fired. A shaft of yellow-red light streaked into the surface of the roadway, at a point about ten meters away, its high-pitched whine loud in the almost-quiet of the empty landscape. Vaughn shot the beam for ten seconds, then released the trigger. The point on the road at which he had fired glowed red. He checked the tricorder and read liquefaction of stone composites and binding materials. It proved little, he knew, though it at least *seemed* to lend credence to the reality of his surroundings.

Turning back toward the tower, Vaughn stepped away, raised the phaser, and fired again. He held the beam for longer this time. When he stopped, a section of the wall glowed red. He worked the tricorder once more, scanning the tower. Again, he read liquefied stone in the affected—

A life-form showed on the display. Vaughn adjusted the scan and located it on the roof of the tower. It read as Vahni Vahltupali.

Vaughn slipped the straps of the water containers from his shoulders, lowering the containers onto the roadway. Then he unburdened himself of the bedroll, also setting it down on the road. He reset his phaser to heavy stun, then strode back to the tower. Cautiously, he moved through the open doorway, his weapon poised at the level of his waist. Inside, the air felt slightly cooler than the air outside, and slightly damp. He waited a few seconds for his eyes to adjust fully to the dimmer lighting, then turned to his left and started up the stone stairs that ran along the wall. The setting matched his recollection of the tower on the Vahni world.

Climbing the stairs as quietly as he could, he took three minutes to reach the top. He stood with his back to the inside wall, beside the open doorway that led out onto the roof. He consulted the tricorder again, verifying the presence of the Vahni. Then he closed and pocketed the tricorder, raised his phaser higher, and stepped through the doorway.

Ventu—or somebody or something that looked just like him—stood on the far side of the roof, a cloth bag at his feet. Vaughn slowly moved forward, observing and saying nothing. As he did, a flash of color and form flowed across the Vahni's body. "Again, you are welcome," came the slightly mechanical voice of the translator. Vaughn peered down at his chest and saw only his tattered uniform under his open coat, but not the optical mesh that had comprised part of the Vahni translation devices. Nor did the interface between the mesh and the universal translator hang in a small casing at his side.

Vaughn looked up. "Who are you?" he demanded.

All at once, the tower thrust sideways, surging to Vaughn's right. He and Ventu were thrown from their feet in the opposite direction. Even as he fell, a sense of déjà vu overwhelmed him, just as it had back in the city with Harriman. He dropped the phaser as he brought his hands up in time to break his fall, but the left side of his forehead impacted the stone floor of the roof. Explosive sounds pounded the air around him, sounds he knew to be the products of a quake. He had lived through all of this before.

The tower continued to shake violently. Vaughn pushed himself up, fighting to rise onto his knees, and to his feet. He looked over at Ventu and saw vacant, white swirls blooming on his flesh, and Vaughn vividly remembered the horrible, silent screams of the Vahni.

He eyed the doorway, and briefly considered bolting through it and attempting to escape the tower before it collapsed. But he had little time, he knew, and if he got caught within the tower when it went down, he might be killed. He looked back at Ventu, but instead of trying to help him, as he had back on the Vahni world, Vaughn raced to the wall that rimmed the roof. Beyond the tower, he saw no Vahni city, nothing but the empty, rolling geography of this gray world. He gazed upward, and saw the sky filled not with the awful sight of a shattering moon, but only the constant cloud cover that haunted this place.

The tower shifted dramatically, nearly knocking Vaughn from his feet once more, but he grabbed the top of the wall and held himself up. He peered over at Ventu—or the masquerade of Ventu—and saw what he had seen a week ago: fear, embodied in the empty whorls cycling across the Vahni's flesh, and the tentacles wrapped tightly around his upper body. Knowing what the next few moments would bring, and not wanting to chance the reality of the situation, Vaughn decided to protect Ventu. If they could make it through the destruction of the tower, then maybe Vaughn could get some of his questions answered.

With the roof moving back and forth beneath his feet, he staggered over to Ventu. "We have to protect ourselves," Vaughn yelled. To demonstrate, he lifted his arms up around his head. "Ventu," he screamed through the din, "protect your head!" Back on the Vahni world, Ventu had died from a massive brain injury. Maybe this time, Vaughn could—

That was when the tower collapsed.

Vaughn could not tell whether or not he had lost consciousness, but the next perception he had was that the quake had ceased, as had the thunderous noise accompanying it. He opened his eyes and raised his head, finding himself atop a pile of rubble that had once been the tower. A veil of dust hung in the air, and the debris beneath him ticked and popped as bits of rubble fell toward the ground. He had been here before.

Slowly, Vaughn moved, taking inventory of his body. He felt familiar aches, particularly in his limbs. *What isn't familiar here?* he thought.

As he began a cautious descent, the urge to call the names of Bowers and Roness rose in his mind; that was what he had done back on the world of the Vahni. But now, when he peered out past the remains of the destroyed tower, he did not see a Vahni city, its pedestrian ways clogged with frantic crowds, smoke flowing skyward from several points, violet lasers shooting up and warning of the emergency. Instead, he spied only a barren landscape, with a narrow belt of roadway receding into the distance.

Moving carefully, Vaughn maneuvered down the mound of debris. Several stones tumbled from the pile, but he managed to avoid a similar fate. Minutes passed, until finally he reached the ground.

Vaughn looked down at himself. His coat was filthy. His uniform, torn open in a few places and covered with dirt, resembled, but did not match exactly, his uniform after the tower collapse back on the Vahni world. Cuts laced his hands, blood seeping from the wounds. He reached up and felt at his temple, his fingers coming away tacky with blood.

Vaughn circled the heap of rubble, looking this time not for Bowers and Roness, but for Ventu. He waved his way through the thick cloak of dust enclosing the scene. A third of the way around, where before he had come across Bowers and Roness and the other Vahni, this time he found nothing.

He continued walking. Farther along, he discovered the body of Ventu. The Vahni lay along the side of the tower wreckage, about three meters up. His tentacles draped lifelessly across the broken stone. Cuts and abrasions covered his body in numerous places, marring his beautiful red-and-blue flesh. And something had clearly fallen onto the headlike projection atop his frame; ichor oozed from a gaping wound that split the ring of his eye.

Vaughn pulled his tricorder from his coat, grateful that it had not been lost. He scanned the inert form of Ventu. The sensor readings confirmed the body as Vahni; there were no signs of life.

A tremendous sense of loss flooded over Vaughn, threatening to pull him down into its dark depths. Despite being convinced that whoever or whatever sprawled dead before him was not truly Ventu, the fact remained that Ventu had perished—not now, not here, but a week ago, on the Vahni world. Ventu, and three thousand other Vahni, and then Ensign Roness, all gone.

Vaughn stepped back away from the wrecked tower, then turned and made his way back to his supplies. He sat down on the roadway beside them, facing toward the wreckage, but averting his gaze, looking down instead. He pulled off his coat, opened one of the water containers, and wet a corner of the fabric. Gently, he wiped the blood from his forehead, then applied pressure to the wound there. He held his hand like that for several minutes, hoping to stanch the flow of blood.

Unable to stop himself, Vaughn thought about the Vahni Vahltupali. Such a lovely species of beings, they embodied what Vaughn had hoped to discover out in the universe. The Vahni stood as the antithesis of what the circumstances of Vaughn's life had left him exposed to. They were bright and joyful, peaceful and calm. Truly, he could not have hoped for a better experience on his first exploratory mission.

And yet I was so anxious to leave, he recalled. While the rest of *Defiant's* crew had expressed their desire to spend more time with the Vahni, Vaughn had looked ahead, to the next discovery, the next wonder, that they might come across. *Charging through the mission as though it were an intelligence operation,* he realized: checking off one objective and immediately moving to fulfill the next, without reflection or satisfaction, but only the intensity for completion. The crew had met the Vahni and embraced them, enjoyed their time with them, as Vaughn had simply categorized the encounter as a success and sought to move on to the next goal, the next discovery. Where had his own joy been, he wanted to know, his own sense of wonder? Somehow, he had missed the whole point of his own desire to explore, and now the cruel truth of that left him feeling empty.

Vaughn withdrew the section of coat he had kept pressed to his forehead. He dabbed at his wound with his fingertips to see if the bleeding had stopped; it had. He looked up and regarded the fallen tower. He felt very much like the ruined structure, shaken until it had torn itself apart.

"Stop it," he said aloud. As he so well knew, he could do nothing about the mistakes of the past. He could only look forward. For now, the chance to explore had gone, leaving a mission in its place. He had to reach the source of the pulse and find some way to save the Vahni Vahltupali. Those were his next goals, and he had to concentrate on accomplishing them.

Vaughn stood up and packed up his few provisions once more. He circled the wreckage twice, searching for his phaser, which he had dropped on the roof before the tower had come down. He didn't find it.

Not wanting to use up any more time, Vaughn put the mass of broken stone behind him, headed once more toward the mysterious pulse.

48

Kira worked the control pad set into the bulkhead. "These will be your quarters while you're on the station, Minister," she said as the door coasted open.

"Thank you," Shakaar said. Kira had met the first minister at the docking bay and escorted him here. Their conversation along the way had been limited to official matters, and had been somewhat strained. It only underscored Kira's feeling that Shakaar had put some distance between them.

Until today, they had not spoken in more than six weeks, since she had returned to the station via the Iconian gateway. And their last significant communication, not too long after she had been Attainted a few months ago, had been contentious. At that time, he had let her know that her excommunication could easily threaten her position aboard Deep Space 9. Although he had never suggested that he wanted to remove her from command, he had tacitly warned that, whatever struggles arose for her, she would have to weather them without him. Since then, she had done just that.

"I'll see you tonight at the reception," Kira said, ready to return to her office.

"Of course," Shakaar said. "Would you like to come in for a few minutes?"

The invitation caught Kira off-guard. Shakaar must have seen her hesitation, because he added, "Unless you really need to get back to ops."

"No," she said, curiosity replacing her surprise. "Not at all." He stepped aside to allow her to pass, then followed her into the cabin. The door hummed closed behind them.

"It's good to see you," Shakaar said, moving past her and farther into the room. "Nerys," he added, with a smile. "You can still call me Edon," he told her, "or have things degenerated that badly between us?"

"No, of course not," Kira said immediately, although she really had perceived an iciness in their relationship. She had initially believed that the distance growing between them had only been natural—they had stopped seeing each other romantically a couple of years ago—but she had lately come to believe it a result of Shakaar's political life. Now, apropos of that, she said, "Unless there are some Bajorans listening to us. Maybe then we'd better argue with each other."

Shakaar laughed, a sound Kira had not heard in a while. "That might actually work best for me," he said. "I think you've got more political enemies than I do."

Kira smiled, but Shakaar's jest bothered her. So far as she knew, the only real political opposition she had came from Vedek Yevir and his followers, who had been the ones to Attaint her. *Well, and maybe from Admiral Akaar,* Kira amended.

"May I get you something to drink?" Shakaar asked, crossing over to the replicator in the small dining area.

"No, thank you," she said.

"Oh," he said. "All right." He looked at the replicator for a moment longer, as though deciding whether or not to get something for himself. Then he walked around the dining table and over to the sitting area. "Please," he said, indicating an easy chair, "have a seat."

Kira walked over and sat down in the chair, and Shakaar sat on the sofa across from her. "You've been well, I hope," she said.

"I have," Shakaar told her. "Busy, but well. I trust the same is true of you."

"It is," Kira said, and realized that she meant it. Despite all of the difficult times she had undergone in the last few months, and notwithstanding the potentially tumultuous days approaching for Bajor, she felt strong in her own life. She recalled the swarm of locusts that had infiltrated her sleep last night, but the concerns fueling her dreams she held not for herself, but for her people. Feeling somehow unburdened by the insight, she returned to her thoughts of a moment ago. "Can I ask you about Admiral Akaar?" she said. She saw what she perceived as hesitation in Shakaar's features, and she quickly added, "Off the record."

Shakaar nodded his head slowly as he seemed to consider this. He leaned back on the sofa, spreading his arms wide. "Off the record, certainly," he said. "What can I tell you?"

"What do you think of him?" Kira asked.

Shakaar shrugged. "He's a Starfleet admiral, like all the rest. Perhaps a bit more serious than some, a little more . . ." As he searched for a word to complete his thought, Kira offered her own observation.

"Secretive?" she said.

"I would've said . . . *guarded* . . . but yes," Shakaar agreed. "Has that been a problem?"

Kira shook her head. "I don't know," she said. "I have a vague uneasiness about the admiral." The apparition of the locusts flew across her mind again, and she wondered if their presence in her dream represented a shadow she felt Akaar might somehow cast over her people.

"Are you sure your feelings are about the admiral," Shakaar asked, "and not about the prospect of Bajor joining the Federation?"

Kira thought about the question before answering. The Prophets only knew that she had been asking herself similar questions for days. But she arrived at the same answer now as before. "I think I've come to terms with Bajor's membership in the Federation," she said seriously. "I even believe that it will benefit our people. But I also think that for those in our generation, so many of whom have been horribly wounded by the Occupation, this step might be exceedingly difficult."

"I understand," Shakaar told her. He pulled his arms in and stood up. "I've had similar thoughts. But I'm confident that we can do this, and that it can be a great boon to all of Bajor."

"I think so too," Kira said. "It's just that, with all the rapid changes Bajorans have experienced in the last century—even in the last decade—we've had to struggle to retain our character. I just wonder what will become of our . . . unique identity . . . once we become just one small part of something so much bigger."

"Is that what you're worried about?" Shakaar asked, walking back over to the dining area as he spoke. "That Bajor will join the Federation and become somehow homogenized? Because my experience is that their member worlds are very different, one from another."

"I don't know," Kira admitted. "Yes, that does worry me. But I also think I'm even more concerned about Bajor *not* joining the Federation." If the locusts had represented Akaar to her, Kira realized, then perhaps the shadow that had so frightened her in her dream had not been the Federation descending on Bajor, but Akaar separating Bajor and preventing its membership.

"I've been dealing with this issue for months," Shakaar said. "Believe me when I tell you that there's nothing to worry about. Everything is proceeding exactly as I'd hoped." They were mere words, Kira knew, and perhaps even hollow promises, but despite the prickliness of her recent dealings with Shakaar, she still trusted him. "We're going to need you in the next few days and weeks, and past that."

"I'll be here," Kira said.

"Are you sure I can't get you anything?" he asked, pointing at the replicator.

"No, I'm fine," she said.

"*Moba* juice," Shakaar ordered. Kira could not see the device past him, but she heard its hum. Shakaar turned back toward her after a moment, a tall glass of the purple beverage in one hand. He sipped from the glass, and then said, "There'll be a great deal of work beyond Federation membership. We'll want to diversify, to *enhance* the usefulness of Deep Space 9, especially once the wormhole is reopened to commercial and exploratory traffic. I imagine the Klingons and the Romulans may push for a bigger role in those affairs this time." He started back across the room.

Kira could only imagine how troublesome it would be to have to deal with both Klingon and Romulan officials as permanent residents of the station, but she also understood why those powers would want a hand in occupying such an important area of space. Even discounting any possible threat from the Gamma Quadrant, Bajor and the wormhole had become a virtual crossroads of the galaxy, a place where everybody's interests could be impacted.

Shakaar sat back down on the sofa. He talked about other governments who had expressed a desire to be represented on DS9, rushing through a list that included the Ferengi, the Tholians, and the Gorn. At one point, she thought he even mentioned the Breen—allies of the Dominion during the war, and a people who had shown nothing but animosity toward Bajor and the Federation, even since hostilities had ended—but realized that she must have misunderstood him. Eventually, Shakaar said, "I did ask you in here for a reason, though. Actually, I wanted to ask for your opinion."

"About what?" Kira asked.

Shakaar put his drink down on an end table beside the sofa, then leaned forward. "I wanted to know who you favor as the next kai."

"Oh," she said, not prepared for the question. "Well, I guess it's a foregone conclusion at this point that Vedek Yevir will be elected."

"I'm not asking for a prediction," Shakaar told her. "I'm interested to find out who you believe would best serve as Bajor's spiritual leader. Or did I misinterpret you, and you think that Yevir is the best person for the job?"

"No," Kira said, too quickly, she thought. Her discomfort with Yevir as kai had less to do with his call for the Attainder and more to do with *why* he had done it. "No," she went on, "I don't think Yevir would be a good kai."

Shakaar regarded her for a few seconds, his eyes peering into hers. Finally, he sat back on the sofa. "It's more than that, isn't it?" he said. "It's not that you don't think Yevir would be a good kai; it's that you think he'd be a bad one."

Kira sighed. "Yes, I do think he'd be a bad kai," she confirmed. "More than that, I think that he might actually be dangerous."

"Dangerous?" Shakaar said. "How? Like Winn?"

"No, not like Winn," Kira said at once. She could still grow agitated and angry when she thought of the former kai, a woman who had been motivated by ego and ambition, a political animal far removed from what Kira considered to be a server of the faith. "I don't think Yevir is driven by ambition," she explained. "He truly has a strong faith and a real commitment to our people. But I also think his faith is . . . voracious."

Shakaar looked at her with a quizzical expression. "Surely you don't object to somebody having a passion for their devotion."

"No, of course not," Kira said. "But Yevir's passion is unbridled . . . *unthinking.* He believes so fully that the Prophets guide his every decision that he doesn't really consider the consequences of his actions."

Shakaar nodded slowly, offering a nonverbal sound of understanding, although Kira could not tell whether he agreed with her assessment. "All right, so not Yevir," he said. "Then who? Ungtae?"

Kira could feel herself making a face, no doubt an expression that conveyed both her affection for the old vedek and her reservations about him being elected kai. "I like Ungtae," she said. "He's a good man, with a long record of good service . . ."

"But?" Shakaar asked.

"I don't know," she said. "He's a man of great faith, humble, maybe even wise, but he's just so . . . plain."

"What's wrong with plain?" Shakaar asked.

"Nothing, really," Kira said. "And I'd probably be perfectly happy with Ungtae. It's just that I would rather see a kai who didn't just satisfy the Bajoran people, but inspired them."

Shakaar smiled at her. "Somebody like Opaka," he said.

"Yes," Kira said, returning his smile.

"You really held her in high regard." It was not a question.

"All of Bajor did," she said. "But yes, I think she was an amazing woman.

Gentle but strong, self-possessed but humble. She was a genuine leader, somebody we could all look to for spiritual guidance."

"I liked her too," Shakaar said.

"I know you did."

"But you still haven't answered my question," he said. "If not Yevir or Ungtae, then who?"

"If I had to choose right now?" Kira asked rhetorically. The irony of the notion vexed her, since the Attainder would prevent her from voting for the next kai. "Vedek Pralon."

"Pralon?" Shakaar repeated, reaching for his glass of *moba* juice. "Really?"

"You don't think Pralon would make a good kai?"

Shakaar sipped from the glass, and then said, "Oh, I think Pralon would be a fine choice, but I just wonder how she would be in dealing with other governments."

Other governments? Kira thought, and realized that he must mean the Federation. The reason he was seeking her opinion became clear; Kira probably had more experience with the Federation, at least in the guise of Starfleet, than any other Bajoran. He must also believe that membership was imminent. "I don't know if Vedek Pralon has had much contact with the Federation," she said. "But I think she could handle it."

"I'm not talking about the Federation government," Shakaar said. "I'm talking about—"

A message over the comm system interrupted him. *"Ops to Colonel Kira,"* came the voice of Ensign Ling.

"Go ahead," Kira replied.

"Colonel, the Alonis ambassador is asking to speak with you," Ling reported. Kira had greeted Tel Ammanis Lent, the Alonis ambassador, over a comm channel when her ship had arrived at the station earlier. Because of the environmental suits that the aquatic aliens required in an atmosphere, Lent had chosen to remain aboard her vessel until the reception.

"Tell her I'm on my way," Kira said, standing from her chair.

"Aye, sir," Ling responded.

"Kira out." To Shakaar, she said, "I'm afraid I have to go."

"Of course," he said, standing up as well. "Maybe we can continue this later."

"All right," she said. "I'll see you this evening." Shakaar nodded his acknowledgment, and Kira headed for the door. She thought that the impromptu meeting had gone well, but as she strode out into the corridor, she found herself surprised that Shakaar still valued her opinion.

49

Bashir reexamined his preparations. Every tool aboard ship that he could conceive of needing, whether it be a device, a drug, or a member of his limited staff, now populated the medical bay. This time, he would be ready for whatever happened to Ezri. This time, he would not permit her life to be endangered.

"Are you all set?" Bashir asked as he checked her condition on the medical display. In addition to all of the other measures he had taken, he had also primed Ezri for her second contact with the object. He had insisted on being allowed a couple of hours to design a treatment that would fortify those areas and processes within her body that had previously been threatened. Now, as he stood beside the diagnostic bed on which she lay, he felt confident that he had provided Ezri the medical reinforcement to safely withstand the coming trauma.

"I'm ready," Ezri said. She peered up at him, an expression of determination set into her features. Bashir thought that he also saw a speck of fear in her eyes, an observation that actually pleased him. No matter how strongly Ezri believed that she had to take this course of action, her fear indicated that she had not made the choice without the proper consideration. Indeed, her decision to proceed despite her fear seemed heroic. As he looked down at her adorable round face and into her beautiful deep eyes, an intense feeling of pride surged within him. The emotion filled him up, and all he could think was how much he loved this woman.

"All right, then," Bashir said. He reached up and tapped his combadge. "Bashir to Bowers."

"Bowers here."

"We're ready to begin," Bashir told him. As long as Ezri remained in the medical bay, and Commander Vaughn on the planet's surface, Bowers would be in command of *Defiant*.

"Acknowledged, Doctor. Keep me informed," he said. *"Bowers out."*

Bashir looked across the room to where Nurses Richter and Juarez sat at neighboring consoles. During Ezri's contact with the object, Richter would monitor the condition of the Dax symbiont, and Juarez Ezri's condition, both backing up Bashir's own observations.

"Well, then," Bashir said. "Let's get started." He reached to a shelf beside the bed and retrieved a tricorder. "I'm lowering the containment field." On the other side of the bed stood the portable stand, and atop it sat the mysterious object. After the attempt to transport the object had failed, Nog had devised a means of physically moving it via a magnetic containment field. The operation had been delicate work, but an engineering team had managed to remove the object from the Jefferies tube and load it onto the stand.

Bashir worked the tricorder, which Nog had configured as a control interface for the containment field. Around the object, a curtain of blue pinpoints flashed into view, accompanied by a low buzz. In a second, the pinpoints and the hum had gone, as had the containment field.

He looked back down at Ezri. He felt a sudden urge to stop her from doing this, but he fought the impulse. Last time, Ezri's contact with the object had been accidental and unexpected. This time, he would be with her from the very beginning, and that and his careful preparations would see to it that she made it through the experience.

"I'll see you soon," she said, and smiled.

"You bet you will," he responded, forcing his lips into a thin smile of his own. He thought to say something more, but phrases such as *Pleasant journey* and *Bon voyage* seemed insufficient. Instead, he simply said, "Good luck."

Ezri reached up, found his hand, and squeezed. He squeezed back, and then she let go. She took a deep breath, lifted her other hand, and reached out above the portable stand and the object. She glanced up once more at Bashir, then lowered her hand. Although the dark substance appeared liquid, no movement rippled across its surface as Ezri's hand came to rest within it.

Immediately, a rush of air escaped Ezri in a grunt, her eyes fell shut, and her head lolled to the side. Bashir looked up at the diagnostic panel. As he watched, Ezri's heart rate decreased and her respiration slowed, and her neural activity started to ebb. Juarez called out the changes from his console.

"I see," Bashir said, more to himself than to Juarez. *I see, and I'm ready.* He set the tricorder back down on the shelf, exchanging it for a hypospray he had previously prepared. Out of habit, he checked the drug in the ampoule—delactovine, a systemic stimulant, since cordrazine had not been completely effective last time—as well as the dosage setting. Then he turned his gaze back to the diagnostic panel, set to act once Ezri's readings had fallen beneath a certain threshold. But that did not happen. Both her heart rate and her respiration reached a plateau, leveling off well above where they had during Ezri's first contact with the object. Again, Juarez reported the changes.

Bashir watched the readings remain stable for a few more minutes, then set down the hypo. He checked Dax's readings, and saw that they remained within a normal range. Bashir's preventive measures appeared to be working. He would have to keep an eye on Ezri's neural activity, but at the moment, neither host nor symbiont seemed to be in any danger.

Bashir inhaled deeply, then let the breath out slowly, releasing some of the tension in his body. He peered down at Ezri's inert form, at the shallow rise and fall of her chest, and wished that he could do something more for her. But for now, all he could do was wait.

Bashir paced. He moved back and forth past the foot of Ezri's bed, his gaze shuttling between her face and the diagnostic panel. During the past hour, her vital signs had begun to slip again, though not yet in a way that threatened her health. The most significant changes had been in her neural activity and isoboramine levels. Bashir had worked to keep both from diminishing too much, employing a cortical stimulator and a round of benzocyatizine injections. The measures had succeeded in slowing, but not stopping, Ezri's decline. Soon, if the decreases continued, he would put an end to this.

He stopped, then walked forward until he stood beside the head of the bed. He picked up the tricorder from the shelf, then peered down at Ezri's soft face. Her skin had paled, he saw, leaving the ribbon of spots down the sides of her face and neck contrasting starkly with her pallor. The cortical stimulator sat affixed to her forehead, the blinking green and red lights of the small device indicating its functional status.

"Neural activity down another tenth of a percent," Juarez reported from across the medical bay.

Bashir glanced up at the diagnostic panel and confirmed the reading. "Acknowledged," he said, and looked back down at Ezri.

He hated seeing her like this. Even though it had been her choice to take this action, it troubled him. He understood that if her interpretation of events had been correct regarding her first contact with the object, then Ezri's declining neural processes and isoboramine levels coincided with Dax's mental contact with—

With what? Bashir asked himself in a burst of anger. With a pool of unimpressive slime that somehow extended into other dimensions? He felt his jaw clench and his hands tense. *How could she have done this?* he thought. How could she have so obviously risked her life—and her life with him—for this speculation?

Bashir squeezed his eyes closed, suddenly furious with Ezri. And with himself, he realized. Why had he agreed to this? For Ezri? For the Vahni? The Vahni would not be served by the unnecessary and avoidable death of Ezri Dax.

Pain coursed through his palm. He looked down and saw his hand gripped so tightly about the tricorder that his flesh had gone white. He opened his hand and dropped the device back onto the shelf, where it rattled among other equipment. A hypospray skittered off and fell to the floor.

He stared at his hand. Indentations decorated the fleshy part of his palm, tinged red now as blood flowed back to the areas. He tried to bring his anger under control, but instead, his ire rose, and he imagined sweeping his arm across the shelf in front of him, knocking everything to the floor. *No, not the shelf,* he thought, and looked over at the stand, and at the bizarre object resting upon it. He saw himself pulling Ezri's hand from the substance, and then upending the stand . . . aiming a phaser . . .

Bashir raised a hand to his face, wiping it across his eyes. He felt pressure in his temples, and a wave of exhaustion washed over him. He suddenly wanted nothing more than to sleep. If he could just—

"Doctor," Juarez called, and Bashir recognized the note of concern in the lieutenant's voice even before the alarm sounded. Bashir dropped his hand and opened his eyes. He looked up at the diagnostic panel, the source of the warning tones, and saw that Ezri's neural activity had dropped precipitously, her other vital signs following it down. He acted at once, almost without thought, a product of his training and abilities. He reached for the hypospray of delac-tovine, but could not locate it on the shelf. He quickly crouched and looked on the floor, recalling the hypo that had fallen, but he did not see it.

"Edgardo," he called, standing back up, "prepare a delactovine injection." As Juarez acknowledged the order, Bashir pulled the tricorder from the shelf. He did not even realize the decision he had made until he reached across the bed and pulled Ezri's hand from the object. He lowered her arm down beside her body, then worked the tricorder. The haze of blue dots that indicated the activation of the containment field buzzed on around the object.

Juarez raced over, a hypo held up in his hand. Bashir took it, verified the drug, and set the dosage. Quickly, he applied the nozzle end of the hypo to Ezri's neck. The short hiss of air was a welcome sound. He peered up at the diagnostic panel, waiting for the changes that would come. And they did come: heart rate, respiration, blood pressure, and numerous other readings. And still her neural activity remained dangerously low, so low that her autonomic func-tions could be endangered. If her brain ceased to function above a certain minimal level, Ezri's body would no longer sustain itself: her heart would cease to beat on its own, her blood would cease to flow through her veins, her lungs would no longer expand and contract.

Bashir reached up to the cortical stimulator and touched a control. At once, the blinking of the green and red lights sped up. He looked to the diag-nostic panel again, but after a few seconds, only a marginal increase marked Ezri's neural activity. Bashir shook his head, a calmness settling over him as he considered the next steps he would have to take. He reached for the hypos and other medical equipment on the shelf by the bed. He had prepared for this contingency. Now he could only take the actions he had planned, and hope that they would be enough to save Ezri.

50

Charivretha sat at the dining table with Thirishar's bondmates, a tall glass of Andorian ale in her hand. She had arrived just as Thriss, Anichent, and Dizhei had been starting dinner. At Dizhei's invitation, Charivretha sat down at the table with them, although she would not join them in their meal; in just a few minutes, she would be leaving for the ambassadorial reception.

It had been an arduous, tiring day, spent in meticulous preparation for the summit tomorrow. Charivretha did well with details, able to master massive amounts of facts, allowing herself to recall them effortlessly as needed; she could sometimes even cull unexpected and valuable conclusions from previously unvisited juxtapositions of information. But for all of that, she cared less for the preliminaries and more for the actual job. She enjoyed politics, not paperwork.

Throughout the long day today, Charivretha had looked forward to a glass of ale. She could not abide replicated versions of the drink, but Anichent had discovered that the barkeeper on the station possessed a couple of bottles in his stock. She had asked Anichent to purchase them, as good an excuse as any to visit Thirishar's bondmates this evening. Thirishar had offered the three of them the use of his quarters just before departing on his mission, and they had all moved in here that same day. Charivretha tried to spend as much time as possible here with them, but her responsibilities sometimes interfered, as had been the case during the past few days.

Now, she smoothed the white, thickly textured fabric of the formal dress she wore, and then raised her glass in salute. Anichent sat across from her at the table, the tall, hardy figure putting her in mind of Zherathrizar, one of her own bondmates. Dizhei, already old for her years, but very sweet, sat to her right, and Thriss, usually so lively, but quiet right now, sat to her left.

"To family," Charivretha said as she lifted her glass. Only Anichent and Dizhei followed her lead—Anichent had ale; Dizhei's glass contained water—and matched her toast. Thriss continued eating her meal, not looking up. Charivretha chose to let the discourtesy pass. She sipped at her drink, the fiery liquid tumbling down her gullet like warm gravel, heating and rasping her throat, and leaving behind a delicious warmth and fullness.

Anichent smacked his lips and delivered a husky sigh after taking a healthy gulp of the ale. He really did resemble Zherathrizar in many ways, Charivretha thought, from some of his mannerisms to his mode of dress; the brown leather vest he wore over a pale green tunic and brown pants gave him the air of an outdoorsman, though she knew his aspirations actually leaned toward politics. "I thought I was overcharged for the ale," he said in a voice made deeper by the Andorian drink, "but now I'd have to say it was worth it."

"And I'd have to agree," Charivretha said in a bass whisper. She cleared her throat, and then looked over to Dizhei. "Are you sure you wouldn't like some?" she asked the prim schoolteacher.

"Thank you," Dizhei said, "but I don't want to change the sound of my voice." She smiled, a clear signal that she understood and accepted the good-natured teasing.

"So, what have you been doing during the past few days?" Charivretha asked. She looked from Dizhei to Anichent to Thriss, including all of them in her question, although again, Thriss did not look up from her dinner.

"Actually, we've begun touring the station," Anichent said around bites of his meal. "This is a very interesting place."

"Really?" Charivretha said. She did not care much for Deep Space 9 herself, finding it a sterile and unwelcoming environment. The unfriendly Cardassian architecture certainly contributed to that feeling, and the Bajoran climate bothered her even more. Here, in Thirishar's quarters, the temperature and humidity had been elevated to sufficiently high levels, but in the public areas of the station the coldness and aridity made her constantly uncomfortable.

"We wanted to acquaint ourselves with Shar's new life," Dizhei explained.

"That's a lovely sentiment," Charivretha said. She admired the forgiveness Thirishar's bondmates managed for him, despite his continually selfish behavior. She loved her *chei,* but he embarrassed her at times, even shamed her, by the self-centered way in which he had chosen to live his life.

With her thoughts, a seed of anger began to form deep within her. As she felt it grow, she very deliberately put her glass of ale down on the table. As an ambassador, she always searched for ways in which she could effectively hide and then restrain her emotions, and she found that concentrating on specific movements could serve that purpose.

"Today, we went to the operations center," Anichent said. "We contacted Lieutenant Ro, and she got authorization for us from the station commander."

"A young Bajoran man escorted us around while we were there," Dizhei said. "He was kind enough to show us where Shar works. It was very exciting."

"I'm glad that you're enjoying your time here," Charivretha said. Then, as casually as she could, she asked, "Did all three of you visit the operations center?"

Dizhei cast her eyes downward, immediately conveying an answer to Charivretha.

"No," Anichent said, keeping his tone light. "It was just Dizhei and me."

"I see," Charivretha said. She reached forward and picked up her glass, again allowing the small physical action to cover and redirect her rising emotion. It concerned her that Thriss had not accompanied her bondmates on their tour, particularly considering the young woman's dour mood this evening. Of course, Thriss's emotions had always run at speed, and sometimes out of control—it remained a wonder to Charivretha that Thriss had managed to complete her studies and become a physician—and so perhaps today represented an isolated incident. "So where else have you been on the station?" she asked.

"Well, we've certainly spent plenty of time on the Promenade," Anichent said, and then added, rather melodramatically, "shopping." He raised his eyebrows and sent a sidelong glance at Dizhei.

"Oh, I haven't been that bad," Dizhei protested. The two began to bicker playfully, obviously a comfortable scene the pair had acted out on many other occasions. Charivretha liked these people, and she felt gratified that Thirishar had been so fortunate with the bondmates who had been selected for him. During the confrontation she had engineered before he had departed on his mission, Charivretha had wondered whether she had made a wise choice in bringing all three of them to the space station. She had initially considered sending only for Anichent, with whom Thirishar had formed his first romantic bond; ch'Thane knew that her *chei* found stability and peace in that relationship, but she had also realized that any chance of convincing Thirishar to return to Andor would require something other than a promise of constancy. And in the end, it had been the emotionalism and volatility of Thriss that had finally compelled his agreement to come back home.

Anichent and Dizhei had moved past their lighthearted raillery about shopping and returned to the subject of where they had been on the station during the last few days. Anichent mentioned the mid-core science, engineering, and administrative facilities, the runabout bays, and the docking pylons. Charivretha took another drink of her ale—a gulp this time, and not just a sip—and set her glass back down. "Thriss," she said, attempting to remain conversational, although her voice had been roughened by the ale. "How have you enjoyed these places?"

At last, Thriss looked up from her meal. "I've stayed here," she said. "I wanted to stay close to Shar."

"I can understand that," Charivretha said carefully, "but really, you should occupy yourself until he returns."

"I miss him," Thriss said simply.

"I do too," Dizhei said. "I just want Shar to come back from his mission and then come home with us. I want our *shelthreth* . . ." If there was more to her thought, she did not give voice to it.

"You know me," Anichent said, shrugging. "I encouraged him to join Starfleet, because I knew that's what he wanted." He paused, and Charivretha thought he was deciding just how much he wanted to say about how he felt. "I just never thought he'd leave Andor so soon. Or stay away so long. I miss him too."

"I know," Charivretha said. She thought of her own bondmates, and how unthinkable—how unlivable—it would have been for any one of them to do to their group what Thirishar was now doing to his. "But at least he finally promised to come home," she said, trying to focus on the positive. Both Anichent and Dizhei nodded and smiled, and Thriss returned her attention to her plate. Charivretha could see that none of Thirishar's bondmates felt all that sure of his pledge. Either they doubted his word, or they doubted Thriss's account of his giving it. Whichever the case was, Anichent and Dizhei at least seemed to be dealing well enough with their misgivings; Thriss evidently was not.

"I know Shar promised to come back to Andor with us," Anichent admitted, "but I'm just not so sure that he actually will."

"Of course he will," Charivretha pronounced. "I won't allow his Starfleet career to stand in the way." She regretted the strength of her words at once; she thought that a lighter touch was required here.

Anichent put his fork down on his plate and folded his hands together, resting his elbows on the table. "Shar didn't leave Andor to join Starfleet. He didn't leave *us* for Starfleet." A strange quality in his tone made it seem as though he had discovered an unpleasant truth. "I know we talk that way, but Shar's told us many times why he left."

"What Thirishar may say and what may be true," Charivretha said, peering across the table at Anichent, "are not necessarily the same." No words and no reasons, she knew, could explain away the irresponsibility of what Shar had done.

"I know that," Anichent said, meeting Charivretha's gaze, almost challenging her. "But I've been wondering if he might be right about our people. Maybe the way of life we've chosen as a race won't save us after all."

"That's absurd," Charivretha said, no longer concerned about the force of her tone. "Since the reforms, the death rate has decreased significantly."

"We're not dying as fast as a people," Anichent allowed, "but maybe . . . I don't know . . . maybe some of us are dying a lot faster as individuals."

"What do you mean?" Dizhei wanted to know.

"What he means doesn't make any sense," Charivretha said. "It's simply doubletalk to allow Thirishar to obviate his responsibilities." She felt angry not only at the negativity of the conversation, particularly in front of Thriss, but that anybody at all could try to justify her *chei*'s actions. She fought to keep her emotions in check.

"No, it's not doubletalk," Anichent said. "Shar wasn't happy on Andor. He didn't like not having choices about some important things in his life. To stay there would only have continued to hurt him."

"He did—and does—have a choice about loving you, Thavanichent," Charivretha said. "And about loving Vindizhei and Shathrissía. And he does love all of you."

"I know he does," Anichent said. "I know."

"And with love come certain obligations," Charivretha told him. "And that's true whether you're an Andorian or a Klingon or a Tholian."

"Obligations, yes," Anichent said. "But I'm not sure love—real love—makes *demands*. An obligation is something Shar should want to fulfill, but our demands . . . the demands of our society . . . I think maybe we've been asking too much of Shar."

"That's ridiculous," Charivretha said. She pushed her chair back and stood up, unable to remain still. "Nothing has been asked of Shar that hasn't been asked of generations before him."

"Then maybe we've been asking too much of all of us," Anichent suggested.

"It doesn't matter," Thriss said suddenly. All eyes turned toward her. She still sat with her head down. "Nothing will matter if Shar doesn't come back from his mission."

"Thriss, don't," Dizhei said, obviously saddened by her bondmate's despondency.

Anichent reached over and tenderly put his hand on Thriss's forearm. "He *will* be back," he insisted.

Thriss slowly withdrew her arm from Anichent's touch. She stood from her chair. "Excuse me," she said, and Charivretha thought she saw tears in the young woman's eyes. Thriss walked from the dining area and across the room, disappearing into the bedroom.

Dizhei looked over at Anichent. "I'm going to go to her," she told him. He nodded, and she followed Thriss through the bedroom door.

Charivretha and Anichent regarded each other across the table. "I'm not sure what any of us are going to do if Shar doesn't come back to Andor this time," he said quietly.

"He'll come back," Charivretha said, as though stating a fact. "I've got to get to the reception. Thank you for the ale." Anichent nodded, and Charivretha rose and headed for the door. She expected that he might say something more to her, but then she had entered the corridor and the door had closed behind her.

As she strode toward the turbolift, she realized that, if Thirishar did not come back to Andor this time, then she had no idea what she would do either.

51

Vaughn watched his daughter die, and in that terrible instant, he relived the moment of their separation, felt the weight of the years since, and regretted everything.

Prynn's body landed in a heap beside the captain's chair. The air grew heavy with the awful smell of her burned flesh. Vaughn stood in front of the chair and looked down at her, his heart aching. He studied Prynn's inert face, her slack features a harsh contradiction to the horrific injuries she had suffered.

Vaughn felt the need to move away from his daughter, and to reach the console she had just been operating. He wanted to suppress his emotions and focus on keeping *Defiant* intact and headed away from its attackers. Prynn was dead, but the rest of the crew were not.

Except that there was no flight control console, no *Defiant*. There were no crew, and no attackers. And so Vaughn crouched down next to Prynn. He reached out to touch her, but stopped as a memory drifted through his mind. He turned his hand up, and was actually relieved when he saw that his palm had not been scorched.

There's no conn for me to burn my hand on, he thought, but the notion floated through his consciousness like vapor, there one moment, dissipated the next. He stretched his arm out toward Prynn again. His fingers alit on her shoulder, pressing lightly. The texture of her uniform, the resistance of the unmoving body beneath, all seemed real—though he knew none of it could be.

Vaughn reached down and dipped two fingers into the pooled fluid atop Prynn's mangled midsection. He brought his fingers up to his face, and saw that they were red with blood. His daughter's blood. The realization slammed into him with incredible emotional force. Anger, heartbreak, and guilt filled him.

Why are you doing this? he asked himself. *Why are you reliving this?* He believed that this could not be real. He had not traveled back six weeks to this moment, nor had the moment traveled forward to him. But no matter the explanation, he had no time for this; he had a mission to accomplish.

Vaughn stood up and peered down at his daughter. Peered *past* her. Beneath Prynn's body, the decking appeared as it should, covered with a light gray carpet. But just beyond her, the carpet faded away, blending along an irregular border into the surface of the road. Vaughn looked up and saw this dead and deadly planet stretching away from him in all directions. And yet he also stood on one small section of *Defiant*'s bridge, around the captain's chair. And though he knew that Prynn would not die—had not died—and though he knew that this could not be real, his heart still grieved for the loss of his daughter. Grieved as it had when this had actually happened. He felt the familiar rage and anguish, the enormous guilt, and he wondered how this could have happened again.

It's not happening again, he forced himself to think. Prynn was not dying—not almost dying—again. Ruriko was not dying again.

Vaughn pushed himself back into the moment, back onto the empty planet from which waves of destruction had been launched at the Vahni. He looked out at the vacant landscape, and with an effort, walked from the fragment of *Defiant*'s bridge and back onto the road. He examined his fingertips again, and saw them still wet and red with blood. He turned, expecting—not expecting; *hoping*—that the scene had vanished. But the incomplete center section of *Defiant*'s bridge sat incongruously in the middle of the road.

His mind reeled, vainly attempting to make sense of what he saw. Of what he knew. Of what he felt. For real or not, explicable or not, his emotions were genuine, more than mere echoes of what had come before. Profound sadness held him in its grip. Prynn had not died, and yet he felt as he had in that moment when he had believed that she had been killed.

Vaughn seemed trapped, encaged by his own sorrow. He had lost any sense of time, he realized, and conscious thoughts not born of his feelings had become difficult to manage. Everything had slowed down around him, as though this instant when he had thought Prynn dead would never end.

Is that what this is? he forced himself to think. An effort to slow him down, to prevent him from reaching the pulse and trying to shut it down? And if so, would not a phaser blast, or even a well-thrown stone, have sufficed?

Vaughn wanted to turn from the scene of Prynn's near-death, but found that he could not tear his gaze away. He stood there for long moments, struggling. Finally, he allowed the kilometers that had passed beneath his boots to take over. Tired from the physical efforts of the last day and a half, Vaughn let his eyelids close. The heartache remained, but with Prynn's still figure no longer visible, he found enough will to employ an old mantra and try to rein in his emotions: *You have a mission*.

Vaughn turned, then opened his eyes. The empty road extended away from him, and he started walking again.

The sky reached down. Vaughn watched as, maybe two kilometers ahead, the clouds swirled above and funneled down to the road like a tornado. He pulled out his tricorder, although he was no more certain of the device than he was of his own senses anymore. He attempted a scan, but the interference from the energy made it impossible.

As Vaughn walked on, he saw a piece of his past come alive. The whirlpool of gray clouds withdrew from the road by degrees, eddies of energy spinning the matter beneath it into a different form. The effect reminded him of a transporter or a replicator, but not working all at once, instead rebuilding from the bottom up.

Even when it was only partially completed, Vaughn recognized the structure the clouds were creating. Tall—and he knew it would grow taller still—it spanned the roadway and well beyond. A complex steel framework sat perched atop a concrete base.

So this is what's happening, he thought. *And this is how it's going to be.* Harriman, Ventu, Prynn, and now this—not time travel, not holograms, not illusions or delusions. Not real, exactly, not *authentic,* but real enough, the energy clouds somehow reorganizing matter into people and places and events from his past—and probably recreating the corresponding sensor readings on his tri-corder. Someone or something was peering into his mind, into his memories.

But why?

Vaughn walked on, determined to reach the site of the pulse. By the time he reached the steel-and-concrete structure, its construction had been completed, the funnel of gray energy withdrawing back up into the cloud cover. The gantry towered above him. The tangled mass of metal gave the impression of architectural confusion, but Vaughn knew that every beam, every conduit, every joint, had been meticulously planned and constructed. The launchpad looked no different now from when he had visited here as a teen.

Vaughn strode through the flame trench, the channel between the two huge concrete slabs on which the tower complex sat. When humankind's early spacecraft had lifted off from here, taken into orbit by massive, controlled explosions of fuel, the initial fires had been diverted here. Up ahead, the huge steel wall that had directed the flames reached from slab to slab. At the bottom of one side of the wall, daylight peered through an open doorway. Vaughn headed there at a steady gait, determined to put this slice of his past behind him as quickly as possible.

Vaughn had read about this place as a boy, captured as he had been by the promise and wonder of exploration. But he recalled now that the joy he had expected to feel when he had first visited this place had never materialized, supplanted by his knowledge of the tragedy that had begun here. As it had then, melancholy now swept over him.

The heels of his boots clicked along the concrete that had replaced the roadway, the sound reverberating hollowly between the walls of the slabs. Vaughn tried to concentrate on humanity's first steps out into the cosmos, many of which had been taken from this very place. But he could not remain focused on such thoughts, his mind being pulled back again and again to his first trip to Cape Canaveral. And back to Prynn lying nearly dead on the bridge of *Defiant.* And to Ventu, killed in the collapse of the tower. And to Captain Harriman, back on that fateful day.

Vaughn kept his eyes on the open doorway in the steel wall at the end of the flame trench. The rectangle of light sat dwarfed by the black wall. Vaughn felt insignificant amid his massive surroundings, and a sense of the helplessness and fear that must have enveloped the people whose deaths had begun here closed in around him.

As he neared the doorway, Vaughn told himself that he should not stop beyond it. That he *would* not stop beyond it. He knew what was there, had seen it all those years ago, and he did not need to see it right now. *You have a mission,* he thought again, and began repeating the phrase over and over in his mind.

It did not matter. He passed through the doorway, saw the roadway reappear beyond the launchpad, and then peered to his right, as though he had no control over his own body. The plaque hung there on the concrete slab, brass letters raised on a darker background. Vaughn stopped and read it.

LAUNCH COMPLEX 39, PAD B
TUESDAY, 28 JANUARY 1986
1139 HOURS

DEDICATED TO THE LIVING MEMORY OF THE CREW OF
SHUTTLE ORBITER CHALLENGER, OV–99

COMMANDER FRANCIS R. "DICK" SCOBEE
COMMANDER MICHAEL J. SMITH, PILOT
RONALD E. McNAIR, MISSION SPECIALIST
ELLISON ONIZUKA, MISSION SPECIALIST
JUDITH A. RESNIK, MISSION SPECIALIST
GREGORY B. JARVIS, PAYLOAD SPECIALIST
S. CHRISTA McAULIFFE, PAYLOAD SPECIALIST

"THIS DAY"
SEVEN EXPLORERS
SAILED ON A FLAME OVER
THE EDGE OF THE WORLD

The words struck Vaughn like a punch to the face. He felt dazed and sad and alone. His knees wavered beneath him, and he thought for a second that he would go down. He looked skyward, the gray launch tower pushing up toward the gray clouds above.

"Stop it," Vaughn yelled, elongating the vowels. "Stop it." Somehow, he kept his feet. He dropped his head back down, and said, "You have a mission. Stop feeling what you're feeling." He peered to his left, at the road as it headed away. "You have a mission," Vaughn said. "You have a mission."

He repeated it another fifty times before he was finally able to get himself moving again.

Vaughn walked on.

He walked through a section of battlefield on Beta VI, where he and his team had been unable to do anything but watch as more than eleven thousand men had beaten each other to death with rocks and sticks. Today, he saw only one member of his team, and perhaps only a dozen men attacking each other, their boots sloppy with the blood of the corpses lying at their feet.

He walked past the dark, stale cell—not much more than a box—in which the Breen had once kept him for seven weeks. He had survived only by licking at the damp stones of the walls, and by killing and eating the *aurowaqqa*—furry, ten-legged creatures, larger than his hand—that had occasionally found their way into his prison. He killed an *aurowaqqa* today, beneath the heel of his boot, unable to stop himself, and then felt . . . diminished . . . for having done so.

He walked down the streets of Pentabo, on Verillia, amid throngs of emaciated children, orphaned by war and living in the wreckage of their world. The desperate, hungry faces he saw today reflected more sorrow and pain than should have been possible for young people to feel. The scene broke his heart anew.

He walked along the corridors of *Kamal,* the old Cardassian freighter lost in the Badlands. Bajorans, whose gaunt bodies betrayed their horrific lives under the Occupation, sprawled dead throughout the ship, their Cardassian oppressors dead beside them. He looked for the Orb, speculating about a connection to this haunted planet, but his experience did not extend to that portion of the freighter.

And finally, as the already pale sky faded toward the onset of night, Vaughn stood on the bridge of *T'Plana-Hath,* staring at the viewscreen, living again that terrible moment when he had first known for sure that Ruriko was gone. Part of him died with her.

Vaughn walked on.

The light would be gone soon. Because of the amount of the energy interference, the tricorder could not tell Vaughn how far he had traveled today, but it did not matter. Either he would reach the pulse, or he would not. Less than a day remained now before the next destructive wave would launch into space.

Vaughn's legs, very tired now but still strong, had held up remarkably well to this point, and he felt confident that he would not falter physically. On an emotional level, though, his strength had waned greatly. That the people and places he had seen on his journey had been re-creations and not precisely genuine was irrelevant, because his reactions to those people and places had been genuine—both whenever they had first occurred and again today.

As Vaughn marched up another rise, he dreaded what he would find on the other side. The experiences of his past had been appearing closer together, and he expected another incident shortly. "You have a mission," he said, despite the uncertainty of his emotions and of his ability to control them.

As he reached the top of the rise, Vaughn tried to brace himself for whatever lay beyond it. It did not work. He stopped, his eyes narrowing as he regarded what he saw before him.

In the distance, a complex of neglected structures spread across the landscape. From this height, Vaughn could see into their midst. No buildings stood in the center of the complex. There was only a circle of darkness.

The site of the pulse.

52

The wardroom hummed with the sounds of many voices. Kira stood near the doors and surveyed the reception. The Bajoran, Alonis, Trill, and Andorian delegations, all clad in formalwear, continued socializing warmly with each other. Kira had earlier decided to stop speculating about what the future would hold, but if the smiles among the guests were any indication, then Bajor would be a member of the Federation within the next couple of minutes. The mood here had been so positive throughout the evening that even the normally austere Akaar seemed to be enjoying himself. That had seemed like a breakthrough for the unapproachable admiral, and Kira elected to take it as a promising sign. Overall, she thought, the event had been a rousing success.

Not typically enthusiastic herself about mingling with government figures, Kira had actually spent time tonight doing just that. She had moved about the room with relative abandon, drawing both the ambassadors and their staffs into conversation. She supposed that she had wanted to put on Bajor's best face, though she of course knew that her behavior here would have no bearing on the talks. Still, she liked being positive.

A few meters in front of Kira, Shakaar, and the Trill ambassador, Gandres, were speaking with one of the two officers Kira had introduced as her aides. The two—Sergeants Etana and Shul—were actually Lieutenant Ro's deputies, and the only signs visible to Kira of what she knew was incredibly tight security. As she watched, Shakaar, Gandres, and Etana moved to one side, allowing Tel Ammanis Lent, the Alonis ambassador, to float past them in her antigrav chair. Lent thanked the trio for their courtesy as she went by, and then glided over to Kira.

"Ambassador," Kira greeted her, smiling. "I hope that you're having a pleasant evening."

"I am, thank you, Colonel," Lent said, her words passing through a level of conversion even before reaching Kira's universal translator. The water-breathing Alonis, when not in an aquatic environment, wore formfitting suits that held a layer of water suspended against their scales. The helmets they wore contained a device that transmitted the sounds of their underwater voices out into the air. "And the food," Lent went on, "is the best I've had at a foreign facility." Kira did not know exactly how the Alonis ate while wearing their environmental suits, but obviously they somehow managed the feat.

"I'm glad you like it," Kira said. "It's just Bajoran hospitality."

"And you are certainly very welcoming," Lent said. "By the way, the kelp is truly delicious."

"Good," Kira said. "I'd heard it was flavorful." While it surprised her that Quark had actually been telling the truth about the exorbitantly priced kelp, what intrigued her more were the Alonis themselves. They physically resembled the creatures of myth that possessed the head and upper body of a Bajoran and the tail of a fish. The silvery bodies of the Alonis were not precisely like that, but similar; their head and torso were more or less humanoid in shape and function, but they had a long tail structure instead of legs, and short fins in place of arms. They had no opposable digits, but had developed an advanced civilization via their short-range psychokinetic ability, which they used to manipulate water into essentially solid tools. They had joined the Federation forty years ago, and were widely regarded as a kind and peaceful people.

"So I'd like to know, Colonel," Lent asked, "have you ever been to Alonis?"

"I haven't," Kira admitted. "But I have been reading about your people and your world. It sounds like you have a beautiful civilization." The ambassador flipped up the bottom of her tail. Kira had learned just a few minutes ago from one of Lent's aides that such a gesture indicated grateful acknowledgment. "Have you ever been to Bajor?"

"I have not," the ambassador said. "But the rich green of your oceans seems like quite an exotic setting." The waters on Alonis, Kira had read, were colored a deep purple, like those on Trill. "I look forward to visiting them one day."

"Well, there are no underwater cities—" The doors to the ward-room whispered open behind Kira, and she glanced over her shoulder to see who had entered. Quark stood there, carrying a tray of what appeared to be Bajoran fruits in a *jumja* glaze. He quickly scanned the room, as though searching for somebody. When he spotted Kira nearby, he immediately stepped over to her.

"Colonel, have you seen Lieutenant Ro?" he asked. He seemed agitated to Kira, and she could only imagine what sort of trouble he had caused this time.

"No, I haven't," she told him, but Quark's attention had already left her. He moved his head from side to side, apparently trying to see past some of the guests.

"Is that her?" he said suddenly, and he thrust the tray of desserts at Kira. She instinctively put her hands up and took the tray, and Quark hurried away.

"Quark," she called after him, but he was already halfway across the room, weaving a path through the guests. Both exasperated and a bit embarrassed, Kira looked back at Lent. "Ambassador, if you'll pardon me," she said.

"Of course, Colonel."

Kira strode in the opposite direction Quark had taken. She went to the end of the room, where tables had been set up for the food. She found an empty space and set the tray down, then turned to look for Quark. Before she located him, though, the doors to the wardroom slid open once more. This time, Ro Laren entered. "Lieutenant," Kira called as she made her way over to the security chief.

"Colonel," Ro said. "Is there something wrong?"

"No, not at all," Kira said. "In fact, I'd like to compliment you on security. You've really done a fine job."

"Thank you," Ro said. The lieutenant seemed distracted, her gaze constantly moving about the room—part of her security training, Kira assumed.

"Quark just came in here looking for you," Kira warned her.

"Quark?" Ro said. "Did he say—"

A blur of movement occurred at Kira's side. "Laren," Quark burst in. "I need to speak with you."

Laren? Kira thought, and she wondered when Quark had developed the nerve to address the security chief by her given name.

"Not now, Quark," Ro said, her eyes still moving about, studying the room. "I'm on duty."

"Laren, listen," he said, dropping the volume of his voice down to what Kira thought of as a conspiratorial level. The Ferengi drifted sideways, insinuating himself between Kira and Ro, his back to Kira. "I need to know what's going on here."

"Did you ever think that if we didn't tell you about it," Kira said over his shoulder, "that it might not be any of your business?"

Quark ignored Kira and continued talking to Ro. "Please," he implored her. "I need to know—"

"I said not now," Ro told him, her tone firm. She stopped scanning the room and peered down at Quark. "The colonel is right: this isn't your business."

Quark staggered back as though Ro had struck him. Kira jumped back, only narrowly avoiding him stepping on her feet. Ro looked up at Kira. "Colonel, if everything's under control here, there are other security matters I need to tend to."

"We're fine here," Kira said. Ro nodded, then quickly turned and left. Quark stared after her for a moment, then started for the doors. Kira stopped him with a hand on his shoulder. "I believe you were about to serve more desserts," she said. Quark looked back at her, out of the corner of his eye, and then back at the closed doors. Kira wondered what had happened—what Quark had probably done—to cause him such anxiety with Ro. She would have to remember to ask the security chief about it later.

When Quark still did not move, Kira leaned in toward his ear. "If you don't start serving again," she said, "then I'm going to have to penalize your breach of contract by closing the bar down for a few days." She noticed that she did not smell the rancid cologne that he often wore.

Quark turned and looked her in the eyes. He muttered something under his breath and moved past her, headed for the food tables.

As Kira watched him go, she saw Akaar standing by himself. He had a drink in his hand, and he seemed to be observing the rest of the guests. Kira decided that the time and place were right for her to try to establish a rapprochement with the admiral. She strode over to him. "Good evening," she said. "I hope you're having a pleasant time."

Akaar regarded her in a manner to which she had become accustomed by now, with an aloofness that suggested judgment and suspicion. She chose not to react to it, instead simply continuing to smile and wait for his response. "I am having a pleasant time," he said at last. "Thank you for inquiring."

"You're welcome," Kira said. "I'm glad that you're enjoying the reception." She paused and debated what to say next, then plunged ahead. "I hope that your time on the station continues to be productive," she said.

Akaar sighed, then leaned down toward Kira. "I'll tell you something, Colonel," he said. "I do not care at all for—" He glanced around the room. "—Cardassian architecture. However, I have so far been impressed with . . . Bajoran hospitality."

As Akaar stood back up, Kira felt her mouth drop open in surprise at the echo of her own words to Ambassador Lent. She began to say something in an attempt to cover her surprise, but somebody called to Akaar from somewhere behind her. Akaar raised a hand and gestured, then looked back at Kira. "Excuse me, Colonel," he said, and walked away.

Kira turned and watched Akaar move across the room, over to Councillor zh'Thane. She thought about her comment just a little while ago to Ambassador Lent about "Bajoran hospitality," and she wondered if Akaar had just tried to tell her something.

53

In the full darkness of night, the soft flurry of white light stood out like a lone star in the void. The materialization sequence finished, and Prynn walked from *Chaffee*'s aft section and over to the site. She shined her beacon down at the small section of decking she had transported away and then back. It had been reduced to a mass of disfigured metal.

"Well, that's it then," she said. Throughout the day, she had managed to cobble together a working transporter, utilizing the parts of the primary system that had survived the crash, along with elements of the two backups. She had been running tests for the last hour, beaming objects in increments both toward the source of the pulse and in the opposite direction. She had ascertained now the effective ranges of the transporter in this environment: one hundred seventy-five kilometers away from the pulse, but only seven kilometers toward it. Beaming in either direction would not help them much, if at all.

Prynn returned to *Chaffee*'s aft section and powered down the transporter, frustrated. She had struggled with the patchwork machinery all day, not just to get it functioning, but to increase its range. But the problem stemmed from the local effects of the energy produced at the source of the pulse, not from the equipment. Even if Prynn had access to a perfectly maintained transporter, nothing short of extremely powerful pattern enhancers would—

Pattern enhancers, she thought. She raced into the shuttle's rear compartment and pulled open the compartment doors in the port bulkhead. Several environmental suits sat within, all intact. Prynn took out two of the full-body suits, along with a pair of helmets. She could use an old test pilot's trick, she had realized, and reconfigure the suits to function as pattern enhancers. That might increase the transporter range significantly.

Prynn spent an hour working on the suits, another idea occurring to her as she did so. She had not quite completed the task she had set herself, though, before exhaustion took firm hold of her. Reluctant to stop, but knowing that she would accomplish nothing by pushing herself too far beyond her limits, she headed back to the encampment. She considered using a stimulant from the medkit, but decided that the best thing would be to get a few hours' sleep and then resume her work.

As she walked, Prynn swung the beacon out along her path in wide arcs. There really was little need to light her way, she reflected, considering that the ground here lay so completely flat and featureless. She wondered about the land that Vaughn's journey had taken him across, and about how far he had gotten.

Vaughn. To Prynn's aggravation, her thoughts had come back again and again to her father today, and not just with respect to the mission here. Her mind had continued conjuring up the image of him walking away from the camp yesterday, which in turn had inexplicably engendered feelings of abandonment in her. It made no sense. Vaughn's attempt to reach the source of the pulse on foot had been the proper command decision, and leaving her behind to work on the transporter and to tend to Shar had also been right. And still, she could not seem to reel in her thoughts and emotions. In her mind's eye, she repeatedly saw him deserting the camp.

Not deserting, she chastised herself. *Departing.* She found it strange and disconcerting that she should be fixated on something that she did not even believe to be true. But then, the pulse, this planet, the crew's experiences here—all of it had been nothing if not strange and disconcerting.

A memory from earlier today occurred to Prynn. While she had been working on the transporter, she had vividly recalled lying wounded on *Defiant*'s bridge, back during the attack by the Jarada. Except that she could not have recalled such a thing; the explosion and the extent of her injuries had knocked her unconscious, and Dr. Bashir had explained to her how it would have been impossible for her brain to imprint and retain memories of the event. And yet today, she had remembered lying on her back beside the captain's chair, and remembered somebody touching her shoulder and midsection. That person would have been Dr. Bashir, of course, who had treated her on the bridge—except that she kept feeling somehow that it had been Vaughn there, and not the doctor. And the sense she had gotten from Vaughn had been one of intense guilt and sadness, and the memory—or daydream, whichever it had been—had left her temporarily feeling sorry for her father.

Prynn passed the shuttle's forward section and headed for the camp. She slowed her pace, trying to be quiet so that she would not wake Shar. He had come to this afternoon, and had been sheepish and apologetic for his outburst this morning. She had waved the incident away, then checked his injuries and provided him what little care she could. He had at least been able to eat and drink, which she hoped would allow him to retain whatever strength he had right now.

Prynn put down the beacon, stripped off her jacket, and flopped down onto her bedroll. Fatigue affected her both physically—she had spent a lot of effort digging through the shuttle wreckage—and mentally—the reconstitution of a working transporter had been far from a trivial matter. And she also supposed that she had been taxed emotionally, with the—

"Prynn?" Shar's voice sounded very small in the night.

"I'm sorry," she said. "Did I wake you?"

"No . . . well, yes, actually," he said. "I've been lying here falling in and out of sleep, thinking and dreaming." Shar's voice, though low, sounded fairly strong. Prynn squinted through the darkness in his direction. She had not yet extinguished her beacon, and he was just visible in the fringes of its illumination. He lay on his back, his head turned toward her, and though she could not tell anything about his complexion in the dimness, he eyes appeared more alive than she had seen them in the last day and a half.

She reached over to where she had set the beacon down. "I'm going to turn the light out," she warned Shar.

"Would you leave it on?" he asked. "For a few minutes?"

"Oh," she said, surprised at the request. "Sure." She pulled a blanket over her body.

"Did you have any success with the transporter?" Shar asked.

"Yes," she said. "I actually got it working, but because of the interference from the energy, the range is limited." She told him the distances to which she had successfully been able to beam objects. "I've started to reconfigure the environmental suits as pattern enhancers in order to address that," she continued. "It should help, but I'm not sure how much."

"You're trying to use the environmental suits as pattern enhancers?" Shar asked. "I didn't know you could do that."

"It's not a common practice outside of flight testing," she explained. "I also have another idea. I'll need your help with it, though."

"What do you want me to do?" Shar said.

"The primary power cell for the shuttle's internal systems was destroyed," she said. "The backup's intact, but it's not working, either. Fortunately, the secondary backup is working, and that's what I'm currently using to power the transporter."

"All right," Shar said.

"If we can get the primary backup cell to function," she went on, "then I think I might be able to construct another working transporter out of what's left of the primary, its backups, and the environmental suits."

"If one transporter won't help us," Shar asked, "then what good will a second one be?"

"We can beam ourselves and the second transporter and power cell," she explained, "and then use the second system to beam the first one to our new location. Then we can keep doing that, sort of skipping across the planet until we reach the far side, where there are breaks in the cloud cover."

Shar seemed to think about that for a moment—Prynn wondered whether he might have drifted back to sleep—and then he said, "That could work." Even though his voice remained quiet, Prynn thought she heard some excitement in it.

"I think so too," she said. "But the problem is that primary backup cell. I can fix it, but it's going to take me a while to finish modifying the suits and piecing together a second transporter. I won't have time."

"I can do that," Shar said. "If you tell me how to reconfigure the environmental suits, I can help with that too."

"Good," she said. "We'll start on it first thing in the morning."

Shar said nothing more, and the silence of this empty world pushed in on them. After a few minutes, Prynn reached out from beneath her blanket and switched off the beacon. The darkness descended at once, nearly suffocating in its completeness. Prynn closed her eyes, anxious for sleep to welcome her into its fold. To her surprise, though, she was still awake fifteen minutes later when Shar spoke.

"I wonder how Commander Vaughn is doing," he said.

"I don't know," Prynn responded, and she heard a coldness in her voice she had not intended. "I don't know," she said again, holding her tone level.

"Whatever happened between you and your father," Shar said, "I'm sorry. I know what it's like to be at odds with a parent."

Prynn laughed, a loud, ugly sound that she regretted at once. It seemed as though the tension of their circumstances had caused her to lose the full control of her emotions. "I'm sorry, Shar," she said. "I didn't really mean to laugh."

"It's all right. I'm sorry that I said anything."

"No," Prynn told him, not wanting him to feel bad. "It's just . . . you don't know what my father did to me." *Did to* me? Prynn asked herself. She must have been tired to have misspoken like that. "I mean, what he did to my mother," she amended.

"You're right," Shar said. "I don't know." He said nothing else, neither inviting her to say more, nor stopping her from doing so. Prynn did not like talking about this, but then . . . after tomorrow, she might never have a chance to talk about it again.

"My mother was a Starfleet officer," she said. "She and my father worked together a lot before I was born, but then Mom decided that she'd had enough of a soldier's life." Prynn felt pressure behind her eyes, and the gentle sensation of tears forming. Still, she found herself wanting to go on. "She wanted children, but Vaughn . . . Vaughn could never let go of the job, even after I was born. We could never really be the family Mom wanted, but she and Vaughn never fell out of love." She could see her mother in her memory—her mother and Vaughn. Tears spilled from her eyes now, sliding coolly down the sides of her face. "I loved them both. I missed Vaughn so much when he was away, and loved it when he came home. I always wanted to be closer to him. That's why—" She stopped, stunned at the words she had been about to say. The revelation had come to her simply and powerfully. "That's why I joined Starfleet," she finished. "I just wanted to share more of his life."

When Prynn paused, Shar said, "That's nice, that you wanted be with your father that much. But I guess something happened."

"My mother ended up on a mission with my father again," she said. "He ordered her away team to . . ." Prynn wiped a hand across her eyes, trying to dry her tears, but smearing them across her face instead. She had not spoken about this—had not *thought* about it like this—in such a long time. It was still hard. "The away team never returned. Vaughn knew the danger, but he made the decision to send them anyway."

"Was it the wrong decision?" Shar asked.

The question astounded Prynn. *Was it the wrong decision?* It had resulted in the death of her mother; how could it be anything but wrong?

"I mean . . . are you angry with your father because you were almost killed when the Jarada attacked us at Torona IV?" Shar asked.

"No, of course not," Prynn answered immediately. "That wasn't his fault."

"On his order," Shar said, "we didn't defend ourselves."

"Because if we had, it would have put a hundred thousand Europani in danger. The Jarada would have attacked the convoy."

"That's right," Shar said. "So maybe there was also a good reason for the order he gave your mother's away team."

No, Prynn thought. No reason could justify the death of her mother. But what she heard herself tell Shar was, "I don't know." And she realized that she had never known. Vaughn had never talked about his decision to dispatch the away team. He had always simply taken the responsibility for her mother's death—and she had always let him take it. "I don't know," she said again, wondering for the first time whether Vaughn's guilt had been because he had given the *wrong* order, or because he had given the *right* one.

"Good night, Shar," she said, unable to talk about any of this anymore right now.

"Good night," he said, and she was grateful that he did not choose to pursue the conversation further.

She had been seventeen when her mother had died, and she had been devastated. They had been not just mother and daughter, but the best of friends. Prynn remembered so vividly when Vaughn had told her . . . the horrible words, the look of pain and guilt on his face, and her tears, flowing as though they would never stop . . .

How could it have been the right decision? she asked herself. If her father had to give the order again, would he? Prynn had never asked him that, had never thought to ask him. And seven years ago, there had not been an opportunity to ask such a question anyway. Mom had died, and her father . . . her father had been there with her for a while, but she had never been able to approach him; the enormity of his guilt and the depth of her anger had been obstacles too great to overcome. After he had told her, they had never really spoken of it again, other than her blaming him, and him saying how sorry he was. He had abandoned her—

Abandoned?

Once more, Prynn saw in her mind the figure of Vaughn walking away from the camp. For a day and a half now, the image had refused to leave her. *Do I hate him because he was responsible for Mom's death,* she asked herself, *or because he wasn't really there to help me through that terrible time?* Although it was not a question that she had ever asked before, she'd been sure of the answer to it for the past seven years. Until today. Until right now.

Prynn wondered if her father knew the answer, and she resolved to ask him—to *talk* to him—about it.

If I ever see him again.

A tremendous sense of sadness and loss engulfed her. And as she fell asleep, all Prynn could think about was how much she missed her father.

54

Kasidy strolled down one of the cobbled lanes that led from the local transporter facility. The night had remained as balmy as the afternoon, an agreeable change from the first few days of the winter. Only a week ago, she had been peering out the front windows on a landscape frosted white by snow. And according to the Bajoran comnet, the weather forecasters were predicting another winter storm just a couple of days from now. All of which had helped her choose to take this opportunity to get out of the house, enjoy a change of scenery, and take in some fresh air.

Yellowish flickers of light danced along the cobblestones, thrown by the traditional oil lamps hanging from poles along the lane. Kasidy ambled along, not rushing despite the lateness of the hour. She knew that the shops would be closing shortly, but hurrying would have defeated her desire for a relaxing walk. She would stop in whichever of the shops she could, and then come back some other time to see the rest.

Except that's not really the whole story, is it, Kas? she asked herself. She had been thinking about coming into town for a week now, ever since Prylar Eivos had called on her. The warmth of the man, his amiable demeanor and genuine thoughtfulness, the ease and humility of his faith, all had reminded her of how Ben had always spoken of the Bajorans. Working with the Commerce Ministry here, before she had become the wife of the Emissary, she had certainly met some nice people, but few who had inspired her to view Bajorans in quite the way Ben had. But, already determined to see out her pregnancy here because that had been what she and Ben had planned, she had now resolved to try to see in these people all that he had seen. Even so, she understood that she had not chosen to visit Adarak at this time of night by accident. Despite her optimism after seeing Eivos, she still had difficulty dealing with her prominence among the Bajoran people.

As Kasidy neared the main avenue of shops, she felt herself tensing. She had already been recognized during the few minutes she had been in town, and she worried that, even this late in the day, she would be faced with the misplaced veneration of strangers. Back at the transporter facility, the young man operating the pad had stared wide-eyed at her as she had stepped down from the platform. The attention and awe had made her uncomfortable, although she had to admit that the young man had recovered quickly. He had welcomed her to Adarak, and then offered to direct her to her destination or answer any questions she might have. She had thanked him, but declined his assistance. She had been to the town before—though not since she had first moved to Bajor—and she knew where she wanted to go.

Kasidy reached the avenue, which intersected the lane at a right angle. She stopped and peered both ways down the wide pedestrian thoroughfare. The old-fashioned oil lamps lined both sides of the way here too, and large trees marched down the center. The yellow lamplight wavered across the leaves, making them appear to move, as though blown by a breeze. At random, Kasidy opted to turn to her left.

The first couple of shops she passed had already closed for the night, though their storefronts remained lighted. Kasidy only glanced at the wares displayed as she walked by, thinking that she would window-shop on her way back. The next shop was open, though, and she stopped to look inside. A pair of paintings stood on easels at either end of the front window, with several interesting bronzes and other sculptures on pedestals between them.

As she gazed at the artwork, the door of the shop opened. A tall Bajoran man emerged carrying a bag in his arms, probably containing something he had just purchased. While the man held the door open for a woman following him out, he looked over and saw Kasidy. "Pleasant evening," he said with a smile. To her surprise, she saw no hint that he knew her identity.

Not quite as renowned as you thought, she joked to herself. "A pleasant evening to you," she said to the man. His companion, also a Bajoran, stepped past him and out of the shop. The woman nodded and smiled at Kasidy, then did a rapid double take, obviously recognizing her.

"Excuse me," the woman murmured, quickly looking away, apparently abashed by her own reaction. The woman linked her arm with the man's and guided him down the avenue.

Now, that's more like it, Kasidy thought, chuckling. She entered the shop, still amazed that she could cause such a response in people, but not feeling quite as tense now as she had just a few minutes ago. After all, the woman had been embarrassed at her blatantly visible recognition of the wife of the Emissary. After Kasidy's experiences with so many well-meaning Bajorans appearing on her doorstep when she had first moved to Kendra Province, perhaps the locals had decided not only to protect her from such attention, but to make sure that they did nothing themselves to discomfit her.

Inside the well-lighted shop, paintings lined the walls, and sculptures sat displayed atop narrow tables in the middle of the room. "Now, you're out late, dearie, aren'tcha?" came a loud, friendly voice. Kasidy looked around and saw a Bajoran woman, older and a bit stocky, waving to her from the rear of the shop.

"It's a nice night for it, isn't it?" Kasidy said. She walked over to the first table, on which stood two bronzes. Both were tall, each about half a meter high.

"That it is, dearie, that it is," the woman agreed. "It's gonna be a cold winter, so I'll enjoy as many of these days as we can get."

"Me too," Kasidy said, tickled by the woman's gregarious nature. "Is this your gallery?"

"That it is," the woman said again.

Kasidy moved around the table, studying the sculptures. One depicted a robed Bajoran woman in mid-stride, her hands oddly crossed in front of her waist; the other showed a bare-chested Bajoran man leaning forward, struggling to haul something unseen, by ropes he held over his shoulders. Kasidy appreciated the technique of the two pieces, which seemed rough and kinetic, and yet also somehow graceful.

The robed woman, Kasidy decided, did not really appeal to her, although it took her a moment to determine why: despite being completely different in composition and material, the work reminded her too much of the jevonite figurine that Eivos had given her. While she remained grateful for the prylar's thoughtfulness, the statuette's tie to B'hala had come to bother her. She had not yet taken it down from the mantel in the front room, but she had begun to consider doing so. If *City of B'hala* had not been Ben's favorite print, she would have thought about taking it down as well.

"Those are by Flanner Posh," the shopkeeper called. "Only twenty-six years old. Lost his father in one of the camps."

Kasidy glanced over at the woman and nodded, not really sure of the significance of the comments. "I'm sorry to hear that," she offered.

"We're all sorry," the woman said, though without any animosity. "I just mention it 'cause what happens to a person informs their art." Kasidy nodded again, not really paying much attention, but when she looked back at the sculptures, a story unfolded in her mind. The man—the artist's father—worked to death by the Cardassians during the Occupation, made to plow fields in the high heat of summer; the woman, a cleric of some sort, also imprisoned in the camp, and somehow a source of strength for the boy—the future artist—allowing him to make it through. She had no idea whether any of that was even close to the truth, but the artwork had that quickly taken on new weight, new meaning, for her.

Kasidy roamed deeper into the gallery, peering at the paintings and the other sculptures, and occasionally exchanging remarks with the shopkeeper. Quite a few different artists were represented here, and Kasidy found that she really liked the work of several of them. As she reached the rear of the gallery, she asked the woman, "Did you do any of these?"

"Oh, my good word, no," the woman said. "My contribution to the world of art isn't as a sculptor or a painter; it's as a critic."

Kasidy laughed. "Me too," she said. "I can't draw a blade of grass."

"But you know a good picture of one when you see it, don'tcha?"

"That I do, dearie," Kasidy said, good-naturedly mimicking the woman's way of speaking.

To Kasidy's delight, the woman threw her head back and laughed heartily. "Ah, you're a kidder, darlin'," she said. "I like that."

"Good," Kasidy said, unable to keep from smiling. "Maybe you'll give me a good deal on this painting then." She gestured to her left, at a pointillist landscape.

"Everybody gets the same deal, dearie," the woman told her, "but they're all good ones."

"I'm sure they are," Kasidy said. "Actually, this piece . . . it's not quite right for me, but I love the style."

"That's Galoren Sen's work," the woman said. "Really maturin' these days.

I like that one myself. Course, I like 'em all, otherwise they wouldn't be hangin' in my gallery."

"Will you be getting in any more of his work?" Kasidy wanted to know.

"Well, lemme see . . . Sen'll probably bring me more of his work . . . oh, in about two months, maybe three."

"All right," Kasidy said. "I'll be sure to come back then."

"I hope I'll see you sooner than that," the woman said. "I do have a pretty good turnover."

"All right," Kasidy said. "I'll be back sooner." And she meant it. This woman had put her at such ease. Even though people had recognized Kasidy tonight, the man leaving the gallery had not, and now neither had this shopkeeper. Plus, now that she thought about it, the two who had recognized her had treated her with common courtesy, but not with reverence; they had even seemed to try to avoid being reverential. Maybe the people of Adarak would allow Kasidy—maybe she would allow herself—to look beyond the place the Bajorans claimed for her in their culture. Somehow, in just a few minutes, this loud, genuine woman had brought Kasidy a lovely sense of calmness and acceptance. "You have a very pleasant evening," she told the woman. Then she thought to ask, "By the way, what's your name?"

"I'm Rozahn Kather," she said. "But everybody calls me Kit."

"Well it's very nice to meet you, Kit. I'm Kasidy."

"Of course you are, dearie," Kit said, and she winked. Kasidy felt her own eyes widen as she realized that this woman had known who she was all along. She also felt sure that Kit had treated her no differently than she treated anybody else.

Kasidy left the gallery feeling more comfortable here on Bajor than she had since moving here. When two women passed her on the avenue, she offered them a big smile. "Pleasant evening," she said. The women returned both the smile and the greeting.

Bajor still did not feel like home to Kasidy, but she suddenly thought she could see a time when it would.

55

Vaughn awoke to the sound of fire.

Earlier, after he had sighted the complex surrounding the source of the pulse, he had descended the hill and walked the final kilometers to the outer walls of the buildings. The veil of night had dropped by then, and considering his exhaustion, he had decided to make camp and get some sleep. He would make his push into the buildings once he had rested and regained some of his strength.

Before laying out his bedroll, Vaughn had paced along the outside of the complex, searching for a way in. He had not needed to search long. The first door he had come to had been not only unlocked, but wide open. Beneath the light of his beacon, the yawning entryway—like so many things on this planet—had projected an air of abandonment.

Now, where he was camped, a hundred or so meters away from the complex, the crackle of flames reached his ears, not from the buildings, but from nearby. He floated slowly up out of sleep at first, until the incongruity of the sound brought him fully awake. In the instant before he opened his eyes, he perceived the flittering light on his closed lids, and felt inconsistent waves of heat breathing across his face.

Recalling that his phaser had been lost, Vaughn did not move as he opened his eyes, wanting to assay the situation before betraying that he was no longer asleep. The small fire grew from within a circular bed of stones, he saw, a couple of meters in front of him. Vaughn waited a moment, looking and listening for anything that might help orient him to whatever new circumstances he now faced. He remembered clearly his mission to stop the pulse, his location on this planet, what he had been through today—

Through the flames, movement caught his eye, just on the other side of the stone circle. Unable to tell what had caused it, he listened for any other sounds beside those of the fire. The movement came again.

"And that's Rigel," a voice said, the seemingly ordinary nature of the words and tone striking in the current context. Vaughn sat up on his bedroll and peered over the flames. A woman sat there, her knees pulled up against her chest, her head back as she gazed at the stars. She had dark hair that fell to the middle of her back, a bit wild despite being tied just below her neck. She looked to be in her thirties—and even younger when the wavering firelight sent an orange-yellow glow across her features—although Vaughn knew that she was older than that. He stared at her, and she looked away from the heavens and over at him. "Do you remember what you learned about Rigel, Elias?" she asked.

Vaughn recited the star's mass, absolute magnitude, and spectral type before he even realized that he had spoken.

"That's right," the woman said, offering him an encouraging half-smile. "It's also one of the most populated systems in the quadrant. Do you know how many planets orbit Rigel?"

This time, Vaughn did not answer. He closed his eyes and tried to concentrate on the ersatz nature of the woman, of the fire, of the moment. He envisioned the clouds whirling down and reconstructing this scene, manufacturing everything before him out of the dust of this lonely world. *This isn't Berengaria VII,* he told himself, *any more than this woman is my mother.*

But somehow it did not matter. Vaughn had lived much of his life in control, but today he had been unable to elude the sentiments of his past. More must be happening here, he believed, than just the re-creation of incidents from his life; he had become too *sympathetic* to feelings of loss and abandonment. Even now, as he attempted to reason his way through this, the moment that had been remade around him pulled at his heart.

Vaughn opened his eyes and said, "Twelve," identifying the number of planets in the Rigel system. He peered around, trying to see more of his surroundings, but the illumination of the fire did not penetrate very far into the darkness. *It doesn't matter,* Vaughn thought again. *This isn't the planet where I was raised. This isn't my mother.*

Except that she looked and sounded so much like her. "That's right, twelve," she said, and there was that half-smile of hers again. Vaughn smiled back. He loved these times. His mother spent so much time out in the wilderness with her work—only occasionally did they do this, heading out to sit by a fire and stare up at the stars.

Vaughn raised his eyes and peered up at the brilliant pinpoints of light that dotted the night. He wondered only briefly how the sea of clouds could have reproduced such an effect, when in reality it perpetually separated the surface of this abandoned world from the rest of the universe. He found Rigel, and shrugged off the fact that the star should not have even been visible from the Gamma Quadrant. He looked back over at his mother, and his heart filled with his love for her. They'd been so close. Genuine or not, he felt grateful for this time, an unexpected gift.

"Elias, I need to talk with you about something."

Oh no, he thought, feeling a terrible jolt, as though he had fallen in frigid water. *No. Not this night. Of all nights, not this one.* And he told her that: "No, Ma. I don't want to talk. I just want to look at the stars with you."

"Elias—"

"No." Vaughn threw off his blanket and stood up. "Tell me tomorrow," he said, knowing that, in so many ways, there would be no tomorrow.

The flames, beginning to sputter now, lighted her eyes. She sat with her hands clasped in front of her shins, hugging her knees. She regarded him with an expression of love and compassion, and he thought that she would allow him the reprieve for which he had asked. Then she said, "I have Burkhardt's disease."

Vaughn said nothing. He had a sudden urge to throw himself on the fire, and thought, *That's new.* He did not remember wanting to immolate himself as a boy. The past had come alive for him, but with the burden of the subsequent years also alive in his mind and heart, this moment had actually worsened.

"Ma, please don't," he pleaded.

"I was diagnosed this week," she said softly, the expression on her face one of empathy. She seemed concerned less with the content of her words than with their effect on Vaughn. "It's a progressive—"

"No," Vaughn yelled, feeling like a boy trying to make something true by wishing it so. "No," he said again, unwilling not only to accept the reality of this moment now, but to have accepted it all those years ago. He turned and walked into the darkness, beyond the reach of the firelight.

"Elias," he heard his mother call after him. He did not answer. He kept walking, allowing the empty blackness of this place to close around him. "Elias," she called again, but he did not hear her follow. He could not remember—he had never been able to remember—exactly what had happened when she had first told him this. Had he bolted like this? Had she come after him?

Now he walked on, the sensation of moving in the consuming darkness strange and unsettling. His mother did not call again, and no footsteps approached behind him. She had obviously decided to leave him alone.

Just as she left me all those years ago, he thought. *Alone.*

Vaughn stumbled and fell forward. His hands scraped against the ground as he went down. He lay like that for a long time, prone, palms flat against the ground, elbows up at his sides. Finally, he rolled over onto his back and stared up at the sky.

There were no stars. He could not even see the clouds for the lack of light. What he did see in his mind was his mother's face, called up from memories not just minutes old, but decades.

She left me alone, he thought again, ancient anger and frustration and sadness accompanying the memories. And then came this thought: *No wonder Prynn hates me.*

Vaughn laughed in the night, more a bark than anything having to do with humor. Somehow, he had never made the connection, although it must have implicitly buttressed the guilt he had felt for the last seven years. Just as his mother had been taken from him, he had taken Ruriko from Prynn. In his daughter's life, he had been no better than a disease.

All those successful missions, he thought, *and yet, when she needed me most, I failed my own daughter. I left her alone.*

He remembered looking into Prynn's eyes a day and a half ago—the white of one made crimson by injury—and then turning and walking away from her. He had not looked back, and now he wished that he had. It seemed impossible, but he had somehow left her alone again. Ch'Thane had been at the camp, of course, but Vaughn had left Prynn with no mother, no father—

No father? he asked himself. *He* was her father. Her mother had been gone for seven years now, but he had not left her.

Or had he? Vaughn had been honest with Prynn about what had happened, about his role in Ruriko's death. He had never even considered not telling her. Prynn had been furious with him, and reasonably so, and from then on their relationship had been defined by the depth of her anger and the enormity of his guilt. They had never really spoken of it again, other than him saying how sorry he was, and her blaming him. He had sought to—

To leave her alone. This time, the thought hit him like a club to the back of the head. He had taken her mother from her, that much had always been clear, but now he realized that he had also taken her father from her. Because of his guilt and Prynn's anger, he had essentially removed himself from her life, because that was what she had wanted—although not, he saw now, what she had needed. And perhaps that had also been the path of least resistance for him, and an opportunity to practice penance. He had always thought that Prynn had a justifiable reason to hate him, but now he also saw that she had another, because he had not really been there to help her through that terrible time.

Vaughn clamped his hands over his face, then let his arms flop onto the ground on either side of him. He had failed Prynn as a father when she had most needed him, and the thought of abandoning her again—permanently, and leaving her truly alone—crushed him. He could not let that happen. He could not.

So thinking, he fell into a restless sleep, filled with dreams of his past, and dreams that were somehow not his own.

56

Kira shrugged out of her dress jacket, pleased to finally be free of the ill-fitting garment. During her years on Deep Space 9, she had often thought to have the jacket altered so that it would sit comfortably on her body, but the idea of Garak touching her clothing had prevented her from ever doing so. Now that the erstwhile tailor had returned to Cardassia, though, a Bajoran seamstress—Hatram something, she thought—had opened a shop on the Promenade. Hatram had even had the good sense to move into a different space than Garak's old shop, which nobody seemed to want to rent. *Anyway, I'll have to bring it in,* she told herself, knowing that she never would. That Garak had owned the tailor's shop had only been an excuse; Kira tended to avoid minutiae such as this, and her life experience had certainly provided her the ability to withstand a little discomfort.

Besides, she thought, tossing the jacket on her bed, *I may never have to wear this again.* If Bajor joined the Federation, then she would be wearing formal Starfleet attire for occasions such as today. Of course, there was no guarantee that Starfleet's dress uniforms would be any more comfortable than those of the Militia.

Kira sat down on the bed and slipped out of her pants. As she dropped them on top of the jacket, she smiled, realizing that she had made a significant decision without even thinking about it. Bajoran membership in the Federation, she knew, would mean that the Militia would roll up into Starfleet. But even with the summit beginning tomorrow, Kira had not really thought about that in terms of her own career—although she had considered the implications for Ro, after Akaar had revealed his disapproval of her. Kira supposed that if she had thought about it, she would have made her choice quickly anyway. As much as she had come to like her position as DS9's first officer, her half-year as the station's commander had proven even more fulfilling. No matter what Vedek Yevir might maintain, Kira believed that she had served Bajor well. She wanted to keep doing so, and it really did not matter to her whether she did so as a member of the militia or as a member of Starfleet; in the last weeks of the war, Admiral Ross and Captain Sisko had commissioned her as a Starfleet commander, and her uniform had fit perfectly well.

Kira stripped off her remaining clothes and pulled on a thigh-length, gold lamé robe, the fabric cool and silky against her skin. She headed out into the living area. It had been a long and tiring day—when were her days anything but?—and she sought a measure of tranquillity.

At the small shrine she kept, Kira lighted a candle and then sat down on the floor, folding her legs together and resting her wrists on her knees, palms facing upward. For a few minutes, she concentrated on the candle's flame, letting its gentle, wavering movement mesmerize her. Then she closed her eyes and tried to empty her mind of thoughts. In place of the flame, she visualized the blue-white pinwheel of light that decorated space when the Celestial

Temple opened, attempting to lose herself within its depths. By degrees, the tension in her body and mind melted away, like a morning frost succumbing to the rising sun.

Thank the Prophets they didn't take this away from me, she thought. In truth, they—Vedek Yevir and the others who had chosen to Attaint her—could not have taken this away. Even had Kira tried to accommodate such a penalty, it would likely have been impossible for her. She spoke to the Prophets too often—virtually every day—and not even in such a structured way as this. Simply walking through the normal course of her life, she maintained a dialogue with the Bajoran gods. It had been her way for as long as she could remember, and it had seen her through many dark times. It was one thing for the Vedek Assembly to forbid her to pray with other Bajorans or to read the sacred texts, and something else entirely for them to try to control her heart.

Of course, Kira still missed temple services, as well as studying the hallowed works. She had read the ancient texts so many times that she could almost recite them—*Maybe more than almost,* she thought—but there was something special about holding the books in her hands and actually seeing the words.

Again she felt that critical times lay immediately ahead for her people. It troubled her that Akaar might have a say in that, and what he had said earlier in the evening recurred to her. He had spoken of "Bajoran hospitality," in a way that she had found difficult to decipher. He had repeated what she had said to Ambassador Lent, but that could easily have been a coincidence. But coincidence or not, he could have intended the words as a compliment or as sarcasm; his inscrutable demeanor allowed for either possibility.

Kira recalled all of the questions the admiral had asked her with respect to Bajor's relationship with Cardassia, and about Bajor in general; she also remembered the discomfort she had felt in answering those questions, and her resistance to his apparent desire to measure the Bajoran people through her. Nobody but Shakaar could speak for Bajor unless the First Minister himself authorized it; according to Kasidy and her friend Prylar Eivos, even the Vedek Assembly seemed on the verge of schism, though Kira had heard nothing more about that in the last week. With Federation membership at stake, though, she knew that Bajoran unity would be more important than ever.

Kira opened her eyes. Her focus drifting, she stared once more at the flame of the candle. She let the minutes pass as she strived to abandon her thoughts, seeking the calmness of her faith. The Prophets would watch over Bajor, she knew. She closed her eyes . . .

. . . and saw the face of Gul Macet. Despite the DNA records provided by Cardassia, Macet still made Kira uneasy. Dukat had played that game too many times, claiming to be something he was not. That face—Dukat's—had haunted her dreams for so many years, and to see those same features now on Macet—

Kira's eyes opened again. *So much for meditation,* she thought. She slapped her hands on her thighs, frustrated, then leaned forward on her knees and blew out the candle.

I have to let all of this go, she told herself. *All of these things that I can't change.* She could only command Deep Space 9, she could only be true to her faith, and she could only deal with Macet as circumstances warranted.

Kira sighed, then stood up. All she wanted right this moment was to follow the path on which the Prophets had set her. She had weathered the last few months—the months since she had been Attainted—relatively well, she thought, but every now and then she lost her way a bit. Although she maintained her faith, and practiced her solitary rituals and prayers, she felt sometimes as though she had been not separated, but distanced, from the Prophets.

And now—right now—she could not even seem to meditate.

She wandered over to the window and gazed out at the location in space she knew the Celestial Temple to be. She wished it would reveal itself. As many times as Kira had seen the sight, it never failed to thrill her in a profound way.

Now, though, only the distant stars and the emptiness of space between them stared back at her. And suddenly an idea occurred to Kira, an idea born of her faith, and of her need to feel close to the Prophets.

"Kira to ops," she said, raising her voice a touch.

"Ops, Selzner here, Colonel," came the reply.

"Ensign, at what time is the *Rio Grande* scheduled to finish maintenance on the subspace relay tonight?" Kira wanted to know. She walked over to the companel and checked the current time on the chronometer.

"Let me check," Selzner said. A moment later, Selzner read off the schedule. The runabout would be returning through the wormhole in less than thirty minutes.

Kira smiled.

As she headed back into her bedroom to don her uniform—her duty uniform—she told the ensign what she intended to do, although not why.

Kira notified ops, checked her equipment a second time, then bent and pulled open the access plate. One end of the plate swung upward, revealing the control panel beneath. Kira keyed in the activation sequence, then grabbed the handle there and twisted it ninety degrees left. Her weight quickly vanished as the local gravitational mat detuned, causing a momentary flutter in her stomach. At once, the pad she stood on began to rise. She flipped the access plate closed, stood back up, and waited.

Slowly but steadily, the launch bay slipped away. Kira peered over at the bow of *Euphrates,* watching it until disappeared from sight. The pad stopped, and she felt a jolt as it locked into place, level with the station's outer hull. She looked forward and saw the arc of the habitat ring sweeping away before her. The Promenade and ops rose to her left, and above, *Gryphon* sat moored to the station at the top of a docking pylon.

Kira turned to her right and gazed out past the docking ring. Her magnetic boots made heavy, metallic thuds against the runabout pad as she moved, the sounds traveling through her environmental suit. Unlike a few weeks ago, the space around DS9 contained no free-floating vessels; the two small ships that had delivered the Alonis and Trill delegations sat along the docking ring, as did Ambassador zh'Thane's ship, and the shuttle that had brought Shakaar and his staff had already departed for the return trip to Bajor.

From her vantage outside the station, Kira noticed that the stars appeared brighter and sharper than when viewed from within DS9. She studied the stars, picking out constellations and orienting herself so that she faced the location of the wormhole directly. After that, she did not have to wait long. Within minutes, the Celestial Temple spiraled into existence, vibrant blue light topping a brilliant white background, with traces of purple moving inside. A sensation of warmth flooded over Kira, and a connection seemed to form, reaching from her small, insignificant body out to the majestic whirlpool of light swirling before her—and reaching back in the opposite direction as well. Kira felt unconditional love and acceptance, for the Prophets and from Them. Her vision blurred, tears pooling in her eyes, as the threshold of heaven began its normal collapse. In a second, the magnificent, churning light had compressed to a point; a flash, and then it had gone completely.

That quickly, Kira had gotten what she had come for. Still, she stood like that, motionless and looking out into space, for a long time. Finally, she went back inside the station.

57

Dax drifted—floated, swam, pushed—knowing that Ezri remained in danger. But they had chosen—as one—this course of action, and Dax would do everything possible to see that they survived this experience—as one. They had a mission, though, and that truth came first right now.

Dax pushed through—

Not the pools this time. Not the Caves of Mak'ala.

Dax pushed through a sea of clouds. A vast sea, reaching not just from pole to pole, but from world to world, and from star to star. Except that there were no worlds, and there were no stars. And yet the sea filled the universe—

And beyond.

The sense of that came to Dax somehow, and Dax knew. *Knew that communication had come, from somewhere, from something. Dax sent out tendrils of thought, seeking to find the link, to enhance it. But only silence returned.*

No, not *only* silence.

Something like a vibration hummed through the universe, electrified the setting. It pealed like a sound almost beyond hearing, glowed like a color almost beyond seeing. Something was there. Something was everywhere.

Dax attempted to communicate, calling to whatever lived out there. Called and waited, but received no response. Tried again and again, in all the ways Dax knew. Still nothing came back.

Time passed without meaning. Seconds might have been seconds, but they might also have been lifetimes, or any interval in between. Or perhaps time did not pass at all.

Dax struggled to exchange thoughts with the inhabitants of . . . what? Of another universe, Dax understood. But the tenuous connection seemed as though it might not have been an actual connection, seemed as though it might have been nothing more than a figment. Dax rested, and waited, listening to the near-silence, but haunted by the voices that faintly disrupted the quiet.

Voices?

Yes, *Dax realized.* Voices. *Dax listened. Strained to listen, and found not only voices, but the beings behind them. The sounds became ideas, and Dax tried to discern perceptions and thoughts. At last, they came, and when they did, they surprised.*

Elias Vaughn lay on the ground, arms at his sides, eyes closed. He could have been asleep or unconscious or dead. Dax understood that the beings had perceived the commander like this, doubtless down on the planet's surface, obviously sometime within the last couple of days.

Dax strived to delve past the image of Vaughn, to contact the beings that had seen him. But communication continued to prove impossible. For Dax, access came for ideas and echoes, but not for a direct link to the minds behind them. Dax could vaguely perceive the beings, but could not apparently be perceived by them.

And so Dax searched the ideas, seeking to understand the intentions of the beings. None were revealed. Dax stumbled mentally, weakening, finding it difficult to maintain the drive to penetrate this alien society. But Dax battled on, turning to the echoes—

Memories, *Dax suddenly realized.* The echoes are memories.

Dax dived down, pushing into the echoes, watching, listening, perceiving. A wall rose up, infinite and impenetrable, but on this side of the wall, Dax saw: this had all begun with the invaders . . . with the saviors . . . with the Prentara.

The Prentara had once populated the world around which the sea of clouds now circled. They had discovered the other realm, and had been astonished by it. Sights and sounds, scents and tastes, sensations and emotions, all had followed with the Prentara, carried along by technology, and all had been magnified. An avalanche of emotive and perceptual experience spread across a universe in which none of this had previously been known. A battle to push outward from the strange realm ensued, and the Prentara fought for their lives.

Just as Ezri fought for hers right now, Dax realized.

The symbiont swooped down into the echoes, hunting for memories and collecting them up. Somewhere, images of Prynn and Shar down on the planet appeared. Representations of Vaughn also arose, although they seemed confused—Vaughn at an ancient launch facility, on a battlefield, on a ship with dead Bajorans and Cardassians. There were the Prentara too, wired in to their machines, wired in to the other universe.

And then Dax pulled back. Drifted upward, floating, swimming, pushing. Again, it was time to find Ezri.

Lieutenant Bowers waited patiently for her to begin, as did Julian. Ezri lay propped up on the diagnostic bed, a glass of water raised to her lips. She sipped, finding the act of drinking both refreshing and strangely foreign, as though she had never done it before now—a consequence, she knew, of Dax's exposure to the other universe.

Ezri handed the glass to Nurse Juarez, who stood beside her. Julian and Lieutenant Bowers waited just past the foot of her bed, and somewhere, Nurse Richter also worked in the medical bay. Ezri took a long, deep breath, gathering herself for the coming conversation. She had reintegrated enough with Dax to have assimilated the symbiont's experiences, but interpreting the images—the *echoes*—had taken some time. Even now, not everything Dax had perceived had bowed to reasonable analysis. Still, she thought that she understood enough that Bowers and the crew had to be told.

As had been the case after her first contact with the object, Julian had wanted her to rest immediately after she had regained consciousness. Again she had insisted on remaining awake, and this time, on speaking herself with Lieutenant Bowers. Julian had relented at once, accepting her claim that she had vital information to impart.

"I saw . . . I *experienced* . . . another universe," she began. She looked to her left, to where she had brought her hand down into the dark gray substance, but both it and the stand on which it had sat had been removed.

"Could you explain that?" Bowers asked. Ezri looked at him, then raised her hand to her forehead and rubbed at her temple.

"Are you all right?" Julian asked. He moved toward her along the side of the bed, glancing up at the diagnostic panel.

"I'm okay," Ezri said, dropping her hand back onto the bed. "It's just that there's so much in my head right now . . . I need to find a coherent way to tell this."

"Take your time," Bowers said. But of course they all knew that time weighed heavily on them right now. As far as they could tell, they were less than a day away from the next pulse.

"Some time ago," Ezri started again, sorting out her narrative, "a humanoid race lived on this planet." That was not new information; the crew had been able to draw the same conclusion from the readings of cities that the probe had returned to *Defiant*. "They called themselves the Prentara, and they developed a sophisticated virtual-reality technology."

"Virtual reality?" Juarez said. "Like holosuites?"

"No, not like that," Ezri said. "They tied powerful computers directly into people's minds."

Julian raised his eyebrows. "That can be very addictive," he stated. "Very addictive, and very dangerous."

"I don't know about that," Ezri said. "But I do know that, sometime later, Prentara scientists discovered this other existence, a pocket universe outside our own that . . . that . . . it was . . ." She grew agitated as she struggled to express the concepts in her mind.

"Easy," Julian said, resting a hand on her upper arm. "Easy." She looked up at him, and he offered her an effortless smile. His obvious support meant a lot to her.

"I'm all right," she told him, and she put her hand atop his. "This other existence that the Prentara found, it was a universe of the mind . . . the very fabric of it supported and nurtured and . . . *augmented* . . . mental activity. The scientists who discovered it reported amazingly profound experiences."

"Like a mind-altering drug," Julian suggested.

"Yes, like that, I think," Ezri agreed, "but far more powerful. They called the other universe the thoughtscape."

"Let me guess. They used it to enhance their VR technology," Bowers said.

Ezri nodded. "They wired their virtual-reality equipment into the interface they had opened between this universe and the thoughtscape. It enhanced their experiences beyond their imaginations, and it worked for them for years. But then something happened." She paused, still coming to understand the horror in what she had learned. "They found out," she went on, "that the thoughtscape was alive."

They all looked at her without saying anything. Even Nurse Richter, across the room, stopped whatever she had been doing and peered in Ezri's direction. The sudden silencing of their voices left the medical bay throbbing with the beat of Ezri's diagnostic scanner. Finally, Julian spoke.

"Did the Prentara know?" he asked. The expression of revulsion on his face reflected Ezri's emotions. The notion of somebody forcibly tapping into another mind, *using* that mind—it was rape of the lowest order. "Did they stop?"

"They did stop," Ezri said, actually relieved about that part of the story. "But I don't know if they ever knew that the thoughtscape was composed of living beings."

"Then why did they stop using it . . . using them?" Juarez asked.

"They stopped when the first pulse emerged from the interface," Ezri explained. "The force of it thrust outward, leaving the planet intact, but we've seen what the pulses have done to the rest of this solar system."

"And to the Vahni's system," Bowers added.

"The Prentara tried to close the interface, but the pulse had widened it considerably and they couldn't do it," Ezri went on. "A substance also came out of the interface with the pulse, and it began forming the cloud cover around the planet. Except that those aren't clouds."

"Is that a manifestation of the thoughtscape?" Bowers asked.

"The Inamuri," Ezri said. "The Prentara called the beings of the thoughtscape the Inamuri. And the clouds aren't the thoughtscape; the clouds are an extension of the interface. That's how Dax could commune with the Inamuri when I touched the substance."

"'Commune'?" Julian asked. "Not *communicate?*"

"No, there was no communication," Ezri said. "Dax could sense the minds of the Inamuri, and their memories, and maybe even Prentara memories imprinted on or swallowed up by the Inamuri. And this story I'm telling . . . Dax didn't learn all of this in this form; we've deduced it from what Dax did learn."

"What happened to the Prentara?" Juarez asked.

"I don't know," Ezri said. "I don't think even the Inamuri know. But we saw the probe's readings. There's nobody alive down there except for our people."

"Maybe the subsequent pulses killed them," Bowers suggested. "But what are the pulses?"

"I think they're the result of the Inamuri trying to push their way into our universe," Ezri said.

"They may still be trying to fight the invasion into their domain," Julian said.

"Yes," Ezri said, the word *invasion* prompting Dax's memory. "The Inamuri considered the Prentara to be invaders . . . but . . ." She searched for the remainder of the recollection. ". . . they also thought of them as saviors."

"I don't understand that," Bowers said.

"Neither do I," Ezri admitted. "But I know what we have to do to prevent any more pulses." Again, all eyes in the room focused on her. "We have to close the interface," she said.

Per Julian's orders, Ezri would remain in the medical bay for at least another day—a recommendation perfectly acceptable to her. She felt fatigued beyond any measure she had ever known, even back during the war. Before she could sleep, though, she needed to complete the information load. Julian had provided her with a mild stimulant so that she could do so, but the effects had now begun to abate.

Ezri operated the padd in her hands and played back the last few sentences she had recorded. The clarity of one piece of data seemed suspect to her, and so she erased that part and rerecorded it. Then she listened to it again. Satisfied, she moved on to the final part of her tale.

While she worked at this task, she knew that Nog and his engineering team worked at another. Within an hour of Ezri's contention that they had to close the thoughtscape interface, Nog had devised a means of doing just that. As she understood it, his plan involved triggering a series of explosive devices to detonate simultaneously in various dimensions of space, including subspace. The idea reminded Ezri of the "Houdini" mines that the Jem'Hadar had used against them at the siege of AR-558.

Nog had explained that each device would destroy a portion of the "walls" of the interface. If enough of the interface was destroyed at the same time, then the surrounding space in this universe would essentially cave in and permanently seal off the realm of the Inamuri. Nog had been specific about the number of devices—thirty-two—because if too few were detonated, then the energy of the Inamuri would be able to overcome the force of the collapsing space, and would instead widen the interface.

Once the devices had been completed, they would be loaded onto a probe, along with Ezri's account of the Inamuri and the Prentara, and then the probe would be sent down to the planet's surface. Keyed to lock on to human and Andorian life signs, or to land beside the interface if bioscans could not locate the crew, it would reach the site about half a day before the next pulse. That left more than enough time for the away team to set the devices in place, and retreat from the site to safety, before the multidimensional explosions closed the interface.

Ezri finished her recording, then worked the padd to transfer it onto an isolinear optical chip. "Julian," she called. With Ezri out of danger, both Richter and Juarez had left the medical bay. Now, across the room, Julian turned from a console.

"Have you finished?" he asked, walking over to her. She held up the isolinear chip, which he took from the tips of her fingers. He slapped at his combadge. "Bashir to Nog."

"Go ahead, Doctor," came the lieutenant's response.

"Lieutenant Dax has finished recording her data," Julian reported.

"All right," Nog said. *"I'll send somebody up for it. Nog out."*

Ezri felt herself outlasting the stimulant Julian had given her, but amid all the difficulties of the last week or so, a moment of playfulness suddenly asserted itself in her. "So," she said.

"So?" Julian asked, looking down at her, his blue eyes peering into hers.

"I told you so," Ezri said, referring to her belief that her contact with the object might help the crew stop the pulse.

"You did indeed," Julian said, obviously picking up her meaning. "I guess that nine lifetimes of experience trump mere genetic engineering."

"I guess so," she said, and chuckled.

"You know, I'm proud of you," he told her. His intense gaze held hers. "Not for being right about this, but for fighting to do what you thought needed to be done. For being strong enough to lead this crew even in the face of your own personal troubles."

His words touched her deeply, because they meant that he had been able to see in her what she had striven to be. "Thank you," she said, and she could not keep from smiling. Her eyes slipped closed for a second, and she forced them back open.

"It's all right," Julian said. "Get some rest . . . Captain."

Captain, Ezri thought, the word like a medal pinned to her chest—or a couple of extra pips on her collar. It echoed in her mind as her eyes closed once more, and she imagined Julian's voice saying it again as she fell asleep: *Captain.*

58

"I'm an idiot," Quark pronounced. The words filled the almost empty room. Quark looked around and saw the few other people here glancing in his direction. He ignored them, and turned back to the person across the table from him.

"Hey, you'd know about that better'n I would," Vic said, shrugging. The holographic singer returned his attention to his holographic breakfast. Quark peered over at his plate, then quickly looked away; the notion of eating flaky, dried-up grain fragments immersed in cow's milk, even when the concoction was made out of photons and force fields, turned his stomach.

Hew-mons, Quark thought, but even as he did so, he knew that his revulsion was misplaced. Nothing and nobody disgusted him right now more than himself. "Yeah, well, trust me," he told Vic. "I'm even more of an idiot right now than my simpleton brother."

Vic lifted a flute of a bright orange liquid that looked quite a bit like *pooncheenee,* though without the reddish tint. Quark knew that the drink could not have been the Bajoran beverage, since this holoprogram ran period-specific. "You mean your brother who's now in charge of the whole shebang back home?" Vic sipped at his drink, then set it back down.

"Not to mention ruining the entire Ferengi economy," Quark moaned. "Thanks for reminding me."

Vic shook his head slowly as he chewed noisily on his breakfast. "So that's why you're upset?" Vic asked. "'Cause your brother's wreckin' the out-of-town books?"

"I'm upset," Quark said, "because there's something going on here on the station, and I don't know anything about it."

"Hey, you can't know everything, right?" Vic said.

Quark leaned forward across the table. "If it happens on this station," he intoned, "I make it my business to know about it." He sat back in his chair. "And if there's profit to be had, then I make it my business."

Vic threw one hand in the air. "So you don't know about this one," he said. "You find out about the next one. No big thing. It's just business."

"'*Just* business'?" Quark repeated, appalled at the combination of the two words. "You don't understand. I'm not just a businessman; I'm a *Ferengi* businessman. Business is my life."

"Yeah, I know that's what you say," Vic offered.

"I'm not just saying it," Quark told him. "Business *is* my life."

Vic nodded and smiled in a way that made Quark uncomfortable. "Hey, pallie, whatever you wanna believe is fine with me."

"I don't just believe it," Quark maintained. "It's true."

"Okay, okay, who's arguin'?" Vic scooped up the last bit of his breakfast and shoveled it into his mouth.

"You are," Quark said.

"Look," Vic said. He set his spoon down in his empty bowl with a clink. "You say business is your life. I just see somethin' different, is all. Since I've been back in business here at the hotel, how many times have you and Julian been in here cryin' in your beer about one dame or another? First it was Jadzia, then it was Ezri, and then the green one. I'm tellin' you, you can't figure the players without a scorecard. I know the doc and Ezri have a thing now, but you . . . you're still in here mopin'."

Quark shrugged and offered a sly smile. "I like females," he said, feeling somewhat sheepish. "I can't help that."

"Course not," Vic said. "I have a fondness for 'em myself. But didn't somebody once say that dames and dough don't mix?" Vic's words sounded remarkably similar to the 94th Rule of Acquisition.

"All right, so I have a weakness," Quark allowed. "That doesn't mean business isn't my life."

Vic raised his glass and downed the last of his drink. "That's right," he said. "Except, what about this?" He put his glass down on the table, then spread his hands out, gesturing at their surroundings.

Quark looked around. "What about what?"

"I don't wanna bite the hand that feeds me," Vic said, "but you're lettin' this light show run twenty-six hours a day. I know we get our fair share of traffic in here from that floatin' bicycle wheel of yours, but not that much."

"I like this place," Quark said meekly, recognizing the truth of what Vic had said.

"Hey, and that's great," Vic told him. He picked up his empty glass and held it up, gesturing toward the bar. "Believe me, I'm happy about that. It just doesn't make the best business sense for a guy who claims business is the most important thing in his life. Plus . . ." He set his glass back down.

"Plus what?" Quark asked.

"Didn't you risk your life to rescue your mother from a bunch of bad guys who snatched her?" Vic said. "I mean, that's great. She's your mom and you gotta do what you gotta do. But you said business is your life, and that ain't exactly business."

Quark nodded, wondering exactly how Vic had learned about Ishka's kidnapping by the Dominion. "My mother . . . she had the Grand Nagus's ear—"

"Yeah, yeah," Vic interrupted, obviously not putting much stock in Quark's purported justification for his actions. "Didn't you also risk your life helping the Feds take this place back from the bad guys?"

"Better customers," Quark said at once. "The Federation and the Bajorans make better customers than the Dominion and the Cardassians." But even Quark did not believe that excuse for what he had done.

A young woman with long red hair and a short skirt appeared at the table, carrying a tray with two bottles on it. "Here ya are, boss," she said, setting the tray down. She poured first from the champagne bottle, and then from the clear, squarish bottle of orange liquid. Vic sipped at the drink while she loaded his empty bowl onto the tray.

"Thanks, doll," Vic said. After she had gone, he looked back over at Quark. "What about all those stories about you runnin' food and medicine to the Bajorans back when the bad guys ran the show?"

Quark felt an unpleasant chill buzz through the ridges along the tops of his ears. "That was at cost," he protested, perhaps a bit too loudly. Trying to settle himself back down, he said in a quieter tone, "That was also a business decision." He repeated his contention that Bajorans made better customers than Cardassians.

Vic seemed to consider him for a moment, and then he leaned forward across the table. In a low voice, the singer said, "I know that's what you say, pallie, but you probably don't realize that there are still some facts and figures from way back when rootin' around inside these walls."

"What?" Quark said. The idea that the station's computer system still retained records of his Occupation-era transactions made his lobes go completely cold. "That's all speculation," Quark insisted, understanding that Vic knew otherwise. "I don't want to hear that outside of this room."

Vic raised his hands up in front of him, palms toward Quark. "Hey, nobody'll hear it from me."

Quark looked away, uncomfortable with where this conversation had gone, but at the same time wanting to hear the rest of what this hologram had to say. "What's your point, anyway?" he asked.

"My point is, you're always in here claimin' to have this ideal of the Ferengi businessman that you wanna live up to, and yet you're always doin' somethin' to mess that up."

"Exactly," Quark said. "So I'm an idiot."

"Yeah, maybe," Vic said. "Or maybe this image they gave you as a kid and that you're always tryin' to fulfill, maybe that's not really what you want out of life."

Quark reached up with both hands and rubbed at the bottoms of his lobes. His ears had gone numb. *Me, not wanting to be a businessman?* he thought, incredulous at the suggestion. *Not wanting to be a* Ferengi *businessman?* The idea seemed preposterous on its face.

"Or maybe you just don't know how to deal with gettin' what you want," Vic went on. "I knew a guy once who wanted more than anything to be a Major League baseball player."

Baseball, Quark thought. *Sisko's game.*

"This guy didn't have all that much natural ability," Vic continued, "but he worked his tail off to get through the farm system and make it to the bigs." Quark had no idea what farms had to do with baseball, but then he had always been mystified by the sport. "So what does he do when he gets there? Drinks like a fish, carouses till dawn, stuff he'd never done before in his life."

"Why?" Quark asked.

"Who knows why," Vic said. "But he makes it to the Majors, and he's only there for a cup of coffee before they ship him back down. Never makes it back up. So he got what he said he really wanted, and he threw it away as soon as he got it. So maybe he didn't really want it, or maybe he didn't know what to do with it once he did get it."

Quark sat quietly for a moment, taking in what Vic had said. The words bothered him, and not because they were untrue. But he also did not know if he had the strength to face them. Finally, he said, "So what's all that got to do with me?"

Vic tilted his head to the side and smiled. "Mr. Quark," he said, "you're not an idiot." He paused, and then said, "You want to know what I think? I think business isn't the only thing you're worried about messin' up these days."

"What do you mean?" Quark asked, although he supposed he already knew the answer.

"What do I mean," Vic said. "Black hair, nice figure, wrinkled nose . . ."

"Laren," Quark said, his heart changing its beat at just the thought of her.

"Laren," Vic agreed.

"I messed that up."

"Doesn't surprise me." Vic grabbed his drink and drained it in one quick pull.

Quark grunted. "She probably wasn't interested anyway."

"I got news for you, pallie," Vic said. He put his empty glass back on the table, then stood up. "The dame digs you."

"You spoke to her?" Quark asked.

"Didn't need to," Vic said. He dug into his pocket and came out with a handful of green bills. He selected several and dropped them onto the table. "I heard her voice when she called you in here a couple nights ago. She's got it for you."

Quark's heart pounded wildly in his chest. He stared up at Vic, unable to say anything.

"Look, Mr. Quark," Vic said. "I hate to eat 'n' run, but I gotta interview some comics this morning. I still haven't found that opening act I've been lookin' for."

"That's all right," Quark said.

Vic smiled again. "Catch you on the flip side, pallie." He walked across the room and climbed the stairs to the stage, then disappeared behind the curtain.

"Catch you on the flip side," Quark muttered, having no idea what the words meant. But he understood the rest of what Vic had tried to tell him.

59

Vaughn's footsteps echoed loudly in the dark corridor. The air here tasted stale, as though it had lain dormant in these buildings for centuries. He did not smell death here, though, only abandonment.

He marched along, his boots kicking up the thick layer of dust that coated the floor. Little galaxies of particles spun through the beam of his beacon. He consulted his tricorder as he walked. This near the site of the pulse and its massive energy, the reach of the tricorder had dwindled to less than two hundred meters, but as Vaughn had hoped, the sensors did function well within that limited range. Now all he had to do was get close enough to the center of the complex to scan the area, then somehow use that information to determine a means of stopping the pulse.

Yeah, Vaughn thought, *that's all.* He laughed, the sound briefly joining his footfalls as they reverberated through the corridor. A doorway stood open in the left wall, and he shined his beacon through it as he passed, interested only in confirming that it was a room, not another corridor.

Vaughn had moved through the complex for almost an hour now, steadily making his way toward its center. Doors had lined most of the corridors through which he had walked, some of them closed, some of them—like the last one—wide open. He had earlier searched some of the rooms, looking for information or tools or anything else that might ultimately aid him in completing his mission here. But all he had found had been more of what he had seen yesterday back in the city: computers, communications equipment, and circuitry junctions. Scans had revealed that the machinery populated many of the rooms here, but also traveled through the walls and beneath the floors. None of it remained active.

Vaughn reached an intersection. A corridor extended to both his left and right, and the one he was in continued ahead. He shined his beacon in all three directions and saw nothing. He performed another scan, making sure that the center of the complex still lay ahead, then strode forward.

Back in the city, Vaughn had speculated that technology had somehow played a part in the extinction of the civilization here. Whether that was true or not, though, he thought that he had begun to see the mechanism by which the inhabitants of this world might have come to their ends. Vaughn had spent yesterday being visited by specters of his past that had evoked brutal feelings of loss and abandonment in him, and his emotions had reeled. If that same sort of thing had happened to the people here, but continuously, if they had been faced each day of their lives with such horrible feelings, then perhaps that had driven them to their destruction. Vaughn did not doubt that living day after day with a *fresh* sense of loss would have been unbearable.

A shape appeared up ahead in the light of his beacon: an empty chair. As Vaughn approached it, he found the sight of it eerie, an apt symbol for this empty world. *This place is haunted,* he thought in a melodramatic and uncharacteristic manner, and he realized just how fragile his emotional state had become. He passed the chair and walked on.

The suggestion of ghosts, though, brought him quickly back to the middle of last night . . . to seeing his mother, hearing again those terrible words, and feeling once more the desperate grief and loss he had first felt as a boy. He had awoken this morning at the first gray light of day, only marginally rested from the interrupted and uneasy sleep he had gotten. Recollections of his dreams lurked vaguely beyond the outskirts of his consciousness, and he had the strange impression that he had dreamed the dreams of others—including those of Prynn and ch'Thane. He also had the sense that he had dreamed of the people who had once lived on this planet, and also, oddly enough, of Ezri Dax. But his first thoughts upon waking had not been of his dreams, or of his encounter with his mother, but of his daughter, and his hope that he would not fail her—would not leave her—again.

Vaughn had padded back to where he had first lain down to sleep last night, and had found almost everything where he had left it. His bedroll and blanket had been there, his food and water, his coat, tricorder, and beacon; he had taken only the latter three objects with him for his foray into the complex. Even the circle of stones had been there, the ashes of a dead fire blackening the ground around which they sat. Only his mother had been missing, a fact for which he had been grateful. He had examined the dirt around the circle of stones, and seen footprints leading away from the camp and back along the direction he had taken to get here.

Maybe she went to join Captain Harriman, Vaughn thought now, bitterly. He had not been on this world long, but he had come to despise it. The intensity of his feelings shocked him, and he tried to push them aside.

Up ahead, the corridor dead-ended against another. Vaughn saw a patch of light on the wall facing him, light not thrown there by his beacon. He stopped—the echoes of his boots diminishing quickly—and switched the beacon off. The darkness within the complex had faded to a dull illumination he recognized too well: the outside light of this shrouded planet. And he perceived something else besides the light: the high-pitched wail at the bounds of his hearing. It sounded louder here, stronger, which did not surprise him.

Leaving his beacon off, Vaughn continued down the corridor. At the intersection, he consulted his tricorder, then proceeded to the left. The light grew brighter, and he walked on until he reached another intersection. He turned again, right this time, following the light. Twenty meters ahead of him, the corridor ended in a tangle of building materials. Past a heap of metal and stone, he could see patches of the dark gray mass that stood at the center of the complex: the source of the pulse.

As Vaughn walked forward, he noticed a heavy curtain of dust hanging in the air, dust that he had not stirred up from the floor. He scanned the air. The dust was primarily composed of traces of stone, sand, and lime, along with some metallic particulates; he concluded that it was the residue of the building collapse up ahead, which must not have happened too long ago. He guessed that this part of the complex had come down during or after the last pulse.

Vaughn stopped at the pile of debris and studied it. It stood close to two meters tall at most points, though lower on the left side and higher on the right. On the left, though, a metal beam hung from the fallen ceiling all the way down to the floor. If he could squeeze past it, he would probably be able to get over the rubble there.

Vaughn set the beacon down, then closed his tricorder and secured it in a coat pocket, fastening a flap across it. Reaching up, he tested the stability of the metal beam; it seemed wedged in place. He ducked down and slowly pushed his body through the space between the wall and the beam, actually making it through without much effort. Just as carefully, he stepped over the debris. He dislodged a few pieces of broken building materials, but quickly got past the heap.

The place where the pulse had been generated stretched before him, a great, dark circle that could have been a reflection of the sky above it. The surface of the circle, perhaps a hundred meters across, roiled and spun, a gray vortex that descended from its edges to a low point at its center. All around the perimeter, the complex had caved in—either blasted by the pulse, Vaughn supposed, or falling in as the zone of energy had expanded over time, loosing the foundations of the buildings. A fine, gray mist hung in the air here, like a thin fog over a lake at dawn.

Vaughn pulled out his tricorder and scanned the vortex. The readings of its surface corresponded to those of the cloud cover, although the vortex was much more powerful. At the center point, sensor readings broke down. Vaughn ran a diagnostic, verifying the accuracy of the aberrant scan. The readings resembled those of a singularity, he noted, with significant distortions in the space-time continuum there, although he saw no compression of matter and no extreme gravitational force. Vaughn adjusted the tricorder several times, attempting to circumvent the conditions, but he could take no better scans.

Finally, he checked the amount of energy that had built up in the vortex, and the rate at which it was now changing. Both measures reached slightly higher than had been predicted by the crew's extrapolations of the probe's data. If Vaughn had harbored any scant hopes that he would reach this place and find the threat to the Vahni Vahltupali gone, or even delayed, those hopes now vanished.

Based on the tricorder readings, another pulse would surge from the vortex in less than four hours.

60

Prynn's emotions seemed heightened today, as though whatever dreams had visited her during the night had somehow made her miss her father more. As she and Shar had worked throughout the morning, she had continually had to force herself to concentrate on what she had been doing. Even now, as they set to complete their final test, her mind drifted to her father, and to the image of him walking away from the camp.

Prynn shook her head, as though the movement could shake the picture in her mind loose. She refocused her attention on the tricorder in her hand, reached forward, and pressed a control. In an instant, white motes appeared before her eyes, and her surroundings faded from view.

She materialized one hundred meters from *Chaffee*'s aft section. She peered back at that portion of the wreckage, and just to the left of it, where Shar lay. She reached to the outside of her forearm, where the controls of her environmental suit's comm system were set. She switched it on, and said, "Tenmei to ch'Thane."

"I read you." Shar's voice sounded tinny in her helmet, with a slight reverb.

"All right," she said. "I'm going to check the equipment."

Prynn turned to her left. On the ground there sat the mass of machinery she had patched together. Two circuitry modules, each about the size of her torso, sat beside each other. Bundles of fiberoptic lines emerged from each in several places, some routing back into the same module, some into the other one. Isolinear optical chips jutted out all across the upper surfaces, sitting amid numerous other components. The tangled collection of technology looked to Prynn like the wreckage of the shuttle itself—twisted, broken, beyond repair— but the modules actually composed the second rudimentary transporter that she had pieced together.

That, along with the environmental suits, she thought. When she and Shar had awoken this morning, she had used the first makeshift transporter to beam him to *Chaffee*'s aft section; with Shar's leg so badly broken, neither one of them had wanted to risk moving him any other way. The two had then worked on the plan they had devised last night, with Shar attempting to repair another power cell and to finish rigging the environmental suits, and Prynn trying to improvise a second transporter. Both had been successful.

Now Prynn set her tricorder to sensor mode. She scanned the extemporized transporter machinery, then executed a diagnostic of it. When she had finished, she told Shar, "The equipment looks good. I'm going to beam you over now."

"Acknowledged," Shar said.

Prynn reset the tricorder to function as a control interface for the transporter, then energized the unit. She lifted her gaze from the display just in time to see the fading sparkle of dematerialization where Shar had been. Several meters in front of her, the white streaks of light reappeared, depositing both

Shar and the other heap of transporter machinery on the ground. Shar lay on his back, also clad in an environmental suit.

"*You did it,*" he told her, the thin sound of his voice still echoing slightly inside her helmet.

"*We* did it," she said, knowing that Shar's part in their accomplishment could not be understated. Despite the painkillers and medication she had given him, his injuries still left him uncomfortable and weak. She found it remarkable that he had been able to concentrate long enough to do the detailed work he had done this morning. "How's your leg?" she asked him now. The process of getting him into an environmental suit had been an arduous one, and even with the anesthetics, she knew, it had been painful for him.

"*I'm all right,*" Shar said.

Prynn nodded, a movement that felt awkward in the confines of her helmet. "Okay," she said. Shar was far from all right, she knew, but she respected his desire to forge ahead in their mission. "I guess we should get started then." They had decided to "skip-transport"—as they had begun referring to it—toward the site of the pulse. Failing that, they would do what Vaughn had ordered: they would use the transporters to get as far away as possible. Although the use of the environmental suits as pattern enhancers had doubled the ranges of the transporters in both directions, they suspected that the amount of interference from the energy at the site would prevent them from getting all that close to it. They could not really know that, though, until they attempted it. They also had no way of knowing whether her father had been able to reach the site by now, and so she and Shar might actually be the last hope for the Vahni. Of course, if they could even get to the location, there remained the matter of just what they could do to—

An electronic thrum interrupted Prynn's thoughts, and she thought at first that it might be feedback in her suit's comm system. She raised her forearm up so that she could see and work the controls there, but as she did, she saw Shar point upward. "*Look,*" he said. Prynn tilted her head back, the movement clumsy because of her helmet. She reached up and unlocked the seals, then twisted the helmet to release it. As she pulled it off, the foreign sound increased in volume. She peered skyward.

Above, an object descended toward them. With only the churning clouds as a backdrop, Prynn could not immediately tell its size. But as it drew closer, she recognized the shape. It looked like a quantum torpedo.

Prynn stood over the object, a sense of optimism growing within her for the first time since the crash. She had set to the tasks she had taken on with determination, but she understood now that, even with the successes she and Shar had managed with the transporters, she had never really believed that they or her father would be able to stop the pulse—or that they would be able to escape this place. Normally confident that she could accomplish anything, solve any problem, she was surprised to realize that she had lacked that confidence for the past few days.

The object had soft-landed five meters from where she and Shar had been with their improvised transporter equipment. It sat lengthwise on the ground, about a half-meter tall, a meter wide, and three meters long. White letters and numbers in Federation Standard marked the black casing in several locations, identifying it as one of *Defiant*'s probes. A gouge penetrated one end of the outer shell, the edges of the gash seared, as though made by an energy weapon.

Prynn bent and released the locks in the probe's casing, then lifted the upper section of it open. Shar had removed his helmet, and she narrated for him what she saw. She could identify the guidance and propulsion systems—which seemed to have taken some damage from whatever had sliced through the outer casing—but where she would have expected sensor equipment, she saw only two small modules, surrounded by a pair of bags that held caches of unfamiliar objects twice as large as her fist. In the center of the probe sat a rectangular container with three words printed on it: VAUGHN CH'THANE TENMEI.

Prynn pulled out the container and opened it. Inside, she found a padd. She carried it back to where Shar still lay on the ground, and sat down beside him. Together, they listened to Lieutenant Dax and Lieutenant Nog describe what the crew of *Defiant* had learned about the pulse, and the solution they had devised to stop it. Prynn could not interpret the movements of Shar's antennae, but if they expressed emotion, then she guessed that they displayed excitement right now; that was how she felt.

"We have to get the explosives to the site," she said when the messages had finished. She wondered whether they should attempt to skip-transport them to the source of the pulse, but Shar answered the question before she even asked it.

"With these type of devices, designed to shift into subspace and other dimensions, I wouldn't recommended transporting them," he said. "The phase change could detonate them."

"All right. Then we'll have to get the probe back in the air," she said. "We'll just have to hope that Commander Vaughn has reached the site, or that we can beam there ourselves."

Prynn walked back to the probe and found the control interface for the guidance system. Reviewing the settings, she saw that the *Defiant* crew had programmed the remaining sensors to scan for human and Andorian life signs, and if unable to find any, then to scan for the energy interference at the source of the pulse. She added a command now to ignore the present location, then set the probe to lift off in one minute. She quickly loaded the container with the padd back inside, then closed and locked the upper casing.

She rejoined Shar, and the two of them waited for the probe to launch. A minute passed, but nothing happened. Prynn used her tricorder to scan the probe, and found that all of its systems had gone dead. Immediately, her optimism faded.

"What happened?" Shar asked.

"I don't know," Prynn said. "It's completely lost power." She returned to the probe and reopened the upper casing. She examined the guidance and propulsion systems. Whatever had penetrated the outer casing had damaged the probe's power cell. She imagined a lance of energy spiking down from the clouds, like the one that had doomed the shuttle. The cell had obviously functioned until the probe had reached them, but the greater power requirements for a liftoff had apparently overloaded it. Prynn knew at once what they would have to do, and when she told Shar, he agreed.

Twenty minutes later, she had replaced the failed power cell in the probe with one of their own. She ran some quick diagnostics, then set the probe to launch. This time, it lifted off and headed away.

Sitting beside Shar on the ground, Prynn watched the probe fade out of sight. She searched within her for her optimism but found it difficult to find now. She knew that she and Shar were essentially back where they had been last night, although the environmental suits now doubled the distances they could transport. With only one power cell, though, they would be able to beam away from here just once, either fourteen kilometers toward the site of the pulse, or three hundred fifty kilometers in the opposite direction.

Either way, she thought, *it won't make much difference.* Either her father would be able to stop the pulse, or he would not. All she and Shar could really do right now was wait . . . and hope.

61

Ro stepped out of the turbolift and started down the Promenade. She weaved through the people, paying them little attention other than to be sure she did not run into anybody. She had just come from Kira's office, where she had briefed the colonel on the station's security status. Now Ro headed back to her own office, where she would continue to coordinate her teams. To this point, all of the procedures and precautions they had put in place for the summit had worked well and without incident.

As she passed the bar, she withstood her inclination to peer inside. She was still angry with Quark for the way he had acted yesterday. They had been having such nice times together recently, and their late-night stroll through the station two nights ago had been tremendously enjoyable—and even, maybe, just a little bit romantic. She and Quark had really taken a liking to each other—or at least, so she had thought.

Ro had not minded Quark's flirtation with Treir when she had first entered the bar. Ro could be something of a flirt herself sometimes. What had made her angry, though, was that he had continued flirting with Treir at the same time that he had ignored her.

Except that you weren't really angry, were you? she asked herself as she approached her office. She had actually been hurt by what had happened. *Of course, what difference does it make anyway?* she thought. The summit had started this morning, and if Bajor ended up entering the Federation, she likely would not be here much longer.

The doors to her office separated and slid open, and as soon as she walked inside, she saw Quark. He stood between the two chairs in front of her desk, apparently waiting for her. He turned, and began speaking as soon as he saw her. "Laren," he said quickly, "I want to apologize for my behavior yesterday in the bar. I don't really know what—"

"Quark," she interrupted, striding across the room and moving behind her desk. She heard the office doors click closed. "I really don't have time for this right now." She sat down in her chair and studied a display. The harshness in her tone and manner carried with it not just her disappointment in Quark, she realized, but also her concerns about her future.

Quark did not move. "Laren," he said quietly. "I'd just like to speak with you for a minute, and then I promise I'll go. You don't even have to say anything." He sounded desperate for her attention, but she also thought that she perceived a seriousness and sincerity in his words.

"All right," she relented, her own voice still severe. "One minute." She sat back in her chair, folded her arms across her chest, and stared up at him.

"All right," Quark said, looking suddenly flustered. She thought that he had probably not expected to be allowed to plead his case to her. He dropped his gaze from hers. "I just . . . uh . . . I wanted to apologize for my behavior yesterday in the bar."

"You already said that," she told him, thinking that he had probably re-hearsed that line before coming in here, but perhaps nothing more than that.

"I guess I did say that." He tapped nervously on her desk with his finger-tips, then seemed to realize what he was doing and stopped. He stepped away from the desk and started moving nervously about the room. "It's just that I didn't mean to do what I did . . . I mean, I didn't . . . I was . . ."

"Quark," Ro said, exasperated at his hesitation.

He stopped pacing and looked over at her. "I'm sorry, I'm sorry," he said quickly. "I just wanted to apologize to you."

"Well, you've done that," she said, let down that Quark could not muster more than the few simple words that he had. "So go on your way." She made a shooing gesture with one hand, then looked down at the display on her desk, although she did not actually read any of the words there. The office doors hummed opened again, and then closed. She sighed heavily and slumped back in her chair, peering after Quark.

Except that Quark had not left. He stood on this side of the doors, looking back at her. "Laren," he said, "I'm sorry." The desperation had left his voice now, replaced, she thought, with forthrightness. He walked back over to her desk, navigating between the two chairs. "The way I behaved with Treir—whether you had been there or not—was wrong," he told her. "But it was especially wrong because I hurt your feelings."

A swirl of emotions surged through Ro, not least among them, confusion. "Why, Quark?" she wanted to know. "Why did you act that way?"

"I'm not sure," he said. "But I think it was out of fear."

"Fear?" That answer did nothing to allay her confusion.

"I've been enjoying the time we've spent together lately," Quark repeated. "And obviously you have, too . . ." He paused, and she realized that he was giving her the opportunity to agree with him.

"Maybe," she said, and then, unable to stop herself, she smiled. Quark smiled back.

"So I think I got scared," he said. "Scared that you might get to know me better and then not enjoy spending time with me. Or scared that . . . I don't know . . . that I might actually get something I want."

To Ro, that answer sounded suspiciously absurd. She leaned forward in her chair and rested her forearms on the top of the desk. "Yeah," she said, "I can see how getting what you want could be pretty frightening."

"Laren, I'm a Ferengi," Quark said. "That means that my entire life has been about trying to get what I want." He stopped and took a deep breath, as though bracing himself for something. "And for most of my life, I haven't got-ten it. So finally getting something I want, particularly something as valuable as . . . well, as you . . . it really is frightening."

Ro looked into his eyes and saw only frankness there. She was moved by that openness and honesty, and by his appraisal of her—which she chose to take in the romantic sense she thought he had intended. "I'm not sure that I completely understand," she said, "but thank you, Quark."

"You're welcome," he said. He waited, and they simply looked at each other for a moment more without saying anything. She realized she was glad he'd come in here, and even more so that he'd said the things he had, in the way that he had.

If only—

Ro stopped her thought, not wanting to think about her unsure future right now, and not wanting her apprehensions to show on her face. Finally, Quark headed for the doors, but again, he did not make it far. He turned back to her. "Are you all right?" he asked, concern evident in his voice. His ability to read her mood so well surprised her, and also impressed her. They had just spent the last few minutes with him basically begging for her forgiveness and her giving it to him, and then him baring his soul, and yet he somehow perceived that something else entirely was bothering her. Still, she did not feel prepared to talk about it right now.

"I'm fine," she said. Seeing doubt in Quark's eyes, she added, "I'm just tired, that's all."

"I see," Quark said, but instead of leaving, he walked back over to her desk. "So, how's the . . . uh, conference . . . going?" he asked.

"The conference, huh?" Ro said, aware that Quark knew nothing about the summit, other than the confluence of officials here at the station. But since Kira had just told her that the first minister would be announcing the meeting and the reason for it to the people of Bajor later today, Ro thought that it would do no harm to tell Quark about it now. "Actually," she said, "they're calling it a summit."

"A summit?" Quark asked.

"Yes," Ro said. "They're meeting about the issue of Bajoran membership in the Federation. They're supposedly going to decide one way or the other—" She stopped talking when she noticed an expression on Quark's face of shock and even pain. For a moment, she thought that there might even be something wrong with him physically. "Quark, are you all right?"

"No," he said, looking off to the side, as though in a daze. He moved in front of one of the chairs at her desk and dropped heavily into it. "No, I'm not."

"What's the matter?" she asked. He continued to stare off to one side. "Quark," she said, beginning to grow concerned. At last, he looked over at her.

"Is it going to happen?" he wanted to know. "Is Bajor going to join the Federation?"

"I don't know," she said. "Why? What difference does it make to you?" She thought that maybe he had surmised her own situation, that since the Bajoran Militia would be rolled up into Starfleet she would be facing the end of her career, and therefore the end of her time on Deep Space 9.

"If Bajor joins the Federation," he said, "then I really am ruined."

"What?" she said, thinking that Quark was once again exaggerating. "Why would you—" But then she saw it. "The Federation has essentially a moneyless economy."

"A moneyless economy," Quark echoed, saying the words as though they had been laced with poison. "I won't be able to make a living running the bar, because this will be completely a Federation facility, and so nobody will be paying."

"I never thought of that . . . I'm sorry," she said, her concern for her own situation now coupled with a concern for Quark. "What will you do?" she asked, a question she had been posing to herself for the last couple of days. "What were you going to do three years ago when Bajor was on the verge of joining?"

"Three years ago, I was a younger man," he said.

"What does that mean?"

"It means that three years ago, I actually celebrated the prospect of Bajor's admittance into the Federation," Quark said. "I was going to stay in the bar and work the angles. Because the one thing that will happen when this becomes a Federation space station is that more ships will come here, and that'll translate to more customers in the bar. More customers means more information, and more information means more opportunity. And as the 9th Rule of Acquisition states, opportunity plus instinct equals profit."

Ro was not quite following Quark. "And you don't have the instinct anymore?" she asked.

"I don't know if I ever had it," he said disgustedly. But then he seemed to rethink that, and said, "I've still got the instinct. But what I don't have anymore is the drive. Not to run the bar without being able to make a sure living at it, not to wait for a piece of information here and there that would allow me to possibly make some small profit somewhere." Ro did not say anything; she was not sure what to say. "I don't know," Quark went on. "I guess maybe the war had an effect on me."

"It had an effect on all of us," Ro offered.

"Yeah," Quark agreed. Again, he looked off to the side, his gaze seeming to see something beyond the office. "When my nephew's leg got shot off . . . I think maybe I've just realized that I value stability. Chasing profit based on gathering speculative information . . . you can make a killing, but there's just so much uncertainty in it." Quark looked back over at Ro. "I'll tell you something, Laren," he said in a voice so quiet that it was almost a whisper. "The bar's not the most profitable it's ever been right now, but—and don't ever tell anybody I said this—that's all right."

"Because you have stability," Ro said.

"Yes," Quark said. "I'm not making much of a profit, but I am making a living." He stood up from his chair, apparently preparing to leave. "I think I've known for a while now that, whenever Bajor did join the Federation, it would finally be time for me to move on."

She looked up at him, and said, "I know the feeling."

"What do you mean?" Quark asked.

"Starfleet," Ro said. Quark's eyes widened in understanding. He sat back down in the chair, and Ro started to talk to him about her own uncertain future.

62

Vaughn leaned against a broken wall, the gloom of the gray mist about him, and listened three times to Lieutenant Dax's account of her contact with the thoughtscape. Each time, he felt a greater sense of the nature of it, and of this world as well, although precise understanding still eluded him. It seemed as though a lot of disparate facts almost fit together to form a greater knowledge, but he could not quite move the facts around to their proper places.

The probe had arrived here as Vaughn had been searching the perimeter of the vortex—the interface with the thoughtscape—attempting to find anything that would help him understand or defeat the pulse. The probe had hovered overhead for a short time, before finally alighting on one of the few patches of ground between wrecked sections of the complex. It had landed about a third of the way around the vortex, and it had taken Vaughn twenty minutes to reach it, crawling through and around the debris of the fallen buildings.

Vaughn had hoped that the probe was more than simply a probe, that the *Defiant* crew had developed information vital to his mission, possibly even a means of stopping the pulse. His heart had raced at the sight of the devices, which he had immediately assumed to be some sort of a solution. Each was metallic, with an ovoid body, and two panels set parallel to its surface, attached by rigid filaments. The devices had been completely unfamiliar to him.

He had listened first to Dax's account, and then to Nog's explanation and instructions about deploying the devices. Vaughn had paid particular attention to the engineer's caution to use all of them. If too few of the interdimensional explosives were detonated, Nog had warned, the interface would not be closed, but only widened. Then Vaughn had listened to Dax's account two more times.

Now, just two hours before the next pulse, he worked his way around the outside of the vortex, positioning the thirty-two devices at intervals of roughly ten meters. He set each one to detonate at the same time, one hour from now. The crew had included two satchels in which to carry the explosives, and he had slung them over his shoulders. He had already emptied and discarded one bag, and had now almost gone through the second one.

As Vaughn circled the vortex, waving away the gray mist suffusing the air, he felt strongly that he stood at the brink of understanding all that was happening—and all that had happened—here. He reviewed everything that he now knew about the thoughtscape and this world. According to Dax, the pulse resulted from the thoughtscape—the Inamuri, she called them—attempting to enter this universe. That did not necessarily imply hostility, he knew. The question he had to answer was, *Why?* Why did the Inamuri want to cross into this universe? The Prentara had violated their space—had violated *them*—via their virtual-reality technology, so perhaps they wanted to counterattack. But Dax had said that the Inamuri considered the Prentara both invaders *and* saviors. How could that be? And whether invaders or saviors, or somehow both, the Prentara had died out long ago, something the Inamuri must know.

Vaughn stepped over a girder that had fallen in such a way that it now hung out over the vortex. He looked back and saw that he had come about ten meters, and so he pulled out another device. He armed it, bent down, and set it in place. Then he moved on.

His own experiences here must tie into all of this, Vaughn thought. As he recalled the various scenes he had encountered, he reflected on the fact that they shared a common thread beyond simply being past events from his life. All of the incidents—from Captain Harriman to Prynn to his mother—had engendered a profound sense of loss or abandonment in him. And the Inamuri, through the energy clouds, had caused that. They must obviously have sensed his mind, his memory, in some way.

Vaughn remembered thinking this morning that he had dreamed dreams not his own, and he wondered now if that might have been an indication of some mental or emotional connection—a *communing*—with the Inamuri. But he had also felt as though he had dreamed Prynn's and ch'Thane's dreams, so perhaps this entire planet was connected to the Inamuri, united by the energy that circled it. He recalled the high-pitched sound he had thought of as the voice of the clouds, and he realized now that he might have been more right than he had known.

Ten meters to the next location. Device, arm, set.

Vaughn continued around the vortex. He waved idly at the gray mist, and thought about the mechanism by which bits of his past had been re-created. The energy from the clouds had reorganized local matter into different forms, but again, the question was, *Why?* Had Vaughn's experiences been intended as an attack on him? As communication? And if the—

Awareness surged in Vaughn's mind. He dropped to his knees, his hands coming up to the sides of his head. His consciousness felt as though it had been split open.

The mist, he understood at once, and knew that the understanding was not entirely his own. The mist, like the cloud cover, was an extension of the interface with the thoughtscape. And he stood within it, and sensed a tenuous connection with—

The Inamuri.

And suddenly Vaughn grasped it all. The Inamuri had not been attempting to navigate through the interface into this universe, although they eventually would. They had been sending the energy clouds through the interface, and all of that energy squeezing through the relatively small interface had caused the pulse. And the sea of clouds, the energy within, had been sent here to reorganize the matter of this world into a form that the Inamuri could inhabit.

"Why?" Vaughn asked aloud. "Why?"

Still waiting for answers, he staggered to his feet. He knew that he had to keep going. *You have a mission,* he told himself. He moved on.

Tell me, Vaughn thought, exhorting the Inamuri to give him more. *Why did you re-create events from my past? And why events of loss and abandonment?*

Because the Inamuri knew loss, Vaughn realized, because it knew abandonment. The re-created events of his life had been either its attempts to communicate or manifestations of its thoughts and emotions.

It, Vaughn thought. Not *they.* The thoughtscape, the Inamuri, was not a race of beings; it was a singular entity. One being that had known only one reality, that of its own "pocket universe," as Dax had called it. It had known only its own existence, and nothing beyond that.

Until the day that the Prentara had connected their technology to it. Connected their minds to it through their virtual-reality systems. They had invaded the living mind of the Inamuri.

Vaughn saw the first device he had set up sitting just ahead, and he turned to see the previous one. Standing an equal distance from each, he pulled out the last device. Armed it, bent, and set it down.

Still crouching, Vaughn gazed through the mist around the perimeter of the vortex, at the interdimensional explosive devices that now surrounded it. Then he looked out into the vortex itself, at the sweeping, twisting surface that so closely resembled the sea of clouds above. The private domain of the Inamuri had been *invaded* by the Prentara, but then the Inamuri had come to understand that *they* were other beings, that there *were* other beings, and therefore that there was more to existence than only itself. In some sense, Vaughn saw, the Prentara had *saved* the Inamuri, adding unexpected knowledge and sensation to its solitary existence. It had tried to establish contact with the Prentara, had tried to enter this universe, not understanding the destruction it caused by doing so. After the first pulse, though, the Prentara had withdrawn from the vortex, from their connection with the Inamuri, leaving it alone again.

No, Vaughn thought. *Not* again. The thoughtscape had been left alone for the first time in its life. Before then, it could not have understood the concept of being alone, because such a thing had been outside of its experience. But then the thoughtscape had learned what it meant to be alone, in the most profound way. And so it continued trying to enter this continuum, and to find other beings.

And now Vaughn was going to seal it back in its own universe. Alone. Forever.

Vaughn had agonized, but he had made his decision, and now he had committed to it. He stood at the edge of the vortex, peering down into its center. Nog's interdimensional explosives would detonate in fifteen minutes. Even if Vaughn changed his mind now, he could not possibly make his way around the vortex again and undo what he had done.

Predictably, he thought about Prynn. She had always thought of herself as being so much like her mother, and he had always thought that too. Certainly she carried a great deal of Ruriko in her, but he saw now that there was also a lot of him within her as well. That might or might not have been a good thing, but it provided him a small sense of peace right now. He was very proud of his daughter, and he loved her. Just moments from his own death, he hoped that his last desperate act would somehow manage to save her. He should have thought of it as a long shot, but he found that he actually believed that he would be able to communicate directly with the Inamuri, and convince it to save Prynn and Shar if it could.

What bothered him most right now was that, if she lived, he would be leaving Prynn alone again. He felt more than foolish for not having seen how much she had needed him since Ruriko had died. He had selfishly allowed his guilt to override his paternal responsibilities—and that his guilt had been justifiable provided him no solace, and no pardon. He had failed his daughter, and his only regret about his attempt to save her now was that he would definitely fail her again; either she would die with him, or she would live, and be without him.

Vaughn checked the chronometer on his tricorder. Thirteen minutes left now. He turned toward the complex and headed for the corridor from which he had first seen the vortex. He climbed over the rubble, then squeezed past the beam, holding his burden out in front of him. Once past the beam, he found the beacon where he had left it. He picked it up with his free hand and switched it on, then strode the twenty meters down the corridor to the intersection there. He bent down and deposited the bag on the floor. Then, one by one, he examined the eight interdimensional explosives he had removed from around the vortex, and he verified that all of them had been disarmed. When the others detonated, he supposed that the force might set these off as well, but without being armed, they could not slip into other dimensions and have the effect Nog had intended. The vortex would not be closed.

Vaughn stood back up, leaving the explosives and the beacon there. Then he strode back toward the vortex, thinking once more about Michael Collins, the astronaut who had circled the moon alone. He also thought about the tendril from the clouds that had struck down *Chaffee.* Vaughn wondered if the Inamuri had been trying to communicate with them all along. He did not know for sure, but he understood that all of this was true, that in some rudimentary way, he and Dax, and maybe even Prynn and ch'Thane, had been in contact with the Inamuri through the energy that now covered this planet and permeated its atmosphere. Dax had touched the fragment on *Defiant,* and Vaughn had experienced the matter that had been reorganized for him here, and he had also walked through the mist around the vortex.

After disarming the devices, he made his way back outside, past the beam and over the pile of debris. Outside once more, he strode directly over to the edge of the vortex. Vaughn checked the tricorder again, and saw that the interdimensional devices would detonate in two minutes. He looked up and watched as many of the devices faded out of sight, slipping into subspace or some other dimension.

If Vaughn had started away from here as soon as he had finished deploying all of the devices, he might have been able to escape the effects of the explosions. But after having come to understand the monstrous loneliness of the Inamuri, he had found himself unwilling to consign the creature to a lifetime of such an existence. As he had been reminded so vividly in the last day, Vaughn had known his own moments of loss and abandonment; he could not imagine a life in which such moments occurred unendingly, with not the slightest reprieve.

From his contact with the Inamuri, however tenuous, Vaughn had gained an understanding of what would happen once the interface was thrown wide: the planet would be transformed, and then the Inamuri would emerge into this universe. Once here, it could contact other beings, putting an end to its isolated reality.

Prynn and ch'Thane would be put at risk, he knew, but with the interface expanded, there would be no pulse, and *Defiant* and the Vahni would be safe. And with the Inamuri in this universe, there would never be another pulse. Vaughn's own life, he thought, was a small cost for all of that.

He checked the chronometer again. Thirty seconds. He tossed the tricorder aside, then peered down into the churning gray depths of the vortex.

Vaughn spread his arms wide, breathed in deeply, and then dived into the twilight maelstrom.

63

Kira looked up when the door signal sounded. Admiral Akaar waited outside. "Come in," she said, and the office doors parted to allow him entry.

Kira remained seated and looked up at the admiral, his enormous size still noteworthy even after all the weeks that he had been on the station. "Good evening, Colonel," he said.

"Good evening, Admiral," she said. "I imagine the summit has been adjourned for the day."

"No," he said. "We are taking a break at the moment, but we will meet for a few more hours later tonight." He paused, and then added, "And of course, we will be here for at least several more weeks."

Kira could not tell, but she thought Akaar might be attempting to bait her with this information. He clearly must have perceived the coolness between them—he had been the source of it—and he would have known that his continued presence on the station did not particularly please her. *He can't even use the word* hospitality *without me suspecting his motives.* Right now, though, she decided not to allow him to bother her.

"Well, you've got important work to do," she said. "What can I do for you this evening, Admiral?"

"Nothing," Akaar said. "I came here to inform you of the break in our session." At first, Kira thought that he must have been joking—why would she need to know about that?—but then he went on. "During the interim, First Minister Shakaar will be addressing the people of Bajor."

"Yes, that's right," Kira said. Shakaar had mentioned the address to her at the reception last night, and she had ensured that he had been provided access to a dedicated comm channel today. "He wanted to announce the summit and its purpose to all of Bajor."

"The first minister will be on the Bajoran communications network five minutes from now," Akaar told her. "I suggest that you watch him." As had been the case since the admiral had first arrived on the station, what he claimed to be a suggestion seemed to carry the weight of an order. In this case, it also sounded rather ominous.

"All right, I will," Kira said. She considered asking Akaar why he wanted her to watch Shakaar's address, measuring her curiosity against the difficulty of extracting even basic information from him. Before she had even decided, though, the admiral bowed his head and started to leave.

Kira watched him go. She waited a moment after the doors had closed behind him, and then said, "Kira to ops."

"Ops, Selzner here."

"Ensign, First Minister Shakaar will be addressing the Bajoran people on the comnet in a couple of minutes," Kira said. "I'd like you to patch it into the station's comm system."

"Yes, Colonel," Selzner said. *"I'll tie us in right now."*

"Thank you. Kira out." She stood up and walked over to the replicator. "Tarkalean tea," she ordered. "One-half measure of *kava*." She preferred her tea not nearly as sweet as she liked her *raktajino*. The replicator hummed, and a cup of the hot beverage materialized on the pad. She picked it up and walked over to a companel set into the bulkhead. She activated it with a touch, and saw the elliptical symbol of Bajor hovering in the center of the screen. She backed up and sat down on a padded seat along the wall, then sipped at her tea and waited. Shortly, the companel blinked, and the image of Shakaar appeared on the display. He wore a formal, dark brown Bajoran jacket over a white shirt. He was seated, with his forearms at right angles to his body and resting on the table in front of him. A padd sat between his arms. Kira recognized the ward-room behind him.

"Good day to all of Bajor," he began. *"For years now, since the first days after the end of the Occupation, many of us have discussed the possibility of our people joining the United Federation of Planets. Opinion has long been divided on the matter, and likely always will be, but in recent years, a large majority of Bajorans have come to favor aligning with the member worlds of the Federation, and becoming a part of a larger community. As we embark . . ."*

How far he's come, Kira thought, her attention wandering from the speech. Shakaar had never lacked for confidence or charm, but he had never cared much for politics, even after being elected first minister. Only his love for their people, and his sense of responsibility to them, had caused him to seek his office, and then to sustain it. For a long time, though, Shakaar had practiced his public service in a homespun sort of way, and although he had not entirely lost that simplicity and lack of pretension, Kira had seen a sophistication grow in him—particularly in the last few months, as he had been dealing with the Federation.

". . . three years ago, the Federation approved Bajor's petition for membership, but at the counsel of the Emissary of the Prophets . . ."

Kira sipped at her tea again, thinking back to her days in the resistance. Shakaar had always been such a strong and effective leader, never wavering from his purpose to free their people. As a girl, Kira had been awestruck by the man, and as a young woman, absolutely dedicated to his command. Only later, as an adult, when she and Shakaar had become romantically involved, had she truly learned how sensitive and solitary he actually was, and how much of a price he had paid—and continued to pay—by choosing to lead their people.

". . . spent time touring Federation worlds. I have spoken with their representatives, as well as . . ."

Kira's romantic relationship with Shakaar had ended abruptly, but amicably. It had been later that they had drifted apart, the gulf seeming to widen especially in the last few months. Although Kira still loved Odo—since he had left, she had not seen anybody, and she did not know when, or even if, she ever would—she also missed her closeness with Shakaar. Not their romance, but the closeness that had come from having a shared history and shared values. When they had talked alone in his guest quarters yesterday, the distance between them had been apparent to her, though the conversation had gone perfectly well. And since it had not been Kira's inclination to diminish their friendship, it must have been Shakaar's choice. And sometimes that saddened her.

". . . and on behalf of the Bajoran people, I officially requested the renewal of our petition for membership in the Federation. Today, here aboard Deep Space 9, a summit commenced to consider that petition. Attending are ambassadors from . . ."

Kira turned her full attention to Shakaar, now that he had come to the official announcement of the summit. She wondered what the reaction on Bajor would be, and just how long it would take the Federation representatives on the station to come to a decision.

"There have been many struggles for our people in the past," Shakaar continued, "but now we look to a bright, positive, and peaceful future." He paused, seemingly to underscore the words he was about to say. "Today," he went on, "I am happy to report to you that Bajor's petition for membership in the Federation has been approved."

Kira was startled. She had believed that there was a good chance that this would happen within the next few months, but for it to happen so soon . . .

"The summit will continue, as there are many issues still to be resolved, but the official signing ceremony will take place six weeks from today. At that time, Bajor will become a member of the United Federation of Planets."

Shakaar continued speaking, but Kira heard nothing more. She felt dazed by the rapidity with which this had happened.

The quaver of the companel drew her eyes back to the display, and she saw that Shakaar had finished his speech, and that his image had been replaced by a Bajoran icon. She put her teacup down on the arm of the seat, then stood up and paced over to the companel. She switched it off. Still feeling stunned, she peered aimlessly around her office. Her gaze came to rest on the bookshelf, and then to the large, red tome there. She walked to the shelf and pulled *When the Prophets Cried* down.

" 'Anew will shine the twilight of their destiny,' " Kira quoted the ancient prophecy. "Not the end of the day," she whispered. "The beginning." Holding the sacred text flat in one hand, she ran her fingers across the faded gilt letters of the title inlaid into the cover.

Alone in her office, Kira smiled, knowing that a new dawn had come to the people of Bajor.

PART FOUR

A NEWER WORLD

The lights begin to twinkle from the rocks;
The long day wanes; the slow moon climbs; the deep
Moans round with many voices. Come, my friends.
'Tis not too late to seek a newer world.

—ALFRED, LORD TENNYSON, "ULYSSES"

64

"Do you have regrets?"

Prynn raised her head and peered over the open top of the survival locker at Shar, not surprised by his question. Her own thoughts had turned to many subjects over the last hour or two, and regret had certainly been among them. Still, even considering the uncertainty of their situation, she did not wish to discuss such matters right now. *What's the point?* she thought. Instead, shrugging and attempting to change the subject, she said, "Well, I've never been surfing on the Canopus Planet."

Shar smiled, but in a way Prynn had noticed before, like a mask with no emotion behind it; she had always taken the empty expression to be his form of a polite response. She had wanted him to ask her what *surfing* was, but he would not let go of his question to her. "I think you know what I mean," he said.

"Yeah," she said, nodding, "I do." She ducked back down and pulled a ration pack from the survival cache. Holding it up so that Shar could see it, she asked, "Would you like something to eat?"

"No, thank you," he said.

Prynn walked around the locker and back over to where Shar lay on his back atop his bedroll. On the way, she decided that she was glad they had opted to transport. Unable to get much closer to the source of the pulse, they had done as her father had ordered and beamed in the opposite direction. She did not believe that it would do them any good, but she was pleased that she no longer had to see the shuttle wreckage. The rest of their new surroundings appeared the same as the old—flat and featureless—just without the embellishment of the crash site. *Now there's a regret for you,* she thought. *If I'd only been able to land the shuttle. . . .*

Shaking off the thought, she sat down on her own bedroll, awkwardly lowering herself onto it. Though they had taken off their helmets, neither she nor Shar had removed their environmental suits since they had transported. In Shar's case, with his mangled leg, the process would have been unnecessarily painful. And since he had not been able to take off his suit, Prynn had simply not bothered to take off hers.

She began to unwrap the ration pack. Beside her, Shar said, "I should have gone home sooner." Prynn looked over and saw him staring up at the sky. She did not say anything. If he needed to talk about this now, then she would let him. "I could have taken a leave of absence from Starfleet," he went on. "I could have even gotten posted to some planetside assignment on Andor." He paused, and when the seconds began to stretch out, Prynn felt that she should say something.

"I'm not so sure how easy it is to get Starfleet to transfer you wherever you want to go," she offered.

Shar turned his head to the side and looked over at her. "I was selfish," he said flatly.

Prynn looked at him for a moment, and then said, "I don't know you very well, Shar, but you don't strike me as a selfish person. I suspect that if you were, then you wouldn't be feeling such remorse right now." She glanced down at the partially unwrapped ration pack in her lap, and found that she really was not hungry after all.

Shar turned his head back and stared up at the sky again. "I just wish I had done things in a different way," he said.

"We all make choices," Prynn told him. "And they're not always the right ones." She thought she had come to understand that in the past few days better than she ever had. "Look, you can't change the past," she said, and the picture of her mother's face rose immediately in her mind. Not wanting to risk any painful emotions following after it, she quickly pushed the image away. "At least, you can't change it," she said, seeking to lighten the moment, "without getting paid a visit by the Department of Temporal Investigations."

Shar smiled again, but in a way that seemed genuine this time. "Have you ever had to speak to one of their investigators?" he asked, his tone a strange mix of curiosity and disdain.

"Not personally," she said, "but one time, when I was on the *Sentinel*—" Something moved quickly to Prynn's right, and she looked in that direction. In the distance, a huge plume shot into the air, a thick, agitated column of smoke—

Not smoke, Prynn saw as the rising mass joined seamlessly to the gray sky above, both obviously of the same composition. She quickly stood up, the ration pack falling to the ground from her lap. As she watched, the column expanded outward, like the result of a massive explosion. "The pulse," she speculated, but then wondered if her father had managed to detonate the devices—

Dad, she thought, and then realized that she had opened her mouth and screamed the word. She stared in horror at the scene. The gray mass continued to spread outward.

"Prynn," Shar called. "Prynn!" She tore her gaze away and looked down at him. "The helmets," he said, and pointed past her. She turned like an automaton, stiffly, not really conscious of her movements. *"Prynn!"* Shar called again, and she looked out and saw the middle third of the horizon filled now, and the column advancing in all directions. She shook her head, as though waking herself from a dream.

The helmets, she thought, and she finally moved, picking them up off the ground. She raced over to Shar and gave him one. He pulled it on over his head, and she bent and helped him twist it into position and then lock it into place. Then she stood back up and did the same for herself.

The instant before the shock wave struck her, she saw the lid of the survival locker crash closed. Then a wall of increased pressure slammed into her, knocking the wind out of her and carrying her backward off of her feet. She flew through the air like a leaf before a hurricane.

At least five seconds passed before she hurtled back onto the ground, hard. Her head snapped back, hitting the back of her helmet. She gasped for air, trying to catch her breath. The gale rushed past, clawing at the contours of her environmental suit, and roaring loudly in her ears. Below her, the ground began to shake violently.

Prynn inhaled great, desperate gulps of air, involuntary attempts to return oxygen to her lungs. She struggled up onto her elbows, and saw blue electrical charges arcing across the metallic portions of her suit. Ahead, she saw nothing—not Shar, not the bedrolls, not the survival locker, nothing but a great, writhing wall of gray bearing down on her. Her gaze followed it upward, and she saw the cloud cover above descending rapidly toward the planet's surface. Instinctively, she threw her arms up in front of her face.

Suddenly, she was surrounded by the thrashing, penumbral mass. The pressure around her increased, and she felt her environmental suit pushing in on her on all sides.

Her last conscious thought was of her father.

65

Quark stood behind the bar, motionless and staring at the display on the companel. He knew what was coming.

"During the past half-year," Shakaar said, *"I have spent time touring Federation worlds . . ."*

This evening, the bar was busier than it had been in a long time, with a virtual mob surrounding Hetik at the dabo table. Earlier, the hum of voices, the ring of glassware, and the delicious clink of gold-pressed latinum had combined in a way Quark had come to think of over the years as the sound of success. But after Shakaar had begun his speech, the mélange of noises had dulled as the attentions of his customers had been drawn first to Shakaar's voice, and then to his image on the companels around the bar and out on the Promenade. Bajorans had mostly been the ones initially distracted from their drinking and gambling by the first minister, but before long, almost all of the bar's patrons had stopped to watch and listen to Shakaar.

"Today, here aboard Deep Space 9," the first minister continued, *"a summit commenced to consider that petition. Attending along with me are ambassadors from Alonis, from Trill . . ."*

"Yeah, yeah," Quark said, waving his hand in front of the display. "We know who the players are."

"Shhh," Treir said beside him, slapping him lightly on the arm.

Quark's mood plummeted by the second as he watched Shakaar delivering his address from the station's wardroom. *I can't believe I served that man drinks there,* he thought.

"There have been many struggles for our people in the past," Shakaar went on, *"but now we look to a bright, positive, and peaceful future."* He paused—rather melodramatically, Quark thought—and Quark knew that the moment was at hand. The summit had only begun today, he had only found out about its purpose a few hours ago, and yet here the first minister was, already making the announcement. After all these years in the bar, and after all that he had been through on the station, Quark's time here was finally at an end. *"Today,"* Shakaar droned on, *"I am happy to report to you that Bajor's petition for membership in the Federation has been approved."*

The bar erupted, cheers and applause going up from the Bajorans present. *And probably the Starfleet types too,* Quark thought bitterly. He did not bother to look around or listen closely enough to find out. He remained frozen behind the bar, glaring at the image of Shakaar on the display. Amazingly, the oaf kept talking, obviously not understanding either the value of a good exit line, or the dreariness of an anticlimax.

At last, Shakaar finished speaking, and the companel blinked into standby mode. Quark continued to stare at the screen. "I guess that's really something," Treir said next to him, reaching up and touching him on the arm. Quark shrugged her hand away, then reached forward and jabbed at the companel's controls, deactivating it.

"I'm sorry," a voice said softly behind him, perfectly audible through the buzz that now filled the room. He turned to see Laren sitting at the bar, her hands folded together in front of her. He had been so preoccupied with the announcement that he had not even heard her come in. An expression of concern dressed her features, which touched Quark. Even with the difficult decisions that lay ahead in her own life, she still managed to feel badly for him.

Laren looked at Treir, who still stood next to Quark. There seemed to Quark to be no animosity in the look, but it also seemed clear that Laren wanted Treir to leave the immediate area. "Uh, I need to go see if Hetik needs any help," the dabo girl said at once, and she quickly moved away.

"So," Laren said once Treir had left, "what are you going to do?" They had each asked the same question earlier, when they had spoken in her office, but neither of their answers had been terribly specific.

Quark regarded Laren for a long moment, appreciating her strong features, the girlish cut of her hair, and the closeness that he had begun to feel with her. He suddenly felt the urge to make a bold gesture, not to impress her—not for her at all, really—but to symbolize for himself the new and indeterminate path down which his life had just begun to travel. He smiled broadly, then reached back and touched a control on the companel. Two loud chimes rang through the bar, and the lively hum of conversation faded. "The next round of drinks," he called loudly, locking his gaze with Laren's, "is on the house." Another cheer went up in the bar, actually even louder than the one following Shakaar's announcement.

Laren smiled back at Quark, apparently delighted by his gesture. The moment seemed to stretch out as they stared into each other's eyes. Everything around Quark seemed to wilt out of existence, and he and Laren together seemed to make up the entire universe. Then a tall, ribbed metal mug came streaking down between them, slamming onto the bar and ending the moment.

"Yridian brandy," said a loud, slurred voice belonging to the Yridian whose hand gripped the mug. Laren turned her head slowly toward the bleary-eyed drunk. Quark watched as she reached up and, just as slowly, slid the mug out from between them.

"Sorry," she said. "Quark isn't working right now. Find one of the waiters to help you."

"But . . . but . . ." the Yridian stammered.

Laren reached out quickly as Grimp raced past, headed for the bar, a tray of empty glasses in his hands. She stopped him with a touch to his arm, and said, "Grimp, would you please find this—" She paused and glanced over at Quark, offering him a comic expression. "—*gentleman* a table to sit at."

"Uh, okay," Grimp said. "I just need to—"

"Do it now," Quark ordered the waiter.

"Here," Laren said, and she took the tray from Grimp, then passed it over the bar to Quark. Quark turned and put it down beside the recycle shelf, then turned back to see Grimp leading the staggering Yridian away.

"Thanks," Quark said to Laren, and he knew that his gratitude carried well beyond her relocation of the drunk.

"Believe me," she said in a soft tone, "it was my pleasure." Then she asked, "Are you all right?"

Quark considered the question briefly, and then shrugged. "Not everything always turns out the way you expect it to," he said. "And you know what? That's not always a bad thing." To his great surprise, he realized that he actually believed that.

"I think you're right about that," Laren told him. Then she leaned in over the bar, and Quark moved forward and leaned in himself. "Now then," she said, "can I buy *you* a drink?"

Quark smiled again, already feeling intoxicated.

66

Vaughn was drowning.

He had struck the surface of the vortex and felt an immediate series of sensations. His body seemed buoyant within the gray eddies, as though floating in muddy light. Electrical currents streamed across his flesh, and blue jags of radiance filled the null vision of his closed eyes. Unexpected warmth surrounded him, and acceleration gathered him in its grip. The force, smooth and circular, carried him down and around—somehow pushed him down—until, at last, he fell from the universe.

And had continued falling. The warmth vanished, leaving him not cold, but empty. Gravity, too, disappeared, and still he fell. His lungs hungered for air, but feeling the void about him, he resisted the impossible attempt to breathe.

Vaughn had forced open his eyes. In the dusky absence of reality, he saw himself plunging down. The other-Vaughn tumbled away, unseeing, and then his *eyes opened.*

Does he see me? *Vaughn had thought, and knew that the other-Vaughn could not. The other-Vaughn was from the past, from moments ago, had only just now opened his eyes.* But what does he see? *Vaughn asked.* Another-Vaughn, from further back in the past? *Vaughn did not know, but he saw fear in the other-Vaughn's eyes, and knew that it must also surely be in his own. He closed his eyes, unwilling to see.*

Vaughn's lungs had formed their own version of the void by then, and he exhaled in an explosive burst. His body went through the motions of breathing in, but there was no air here. His muscles moved anyway, trying to inhale, trying to help sustain him.

The gray existence had surged into Vaughn, through his mouth and throat, down into his lungs. Filling his lungs with the pseudomatter of the thoughtscape. A spasm closed his larynx.

Vaughn was drowning.

Vaughn was dying, but he did not wait to die. For almost as long as he could remember, he had gazed up at the stars and yearned to explore. And for nearly as long, he had been forced, had been requested, had been constrained, to fight. He could not say that the fighting had come to nothing, because it had not; it had been necessary, always necessary, sometimes for the greater good, sometimes for the smaller, and still other times, merely for survival. But now, in the end, he chose not to battle, for he saw no enemy. Instead, he would do what he had always wanted to do; he would explore.

Vaughn opened his mind. He threw off the walls, he threw off the secrecy, the denials and rationalizations. As his long day waned, he searched for the truth, for the essence of himself.

He opened his eyes again, and saw himself . . .

. . . setting the interdimensional devices around the vortex, ready to die alone, unable to have made peace—to have made a bond—with his daughter . . .

. . . on a battered starship, engaged with a mystical object that showed him how much death he had been privy to, and that death had been no companion to him . . .

. . . standing in a transporter room and watching the love of his life leave, pretending that she would return, knowing that she would not . . .

. . . *leaning over the corpse of a person he had killed, in the name of saving others, and realizing in that moment that he had sealed himself off from the rest of humanity* . . .

. . . *listening to the words of the officer who had set him on his path, allowing himself to be extracted from the fellowship of the innocent* . . .

. . . *sitting in a sickroom, holding on to the hand of his mother, who had filled his world and left him too soon* . . .

. . . *being born into an existence that promised true connection—of the mind, of the body, of the heart—but in the best of circumstances, delivered isolation in almost every instant* . . .

. . . *and from all those moments, all those Vaughns peered back—peered forward—at him right now, as he fell within the thoughtscape, gone from one universe and into another, alone as always, and yet alone as never before. Vaughn's consciousness stretched across all those moments, existed at the same time in all those moments, and in all those in between. And he witnessed all at once, as he thought no one should, the extent to which he had existed, did exist, and would always exist, separated from every other being in the universe.*

The loneliness extended from the instant of his birth, across uncounted—billions, trillions—of instants, to now. Not every instant, but almost all of them. The understanding crippled him.

Vaughn was dying, and now he would wait to die.

Waiting, Vaughn understood that the loneliness was a lesson, and he learned from it. He could not have done otherwise, not as he searched for the truth of a life that stretched away behind him. And not as the life that surrounded him, and occupied him, cried out in the pain of an isolation it had never known until inadvertent invaders had brought it the unintended gift of companionship—and then taken it away. The thoughtscape had considered the Prentara both invaders and saviors, Dax had said, and Vaughn now grasped precisely why. Even a tormentor could provide company.

Waiting, Vaughn considered the prison that the home of the Inamuri had become. Still existing in every moment of his life, he closed his eyes on the thoughtscape, and opened them on the morning he left home—after his mother had already gone, and really, had she not taken home with her when she had? Vaughn had always wanted to explore, and now he saw that he had left home a long time ago, and that he had been looking for it ever since.

Waiting, Vaughn realized that these lessons and the learning were connections. The teacher and the student. The thoughtscape had tied itself to him.

Hear me, *Vaughn screamed without words.* I am here.

Vaughn searched for the right moments of his life. He peered across the thoughtscape and saw everything he had ever been, everything he had ever done, all laid out before him, each instant distinct from the next. He closed his eyes, and opened them on the bridge of Defiant, *returning again to the moment when he knew Prynn had gone.*

Not this, *he said as his heart ached.* Not this.

He closed his eyes, and opened them on the distressed figure of Ensign ch'Thane, thrown onto the desolate plain of a dead planet.

Not this, *he repeated.*

Vaughn stopped waiting to die, accepting that he had decided to fight again, to struggle for even the smallest connection, for as many moments out of a lifetime that he could. No longer waiting to die, he saw that those moments, no matter how few, no matter how fleeting, were all worth fighting for. They were worth dying for.

His last conscious thought was of his daughter.

67

Kira strode purposefully down the corridor, the bright illumination and openness aboard *Gryphon* a noticeable contrast to the dark, cramped corridors in Deep Space 9's habitat ring. She read the room-identification plaques as she passed sets of doors, until at last she found the one Commander Montenegro had provided her. She reached up and touched the door chime set into the bulkhead there, and a moment later the doors parted and slid open.

Kira stepped inside, and although she saw Akaar immediately—across the room, seated in a chair—she could not resist looking around. The cabin was spacious, easily twice the size of most of the crew accommodations aboard the ship, she was sure. Unlike standard guest quarters, it had been decorated with more than a few adornments, and not just in a generic manner. *Why wouldn't he make these quarters his own?* Kira thought. Akaar had been living here for several weeks now, and who knew how long would be here after today?

Some of the items she saw—including what appeared to be primitive ceremonial masks and totems—reminded her of similar items that Captain Sisko had kept in his quarters. In addition, though, numerous textiles hung on the walls: sashes, headdresses, capes, many of them in brocaded fabric, and in a mixture of both muted and vibrant colors. She also saw an object that appeared to be a weapon: three curved blades arranged in an essentially triangular shape, with a circular hole in the middle that she guessed functioned as a grip.

"Colonel," the admiral said. "This is unexpected." He did not stand.

Kira stepped farther into the room. She had come here after the summit had finally adjourned for the day. Now, in a moment of spontaneity, she raised her right fist to the left side of her chest, then opened her hand and held it out in front of her. "I come with an open heart and an open hand."

Akaar's eyebrows slowly rose. "Indeed," he said, and now he did stand. "Then I certainly must welcome you with an open heart and hand." He returned her gesture.

Kira smiled, skeptical. "Admiral," she started. She brought her hands together in front of her and paced to her left. "I have to tell you," she said, "I'm not really sure what to make of you."

Akaar's shoulders moved slightly, his equivalent, she supposed, of a shrug. "I am a Starfleet admiral," he said. "I am here simply executing my duties."

Kira stopped and faced him across the room, folding her arms across her chest. "And your duties included interrogating me?"

"Interrogating you?" Akaar said. "Yes, they did."

"Why?" Kira demanded, throwing her hands up and out, and then letting them fall to her sides. "To understand Bajor through me? That's not really fair. I'm not an elected representative. I don't speak for my people. I *can't* speak for my people."

Akaar nodded. "Is this the open heart you come with?" he asked her.

"It's the open hand," she said.

"I see." He moved across the room, away from her and over toward a replicator set into the far bulkhead. "May I get you something to drink, Colonel?" he asked. Looking back at her over his shoulder, he added, "To celebrate."

Kira did not know what to say. She did not particularly want to share a drink with this man, but she also did not wish to give the impression that she was not pleased about Bajor's acceptance into the Federation. Before she could formulate a response, Akaar spoke again.

"Colonel Kira," he said, turning to face her directly, "did you think that my questions to you, and your answers, would prevent me from fostering Federation membership for Bajor?"

"'Fostering'?" Kira echoed. She found the claim that Akaar had been a proponent for Bajor difficult to believe. But then, she had come here looking for answers from the admiral, wanting to identify and understand his motives. She said, "I will toast Bajor joining the Federation."

Akaar nodded once, then turned toward the replicator. Instead of ordering something there, though, he picked up a short, bulbous bottle from a shelf. Kira watched as he pulled the stopper from the dark green bottle and poured a clear liquid into two glasses. He carried the glasses back across the room and offered her one. "This is *grosz,*" he told her. "From my native Capella." Kira accepted the glass. Akaar held his up and said, "To Bajor joining the Federation."

Kira lifted her glass, and saw that the drink was not perfectly clear, but had a purple tint. "To Bajor joining the Federation," she echoed. Akaar moved his glass forward, touching it to Kira's with a soft ring. He drank deeply, and she took a gulp herself. The drink fired her throat as it went down, leaving behind an acerbic taste as the burn faded. She breathed out loudly through her mouth. "That's a powerful flavor," she said.

"Perhaps I should have forewarned you," Akaar said. "I understood that, as a rule, Bajorans liked 'powerful flavors.'"

"I wasn't complaining," Kira said, and to support her declaration, she took another swallow. Again, she exhaled loudly. "Just offering an observation."

"Observation noted," Akaar said. Motioning toward the sitting area, he said, "Would you care to sit, Colonel?" Kira walked around a low table and sat on the sofa below the windows. The admiral's cabin looked out, not on the station, but on open space. Akaar sat back down in the chair he had been in when Kira had arrived. He drank even more of his *grosz,* and then said, "Am I correct in saying that you believe I have been attempting to judge Bajoran society through you?"

"Haven't you been?" Kira asked, trying to keep any antagonism out of her tone, if not out of her words.

Akaar reached forward and put his almost empty glass down on the table. "No, Colonel, I have not been," he said. "What I have been doing is attempting to judge *you* through your feelings about your people and through your relationship with them."

"You've been judging *me?*" Kira asked, not sure that the revelation actually made her feel any more comfortable with the admiral.

"I believe that how a person sees their society, how they fit in and do not fit in, how they deal with internal strife, can say a great deal about them." Kira supposed that there must be some truth to that, but—

"The Attainder the Vedek Assembly imposed upon me . . ." She let her words trail off.

"The Attainder is the result of how some Bajorans view you," Akaar said. "Or perhaps it is not even that, but a form of political expediency. But with respect to you, Colonel, it is not the Attainder that interests me, but how you have dealt with it. You have carried on, and not just for yourself, but in continued service to your people." The words surprised Kira, not because they were not true—they were—but because they revealed an opinion she would never have guessed Akaar to possess.

"Perhaps I owe you an apology, then," she said. But then, recalling that the admiral had certainly not made his stay at Deep Space 9 an easy one for her, she added, "Or perhaps you owe me one."

"Perhaps neither," Akaar countered. He reached forward and picked up his glass of *grosz,* finishing it. "Would you like another?" he asked.

Kira held up her glass and saw that it was still half full. Quickly, she raised the glass to her lips, threw her head back, and downed the rest of her drink. Then she held the glass out to the admiral, and said, "Yes, thank you."

For the first time that she had seen, Akaar smiled. He took her glass and walked back across the room, returning a moment later with two new drinks. He handed one to Kira across the table, and remained standing. "Colonel, I believe that you and I have similar feelings about our peoples," he said. He paused, and then added, "Although I may have more frustrations with mine."

"Oh, I've had plenty of frustrations myself," Kira said. "Back in the days of the provisional government . . ." She did not need to finish the sentence.

"I understand," he said. He seemed to consider something very seriously for a moment, and then he said, "On my world, the Ten Tribes have warred sporadically for most of my life." Kira wondered how long that was, and suddenly had the sense that Akaar was a great deal older than she had assumed from his appearance. "Numerous leaders have stepped forward through the years," he went on, "and attempted to unify all the people. Some succeeded, but only for short times. Many of Capella's greatest leaders were deposed, others were . . . others were killed." Genuine emotion appeared on Akaar's features, an expression of terrible sadness, Kira thought. The admiral absently sipped at his drink, and then said, "I was the victim of a coup myself."

"You?" Kira asked.

He moved back to the chair and sat down. "I was a boy," he said. "Born into leadership, a teer at birth." Kira gathered that *teer* was the title given to Capellan leaders. "My mother served as my regent, and it was she who took me from our world and got me to safety when our government was overthrown."

"Have you ever gone back?" Kira asked.

"Many times," Akaar said. "I have had a long life, and my people are a good, strong people . . . perhaps too strong in some ways. The unity we need eludes us."

"I'm sorry," Kira said. "I think I understand."

"I believe that you do, Colonel," Akaar agreed. "For more than a century, the Federation has provided my people with food and medicine . . . they have dramatically improved the quality of health care. Before my birth, Starfleet officers even saved my mother's life. For a long time, I have wished for the opportunities for my people that Federation membership would bring."

"Will it ever happen?" Kira wanted to know.

"I hope so," Akaar said, melancholy tainting his voice. "But certainly not in my lifetime. I've had to admit to myself that we Capellans have not matured enough as a society to become part of a greater community." It seemed a difficult admission for him. "I'm envious of your people," he said, holding his glass up again, "Bajor has come far since the Occupation, and you should be proud of that, Colonel."

"I am proud of that," Kira said, but she heard a hesitancy in her tone. "I am," she repeated, stronger.

Akaar must have sensed her momentary uncertainty, because he asked, "Do you have concerns?"

"Yes," she confessed, "but not exactly about my people. I favor Federation membership, but tonight, after the first minister's announcement, I found myself worrying about Bajorans being able to retain their identity now."

"The Federation has chosen to invite and accept Bajor into our community because Bajorans offer their own uniqueness," Akaar told her. "There will be no need and no desire to change that. This union is not about how Bajor can be made to fit into the Federation, but rather how the Federation can be made into a part of Bajor."

Kira smiled, those ideas precisely what she had hoped for, and the words precisely what she had needed to hear tonight. "Thank you, Admiral," she said.

"You should be proud not only of your people," Akaar said, "but of yourself, and your part in leading them."

"I feel privileged to serve."

"And you will continue to do so," Akaar said. "I am not supposed to tell you this, but when the Bajoran Militia is absorbed into Starfleet, not only will you be offered a captaincy, but you will be asked to remain in command of Deep Space 9."

Kira smiled again, realizing that she had never really considered the possibility that she could be reassigned elsewhere once Bajor joined the Federation. "Thank you," she said again.

"It was not completely my decision, Colonel," Akaar said, "but those were my recommendations."

Kira regarded the admiral, amazed at how completely she had misread his motives and judgments. At the same time, she remembered how easy he had made it for her to do so. Something else occurred to her, and she immediately asked the question that rose in her mind. "What about Lieutenant Ro?"

In an instant, Akaar's demeanor changed. His face seemed to harden, his body to tense. "A determination about Lieutenant Ro has not yet been made," he said.

Kira persisted, convinced, after serving with Ro for months, that the station's security chief was being unfairly judged. "And what were *your* recommendations about Ro?" she asked.

"They differed considerably from my recommendations about you, Colonel," Akaar said. "My opinions about Ro Laren have been on record for a long time."

Kira nodded, understanding, but also realizing that people changed. Captain Sisko had shunned the title and responsibilities of the Emissary at first, and then had come to embrace them. Damar had been an ugly, hateful man, who had come to acknowledge and regret the terrible things he had done, and had become a strong and worthy leader. And even Kira herself . . . after the Occupation, she had for a long time resisted the prospect of Bajor joining the Federation, but now . . .

"Opinions about Capellans have existed for a long time too, I imagine," Kira finally said. "But maybe in the future, how they learn to comport themselves going forward will matter more than how they did in the past." Her message to the admiral was clear: Ro deserved another chance, or at the very least, another evaluation.

"Maybe," Akaar said, the analogy obviously not lost on him. But he appeared unconvinced about either Lieutenant Ro or his own people.

Kira held up her glass of *grosz* once more. "To Capella," she said.

Akaar did not smile, but he regarded Kira with what seemed to be an expression of appreciation. He lifted his glass. "To Bajor," he said.

Kira leaned forward in her chair, holding her glass out to the admiral. He leaned forward himself, and touched his glass to hers. "To newer worlds," she said.

68

The door opened, and Ezri stepped onto the bridge. Julian stood at her side, wanting to assist her, she suspected, but respecting her need to walk onto the bridge unaided. She was still recuperating from her latest experience with the thoughtscape, but when she had received word from Bowers that something was happening on the planet, she had wanted to be here. Julian had understood, and had put up no argument.

As they made their way toward the center of the bridge, passing Nog at the engineering console, Ezri saw the eyes of all the crew directed forward. She peered up at the main viewscreen. The clouds surrounding the planet had erupted in one area, as though forced up from below. The movement of the cloud cover had become far more violent, she saw, even causing numerous breaks through which the planet's surface was now visible. The effects could not have been the result of the pulse, Ezri realized at once, because if they had been, then Bowers would already have ordered *Defiant* away. "What's happening down there?" she asked as she and Julian came abreast of the command chair.

"We're not sure," Bowers said, vacating the chair and allowing Ezri to take it. "But we're seeing some breaks in the clouds, big enough to allow us to scan through them. The energy buildup at the source of the pulse appears to be dissipating there and spreading out into the atmosphere."

"Is the pulse still a danger?" she asked.

"Not as far as we can tell," Bowers reported. "At least, not right now."

Ezri turned and looked past Julian, over toward the engineering station. "Nog," she said, "you did it." The away team must have succeeded in deploying the devices Nog and his engineers had developed and sent down to the surface. For the moment, it appeared that four billion Vahni Vahltupali would be safe.

"Not me," Nog said, turning in his chair toward her. "The explosion should have sealed the interface. The energy should have been trapped on the other side."

She looked to Bowers. "Has the thoughtscape emerged onto the planet?"

He shook his head. "We can't tell what happened."

Quietly, so that only Bowers could hear, she asked, "Has there been any sign of the shuttle?"

"We've been scanning outward from the site of the pulse wherever we can," Bowers said, lowering the volume of his voice to match hers. "So far, nothing."

Ezri considered their options. She eased herself up out of the command chair and walked over to the engineering station. "Nog," she asked, "how long until the *Sagan* will be repaired?"

"At least two more days," he said.

She turned and looked back at the viewscreen. Even if *Sagan* were available right now, she did not know if she would order it down to the surface. As much as the cloud cover had been in motion when *Defiant* had first arrived here, there had been enough stability in it that, when openings through the clouds had formed, the crew had been able to safely send both a probe and the shuttle through and down to the planet. But now the scene on the main viewer showed an atmosphere in complete turmoil. The idea of putting more lives at risk—

"I've got the shuttle," Ensign Merimark called from the tactical station.

Ezri heard reaction from the bridge crew, but she ignored it, instead pacing over to stand beside Merimark. "What are you reading?" she asked.

"I'm picking up *Chaffee*'s transponder signal," Merimark said. "I'm trying to scan the location . . . it's difficult, there's still energy in the clouds, and they're moving so—wait . . . there . . . it's on the surface . . . I'm reading hull plating—" When the ensign suddenly stopped speaking, a sense of dread filled Ezri.

"What is it?" she asked.

Merimark looked up with a weary, pained expression on her face. "The shuttle crashed," she reported. "There are no life signs."

Ezri felt whatever strength she had left in her drain away. She looked over at Julian. He stared back, the anguish he felt apparent on his face, as it must have been on her own.

"Lieutenant Nog," she said firmly, finding strength in her responsibility to the crew. "I want the *Sagan* ready as soon as possible, crews working on it around the clock."

"Aye, sir," Nog said.

"Lieutenant Bowers, I want options," she told him. "I want to find the away team." She did not need to add *alive or dead*.

"Yes, sir," Bowers said.

Ezri had already lost Gerda, and now maybe she had lost Vaughn and Shar and Prynn, but she would not leave this planet until she knew that for sure.

Ezri sat in the command chair, watching along with the rest of the crew as the planet below was transformed. Above the area from which the pulse had once originated, a huge mass of unidentifiable gray matter burst up into the atmosphere. Like the darkened image of a nuclear detonation, the mass emerged kilometers wide through the cloud cover. The clouds themselves fled from the explosion of matter, pushed aside by the enormous displacement of air.

The gray mass spread as it surged upward, and at its edges, began to turn back toward the planet, as though gravity had only just prevented it from surging out into space. Its surface whirled at uncounted points, a collection of spinning vortices impossibly bound together. The mass seemed to hover as it unfolded, as if now defying gravity.

And then it plunged down, not falling back to the planet, but diving toward the surface. The mass hurtled earthward, streaking down faster than it had climbed up. It struck the ground with phenomenal force, instantly liquefying rock at the points of impact, and sending expanses of ground blasting outward. The mass pushed along the surface, dislodging the crust to a depth of ten kilometers.

The clouds, tossed away earlier, now returned and joined the maelstrom, swirling into the mix of gray matter and rocky debris. Energy surges forked like lightning across the exterior of the enormous amalgamation. The mass grew across the surface.

And then the planet became shrouded once more, buried beneath a churning gray shell that hovered between solid and liquid states. The mass undulated like a living thing. It reached unbroken from pole to pole.

Ezri watched all of this, something she had not witnessed in nine lifetimes of experience, and thought, *Vaughn and Shar and Prynn are down there.*

Or at least, they had been.

Over the course of hours, the great, gray shell smoothed and calmed, but sensors could not pierce even its outer layers. Through breaks in the cover that had occurred during the transformation, though, scans had indicated that the energy level at the site of the pulse had dropped to zero. Whatever had happened down on the planet—and whatever price had been paid to make it happen—the pulse had been neutralized.

The science and engineering teams continued searching for a means of penetrating the shell, either with sensors or with *Sagan,* once it had been repaired. While the crew held out little hope of finding the away team alive, Ezri refused to accept that—felt that it was her duty to refuse to accept that. She had briefly thought about the eulogies she might have to deliver for her crewmates, not much more than a week after the service for Gerda Roness, but she had quickly scuttled such morbid—and inappropriate—notions. As the acting captain of the ship, Ezri remained dedicated to doing all that she could to save the away team, and she would presume them alive until it had been proven that they—

"Something's happening on the planet," Ensign Merimark announced. "I'm reading a break in the shell . . . two breaks . . . both sizable."

"Put it on the viewer," Ezri said. The main screen blinked, and one view of the planet was replaced by another, targeted view. On the surface of the gray shell, two small, circular holes had appeared.

"The openings are both fifty-three-point-three kilometers in diameter," Merimark reported. "Depth . . . they reach all the way down to the planet. I've got full sensor contact down to the surface."

Foreboding suddenly washed over Ezri, the narrow cylinders in the shell uncomfortably reminiscent of the barrels of weapons. She recalled the simulation of the pulse that Nog had shown her down in engineering, and she now envisioned the destructive energy hurtling through the cylinders and out into space. "Are there any energy readings?" she asked.

"Negative," Merimark said. "Energy readings are minimal. There doesn't seem to be—" The ensign stopped speaking abruptly, and Ezri spun quickly around in her seat to face her. "I'm reading two life signs at the bottom of one well, one life sign at the bottom of the other."

Ezri vaulted out of the command chair and raced to Merimark's station. "Are they human?" Ezri asked, looking for the answer on the console. "Andorian?" She felt her heart pounding in her chest, a desperate hope forming in her mind.

Merimark's fingers flew across the panel, causing words and numbers to march across her display. "One Andorian," she said. "And two humans. Two of them are in environmental suits."

"Transfer the coordinates to the transporter," Ezri said at once.

"Aye, sir," Merimark said.

"Dax to medical bay."

"Go ahead," Bashir replied.

"Julian," she said with barely restrained excitement, "we've located an Andorian and two humans down on the planet. We'll have them beamed directly to you." She felt absolutely astonished at the unexpected turn of events, both disbelief and joy coursing through her.

"Acknowledged," Julian said, and she could hear his excitement even in the single word. *"I'll keep you posted. Bashir out."*

"Dax to transporter."

"This is Chao," came the voice of the transporter chief.

"Chief, we need an emergency site-to-site transport from the planet's surface directly to the medical bay," Ezri said, the words spilling from her. "One Andorian, two humans. Ensign Merimark is transferring the coordinates."

"I see them," the chief said. *"Transporter locks . . . established."*

"Acknowledged," Ezri said. "Bring them home."

69

Ro Laren stepped out of her office and set the lock. It had been quite a day, and she looked forward to crawling into bed, pushing away all thoughts of Bajor and the Federation, and getting some sleep. Of course, she had not been able to do that for the past couple of nights, which certainly contributed to her exhaustion right now.

"What a coincidence," a voice said from just down the Promenade.

Ro turned and looked in that direction, the figure of Quark difficult to see clearly in the shadows of DS9's simulated night. He stood at the entrance to the bar, evidently just closing up himself. "I don't know if I believe in coincidences," she said, and began walking toward him.

"Oh no?" Quark said. He waited until she reached him before continuing. "Are you suggesting that I planned this?" he asked in obvious mock offense. "Are you suggesting that I stood right here, staring over at the security office and waiting for you to come out, when I could have closed up half an hour ago?"

"Well, didn't you?" she asked, playing along. Ro realized that one of the things she particularly liked about Quark was simply that he was fun.

"Actually," he said, reaching down and setting the lock on the bar entrance, "it was more like forty-five minutes."

Ro laughed, which felt especially good after the stress of this week. That was another thing she liked about Quark: he was funny.

"May I walk you to your quarters, Laren?" he asked.

"Well," she said, drawing the word out as though having to seriously consider her answer, "I suppose since you've been waiting here *so* long . . ." She started for the turbolift, and he fell in step beside her.

"Now that's what I like," Quark said. "A female who knows her own value."

"What do you mean?" she asked him.

"I mean, if I'd only been waiting for you for fifteen minutes," he said, "you probably would've left me standing there."

"Probably," she agreed with a smile. They reached the turbolift, and Quark pressed the control panel in the bulkhead beside it. The door retracted, and she and Quark entered the car. "So, Quark," she said after the door had closed and she had specified her destination, "were you really waiting for me?" The lift began its descent.

"Not really," Quark said, and Ro felt a twinge of disappointment. "I could have closed up an hour ago, but Morn kept going on and on about the political situation on Beta Antares IV. Turns out one of his sisters is a top boss there."

" 'Boss'?" Ro said. "Isn't that sort of an odd title for a politician?" She had heard of government officials being called many things, but *boss* had never been one of them.

"With Morn," Quark said, "I don't ask questions."

"Why not?"

"Because he might answer them," Quark moaned, "and then another hour of my life would be gone." Ro chuckled, well aware of Morn's penchant for seemingly endless conversation.

As the lift changed direction, Ro noticed something. She looked over at Quark, and said, "You're not wearing that cologne anymore."

Quark offered a little shrug. "You didn't like it," he said.

"That's very considerate."

"That's the 305th Rule of Acquisition," he told her. " 'Always be considerate.' "

"No. Really?" she said, and felt immediately foolish for having asked. She may not have known all the Rules of Acquisition—or any of them, for that matter—but she could have guessed that being considerate was not a business principle widely held by the Ferengi. She really must be tired. Quark apparently saw her embarrassment, because he did not bother to say anything, but only raised the ridge above his eyes. "Don't laugh," she warned.

"Who's laughing?"

"Well, how was business tonight anyway?" she asked, clumsily changing the subject.

"Good," Quark said. "Except for me buying a round for everybody."

"At least you got one back," Ro said, referring to the drink she had bought him earlier, after Shakaar's announcement. She had enjoyed that, although she had been called away on a security matter soon after.

"Best drink I ever had," he said, his appreciation clearly genuine.

The turbolift decelerated to a stop, and the door slid open before them. Ro stepped out into the habitat ring, but when she looked around, she saw that Quark had remained in the car. "Aren't you coming?" she asked. "I thought you were going to walk me to my quarters."

He did not move, but looked at her with a serious expression on his face. "May I ask you a question, Laren?"

Ro suspected she knew what the question would be, and she made a decision she could not entirely believe she was making. "The answer is *yes*," she said.

Quark's lips parted in a big smile, his eyes wide with surprise. "You haven't even heard the question yet," he said.

Ro reached out to the side of the doorway, then leaned back into the turbolift, holding Quark's gaze. "I trust you," she said.

Quark looked into her eyes for a few seconds, but then he said, "You might want to wait for me to ask this question before answering."

"Okay," she said. "Go ahead."

"I, uh, I wanted to, uh, know," he said, stumbling along. "I wanted to know if you would like to go out with me?"

"You mean on a date?" she asked solemnly. Quark nodded. "Then the answer is *yes*." She pushed away from the side of the doorway and swung back into the corridor. "Now, walk me to my quarters," she said. "I'm exhausted and I need to sleep."

Quark exited the car, and the two began walking toward her quarters, side by side. They were both quiet for a few moments, a silence Ro found very comfortable, something she had not experienced in quite some time. Even with Bajor joining the Federation, and her future filled with nothing but uncertainty, she felt content right now. And before she realized she was doing it, she reached over and took Quark's hand in her own.

They walked like that all the way to her quarters.

70

Prynn opened her eyes as though from a long and restful sleep. She had no conscious thoughts as she lay on her back, staring up in the dimly lighted room. After a few seconds, for no good reason, she turned her head to the right. When she saw Shar lying on the diagnostic bed next to her, she bolted up, leaning on her hands. In an instant, she recalled everything that had taken place on the planet, up until the moment Shar had yelled at her to get the helmets. It seemed impossible that they had not been killed, but—

Dad, she thought, remembering the great gray column, expanding outward, obviously from an explosion—an explosion where he had been. Prynn spun quickly around to look at the diagnostic bed to her left. It was empty. *Dad,* she thought again, calling to him in her mind, but she knew that he was gone. She dropped down onto her side on the bed. Tears blurred her vision and rolled down her face. She felt hollow. She had lost her father, and to make it worse, she had also lost the last seven years with him.

At the periphery of her perception, Prynn heard the whisper of a door. She ignored it, unable to focus on anything but her sorrow. She squeezed her eyes shut as she began to sob.

"Ensign Tenmei?" Through the sounds of her grief, she heard the voice of Dr. Bashir. She felt a hand on her shoulder, and she opened her eyes. Before her, she saw the shape of his face, though she could not make out his features in the shadowy lighting. "Are you in pain?" Bashir asked.

Pain, Prynn thought, and could not begin to describe the agony that consumed her. She tried to answer, but she could not stop crying. Finally, she managed to say, "My father."

"Oh," Bashir said. "Ensign, your father's going to be fine."

Her tears seemed to stop immediately. "What?" she asked, raising her head. "What?"

"Your father's here in the medical bay," Bashir told her. Prynn stared at him, unmoving. She felt him exert pressure on her shoulder, trying gently to push her. She allowed him to guide her, and she peered into the gloom where he pointed. "Computer," Bashir said, "lights up one-quarter."

As the illumination in the medical bay increased, Prynn looked up at Dr. Bashir's face for a moment. Then she peered back to where he was pointing, at a diagnostic bed halfway across the room. She saw the figure of a man lying atop it and recognized her father's profile at once. The sheet covering him up to his shoulders rose and fell at his chest, confirmation of his breathing.

Prynn laughed, a sharp, involuntary noise as uncontrollable as her crying had been. "He's alive," she sputtered. She laughed again, even as tears began streaming down her face once more.

"Yes, he is," Bashir said. Prynn leaned backward, ready to fall onto the bed, but the doctor put a hand behind her and lowered her down. "Computer, night lighting," he said. The shadows returned, the doctor's face fading from sight once more. "I'm going to get you something to help you sleep," he told her.

"Wait," she said, grabbing his arm as he started to go. "How did we get here?"

"I wasn't on the bridge when it happened," he said, "but I believe that the clouds cleared above you, and we just beamed you up. You and Ensign ch'Thane were wearing environmental suits, so you were able to survive down on the planet during its . . . transformation." He tapped at her hand, then softly pulled it from his arm and set it beside her on the bed. "I'm going to get something to help you through the night," he said again, and he walked away.

Before he returned, Prynn had already fallen back to sleep.

71

As Kira prepared to leave her quarters for her office, she thought again about contacting Kasidy. She had tried to reach her last night, right after Shakaar's announcement, but Kas's comm system had not been accepting incoming transmissions. She knew that Kas sometimes shut down her comm when writing letters, not wanting to be distracted. Kira had not bothered to leave a message.

Now, even though it was still early—more than an hour before the start of the day shift—she decided to try again. She sat down at her companel, opened a channel, and sent a greeting. After only a few seconds, the display blinked and Kasidy appeared. *"Nerys,"* she said with a bright smile. She looked as though she had been awake for a while.

"Good morning," Kira said. "It looks like I'm not contacting you too early."

"Not at all," Kas said. *"I always love hearing from you. Of course, if I could only get you to come for a visit . . ."*

"I know, I know," Kira said. "As soon as I can get away . . ."

"Nerys, if I have to wait for a day you're not working, then this child—" Kasidy reached down below the view on the display, obviously running her hand across the swell in her midsection. *"—will probably have a command of their own by then."* Kira chuckled, and resolved again to find some time to visit Bajor. *"So how are you?"*

"I guess . . . I'm pretty excited," Kira said, putting her anticipation into words for the first time.

"'Excited'? Now that sounds good," Kas said. *"About what?"*

"About Bajor." Kira realized that Kas did not know what had happened yesterday. "You haven't heard, have you?"

"Apparently not," Kasidy said. *"Why don't you tell me?"*

"Kas, Bajor's been accepted into the Federation." The words actually sounded like something out of a dream to Kira. This time had been in Bajor's future for so long now that it seemed strange for it to finally be in the present. "The official signing will take place in six weeks."

Surprise showed on Kasidy's face. *"When did this happen?"* she wanted to know. Kira told her about Akaar and the ambassadors and the summit, and then about the first minister's speech. When she had finished, Kasidy said, *"I didn't realize this was so close to happening."*

"I don't think any of us did," Kira agreed, "other than Shakaar." She noticed that Kas's expression had slipped from surprise to what looked like discomfort. "Are you all right?" Kira asked. "Does this bother you?"

"I'm fine," Kasidy said. *"It's just . . . I'm not exactly sure how I'm supposed to feel about this."* She paused, and then said, *"I mean, I'll be living in Federation territory, so that's a good thing."*

"It will all be good."

"I know, you're right," Kasidy said. *"It's just that . . ."*

Just that Captain Sisko should be here, Kira thought. "It's all right, Kas. You had a sacred vision, so you know that Benjamin is with the Prophets. And that means he must know about this."

"Of course," Kasidy replied, a forced smile appearing on her face. *"You're right. I'm sure Ben's very happy about this."*

"I'm sure he is," Kira said. "He worked hard for this, against a lot of opposition and through some difficult times. But this is all happening because of him."

Kasidy smiled again, and this time, it seemed genuine. *"He really was—he really is—something."*

"Yes, he is." For the next hour, they talked about Benjamin Sisko.

72

"I'll see you on the bridge, Captain," Nog said.

Before Vaughn could respond, Dr. Bashir offered his own opinion on the matter. "Not for at least a day or two, you won't," he said, walking over to Vaughn's biobed. The doctor held a padd in one hand, which he referred to as he checked the diagnostic panel.

"I'll be there soon enough," Vaughn told Nog. The engineer smiled and nodded, then left. This had been Nog's second visit today—earlier the lieutenant had also gotten the opportunity to speak with Ensign ch'Thane—and he had not been the only crew member to stop by the medical bay. In fact, the only person among *Defiant*'s small crew who had not come by, not surprisingly, had been Prynn.

Vaughn might have had a profound experience down on the planet, and come to a deeper understanding of his relationship with his daughter and of the troubles between them, but he had no reason to expect that she had done the same. According to Dr. Bashir, who had clearly noticed Prynn's conspicuous absence, he had released her to her quarters this morning, with orders to remain off her feet until tomorrow. Of the three members of the away team, Prynn had been in the best condition after their ordeal, but even she would need time to recuperate. Vaughn had tried to accept what the doctor had told him, but it seemed less like a real explanation for Prynn not visiting him, and more like wishful thinking. And the truth was, no matter the troubles between them, it hurt him that she had not come in to see him.

"So how are you feeling?" Bashir asked.

"Tired," Vaughn said, and though that was certainly true for him physically, it was in an emotional sense that he felt most drained. Since he had regained consciousness, he had attempted to shake off the effects of his experiences down on the planet, but he had not been completely successful. All those memories of loss that he had carried with him through his life, most dulled by the passage of time, had been made current again for him, and all at once. He suspected that only time would help him mend the reopened wounds. He would be able to get through it, he believed, but he did not expect the process to be particularly pleasant.

Not wanting to dwell on all of that right now, though, he asked the doctor, "How's Ensign ch'Thane?" Bashir glanced across the medical bay to where the young man lay sleeping.

"He's doing well," the doctor said. "He's got a strong constitution. I'll probably release him tomorrow morning." Vaughn had already learned that ch'Thane would not lose his leg, although Bashir had noted that if the ensign had gone without major medical treatment for another few hours, not only might he have lost his leg, but his internal injuries might have killed him. "You, on the other hand," the doctor continued, "I may want to keep here for two more days."

"I understand." What had physically happened to Vaughn during his time within the thoughtscape, up until his eventual rescue, remained something of a mystery. Vaughn had hypothesized that, although he had dived into the vortex, he might never have actually passed into the universe of the Inamuri, or if he had, that he might have been carried quickly back into this one when the Inamuri had made the transition itself. Either way, he had guessed that the thoughtscape, sensing his plight via their strange mental and emotional connection, had formed an atmospheric pocket around him.

Dr. Bashir, on the other hand, had developed a different theory. He had detected residual energy readings within Vaughn's body, leading him to conjecture that the Inamuri had actually reorganized matter within Vaughn's lungs into respirable air. And because the residual energy spread throughout Vaughn's body, the doctor also thought that the Inamuri might have essentially pressurized him from within.

Whatever the explanation, Vaughn felt confident that his survival had been the result of action taken by the thoughtscape, and Bashir concurred. Because of the uniqueness of that situation, Vaughn understood why the doctor wanted to keep him in the medical bay for a couple of days. While there appeared to be no deleterious effects on Vaughn—other than to his emotions—he agreed that remaining under direct medical observation for the time being seemed like a good idea.

To Bashir, he said, "I trust your medical judgment, Doctor."

"Well, I guess somebody has to." Vaughn and Bashir both looked toward the door on the other side of the medical bay, where Lieutenant Dax had just entered.

"You keep talking like that," Bashir said as the lieutenant walked over, "and I'll have grounds to declare you mentally unfit for duty."

"And you can write those orders from the brig," Dax retorted. Vaughn enjoyed the lively banter, a welcome change in tone for him from the last few days.

"I like the brig," Bashir joked, checking the diagnostic panel again and making a note on his padd. "Less work to do." He held up the padd, obviously to demonstrate how overworked he was. He finished what he was doing, then discreetly withdrew across the room to a console, leaving Vaughn and Dax by themselves.

"How are you feeling, sir?" Dax asked.

"Like an old man."

"Hmmm," Dax said. "That doesn't really fit with the crew's view of you as being indestructible."

"Indestructible?" Vaughn said.

"Prynn and Shar were at least wearing environmental suits when we recovered them," Dax explained with a smile. "You made it through two universes in a torn Starfleet uniform and a field coat older than most of the crew."

"Take my word for it, Lieutenant, there are better ways to travel," he said. Then, curious, he asked, "What's the status of the thoughtscape?"

"It's difficult to know for sure without direct communication," Dax said, "but it appears to have transformed a great deal of matter into a form that it can inhabit in our universe. So far as we can tell, the entire thoughtscape emerged through the interface and now surrounds the planet, in normal space and in several other dimensions."

"It's been trying to do that for centuries," Vaughn said. "The energy clouds were the mechanism for that. The thoughtscape—" Vaughn searched for the right word. "—*pushed* them through the vortex . . . the interface."

"And the energy released with each push was the pulse," Dax said.

Vaughn nodded. "And each time, the interface widened," he went on, "allowing the thoughtscape to push more through the next time, and faster, which increased the size of the pulse. But it hadn't yet been able to get enough energy through to transform enough matter . . . not until Nog's devices widened the interface."

"You know all of this from communicating with the Inamuri," Dax said. Though she had phrased it as a statement, it was clearly a question.

"I wouldn't say 'communicating,'" Vaughn told her. "I liked your word, Lieutenant: *communing*. Except that where you only seemed to have a one-way communing, I seemed to have had it in both directions. Obviously, I was able to make the Inamuri understand the danger to Ensign Tenmei and Ensign ch'Thane."

"And to yourself," Dax noted. "It was quite a sight to see the holes in the shell around the planet, especially when we found the three of you at the bottom."

"I'm sure it was," Vaughn said. "I also sensed that, when *Defiant* and *Chaffee* were hit by energy from the clouds, the Inamuri wasn't attacking."

"It was trying to communicate," Dax surmised.

"Yes," Vaughn confirmed. "As we both found out, the substance of the clouds also functioned as a conduit for thought."

"When I . . . when Dax . . . communed with the thoughtscape," the lieutenant said, "it wanted to keep that connection . . . it *cherished* that connection." Vaughn nodded, understanding the terrible loneliness of the Inamuri, and how desperately it craved companionship.

"What about the fragment of the clouds aboard the ship?" Vaughn wanted to know.

"It's gone," Dax said. "As best we can tell, it withdrew into another dimension and . . . rejoined . . . the rest of the clouds." She paused, then asked, "What about the Prentara? How did they die?"

"I'm not sure," Vaughn said. "But my experiences on the planet . . . I still don't know if the Inamuri was trying to communicate its sense of loss to me, or if somehow the feelings of loss in my own life caused the experiences. Either way, I think that same sort of thing must have happened for every Prentara, every day. And living with that sense of loss, being faced with it all the time . . . I can understand how that could have driven them to their own destruction."

Dax stood quietly for a moment, no doubt contemplating the enormity of it all. Finally, she said, "I sent your message to Starfleet Command." Vaughn had earlier asked the lieutenant to contact Starfleet, detail what had transpired here, and request that they immediately send a scientific team in order to find a means of communicating directly with the Inamuri.

"Did you tell them the promise I made?" Vaughn asked.

"I did," Dax said. "I also contacted the Vahni Vahltupali and explained to them as best I could what happened here. They're going to try to make contact with the thoughtscape."

"Good," Vaughn said. "Thank you, Lieutenant. You did a good job up here. You took risks, but they paid off. Your actions in attempting to contact the Inamuri not only saved it, but saved the away team and the Vahni."

"Thank you, sir," she said. "It was a challenge, but . . . I like command."

"I knew you would," Vaughn said. "When we return from the Gamma Quadrant, I intend to recommend you for the Pike Medal of Valor."

Dax smiled. "Thank you, Captain."

"Now, unless there's anything else, Lieutenant, I think I'd like to get some sleep."

"Certainly, sir," Dax said. She crossed the room to speak with the doctor for a moment, then left the medical bay, presumably headed back to the bridge.

Vaughn adjusted his position on the bed, trying to make himself more comfortable. His body still ached from everything he had been through. *That ache is nothing,* he thought, *compared with what the Inamuri has been feeling for centuries.* He did not regret the promise he had made to the strange being, despite that he had taken it upon himself to speak for the Federation. And he vowed to himself to make sure that Starfleet kept his word.

We'll be back, Vaughn had promised. *And we won't let you be alone.*

Vaughn sat in a chair in his cramped quarters, a padd in his hands. He read the last sentence that he had written—*The joy of life is connection*—and then erased it. It was not quite right. And he wanted to get it right.

A hundred years old, Vaughn thought, *and I'm still learning.*

And what he had learned now had come from those hundred years, from the immeasurable number of moments he had lived within them. What had happened to him within the thoughtscape had been both a curse and a gift. He remembered that he had somehow been conscious, all at once, in every moment of his life, and though he could no longer feel precisely what that had been like—and was thankful for that—he understood that he still carried the loneliness of that experience within himself, and that he probably always would. The curse had been sensing the extent to which he had been alone— *without connection*—in so many moments of his life. The gift had been in the understanding that had come with that, the realization that the moments when he had made a connection—to Ruriko, to his daughter, to his friends and co-workers, to the human race itself—had redeemed the aloneness. Each moment, he now saw, came with a choice, and too often he had not chosen to *connect*.

Vaughn looked at the padd again, then dropped it into his lap. Dr. Bashir had released him this morning from the medical bay, but had suggested that he not work a full shift today. Vaughn still felt tired, but the fatigue was an emotional fatigue, not a physical one, and he knew that he would simply have to bully his way through it. He would follow the doctor's advice and work a half-shift today, but he would resume his full schedule tomorrow.

Defiant, Vaughn knew, had departed from the world of the thoughtscape, and now continued on its journey through the Gamma Quadrant. He had felt uncomfortable leaving the Inamuri, and a couple of the crew had actually volunteered to stay behind. *Sagan* had now been repaired, and the volunteers had suggested remaining in orbit about the thoughtscape until the science team arrived from Starfleet. Vaughn had been impressed by the offers, but there would have been little point in being here until a direct and safe method of communication could be devised, and *Defiant* simply did not have the resources to be able to do that.

Vaughn picked up the padd again and started to reread what he had written, but his mind quickly wandered. He was anxious to see Prynn. He had not had any contact with his daughter since he had walked away from her on the planet's surface, headed for the pulse. *Actually,* Vaughn thought, *that might not be true.* He remembered his feeling that the energy surrounding the planet had somehow connected everything on it. He had never sensed a direct connection with her, although he had felt some sort of a link with her through her dreams. If she was willing, he would talk with her about that, and about whatever experiences she might have had during their ordeal.

Ultimately, though, Vaughn wanted to express to Prynn his newfound understanding of how he had failed her. He hoped, now more than ever, that they could work toward a reconciliation. They would need to delve into what had happened in their lives and in their relationship, and into how and why they had become separated. It would probably not be easy, he knew, but they would have to search for answers together. For him, their circumstances had changed, and he hoped that they could be changed for her too. But in the two days he had spent in the medical bay after regaining consciousness, Prynn had not visited or contacted him once, and so he had decided not to force matters with her. Perhaps after they returned to Deep Space 9, he could—

The door chime sounded. "Come," he said. Across the room, the door slid open to reveal his daughter.

"Prynn," Vaughn said, stunned to see her. He stood from the chair, dropping the padd onto it. She stepped into the room, and Vaughn felt suddenly awkward, and even lost. He thought, *Connect,* but he could not find the right words to begin.

"Dad," Prynn said, and he realized that she had not called him that in years. He saw tears in her eyes, and he started toward her. She raced forward too, and they threw their arms about each other, hugging tightly. "I'm so glad you're all right," she said.

Tears pooled in Vaughn's own eyes. "Oh, Prynn, Prynn," he said. "I'm so sorry." He meant it in a way he never had before, although he knew that she would not know that. He felt his daughter's body shaking as she wept. He cried with her, and they held each other like that for a long time.

When they parted, he looked into her eyes in a way he had not been able to for so long. He reached up to the side of her face and brushed away a tear. "Your eye," he said, remembering that the last time he had seen her, the white had been injured and discolored.

"Dr. Bashir," she began, but did not finish the thought. "I couldn't see you in the medical bay because . . . this . . ." She made a motion that seemed to include the two of them, their tears, the intensity and importance of this moment, and he understood that she had wanted this reunion to be private.

"I know," Vaughn said. "It's all right. I'm just glad that you're here now."

"I am too."

"I'm sorry," he said again, knowing that she would mistakenly think that he was apologizing for Ruriko's death. "After your mother died . . . I should have been there for you." He did not expect her to understand immediately. "When we were—"

"I know," she interrupted. "Dad, I know. I don't blame you for what happened to Mom. But I see now that I needed you back then, and when you weren't there . . ." She let her words trail off. "But I understand what happened . . . you lost Mom too."

"Yes," Vaughn agreed, "but I'm your father. I failed you, and I'm sorry."

"I know," she said. "But you're here now. And I still need you."

"I need you too, Prynn," Vaughn said, and he pulled her close once more. When they parted this time, she smiled, and all at once, Vaughn felt connected to his daughter again. There were so many things that they needed to search through together, to understand together.

They sat down and talked for hours, as they had not done in a very long time.

Finally, Vaughn had begun to explore.

THIS GRAY SPIRIT

Heather Jarman

For my husband, Parry, and my father, Jeff—
because they handed me the key
and
In memory of my brother Tad:
"Not all those who wander are lost."

Acknowledgments

If it takes a village to raise a child, it takes a family to write a book. Many deserve thanks.

First, I would be remiss if I didn't express gratitude to the *Deep Space Nine* family of actors and writers who gave us this incredible universe to play in. Long after this book is garage sale fodder, *DS9* will endure.

My husband continually pushed me to aim higher; without his encouragement I never would have tried, let alone succeeded. He and my daughters—Sara, Ally, Rachel, and Abby—showed admirable patience and positive attitudes throughout this process. My parents, Marge and Jeff Clayton, must have wondered how they grew a geeky daughter in the midst of my cheerleader sisters, but they have always supported me with enthusiasm. My siblings deserve notice as well: Laurie reintroduced me to *Star Trek* after years of hiatus; Jane was my steady support; Tad shared my love of sci-fi and fantasy; and Julie was a bud. My brother Peter is a marvelous thinker, genetics researcher, and social policy innovator who gave me the tools for the Andorian backstory. My sister-in-law Amy inspired me with her bravery. Peter Jarman's loan of his laptop assured there would be a book.

A tender thank you to my fellowship of writers, all of whom own part of this book. My incredible writing partner, Kirsten, might not have co-written this with me, but she's been with me in the trenches the whole way—middle of the night, weekends, deadlines. She's the godmother of the project. Jeff Lang, whose wit, wisdom, and open arms saw me through rewrites, incessant whining, and everything else. A gifted writer in her own right, Bethany Phillips is the reason the outline was eventually completed. Thanklessly, she proofread, talked plot points, and offered advice whenever, wherever. Jim Wright, a comrade in arms, who, in a way, started me on this road when he said, "You should write a column for *The Starfleet Journal*." Keith DeCandido was the voice of pragmatic experience who talked me off a few proverbial ledges!

Dena's blanket hugs and prayers kept me warm through long hours at the computer. My dear MIA Mikaela brought the funny whenever I needed it. Both of you deserve smooches.

The amazing Susannah just gets it: *Law, hîr nín, ú dollen i Rîw. Anírach, nui lû, gwannad uin gwaith lín?* Cathy, Marsha, Betsy, Eden, and the toytrucks gang supplied the cheering section. The team at Oak Hills School that supported the girls has earned special thank yous—Wendy, Chris, Heidi, Ashley, Tammy, and Cynthia. My resident genius, Dr. Fraser Smith, brought the tech hooks that made me look good. Without Patti Heyes, Katie Fritz,

Sara Wilcox, and my friends in PTF—D'Alaire, Julie, Monica, Janet, and Marianne—I never would have made writing *Star Trek* fiction a priority.

To the "father" of this project, Marco Palmieri: for your brilliant instincts, incredible talent, unfailing patience, and daring to take a chance on this new kid, I owe you my deepest gratitude. Thank you for giving me the chance to build foundations for my castles in the air.

"What do you fear, lady?" he asked.
"A cage," she said. "To stay behind bars, until use and old age accept them, and
all chance of doing great deeds is gone beyond recall or desire."
—J.R.R. TOLKIEN, *THE RETURN OF THE KING*

I am a part of all that I have met;
Yet all experience is an arch where through
Gleams that untraveled world whose margin fades
Forever and forever when I move....
...And this gray spirit yearning in desire
To follow knowledge like a sinking star,
Beyond the utmost bound of human thought.
—ALFRED, LORD TENNYSON, "ULYSSES"

1

"qablIj Hi'ang!" *Ngara snarled the traditional challenge at the approaching son of T'Mokh. She crafted a dance of fast precise spins to the tempo of her anger. Sweat dripped off the glistening ridges of her forehead, beading on her eyelashes.* "I will toast my father's honor over your corpse, you sniveling p'takh!"

A master of the spear, Lughor did not fear her. Blow for blow, he would match her dazzling display of warrior craft. "qabwIj vIso'be!" *he growled, revealing himself as one well schooled in the ways of battle. In one deft motion, he rent in twain her sleeve from shoulder to wrist. She roared in anger.*

Weapons clashed. Lughor pushed against her. Ngara deflected each blow. Grunting, she gained ground on him. She raised her spear over her shoulder, heaving the point into Lughor's thigh. In pain, he staggered backward. Calling upon Kahless, he found the strength with which he could combat her fiery fury.

The struggle began in earnest: thrust, parry, spin away. Weapons locked as the combatants matched rippling muscle against rippling muscle.

Her pulse, pounding through her ears, deafened her to Lughor's mocking provocations. She cried, "On this night, I will stand in hot black pools of your blood, spilled when I slit your throat!" *Ngara flew through the air, her spear before her, aiming for his throat.*

Lughor's eyes narrowed. In a feline crouch, he leaped up to intercept her chonnaQ *with his own. Ngara's weapon snapped in two. Roping his arm around her waist, Lughor wrested her to the ground. In one swift movement, he stripped her of the knife strapped to her thigh.*

A battle cry rang from her throat. Ngara broke free of Lughor's grip. Flipping him onto his back, she straddled his waist, curling her sharp fingernails into his skin. Lughor bucked, but Ngara bore him down, pressing his shoulders to the ground. The sticky sweat-slick cohesion of their bare limbs fused their bodies together as they wrestled on the forest floor. Pungent air, heady and thick with their mingling musks, fed their desire.

The smell of Lughor's blood on her hands suffused Ngara's senses; she longed to flick her tongue in his wound, greedily lapping the droplets from his skin. Hunger for her burned in his dark eyes. Pinning her arms above her head, Lughor slid his d'k tahg *beneath the lacings of her leather corset, blade against breast.* "I will have you!" *he growled. And with a swift upthrust—*

"Nog, what the hell are you reading?"

The padd Nog had been holding with white-knuckled intensity almost flew out of his hand when he heard the voice in his ear. With a clatter, he slammed the padd facedown on the mess hall table and rested his arm on it protectively. All things considered, *Defiant's* embarrassed chief engineer felt like he'd come precariously close to leaping out of his own skin.

Nog looked up to see Ezri Dax's upside-down face smiling mischievously at him as she leaned over the top of his head. "At ease, Lieutenant," she said. "I can only assume that wasn't the engineering status report I asked for."

Eyes still fixed on Dax, Nog felt around the top of the table with his free hand, past his bowl of tube grubs and his Eelwasser, and found the padd in question. "Umm, no. That would be this one," he said, handing the padd to Dax. *Blessed Exchequer, please spare me this humiliation . . .*

"Thanks," Dax said, straightening up to examine the contents of the report. "I've got Bowers running a diagnostic from the tactical side. With any luck, we can identify where those false readings are coming from when we line this data up with his."

"I'm sure we will," Nog agreed. *She's not gonna embarrass me! Oh, thank you, thank you, thank you . . .*

"That must have been some fascinating reading on that other padd," Dax said at length. "You don't often encounter references to leather corsets in Starfleet's engineering manuals."

Ears flushing, Nog winced. *The jig, as Vic might say, is up.*

"Oh! *Burning Hearts of Qo'noS!*" exclaimed Engineer Bryanne Permenter, pointing at Nog from across the mess hall. Bringing her tray with her, she plopped down in the chair beside her boss. "Have you gotten to the part where Ngara has the *bat'leth* duel with the minions of the House of Rutark?"

Nog looked up at Dax. She folded her arms and raised a teasing eyebrow as she waited for Nog's answer.

"Yes, all right! I'm reading *Burning Hearts of Qo'noS!* There, I said it! Are you happy?" Turning to Permenter, he said excitedly, "That was great! I never thought she'd make it past the bewitched targs guarding the moat, did you?"

Dax rolled her eyes and shook her head. "Is this what all engineers do between duty shifts?"

"Hey, not fair, Lieutenant," Permenter said. "I got it from T'rb in sciences. So they started it. And if the text was in the library computer and not copy-protected, none of us would need to pass the same padd around from one person to the next." Turning to Nog, she said, "Didn't Richter have it before T'rb?"

"No, Richter asked me to pass it to her when I was done," Nog said. "Ensign Senkowski gave it to T'rb."

Retrieving his chef's salad from the replicator, Jason Senkowski announced loudly, "Don't you dare bring me into this. I wouldn't waste time on that poorly written excuse for a novel. Imagine it, Lieutenant," he said, addressing Dax, "a Klingon *bodice ripper.* I tell you, it's the end of literature as we know it."

Permenter snorted. "This from the man who practically begged me to read *Vulcan Love Slave.*"

Nog looked at Senkowski, surprised. "Really? Which version?"

"The classic original, of course," Senkowski said. "By Krem."

"That's never been proven," Nog pointed out.

Senkowski shrugged as he sat down, one table over from the group. "Never been *dis*proven, either. I know Iskel is the popular favorite, but I'd say the evidence that Krem was the original author is compelling. Regardless of who actually wrote it, though, I'll take *Vulcan Love Slave* over *Burning Hearts of Qo'noS* any day." Senkowski turned his attention back to *Defiant's* first officer. "And for the record, Lieutenant Dax, I happen to *like* Starfleet's engineering manuals. I find them pithy, concise, and thorough."

"I appreciate your candor, Ensign," Dax intoned solemnly, trying not to smile. Senkowski had made no secret of his ambition to earn a second pip by the mission's end.

"Still miffed Mikaela got the shift chief promotion, eh, Senkowski," Permenter noted.

"I take my engineering duties seriously," he said, raising a forkful of salad.

"As well you should," Dax said, elbowing Nog.

Taking the hint, Nog added, "You're an invaluable member of the team, Ensign." Pulling the padd close to his chest, he sneaked another look.

Ezri laughed.

"What!" Nog protested. "I'm at the good part!"

The mess hall doors opened, admitting Lieutenant Sam Bowers. "Lieutenant Dax," he called when he saw her, waving a padd.

Whew. Dax can bug someone else for a few minutes. Nog returned to his novel. *I just need to see what happens when Lughor's brother . . .*

"Results of the tactical systems diagnostic?" Dax asked, weaving around several empty tables to meet Bowers halfway.

Reluctantly, Nog tore his attention away from Ngara and Lughor's heated encounter. Though he was off duty, the weapons systems problems could spill into the next shift; an advance notice of what he was facing could be helpful.

Holding up the padd triumphantly, Sam told Dax, "Turns out we had a redundant programming problem. Nothing serious after all."

Dax took the padd and scrolled through the data. "That's a relief. Last thing we need in a firefight is a malfunctioning torpedo launcher," Ezri said.

Sam nodded in agreement. "Tell me about it. I like to think I'm good at improvising, but I prefer having a full arsenal at my disposal."

Satisfied that the *Defiant's* most pressing problem had been resolved, Nog settled in to find out whether Lughor had yet managed to break Ngara's clavicle. Permenter leaned over to see what part he was reading, "oo-ing" and "ah-ing" appropriately.

Unexpectedly, the lights dimmed. Every crewman in the mess hall froze in anticipation.

Nog's sensitive ears heard EPS conduits changing amplitude before they plummeted into unhealthy silence. With *Burning Hearts of Qo'noS* tucked under his arm, Nog was on his way to main engineering before the call from the bridge rang out over the comm system: *"Red alert! All hands to battle stations! We're under attack!"*

• • •

Acrid smoke filled the corridor, stinging her eyes. Half blind, Dax and Bowers rushed onto a bridge in chaos. Along every wall, stations flickered and sparked as crewmen worked to contain fires and route control of key systems to other consoles, only to contend with new malfunctions at those stations. "What the hell happened?" she muttered, unable to hear her own words over the cacophony.

Through the smoke, she made out Vaughn standing in front of the command chair, issuing orders to engineering over his combadge. She stumbled over burned panels thrown aside to facilitate repairs, crunching pieces of shattered control interfaces and carbonized isolinear circuitry. The dim lighting wasn't making it any easier. She heard Sam curse when he saw the condition of tactical.

"Captain," Ezri said, raising her voice to be heard over the klaxon.

Vaughn pointed toward one of the pulsing red alert lights as he struggled to hear the report coming in. Ezri got the message and found a working panel from which she could mute the klaxon.

Nog's voice was suddenly audible to her, but he sounded frantic. "—targeted our energy systems with millions of nanobots. They're eating through our EPS system like acid, bleeding our power. Warp core's down and we're running completely on the auxiliaries. But at the speed the nanobots are working, it won't last long."

"Understood," Vaughn said. "Do what you can, and keep me posted on your progress. Vaughn out."

"What do we know so far?" Dax asked.

"We tripped some kind of sensor web. The instant we penetrated the field, the nanobots just shifted out of subspace and converged on *Defiant,* entering through the plasma vents. We didn't know what hit us until it was too late. I want a shipwide status report immediately." Turning to Bowers, Vaughn said, "Sam, make sure that whatever we've stumbled into is the end of something and not the beginning."

Seeing that sciences was vacant but at least partially functional, Ezri took a seat and attempted to assess the scope of the damage. Nearby, Prynn Tenmei knelt beside an unconscious Ensign Leishman, the bridge engineer on duty when the attack came. Judging from her injuries and the condition of her station, Ezri concluded at a glance that Leishman's console must have blown right in front of her.

Ezri moved to initiate a site-to-site transport to sickbay, but discovered transporters were down. She relaxed when Ensign Richter entered the bridge, carrying a medkit. Tenmei moved aside to give the nurse room to work. Satisfied that Leishman was being taken care of, Dax returned her attention to coaxing information from the uncooperative ODN.

"Lieutenant Dax," Richter said, removing hyposprays from the kit. "Doctor Bashir wanted me to let you know that high-level radiation is flooding every deck. The whole crew will need hyronalin inoculations. But we don't have the medical staff to cover."

"I'm not sure who's available," Ezri said.

"I can help," Tenmei offered.

Richter gingerly eased Leishman up off the floor, attaching a neuromonitor to the back of her head. "I don't think she'll need surgery, but Doctor Bashir will have to make that call."

Dax called to two crewmen working by the aft wall of the bridge. "Rahim, M'Nok—get Leishman to the medical bay." Dax looked at Tenmei. Her face and hands were smudged black, and she looked as though she had a nasty burn on her jawline. "You sure you're up to volunteering, Prynn?"

"I'm fine. Honest," Tenmei said.

Richter shrugged at Dax. "It's her call."

Ezri nodded to Tenmei as the two crewmen saw to Leishman. With Rahim on one side and M'Nok on the other, they lifted the unconscious engineer between them and draped her arms around their shoulders. Richter followed right behind them after handing a hypospray to Tenmei, who stayed just long enough to administer hyronalin to Vaughn, Dax, Bowers, and the remaining bridge officer, Ensign Cassini.

Ezri finally succeeded in calling up the engineering stats. Preliminary readings indicated that the nanobots had become inert. *So they were designed to cripple us, not necessarily to kill us,* Dax mused. *The question is, how much damage have the little monsters done?* The diagnostic results, illustrated by green bars, one block stacked upon another, flashed onto her screen, but the data stream stalled with only two or three bars lit. "Come on, you can do it," she urged the damaged *Defiant*. She watched, waited, and after a few moments that felt like eternity, her heart sank. "Captain," she shouted, trying to keep the panic out of her voice. "We've got a situation."

Vaughn, working with Bowers on tactical, crossed over to the science station.

"Report," he said, resting a hand on the back of Ezri's chair.

"What you're looking at on this screen is the sum total of our power resources, including all backup and auxiliary systems," she said soberly.

Vaughn frowned at the readings. "Three or four hours tops?"

"I'd put it closer to three, but if we shut down all nonessential systems, we might be able to squeeze out a bit more time."

"Do it," he ordered. He returned to the captain's chair. "Mister Bowers?"

"Yes, sir," Sam responded.

"Send out a broadband distress call—"

"Sir," Cassini said, working from a sensor display. "There's a ship approaching, four-hundred thousand kilometers and closing."

"On screen."

The viewer sputtered reluctantly to life, and Dax's first thought upon seeing the starship was that it looked like a fat metal wheel preparing to roll over them. An oddly configured drive unit formed two flat slabs mounted on the aft curve of the wheel, one atop the other. The part of Ezri that was Torias and Tobin, a pilot and engineer respectively, began to appraise the ship's design for visible signs of its strengths, weaknesses, and functions. *How fast can it fly? Are those weapons ports? Friend or foe?*

"They're deliberately skirting our trajectory, sir," Bowers reported. "My guess is that they're trying to avoid triggering the sensor web that got us. That may mean they're the ones behind it."

"They could have seen what happened to us and are just looking to avoid the same fate," Cassini pointed out.

"Except that they're closing on us. Down to one hundred fifty thousand kilometers and slowing."

"Hail them," Vaughn ordered.

Sam tapped in commands, waited, and tapped in more commands. He slammed his fist into the console. "Our transmitters are off-line, Captain," he said.

"We're being scanned, sir," Ezri announced, watching the *Defiant*'s internal sensors register the probe.

"What's our tactical situation, Sam?"

"Phasers and torpedo launchers offline. Cloaking device and deflector shields nonfunctional. I'd have to say we're sitting ducks, sir."

Vaughn scowled and tapped his combadge. "Bridge to engineering. This would be a good time to tell me our propulsion systems are back online, Nog."

"Eighty-five percent of our EPS system is shot, sir, and power levels are plunging. We're doing what we can, but the truth is, we're not going anywhere anytime soon."

"Unknown ship now ten thousand kilometers and closing," Bowers said. "They're hailing us. Receiving a message, but I can't make heads or tails of it. If we have the algorithms necessary for decoding, the universal translator can't find them."

"Audio," Vaughn ordered.

The guttural gibberish blaring over the comm system sounded like no language Ezri had heard in any of her lifetimes. Intermittent static contaminating the stream didn't help matters.

"Unknown ship is coming to relative stop above us, *z*-plus three hundred meters away, matching our momentum. Distance is now constant." Bowers suddenly cursed and announced in a rising voice, "Transporter signal detected inside main engineering!"

Phaser in hand, Vaughn was headed for the door before the word "engineering" had escaped Bowers's lips. "Dax, you have the bridge. Sam, you're with me."

Cold and dark as a tomb, thought Nog, wishing he could trade his hypersensitive hearing for better night vision. Between the plasma coolant leaks and the EPS system, Nog had enough work to keep his entire staff—hell, the whole crew—busy for a week.

"I need more light here," Nog said, up to his elbows inside an access panel alongside the main engineering console. If he could get the primary EPS junction functional, the *Defiant* might stand a chance. Flat on his back, he gazed up at the singed circuitry, searching for reasons to be optimistic. A sharp, barky cough caused his hands to shake; the hyperspanner clattered to the floor. "Dammit!"

Lying beside him, Ensign Permenter flashed her own light in his direction. "You doing okay, boss? That last burst of plasma got you in the face," she said, concerned.

He coughed. "Without power, coolant is the least of our problems. Pass me that laser drill."

She slapped the tool into Nog's hand, retrieved the hyperspanner from where he dropped it and replaced it in the toolkit. "Heard from Nurse Juarez. Mikaela's gonna be fine."

"One piece of good news," Nog sighed deeply. "See if Senkowski and his team have managed to shore up the auxiliary power."

"Yes, sir," Permenter said, scrambling to her feet.

In the midst of the hum of tools and engineers speaking in hushed whispers, a shimmering light appeared, emitting a metallic buzz.

"Transporters!" Permenter shouted, slapping her combadge. "Intruder alert! Security to engineering—!"

Two tall alien figures in luminescent environmental suits materialized, carrying a coffin-size box between them. Nog peered in the half-light, trying to see behind the dark-tinted face shields.

One of the aliens panned the room with what to Nog's eyes looked like a scanning device, then pointed at the primary EPS junction where Nog had been working. They lifted the box between them and started forward.

"No you don't," Permenter said through gritted teeth. She held her phaser threateningly before her and stepped in front of the aliens, blocking them from approaching the junction. "Drop that thing and back up. Now."

The aliens stopped and looked at each other. One of them jabbered something incomprehensible to Permenter. He unhooked something from a utility belt and pressed a button, causing the device to glow green.

"Turn that off!" Permenter shouted.

Dammit! Nog stepped forward, drawing his own weapon. "Stay back," he warned. "Take another step and I'll fire." The alien continued to speak in its unknown language as it eased closer to Nog. *I don't want to do this, I don't want to do this,* he chanted in his mind.

The alien kept coming.

He fired his phaser. The intruder approaching him jerked and collapsed to the ground.

The shot distracted Permenter, giving the intruder she was covering the opportunity to lunge forward and spin her around. The alien hooked an arm around the engineer's neck, pulling her head back against his shoulder, using his free hand to wrestle the phaser out of Permenter's hand. Suddenly the phaser was pressed against her temple. Nodding his head toward Nog's phaser, the alien made a guttural noise. The message was clear. *Drop the weapon.*

Unwilling to risk Bryanne's life, Nog complied, then kicked his phaser off to the side.

The main doors suddenly opened and every face turned.

"Stand down!" Vaughn barked.

Bowers pivoted into the room after Vaughn, holding his phaser out in front of him. Three security officers and Dr. Bashir came racing in after Bowers. Perhaps overwhelmed by the superior numbers, the intruder threatening Permenter dropped the phaser, released her, and dove for cover behind the warp core.

Dropping to his knees beside the wounded alien near Nog, Julian Bashir opened his tricorder and performed a scan. "Our environmental conditions are suited to his physiology," he reported, easing off the alien's helmet. "Their biology is . . ." Bashir frowned and trailed off, looking as if he'd just seen something on the tricorder that puzzled him. The doctor abruptly removed a hypospray from the medkit, applying it to the alien's neck.

"Will he be all right?" Nog asked, crouching beside Bashir.

"Should be. I'll know in a minute," Bashir replied.

Okay, so who or what did I just shoot? Nog wondered. From what little he could discern in the half-light, their alien guest had leathery, hairless brown skin, a mouth as wide as his eyes were apart, and filmy membranes over his eyes. He looked amphibious, down to the ridges of cartilage where humanoid ears would be. *Weird.* Earless humanoids always looked odd to Nog.

"The stun hit him pretty hard," Julian announced to his shipmates, all of whom watched him intently. "It was close range, but fortunately his environmental suit diffused most of the blast."

Hidden in the shadows behind the warp core, the alien who had assaulted Permenter had found a ripped-out section of damaged EPS conduit and hefted it over his shoulder, obviously screwing up his courage to attack anyone who approached him. He jabbered away incoherently.

"Why are you here?" Vaughn asked, cautiously approaching the agitated alien. "What do you want with us?"

The alien responded by swinging the conduit out in front of him and shouting something long but totally incomprehensible. Vaughn backed off, maintaining a respectable distance between them.

Bashir's patient inhaled sharply, sputtering and coughing; the membranes over his black-brown eyes lifted. He lurched up, bent over and retched on the floor. Soothingly, Julian patted his back.

"I'll give you something for the nausea." He scanned his patient once more with the tricorder, frowning again before applying another hypospray. The intruder's head swayed and tipped backward. Julian braced his fall, easing him back onto the floor. Searching the medkit, he found an emergency blanket to cover the alien. "You're going to be fine. When your temperature stabilizes, you'll feel better."

"*Nijigon boko nongolik* attack us?" the alien gasped, wiping its mouth with the back of its gloved hand. "We were trying to help."

"Finally," Bowers muttered, relieved that the universal translator had succeeded in decoding the aliens' speech.

"We haven't understood your language until now," Vaughn explained to the pipe-wielding alien. "Our ship has recently come under attack. For our own protection, we had to assume that you set the weapon that damaged our vessel, and that you and your companion had hostile intentions. I'm glad to find out we were wrong. We have no desire to hurt anyone." Vaughn holstered his phaser and spread his hands, stepping forward. "I'm Commander Elias Vaughn of the *Starship Defiant,* representing the United Federation of Planets. We're on a peaceful mission to this part of the galaxy."

The armed alien dropped the conduit and detached his helmet from his environmental suit. No, Nog saw, *her* spacesuit. Save her greenish-gray skin, she closely resembled her colleague. She ran long, knobby fingers through a profusion of violet colored braids attached to a headpiece. Skin pockets hanging off her jaw alternately inflated and deflated with each breath.

"We saw what happened to your ship," she said, her voice low and percussive. "When the snare activated, it registered on our sensors. We're quite familiar with what these weapons can do, so we came to assist you. We brought with us an energy source and were about to integrate it into your power systems when that one—" she pointed at Nog "—attacked my partner."

"Lieutenant Nog, chief engineer," he said. "And I'm very sorry. After what we'd just been through, I had no way to know you were trying to help us."

A long silence elapsed. The alien riveted her attention on Nog. She took a cautious step toward him. "If you couldn't translate our message, it was an understandable error." Her lashless lids moved up and down over her eyes several times. "I, also, am my vessel's technologist. My name is Tlaral."

Nog grinned. Her statement told him all he needed to know. Suddenly he was at her side, examining her equipment. "As engineers, we already speak the same language. Show me how this device works," he said, tipping his head back to look up at Tlaral. "Is this a duranium casing?"

"Looks like we're done here." Bowers shrugged.

Folding his arms, Vaughn chuckled and shook his head as he watched Nog and Tlaral commiserate. "Witness here, first contact—engineer style."

Within the hour, the alien technology poured energy into *Defiant*'s auxiliary systems. As Vaughn learned from Tlaral, the temporary fix would power environmental and computer systems until they could reach a safe port. What would come after? Vaughn called an impromptu strategy session in his ready room to make that determination. He invited Tlaral to join them while her companion, a "technologist" named Shavoh, recovered in sickbay under Julian's watchful eye.

As the meeting progressed, Vaughn realized their options were slim.

"Other than your world—" Vaughn began.

"Vanìmel. Where there are repair facilities, supplies—whatever resources you might need," Tlaral interrupted. "I've been authorized by my chieftain to offer your ship and its crew our world's hospitality. He awaits your decision."

"You've stated my crew has few alternatives beyond Vanìmel," Vaughn said, repeating Tlaral's assertion. The technologist had been adamant that the *Defiant* come to her homeworld. From Dax's review of the sensor logs, Vaughn had learned of multiple M-class worlds with warp-capable civilizations located within a few days of their current locale. Why Vanìmel and not one of the others was a question Tlaral had yet to answer.

"Of course there are other worlds—most are some distance from here—that might be willing to offer aid to strangers. Assuming they didn't first shoot you down for trespassing." Tlaral left her chair to point out several planetary systems on the starchart displayed on Vaughn's viewscreen. "Here, and toward the Wiiru system. And that's hoping you make it that far without encountering another one of the weapons that caught you today."

From a padd, Bowers examined the preliminary data Tlaral had provided on the web weapons. "What are the odds of us being hit again?"

Tlaral explained patiently, "This whole sector is webbed. Vanìmel and my people, the Yrythny, are under siege. That's how we know these weapons so well. They are meant to ensnare *us,* but they do not distinguish between our ships and others. You might not see any ship-to-ship combat, but make no mistake, this is a war zone."

Vaughn folded his hands together, rolling the day's cumulative knowledge around in his head. The stopgap power bridge Tlaral had installed in engineering had already proved the effectiveness of Yrythny technology. Even Nog had been impressed. Pragmatically, the *Defiant* was days away from the closest advanced civilizations, assuming they could restore warp drive without further assistance. Vaughn disliked having limited options to choose from, but from appearances, Vanìmel was a solid one. He made his decision. "We gratefully accept your chieftain's generous invitation, Tlaral. From there, we'll determine how to go about repairs."

"Our government will be very accommodating," she said earnestly. "The present struggle has isolated us from our neighbors. I know our leaders will be grateful to have an ally."

Ally, Vaughn thought, musing on Tlaral's word choice. *Perhaps these Yrythny have motives beyond offering aid and comfort to weary travelers. Which begs the question . . . what will they expect in return?*

2

Before Colonel Kira Nerys opened her eyes, she resisted the impulse to thump the walls or kick the panels of her quarters, though part of her suspected that if she uttered the phrase "Computer, end program," the world as she sensed it would dissolve in an instant. Or that she would awaken from an exhausted sleep on the frozen Dahkur ground to be told it was her turn on watch. Or, even better, that she had dozed off, midconversation with Odo, and when she finally emerged to consciousness, she'd feel the warm flow of his embrace.

Sprawled diagonally across her bed, mussed covers tangled around her legs and pillow smothering her nose, Kira rightly guessed that whatever reality she was in, she slept solo. Her own smells and the definitive silence testified to her aloneness. But maybe, just maybe she wasn't actually on the station any longer, maybe she was . . .

"Ops to Colonel Kira."

So maybe she was still at home.

Deep Space 9, home? That was a place her mind couldn't go this morning.

Throwing aside the pillow, Kira sighed, rolled over, twisted her shoulders to loosen the stiffness and spoke to the ceiling. "Kira. Go ahead." She could hear a hint of a tremor in Ensign Beyer's breathy voice. The coolest heads had gone with Vaughn to the Gamma Quadrant, leaving the jumpy ones behind; Kira was learning patience.

"Um, we've just received a subspace transmission from the Cardassian ship Trager, *sir. Its captain has requested to speak with you."*

"Put it through to my quarters, Ensign. Audio only." She suddenly felt remarkably alert for having not yet partaken of her morning *raktajino*. She addressed her unseen visitor, steeling herself for her stomach's inevitable lurching. "Colonel Kira, here. Go ahead, *Trager.*"

"Colonel." The rich baritone voice poured into the room, and despite being braced for it, Kira found she still had to rein in her emotions.

"Gul Macet," she said evenly. "What can I do for you?" Kira reached for her robe and cinched the waist tie extra tight. Ruffling the hair on the back of her neck with her fingers kept her hands occupied. Intellectually, she knew Macet wasn't Gul Dukat, the hated former prefect of Cardassian-occupied Bajor. Cardassia's provisional government had vouched for him, even sent her his DNA scan in an effort to reassure her and any others who might question his identity; unfortunately, scientific technobabble failed to overwrite years of conditioning. She tried repressing her gut reaction to Macet, but instinct was not easily assuaged by intellect.

"And how is life on Deep Space 9 this morning? All's well, I presume?"

"Nothing out of the ordinary. Why?" Kira took a seat in front of her companel, hastily skimming the last shift report. The tone in Macet's voice made her wonder what he knew. Like something awful might be hurtling toward the station at warp speed and he thought he'd give her a friendly heads-up.

"With all that's gone on lately—resettling the Europani, Fleet Admiral Akaar and his group coming to Bajor, your first officer leaving for the Gamma Quadrant—I know you've had your hands full."

"Goes with the territory, Gul Macet. We're a busy outpost."

"Busy supplying aid to my people among your many tasks, Colonel. We certainly appreciate all that Bajor has done for us. The last shipment of medical supplies could not have had better timing."

"I'll convey your gratitude to First Minister Shakaar the next time I speak with him." No point in telling Macet that after the Europani had been resettled on their planet, Kira had worked to bring the Cardassian relief efforts back up to their previous levels. *There must be a point to his contacting me,* Kira thought. *I hope he gets to it soon.* Chitchat wasn't typically Macet's style. On the other hand, she didn't really know what Macet's style was.

"Perhaps I can offer my thanks in person."

Abruptly, Kira straightened up. "You're on your way to Bajor?" *So much for today being uneventful.*

"To the station, actually. We should be arriving this afternoon."

"We?" Alone, Macet would be tricky; if he brought a battalion of soldiers with him, Kira might be facing a logistical nightmare. Such as how to prevent a station full of Dukat-loathing Bajorans from killing Macet on sight.

"Myself, my men, Ambassador Lang, her staff—"

"Ambassador Lang," Kira repeated. "Natima Lang?"

"Ah, you remember her."

"You could say that." Once a resident of the station, Lang had been a correspondent for the Cardassian Information Service during the Occupation. After the withdrawal, Lang's advocacy of controversial reforms on Cardassia had forced her and her students to seek political asylum back on the station. Familiarity with Lang's virulent anti-Occupation stance had always lent her a modicum of respect in Kira's mind. And then there was the Quark factor: Lang had exhibited a knack for bringing out the latent nobility lurking beneath Quark's profit-oriented paradigm. *Now she was returning as an ambassador from Cardassia's fledgling democratic government.*

"Ambassador Lang is on an errand from Alon Ghemor. She requests a meeting with First Minister Shakaar at his earliest convenience. You can arrange that, can't you, Colonel?"

"I'm not his secretary, Macet," Kira said tersely. "And I should probably tell you, he isn't on the station. He's in Ashalla working out the details of Bajor's admission into the Federation."

"I think if you conveyed the news of our visit to Admiral Akaar, he would be pleased that Minister Shakaar has accommodated us. It's possible the Admiral might appreciate the opportunity to discuss the status of the Federation's protectorates in Cardassian territory."

Kira's eyes narrowed. "I'll be happy to pass word along to the first minister and the admiral, though I believe they might be better able to accommodate you if they knew what Ambassador Lang's business was."

"It's not my place to explain Ambassador Lang's mission. I'm merely serving as her transport and protection at the behest of our government. She will make her purpose known to the appropriate parties in due time. Meanwhile, if you could present our request to Minister Shakaar, we would be in your debt."

"I'll do what I can." *Though how willing Shakaar will be to reorganize his life around a surprise Cardassian visit is yet to be seen,* Kira thought, grudgingly giving Macet credit for excellent timing. Shakaar risked appearing to be unwilling to forgive old grudges if he failed to give the Cardassian diplomats proper attention, something the Federation delegation would certainly frown upon. "Meanwhile, why don't you transmit the specifics as to when you anticipate arriving, what kind of accommodations you'll require, supply needs and so forth."

"You're most gracious, Colonel. Transmitting requested specifications now. And I look forward to seeing you again."

"Good day to you, Gul Macet. Kira out." Kira waited for the light on her communications panel to indicate the termination of the subspace link before she contacted ops. "Ensign Beyer, how is the station's workload looking around 1400?" Kira tapped an inquiry into the computer requesting the arrival and departure schedule even as she waited for Beyer to provide the big picture. "Pull together stats on docking crew support staff, available security officers—whatever it takes to host a vessel the size of the *Trager.* And check the habitat ring for vacant guest quarters. I know a lot of our meeting spaces have been appropriated by the Federation delegations, so long-term conference room availability might be a concern."

"The Chamberlain—"

"The Cardassian relief vessel?" Kira read aloud from her desk screen.

"Yes, sir. The Chamberlain *is set to leave at 1245 off upper pylon one. Starfleet's* Kilimanjaro *is off at 1315 from lower pylon three,"* Beyer prattled on. *"Regularly scheduled Bajoran shuttles leaving for—"*

"Ensign."

"Yes, sir?"

"I can read the schedule. What I need you to tell me is whether or not the station has the resources to accommodate the *Trager* based on the specs just transmitted to ops."

"I think we're good to go, sir."

"Transmit the appropriate docking specs to the *Trager* and notify Lieutenant Ro about its arrival. Wait. Belay that last one. Have Ro meet me at my quarters in twenty minutes."

"Yes, sir."

"Kira out."

Kira leaned back in her chair, steepled her fingers together and brought them to her lips. *The* Trager *comes to pay a social call . . . whatever the Ghemor government has in mind must be explosive, otherwise Macet wouldn't have been so cagey about Lang's mission . . . and what if Macet has his own ulterior motives? Time to plunge in and hope I'm not drowning in palace intrigue by day's end.* She sighed and headed for the shower, for the moment satisfied by the reality thrust into her brain by coursing adrenaline.

Accustomed to briskly exiting her quarters, Kira avoided spilling her double *raktajino* by instantaneously thrusting the mug away when her boot nearly connected with Lieutenant Ro's skull.

"You mind telling me what the hell you're doing down there, Lieutenant?" Kira asked.

Ro looked up at her. "I'm sorry, Colonel. You obviously haven't been out yet."

Kira crouched to see what held Ro's fascination: a small, opalescent ceramic urn with a torn piece of parchment sticking out of it; two spent sticks of incense and what looked like a cheap, bronze religious icon—something one might find in the marketplace stalls around the temples. She removed the parchment from the urn and immediately recognized the ancient Bajoran calligraphy. Scanning the words for something identifiable, she felt puzzled until her eyes locked onto the characters for the word "Ohalu." She looked over at Ro whose tight-lipped expression indicated she, too, had recognized the text.

"I take it these things don't belong to you," Ro observed.

"No," Kira confirmed. "But it might be a good idea to know who they do belong to."

"My thoughts exactly," Ro said. Removing a tricorder from her belt, she scanned the items for DNA and stored the readings in the tricorder's memory. Then she touched her combadge. "Ro to Shul."

"Go ahead."

"Send someone with an evidence bin to Colonel Kira's quarters. There are some religious artifacts sitting on the floor outside her door that I want collected. Return the bin to my office and I'll handle it from there. Ro out." To Kira, she said, "It's probably nothing, but better safe than sorry."

Some minutes later, after Corporal Hava arrived to gather up the items, the two women walked toward the crossover bridge. Kira wasn't surprised by Ro's familiarity with her routine; Kira's alpha shift walks to ops were part of the station's rhythm. The walks began many years ago, taking on special significance when a stop by Odo's office became more than an excuse for exchange of gossip. Though Odo's departure might have given her a reason to take a turbolift, Kira found comfort in going through the same motions she always had, as if holding on to this one remaining vestige of an old routine would somehow help keep her grounded.

"Any idea who might have left those items?" Ro asked as they walked.

"How would I know? Since I made Ohalu's book public, I've more or less been out of the religious loop," Kira said, more testily than she intended. "Maybe an extremist crackpot thinks his tokens will prevent my evil influence from tainting the faithful."

Ro appeared to be exerting effort not to answer Kira's annoyance in kind.

"Sorry, Colonel. I assumed that perhaps this had happened before. That maybe we're dealing with a precedent."

"No. I'm just as puzzled about it as you, Ro," Kira said. "But I don't plan to lose any sleep over it."

"Wasn't suggesting you should, sir. Like I said, it's probably nothing. But you do understand that nocturnal visits to the door of the station commander's quarters need to be investigated?"

Kira nodded. "Fine. Just keep it discreet. Last thing we need around here is another religious crisis."

By the time they made their way to the Promenade, the place was already crowded and noisy with merchants opening their storefronts, parents hustling reticent children to school, Bajorans heading for morning shrine services, Starfleet personnel attending to the business of bureaucracy and overnight shift workers flooding into Quark's. Earthy smells of roasting Andorian flatroot, a delicacy presently popular with the ops staff, seeped onto the walkway.

Kira observed Ro's apparent obliviousness to the confusion swirling around her and wondered what the security officer might be mulling over. Ro's brow wrinkled more deeply as she studied the floor.

Her head came up and she looked at Kira. "It occurs to me that since I'm not in the religious loop myself, maybe in-depth surveillance of our local faithful might be a gap in our intelligence. I'll find one of my deputies who isn't offended by my agnosticism or your Attainder to keep us briefed as to the goings-on among the prylars and vedeks," she said, with thinly veiled sarcasm. "We could be facing a religious uprising and neither of us would know about it."

Kira smiled grimly. "All right, Ro. Point taken." At least Ro felt comfortable enough to make light of her current predicament. It wasn't as if *not* talking about the Attainder would make it vanish. She paused, stopping in her tracks when a fact she'd dismissed a week ago suddenly seemed relevant to the present. "Maybe I do know something."

"Oh?" Ro said as she nodded to Chef Kaga, who was carrying a basin filled with a squirming mass of *gagh* as she and Kira passed the Klingon Deli.

Kira continued. "When I was talking to Captain Yates a few days back, she mentioned something about rumors of a schism in the Vedek Assembly."

Ro's eyebrows shot up. "Really? That's interesting. At least I know what to listen for during the next week or so."

"You could always put Quark on it."

"And give him one more reason to think he knows more than the rest of us?"

"Bad idea."

"Agreed."

Kira noted that as she and Ro walked the crowds parted a bit too quickly to be spontaneous. She never thought she'd miss the jostle and muttered under-the-breath "excuse mes" that used to mark her morning strolls through the Promenade. Now, it was the station visitors who offered polite pleasantries. When she appeared, Bajorans averted their eyes, finding that the goods in their arms, the padds in their pockets or the posted station schedules required their immediate attention. Kira understood they had no malicious intent; were she in their position, she couldn't honestly say that she wouldn't do the same. But she missed the smiles in their eyes, the wave of a hand, the sense of community that united them.

"Ensign Beyer mentioned a Cardassian ship arriving this afternoon?" Ro asked.

"Yes," Kira answered, grateful for the diversion from her thoughts. "A Cardassian warship called the *Trager* bearing a diplomatic delegation will be visiting the station. Its commanding officer is a Ghemor-loyal gul named Macet."

"We have semiregular visits by Cardassian ships. This one warrants special attention because—?"

How do I say this delicately? Kira thought. "Let's say that Macet bears an *extraordinary* resemblance to his maternal relatives, the *Dukats.*"

"I see," Ro said. "Exactly how Dukat-like does he—?"

"Nearly identical," Kira said grimly. "On his previous visit, understanding our people's sensitivity to his appearance, he stayed aboard his ship."

"Thoughtful of him."

"Send out a security notice alerting station residents of Gul Macet's arrival. Include a picture from his file. Explain that he's here on official business." Kira imagined panicked Bajorans stampeding to Ro's security office or whispered gossip wafting about the station causing needless fear.

"Our residents are generally reasonable people, but Macet's appearance is a surprise I doubt they'd handle very well."

"Agreed. Another layer of security presence might be a precaution worth taking."

Ro rolled Kira's words around in her head. "Plainclothes deputies. Specifically assigned to areas being utilized by the Cardassians."

"A good place to begin," Kira said. "When Ensign Beyer finishes assigning quarters, I'll have the details sent to your office."

They arrived at a turbolift. "Then with your permission, Colonel, I'll take my leave of you here."

"Dismissed, Lieutenant," Kira said. She watched Ro head off for the security office, waving to Quark who was posting the morning specials near the front door. Why her security chief would consider seeing the Ferengi socially in any capacity puzzled Kira. Maybe it had to do with keeping your enemies close.

Maybe.

Or maybe not?

Another thought she couldn't wrap her brain around this morning. At least not until she'd had another *raktajino.*

As soon as Kira stepped into ops, Ensign Beyer thrust a padd containing the minute details regarding Macet's visit into Kira's hand and began a recitation of her most recent accomplishments. Instead of waving her aside, Kira commended the anxious ensign's efforts and hastily retreated to—

—*my office,* she thought, still amazed by the twists and turns of her life that had brought her here. The more Kira flexed the muscle of her position as station commander, the more she enjoyed it. Hell, she'd be happy if the only perk of being in charge was not having to indulge every whim of the egomaniacs populating the upper echelons of the Bajoran Militia and government. Most days, her job title allowed her to skip implementing stupid directives passed down by bureaucrats. On Deep Space 9, *her* word was law.

Still, she marveled at how quickly self-interest supplanted concern for the collective good that marked the Occupation era. Former comrades-in-arms who, in earlier days, would have shared food off her utensils wouldn't bother to acknowledge her pleas for personnel or supplies if it didn't benefit them personally. As hard as the resistance days were, Kira missed how basic Bajor's needs were then—how simple the goals. Shakaar's tireless efforts since the end of the war to make Bajor a more active participant in the community of the Alpha Quadrant were steering the people into a new and much more complex age, compelling them to face the question of how to move forward anew as Federation citizens. Bajor could reclaim its former greatness, of that Kira was confident, but not without the growing pains innate to any change. Part of Kira's job, as Deep Space 9's commander, was to help ease those pains by tackling her share of unpleasant tasks. And she knew as soon as she signed off with Macet that one of those unpleasant tasks would be awaiting her arrival in ops.

She sighed: she couldn't put off contacting Shakaar any longer. Kira took a seat behind the desk, cleared her throat and told Selzner to open a channel to Bajor.

After several annoyingly long delays as her request to speak to the First Minister went up the chain of government underlings, Shakaar appeared on the viewscreen, frowning. *"Nerys,"* he said, curtly. *"We're quite busy here."*

Kira understood his unspoken message: you'd better have a damn good reason for disrupting me during these delicate and politically sensitive negotiations. *Well, things are about to get more delicate,* she thought.

"First Minister," she began, proceeding to outline what little she knew of Macet's mission and a few of the details of his impending arrival.

Shakaar absorbed her report without surprise. *"Thank you for this news, Colonel. I admit we suspected something like this was coming. The timing is rather unfortunate; whatever the Cardassians want, it will best be dealt with on the station, I think. The talks with the Federation could easily be upstaged and we can't risk that. Make whatever preparations are necessary to properly host them."*

"Of course. Can I tell them when you'll be available to meet with them?" Kira crossed her fingers, hoping Shakaar wouldn't expect her to babysit Macet's group for an indefinite period of time.

"Give me a few days to wrap up some loose ends here. I'll be back on the station before the end of the week."

Kira hoped she didn't look too relieved. "Thank you, Minister. I'll get back to you when—"

"Come to think of it," he interrupted, *"a reception would be the polite way to receive them."*

"Excuse me?" Kira said, uncertain where Shakaar was taking this line of thinking.

"We need to facilitate their introduction to Admiral Akaar, Councillor zh'Thane, and the other dignitaries in the system. We can't assume they'll randomly bump into each other in the habitat ring." Shakaar was gesturing animatedly with his hands, a trait Kira recognized as something he used when he was conveying his plans for a surprise assault on a Cardassian patrol. *"We need to do this properly. Show how we've mastered the finer points of diplomacy. Bajor, after all, is a citizen of the quadrant."*

"That's a fine idea, First Minister. Just let me know what kind of support you'll need from my staff. I'm assuming Lieutenant Ro will provide security—"

Shakaar smiled broadly. *"No, Nerys. I believe you're misunderstanding me. I'd like you to take charge of this event."*

Kira stared. *Be calm, Nerys. Don't let him dare you into saying something you'll regret,* she thought, biting back a curt reply she longed to deliver coupled with a vivid scatological epithet. "I'm hardly qualified to work on issues of interstellar protocol. I'd probably end up seating the Romulan attaché next to the Klingon delegate and then where would we be?" She smiled insincerely, curling her fingers into tight fists.

"Colonel, I don't need to remind you how fully occupied my own staff is at this time. Not to mention that most of the Militia is still cleaning up the vestiges of the Europani matter." Shakaar shrugged his shoulders. *"At the moment, I can't spare the personnel. You're familiar with the parties involved—you and your people have had more direct dealings with Lang and Macet than any of us—I think that qualifies you perfectly."*

Taking a deep breath, Kira rose from her seat and laced her hands behind her back, keeping her expression as neutral as she could. "Really, First Minister, I have to protest. I believe this is a case of misplaced belief in my abilities."

"My aide Sirsy will be at your disposal. She'll contact you with the list of Bajorans I believe should attend. She'll also give you our tentative schedule over the next week or so," Shakaar said. *"Have some faith, Nerys. Shakaar out."*

When her desk screen abruptly reverted to its standby pattern, the most profane word Kira knew tore itself from her throat. *He's not going to let me forget who's really in charge here. That he could use my religious situation to punish me. On his whim I could be back on Bajor planting crops before the next moon waxes.* She gritted her teeth. *And who in the hell decided I needed to moonlight as the station's social secretary?* As she touched her combadge, the inklings of a plan began forming in her mind. What was the first rule of leadership? Know how to delegate. Ensign Beyer seemed anxious to please. A crash course in diplomatic reception planning would keep her busy and out of Kira's way. And the Cardassians?

She'd be damned if she had to be the only one yanked around by this unexpected visit. "Kira to Ro."

"Yes, Colonel?"

"You learned something of diplomacy when you served on the *Enterprise?*"

"Excuse me, sir?"

"The Cardassians, Lieutenant. You've been appointed to head Deep Space 9's welcoming committee."

When Beyer notified Ro that the *Trager* would be docking within the hour, the lieutenant used her remaining time to review any information Odo might have accumulated about the ship's passengers. Only Lang and Macet proved to have substantive entries in the station's database.

Because Macet's military career apparently had never taken him to Bajor until recently, the most information she found on him was in a Starfleet Intelligence file that had recently been uploaded to the station from Command. Presumably Kira had requested the file following her encounter with the gul during the Europani evacuation. Among other things, it included Captain Picard's official report on the *Phoenix* affair that Macet had been involved in, plus some recent updates by Kira and Vaughn. But little else.

Lang was another matter; Ro found the name cross-referenced in more than a dozen files outside her own. While Ro appreciated Odo's thorough but terse summaries of facts and observations, she found his subtext most illuminating.

For example, the contents of Odo's "Natima Lang" file, compiled during the ambassador's second visit to the station, fascinated Ro. She was impressed by Lang's unorthodox political views and active resistance against Cardassia's Central Command. Why the Ghemor government had selected her to run errands to Bajor was obvious. What took Ro a moment to figure out was the relevance of Odo's inclusion of cross-references to stationwide crime reports in Lang's file. She focused on a few specific items that caught her attention.

Forty-two percent reduction in illegal trafficking linked to Quark's

Six complaints regarding quality, swindling or thievery re: bar service (twenty-seven in same time frame previous year)

Dr. Bashir: dabo girl w/sprained finger from stuck dabo wheel; no harassment involved

The conclusion was obvious: Odo attributed the crime rate drop to Lang's influence on Quark. So Quark had ties with Ambassador Lang, probably romantic ones. *What did Lang have that he wanted?* she wondered. Ro might be considering her possibilities with Quark, but she wasn't stupid about him. Quark, characteristically, wasn't one to plunge into a relationship without a profit motive hovering in the background. If some mutually beneficial emotion passed between interested parties, so much the better, but love alone never justified any transaction. His steadfast belief in the 229th Rule of Acquisition, "Latinum lasts longer than lust," assured that.

She considered Lang's holo. Unless one found exotic reptiles desirable, Ro never understood what might make Cardassians attractive to anyone outside their own species: she found them brutes who gloried in the slow, sadistic kill. Never distinguishing between those who could defend themselves and the sick, weak or young, Cardassians in Ro's experience gloried in calculated brutality simply because they could.

But Lang . . . If the eyes, indeed, were the windows to the soul as the old Terran adage went, Lang's eyes lacked the chilly veil of superiority all Cardassians seemed schooled in. Rather, Lang evinced a steely softness Ro believed characterized those who knew and practiced compassion, but understood that protecting goodness required a willingness to go into battle when circumstances required it.

Her viewscreen's chronometer reminded Ro that she had less than twenty minutes before the *Trager*'s arrival—and she still had an errand to run before she greeted the station's latest guests, if "guests" was the right way to reference them. Usually guests didn't require more than uneventful arrivals, pillow pastries and quiet quarters to find comfort aboard DS9. The Cardassians might be comfortable, but the rest of the station was another matter.

After reviewing the potential pitfalls of hosting a warshipload of Cardassians, Kira and Ro determined that the station status would have to be pushed up to security level yellow. Impact to the day-to-day tasks occupying most civilians would be minimal: other than permitting only scheduled trips to and from the station, internal communications, commerce and activities would continue as normal. Those affiliated with the diplomatic delegations, Militia members and Starfleet personnel, would have to provide retinal scans in addition to the usual voiceprint ID in certain secured areas. All ships would be subject to random security checks and no last-minute flight plans would be authorized. The cargo pilots would complain, but Ro felt the inconvenience would be mitigated by the decreased likelihood of some militant anti-Cardassian group deciding to use the station as a staging ground for an act of revenge.

Reassured that her people were in position and that all available measures had been taken to guarantee an uneventful remainder of shift, Ro closed Lang's file, hoping she could glean a final insight into her guests by visiting the one person on Deep Space 9 who might know more than Odo.

Quark polished the last in a set of exquisitely crafted Gamzian crystal snifters (an idea he'd thought of after reading last year's bestseller on Ferenginar, *Packaging Your Way to Easy Profits*) when Ro sidled up to the bar. She smiled cryptically.

"After we talked the other day, I went ahead and reserved the holosuite for tonight. Hope that wasn't too forward of me," Quark said.

Ro shook her head and shrugged. "Tonight isn't going to work. Station business."

"Come on, Laren. Tell that slave driver of a boss of yours that all work and no play makes for perpetually irritable employees," Quark said, and muttering under his breath added, "and if she's not walking evidence of that truism, I don't know who is."

"I have a feeling you'll want to be behind the bar tonight, not in a holo-suite."

"Hmmmm. Must be some kind of show you've got planned if it's better than gazing at you across a candlelight dinner for two, the moonlight etching your profile in silver against the velvety night sky."

"Quark," Ro warned, her eyes narrowing.

"Fine, fine," he groused. "I'll have to unload the holosuite time, though at this late hour that might be hard to do without deep discounts . . . Then again . . ." He craned his neck around the corner and hollered into the store-room. "Hey you, Treir!"

Treir appeared in the doorway, a two-meter statue cut from jade. "Try again," she suggested, gazing placidly down her green nose at her boss.

Rolling his eyes, Quark gestured for her to come closer. "Check the atti-tude in the back, Treir. This is business." He waited, looked back over his shoulder and saw his number one dabo girl still fixed in the doorway, clearly unimpressed by his dictum. And what was with the outfit? Wearing scanty and provocative exercise attire instead of scanty and provocative work attire. Dis-gusted, he dropped his hands to his hips. "I could fire you for being out of uniform during business hours."

She folded her arms across her chest, yawning. "Try again, Quark."

"I don't—This isn't—I refuse to—" he sputtered. Glaring, he gave an annoyed sigh, squared his shoulders and took a deep breath.

Resting her chin in her hand, Ro's eyes danced with amusement; she un-successfully suppressed a smile.

Insulted, Quark spun around and said, "Try to remember you're on my side, Laren." He turned back to Treir and said very slowly, "If you have a mo-ment, Treir, I have a business proposition I'd like your input on," he punctuated his amiable sentence with a decidedly sardonic smirk.

"Sure, I have a sec. What do you want?" she said, hopping up on the coun-ter. She threw her bare green legs out in front of her, braced her hands behind her and arched her back in a stretch.

She's trying to distract me—and it's working, Quark thought, noting how equally effective she'd been in blocking his preferred escape route. "As your employer, I shouldn't have to recite a damn sonnet to get answers to my ques-tions. You signed a contract. I could fire you—without cause."

"Yeah, but we both know you won't. I'm too valuable to the bar," Treir said pleasantly, removing a pair of metal bracelets from her pocket and bending to snap them around her ankles.

"Hey!" Ro jumped up from her stool and circled round to where Treir perched on the bar. "Are those new grav weights? I saw some of the Starfleet people using them during their rec periods."

Treir nodded affirmatively, unsnapped one and handed it to Ro. "They're great for extra resistance. Improves the workout like you can't believe. Just press this button here and it enhances the artificial gravity by—"

"Ahem," Quark cleared his throat. "Were we not having a discussion, Treir?"

Pressing her face between her calves, Treir grabbed her ankles and flattened her back. "You were talking. I wouldn't call that a discussion."

Quark looked pleadingly to Ro for support, but Laren was preoccupied tinkering with the grav weights. *So it's just me and Treir's fantastically pliable limbs . . .*

"Be careful with that, Ro. It can be tricky if you aren't used to them. Increase the resistance gradually," Treir advised.

Ro nodded in acknowledgment and locked one of the grav weights on her wrist.

Distracted by Treir's point-flex-bounce rhythm, Quark paused, straining to recall what started the discussion in the first place. He admired Treir's unapologetic advocacy of her own interests, but her unpredictable demands certainly slowed the pace of doing business. Then his brilliant idea reoccurred to him. "Due to an unforeseen change in plans, the bar has three hours of available holosuite time."

"Didn't I tell you that last-minute date scheduling is a surefire way to end a relationship before it starts?" Treir rolled over onto her stomach, grabbed her foot with her hand and pulled it up to her shoulder. She repeated the stretch with the other leg, maintaining her balance between the counters all the while. "Ro, I think you might have the setting on that weight too high . . ."

"My evening with Lieutenant Ro has been *rescheduled*," Quark clarified. "Leaving us with a prime business opportunity."

Ro activated the grav enhancement field with a quick flick, sending her arm plunging to the floor like a falling rock, dragging her along with it. "That was predictable," she said to the tile pressed against her cheek.

"Can we please focus?!" Quark growled.

An uncharacteristic silence descended on the bar. Servers paused, protectively hugging their drink-filled trays since Quark deducted broken glassware and spilled beverages from their salaries; gamblers peered from behind the *tongo* wheel and over the *dom-jot* table, hoping for a front-seat view of any fight that might break out; diners tossed tips onto tables, eased out of their chairs and closer to the door. Even big, brawny Hetik froze over the dabo wheel.

"As you were, everyone!" Treir said, dropping off the counter. "The house announces a complimentary round of Orion ale!" A cheer went up through the bar as she ordered several pitchers from the replicator and began filling mugs. Servers whisked by to collect the libations as swiftly as Treir poured.

Quark extended a hand to Ro and helped her up off the floor. "We'll send out a stationwide notice advertising that we're auctioning off this rare and valuable holosuite time—" he said to Treir.

"In half-hour increments," Ro suggested, brushing smudges off her uniform.

Quark continued, "Highest bidders have the company of the dabo girl—"

"Or boy," Treir said.

"Yeah, yeah. Whatever. The dabo *person* of the customer's choice. We'll have a stampede by day's end."

"Good idea. If you want me to proofread the notice, let me know." Treir finished pouring the last round of complimentary drinks and strolled toward the door.

"The idea was for you to write the notice!" he shouted at her back.

"Break time," she said apologetically. "I've got a few laps around the docking ring to cover before my next shift."

Watching as Treir disappeared into the Promenade crowds affirmed Quark's deep belief in the incompatibility of females and finances. No sense of timing in females. A business proposition required tending, to be cultivated like a rare cheese. How typical for Treir to run off, just as the real work started. She confirmed why females proved most useful when naked, in the mud, wombs rented out. Quark retrieved another Gamzian glass snifter from the box and began polishing it. "I do *not* need my notices proofread." Ro would validate him. As females went, Ro was surprisingly like a male.

Ro shrugged. "Last time—"

"Weren't you here on business, Lieutenant?" Quark said, irritably. Maybe she wasn't as malelike as he'd hoped.

"Right. Business." She checked her chronometer. "Damn! I'm running late," she said, rising from her barstool. "Wanted to give you a heads-up. The *Narsil* won't be able to dock until tomorrow."

Quark blessed his excellent eye-hand coordination when the glass he held threatened to slide out of his grip. "What is it with bad news and station management today? You collectively wake up on the wrong side of the bed?"

"The captain of the *Narsil* didn't file a flight plan until an hour ago. We're not permitting any unscheduled dockings or departures until further notice," she said as she headed for the exit.

He followed after, walking beside her. "I have a load of Matopin rock fungi on that ship, Ro. It festers if it isn't put into proper storage so if the *Narsil*'s cargo bay needs decontamination—"

"Oh, yeah," Ro said. "Speaking of food, Colonel Kira requested that you send up a catering menu to Ensign Beyer. Minister Shakaar assigned her to oversee the planning of a diplomatic reception."

The portrait of Kira as a domesticated female doing female business—for once—at the bidding of her male superior had a certain appeal to Quark. "What's the occasion?"

As Ro outlined the parameters of Kira's latest assignment, Quark ran his thumb up and down the glass stem, mentally calculating the number of VIPs and high-powered individuals likely to be in attendance; he found the potential bottom line very attractive. "We're talking a lot of guests then. Starfleet,

Cardassians, Bajorans, Trill, Andorians, Alonis. . . . Numbering in the two- to three-hundred range?"

"More or less. I suppose," she answered.

The list of high-priced, exotic delicacies he could dazzle the delegations with boggled the mind. And the bill? The Bajoran government would have to loot the temple treasury to cover his costs . . . unless . . . unless he could parlay this catering job into a more lucrative business opportunity.

So what if Bajor succumbed to all the money-free, hearts-and-flowers flourishes forced upon them by joining the Federation? Quark was confident that Cardassia would never embrace the Federation's do-gooder ideals. The Great River wasn't dammed up, merely diverted. Granted, there were issues with starvation and disease, but soon enough the Cardassians would be ripe for the picking. He'd dealt with them before (a bit on the chilly side—every client had its quirks) and being a good Ferengi, he'd adapted. Ply them with a little *kanar* and he could sell them anything.

This could work.

If Ghemor—or Shakaar for that matter—planned on hosting many more occasions like these, their governments certainly would want the finest food services in the sector. Quark's Bar: Official Hosting Services to Wormhole Worlds. Had a nice ring to it. He could have a snazzy logo designed. Maybe wrangle an honorary title of some kind or another. This little party had the potential to provide a means of securing his future (not to mention unloading more than a case or two of *yamok* sauce that wasn't too far past its expiration date to be palatable). The Material Continuum always provided to those willing to navigate its rapids. A toothy smile spontaneously filled his face. "I'll send the menu up immediately. I'm certain I can come up with something especially pleasing to all the parties."

"Thanks, Quark." She took his free hand and squeezed it appreciatively.

"You know, Laren, I'm acquainted with more than a few Cardassians," he said, hoping he already had an "in." "Who's Ghemor got coming?"

"Someone Colonel Kira worked with in the Europani crisis, a Gul Macet," she paused, studying Quark's face closely. "But the delegation is being headed by a woman, Natima Lang."

He gulped, glanced at Ro, and hoped he'd had the presence of mind to avoid gaping at the mention of *her* name. *Of course she knows about my special connection with Natima. She's playing me like a Trill syn lara and doing a damn fine job of it to be sure,* he thought, shivering in delicious anticipation of their upcoming night out. The potentialities of a woman who could outmaneuver him had a powerful allure.

"You might want to take care of that," Ro said, gesturing at his palm.

Quark looked down and discovered he held a handful of shards, the rest of the snifter a pile on the floor. Glass-punctured fingers drizzled blood onto his ruffled shirt cuffs. "This is a custom-made suit of the finest Tholian silk, I'll have you know. I hope you're handy with mending, Lieutenant, because I'll be dropping this suit by your quarters as soon as this shift ends."

Treir, sweaty and panting, jogged past Quark, carefully sidestepping the broken glass. "Had a bit of an accident, huh?"

He gave his star dabo girl a look. "Break time over?"

"I needed my other weight," she said, by way of explanation. "Then I'm going back out."

"On the bar," Ro said. She flattened a palm on Quark's chest, straightened and smoothed his shirt ruffles, and smiled. "I'll send Doctor Girani if you don't get that hand attended to."

And she left.

Quark watched Ro walk away, finding the confident way she threw her legs out in front of her, her hips swinging steadily, oh so alluring. When the turbolift doors closed behind her, Quark turned back into the bar, his wound reminding him of unfinished business. He retrieved a napkin from the countertop and fumbled behind the bar for a medkit. Hopefully, that stupid dabo boy had recharged the dermal regenerator after that exquisitely tasteless episode with the fingernail lady last week.

"Treir! Get this glass mess taken care of!" Quark shouted.

"Try again, Quark," Treir said sweetly, dabbing at her forehead with a bar towel.

3

Captain's Log, Stardate 53471.3

The Defiant *has taken up temporary residence in the main storage bay of the transport ship,* Avaril. *Our hosts, the Yrythny, have offered us their resources and supplies to help restore* Defiant *to full functionality. According to the Yrythny, the "web weapon" we encountered was designed for the express purpose of disabling Yrythny ships.*

The Yrythny are embroiled in a conflict with the deployers of the weapon, the Magisterial Cheka Kingdom. The Yrythny describe the Cheka as militant imperialists who dominate this region of space. The Cheka employ a twofold strategy in maintaining their civilization: they enslave species to serve their empire, and subsequently augment their technology base through their conquests of those species. The Cheka apparently have neither the ability nor the motivation to innovate, relying primarily on the inventiveness of other species. Thus far, the Yrythny have successfully resisted Cheka conquest.

The Cheka's current goal is to genetically engineer a servitor species to act as their army (possibly as the Founders created the Jem'Hadar), and this seems to be the source of their fixation with the Yrythny. The Yrythny, they believe, hold the key to the genetic breakthroughs the Cheka seek. And because the Cheka have no compunctions against experimenting on living subjects, the Yrythny understandably refuse to cooperate.

Doctor Bashir has informed me that the Cheka have likely chosen the Yrythny for experimentation due to the unusual nature of our hosts' DNA. His scans have revealed that Yrythny genetic material is artificially enhanced, and Bashir has hypothesized that at some point in the Yrythny's distant past, an advanced species such as the Founders or the Preservers tampered with Vanìmel's evolutionary process with chromosomal segments that hastened their evolution from amphibious animals to sentients. The Yrythny call it the "Turn Key."

In an effort to coerce Yrythny cooperation, the Cheka have mined all the sectors around Vanìmel with their web weapons. They've succeeded in destroying numerous Yrythny starships as well as cutting them off from most interstellar commerce. The long-term impact of such isolation could be dire for the Yrythny, and they eagerly seek peaceful, cooperative solutions to their present dilemma. We hope our exchange of information will allow both our peoples to better detect and defend against this unseen enemy. Our ability to safely resume our mission may depend on this alliance.

Standing before the observation window, Vaughn watched Vanìmel, a sparkling aquamarine gem of a world, become progressively more distinct as the *Avaril* advanced. The planet's ring glowed luminously beneath the light of its sun. Expecting the ring's ice, rock, and frozen gases to soon come into focus, Vaughn gasped aloud when a structure of modules, domes, and towers resolved instead.

"A city!" he said, feeling childlike awe.

Tlaral nodded. "Almost half our population inhabits Luthia. Our seat of government, our universities—all of it resides within the ring."

The closer the *Avaril* drew to Luthia, the more astonishing the ring city's design became. As civilizations build atop one another, so had the Yrythny built the ring. Older, crudely crafted units comprised Luthia's interior with little segue to the elegantly designed units mounted along the ring's exterior. Docking platforms fixed on elongated spindles extended from the edges, defining the farthest perimeter.

Doors buzzed open admitting a pale-green Yrythny who wore a headpiece of cascading rainbow-colored braids, interwoven with crystal beads and metallic ribbons. His three Yrythny escorts resumed positions in the corners of the observation deck, eyes trained deferentially on the ground.

"Chieftain J'Maah," Vaughn addressed the *Avaril's* captain. "Thank you for allowing me to take in this stirring vista."

"I wish I could have brought you to the bridge, Commander Vaughn, but I assure you the view from here is equally magnificent," J'Maah said, walking toward Vaughn, arms extended. In greeting, he grasped Vaughn by the elbows; the commander reciprocated the gesture.

Stepping behind Vaughn, Tlaral bowed her head subserviently, waiting to be addressed by her superior. The chieftain rapidly tapped his tongue against his teeth, a signal to the technologist, Vaughn guessed, that she could resume her former stance.

"We have word from our leadership. Assembly Chair Rashoh bids you and a group of your officers join him for a meal," J'Maah said, officiously. "You will dine while the *Avaril* docks, clears quarantine and other such matters. Our crews will relocate the *Defiant* to a docking bay at the port, where your people may undertake repairs. Our government is also arranging accommodations for your crew within the city."

"Your generosity is deeply appreciated, Chieftain."

"Tlaral will take you to our shuttlebay as soon as you have assembled your team."

"We'd be happy to transport down if it would be easier," Vaughn offered.

Sternly, J'Maah shook his head, vibrating the skin pockets hanging off his jaw. "Our transporters have limited range. It was the reason *Avaril* needed to come so close to your ship before our technologists could be beamed over. The assembly chair's private shuttle has been sent for you. Quite an honor. Quite an honor. Go on then." J'Maah shooed Tlaral and Vaughn toward *Avaril's* tremendous cargo bay where *Defiant* and her crew were ensconced.

Vaughn exited without protest, rightly sensing that J'Maah was accustomed to calling the shots. As per J'Maah's instructions, he would gather his senior staff and he would meet with the government leadership. But, like it or not, he would return to his mission as soon as possible.

On *his* terms, naturally.

• • •

After what seemed like a protracted trek down the docking spindle, the transport doors opened, admitting them to a customs-security area. With a Yrythny escort on either side of each member of the away team, Ezri followed behind Vaughn, Shar, Julian, and Lieutenant Aaron McCallum, security officer, as each of them submitted to full body scans and routine medical screening. For a passport, the Starfleet officers had retinal patterns entered into the Yrythny database. When security issued an "all clear," their guides led them into the public square, crowded with the trappings of Yrythny life. Merchants hawking bleating animals; food vendors with copper frying vats, their aprons splattered with oil and batter; students clustered around a fountain in heated discussion.

Ezri was content to allow "her" Yrythny to guide her through the sea of bodies, jostling this way and that. Her attention was drawn above the confusion to the lacy, carved arches, lined with enameled tiles, and the delicate curlicues painted up the pillars. Squinting, she could make out dainty flowers and vines twining around the base of the domes, made translucent by the warm light of Vanìmel's sun. She wanted to pause for a moment, to study the graceful lines and forms, but her Yrythny escorts continually ushered her along.

Choruses of Yrythny voices thudded around her, punctuated by grunts and moans as bodies crashed into each other. With Julian in front of her and her tall Yrythny guides to the side, Ezri was effectively blocked in; she allowed the crowd's momentum to propel her forward. Other than ceilings and heads, she saw only the walls, seemingly carved out of rose-colored sandstone instead of forged metal. She continued to walk, face upturned, until she crashed into Julian's back.

"Sorry, Julian, I wasn't paying . . ."

Piercing screams cut through the plaza. A crash of a tipping cart. Weapons fire.

Throwing arms out, their Yrythny escorts turned their backs on their Starfleet charges, shielding them from whatever was going on. Blocked by the wall of tall Yrythny, Ezri ducked to look beneath their linked arms.

Up winding staircases, through ornate doors and elaborate archways, panicked Yrythny fled, tossing aside whatever they carried. But as many Yrythny swarmed out of the plaza, others streamed in through adjacent streets wielding anything from crude metal bars to beam weapons.

A mob. Heading directly for the away team.

More weapons fire. An escort next to her went slack, tumbled to his knees and toppled to the ground. Then another. Then still another. Whipping out his tricorder, Julian went to work. Vaughn shouted. Ezri couldn't understand him over the din. She heard another of the escorts trying to reason with the rioters, screaming, "Stop! These are our guests, not our captives!" But his appeals were ignored as one of the rioters clubbed him across the head with a pipe. The escort fell, whether unconscious or dead, Ezri didn't know which.

So it's a lynch mob, Ezri thought. *These people are so eager for Cheka blood, they'll do anything for a taste of it, even turn against each other.*

She spotted one of their attackers making a beeline for Shar.

"Shar, watch out!" she shouted, spinning around and reaching instinctively for her empty holster. *Damn diplomatic protocols.* Weaponless, she charged forward. A Yrythny forearm hooked around her neck, yanking hard against her throat.

Complying with the beam weapon pressed against his temple, Shar swallowed hard and dropped to his knees, clasping his hands behind his head, his antennae tensed. Fury and the smells of fear stimulated his senses. The click of safeties being released seemed unnaturally slow and loud in his ears.

A guttural exclamation. The metallic sound of weapons fire. More screams. Blue gray smoke obscured his view.

Several Yrythny off to his side argued. "—reports said our defense perimeter was compromised—"

"—Cheka sending their spies—"

"—our chance to make an example—"

"—say we kill them now—"

Shar fought not to be sickened by the dull thud of metal against tissue and cracking bones. Senses threatening to overload, he fought to ignore the scent of singed flesh, the sweat-sour clothes worn by assailants, the bioelectric surges of pain.

Shar looked around him. The away team's escorts had suffered a brutal assault. Vaughn and McCallum appeared uninjured. He glanced behind him to check on Julian and Ezri, but his assailant swung the butt of his weapon across Shar's face. Blood, warm and sticky, drizzled down his cheek. His breathing became a hiss.

"Move again and I'll blow your head off," his assailant said, pressing the weapon into Shar's wound.

A companion grunted approvingly.

His emotions intensifying toward violence, Shar's eyes panned up to his assailant's face. The Yrythny was slow, clumsy. Shar's antennae spread wide, triangulating on his target—

"Fire that weapon, U'ndoh," a new voice rang out, "and I vow you'll never see the light of day again. The same goes for anyone who harms these innocent people."

His assailant paused. Shar remained still. The gun fell away from his cheek, and his assailant abruptly ran off. Slowly, Shar's need for violence receded and his breathing returned to normal. He searched the nearby crowd for his rescuer, but it seemed she had departed.

"Listen to me, Wanderers!"

Shar jerked toward the now-familiar voice, distinctive among the angry rumblings.

A Yrythny, about his height, hair twisted into a topknot, shoved authoritatively through the crowds. Ignoring their taunts, she slapped away hands and shrugged off any who dared try impede her. When she reached a pillar near the plaza's center, she flattened and rubbed her palms against the pillar's smooth surface to attain adhesion, and without a backward glance, shimmied up, kicking away a rioter who grabbed at her ankle. When a solid meter separated her from the tallest Yrythny, she anchored her legs around the pillar, tightly linking her ankles. Her coarsely woven skirt rucked up around her knees.

Cupping her hands in front of her mouth, she shouted, "Listen to me or suffer the consequences! As your Lower Assembly delegate, I speak as the law. This gathering is illegal!"

One by one, the mob turned their gazes upward. Pottery and fruit hurtled through the air, smashing against the pillar. Rioters shouted protests; others watched warily.

"Wanderer caste caught bearing weapons may be subject to punishment by death," she continued, ignoring the glass shattering above and below her.

In response, some Yrythny cast aside weapons; pieces of pipe, tools, and sidearms fell like stuttering raindrops. A few rioters disbanded, but others persisted in catcalls.

From her high perch, Shar's defender surveyed the remaining agitators haughtily. "Disperse now if you wish to avoid arrest!" she cried. "An armed patrol is on its way and is prepared to take all of you into custody. Save your energies for actions that will change our world for the better, not ones that will doom your cause and yourselves."

Her pronouncements ignited quarrels, both with her and among themselves. Primitive, hivelike contention heated the plaza as Yrythny fought with Yrythny. Head swimming, Shar saw coal eyes dark with rage; knobby fingers, grabbing, scratching; wide, gaping mouths rimmed with glistening teeth. Fevered chaos spun faster and faster around him . . .

The distant, rhythmic thud of boots thundering toward the plaza proved their leader's claim. Panicked, the crowd pushed and shoved every which way, stampeding over the fallen. Terrified shouts drowned out cries for help.

Fear reigned.

Holding her post on the pillar, the Yrythny leader watched closely, waiting for the ground situation to stabilize. Slowly, the mob dispersed, leaving only the injured and infirm. She eased her way back down, waiting, her eyes turned toward the patrol pounding slowly closer, ever closer. The mob retreated. Shar discovered that, like Vaughn and McCallum, Dax and Bashir had survived, unharmed.

Rushing down the stairs with weapons drawn, the patrol peeled out of formation to secure each arched entrance into the plaza.

"No one move!" the patrol leader bellowed. "You there," he pointed. "Stop what you're doing!"

Shar followed the gesture to Bashir, who crouched beside several of their fallen escorts. Pale, but unscathed, Ezri sat close by, monitoring one of the wounded Yrythny with the doctor's tricorder.

"I'm a physician. These are your people I'm treating," Bashir snapped, clearly agitated after their ordeal. "They sustained their injuries protecting us, so you'll have to arrest me to make me stop," he said, and continued mending a laceration.

That seemed to bring the patrol leader up short. "Fine, then." Carelessly, he kicked away refuse cast aside by the fleeing mob. He approached Commander Vaughn, who was facing him expectantly. "Are you the leader of your group?"

"I'm Commander Vaughn."

"Chief Enforcer Elkoh," the patrol leader said. "Can you explain what happened here?"

"I was going to ask you the same question."

The patrol stopped all Yrythny lingering in the plaza, demanding identification and conducting spot searches. With arms straight up in the air, civilians suspected of lawbreaking waited their turn to have their belongings inspected. Other enforcers retrieved the weapons thrown aside by escaping rioters.

Vaughn provided what answers he could to Elkoh's inquiries; perhaps they looked to him, as an alien, to offer an objective account of the incident. For his part, Vaughn was more interested in what the Yrythny female who dispersed the mob would have to say. She stood by quietly, watching, awaiting her turn. She'd removed a small computing device from her shoulder pack and was clicking through the contents when the chief enforcer thanked Vaughn and turned to her. "Delegate Keren?" he asked.

She nodded, unruffled, and replaced her computer in her shoulder pack. Shoving her hands in her pockets, she said, "Enforcer?"

The officer subvocalized something into a metal nodule mounted on his throat and then paused, listening intently to his earpiece until frown wrinkles creased his spotted forehead. "You had something to do with this?" he said accusingly. "After the last time, Assembly Chair Rashoh said that if you were discovered to be involved, directly or indirectly, with any act of Wanderer rebellion—"

"I read the censure," Keren said, raising a hand to hush her inquisitor. "I caught word that there might be trouble, after the Assembly received the news of the aliens' visit. I came here to greet the Assembly Chair's guests."

"From whom did you 'catch word'?" the officer sniffed.

"That doesn't matter," Keren dismissed him breezily.

"Assembly Chair Rashoh will beg to differ. He—"

"Stop, Elkoh. *I* speak on behalf of our esteemed leader," said a Yrythny newly arrived on the scene.

To Vaughn's eye, the towering, dark-skinned newcomer resembled the chieftain of the *Avaril* in mien and garb. But where J'Maah had been thick and stumpy, this Yrythny was lean and tall, his neatly braided chestnut hair falling out of an elegant headpiece, adorned with bronze and silver embroidery.

"Yes, sir, Vice Chair Jeshoh." Elkoh offered his superior a bow before ducking away. "I may need to question you and your people further," he cautioned Vaughn.

"I'm not going anywhere," Vaughn said mildly, keeping his attention fixed on Vice Chair Jeshoh, who had turned toward the away team's benefactor.

"Ah! Delegate Keren. Why am I not surprised to find you here?" Jeshoh trained his ebony eyes on the smaller Yrythny.

"You owe these strangers your gratitude, Jeshoh," Keren said, pointing at Vaughn's crew, who continued to see to the injured escorts. They'd been joined in the last few minutes by several Yrthny medics. "The honor guard you sent to bring them to the dining hall would all be dead were it not for their medical assistance. Your own enforcers are more interested in finding the guilty than helping the wounded." Keren tossed her cloak off her shoulder.

Jeshoh turned back to Vaughn, and in a gesture Vaughn was beginning to know well reached for the commander's elbows. Vaughn responded in kind. "I bring the deepest apologies of our leadership. Please know we will do all we can to assure your continuing safety."

Before Vaughn could reply, another enforcer tapped him on the shoulder. More questions. Could he identify any of the agitators from a digital image? The soldier handed Vaughn a tablet and showed him how to scroll through the contents. While he perused the Yrythny "Most Wanted" lineup, Vaughn listened to the conversation resuming between Jeshoh and Keren.

"You risk violating your censure, Keren."

"My fellow Wanderers listen to me! The violence could have been much worse."

"For your sake, I hope an investigation proves you right."

"It will. The truth bestows confidence, Vice Chair Jeshoh."

"So you always say. I still win our debates."

"That's a matter of opinion," she countered.

"You haven't passed a single resolution this legislative session."

"My most recent is stalled in *your* committee."

"If it was a good law, wouldn't we pass it?" Jeshoh walked away before Keren could protest. "Commander . . . Vaughn, is it?"

"Yes," Vaughn said.

"The leadership awaits us. Several of these enforcers will escort us to dinner." Taking the tablet from Vaughn, he called out to Elkoh, passing the device to him. "You will proceed without further inconvenience to our guests, Chief Enforcer. Assign your best people to accompany us."

Silently, Shar and Keren walked side by side down Luthia's long, streetlike tunnels past shops, laboratories, supply depots and military checkpoints to a pathway that ran along an artificial river. Swift currents hurried along beside them, foaming and crashing against red coral barriers and boulders, which were weathered smooth. He found the soft random sounds of the water calming. With each twist of the path, with each bridge they crossed, Shar became increasingly amazed at how much more of a "city" Luthia was than any of the Federation's space stations. No matter how much time he spent on Deep Space 9, he never forgot that he was swaddled in metal and conduits. Here, the life pulsing through the city might wholly push aside his disbelief.

A dense, mixed population of civilians, government and military personnel created a stimulating mix of textures and scents: salt-water-filled bins of fish; tangy, unwashed clothing and rotted wood; butter-soft slippers made of skins; homespun cloaks, gaudy baubles, tubs of congealed cooking fats. He was reminded of some of the more rural communities of Andor.

Shar avoided looking directly at Keren, trying instead to study her unobtrusively. Not nearly as muscular as many of the Yrythny they'd encountered so far, she had a slender build. Her charcoal and cocoa-colored facial stripes blended in with the nondescript headpiece she wore. Her clothes were suitable for farm work, and yet apparently she was some kind of government leader.

Keren shoved her hands into her pockets and hummed a discordant tune while she walked. Shar lengthened his stride so he could keep up. Surprisingly, he felt not the slightest bit winded as he chased alongside Keren; he'd grown accustomed to his body taking time to adjust to the gravity or the atmosphere of a new world, but Luthia already felt comfortable to him.

"Thank you," he said finally.

She raised calm eyes to Shar's frankly curious face. "Are you addressing me?"

"You saved my life," Shar offered by way of explanation. "Thank you."

She shrugged, adjusted the ties on her blouse. "The fools who attacked misunderstood the news from the *Avaril*. They thought you were Cheka spies, captured when you encroached on our perimeter. Of course, it may be that you *are* spies, but we've no proof of that. I'm afraid that our ongoing conflict with the Cheka has many of our people on edge. The helplessness, the anger sometimes feeds the mob mentality and overwhelms common sense."

"I see. Then, may I ask ... Why me, Delegate Keren? My shipmates—"

"You have me at a disadvantage," Keren interrupted. "While you know me, I don't have the benefit of your name."

"I beg your pardon. Ensign Thirishar ch'Thane, science officer, *U.S.S. Defiant.*"

"Thank you. I liked the look of you, Ensign ch'Thane. Kneeling there, you didn't seem fearful." She studied Shar. "More curious."

"I have many questions," Shar said honestly.

"As do I. In exchange for your life, may I ask the first?"

When he realized Keren appraised him as candidly as he did her, he felt his face become flushed. *For what other reason have I come on this journey, than to ask questions and seek answers?* "Please," he said.

"Dammit!" Ezri whispered, hopping on one foot. The thud of her boot resonated through the cavernous hall of the massive government building into which the away team had been led.

Startled, Julian looked up from his tricorder. "Are you hurt?" He glanced at their soldier-escort, offering a smile. No need to panic the local constabulary.

Wearing a pinched expression, she grunted, "I walked into that bench over there. My shin hurts like hell." She shook out her leg, rolled her shoulders.

Julian scrutinized her nervous fidgeting. Yes, Ezri had assured him, several times, that she felt fine. Aside from heightened adrenaline—entirely normal, considering—and a few minor bruises on her throat, his tricorder readings bore her out. Maybe. Her blinking, her jerky movements—uncharacteristic clumsiness . . .

"Don't say it," she said perfunctorily.

"What?"

"I could tell you were going to say it."

"Say what?"

"You had that look," she said, screwing up her face. "The look you reserve for an infected specimen."

"Not fair," he protested, shaking his head. "I'm always concerned about you." He suppressed the desire to put his arm around her. *One doesn't squeeze the X.O. on duty,* he reminded himself. By mutual agreement, he and Ezri were keeping their relationship in their quarters for the duration of their mission. "We've had a rough day. We're all exhausted. We're on an alien planet in a strange environment—"

"So why aren't you looking at Commander Vaughn that way? Or Shar? Or Aaron?" she challenged.

He considered her, and by some not-genetically-enhanced instinct, Julian knew that Lieutenant Colonel Travis had stood a better chance of defeating General Santa Anna at the Alamo than he, in this moment, had in winning an argument with Ezri Dax. "Shall we go to dinner?"

"You're trying to change the subject."

"As a matter of fact, I am," he admitted, following their group into an expansive dining hall. Rich, spicy smells instantly assaulted him, very reminiscent of a victory celebration General Martok had once hosted aboard the *Rotarran.* A few of his non-Klingon guests had lost their appetites (and their earlier meals) after prolonged exposure to the gamey buffet. He hoped his crewmates could avoid such queasiness now, especially Ezri, who in the past had struggled with nausea.

The thought reminded him of something. "Being in Luthia doesn't make you spacesick?"

She snorted indelicately. "I beat that months ago."

"So far above a planet's surface, with all these twisting hallways? And that bowl over there appears to be filled with something akin to *gagh. "* He peered more closely at a passing plate. "Possibly a tangerine-colored sea anemone."

"Keep it up and you just might *make* me sick."

Modestly dressed in rough linens and bland earth tones, Yrythny attendants guided the Starfleet guests to the head tables. Twenty or so Yrythny, dressed similarly to Jeshoh, stood beside benches waiting for their guests.

When the officers from *Defiant* assumed their places, the attendants scurried to the back, eyes cast down.

The strong social parameters he'd observed since meeting the crew of the *Avaril* led Julian to believe that the Yrythny were a caste-based society. The basis of those castes wasn't readily obvious; he wondered if their unusual genetics figured into their designations. Headwear, it seemed, denoted rank. Turbans, hairpieces, skullcaps and scarves in vivid colors, some with beads, others with elaborate embroidery, contrasted sharply with the nondescript veils and hooded cloaks he'd seen in the plaza and streetways of Luthia. Thus far, everything he'd learned about the Yrythny, whether from observation or while treating their wounded, intrigued him.

At the front of the room, an Yrythny wearing sky blue robes clapped his hands together three times. He lifted his arms to the heavens and chanted an invocation. Joining hands, the other Yrythny focused eyes upward in imitation of their cleric. When the chant concluded, hosts and guests alike sat down.

Servers with heads swathed in scarves carried in plates of cold yellow and green vegetables drizzled in creamy sauces, flat, wide noodles and pots sloshing with shellfish broth. Commander Vaughn directed the servers to Julian, who scanned each dish for metabolic compatibility. After a brief analysis, he signaled Vaughn with the all clear. The commander scooped a generous helping of noodles tossed with pieces of a purple squidlike life-form onto his plate; the others followed suit.

Ezri reached toward a plate of kelp-colored fishcakes.

Julian cleared his throat sharply.

She sighed. "What now?"

"If you feel your spots starting to itch . . ."

Ezri rolled her eyes. "I know the drill, Julian. I don't need you to mother me."

He frowned. "Did it ever occur to you that I'm simply looking out for the welfare of *Defiant*'s first officer?"

She scooted over, placed a quick kiss on his cheek and whispered, "Tell you what. After food and a shower, we can climb into bed and you can conduct a thorough examination of *all* my spots. In the meantime, *relax.*"

Julian laughed and shook his head. Admittedly, he tended to overcompensate where Ezri was concerned, but he had no desire to embarrass her or undermine her authority. Perhaps he could ease up. He kissed her back, pleased by the prospect of a leisurely late night. And spot #514 was a particular favorite.

Copying the Yrythny, Ezri used her hands and fingers as utensils, rinsing them in the water basins when she changed from one item on her plate to the next. The efficient servers periodically passed by to swap out dirty basins for clean ones. The food supply, comprised mostly of marine life, seemed endless. Whenever she cleared one plate, another appeared. Julian had escaped to speak with Vaughn three plates ago. Finally, she cleared a plate filled with pulpy fruit and syrup-soaked biscuits and no plate replaced it. Grabbing her stomach, she slumped over. *I've eaten enough to last me the rest of the day,* she thought, *and considering that the replicators on* Defiant *won't be working anytime soon, that's not a bad thing.*

On her immediate left, the Yrythny she remembered as being called Jeshoh was finishing his own meal.

"If you don't mind, I'd like to know your people better," she began, hoping he wouldn't find her curiosity offensive. "Vice Chair Jeshoh, isn't it?"

Dipping his fingers in the basin, he rinsed the last of his meal away and dropped his hands to his thighs. "Yes. I understand we have similar roles."

"Oh?"

"Like you, I am—" a filmy lid dropped over his dark eyes before abruptly opening "—second in command. Talking may prove enlightening for both of us."

The servants cleared off the tables, brushing crumbs to the floor and wiping the surfaces in front of the guests. Jeshoh spun away from the tabletop, giving the workers more room; Ezri did the same, so they sat knee to knee.

"I heard Delegate Keren use the term 'Wanderer,' and call them 'her people.' To what was she referring?" The slavish servility she was witnessing piqued her interest. She respected the cultural values of other worlds, but being fawned on by attendants who didn't dare meet her eyes or accept "thank yous" made her uncomfortable.

"You're perceptive," Jeshoh said, bemused. "We are two peoples. I am Houseborn, meaning after my sea time as a hatchling, I returned to the place where my parents laid me. I was reared in House Perian, the First House of the Yrythny, on the shore of the north continent off the Black Archipelago.

"The Wanderers have no home. Like the Houseborn, they, too, are swept into the sea as hatchlings, but when the time comes to make the transition to the land, they fail to return to their place of origin. Lacking the proper instincts to heed the voice of the water, the Wanderers are proven to be weak. They work harder to attain the same knowledge we Houseborn come by naturally."

Ezri refrained from commenting. Instead, she asked, "But where do Wanderer hatchlings end up, if not at their own Houses?"

"They come ashore to other Houses, where they are taken in and raised as servants."

"And this Delegate Keren," Ezri said, recalling the slightly built, feisty Yrythny leader who scaled the pillar and effectively dispersed the mob. "She is—?"

"Delegate Keren is a Wanderer. A representative elected to voice Wanderer interests in the Lower Assembly. She is also trouble," he added quietly. "Over time—in the last two centuries especially—the Wanderers have attained more rights and privileges. Keren, I'm certain, would try to convince you otherwise."

"I wouldn't mind hearing both sides of the story," Ezri said truthfully.

Jeshoh smiled and shrugged. "I suspected you wouldn't. You seem very inquisitive, which is a trait my people admire. But I feel I should warn you, she'll make it sound worse than it is. With their advanced educations, Wanderers have earned positions in the sciences and arts. They were chiefly responsible for the building of Luthia, originally as an escape from planetside living. Now, Luthia hosts half our population. Wanderers still live separate, primarily congregated in the oldest part of the ring. They call it the Old Quarter."

"I take it the mob in the plaza were unhappy Wanderers." *Unhappy was putting it mildly. Maybe enraged? Perhaps even seething with retribution?*

"The Wanderers believe the Houseborn will use the war with the Cheka to rescind their rights—or use it as an excuse to avoid advancing their rights. Either way, they're misguided." While he spoke, a servant knelt beside Jeshoh, poured oil from a small pitcher onto his arms and massaged it into his skin. He carried on without acknowledging her presence.

Ezri pursed her lips, considering the best way to phrase her next question. "From what you've said, it sounds like the Wanderers have tremendous opportunities. What else do they want?"

Jeshoh sat silent, submitting his limbs to the servant's ministrations: the other arm, a lower leg, the other leg. Ezri hoped his silence meant he was considering her question, not that she had overstepped her bounds.

Finally, he clicked his tongue, dismissing the servant. He said softly, leaning closer to Ezri, "They want arms—to serve in our military. They don't trust the Houseborn to defend them." He shook his head. "They want to join the Houseborn in the waters and have offspring. But they fail to see that passing on their flawed instincts will weaken our species."

"And in spite of progress toward more equal rights for the Wanderers, you still have a hard time living together, I take it?" *If the groups in the front and back of this dining room not mingling are any indicator, I'd have to say the answer is "yes,"* Ezri thought.

"The Cheka barricades magnify the problems. Since we began associations with other species, our society has reconfigured itself around interstellar trade. Supply shortages and economic setbacks make people afraid and angry." Jeshoh paused, looked around to make sure no one was listening before whispering, "Rumors of a Wanderer underground movement are being voiced in committee meetings, not just gossiped about in the marketplace."

And the real reason we were almost killed in cold blood starts to emerge. "That's a very serious situation."

"And we've yet to find a practical way to resolve it. Neither side trusts the other," he paused again, looking around to see who might be listening in on their conversation. "We haven't had war on Vanìmel in 200 years, but . . ."

Ezri grasped the Vice Chair's meaning. Though the Yrythny had lived in relative peace for two centuries, Jeshoh feared conflict was imminent. *What have we stumbled into?* She wondered what Vaughn and the others had learned.

Unbidden, she remembered how Curzon's deft maneuvering had prevented one of the early Proxcinian crises from exploding into war. "You say you traffic with other species routinely. Have you thought about utilizing third party mediation to open up talks with the Wanderers?" she said finally.

"Explain," Jeshoh said, puzzled.

"Bringing in a neutral party to facilitate talks between the warring sides. Oftentimes, someone from the outside—one who isn't invested in one side or the other—is better at determining what points are negotiable and what points each side needs to be flexible on." As she spoke, she drew an imaginary diagram on the tabletop with her fingers. "A third party functions as the apex of a triangle, balancing the single line binding the conflicted parties together by drawing lines among all three."

Jeshoh smiled indulgently. "Unfortunately, economic relationships being what they are, our neighbors may be counted upon only to act in their own best interests. Actively helping to stabilize the situation on Vanìmel would damage their standing with the Cheka, who are the dominant economic power in this region."

From the table behind Jeshoh, the Yrythny cleric turned around abruptly, throwing aside a bowl of fish noodles to gape at Ezri. "A third between the Wanderers and the Houseborn," he said, eyes wide with excitement. He didn't bother to plunge his dirty hands into the basin, instead electing to rub them on his robes.

Sipping from a water glass, she reiterated, "Third party mediation is hardly a new idea."

"The third forges a whole peace?" the cleric persisted.

Ezri looked at the cleric, then at Jeshoh for clarification—he had none—and then back at the cleric. "I suppose," she said, wondering what he was getting at.

The cleric grabbed Jeshoh by the shoulder and shook him. "It's the Other. What she says follows the pattern of the Other."

Jeshoh's confusion gradually dissipated. "Perhaps," he said, prying the cleric's fingers off his shoulder. "It may be worth considering, at least."

By now, loud Yrythny voices clamored on all sides of Ezri; benches were shoved back as individuals of all ranks squeezed into the spaces around her, and with shoulders and elbows bumping, gesticulated madly. Julian shot her worried looks; she ignored him. Contrary to what he might suppose, she did not start whatever this thing was and she wasn't about to be blamed for it. He was a little too quick to fall in with Benjamin and his "She's a Dax. Sometimes they don't think, they just do" aphorism. *Had Benjamin ever had the nerve to say that to my face? Hah!* No matter what anyone might think, she didn't go looking for trouble all the time. Especially not *this* time.

Another Yrythny beside Jeshoh stood up, raising a hand, asking for acknowledgment from the Yrythny leader, Rashoh, who was seated beside Vaughn. "Assembly Chair, our good cleric has a rather startling idea that merits immediate consideration!"

With one swift movement, the cleric hefted Ezri to her feet, threw a food-speckled arm around her shoulder and clutched her to him as he approached the head table. "Good Master, Lensoh speaks truly. This one—this visitor from far away—has been sent by the Other to finally bind together our fractured world." He squeezed Ezri for emphasis, his fingers bruising her upper arm.

"I never said that," Ezri protested. "That's *not* what I said. I said that the Wanderers and Houseborn should consider third-party mediation . . ."

Vaughn looked at Ezri quizzically; she shrugged her shoulders as if to say, *I swear to you I don't know what he's talking about.* Still, with virtually every pair of Yrythny eyes fixed on her, she knew she'd be doing some accounting to Vaughn later but she hoped it would be for laughs. Vaughn had a decent sense of humor. Usually.

To the cleric, Rashoh said, "Explain further." But his frown remained focused on Ezri.

"This one has suggested the introduction of a Third. To complete the triad of Wanderer and Houseborn. To balance our people and facilitate peace," the cleric said. "And I believe this one, this Ezri Dax who stands beside me, has been sent from the Other to help us. She will be the Third!" In benediction, the cleric raised his arms to the ceiling. "Praise the Other!"

The crowd murmured a disjointed chorus of honorifics to the Other before the drone of chatter consumed the room. Trays clattered to the floor and benches toppled as they eagerly discussed this latest development.

"There must be a misunderstanding here," Vaughn said, attempting to quell the excitement in the room before it spread any further. "Lieutenant Dax will share our knowledge and experiences with you, but any other role would be inappropriate." He gave Ezri a meaningful look.

"I have to agree," Ezri chimed in at once. "It wasn't my intention to involve myself in your internal affairs."

"You cannot deny the Other's intervention," the cleric insisted.

Many Yrythny politicians, including Keren, had left their tables to assure themselves a position where they could better hear and be heard. A few tried to worm their way closer to Ezri, hurling questions at her faster than she could answer them. She rotated toward each voice in succession, trying to match what was being said with the speaker. *What I wouldn't do for Jadzia's height about now,* she lamented. Ezri saw Vaughn's hand above the crowd, as he jerked his thumb back to indicate he wanted her at his side, posthaste. Squeezing her way past the servants and politicians and clerics, she walked up to her CO, carefully placing her back to the crowd.

Vaughn said, over the cacophony of Yrythny voices, "If you'd excuse me, Assembly Chair, Vice Chair, Honorable Cleric, we must take leave of you and your good people at this time." The murmuring quieted, the Yrythny waited respectfully for Vaughn to continue. "My officers and I need to check on the status of our ship and those we left behind. Please accept my thanks on behalf of all of my crew for your gracious hospitality."

Perhaps realizing the uncomfortable position their guests were in, Rashoh and Jeshoh interposed themselves between the away team and the crowd as Vaughn led his people toward the exit. The cleric, who originally fingered Ezri, included himself in the leadership, staring after her with reverential wonder. She groaned inwardly. At least the other Yrythny were clued in that they needed to allow their leaders—and their guests—to proceed without interference.

In the spacious hall beyond the dining room, the Yrythny leaders offered the entire *Defiant* crew guest quarters, far removed from the civilian areas; reduced trade and tourism in the wake of the Cheka conflict had left their hosting facilities completely empty. The away team learned that one of Rashoh's aides would escort them to the docking bay harboring *Defiant,* where further instructions would be provided.

The discussion proceeded without Ezri commenting. She thought that was best.

On their way back to the *Defiant,* Ezri related her conversation with Jeshoh and how her neutral comments had been seized on by the cleric and twisted into something unintended. "At least I haven't been elevated to an Yrythny deity," she quipped. *Though godhood would have appealed to Curzon.*

"For all our sakes," Vaughn replied, "you'd better hope it stays that way."

In the complex of guest accommodations where the bulk of the *Defiant* crew had been housed following the away team's return to the ship, Shar tried to concentrate on the database terminal his hosts had provided each member of the crew. Unfortunately, he was finding it hard to focus.

Shar gave up counting the number of times he'd heard Vaughn, Dax, and Bashir's doors open and close over the last hour. He didn't need to eavesdrop on their conversations to miss the tension in the air; his antennae hadn't stopped itching since Vaughn and Dax had met with Nog back at the ship.

Working with Yrythny engineers and his own team, Nog had made supply lists for the *Defiant*'s repairs. The Yrythny had—or could get their hands on—most of what Nog needed to fix the ship. How to defend the *Defiant* against the Cheka nanobots was proving to be the challenge, one that might take longer than the actual repairs. Even their hosts admitted they didn't know how extensive the web network was in this sector; the Cheka apparently redeployed the webs frequently at random coordinates in order to make space travel as dangerous as possible for the Yrythny. The only reason *Avaril* had been able to come to *Defiant*'s aid at all was that the particular web that had snared *Defiant* was one the Yrythny had recently discovered. With the web weapons invisible to sensors, the commander didn't want to make a move until they developed a workable countermeasure.

Not one engineer had yet shown up at the guest quarters. When it became clear Nog wasn't planning a dinner break, Vaughn finally sent Lankford and T'rb up with food. Shar expected that Nog would catnap on a cot by the ship: the situation was that critical.

Everyone without a specific assignment had been ordered to comb the Yrythny database for information on the Cheka and their web weapons. So once Shar had retired to his quarters for the evening, he settled in front of his terminal and tried to go to work—except that the continuing discord among his senior officers had proven very distracting.

Of course, he knew that something else was causing his mind to wander this evening, something that had nothing to do with the stir Lieutenant Dax had inadvertently caused. Ever since he'd examined the tricorder readings Dr. Bashir had taken of the Yrythny back aboard *Defiant,* Shar had been preoccupied with their genetic "Turn Key." The opportunity to research it in the Yrythny's own database was proving too great a temptation. In delineating its nature to Commander Vaughn, Dr. Bashir had described it in human parlance as a "skeleton key," designed to unlock any gene, even reconfigure it, to hasten the evolution of a species. The implications of the Turn Key had a particular allure for any scientist with an interest in cytogenetics. Especially one from Andor.

The climate of Luthia suited Shar well. Healthy Yrythny skin required high levels of humidity, he'd learned, an environmental condition that also suited Andorian physiology. Though the Yrythny didn't sleep in beds, but rather, cushioned depressions in the floor of their sleeprooms, Shar found the accommodations lavish, almost decadent for a species whose technology was still about two hundred years behind that of the Federation. Overstuffed couches and planter boxes flowing with flowering vines were mounted on every wall except the one that opened into a round courtyard. A burbling, multitiered fountain surrounded by gardens textured with ferns, trees and lacy crimson ground cover provided a pleasant view from every apartment.

The three stories of the *Defiant* crew's rooms extended off the courtyard like spokes of a wheel, providing them easy, private access to each other. Dax and Vaughn's quarters were on the level above Shar. Several times already, the commander and the lieutenant had ascended and descended the stairs situated off to the right of Shar's courtyard wall. Many of his crewmates had lounged by the fountain reading or chatting, enjoying the view of the stars through the clear dome overhead. General consensus seemed to be that the housing conditions were making this unplanned mission detour more palatable.

As had tended to happen on this mission, Shar's thoughts strayed home whenever he had empty time. Every day since last seeing his bondmates on Deep Space 9, he found himself yearning for them, and for the intimacy of the *shelthreth* that he'd denied the entire bondgroup by accepting this assignment to the Gamma Quadrant. And Thriss . . . if he allowed his thoughts to linger too long on her, he knew he'd lose his ability to think. *Thriss would love it here on Luthia . . .* He stopped that thought before it went any further: staying focused on his research into the Cheka and their weapon was his best recourse against loneliness.

The courtyard doors parted, admitting the sounds of bleeting avians, trickling water and the brush of soft footfalls. Shar expected to see Nog and started when he recognized his rescuer from this afternoon, the Yrythny delegate. In the lavender light of Luthia's dusk, Keren stood in shadow, the edges of her face eerily translucent, but her energy—unmistakable. *What could she possibly want? Maybe she's mistaken my quarters for Ezri's, right above me,* he thought.

"I've come with answers, Ensign ch'Thane," she said airily, her draping clothes rustling as she walked. She first opened the sleeproom door and then the closet.

"My roommate isn't here, Delegate," Shar told her, wondering what she'd come to tell him that required privacy.

"Excellent. Then you can come with me without being missed."

After the dinner-hour controversy, Vaughn had ordered all personnel to minimize unsupervised contact with the Yrythny until the "Lieutenant Dax situation," as it had come to be referred to, was resolved. "I need to check with my commander, he'd—"

"Don't." She held up a hand. "Please trust me. All I want is for you to see the other side."

"The other side of what?"

"Of this. Of Luthia. Of my people." Keren dropped down on the couch beside him. "Our city is abuzz with talk about the Other sending a Third. There are those who see it as a sign, others as a Houseborn trick. It's not your commander's fault that you've only dealt, thus far, with the Houseborn leadership. They know little of my people's truth, our history, our concerns. And that's why I've come."

Shar could see why she was a politician: she was a persuasive orator. Perhaps this was what his *zhavey* had been like when she was younger. She didn't seem duplicitous, and she *had* saved his life. Commander Vaughn's instructions notwithstanding, perhaps this was an opportunity to find other resources in Luthia, outside official channels, that might help his shipmates. Shar decided to trust her.

"Very well," he said.

She tossed a thin, heather-brown cloak at him; like hers, it featured a large hood and fastened at the neck. She also provided him with Yrythny-style footwear in lieu of his boots. The thin slippers, comprised of fabric tops laced together with roughened, leathery skins for the sole, would be virtually soundless as they walked. The need for such attire was obvious: to avoid drawing attention to himself or to Keren. Once he'd fastened the cloak and pulled the hood up over his head, flattening his antennae among his locks as he did so, Keren brought a finger to her lips and gestured for Shar to follow her. Slipping through the courtyard, the leaf fringes of rangy trees provided additional cover. Vanìmel's second moon had risen, casting cold pale light over their path.

"You can't seriously think this idea has merit, Dax," Vaughn said, extending his legs onto the coffee table. He sipped his brandy and waited for her reply.

Ezri, hands knotted behind her, walked the room.

Was this the third or fourth time through this conversation? For his part, Julian seconded Vaughn's opinion, but wasn't about to do so in front of Ezri. She would see it as a personal betrayal, when in reality it was a question of propriety. Starfleet regulations, to say nothing of the Prime Directive, provided narrow criteria for any kind of intervention in a non-Federation world. Because he outranked her, technically, Julian could voice his objections without subverting her position, but he knew Vaughn would do a far better job than he would at pointing this out.

"Look, I know this is a little out of the ordinary," Dax said, continuing to pace. "But I've been going over this in my head since dinner, and I'm just starting to wonder if maybe we're being a little too quick to dismiss the idea. After all, they were the ones asking for my help. Given the aid that they're providing us, is what they're asking really so out of the question?"

"You're talking about helping to facilitate a fundamental change to their societal structure," Vaughn said. "There are protocols in place for such an undertaking, and for good reasons."

"But according to Jeshoh, that change has already been taking place for centuries. Whatever the underlying reasons for this schism between the Houseborn and the Wanderers, these people know they have a problem. They want help solving it. All I'd be offering is the benefit of an outside perspective."

Vaughn sighed. "Let's not kid ourselves, Dax. Your 'outside perspective' is going to be viewed by these people as *guidance*. They already see you, you'll pardon the expression, as a prophet. Someone who's come to impart otherworldly wisdom. That just seems like the wrong place to begin a relationship with the Yrythny. If there's to be a solution to their internal dilemma, wouldn't it be more meaningful for them to find it, rather than as a pronouncement from on high?"

"The Yrythny are facing crises on many fronts," Ezri persisted. "We're already working with them to develop a defense against the Cheka. How is what I'm proposing to do any worse? And besides—if Julian's right, the Yrythny species owes its very existence to outside intervention. Hell, we all do, don't we? As individuals and as entire species, the people of the Federation are who they are today because of how they've influenced each other. That's not interference, that's *life*."

Vaughn rubbed his temples. "God, I hate arguing about the Prime Directive." He looked across the room. "Well, Doctor? You've been uncharacteristically quiet this evening. Do you have an opinion on this?"

From the look on Vaughn's face, the commander knew precisely what he was doing in asking for Julian's opinion. Without meeting Ezri's eyes, Julian cleared his throat. "I think there are valid points on both sides of the argument," he said neutrally. "If we go forward with this idea, I believe the best course would be simply to make the Yrythny aware of their options by showing them historical precedents from our own databases, and then leaving the decision up to them as to whether any of those is right for Vanìmel."

Vaughn looked back at Ezri. "That actually sounds reasonable to me. Dax?"

Ezri was frowning at Julian. "If it comes up tomorrow, sir, I'll follow the plan we've discussed."

"Thank you, Lieutenant," Vaughn said, rising from the couch. "I'm going to check in with Nog before I call it a night. Get some rest, both of you. Tomorrow will be a long day." He let himself out the balcony door.

Julian steeled himself, waiting for Vaughn's footsteps to fade away, knowing as soon as they did . . .

"Thanks for your support there, *Doctor!*" Ezri slouched into an overstuffed armchair designed for the long-legged Yrythny. Her feet dangled above the floor.

"Let's distinguish between my support for you as my first officer and my support for you personally—"

"Don't you dare hide behind our relationship! You should have more confidence in me!"

"What are you talking about? Of course I have confidence in you. But what does that have to do with ... wait a minute." Julian stared hard at Ezri; he could almost see her mind spinning a plot. "You think you could mediate this conflict, don't you?"

Ezri didn't answer.

"You do!" Julian exclaimed. "I can't believe this. You really think you can do it, don't you? No challenge is too great for Ezri Dax."

"I don't know what you're talking about."

"Oh, I think you do," Julian said. "This whole thing started when Commander Jast was killed. Ever since then, you've been relying more and more on your past lives. This isn't you, Ezri!"

"And just how the hell would *you* know?" Ezri snapped. "Let me clue you in on something: Before I was joined, I was a damn good officer. Maybe not as stellar as the superhuman Doctor Julian Subatoi Bashir, but as Ensign Ezri Tigan I was levelheaded, assertive, even ambitious. Then I become the unplanned ninth host of Dax, and for the first time in my life, I don't know who I am anymore. *That's* the Ezri you got to know, my love. And now, when I've finally figured out how to integrate my past lives and apply them to my own personal evolution, you think I'm not myself. But what you're not getting is that the Jadzia you were getting to know that first year, the one who hesitated, and got nervous and spacesick all the time—*she* wasn't me."

Julian looked away for a moment, then forced himself to meet her eyes. "You said Jadzia," he said quietly.

"What?" Ezri snapped.

"You referred to yourself as Jadzia just now."

Ezri stared back uncertainly, obviously replaying the conversation in her mind. "That was an honest mistake."

Julian nodded. "I know it was. Because as a doctor who's spent years studying Trill symbiosis, I know that in an unplanned joining, it can take quite a while for the host to find her equilibrium. So I'll ask you just one question, and then I'll let the matter drop. Do you really think you've found yours?"

When Ezri declined to answer, Julian wondered if he'd made a mistake confronting her with this tonight. "Look, it's been a stressful day for both of us. Maybe we're both not ourselves tonight. We'll be more clearheaded in the morning. Let's go to bed."

"Excellent suggestion." She shuffled off to the sleeproom.

Julian waited for a proper interval to pass before following after her, knowing he probably wouldn't be counting her spots tonight. He heard her toss her combadge on a table, kick off her boots, unfasten her uniform. *Now would be good.* When he reached the doorway, Ezri was waiting. She threw a cushion at him.

"What?" He clutched the pillow against his chest.

"Get some rest. Captain's orders," she said, and locked the door.

Shar tripped on the uneven floor gratings. Every other step, he bumped into cloaked Yrythny, streaming out of homes and work. The Old Quarter hummed with night activity. Shar and Keren descended a wide stair into a central plaza, joining the sea of people flowing in and out of archways. Shoppers lined up at merchant stalls and booths; artisans and performers squeezed into spaces not occupied by food carts boasting leaf-wrapped fish grilling over sage-fragrant coals or ropes of bulbous root vegetables dangling on hanging racks. A hidden puppeteer manipulated his carved, brightly painted creations for a group of enraptured children, while a lute-playing musician accompanied his tale. With their hoods up and in the poor lighting, no one noticed Shar or Keren.

He followed Keren to a tapestry shop tucked in a crooked back alley. Pushing aside the weighty rug-door, Keren and Shar ducked inside the dusky shop. With tables and cabinets piled high with fabric wares, Shar could barely see around the pyramids of dry goods emanating mildew and dust. The Yrythny attending the virtually empty store ignored them, continuing to enter information into a computer terminal on his countertop. Keren picked through hanging tapestries lining the back wall, lifting a particularly worn-looking one, examining a price marked on the back and moving to the next one. What she hoped to accomplish by taking him shopping wasn't yet clear to Shar. He opened his mouth to tell her so, when, after she'd studied a massive, wall-size tapestry with rotted-out fringes, she vanished. Peering under the tapestries on both sides and behind him, Shar failed to locate her. He duplicated Keren's actions: lifting a corner of the massive, moss-green tapestry, tilting his head to read the price and—*swoosh*—the floor spun, and he found himself standing in a corridor crammed with Yrythny, cloaked like him.

Uncertain as to what he was supposed to do next, he hung back until he felt Keren's hand gripping his arm. The crowd propelled them into what must be the tapestry shop's warehouse, where the Yrythny sat on a dozen or more metal benches. Other than the scrape of bench legs on the floor, the rustling of cloaks and the occasional whisper, the room was quiet. Though the mottled light obscured his ability to distinguish bodies, Shar guessed there were almost a hundred in the room.

He and Keren secured a spot near the back, and waited as the seats slowly filled to capacity. Finally, when it appeared that not one more body could be squeezed into the musty room, an individual seated close to the front rose.

"Aliens have come to Luthia," the leader began. "We have been assured that these strangers are not agents of the Cheka, and there are those who believe the strangers—one in particular—have been brought here by the Other to help us find peace with our Houseborn siblings. I for one am skeptical. This could very well be yet another Houseborn attempt to lull us into passivity so they can find our group and institute a crackdown. We need to have a strategy in place for dealing with either possibility."

A woman in front of Shar stood up. "We should at least consider the possibility that the situation is exactly as it's been described to us—that these aliens have come to us in need after being caught by one of the Cheka traps meant for us. As strangers to this region of space, they're uniquely positioned to view our dilemma impartially. Perhaps the Other did indeed lead them to us. In which case, the rash actions our people took when they arrived may have already damaged our cause. Perhaps as they learn more about our plight—"

"And how precisely will they do that?" someone else jeered. "The strangers won't be allowed to see us. The Houseborn will keep them away from the Old Quarter because it is squalid and dirty. The strangers won't talk to the house servants and the *shmshu* herders and the fishers. They'll be trotted around to the intelligentsia who, fearing the loss of their lifestyles, will minimize the seriousness of our plight."

For the first time, Shar wondered who from the mob was in the room. He hunched over, tucked his feet under the bench and hoped his alien presence would go unnoticed. His antennae twitched with the conflicted emotions in the room.

A new speaker began, "I came out of House Fnorol in the East Sea. Until twenty years ago, the Elders eviscerated Wanderer females as they came of mature age, justifying their actions because it prevented them from joining their 'superior' Houseborn sisters in the spawning waters." Shar could hear the sneer underlying his bitter words. "Those that weren't maimed, died. There's no way our esteemed Assembly Chair will share that part of our history with the strangers." And he sat down.

"What about the burnings! They came through our villages and burned them to the ground!"

"Our younglings were starved—"

"—beaten with clubs when they were found to be Wanderer young—"

One after another, speakers rose, testifying to mutilation and slaughter with such matter-of-factness that Shar could barely imagine the scope of their experiences—their histories. As quick as his mind was, Shar found himself struggling to process what he heard. He searched for something inside himself that would allow him to understand such atrocities.

"Information about atrocities committed against us can't come from us directly," the meeting leader argued. "The Upper Assembly can discredit it as the ranting of militants, and not history. The fact that we can't carry arms or defend ourselves, even when we serve on starships—is obvious. Starvation, repression—during the Black Time, slavery—those things will be even harder to bring to light."

A Yrythny sitting several benches away from Shar sprang to his feet and rushed to the front of the room, his body quivering with anxiety. "I say we forget about the strangers. They're of no consequence. We may have another Black Time if the Cheka barricades don't come down soon. The Houseborn *will* starve us to save their own, be sure of it."

"Or they'll kill us. Round us up and slaughter us so our hungry mouths don't take food from theirs," another agreed.

The last comment provoked a wave of whispering, stopped only when the meeting leader demanded order by rapping a scepter against the podium. "Enough! We have eyes and ears in many places. Mass murder won't come upon us unawares, but the Houseborn may appoint these strangers to decide our fate before tomorrow if we aren't careful."

Keren stirred beside him. Shar wasn't surprised when she worked her way down the row, through the center aisle and to the front. She threw back her hood, revealing her face. Audible gasps sounded from every corner.

"I make no pretense as to my identity. You all know I am one of you," she said, calmly. "I believe that the strangers coming may be for our good. We have struggled since the Archipelago Wars to wrestle rights away from the Houseborn and we are still far from finding equality with them." She paused, directing her gaze at the floor for a moment before returning her attention to the crowd. Her eyes moved from row to row, seeking personal contact with each listener as she spoke. "My time to go into the waters is coming, but because I am a Wanderer, I will be denied that opportunity during the Homecoming fifteen days hence.

"Instead, I will present myself to the physicians, receive my injection and go about my life pretending that I don't want or need to go into the waters." Keren's steady voice was heavy with sorrow. "And I will be living a lie. I deserve to take a consort, to add to the next generation. I believe our contact with the strangers may make that and many more things possible."

"How do you know they can be trusted?" the leader asked.

She stepped behind the podium. Resting a hand on each side of the rostrum, Keren surveyed the crowds. "I've dealt with them. They don't even come from this part of our galaxy. They live tens of thousands of light-years from here. Knowing nothing of our history, they can look at both sides impartially. Who else among those that we trade with, that we exchange culture and knowledge with, can make that claim? None." Her eyes finally found Shar, willing him to lift his eyes and meet hers; he complied and held her gaze, unwavering.

"Who knows if these strangers have been brought here by the Other? There's no question that we face perilous times. The blockades may turn Houseborn against Wanderer after centuries of relative peace. We have neither the arms nor the resources to fight them, but we are being swept by currents that will decide our fate, one way or the other. The strangers may be our last chance." Keren spoke as if to Shar directly, as if she sat at his elbow and whispered her words for him alone. He was transfixed.

4

When the turbolift doors closed, Ro requested the Promenade. She scowled at the universe in general, wanted to bang her forehead a few times, but settled for resting her head against the wall and closing her eyes. Seeing Gul Macet, Ambassador Lang and their "delegation" of soldiers had triggered a brain stem reaction: being hunted like prey. That her next turn would find her face-to-face with a resettlement camp guard prepared to clamp holding irons on her wrists and haul her off to be beaten. It was easier with the Maquis because she'd rarely had to stare down her enemy; the covert, anonymous nature of their war assured that. Now, she counted on the traveling time between the outer edge of the habitat ring and her upper core office to cushion her jangling nerves.

Conditioned response, Ro reminded herself. The reason her advanced tactical instructors gave repeatedly while drilling the class through every permutation of every worst-case scenario conceivable—so when you're staring your worst nightmare in the face, your training, not your instincts, takes over.

"Welcome to Deep Space 9, I'm Chief of Security, Lieutenant Ro," she recalled saying as she nodded a courteous greeting to the Cardassian, Macet. *Kira wasn't kidding about the family resemblance.* When he opened his mouth to speak it was every propaganda holovid from her childhood. The same elongated syllables she'd heard announcing "the unfortunate need for ration cuts" or that "strained resources forbade the distribution of vaccines to afflicted provinces." And she pushed back an instinctual inclination to spit at his feet.

This. Isn't. Dukat. She'd repeated the words in her mind each time she found herself staring at him. She tried focusing on the tufts of hair on his chin, as if the cosmetic difference could trick her psyche into accepting Macet. Her mouth had parroted all the proper polite inquiries she'd heard employed on occasions such as these. Maybe she'd picked up niceties via osmosis from Troi and Picard. The whole *Enterprise* crew had been so damn polite! *"I hope your trip went well." "Radiation in the Denorios Belt often sends false sensor readings this time of year." "We've secured quarters in the habitat ring for the senior members of your party—oh no, it isn't any problem. More convenient access to the meeting rooms than having to come down from the docking ring every few hours."* What she wanted to say was "Get the hell off my station and stay off."

She had searched Macet's face for evidence that justified her fears and found nothing there but even-tempered professionalism—maybe even good humor. Did those traits prove he wasn't Dukat? She'd seen the propaganda. Dukat allegedly loved children and small animals. He was an excellent father. Surely he couldn't authorize the wholesale slaughter of an entire camp accused of aiding the resistance? Hah! Wasn't Lang a former member of the Cardassian News Service, a.k.a. the empire's propaganda machine? All of it felt a bit too coincidental for Ro to be comfortable.

Give her a day alone with him. Hell, give her an *hour* alone with him and she'd figure out the truth. Assurances from the Ghemor regime and DNA tests might support Macet's claim to be who he said he was, but in a universe that already contained changelings, mind-altering entities, and even less explainable phenomena, how could anyone ever be truly sure of him?

Ro's stare must have lingered on Macet for a long while before she noticed the small, slender figure clothed in a vivid periwinkle blue gown standing beside him. She didn't recoil from Lang's proffered hand. The gesture surprised her: Cardassians didn't, as a rule, shake hands. In Ro's experience, such a greeting came more commonly among Federation types than from the austere Cardassians. Clasping both her hands around Ro's, Lang thanked her for accommodating them on such short notice. Strangely, the ambassador's fingers on Ro's wrist recalled the pleasant touch of cool water. In her experience, cold Cardassian hands usually meant death, or at least the promise of it.

Lang had issued the order to Macet's men to disarm before she would permit them to continue beyond the airlock. Ro had witnessed their puzzled expressions as Macet walked down their line, equipment satchel proffered— their barely camouflaged resentment when he sealed the bag and sent it back into the *Trager* with one of his men. Understanding that Macet could have just as easily disarmed his men while shipboard, Ro recognized the gesture for what it was: a move to placate her defenses. They had submitted, Ro imagined resentfully, to Lang's demand for absolute silence while the party moved from the disembarking area to the habitat ring. As she guided the group through the least traversed corridors, Ro observed the ambassador surveying each doorway and dark hall ahead of them. And while Lang's hands rested, deceptively relaxed, at her sides, the tension in her thumb and forefinger indicated she wasn't quite as willing to embrace the passivity she required from Macet's men; Ro would bet the house that hidden beneath the rustling folds of her gown, Lang had a weapon. *She's on as high alert as we are. She's as concerned about Bajorans coming unhinged as Kira is about possible Cardassian treachery.* Ro had made a conscious decision to let her guest's infraction of protocol pass without comment—carrying weapons aboard the station was forbidden save for Militia and Starfleet personnel, and authorized visitors.

Ro had found her guest's wariness reassuring: at least neither party labored under the pretense that a meeting between former enemies was anything normal.

Lang must have noticed Ro's scrutiny because she had quickly said, "Reconnaissance is an old habit. You don't live most of your adult life under the threat of arrest or assassination without assuming an enemy with a weapon lurks in every shadow."

"I know something of that myself," Ro had answered.

Lang's expression had softened, a touch of humor in her eyes. "Somehow, that doesn't surprise me."

A smile crossed Ro's face now as she replayed the scene in her mind, realizing that was the moment she decided that she liked Lang. Once their mutual mistrust had been established, Ro had felt freer to make small talk, mention Lang's previous experience on the station. Traversing a particularly obscure access tunnel crossover bridge, Lang had recalled how she used this route to deliver confidential reports to her underground contacts. Ro made a mental note to add semiregular sensor sweeps of the corridor to the surveillance profiles. In her turn, Ro reciprocated with an anecdote or two about her Maquis days. Lang had laughed at more than a few of her tales. Fringe rebel groups, regardless of ideology, tended to have characteristics in common.

Macet had remained quiet for the duration of their walk, something Ro felt grateful for. He must have sensed her reaction whenever he spoke; she hoped she didn't physically recoil for that would be an undeservedly rude response to a guest. But until the cadence and timbre of his voice stopped causing her blood to boil, she was glad Macet kept his mouth shut.

Upon arriving at their quarters, Ro had briefed Lang and Macet on the extra security precautions Kira had ordered. Neither seemed particularly surprised; they exchanged a glance that informed Ro the Cardassians had contingency plans of their own. Layers upon layers of fear would have to be peeled away before her people and their former oppressors could have uninhibited rapport. Whatever mission Alon Ghemor had assigned Ambassador Lang must be critical to Cardassian interests. Otherwise, how could he justify a high-profile visit while relations between the two worlds remained tenuous at best? Shakaar's humanitarian initiatives had been a solid first step toward finding common ground, but Ro wasn't sure they were prepared to expand past them, especially with the Federation talks under way. *Damn Cardassians always have the worst timing.*

A metallic hum overtook the almost silent whirr of the turbolift. Ro turned toward the sound to see Taran'atar shimmering into visibility.

Ro frowned. "Don't I recall an order coming down from the colonel about your being shrouded in public places aboard the station? Namely, that you aren't supposed to be?"

"The enemy is here. I needed to assess them," he said, checking the charge on his phaser.

Ro shook her head. "The Cardassians aren't our enemies any longer. They've never been *your* enemy. Your people served alongside them in the war."

"Do you know their minds?" he asked, returning his sidearm to its holster.

"Bajorans aren't telepaths, if that's what you're asking," Ro said, hoping her glib answers would irritate Taran'atar enough that he wouldn't pursue this line of questioning.

If Taran'atar sensed Ro's discomfort, it didn't stop him from peppering her with questions. "Do you have knowledge of their goals—their strategy?" he persisted.

"I'm assuming they're here to meet with the First Minister, but outside that, no, I haven't tapped into their database or spied on their private discussions."

"Then they are your enemy. The unknown is always the enemy, Lieutenant," he said as if there was no arguing with his conclusions.

Much as his cold pragmatism felt far too absolute for these "enlightened" times, Ro had to admit she agreed with him. How else had she survived during her years with the Maquis? Most of her Maquis friends had been slaughtered by Cardassians or arrested by Starfleet. And yet, by the grace of some unknown power that she refused to believe was the Prophets, she stood here, in a Bajoran uniform, alive, free and physically unscathed. It was her steadfast refusal to trust anything or anyone that saved her. Or so she believed.

"All possibilities exist until a choice is made," Taran'atar continued, accepting her silence as a tacit endorsement. "Until the moment of choice, it's strategic to anticipate and plan for any potential outcome. It's how survival is assured."

"The odds of Bajor obtaining a safe, beneficial outcome will decrease if the Cardassians think we're luring them into a trap," she said, playing the opposition card.

"You are naïve, Lieutenant, if you assume that the Cardassians aren't luring *you* into a trap."

A soothing voice announced their arrival at the Promenade. Ro turned to look at the Jem'Hadar before she exited the lift. "Do you have business here? Or do you have more innocent civilians to spy on?"

"There is nothing here that concerns me. I will report my observations to the colonel at a later time." He appeared to be conducting a quick weapons assessment before, presumably, shrouding again.

How could he assume that blatantly disregarding orders was fine? Taran'atar was breaking a dozen rules Kira had laid down for him. "I'm telling her about your clandestine operation during my end-of-shift security briefing." She felt like an older sister tattling on an errant sibling.

"Do you think I would have showed myself to you if I had not wanted you to inform the colonel?"

Damn it all if he didn't just make me look stupid, Ro thought. The turbolift doors closed, leaving Ro a little bit grateful she didn't know where the Jem'Hadar was headed next. She didn't know whether to be comforted that someone, namely Taran'atar, on her side had sidestepped propriety for expediency, or annoyed that she hadn't had the guts to do it first. As she wove through the Promenade crowds toward her office, she continued contemplating his words. The unknown is always the enemy, he'd said. These people weren't unknown ... but everything she knew about them told her they were the enemy.

Sergeant Etana thrust a stack of reports into Ro's hand as she passed through the doors of the security office; Ro barely acknowledged her. Making peace with her own confused thoughts proved harder than wrestling down a Vicarian razorback. She hated admitting that Taran'atar more or less espoused her own suspicions. All her training, her years in Starfleet were supposed to have quashed her xenophobia. Nice to know her enlightened education amounted to something. She found her chair by rote, tapped in her passwords and called up her workfiles.

Inwardly, Ro sighed. She sorted through the memos queued up on her viewscreen. Opening those designated "urgent," she shuttled the others away until she was in the mood to deal with them. She'd always been cynical toward the old Federation philosophy about forgiving and forgetting because there were rarely assurances ahead of time that the enemy had replied in kind. Even the great negotiator himself, Jean-Luc Picard, had been deceived on occasion because he believed that those across the table from him told the truth simply because *he* told the truth. Hadn't she seen his dangerously trusting nature on their first mission together? And hadn't she herself exploited it on their last?

What a strange day this had become! A philosophical alliance between a Bajoran lieutenant and a Jem'Hadar soldier wasn't something Ro could have predicted a year ago. What isn't known is the enemy until proven otherwise. Ro had little experience to prove to her that Cardassians weren't the enemy. Even this group had yet to provide any details about why they had come.

She called up Lang's file to amend it with information about her present visit. Ro now had a lilting alto voice accompanying her mental picture of Lang. The viewscreen picture failed to capture Lang's incisive intelligence, her graceful carriage or ability to elucidate her hopes for the future of her people.

Ro would be lying if she didn't admit to enjoying her brief chat with Lang. After a few minutes of animated discussions with the ambassador, Ro considered that her own view of Cardassians as an aloof, calculating and cruel people might warrant an exception. Lang had a sense of humor; she questioned her people's nearly universal adherence to officially sanctioned views of government, religion and ethics. Her misgivings about Cardassians weren't entirely unlike Ro's concerns about the Bajoran tendency to mindlessly accept whatever the vedeks passed down to them without critically thinking through the rightness of those edicts. She found herself nodding in agreement with Lang's ideas without pausing to consider that these ideas came from a Cardassian.

In an impulsive moment, before she'd left the Cardassians to settle into their quarters, Ro had asked Lang to join her for drinks at Quark's sometime after dinner. She conceded her own naughty curiosity about Quark's reaction to seeing his old flame, elegant and beautiful as ever. But there was also her hope, however small, that she could, once and for all, eliminate the bitter taste of suspicion from her mouth, by proving Taran'atar, herself, and all those who lived in a place of mistrust and ignorance, wrong.

Councillor Charivretha zh'Thane sat taller in her chair, hoping to create the impression that she was listening attentively to the Bajoran trade minister. Her seasoned experience in surviving such meetings aided her attempts to focus, but enduring Minister Kren's nasal monotone for extended periods of time required more than her usual self-discipline. Unwilling to risk appearing impatient, Charivretha deigned to check the time; she guessed Minister Kren's accounting of Bajor's trade relationships with non-Federation worlds had been going on for two hours. His proposed solutions to amending those trade relationships once Bajor entered the Federation would account for another two hours. A suggestion to Second Minister Asarem Wadeen, who peripherally supervised Bajor's monetary and trade policies, that Minister Kren submit his remarks in text for subsequent sessions might be in order. Charivretha's two dozen or so counterparts appeared to be focused on the speaker. Perhaps it was the dual impact of Kren's nervous energy and vocal tones on her Andorian senses that made her restless. Or perhaps not: out of the corner of her eye, she noted the meeting's chair, Trill ambassador Seljin Gandres, dozing off in spite of Gandres's years dealing with the Pakleds on behalf of the Trill diplomatic corps.

Charivretha's antennae alerted her to her aide's presence; Thanis's relaxed energy patterns were distinctive in this tightly wound room. He whispered something in her ear, stepped back and waited for her response. *Damn. We're already working on the station instead of Bajor to accommodate my personal circumstances,* she thought. *If I keep asking for favors, I'll prompt more questions and curiosity—exactly what I'm trying to avoid. But this situation can't be helped.* She raised her placard, asking for recognition from the chair.

Gandres started, too relieved at Charivretha's interruption to be properly discreet. "Excuse me, Minister Kren, Councillor zh'Thane has asked to be recognized."

"A matter of personal concern has come to my attention. I'd like leave for the remainder of the hour, with the chair's approval," Charivretha asked.

Gandres picked up his wand and tapped the bell sitting on the table before him. "Chair calls a recess for all delegates. Session to be resumed at 1330."

While her colleagues and their aides milled around her, some lining up at the replicators, others starting preparations for their own remarks, Charivretha gathered her things and followed Thanis to the wardroom's antechamber where her visitor awaited.

Uncharacteristically, the usually composed Dizhei paced the length of the room. Her antennae tense, eyes bright with worry, Dizhei flew to Charivretha's side as soon as her elder entered. Before Dizhei could speak, Charivretha raised a hand for calm. "I'm assuming we have a situation with Thriss."

"It's not *a* situation, *Zhadi,* it's the ongoing situation. I'm so sorry to disturb you, but there was an incident with the cloth merchant an hour ago and I'm uncertain how to proceed," Dizhei said through short bursts of breath.

Sighing, Charivretha took a seat on one of the benches lining the waiting room. She patted the spot beside her, indicating to Dizhei to join her. Charivretha rested a hand on Dizhei's shoulder, making small, soft circles on her back. "Slow down, Dizhei. You'll faint."

Clenching and unclenching her hands, Dizhei leaned closer to Charivretha, allowing the young one to whisper her concerns. "I thought a distraction would help. She's done little but taunt poor Anichent about the lack of progress in his research—if you were to ask me, I think she's tampering with his data just to see if she can make him as irritable as she is, but I have no proof to support such allegations and even Thriss tends not to be cruel—"

"Dizhei, *shri'za,* " Charivretha implored, hoping her use of the endearment softened what she imagined was her own impatient tone. She also hoped it reminded her son's bondmate that they were not alone in this place, that discretion was paramount. "When your students misbehave, are you always so flustered?"

"I'm sorry, *Zhadi*. I see more than mere misbehavior from Thriss, and I fear where I see these behaviors leading."

"Explain," she prompted.

"We went out shopping today. I had read in the station announcements that a group of craftsmen from the Musilla province would be displaying their wares. I thought it might take her mind off—" she paused "—everything. She likes mingling with those of other cultures. Her *zhavey* is a textile artist and I thought she'd find an outing pleasant."

"And . . . ?"

"She found a piece of cloth—handwoven, exquisitely rich in color and detail. Seeing that it pleased her, I asked the merchant discreetly for a price—I thought I would surprise her with it as a gift. When he tried to take it away from her, telling her at my request that it wasn't for sale, she raged at him. 'How could he deny a soul her burial shroud? Was cruelty to widows part of his way of doing business?' I paid him the litas you left me and removed her from the shop as soon as I could."

"You did well. What do you require of me?" Charivretha squeezed Dizhei's leg affectionately.

"I believe we need to reconsider our plan to wait here until Shar returns," Dizhei answered confidently. "Anichent agrees."

Charivretha imagined how long Anichent and Dizhei had been planning on bringing this proposal to her before Thriss's behavior forced the issue. *The intimate associations of bondmates . . . I miss them,* she thought, remembering her own experiences. But sometimes bondmates lacked the objectivity to perceive the wisest course of action. "Didn't we all decide that being here when Shar comes back will improve the chances of his returning to Andor for the *shelthreth?*"

"Thriss is pained by the reminders of Thirishar that surround us, and yet she wallows in them. She, of all of us, insists on sleeping in his bed every night." Dizhei shook her head. "I can't help but think that perhaps, if we go home, Thriss can lose herself in her studies. Complete her medical training and start her residency sooner."

Charivretha considered her child's mate, imagining not for the first time how effective Dizhei must be in dealing with her pupils' overly concerned families. Not one for impulsivity, Dizhei had the most responsible nature of the four of them. She could be counted on to be rational under the most trying circumstances. And yet, here she sat, her flushed forehead and bloodshot eyes tangible evidence of emotional distress. If gentle Dizhei felt this undone by her predicament, Charivretha could hardly fathom what the moody Thriss might be capable of. One misstep and Shar's future could be jeopardized. The stakes could hardly be higher. *I wonder if all* zhaveys *go through this . . .*

As much as she appreciated the honor of Shar's being matched with a bondgroup, Charivretha found herself wishing, not for the first time, that Shar's DNA might have been compatible with one less volatile than Shathrissía zh'Cheen. Yes, Thriss's willowy fragility, unusual by Andorian standards, suited Shar's tendency for appreciating the unconventional. He enjoyed being unique, embracing the less obvious choices, and Thriss certainly embodied that. Together, Shar and Thriss brought out the best and worst in each other. At the time she met Thriss, a scrawny, wide-eyed thing of seven, Charivretha had no idea what a force to be reckoned with was sweeping into her life.

It was during Shar's Heritage studies. The students were learning the first forms of an ancient festival dance, one they'd be called on to perform at the Time of Knowing. Sitting in on her *chei*'s class, Charivretha had remembered her own Knowing ceremony—the subsequent celebration after she'd learned the names of her bondmates; her life had been redefined during those hours. She had recalled her own youthful excitement while observing her *chei* and his classmates, including Thriss, standing off to the side in the shadows. Considering the group as a whole, Charivretha had noted how Thriss's plainness, her homeliness, distinguished her from the rest. And then, on her cue, Thriss had assumed her place in the form, had risen up onto her toes and had curled her arm over her head with such delicacy and loveliness that Charivretha's breath caught in her throat. Dozens of pairs of childish eyes had focused on the ethereal Thriss, each wondering if she would someday belong to them.

Subsequent years brought Thriss official reprimands for misbehavior in class—mostly for inappropriate displays of temper—but she had remained well liked by her peers, gaining a folk-hero–like reputation for speaking out against perceived injustice. All her peers valued her opinions and desired her approval as they copied her hairstyles and the clothes she wore. When she staged a sit-in protesting Andorian communities encroaching on animal habitats, half the students joined her.

Except Shar.

Shar's seeming obliviousness to Shathrissía ought to have been Charivretha's first clue that he felt differently about her than he did about his other bondmates. He never sought out her company, never invited her to study. For her purposes at the time, Charivretha found Shar's disinterest a relief: it decreased the likelihood that her *chei* would find the trouble that followed Thriss wherever she went.

When, five years later, Shar received Thriss as his bondmate, Charivretha still refused to worry because the bondgroup was a strong one. Shar instantly adored Dizhei, as everyone who met her did; with Anichent, he found a kinship of minds unlike any he'd ever experienced. Anichent and Shar quickly became inseparable. Charivretha often saw Shar and Anichent shyly holding hands during study time; Shar's tender displays of affection warmed Charivretha as few things did.

Though he treated Thriss honorably, Shar appeared indifferent to her company. Because Shar tended to run counter to whatever trends and fads existed among his peers, Charivretha assumed he ignored Thriss because of her popularity. Thriss tried, but failed, to provoke any substantive reaction from him. In retrospect, Charivretha could see that Shar had conscientiously avoided Thriss, taking deliberate steps to assure their school schedules, their extracurricular hours and their mealtimes didn't intersect. *As his* zhavey, *I should have known intuitively why he behaved the way he did: Shar ignored Thriss to avoid confronting the powerful attraction he felt for her. Years, I wasted years that I might have used to derail what proved to be the inevitable explosion between my chei and his lover . . . if I could have stopped them, if I could have foreseen what they would do and how irrational they could be . . .*

Knowing all of the situation's complexities, Charivretha had played a dangerous card in bringing Thriss to Deep Space 9. Ideally, Thriss's ability to insinuate herself into Shar's emotions should have given him an incentive to bow out of the Gamma Quadrant mission. Instead, Thriss's appearance had reinforced the very decision Charivretha hoped to reverse. Shar had accurately perceived that his best chance at pursuing his misguided quest to find an external solution to the Andorians' spiral toward extinction—as if he, brilliant as he was, could solve a problem his people had struggled with for so long—was to go as far from Thriss as possible, as fast as he could travel. *The Gamma Quadrant certainly meets those criteria,* she thought bitterly. *Now what to do with Dizhei? If Thriss's outbursts threaten Dizhei's equilibrium, we might face losing more than Shar. . . .*

Thanis discreetly crouched down beside Charivretha, informing her that the trade agreement transitioning session would be resuming shortly. Did she need to ask for more time from Ambassador Gandres? Charivretha shook her head no. With all the tenderness she could muster, Charivretha gathered Dizhei in her arms, cradling her against her shoulder. Beneath her own trembling hands, Charivretha felt the labored breathing that marked Andorian keening. Resisting the impulse to give into her tumultuous feelings, she focused her energy on reassuring Dizhei, cursing her selfish offspring. Where had she failed in conveying to Shar the seriousness of his obligations? "I will do what I can," she whispered into Dizhei's hair. "I promise."

As Ro prepared her end-of-shift report, she noted grimly that while the Cardassian presence on the station hadn't produced a marked increase in security problems, the imposition of yellow-alert protocols had. One of her corporals had just been admitted to Dr. Tarses's care. The Klingon captain of a vessel loaded with Cardassian humanitarian aid had charged the security officer with a *d'k tahg,* when, under orders, the deputy prevented the *J'chang* from launching. Other than reissuing her earlier statements about changes in station security, adding random, full-body scans, and making certain that all pilots arriving at or departing from the station were aware of those changes, Ro felt there was little else to do until everyone adjusted to the new rules. People typically hated change.

A beep from her console alerted her to the approach of a visitor to the security office. Ro recognized her through the door windows immediately: Councillor Charivretha zh'Thane.

Ro rose from her chair as the councillor entered, but zh'Thane quickly indicated she expected Ro to sit down. The councillor took her place in the visitor's chair, sitting regally straight, hands folded in her lap; she exemplified poise.

Before today, Ro had spoken to zh'Thane only a handful of times, and on all those occasions she found the diplomat to be pleasant enough, but imperious. She could only imagine what Shar must have felt growing up with such a formidable presence to contend with. Even now, in her office, Ro felt zh'Thane was holding court.

"I bring the accolades of Admiral Akaar, Lieutenant Ro. He's pleased with Colonel Kira's decision to increase security. He also admires how swiftly and capably it's been handled," she said, a slight tremor in her voice.

Knowing Akaar's reservations about her competence, Ro found zh'Thane's words to have little more substance than polite pleasantries. What intrigued her was the crack in zh'Thane's perfectly composed veneer when, for an instant, she showed vulnerability. *In good time,* Ro thought. Not wanting to offend her guest, she offered a half-smile.

Zh'Thane replied by deliberately closing her eyes, allowing her long gray lashes to flutter politely. "I'm sorry to hear of your corporal's injuries. I hope it's nothing serious."

Ro was impressed with how in-the-know zh'Thane appeared to be: the incident with the *J'chang* had occurred in the previous hour. "Dr. Tarses will release him to his quarters this evening. Just keeping him under precautionary observation for the time being. Thanks for asking." Assuming zh'Thane had more pressing concerns than passing on Admiral Akaar's compliments, she made the opening move. "Now, what can I do for you, Councillor?"

"The yellow-alert status. It's my understanding that all starship departures and arrivals require a day, sometimes longer, for clearance," she said, perusing a padd she'd apparently had tucked inside her sleeve.

"That's correct. We felt that we needed to screen for potential security risks, biohazards or other illegal activities that might threaten the various diplomatic goings-on." And her staff—already putting in extra shifts since Akaar's arrival—felt burdened by the pressure of their added responsibilities. *Councillor zh'Thane had better not add to their load,* Ro thought defensively.

"A plan must exist to accommodate emergencies. Something involving Admiral Akaar or First Minister Shakaar, for instance." Her antennae curled slightly forward.

"Not going to happen. The same rules that apply to the lowliest scrap scow apply to the admiral and the first minister. Barring full-on military assault or medical emergency—"

Zh'Thane pounced. "I require a medical exception for my vessel, Lieutenant."

"Why?"

"That's a private matter."

Ro refused to budge. "Without signed medical orders, your ship will have to queue up behind everyone else."

"I'm a Federation councillor, Lieutenant," zh'Thane said quietly, though the warning in her tone was implicit. "You can take me at my word." The councillor leaned forward as she regarded Ro challengingly across the desk.

Placidly, Ro met zh'Thane's stare. Tough talk and aggressive body language never fazed her. "If I had a bar of latinum for every VIP who asked for special privileges, I'd be retired on Risa by now. We're in a state of heightened alert." Why was it that important people always assumed the rules didn't apply to them?

"The war's over. I think we're reasonably safe. Aren't you being overly cautious?" zh'Thane snapped.

"If I hadn't experienced an unprovoked Jem'Hadar attack fairly recently, I might agree with you. Our known enemies might be accounted for—it's the unknown enemies we need to guard against." The casualties, the damage to the station's primary systems, and the ensuing panic all loomed large in her recent memory; none of it would Ro want to experience again. If safety required inconvenience, she would happily be the enforcer.

"Perhaps I should speak with Colonel Kira," zh'Thane said.

"That's certainly your privilege. But if you have a genuine medical concern that may require bypassing our security measures, the colonel will require the same answers I do."

Zh'Thane appeared to waver indecisively. "This isn't—" she began, then started again. "Lieutenant, believe me when I tell you I'm not insensitive to the station's security concerns or your responsibilities. But the situation—" She cut herself off again and closed her eyes, then took a deep breath as if to calm herself. When her eyes opened again, they seemed pleading. "Please don't require this of me."

"With respect, Councillor," Ro said gently, "I can help you only if you can help me to understand the situation."

"I know," zh'Thane said. Hands squeezing the armrests, the councillor's upper body and antennae tensed, until she exhaled deeply. "It's simply that I've been trying to convince myself that taking an outsider into our confidence wouldn't be necessary. I realize now how foolish that was. But you must understand that that level of trust doesn't come easily to many of my people, Lieutenant. If I am open with you, can you assure me that what I say will remain between us?"

Ro stared at zh'Thane, a little stunned to see how fragile and powerless she suddenly seemed. *Whatever's going on, it's obviously mortifying her to do this.* "I have no desire to violate your privacy, Councillor. Perhaps you *should* speak with the colonel directly—"

"No," zh'Thane said firmly. "It's my understanding that you're Thirishar's friend. He admires and respects you. That will make this easier for me, but I need to know that you'll keep this in confidence."

With a deliberate move of her hand, Ro tapped in the commands engaging her office's privacy shields. She rarely used the shield, saving it for interrogations or clandestine informants reporting in. "I will, unless doing so somehow compromises the safety of this station."

Zh'Thane nodded. "Acceptable. . . . You're aware of Thirishar's bondmates being aboard the station?"

"Yes," Ro said. "I was the one who arranged for their stay in Shar's quarters during his absence, per his request."

"For which I know they're most grateful. Having any small aspect of his life to cling to has been a great comfort to them these past weeks. You see . . . by accepting his current assignment, Shar has put his well-being, and that of his bondmates, at risk."

Ro frowned. "In what way?"

"He was supposed to come home!" zh'Thane hissed. "I don't speak of a cultural obligation that's at odds with his Starfleet career, although that aspect of it certainly can't be overlooked in all of this. I speak now of biological necessity."

Ro tried to intuit from zh'Thane's hints what she might be implying, and became alarmed. She knew that some life-forms had an imperative to return to their place of birth in order to continue the reproductive cycle of their species, only to die if they failed. "I've heard that Vulcans—"

"This isn't like that," zh'Thane said. "You're perhaps imagining that Shar has put himself in danger by denying an inner drive to procreate, but that isn't the case. In fact, the situation is, in many ways, far more grave than that, with potentially farther-reaching consequences.

"The Andorian species, you may know, has four sexes, none of which is truly male or female as you define them. Our interactions with the many two-sex species that comprise the majority of sentients with whom we traffic has led us to accept male and female pronouns for simplicity's sake, and because it helps us avoid unwelcome questions about our biology.

"Because our procreative process requires chromosomes from four parents, it is, as I'm sure you gather, a very complicated matter for four individuals who are compatible—genetically and emotionally—to come together to produce a child."

Complicated is an understatement, Ro thought. *It sounds damn near impossible.* "Councillor, forgive me, but . . . I don't understand how such a biological system could sustain itself."

"It doesn't," zh'Thane said quietly.

That was when Ro began to understand what the Andorians were facing, even as zh'Thane continued to spell it out.

"Our species is dying, Lieutenant. It wasn't always this way, but certain . . . changes . . . have led to our present dilemma, which neither Andorian nor Federation science has been able to solve. The best we've been able to do is adjust ourselves to our circumstances. Our culture is now defined by the need to do whatever is necessary to ensure the survival of our species. Successful conception requires careful planning. As many variables as can be controlled, are. But matching together the most viable quads is a difficult undertaking. This is so much more complicated than . . . Do you know that within minutes of Shar's birth, his DNA map was entered into our master files with the express purpose of being matched to those he was most compatible with, genetically? He belonged to something bigger than he was before he even had a self-concept!

"Thirishar believes we are simply delaying the inevitable. And he's right. We take our obligation to produce offspring more seriously than any other aspect of our lives because our species is headed toward extinction. We have to do all that we can to assure our kind's survival until a solution can be found."

Ro watched zh'Thane's antennae twitch sharply with her every word, the councillor's agitation palpable.

"That's why you needed Shar to return home," Ro realized. "To join his bondmates in producing a child."

"Yes. In their late teens and early twenties, all fertile Andorians are obligated to return to Andor for the *shelthreth*—a period of time and a ritual akin to a wedding. If all goes well, the *shelthreth* results in conception and the bond-group's obligation to reproduce will be met. But time is an important factor as well. Individually, Andorians have only a five-year window of fertility. Thirishar and his bondmates are nearing the end of theirs. His stubborn refusal to come home and instead waste precious months in the Gamma Quadrant is putting them all dangerously close to missing their last opportunity to conceive.

"Perhaps you're wondering how tragic it can possibly be if one less child is born to us. But to my kind, every birth is important. Every new life is hope. And yet Thirishar, my own *chei*, doesn't see it this way." Zh'Thane shook her head. "There has never been a time in his life that he didn't have these obligations, and yet somehow, he thinks he's the exception. That the needs of his people have no hold on him!"

"Councillor, please—"

The knuckles of zh'Thane's hands turned white-blue. "He goes off on this quest of his, thinking he's doing what's best for all of us, without stopping to think that it might destroy everything his life is about! If the worst happens, all of it—Dizhei's students, Anichent's research, Thriss's medical studies, my career, will be worthless! Our work will have no meaning because we will have failed in our greatest purpose and obligation to our people."

"Has something happened medically with one of Shar's bondmates that compromises the *shelthreth?*" Ro prompted gently.

"My *zhri'za*. One of Shar's bondmates, Shathrissía. The stress of Shar's decision is having unforeseen—consequences. She has become emotionally unpredictable—possibly even unstable. I worry about what she might do if she loses control. If her equilibrium destabilizes any further, she will have to return to Andor."

"Why not make the arrangements and depart now, if you're so concerned?"

"Because it is still the best choice for the three of them to wait here until Thirishar returns," zh'Thane explained patiently. "Should the situation change, however, we might have to move swiftly, without having time to make the proper applications."

"Our medical staff has training in the physiologies of most Alpha Quadrant species," Ro offered kindly. "They might be able to help."

Zh'Thane's voice cracked and a wail-like sigh escaped her throat. "If only it were as simple as asking Dr. Tarses for a hypospray. Or finding a project to keep Thriss busy—perhaps sending her on a cultural tour of Bajor or to Cardassia to offer medical service. She tends to be mercurial, to change her mind at a moment's notice. If we can persuade her to listen to sense, she might agree to go home."

Ro considered how best to handle the situation. She'd always sensed something conflicted in Shar, simmering below the surface of his steadiness. And it was uncharacteristic of someone as skilled in negotiation as Councillor zh'Thane to become so overwrought without good cause. She went with her gut. "Without betraying your trust, I'll take this to Colonel Kira and let you know what she says. I'll get back to you once she's made her decision."

Likely embarrassed by the intensity of her outburst, zh'Thane refused to look at Ro. "Thank you, Lieutenant." She exited without a backward glance.

Ro spent the remaining few minutes of her shift considering how best to present zh'Thane's petition to Kira when her relief reported in. Sergeant Etana Kol nodded to Ro but scarcely said a word as she took Ro's place at the security desk. Etana hadn't been her usual jovial self since the *Defiant* departed; like several others in the station crew, the deputy had someone aboard *Defiant* whom she missed terribly. And from what Ro knew of the relationship, three months would be the longest time Kol and Krissten had been apart since they'd gotten together. *That must be hard. Still, Etana's not stupid. She must have known getting involved with a Starfleet officer might mean prolonged time apart.* "You okay, Kol?"

Etana looked up with a smile. Ro was impressed by how easily it seemed to fall into place. The sergeant shrugged. "Hate sleeping alone."

Ro smiled back. "Don't worry; when she gets back, you'll be annoyed you don't have the bed to yourself anymore."

Etana laughed. "You're probably right. Night, Lieutenant."

"G'night, Kol."

As she left the security office, Ro saw to her surprise that zh'Thane was still just outside, chatting pleasantly with Hiziki Gard, the Federation's security liaison and aide to the Trill ambassador. Ro nodded to Gard as she passed them, and gleaned from the few bits she overheard that zh'Thane's earlier angst had passed.

Was that whole thing an act? Ro wondered, stopping in front of the turbolift. As she reconsidered what she would say to Kira, Ro found herself wondering how much of zh'Thane's performance had been staged and how much had been genuine.

"Lieutenant."

Ro looked over her shoulder and saw the councillor standing alone again near the security office, Gard having apparently moved on.

"Thank you," zh'Thane mouthed soundlessly. Her eyes brimmed with pain for the briefest of moments before the composed politician's facade descended like a mask. Then she turned away, disappearing into the humanoid tide of the Promenade.

5

"Commander, I can't access the Defiant," Nog hissed.

What the hell is Nog doing in my room? Vaughn thought, eyelids fluttering as he bounced back and forth between half-sleep and wakefulness. He couldn't recall his dream save that his hair was the brown of his youth and there were swaying palm trees in the background. He thought Ruriko was there, but as always, he was unable to reach her.

"Commander, are you there?"

Blindly, Vaughn felt his way to the end table, groping for his combadge. When he clutched it in his hand, he pressed it and said, "The door won't open, Lieutenant?"

"Sir, there's a contingent of Yrythny soldiers here—with weapons. And they pointed them at me when I tried to board the ship."

Fully awake, Vaughn swore and sat up, reaching for his uniform. "I'll be right there, Nog. Vaughn out."

What a difference a few hours make! After the night's last debriefing, Vaughn had felt comfortable with how things stood—at least with Nog. The *Defiant*'s problems seemed cut and dried: if it's broken, fix it. Repairs would be complex—taking far longer than any of them desired—but the Yrythny had pledged to be generous with cooperation and resources. Maybe that was his mistake: assuming that the worst was past them. He'd served in Starfleet long enough to know that whenever a situation looked bleak, it was bound to be a veritable black hole before it improved. Nog and his team had even addressed his most pressing concern, the development of a theoretical model for a defense system against the Cheka weapon. *That alone should have tipped me off that this whole thing would be shot to hell before breakfast.*

Vaughn recalled that, after midnight, Julian had wandered up to the repair bay. Bashir, he knew, didn't need as much sleep as most humans, so Vaughn didn't look askance at the doctor's middle-of-the-night proposal to inventory sickbay. Anyone willing to work was welcome. In a flash of inspiration, Julian had suggested using the humanoid immune system as a model for a defensive weapon. The ideas tumbled out from there.

If the Cheka nanobots represented invading viruses and bacteria, then femtobots—even smaller and designed by the *Defiant* staff—could be used like the CD8+T and B cells deployed by humanoid bone marrow to gnaw through the viruses. Nog's plan called for maintaining a cloud of femtobots in stasis just beneath the ship's shield envelope. If *Defiant* tripped another web weapon, the femtobots would activate and attack as soon as the nanobots pierced the shields. Brilliant.

In theory.

The trick, of course, was that although it was well known that molecular cybernetics didn't stop at the nanite level, creating femtobots able to withstand the stress of the shield matrix *and* hard enough to pierce the nanobots was uncharted territory. The *Defiant* simply didn't possess the structural materials Nog and his engineers would need to make the plan work. Their computer simulations, run using variations of readily available materials, had all failed. Either the femtobots disintegrated in proximity to the shields, or the ship sustained critical damage due to delayed or partial deployment. The femtobots required something more resilient than *Defiant*'s replicators or her engineers could fabricate.

Even though a significant challenge awaited Nog, Vaughn hadn't been too worried. Nog's resourcefulness and innovative abilities never ceased to amaze him. Vaughn had instead assumed his biggest problem would be his hosts' hastily conceived notion that Dax should facilitate some mediation process between warring Yrythny factions.

Prime Directive and first contact issues aside—and his concerns regarding those protocols weren't exactly minor—Vaughn had reservations about letting Dax get mixed up in the Yrythny's internal politics. Despite her zeal and seriousness about her transfer to command—and the fact that her past-life experiences gave her unique advantages as his XO—nothing in the lieutenant's Starfleet background or his own interactions with her shouted that she ought to have her responsibilities broadened to include diplomacy. Granted, her counselor training lent her legitimate, professional expertise in the area of xenopsychology, but Vaughn still remembered Curzon Dax's questionable judgment during the Betreka affair, and the choices that had nearly gotten them both killed. Ezri wasn't Curzon, of course—not exactly—and while she was a quick study, Vaughn wasn't about to turn over the fate of a world poised on the brink of civil war to her, no matter what gods appeared to have ordained it.

Sprinting up the stairs that led to *Defiant*'s docking bay, Vaughn saw the problem immediately. Just as Nog had reported, a squadron of armed, uniformed Yrythny soldiers blocked the ship's airlock. Nog was huddled with several engineers some distance away. The chief engineer's face relaxed visibly when he saw his CO; Vaughn hoped the situation hadn't worsened since he left his quarters.

"Report, Lieutenant."

Nog launched into his story at once. "I arrived at 0600 to resume command of the repair team, accompanied, as you can see, by Ensign Senkowski, Ensign Leishman, and Ensign Gordimer."

At mention of their names, auburn-haired Senkowski, smiley Leishman and stocky Gordimer in succession, straightened up and nodded a polite acknowledgment to their commander.

Nog continued, "We discovered the troops you see here blocking the airlock; they denied us access to the *Defiant*. Lieutenant McCallum, Ensign Merimark, Ensign Permenter, and Crewman M'Nok are still aboard. I've already contacted them and they haven't been threatened, or had their work interfered with. They didn't even know they were trapped inside until I told them."

"What do these guards have to say?"

"Nothing, sir, except that they're acting under orders to secure the ship."

There must be a point to this. Even implied threats aren't arbitrary. "Have you contacted the Yrythny authorities?" If Vaughn were to guess, he'd assume that one of their friendly dinner companions was responsible for their armed visitors.

"Sir, we've tried to raise our concerns with the Yrythny government, but our inquiries have been rerouted, ignored or gone unacknowledged," Nog said.

I just bet they have, Vaughn thought. *They want us to stew in our worry a little longer. Makes us more pliable, more readily agreeable to their demands when they finally get around to making them.*

"And for that, I apologize, Lieutenant Nog," Assembly Chair Rashoh's rumbling voice came from behind them. "I had hoped to contact you myself, Commander, before your engineers arrived for duty this morning, but obviously my good intentions came to naught."

So you've decided we've waited long enough, or you've grown impatient. Which one is it? "As you say, Assembly Chair," Vaughn said placidly, turning to face Rashoh and his party. None of their identities surprised him, just the failure to bring their token Lower Assembly member, Keren, along as a spectator. Accompanying the Assembly Chair were Vice Chair Jeshoh and another Yrythny official Vaughn didn't recall meeting. He considered them cautiously, wondering what ill tidings they brought. "Imagine my concern at discovering my crew had been denied access to *our* ship." *Let the games begin . . .*

"*Your* ship, certainly," the Assembly Chair said with a toothy smile, his never-blinking eyes glinting like obsidian. "As your lieutenant has no doubt reported to you, we haven't violated your sovereignty and boarded your vessel. Rather, we have some concerns that we wanted to discuss."

"Concerns?" Vaughn raised an eyebrow. *What trumped-up excuses have you spent the night dreaming up?* He offered Rashoh a warm smile of his own.

"The radiation contamination inside is immense. We require assurance that our own people won't be impacted," the Assembly Chair said soberly.

Vaughn smiled tightly at Rashoh. "Mister Nog?"

Taking his cue, Nog opened his tricorder and panned it in the direction of the airlock. After a moment he turned back to Vaughn and held up the results of his scan.

To Rashoh, Vaughn said, "I encourage you to verify these findings with your own instruments, but according to this, you and your people have nothing to fear."

A pointy-faced Yrythny wearing billowing muted green pants and a gaudy macramé headpiece stepped forward with outturned feet, bowed, and said in a hesitant voice, "I am Science Minister M'Yeoh. Let me come to the point, Commander."

"By all means," Vaughn said pleasantly.

Threading his lengthy, bony fingers together and flexing his fingers rhythmically—as one might tap one's toes—Minister M'Yeoh waddled closer to Vaughn. "As I see it, you have three options," he said. "Clearly, your ship can't fly or sustain life for long. Should"—he gulped—"you decide that it's irreparable you might wish to trade your ship for one of ours. Or you might decide that our world suits you as a place to rest temporarily. Perhaps contact your own people in the Alpha Quadrant and wait for them to come and bring you home."

"Or they can repair the *Defiant* using our resources—personnel, raw materials and so forth," Jeshoh interjected. "As we *promised* our guests yesterday."

At least Jeshoh's not pretending to go along with this charade. "Vice Chair Jeshoh offers the only option I'm willing to take," Vaughn said, waiting for the word he felt certain would follow.

"But that's our problem, Commander."

There it is, Vaughn thought ruefully. *The "but."* Would that someday sentient nature surprised him even a little, but it often seemed as if all species—all thinking beings—functioned on similar paradigms, even this far from home.

Assembly Chair Rashoh clucked, jiggling the pockets of skin hanging off his jaw. "We want to be generous with you, but the reports from your chief technologist indicate that your ship will require extensive—and expensive—resources. Much of what you need we obtain from foreign trade, and as we've already explained, our conflict with the Cheka has limited our supply runs. How can we possibly give you what you need without risking shortages to our own vessels?" Assembly Chair Rashoh's sad expression lingered on Vaughn for a long moment, allowing his words to hang in the air.

"I understand completely," Vaughn said. "Would you consider a trade?"

Smiling, the Assembly Chair took Vaughn by the elbows. "I believe we would be open to such a proposal."

"Hmmm. I have some suggestions, but perhaps you have something in mind?"

M'Yeoh said, "We've reviewed this model for a defensive weapon that your Lieutenant Nog designed and found it has merit. But like you, we lack a raw material suitable for construction of the femtobots."

Hearing mention of his work on the defense system, Nog sidled up close to M'Yeoh. Vaughn had momentary concerns about how the Yrythny government had been privy to Nog's technological innovations, but then he recalled that a group of engineers from the *Avaril* had asked if they could help out. In spite of their rough first contact, the Yrythny engineers had bonded with Nog and his staff.

"Among the trade avenues still open to us, we have a membership in a matter Consortium several sectors away that deals in unique and rare materials," the Assembly Chair explained.

"Matter Consortium?" Vaughn asked.

"A nexus of free trade situated near a natural particle fountain in this sector. The Consortium harvests the outflows of the particle fountain. The matter emerging from the fountain has undergone intense gravitational pressure and temperature fluctuations. Its molecular and subatomic structure is fundamentally altered by these forces. We believe it will meet your requirements."

Nog was rapt with attention. Technology that facilitated particle fountain mining, while found in the Federation, such as the one at Tyrus VIIA, was still primarily experimental. Vaughn could see the cogs in his mind spinning furiously as he processed Rashoh's words. When Nog leaned forward, as if he were preparing to question the Assembly Chair, Vaughn touched his shoulder, wanting him to hold back until he had the complete picture.

"You're saying we can obtain the structural materials we need from this Consortium?"

Rashoh smiled but shook his head. "Unfortunately, trading is closed to nonmembers. However, as members ourselves, we would be willing to act on your behalf. You could travel on *Avaril,* with your ship, allowing your crew time to work on your repairs during the journey. Our long-range probes have recently verified a route to the Consortium that is still free of web weapons."

"A generous offer," Vaughn said, relieved that the game was nearing an end. "But what could we possibly offer you in return?"

"Allow your first officer, Lieutenant Dax, to stay behind and mediate talks between the Houseborn and the Wanderers."

And your first instinct was right, Elias. The situation with Ezri is the real problem here. He exhaled deeply, considered the group standing before him and saw in their faces a resolute determination to do whatever it took to bring their will to pass.

"Agreed," Vaughn said. "Threats weren't necessary, Assembly Chair, Minister M'Yeoh, Vice Chair Jeshoh. Reasonable people negotiate and I am nothing if not reasonable. Your soldiers will now leave and my engineers will go to work." He smiled coldly at his blackmailers.

The Yrythny delegation didn't bother to hide their relief at Vaughn's answer. *Why hadn't they just asked?* In his more than eighty years in Starfleet, whether it was dropping into a war zone or playing cat-and-mouse games with the Tal Shiar, Vaughn had learned that desperation drives otherwise sane people to do crazy things. *The time for asking whether Dax should do this is probably past—the question now is whether Dax* can *do this. For all our sakes, I hope her plucky determination—and the cumulative wisdom of all her lives—will be enough.*

Shar waited impatiently as the troop transport in which he rode crept slowly through the narrow needle, toward the massive docking platform. Through the windows, he could see Luthia's winking lights diminishing as he inched closer to the *Avaril.* Would that he could have joined the others an hour ago when the crew checked out of the guest quarters! But he—along with Candlewood, Juarez, and McCallum—was remaining behind to assist Lieutenant Dax. Loading the shuttlecraft *Sagan* with the away team's supplies and piloting the ship to a bay closer to their guest quarters had left him little time for a pressing personal errand. He still hoped he had enough time to pull Commander Vaughn aside to make a private request. Shar rarely made such requests; he hoped Vaughn understood that.

If Commander Vaughn followed the pattern established thus far, *Defiant* would send its official weekly report to Deep Space 9 while at the Consortium. "Letters" from the crew to their friends and families were transmitted on an "as time and equipment permitted" basis. At present, both were in short supply, but he didn't wish to let another week pass. When the next report was transmitted to Colonel Kira, Shar hoped to include a message to his bondmates: not only because they expected one, but because he deeply regretted the last one he had sent.

His first letter home had been stilted. Still smarting from the sting of his *zhavey*'s ploy, he'd been at a loss as to what to say. She had staged her ambush—bringing his bondmates to the station all the way from Andor to persuade him not to join the *Defiant*'s mission—because she loved him and believed his choices would lead him to unhappiness. But that didn't lessen his frustration with her tactics. There was a fine line between "force" and "guilt" to Shar's way of thinking. Especially since she *had* succeeded in making him feel guilty. He missed the days when their relationship was less adversarial.

All these feelings had filled Shar when he'd recorded his first message to his *zhavey*. He finally settled on a matter-of-fact recitation of his experiences coupled with brief well wishes and words of affection. Had he sent what he had recorded on the first pass, Shar expected that Charivretha might have come chasing through the wormhole after him. Saying the words, however, had been enough to make him feel better, so he erased the inflammatory accusations in favor of his proper letter. He might send his first draft later on, when the *Defiant* was too far away to catch ...

> *Zhavey:*
>   *I am sorry to have disappointed you. Please believe me when I say that I would not have chosen as I did if I didn't believe that I was doing what was best for* all *concerned. Has not your whole life been about the greater good of Andor? Is it too hard to understand that I've become what I am by learning from your example?*

Even more difficult was the letter to his bondmates. All his words were *just* words. Empty. Hollow. Failing utterly to convey the heartache he felt, or to acknowledge the heartache he knew he'd caused them. Why were pain and love coupled so tightly together?

> *Dearest Thriss, Anichent, Dizhei—I love and miss you all, but this mission must come before my return to Andor for the* shelthreth. *I hope that someday you understand my choices and forgive me. While it might seem I'm being selfish, I'm doing this for you, for all of our people. Our people's present course merely postpones the inevitable—we must explore new possibilities if we are to defy our fate. And if a few aren't willing to make sacrifices for the many ... Unfortunately, because you are matched to me, you are among the few. You didn't choose this for yourselves and for that, I'm sorry.*

In the early weeks of the mission, Shar had watched Vaughn and his daughter, Ensign Tenmei, tentatively feel their way back to reconciliation after years of estrangement due to her belief that Vaughn had put his duty to Starfleet before his love of her mother. Shar wondered if someday he would have to make a similar reconciliation with his bondmates.

Early this morning, he had come up empty as he fumbled for the right words to express his thoughts to those closest to his heart. Never mind that he had years of practice recording such messages, having spent so much time away from them, communicating solely through subspace letters. No matter where his Starfleet assignments had taken him in the past, maintaining his ties to his bondmates had been a priority. Infrequent were the times when, as a group or individually, they could take leave from schooling or work.

While Dizhei's teaching responsibilities tethered her to Andor, both Anichent and Thriss left home for personal and professional reasons. Anichent's research and conferences had provided him with opportunities to visit Shar at the Academy. Thriss regularly went from Andor to Betazed with her own *zhavey*, a visiting professor from the Andorian Art Academy to Betazed University. During the war, Thriss had managed to meet Shar for weekend leave on three occasions. In the war's darkest hours, each of her visits had buoyed him up and renewed his resolve to press forward in the face of reports enumerating Starfleet losses. Her dreams of a post-war future underscored his determination to make the most of every duty shift, helped him avoid discouragement when the casualty reports listed the names of friends and officers he had served with.

Damn it, Zhavey! *I had reconciled myself to not seeing them before I came home from the Gamma Quadrant. I had prepared myself and knew I could make it for another few months and then return home for the* shelthreth. *But you couldn't trust me enough to accept my choice without questioning.*

Of all of them, he thought Thriss would have most appreciated this voyage. She never shied away from new experiences, always living close to the edge, plunging into the unknown when the rest of them cowered beneath their covers. Since they were children, she had always been the first to take a dare. More than once, her risks had landed her in the infirmary or before a disciplinary council, but her passion never dimmed. She never ceased to surprise him.

He still remembered the look on his bondmates' faces as they stood by while Charivretha demanded he return with them to Andor.

Ever the optimist, Dizhei had tried to look cheerful, but her cloudy eyes and too bright smile betrayed her true feelings. Anichent's silence during the argument had disappointed Shar. After so many years of closeness, Shar assumed that he, even more than Thriss, would know why Shar needed to join this mission. Anichent had been Shar's first love, the one who, early on, had encouraged his academic pursuits, fed his ambitions to attend the Academy. Hadn't it been Anichent who, in his pragmatic, methodical way, outlined the sacrifices Shar would have to make in following the life path he had elected to take? But in their last encounter, he'd barely said a word.

And Thriss . . .

How many sleepless nights had they spent lying on their backs, mapping the constellations in Andor's heavens, interspersing their stargazing with talk about their goals and dreams? His absurd aspirations didn't sound quite so absurd when she brushed her lips against his ear, whispering words of encouragement. She, more than the others, had always defended his choices, even when those choices were made at her expense. After everything they'd been through together, after he'd opened himself to her incandescent spirit and saw his own yearning for a better future reflected back at him . . . How was it that she, of all people, could come to him making that final desperate appeal as he was about to board *Defiant? Oh, Thriss* . . .

The shuddering transport groaned to a halt. Shar sprang through the barriers and ran up the steps to where the *Avaril*'s crew prepped for launch, *Defiant* once again nestled inside its cavernous bay. Hordes of Yrythny shuttled storage lockers of supplies into exterior hatches; officers with electronic tablets ran through pre-launch checklists. Shar surveyed the crowded platform until he found his own crew. Dr. Bashir was giving last-minute instructions to Ensign Juarez, who would stay behind as medic for Lieutenant Dax's team. Spotting his commanding officers engrossed in conversation, Shar worked his way over to them. He assumed a position at Vaughn's elbow, waiting for his turn.

"Transmit on subspace channel delta—" Vaughn was saying.

Ezri's brow furrowed. "Delta? That requires security encryption."

"Right. I want our communications kept private, just to be on the safe side."

"All right," Dax said, and then smiled. "Any last words of encouragement?"

"Yes. Try not to start a war this time."

"Very funny. I'm not Curzon, you know."

"Try to remember that and I'm sure you'll do fine." Vaughn surveyed the dwindling activity in the launch bay and said, "I expect we'll be departing shortly. Has your team finished offloading your supplies?"

Lieutenant Dax threaded her hands behind her back and stood up a little straighter before turning to Shar. "Ensign?" she said in her firmest command tone.

"Yes, sir. An hour ago."

"Excellent work, Ensign." Vaughn smiled, placing a hand on Shar's shoulder. "Since I won't be here to consult with Lieutenant Dax, feel free to offer any insights you might have gleaned from having a professional politician for a mother."

Never mind that I've spent most of my life trying to avoid being overtly associated with Zhavey . . . "Yes, sir." Shar took a deep breath. "Sir, if you don't mind—"

"Yes, Ensign?"

Shar fingered the isolinear chip in his hand. "Commander, I realize this is unorthodox, but I have a personal request to make. . . " His antennae tightened and twitched.

"If you'll excuse me," Dax interrupted, "I need to say good-bye to Julian."

Respectfully, Vaughn waited until Dax was out of earshot to speak. "You were saying, Ensign."

"When you transmit your weekly report to Colonel Kira, would it be possible to attach a personal letter to my bondmates?"

Vaughn smiled. "Of course, Shar," he said gently. holding out his hand to accept Shar's chip. "Though I can't guarantee that the report will go out on schedule, I'll make a point of adding your message to the data stream. Rest easy, Ensign."

"Thank you, sir," Shar said, flushed with gratitude. "And good luck."

As he walked away to look for Nog, Shar spotted exhausted Ensigns Senkowski and Permenter and knew his friend would be close at hand. Neither officer had been far from the *Defiant* since the *Avaril* docked. Earlier this morning, Shar had observed Permenter curled up on a storage locker, snoring. He turned a corner around stacked cargo canisters and as he suspected, found the chief engineer speaking animatedly. Enthused about the task at hand, Nog didn't notice that both ensigns stared at the padds they held, their bloodshot eyes looking like they were propped open with toothpicks.

"—and make sure that the cables we're running down the new EPS conduits are free of irregularities. The shield augmentation might destabilize if— Shar!" Nog exclaimed. "Want to hitchhike to the Consortium with my engineering crew? Lieutenant Dax won't care."

"You know how clumsy I am with a hyperspanner. I'd probably couple a flat ring to a trisk wire." Shar recalled more than a few near-misses during the Core repairs back at DS9.

"Hey! That was almost a joke. Not quite ready for stand-up at Vic's, but you're coming along nicely."

"Stand-up?"

"Never mind."

Shar had been gradually assimilating his shipmates' sense of humor on this trip. They tended to sprinkle humor into almost every conversation. He supposed that with practice, it would eventually come naturally to him.

"There's someone I want you to meet," Nog said. "Hey, Tlaral! Come over here." He waved her in their direction.

A Yrythny was bent over a communications unit, using a micro-laser to fuse the last array component in place. She lifted her eye-shield. "I'm busy!" Tlaral shouted.

"I want you to meet my friend and shipmate, Ensign ch'Thane," Nog shouted.

Tlaral nodded politely, dropped the eye-shield and resumed her work.

Nog whispered, "She was one of the ones who beamed aboard to help us after we tripped the web weapon. If I could find a way to get Commander Vaughn to let me invite her to stay with the *Defiant* permanently, I would. She's a whiz with the cano pliers—and I've never seen an engineer who could diagnose a circuit board faster. Except maybe my father."

"Is she going with you?" Shar asked, wondering if the glow in Nog's face indicated that he might find true love, or at least serious infatuation, on this journey.

"Her husband—they call them consorts here—is a bigwig in the government. He's going to be on board, too. He's like the science minister or something? Mutters a lot."

"M'Yeoh. Yes, I've met him. Why is he going with you?"

"We need a senior government official in order to be able to trade at the Consortium. He was the only one who didn't need to be here for Ezri's gig."

Shar knit his brow quizzically. "Gig?"

"We need to go to Vic's more when we get back, Shar. You'll pick up the lingo in no time. You need to get into the groove."

Shar felt confident he could live a fulfilling life without knowing what a "groove" was, let alone getting into one.

The *Avaril* had been gone from Luthia for less than a day when the Yrythny General Assembly summoned Ezri to appear before them. She shouldn't have been surprised—they'd been anxious from the beginning.

Vaughn had only just launched when a messenger appeared with her non-negotiable schedule, loaded with committee meetings from breakfast to bedtime. Having only a cursory knowledge of the Yrythny, she hardly had enough information yet to make any substantive pronouncements as to the merits of each case. She had wasted no time in assigning the entire away team to research while she'd locked herself into the makeshift office space provided her by the government. After a few minutes standing on her head (which seemed to settle her nerves) she had begun mapping out strategy, searching Curzon's memories for any relevant experiences he might have had. What she concluded was that whenever circumstances hurtled Curzon into the unknown, he was phenomenally gifted at faking it. *Some help you are, Old Man.*

So she had treated her meetings as she would a surprise exam or a red alert. Focus. Breathe. Study the situation. Act, not react. And try not to panic. It worked for the most part. A thirty-two-hour diet of position papers had filled her head with facts. Whether she could put them together in a useful fashion was another issue altogether.

She was about to find out.

Nothing like having some prep time, Ezri thought, shuffling through the padds loaded with Yrythny history, law, customs and geography brought to her by Candlewood and Shar. She read as quickly as she could, catching the main points and leaving the fine print for later; hopefully, no one would be quizzing her. She'd just finished perusing a treatise on Wanderer rights when Shar appeared in her doorway.

"The escort's here, sir," Shar announced.

"Already? They're early!" Ezri moaned. "Help me gather all this up. And find me something I can carry it in. I don't know when I'll be coming back here today."

Shar quickly procured a shoulder bag and loaded it up with any and all items Ezri might need. *"Coral Sea Wars,* then *Black Archipelago Conflict,"* she pronounced finally. *"First Proclamation on Rights* came with the *Peace Talks."*

"I think *Black Archipelago* comes before the *Coral Sea Wars,"* Shar commented, then added "sir."

"After! Let's go!" She marched out of the office and into the exterior corridor, where the escort to the Assembly Hall awaited her.

Since he'd first set eyes on it, Vaughn knew that the *Avaril* rivaled even a Romulan warbird in size. After living aboard her for only a day, he decided that she conformed less to his notions of a starship than she did to a warp-capable space station. Finding his way around identical spiraling corridors and dozens of transport car tracks proved challenging. If their wide-eyed expressions of confusion were any indication, his crew felt similarly.

Because *Defiant* was still, to all intents and purposes, uninhabitable until repairs were completed, the crew had been provided accommodations aboard *Avaril*. Bowers, who had been supervising the removal of personal crew gear from *Defiant,* had mistakenly guided a group, arms laden with duffel bags, to the *Avaril*'s engine room. Wisely, Chieftain J'Maah had designated several large empty rooms close by *Defiant*'s bay to serve as living space, minimizing the square meters in which the Starfleet crew could get lost. To facilitate intercultural understanding, Chieftain J'Maah had provided them access codes to the unrestricted portions of the ship's database. The voyage to the Consortium was expected to take four days in each direction, so Vaughn had issued a standing order that all *Defiant* personnel were to spend at least two hours daily exploring the political and social contexts of the sectors they were traveling through. In addition, attendance at scheduled inter-crew mixers was mandatory (the exception being Nog and his engineers: repairing the *Defiant* took precedence over all activities for the duration of the journey). For himself, he was determined to memorize the layout of the *Avaril;* he hated getting lost.

But there were practical concerns that required adaptation, such as the sleeping accommodations. Because the rooms given over to the *Defiant* crew weren't actually designed to be quarters, nothing remotely resembling a bed was available. Bashir and Prynn had been assigned to collect sleeping bags, blankets and pillows from *Defiant*. After the first night sleeping on the *Avaril*'s decks, Vaughn expected the crew's tolerance for noise, snoring and quirky bedtime routines to increase markedly.

With Bowers, Bashir, and Prynn still fine-tuning housekeeping and his briefings with Chieftain J'Maah completed, Vaughn was left with a block of time before he was scheduled to join the *Avaril*'s senior staff, including Science Minister M'Yeoh, for dinner and a discussion of what to expect at the Consortium.

From what Vaughn had gathered so far, M'Yeoh, in his ministerial position, would secure credentials for Vaughn to conduct trades under the Yrythny's sponsorship. Vaughn's impression of the science minister since their first encounter was of a sniveling career politician. Descending from one of the oldest and most prestigious Houses on Vanìmel had been enough to secure M'Yeoh a high government position. Developing a constructive working relationship with him over the next few days might prove challenging. Vaughn had never had much use for inheritors of power; they were too often more trouble than they were worth, in his experience.

Checking the time, Vaughn noted that he had about half an hour before he was to present himself in J'Maah's quarters. Having heard that the crew had organized a poker game for later in the evening, Vaughn decided to go on a personal errand now, before the meeting with J'Maah, freeing him up to play a few hands after dinner.

Though he knew unscheduled hours might be infrequent in coming days, he decided to forgo practicality and download the next volume of *The History of Terran Civilization* from the *Defiant*'s library into a padd for recreational reading. He'd finished the volume on Alexander the Great the day before they'd encountered the Cheka weapon; he was eager to revisit the rise of the Roman Empire.

With most of the crew settling into their new living spaces, Vaughn wasn't surprised to find the corridors outside *Defiant*'s bay empty. He entered his personal access code into the doorpad and strode across the bay, the hollow clap of his shoes against the deck-plates echoing through the chamber. Like a recovering patient, *Defiant* rested on her seldom-used landing legs. Supplementary power modules attached to external access ports and long, snakelike umbilicals trickled energy into the ailing vessel's environmental systems. Vaughn patted her hull affectionately, hoping for her quick recovery. He ordered the hatch to open and he climbed aboard. Given the chance, Julian would lecture him about unnecessary radiation exposure, but the hyronalyin would cover him for more than the fifteen minutes the task required. Besides, decontamination was progressing at a good clip, and Vaughn wanted to sit in the captain's chair, feel the armrests beneath his hands, take in the view from the center of the bridge. He might not be *Defiant*'s first love, but he felt their courtship was going well and he missed being in her company.

He hadn't taken ten steps down the corridor beyond the airlock when he swore he heard the sound of a door closing. Tensing, he kept still and waited for any further sounds, but heard nothing. He didn't dare ask the computer for information. At the closest functional companel, he initiated internal and external sensor sweeps; both yielded nothing. As far as the computer was concerned, Vaughn was the only organic being in the repair bay. Still, he couldn't shake the sense that someone or something had been here—if not when he arrived, then certainly just before.

The *Defiant* had been boarded illicitly—he was sure of it. He wished the violation were unexpected, but the only unexpected part was how soon into their journey it had happened. Though his hosts had been gracious since achieving an "understanding," Vaughn knew intuitively that he needed to be wary.

Thus far, all his interactions with the Yrythny, save the manipulative tête-à-tête with the Assembly Chief, had been nonconfrontational and cordial. Vaughn had collided with enough admirals and politicians in his day to recognize that getting a job done sometimes required playing hardball. Since the unpleasantness back in Luthia, the Yrythny had facilitated his every request and resolved every concern he raised. That alone troubled him. Though it wasn't unreasonable to assume that the Yrythny's unhesitating cooperation had been bought with Vaughn's concession to allow Ezri to mediate, Vaughn had become too old and suspicious to take anything for granted. He found himself wondering what the next round of demands would be. *If any more unauthorized visitors come aboard, I need to know how, and why, and who's being so bold—without needlessly worrying the crew. I will not be surprised again.*

With great reluctance, Ezri tore her eyes away from the ceilings, and offered a courtly nod to two door attendants awaiting permission to admit her to the Grand Assembly Chamber. She had assumed upon seeing the hexagonal domes, the vaulted ceilings trimmed in gold, the filigree archways and the kilometer of inlaid marble floor, that she had reached the Chamber, but her escort, with some amusement, had informed her this was merely the lobby. She had gasped audibly when she saw the exterior chamber walls were encrusted with mosaics made of salmon, red, black and melon-colored corals, gemstones and burnished metals. Her escort, upon seeing her interest, explained that the pictures told the tableaux of Yrythny mythology and religion. How the Other had come from a faraway world to stir the primordial oceans of Vanìmel with its magic, thus allowing the Yrythny to leave the dark depths where they had always dwelt and be quickened into warm-blooded sentience. Within the artistic flourishes, exaggerated proportions and motifs, Ezri recognized the various stages of Yrythny evolution from amphibious animals to upright sentients, to a space-faring people who had constructed Luthia and developed warp drive. The picture-book story spread out above her was a helluva lot prettier than the pages of text she'd been force-fed. Certainly studying the mosaics could qualify as job related; she resolved to request the time to do so.

Shar cleared his throat and she realized the door attendants had placed their ceremonial scepters in a wall rack in preparation to admit her to the Chamber. Breathing out, she smoothed her uniform and waited for her cue. She could do this. Of course she could do this. Hadn't she made dozens of presentations before her classes at the Academy? This would be a piece of cake. She could tell that joke about the human, the Klingon, and the Romulan who walked into the Vulcan embassy, and then . . .

Upon seeing close to a thousand stern-faced Yrythny, dark eyes fixed on her, Ezri's mind blanked. She gulped. All the representatives stood in unison—a thunderous sound in the vast chamber—acknowledging her entrance. Those sitting closest to the center dais, the Upper Assembly representing the House-born, wore heavy robes of sapphire; those sitting on the balcony levels rimming the oval-shaped room, the Lower Assembly representing the Wanderers, wore green robes. She climbed a small number of stairs onto a rostrum of the presiding chairs. A backless bench was placed in front of a long flat table where Assembly Chair Rashoh, Vice Chair Jeshoh, Lower Assembly Chair Ru'lal and Lower Assembly Vice Chair Keren sat, soberly waiting for her.

As soon as she sat down, the entire Assembly resumed their seats. Ezri shifted on the bench, trying to remember whether sitting with her legs crossed or tucked neatly together with ankles linked was more dignified.

The Assembly Chair touched a control, illuminating one of the closest representatives. Ezri guessed this was how the chair recognized a speaker. Her guess was confirmed when the delegate stood and addressed the Assembly.

"We have discussed, Assembly Chair, the matter of this outsider, Lieutenant Ezri Dax, functioning as a Third, and both assemblies have agreed by a narrow margin, to accept her input. I propose a resolution, which I am now sending to my fellow representatives." He thumbed a switch, ostensibly sending the text of his resolution to the other desks in the Chamber, ". . . that this Ezri Dax take up residence, planetside, in the House of my birth, Soid, where she can best learn the manner of our people and then render a judgment. I move for a vote."

He hadn't been sitting more than a minute when hundreds of lights began flashing on every level of the room. The Assembly Chair recognized a delegate seated near the Yrythny who had just spoken, but without permission another delegate on the opposite side of the room stood up and began speaking until yet another delegate stood and began speaking over the words of the other. Ezri jerked back and forth, trying to keep track of what was being said, the speakers, the lights, the points of order and resolutions, but found it impossible. The Assembly Chair's fingers flew across his desk panel, his jaw clenched, but none of those clamoring for recognition heeded his points of order. Jeshoh, Keren and the others looked on helplessly.

From what little she did follow, Ezri learned that members of each House protested any House but their own being designated as the one she would visit first. In turn, the Lower Assembly representatives felt that focusing on the Houseborn issues would prejudice her before she had a chance to hear the Wanderer side. As lights from the top of the Chamber went off and on, voices grew more heated, argumentative rhetoric stopped being funneled through the Master Chair and instead went directly toward the "enemy" party. Several delegates, robes catching on balustrades or on chairs, climbed over barriers separating delegations and further punctuated their arguments with their fists. Jeshoh shouted for order, as did Keren, but their calls were ignored.

And Ezri discovered that many hate-infused faces directed their venom at her. Seeing contempt and mistrust wherever she looked, she hoped the leadership had a plan to protect her, just in case she was mobbed. Thinking she could even attempt something of this magnitude was such a mistake. *Have you lost your mind, Ezri? This is crazy!*

And then she remembered. A crumb, a fragment of a memory and she rooted around for the rest of it.

. . . Lela felt their hostility, their scorn, as she made the long trek from the door to her seat. As if being a woman, being young and being her symbiont's first host weren't enough to prejudice them against her, she knew she had a controversial proposal to make. Most of her colleagues would vehemently disagree with her idea, and it stood little chance of passing, but she knew that she had to make the proposal anyway because she couldn't live with herself if she didn't. Further, she knew that she would deserve their sneers and mocking whispers if she couldn't stand on the courage of her convictions. She knew that courage wasn't the absence of fear, but rather, acting in the face of fear. Rising from her desk, she lifted a hand, requesting the president pro tempore's attention, and when he refused to see her, with a shaky voice she said . . .

". . . I am here because I believe in the cause of peace," Ezri began. "Because I believe that my unique perspective gives me the ability to see through the thick forest of rhetoric and rivalry and find the clarity that lies beyond the dark and shadowed path." And as Lela's words flooded back to her, Ezri's confidence increased, her voice ringing out more clear and strong, striking a chord with the quarreling Yrythny until gradually, they settled down, resumed their seats and prepared to listen.

Of course I can do this, she thought triumphantly. *I'm Dax.*

6

"What is this, the eleventh time you've searched Jake's quarters?" Ro observed, the door hissing closed behind her.

Sitting on the couch in front of a storage box, Kira looked up from the antique book she perused. "These items were transported from B'hala. I think I've only looked through them three or four times." She took a sip from a mug sitting on the coffee table. "A fifth time can't hurt."

Ro sat down in a chair across from Kira. "Nothing new, I assume." In the course of her duties, she, too, had examined the contents of every box stacked against the walls. Anything he'd left behind had been systematically analyzed and catalogued. Though foul play wasn't readily evident in the circumstances surrounding Jake's departure, Bajoran and Starfleet security were treating the disappearance like a criminal investigation.

"I thought maybe knowing Jake's frame of mind when he left might give us some clues. I've been thumbing through the book the investigators found on his nightstand, but so far," she paused, examining the spine of the novel and reading aloud, "*The Invisible Man* hasn't proved to be much help."

"The forensic behavioral specialists from headquarters combed through his personal logs, his books, his schedule, who he was eating dinner with—his diet even—and they didn't draw any conclusions."

"But I *know* Jake. I should be able to see nuances that the experts might not," Kira said, dropping the book back into the carton. Replacing the lid, she pushed the carton aside and moved on to open another numbered container. She examined an insert listing the carton's contents. "Looks like work clothes and family pictures in here."

The depth of Kira's loyalty never ceased to astound Ro. To her, it appeared that Kira spent every minute she could spare from her regular duties focused on solving the mystery of Jake Sisko's disappearance. Ro didn't find fault in Kira's single-mindedness. Jake's vanishing coupled with Captain Sisko's mysterious disappearance and Odo's departure made for a major string of losses. Kira's behavior was more than justified to Ro's way of thinking.

"I've followed your updates throughout the day and the situation generally appears to be under control. I'll send a strongly worded memo to the Klingon ambassador reminding him that docking on Deep Space 9 is a privilege, not a right." Kira reached into the box, flipped through a pile of photos, and pushed aside a neatly folded sweater before removing a padd. "What did you think of Ambassador Lang and Gul Macet?"

"Lang surprised me," Ro confessed, smiling as she remembered. "We started talking—even had a few laughs—and we're meeting for drinks in a few hours. I think she's curious about what's going on around the station . . . to see if anyone from the old days is still around."

"You know about her history with Quark?" Kira circled her hand two or three times to indicate "the rest of the story."

Ro shrugged. "Quark doesn't kiss and tell unless it gives him more room to maneuver. The look on his face when I walk through the door with Lang should be pretty revealing."

"I imagine it will," Kira said dryly. "Anything else come out of Macet's presence aboard the station that I should know about?"

"Minor accidents. An unfortunate incident with a *jumja* stick when Macet made an unexpected appearance near the arboretum."

Kira winced. "Prognosis?"

"Dr. Tarses said a few sutures and an analgesic would cover it. A fainting here and there. An irate prylar who swears we're seeing the second coming of Gul Dukat—based on an obscure passage from the *Larish Book of Prophecy.*"

"Macet . . ." Kira said, absently tracing shapes on the coffee table with her finger. "Do you have any thoughts?"

"Yeah. I want to run my own DNA tests because it's too bizarre to be believed." Ro had been eager to say those words aloud since she met Macet. Standing face-to-face with the physical reincarnation of Dukat had catapulted her thirty years into the past. From her days on Bajor, she recalled waiting in the soup line, staring at the screens bearing the prefect's holo, wondering if the image was of a real person or something the Cardassians invented to scare their slaves. The way Bajoran mothers would invoke the *pah-wraiths* to warn their disobedient children. Ro never bought the folklore about the *pah-wraiths* any more than she now accepted what she'd been told about Macet.

"Ro, your reaction's understandable, but—" Kira said, doing her best to sound like she believed what she was saying.

"Colonel, there have been no confirmed sightings of Dukat since your own experience with him at Empok Nor," Ro stated emphatically. Believing Kira was about to protest, Ro pressed on. "And I know the rumors about the fire caves. Without concrete confirmation, they're just that—rumors. Dukat could be anywhere, doing anything," Ro argued. "He's insane! Who's to say he hasn't developed some alternate personality and it's this Macet."

"Akellen Macet was known to the Federation even before the Occupation ended," Kira said patiently. "Starfleet Command sent me his file right after I notified them of his role in the Europa Nova evacuation. And Alon Ghemor transmitted the gul's DNA records as well as his own personal assurance of Macet's identity."

Why Kira insists on sticking to the official party line, I don't get, Ro thought. *But I suppose being in charge means you have to appease the brass. That doesn't mean I have to.* "Asking Gul Macet to submit to a station security ID verification wouldn't be out of line considering our current alert status." Ro wanted her shot at him. Have him in her office on her terms.

Kira's eyes drilled into Ro's. "While I have no doubt that Macet would agree to it, I won't authorize it. Consider this issue closed, Lieutenant."

Knowing the debate was over, Ro pursed her lips and said, "Yes, Colonel."

"Anything else?" Kira took a deep breath and leaned back against the couch.

"In direct violation of your orders, Taran'atar has been shrouding and spying on our Cardassian guests." Ro conveyed the details of the Taran'atar incident to Kira with more objectivity than she felt. Part of her was glad Taran'atar might be out gathering the intelligence that would, with any luck, put her own lingering doubts to rest.

"I'll handle Taran'atar," Kira said, her expression pensive. "But continue to note any disruptive behavior. What's next?"

Kira's lack of reaction to Taran'atar's disobedience surprised her. Ro paused, wanting to ask how Kira planned on managing the Jem'Hadar. How could Kira be comfortable with Taran'atar playing by his own rules? Under usual circumstances, she'd pass off responsibility for Taran'atar without a second thought. This time, Ro had to trust that Kira had a plan to prevent him from provoking the Cardassians. Macet and Lang she didn't worry about. Macet's soldiers were another matter. If Macet's soldiers reciprocated Taran'atar's undisguised animosity, trouble was inevitable.

"Problem, Lieutenant?" Kira asked.

Shaken out of her thoughts, Ro answered, "We do have a delicate situation involving Councillor zh'Thane." Without sharing the finer points of Andorian physiology, Ro explained zh'Thane's end-of-shift visit and the resultant request to Kira.

Kira nodded. "How do you want to handle this?"

"Perform in-depth background checks on zh'Thane's staff. Send a crew to scan every centimeter of her ship. Everything checks out, she gets a pass off the station."

"All right. I'll update Admiral Akaar on zh'Thane's request. He shouldn't have any objections if he's in the loop from the beginning."

"Good point." There came a moment in every conversation when enough had been said; for Ro, it was the mention of Akaar. Until he had shown up, Ro had been able to put off sorting through her issues with Starfleet. His presence triggered many unhappy memories. *At least Kira's dealing with him.* "Will there be anything else, Colonel?"

"You're dismissed. Oh. Wait." Kira looked sheepish. "Just to satisfy my own curiosity, but you wouldn't know how the reception plans are coming along, would you?"

"Would that be why Quark was following Ensign Beyer around begging her to sample his tube grubs with icoberry sauce? Come to think of it, she had tablecloths draped over her shoulders and a mouth full of food last time I saw her," Ro said.

"The tube grubs must be for Ambassador Gandres—he has a fondness for all things Ferengi, or so I'm told."

"I'm impressed, Colonel. You managed to delegate party planning duty pretty quick."

"Shakaar insisted on having the job done correctly. As station commander, it's my obligation to find the individual who can best meet the minister's expectations."

"Whatever you say, Colonel," Ro said, grinning as she turned toward the door.

"Oh—and if Ambassador Lang says anything you think I might find useful—"

Ro paused. From appearances, Kira's evening would consist of replicated *raktajino* and a cold floor. *I bet Kira would enjoy a night out. I should . . . no. I wouldn't want her to feel like she had to accept my invitation, and it might be awkward to turn me down. Maybe another time.* She finally said, "Goes without saying, Colonel."

Kira had removed another box from the stack before Ro made it to the door. Persistent as she was, Ro couldn't imagine starting and restarting the tedious process of searching for answers in those boxes—especially since she was confident there were none to be found.

The difference between a believer and an unbeliever, Ro thought.

When Charivretha entered Thirishar's quarters, Anichent raised his hand to request that she refrain from interrupting his conversation. She recognized the Vulcan on the viewscreen as a well-known scientist. It pleased her to see that Anichent was working on his post-doctoral research instead of frittering away his time, moping as Thriss seemed bent on doing. How capably Anichent navigated his technically dense conversation with his colleague! All their talk of rips in space-time fabric fascinated her, but she doubted she could explain it if called on. Science had never been her forte.

During her student days, Charivretha had taken only the minimum requirements in physics, chemistry and biology, choosing instead to fill her schedule with extra courses in political science and government. Still, she found the physical sciences exciting in a mysterious way. In relaxed, intimate moments, one of her bondmates, a warp propulsion theorist, whispered to her the subtle poetry of swirling galaxies and interstellar fusion—a unique ritual between lovers to be sure. Her devotion to him was not unlike Shar's love for Anichent. In this one way, she and her *chei* were similar.

Anichent deactivated the subspace link and turned to her. "Thank you for waiting, *Zhadi.* I meant no disrespect."

Thinking about how pleased Shar would be to see his bondmate immersed in the work he loved, Charivretha affectionately squeezed Anichent's shoulders. "You amaze me, Thavanichent. You should apply for that fellowship at the Daystrom Institute."

"As you say." He flushed, and looked away, focusing on gathering up the bioneural circuit sheets and isolinear chips scattered over his work surfaces. The Vulcan he'd been conversing with was engineering a device to be retrofitted on starship arrays; Anichent had decided to see if he could build a miniature model of the device in order to verify his own findings.

Charivretha could imagine Anichent, one day, deciding to join Starfleet engineering as a way to facilitate spending more time with Shar. They could request joint assignments. Both of them would be less lonely. Charivretha believed having a bondmate by his side could only help Shar, stabilize him, reinforce his obligations to the Andorian Whole.

Feeling conspicuous for not helping, Charivretha dropped to the floor, working to assist Anichent in gathering his things. "I've come with a plan for the evening. I think it would be good for all of you. Don't give me that look, Anichent. Even you need to rest from your work—to recreate."

"Dizhei must have talked to you," he said sagely. He leaned over the desk and chairs, searching for any components he might have missed.

And that's not the half of it . . . Unwilling to revisit the humiliating discussion she'd had with Lieutenant Ro, Charivretha avoided following up on Anichent's words. He could draw his own conclusion. "How many days has it been since you three did something fun? Dizhei has been correcting her students' projects, you've been tinkering with hyperspanners and laser drills and Thriss has been preparing her residency applications—"

"Not many of them," Anichent muttered.

Those two, quarreling again? Do they ever stop? Poor Dizhei! Taking sides might disturb the precarious bondgroup dynamic, so she resolved to avoid any topic that might result in a conversation about Thriss. "You all deserve to be rewarded!" Charivretha said, reassembling a toolkit. "There was quite a bidding war over these holosuite hours. An attaché I work with was our most eager competitor, but in the end, I succeeded. I'm not about to let such a valuable opportunity go to waste."

Anichent placed the last of his items into a nearby case. "I suppose we should ask Dizhei and Thriss if they feel up to going out."

"Come with me, would you?" Charivretha asked. Anichent nodded stiffly and arm in arm they went to find the others.

No one will notice, Thriss thought, her hand hovering over the control panel. The temptation to increase the volume overpowered her fear of being caught; she made the adjustment. Out of the corner of her eye, she watched Dizhei. When her bondmate continued working without interruption, Thriss relaxed.

From the time they were little, Shar's voice had always hypnotized her. He wasn't prone to long speeches or flowery language but the tone in his voice made her shiver deliciously. She recalled "borrowing" school supplies from his desk just so he would have to ask her where she'd put them. Once, during their exercise period, she'd casually thrown a foot out in front of him during a foot race, sending him sprawling to the floor. Of course she'd volunteered to escort him to the nurse. That was the first time she'd touched him: dabbing a lumpy bruise on his forehead with a cool cloth. Oh, how annoyed he'd been with her! She smiled a little sadly at the memory. *Now he's thousands of light-years away without me to take care of him.* She rubbed her eyes, hoping Dizhei didn't see the beginnings of tears.

Notwithstanding Dizhei's unfailing kindness, Thriss knew she became impatient with the weepiness. The high rounded back of her chair shielded her somewhat from Dizhei, though, so she hugged her legs tight against her body, rested her chin on her knees and settled in to watch the recording.

Several days ago, she'd been browsing through Shar's database when she discovered his journal—what Starfleet people called their personal logs. At first, she watched them after Anichent and Dizhei were asleep, fearing their disapproval, selfishly wanting to hold something of Shar's for herself. Both her bondmates fussed about propriety, about respecting personal boundaries. Thriss knew that delving, uninvited, into these recordings might be construed as a violation, but she couldn't help herself. And it became harder and harder to wait until the middle of the night to spend time with Shar. So she decided to risk viewing them now, even though Dizhei, who listened with earpieces to her students' assignments, was in the room with her.

From what she could see, he appeared happy. This latest assignment to DS9 agreed with him. Seeing his contentment, however, always led her back to questioning why he couldn't be content with *her*. Why not come back to Andor for the *shelthreth* and then she'd go wherever he wanted her to. They simply had to put their obligations behind them.

Voices in the background cued her that others had joined her and Dizhei. *Why did Anichent have to come in now? I want to finish watching this day first, the day he received my gift.* She saw Shar looking at the elaborate model of Andorian DNA, constructed with rounded, highly polished, multicolored crystals. It pleased her to see he kept it on the shelf closest to his bed.

"Thriss!"

Abruptly, she spun her chair around and before she could protest, found herself facing Charivretha.

Dizhei, sprawled on the bed studying childishly drawn maps illustrating Andor's geography, startled when Charivretha addressed Thriss, her earpiece dropping into her hand. Anichent plopped down by Dizhei, leaning over to whisper in his bondmate's ear.

"Computer, halt playback," Charivretha snapped. "Do you have authorization to examine Shar's logs?" she asked Thriss.

"He gave us access to his quarters. Access is access," Thriss explained. She respected Charivretha. Honored her. Feared her. But in this one place, where their personal interests intersected in Shar, Thriss and Charivretha were forever at odds. Charivretha accepted Thriss because she matched Shar's genetics, but his *zhavey* made no secret of her preference for Anichent, or her admiration for Dizhei. Further, Charivretha resented Thriss's unconditional support for Shar's decisions, especially those decisions that conflicted with the priorities Charivretha believed Shar ought to embrace. And with Charivretha, duty defined life. Duty and obligation. When Thriss refused to use her influence to pressure Shar into accepting Charivretha's edicts, the barriers between Thriss and her *zhadi* grew, but Thriss didn't care. She loved Shar too much to see him unhappy, even if it meant sacrificing her own happiness. And there was that little tendency of hers—a tendency to resent being told what to do.

Charivretha specialized in telling people what to do. She had made a career of it.

"Personal logs require passwords." Charivretha grabbed Thriss by the chin and, treating her like a child, tipped her face up.

"I know his passwords," Thriss said. She met Charivretha's pointed stare, her stormy gray eyes revealing nothing.

"You stole his passwords," accused Anichent.

Dizhei placed a steadying arm around Anichent's waist, trying to soothe him.

"I don't steal, Anichent," Thriss snapped, jerking her head out of Charivretha's palm. "I know these things about Shar. He's used the same password for his private files since he was fifteen. If he hadn't wanted me to read them, he would have changed the password. He didn't, so I can do as I please. With his blessing." Because she understood Shar's deep affection for Anichent, Thriss hated arguing with him; she tried avoiding it—another way she honored Shar. Too bad genetic matches didn't mean good personality matches. If it were possible to be more opposite from Anichent than she was, Thriss didn't know how. They were fire and ice.

The antennae on Anichent's head twitched and flexed, his eyes darkened. "You behave as if this blessing extends only to you, and not to Dizhei or myself. How do you know I don't have knowledge of Shar's passwords?"

Why was he always seeking a fight? "View the logs. I don't care."

"I respect my *ch'te* enough to allow him the privacy of his own thoughts," Anichent snapped.

She tossed her hair. "Or perhaps you're afraid that those thoughts aren't of you."

Charivretha shushed them both, sending Anichent into the other room to check on the featured menu at Quark's. Thriss complied with Charivretha's orders to keep peace. One more argument with Anichent would mean ending her day with another headache; Thriss wearied of fitful sleep. She moved away from the desk and dropped down onto the edge of the bed; Dizhei alternated between massaging her shoulders and stroking her hair.

Taking Thriss's place in front of the monitor, Charivretha exited Shar's logs and then explained her intended evening plans.

Thriss bit back a complaint. Well-intentioned as she was, Charivretha always wanted to fix things even when, given time, resolutions might occur naturally. The thought of spending a night pretending to have a good time so Dizhei and Anichent wouldn't have one more reason to be irritated with her ... Anichent especially. "I have applications to finish," she said, offering the first excuse she could come up with. "And you know me and holosuites."

Before Charivretha could retort, Dizhei tenderly placed her head in Thriss's lap, linking her fingers through hers, stroking the back of her hand with her thumb.

Oh, all right. Guilt works too, Thriss thought. "We could visit the Palace of Zhevazha or take roles in one of the Sagas," Dizhei suggested. "You always enjoy swordplay. Or maybe we could visit a favorite spot. You love Casperia Prime. You told me yourself that the days you and Shar spent climbing there were the best vacation you'd had in years!"

On rare occasions, segments of the bond would section off in a pair or trio. Thriss and Shar had gone away together once—after he graduated from the Academy and before he assumed his wartime assignment. She cherished those days as belonging to her and Shar alone, never sharing any details of their time together with either Anichent or Dizhei.

Thriss leaned down to touch her cheek to Dizhei's. "You go, *sh'za*. You and Anichent deserve to relax away from me. I'm not good company right now. Enjoy food that's not replicated. You told me last week you wanted to learn to play *tongo,* this is your chance!"

Almost imperceptibly, Dizhei shook her head. "I'll stay with you. It's not good to be alone. Anichent can go with *Zhadi."*

Thriss eased Dizhei up from her lap. Cupping Dizhei's face in her hands, Thriss touched her forehead to hers. They entwined fingers through each other's hair. Dizhei was like a *zhavey* to her. Thriss decided she could yield—make an honest effort to get along with the group. "I believe the last time we fenced, you beat me. Every game. Don't assume you'll have an advantage this time." Thriss smiled and Dizhei reciprocated.

In the doorway, Anichent appeared holding Quark's evening menu; he sighed, visibly relieved.

Thriss assumed that Anichent was happy he didn't have to take her on; their "discussions" usually ended after heated words or thrown furniture—and it wasn't always her doing the throwing. Neither of them enjoyed being pitted against the other in the battle for Shar's affection; both resented, justifiably, having to defend their places in Shar's life.

She wasn't entirely so self-absorbed that she didn't know what Anichent really thought: he believed Shar's unusually strong attachment to her would fade after the *shelthreth* because he saw her and Shar's relationship as being comprised of physical urges, sexual chemistry. He clung to the hope that in the long run, Shar would choose a mindmate over a bed partner. *What Anichent doesn't see is that I am both,* Thriss thought triumphantly.

Neither she nor Anichent spoke of what would happen to Dizhei, who nurtured and loved them all, regardless of what her own future held. She cared more about their collective concerns than her own. Thriss's own *zhavey* had chastised her once for their overlooking Dizhei's needs, chalking it up to youthful myopia. As time passed, Thriss recognized her *zhavey* was right: Dizhei was the stabilizing influence that held their bond together.

Thank the gods for Dizhei, Thriss thought. *One of us needs to keep their wits about them.*

Quark leaned against the bar, both lobes focused on table 5 where Natima and Ro sat conversing. Normally, the layers of bar noise never interfered with his ability to follow whatever conversations were under way. He'd grown accustomed to filtering out the dings of the dabo wheel, the clatter of latinum at the *tongo* table, clinking glasses and the clicking heels of the servers as they raced across the floor to pick up their drink orders. But tonight, he swore Ro must have brought some privacy device to protect whatever female-talk she had planned with Natima. It was like that nightmare he had where he showed up at his vault to collect his latinum only to discover his vault was a front operation for a Bajoran Orphans Charity Fund. He'd given away everything he'd earned without realizing it. Talk about feeling naked before the universe! That same panicked sensation threatened to wash over him now as, try as he might, he couldn't figure out what those conniving females were up to. *But oh, they're lovely to look at, aren't they?*

Natima, her thick hair sparkling with merlot-colored gems woven into the twist down her back and extending to her waist, wearing that crisp, shimmering red-black gown, the square neckline showing off enough of her fine, feminine assets to bring back pleasant memories of springwine and *oomox*. And Ro, zipped to the neck in some stretchy blue thing that looked far too Starfleetish for Quark's preference, still had that dark, sexy tomboy aura going for her. Too bad Garak wasn't around to offer Ro some off-duty wardrobe advice. He might have been able to persuade her to try something more flattering. Quark shuddered when he recognized the lunacy of that last thought. *A female reduces me to missing Garak?* Quark poured himself a shot of whiskey, threw it back in one swift motion and waited for the burning sensation in his eyes to recede. With all the chattering, he could only pick up the slightest hint of the timbre of Natima's voice or the higher notes in Ro's laugh.

At least she's laughing.

But what if she was laughing at him?

He'd thrown back a second shot before he'd even had a chance to consider how his staff might take advantage of his panic by pocketing their own tips. Quark made a mental note: *Conduct locker and body searches before staff clocks out.*

Several stools away from where he stood, he noticed an unfamiliar Starfleet officer sitting quietly, sipping spoonfuls from a bowl of what looked like plomeek soup and reading the latest edition from the Federation News Service. He scoped her out. A thin, platinum band on her left hand, fine age lines around her eyes and a centered sensibility evidenced by how easily she focused on her reading in this noisy room. Discerning her descent (she was a bit too—pointy?—to be all human) proved challenging. Before he'd drawn any conclusions, he found a pair of steady green eyes fixed on him.

"Hello," she said. "You must be Quark."

"And you must be a new customer I need to impress. Can I get you something to drink?" He sauntered down the bar and cozied up to the new kid on the station. Pretty. Nice hands. Definitely on the curvy side of female. Add a plunging neckline and she'd be a *dabo* girl to be reckoned with.

"Thanks. But the soup is fine until my husband gets here," she said with a polite smile, and resumed reading.

And what in that padd could possibly be more interesting than me? Maybe it was his approach. He tried again. "I've quite a selection of otherworldly delicacies. Can I get something going for you and your husband, Lieutenant Commander—"

"Matthias. Actually, I believe he's already eaten with our children. We're meeting here before we attend Prylar Kanton's B'hala lecture."

"A lecture?" Quark couldn't hide how underwhelmed he was by her choice of entertainment. "A spin at the dabo wheel or a hand of *tongo* wouldn't be more fun? Who knows—you might get lucky."

She tucked a loose amber-blond tendril behind her ear and took another spoonful of soup. "I'm certain the lecture will be very pleasant."

Pleasant. We wake up in the morning so our day can be pleasant? What a sad, sad life. He sighed. *With Bajor about to join the Federation and the Militia poised to be assimilated into Starfleet, the fun quotient around here will plunge. One more reason to search for business options elsewhere . . .*

. . . A search that might be aided by one Ambassador Natima Lang, Quark suddenly realized, and reminded himself that he needed to keep her under his watchful eye.

"My house specialty drinks are the perfect way to toast your *pleasant* evening," he suggested to Matthias. "A Warp Core Breech? Black Hole? Triskelion Tidal Wave?"

"I'll pass. After all, once I'm done with the lecture—a *pleasant* part for him since he's an archeologist—the *excitement* begins in the atrium with a candlelight dinner for two. The Chateau Mouton Rothschild we're being served will be my drink quota for the night."

Quark grimaced. "Why settle for something as pedestrian as a Rothschild when I can offer you the seductive delights of a thousand worlds?"

"That's a risk I'm willing to take."

Quark *tsked* and left Matthias to her soup. *Having Natima around must be throwing my game off,* Quark thought. He couldn't remember the last time he'd gone zero for five on a sale. He resumed his perch within eyesight of Natima and Laren.

"You must be very fond of her," Matthias observed, ostensibly attending to her padd.

Quark twisted toward the officer, but realized she wasn't looking at him. "Are you talking to me?"

"You were involved with the Cardassian at that table, what, five or more years ago." She paused, pondering her next words thoughtfully. "Things didn't end well. You're watching for an opening to go over there to find out what they've been talking about."

Oh please don't let me be dealing with a telepath. I'll never be able to fix the wheels again! Panic threatened to flood him.

Matthias must have noticed his discomfort because she quickly clarified her comments. "I spent five years doing field research in inter-species anthropology. Studying the body language patterns and brain-stem physiological reactions of a number of Alpha Quadrant sentients. Most individuals fail to realize how much their unconscious reactions reveal about them."

Being a man whose work it was to know what his customers wanted without asking, Quark appreciated her area of study. "Remarkable that you can know so much without reading my mind."

"I didn't say that," she teased. "I have some Vulcan ancestry, but it's a few generations back on my father's side. Your secrets are safe, Quark."

"Secrets? I have no secrets. My life is an open book."

"True. Ferengi aren't particularly complicated to decipher."

"Not particularly complicated?" Quark felt like he'd just been insulted.

"No," she said, unapologetically.

"So you can just look at whoever happens to walk into the room and after a relatively short observation figure who and what that person is about."

"More or less. Some sentients are more obscure than others."

"You don't say?" *Now that's a talent a good businessman could learn to exploit.* "What about him?" Quark asked, indicating Morn, who sat in his usual seat, nursing a tall mug of frothy ale. The Lurian turned toward Matthias and blinked blearily.

"He falls into the obscure category," she said.

Impressed, Quark considered asking Commander Matthias if she could share a few tips that would enhance his already formidable skills in the fine art of behavioral profiling, but before he could open his mouth, in walked a Bajoran man with a smooth pate and a thick, but neatly trimmed brown-black beard. Decently tailored clothes for an academic. Quark watched as the man cast a glance around the room, smiling when he spotted Matthias; he moved speedily to her side. *The husband, I presume.*

Their animated whispers held no interest for Quark. Before he could ask the husband if maybe he wanted a spin at the dabo wheel, Matthias pushed away her half-emptied soup bowl. *Holding hands like newlyweds,* Quark thought cynically, as they left the bar presumably to hear Prylar Kanton's scintillating lecture on the wonders of B'hala.

Morn watched him, straight-faced.

"What are you looking at, Mr. Obscure?" Quark snapped, sending his best customer scurrying off for cover behind the new dabo boy, guessing correctly that Quark's glare wouldn't find him there. Quark spent a good part of his day pretending he didn't have a dabo boy.

"Table 6 wants the Dabo-Dom-Jot Special," Treir said, sidling up beside him.

Quark also spent a good part of his day pondering those staff members most likely to exploit any weakness on the part of management. "We don't have a Dabo-Dom-Jot Special," he answered, waiting to see what angle Treir was coming from. She had to have one: she wouldn't be Treir if she didn't.

"I invented it after I realized that the gentleman at table 6 will cough up one bar of gold-pressed latinum for the Dabo-Dom-Jot special." She indicated an assorted group of humans, smuggler or mercenary types, huddling in a corner of the bar.

Quark grinned. Holosuites going for five times their usual rates. Latinum for bogus package deals, and two gorgeous females sitting right in his eye line. Maybe things weren't going so bad, even if he couldn't understand *a single word those females were saying!* He composed himself. This was business, after all. "By all means, offer them the Special."

"See, the thing is, if I become the Dabo part of the Dabo-Dom-Jot special, I want fifteen percent instead of my usual five percent," she said, dropping seasoning tablets into half a dozen Black Holes.

Treir, there isn't a tar pit big enough or dark enough to hold your evil mind. "No deal." He wasn't in the mood to take more punishment at female hands than he had to. He'd figure out his own bogus package deal and charge more.

"Fine. I'll tell them to check out the Fifth Moon Casino on their way home to New Sydney. Their Dabo-Dom-Jot special is only 45 strips, anyway."

"Ten percent," he countered.

"I would have settled for eight, but thanks for the bonus."

An incongruity in Treir's tale occurred to him. "How could the Fifth Moon Casino charge 45 strips for their Dabo-Dom-Jot special if you invented it?"

Her white teeth shone against her jade complexion.

Whatever temporary stupidity was afflicting him had better go away in a hurry. He'd be giving every dabo girl vacation days before the night was out. And there was the legitimate possibility he was worrying about nothing. He needed intelligence, but he wasn't about to waltz over there and talk to Natima and Ro directly. *"Excuse me, ladies, somebody here mention my name?"* What an idiot! If they weren't laughing about him already, they'd certainly be laughing about him after that.

Quark needed a spy.

"Treir, you haven't had a chance to see if table 5 needs their drinks refreshed. I happen to know the Cardassian ambassador has a fondness for Samarian Sunsets."

"Translated: Have I heard any good gossip eavesdropping on your girlfriends?"

"You got your extra five percent. I'd say that's worth something."

Treir sighed. "Natima said something about someone never guessing that she was faking it because if she let things go any further, he'd find out that—"

Quark held up a hand to silence her. "I've heard enough, thanks. Go be the Dabo part of the Dabo-Dom-Jot special."

"I need to change first," she said. "Oh. And Councillor zh'Thane's party is up next for the holosuites. You might want to send a ten-minute warning to the group in there now. Never know if they're in a compromising position." She sauntered into the backroom.

He mulled over Treir's tidbit. His stomach tightened. He imagined every possible permutation of conversation that might lead to those comments from his former lover and the object of his present pursuit and he liked none of them. From the rear, the sounds of the cellar hatch slamming closed and storage clattering to the floor gave him one more reason to worry. *What was Treir doing back there?*

Treir emerged, a fluorescent pink hairpiece mounted on her head, a short spangled dress dangling beads and pearlized bells. The outfit had much in common with an exploding wedding dais.

"Um, Treir. About what you're wearing . . ." Quark began.

"They were talking about the oddest place they'd ever hid a weapon, by the way," she whispered in his ear as she pranced by.

In that moment, Quark had enough. Either that, or the whiskey had finally unbound his courage.

A Ferengi's gotta do what a Ferengi's gotta do, Quark recited in his mind, steeling himself to face Natima. The 100th Rule of Acquisition. He slid a tray off the rack, ordered up a couple of drinks and started off on what he hoped would appear to be a leisurely stroll across the floor.

"He's coming," Ro said, quietly. Because Lang's chair only half faced the bar, Ro had kept Quark under surveillance. Once they'd transcended the usual swapping of histories and small talk, the status of their dealings with Quark had come up. Ro explained her still ambiguous intentions toward him; Lang related the story of their affair. Resolving that neither woman had any reason to compete with the other, they closed the book on Quark in just under five minutes by placing a small wager on how long he would be able to endure watching them from a distance before his curiosity—or anxiety—drove him to check on them.

"He lasted longer than I thought he would," Lang said.

"You think he's built up a good head of paranoia?"

"Probably. I'll pay you after we settle up our bill."

"That's all right. Winning's enough for me."

"Ah! You enjoy the game more than the prize. I respect that." Lang grinned, raised her glass of *kanar* and clinked a toast with Ro.

"Ladies," Quark said, sliding the drink tray onto their table. "Thought I'd bring over a little theme drink I've concocted for the reception. See if you think the diplomatic corps will approve. I call it a Peace Treaty. Starts off provocative, ends on a smooth note."

"Thanks, Quark," Ro said, taking a drink from the tray and passing it to Natima before taking one for herself. Ro choked, barely avoiding spitting up. "A bit heavy on the syrup."

Thoughtfully, Natima palmed the glass, swirling the liquid around, and delicately smacked her lips as if to contemplate the drink's overtones. "The sweet juxtaposes the fire of the whiskey nicely."

"Sounds like the dealings between your governments could take awhile, eh, ladies?" Quark said, bussing empty appetizer dishes onto the drink tray. "Consensus can be hard to come by."

"No, I think we've found consensus on many things," Natima said, her sparkling eyes searching out Ro's.

Taking her cue, Ro nodded in agreement. "Absolutely. I think Bajorans and Cardassians can find a lot of common ground."

"Oh. I suppose that's positive," Quark said, glancing between the women. "So . . ."

"So . . ." Natima echoed.

He stood in front of the table, tapping his foot, waiting, and clearly hoping that one of his guests would say something. Ro felt no obligation to rescue Quark. His seeming inability to string together a snappy comeback was a rare enough occurrence to be novel to her. She contented herself with surveying the crowd; playing security chief for a minute or two couldn't hurt anything. Besides, if anything was going to get out of hand tonight, she'd like advance notice. A large cluster of off-duty Starfleet personnel moved aside, giving her full view of Councillor zh'Thane accompanied by Shar's bondmates. Now was as good a time as any to update zh'Thane's party regarding her special request.

And let poor Quark off the hook.

"Quark, why don't you have a seat? I have an early shift and some business to take care of," Ro said, rising. "And put all this on my tab, would you? Ambassador, it's been a delight."

Lang raised her glass again as Ro stood up. "The pleasure was mine, Lieutenant."

"We still have our evening together, Laren?" Quark said, a bit too loudly.

Lang covered her mouth with her hand, but not before a guffaw escaped.

Ro sighed. "Once everyone's adjusted to the new security protocols and the reception is over, I'll be able to make definite plans," Ro explained. "But I think I'll be ready to put in a holosuite reservation soon." She gave Natima a little wink and headed off to meet with zh'Thane.

"Lieutenant Ro and I are exploring the possibility of a social relationship," Quark said after she'd left.

"She mentioned that you two got along pretty well," Natima said.

He watched Ro cross over to where the Andorian party—all four of them—waited for their holosuite. He'd heard rumors about some of the unique quirks of Andorian biology and was—intrigued?—by the commercial possibilities. "Hmmm. Now there's a holoprogram I'm certain would be a big hit: 'Andorian Ecstasy: Good Things Come In Fours.' Never occurred to me before now, but it might have more wide-scale appeal than just for Andorians. Few people know about Andorians and how they, you know." He grinned luridly. "Very hush-hush."

Natima rolled her eyes. "And is it possible that they tend to be a private people precisely to avoid having their intimate relationships exploited by entrepreneurial Ferengi?"

"All sentients are motivated by the need to eat and the need to reproduce. It's variety in both that keeps life interesting."

"So you see yourself as the host at a buffet table of exotic delights of all shapes and sizes?"

"Precisely."

"Quark, as much as the universe changes, you always somehow manage to stay the same." Natima shook her head.

Quark stopped smiling and found himself staring deeply into her eyes. "Another thing that hasn't changed is how much you mean to me, Natima." Quark reached over, placing his hand over hers. "Every bit of news out of Cardassia, every report, I looked for your face—your name—hoping you were safe."

"I have to confess even with everything that's happened to my people in recent years, my thoughts have often traveled back here, because I was worried about you, too. I had a feeling you'd make it."

"Takes more than a few wars to kill me off."

"I believe that."

Quark sighed. "I'm happy you're here, Natima."

She smiled, and placed her hand over his. "Me, too."

Other than when she'd first admitted them to Shar's quarters, Ro had never seen his bondmates all together. A pair might go shopping on the Promenade; from time to time she'd pass by one in the habitat ring, or while crossing over the various bridges to different levels of the station, but never in a group. She suspected they avoided it deliberately. Wherever they went people would talk simply because, to a person, they were striking.

The one sitting next to zh'Thane had an angular handsomeness he emphasized by wearing his hair pulled back tightly from his face. His choice of clothes—a shirt in a vivid hue of teal coupled with an ornately embroidered vest—reflected fashion sensibility Quark would appreciate. In the middle sat the bondmate Ro had met one day in the Replimat—a talkative, friendly individual, especially compared to Shar, who said little unless he was spoken to. Having explained that she was a teacher, she'd inquired about sitting in and observing the station's classrooms and Ro had forgotten she'd promised to get back to her. Ro made a mental note to add that to her task list for the morning. If she had to guess, she'd pick the Andorian who sat, just a bit apart from the other two, as the "problem" zh'Thane had come to see her about.

Unlike the congenial stockiness of the chatty one who sat beside her, she had a lean, willowy look, emphasized by her choice to wear her long white hair straight and smooth. She must have sensed Ro's scrutiny because suddenly Ro found herself facing a pair of piercing gray eyes.

"Lieutenant?" she said, her voice silvery toned.

"Umm. Yeah." Ro grabbed an empty chair from a close-by table, placed it in front of the Andorians' booth, threw a leg over and straddled it. "Yes. I apologize for interrupting your night out, but I've got good news regarding your trip."

Her eyes narrowing on Ro, the willowy one said, "Trip? What trip?"

"Thriss," zh'Thane warned.

Puzzled glances passed between the other two bondmates and Ro wondered if zh'Thane had told them about her request for an exemption. *Maybe this was a mistake and I should have handled this one-on-one with the councillor.*

Zh'Thane must have noticed their apprehension because she quickly said, "Remember we talked yesterday about the timetable for your return to Andor? I'm anxious to hear what you've learned, Lieutenant."

Warily, Thriss watched Ro, her expression flinty.

Ignoring Thriss, Ro took her cue from the senior member of the group and proceeded. "Colonel Kira paged me a short time ago with her approval for your emergency departure exemption. Everything checks out—your ship, Councillor, will be free to leave the station on an 'as needed' basis."

Confusion erupted.

"Dizhei, you discussed this with *Zhadi?*" one of the Andorians said, anxious. "I thought we'd decided to keep it to ourselves—"

"I thought after what happened this morning—"

"—believed you and Anichent were in agreement—"

Shathrissía kept silent, her eyes solemn. Ro saw her hands curl around the edge of the table, her breathing deepen.

"We can't risk—"

"—room for last-minute—"

"Wait!" Ro said, bringing her palm down on the table, a little harder than she intended. At the sound, four pairs of eyes fixed on her.

"No one said you had specific plans. Your situation isn't much different, except now you have the option of leaving on short notice without having to go through all the procedures required by a yellow-alert status." She turned to zh'Thane. "I have the codes at my office. I'll have them sent to your quarters, Councillor. Provide them to ops and you'll be allowed to depart without question."

"So you all conspired to return to Andor without talking to me about it," Thriss said softly. "When was this decided? You and Anichent have a little pillow talk, Dizhei? Or was it your idea, *Zhadi?* Trying to control us, as usual." Thriss jerked around to face zh'Thane, tipping over a mug filled with Orion ale; liquid drenched the table.

Flustered, Dizhei jumped up. Thriss sat fixed, unbending, ignoring the disturbance she'd caused.

"We hadn't decided anything without discussing it with you, Shathrissía," Anichent said. He draped an arm around her shoulder and hugged her reassuringly. "We had to make sure the proposal was feasible. All is well, *zh'yi.*"

"I am not some addle-minded child you can lie to," she snarled. Prying his arm from around her shoulder, Thriss scooted away from her bondmate. He caressed her cheek; she slapped his hand away. "Don't. Touch. Me."

Uh-oh. Looks like we might have a situation here, Ro thought. She needed to turn down the heat before it became a meltdown. "How about we take this to the holosuite? You can talk privately, work through—"

"What's this 'we'? And why are you still here?" Thriss turned on Ro, eyes blazing. "Oh I see. You're one of *zhadi*'s lackeys doing her dirty work."

"Watch your impertinence in public," zh'Thane warned.

Ro shot zh'Thane a look, discouraging her from speaking further, and addressed Thriss and her bondmates. "As station security chief, I answer to Colonel Kira, not Councillor zh'Thane and certainly not you. When I suggested you take this to the holosuite, that was a polite way of asking you to resolve your disagreement elsewhere," Ro said evenly. "If you intend to use your holosuite time, I suggest you do it now. Otherwise, there's the door." Pushing her chair back from the group, Ro made it halfway to Quark and Natima's table when the sound of shattering glass caught her attention. She spun around in time to see Thriss brandishing half a broken drinking glass, the razor-sharp edges within centimeters of Anichent's face. Ro started back toward the Andorians at a brisk clip. *Dammit!*

"You push and you push, but I'm not giving in this time," Thriss threatened, loud enough to be heard at the surrounding tables. "I'm not leaving the station without Shar!"

Ro watched, horrified, as Anichent grabbed at Thriss's arm, trying to wrest the makeshift weapon away from her with his free hand. She threw an elbow into his stomach; he grunted, released his grip on her wrist and toppled into her. In lifting her weapon-arm out of Anichent's way, Thriss caught her gown on a chair and her arm fell reflexively, thrusting the jagged glass edge into his shoulder. Shaking uncontrollably, Thriss gasped, stumbled backward.

Raising his hand to his wound, Anichent's face blanched gray. He teetered, tipped, his eyes rolled back into his head and his hand, smeared in dark blue, hung limply.

Dizhei screamed, bracing her weight on the table. Startled, she threw up her hands, bits of glistening glass embedded in her palm.

Ro slapped her combadge. "Security, send a team to Quark's! And alert the infirmary to expect company!" Shoving past zh'Thane and Dizhei, Ro hastily examined Anichent. He drifted in and out of consciousness, his clammy skin shone with sweat. Not being familiar with Andorian physiology, she could only guess he was in shock.

"Councillor!" Ro ordered. "Snap out of it, I need you to help him to the infirmary." Zh'Thane regained her composure, slid her arm around Anichent, and with him propped against her, helped him away from the table. Dizhei followed after zh'Thane, quaking with each step. Within minutes, medical help would arrive to tend to Anichent, but her job wasn't done yet. Ro turned to face Thriss.

Agitated, Thriss, in her blood-spattered dress, huddled against the wall, thrusting the broken glass out in front of her. Upper body hunched, she jerked toward each sudden movement in the crowd.

Her voice low and steady, Ro said, "Put down the weapon." She walked slowly, focusing her energy on capturing Thriss's attention. "Put it down and we'll talk."

"No," she whispered. "I won't."

7

Vaughn plunged his sticky fingers into the washbasin, swishing them around until the remains of the nut-syrup pastries washed away. A servant standing at his shoulder snatched the basin and replaced it the instant he finished. *And I thought Starfleet brass were pampered.* The Yrythny military chieftains, if J'Maah was representative, had a lot in common with feudal lords with their rugs and embroidered couch cushions. Vaughn had vacationed at luxury resorts whose accommodations paled in comparison to these.

"Excellent dinner, Chieftain J'Maah. I enjoyed the roasted shellfish especially," Vaughn said. The *Defiant*'s replicators were good, but having a fresh-cooked meal was definitely appreciated.

Chieftain J'Maah stretched out on the floor, rubbing his full stomach with satisfaction. "Myna is a good cook. She served my House when I was growing up. I took her off Vanìmel when the promotions began. My consort consented to letting Myna come on this journey because of you, Commander Vaughn." He closed his eyes, breathed deeply and relaxed.

Vaughn wondered if this was some kind of mealtime ritual the Yrythny followed and waited to see if M'Yeoh, First Officer Meltoh and Navigator Ocah dropped to the floor. J'Maah's officers remained seated, sipping at goblets of wood wine. Vaughn followed their lead. "My best wishes to your consort, then," he said. "And my compliments to Myna."

A servant had brought J'Maah pillows for his head and feet. Another combed and braided his hair, interweaving crystal beads and ribbons as she worked. She hummed softly.

"Not the rinberry oil, Retal." J'Maah backslapped the servant's cheek. "Takes the color out of the headdress." He shook his braids, his face puckered in resentment. "Go on now, find the right one."

Vaughn was finding it increasingly difficult to stomach the scene playing out before him.

Murmuring apologies, the servant's yellow-green skin blanched; she crawled away on hands and knees. She huddled in the corner, rubbing ointment into the scrape she'd received from the chieftain's chunky rings.

Vaughn wanted to ask if she required medical assistance, when J'Maah explained, "Very loyal, that Retal. But not smart. Can't expect too much from a Wanderer."

Without a word, Retal returned to her ministrations, dabbing J'Maah's scalp with oil, her long graceful fingers deftly weaving the strands.

Vaughn watched, his chest tight. *I think I'd like to be excused from the table.*

Minister M'Yeoh materialized in the chair beside him. "Tell me, Commander, how are the repairs on your ship going?" he murmured. Seated at the foot of the table, he had said little during the meal.

Turning away from his view of J'Maah's pedicure, Vaughn sipped from his wood wine. "The extra hands from the *Avaril*'s engineering staff have helped tremendously." After his concerns about the *Defiant*'s security, he'd reviewed a list of all non-Starfleet personnel allowed to access the repair bay and requested that their bioscans be entered into the security identification system. If he had Yrythny coming and going with Nog's crew, he wanted to keep track of them.

"We've received word from Luthia," J'Maah said. "Your Lieutenant Dax did an excellent job at the Assembly Chamber today."

Perhaps luck hasn't completely eluded us, Vaughn thought, relieved. *Or maybe this Other of the Yrythny is watching out for our mission.*

J'Maah burbled contentedly. "I should have asked you, Vaughn, but Retal here has an excellent way with hair. You're welcome to have her attend to that—that hair on your chin even."

"Thank you for the offer," Vaughn said politely. "Another time, perhaps." Watching this slavish attention to J'Maah was setting Vaughn's teeth on edge and he hoped he'd be given leave to return to his crew shortly. Too bad Quark wasn't here—he would love all this decadence.

"As you wish," J'Maah wheezed, his barrel stomach rising and falling in a relaxed rhythm. "We have the whole way to the Consortium and the whole way back to Vanìmel."

Here comes the part where I might provoke animosity, Vaughn thought. "Chieftain, a point of clarification. The *Defiant* should be spaceworthy by the time we reach the Consortium. Once we obtain our matter load, we plan on flying back to pick up Lieutenant Dax and her team."

"Of course, of course. The needs of your crew come first. I'm sure they're anxious to get on their way," J'Maah said.

"We still hope to explore a great deal of territory before we return home."

"Whatever we can do, Commander. We're here to help." The chieftain's breathing deepened, his body relaxed and finally his membranous lids dropped over his eyes.

The senior staff sat quietly, watching their captain's still figure for a few minutes. Finally, First Officer Meltoh whispered, "This is when we go. You first, Commander."

Hastily, Vaughn made for the exit, grateful for tinny replicated food and sleeping on the deck—without the services of a head masseuse.

"A pillow is a legitimate bet," Tenmei protested.

Julian examined her more closely and determined she was being sincere. "Fine then, I'll take a look at it, decide what it's worth."

Without sitting up, she reached back and grabbed the pillow from where it sat at the foot of her sleeping bag. "Can you put a price on a non–Starfleet-issue pillow at a time like this?" she asked, tossing the pillow at Bashir. "Besides, if Cassini can bet his slippers—"

"They're self-heating!" came Cassini's muffled protest. He'd tunneled into the sleeping bag two across and one down from Tenmei, having retreated there after being soundly thrashed one round back.

"—then I can bet my pillow," Tenmei concluded.

Since Nog, the commerce expert, was otherwise occupied, assigning value to crew members' bets had fallen, by default, to Julian. He preferred to play poker; running the statistical probabilities and plotting strategy was very entertaining. His crewmates, however, determined there wasn't a way to handicap him in cards and none of them enjoyed losing every single round. Either Julian dealt the cards or he watched. "Take it or leave it," Tenmei had told him.

It wasn't fair, really—he didn't consciously choose to win every contest he'd entered—he just did. During their first week into the mission, engineering sponsored a casino night in the mess. Any game that wasn't random, Julian won. After that, it became an unwritten rule that the advantage bestowed on Julian by his genetic enhancements required handicapping or elimination. No one resented his abilities, but no one would play cards with him either. In this round of poker, Julian represented the house. He sat cross-legged on the floor between Chao and Lankford and knew, from his glimpses at their cards, that they'd be joining Gordimer in the "broke" department very soon. Chao might figure out that Tenmei was bluffing—there was no way she could have better than three of a kind—but he doubted it.

When they were on the *Defiant,* the crew usually bet whatever personal items they'd brought with them that didn't exist in the replicator database. Ezri, swearing she had a sure thing, had begged him to loan her Kukalaka after she lost her last bag of *jumja* chews to Bowers. Their present resource scarcity required they be even more innovative.

Gordimer offered his sleeping spot in the darkest, least trafficked corner of the room for the night. Bashir wanted to play for that bet alone. Chao threw in a headset that emitted wave frequencies that improved REM sleep. After coming up empty, Rahim raided Leishman's candy supply, reasoning that Nog wouldn't give his engineers long enough breaks to come back to quarters and *take* a candy break. For her part, Tenmei had a Tholian silk nightshirt Chao and Lankford coveted. Bowers, who won the last hand, currently had possession of the best sleeping spot in the room, the headset, Leishman's candy and Prynn's nightshirt. If Julian didn't sign off on Tenmei's pillow, she was out of the game.

Bashir punched and hefted it, rested it in his lap, raised it to his nose to take a whiff. "Ah! Lavender. Very nice."

"Thank you, Doctor," Prynn said hopefully.

No one made any cracks about Tenmei's relationship to Vaughn earning her Julian's favoritism. Her fellow crewmates were smart enough to know they'd be talking to Julian about mending a deviated septum if they did. Squeezing Prynn's pillow, Julian had to assess its value under the present circumstances.

"Fine. The house agrees to accept Ensign Tenmei's pillow as a raise," Bashir said. "Lieutenant Bowers?"

"Fold," Bowers said with a sigh, tossing in his cards.

Tenmei chuckled contentedly and gathered up her winnings. Cassini emerged from his sleeping bag, retrieved her cards and looked at them. "Two pair? I gave up my self-heating slippers for three of a kind and I could've beaten you."

Tenmei shrugged. "Take my advice, Cassini, stick to dabo. Poker's not your game."

Before Cassini could fire off a retort, the door slid open, admitting the two Yrythny technologists who'd been helping the *Defiant* crew, Tlaral and Shavoh. "We finished our shifts and wondered if there was anything—" Shavoh began. Puzzled, he looked back and forth over the unoccupied dining area and computer station, which blocked their view of the poker game.

"Over here," Bashir called out.

Grabbing Tlaral's arm, Shavoh guided his friend to the rear of the room where the cots and sleeping bags were laid out. Both Yrythny engineers looked confused.

"You'd better have a seat before Lieutenant Nog notices you're here," Tenmei said, patting the spot on Senkowski's mattress pad next to her. Like Leishman, Senkowski wouldn't be back any time soon to use it. The redshirts and blueshirts had begun their joking predictions as to what the yellowshirts would do when Nog finally eased up. While everyone did what they could to help, Nog allowed only the nonengineers to leave at shift's end.

"We're here to help," Shavoh offered. "To work on the *Defiant*."

"Of course you are, but we've all been ordered to mix and mingle. Cultural exchanges and all that. Consider sitting for part of your duty," Tenmei said. "Right, Doctor?"

"Absolutely," Julian confirmed. "We're glad to have you, especially since I think several of our players are going to be tapped out in a minute. Are you interested in learning to play cards?"

Tlaral and Shavoh exchanged glances and Tlaral said, "You'll teach us?"

"Happy to," Tenmei said with a small smile.

Julian winced, knowing *Defiant*'s conn officer was eager to teach their "green" alien friends a thing or two about Alpha Quadrant gambling. That, and to further line her coffers.

The two Yrythny engineers cautiously eased down on the floor, trying to situate their legs comfortably. Both settled for lying on their sides and draping their legs out behind them.

"I believe it was your turn, Ensign Lankford," Julian said.

Wrinkling her nose, she shuffled and reshuffled the cards in her hand, allowed Tenmei to cut the deck, then dealt. "First bet goes to Mr. Bowers," she said after everyone anted.

"I'll open with *Burning Hearts of Qo'noS*."

Chao groaned. "The Klingon bodice ripper? I'll fold." She threw her cards into the pile.

"I take exception to the characterization of that novel as a bodice ripper, Chief," Bowers said with a wink.

"What would you call it? A face biter? I just can't believe someone finally pried it away from Nog."

"Lieutenant, Chief," Julian said, holding up a hand in the direction of each woman, "by the end of this journey, I suspect everyone on *Defiant* will have read *Burning Hearts of Qo'noS* so I'd advise you both to—Tlaral? Are you all right?"

The Yrythny technologist swayed where she sat, her lashless eyelids flickering. "I'm sorry—I feel a little unwell."

Grabbing the tricorder beside him, Julian performed a quick scan. "Obviously, I'm not well versed in Yrythny physiology, but I doubt the level of fluctuation I'm seeing in your readings is normal. Electrolytes, pulse, temperature, hormones . . ."

Tlaral tipped again, this time forward. She threw down her hands to prevent a fall. "I think I need to lie down," she whispered.

Shavoh helped Julian ease Tlaral onto her back. Prynn shoved the pillow beneath her legs, elevating her feet. Bashir ordered Bowers to retrieve his medical bag while Chao doused a cloth in water and draped it over Tlaral's forehead.

"I probably haven't eaten enough today and I've worked a double shift," Tlaral said weakly. Her eyes rolled, her lids dropped and she went limp.

Julian scanned Tlaral with his tricorder. "Prynn, help me examine her for any external injuries."

While Tenmei went to work removing the Yrythny's tunic, Bashir rechecked his tricorder readings before turning his attention to Tlaral's back. "What's this on her shoulder—a birthmark, an old injury?"

Shrugging, Shavoh covered his eyes, worried. "I don't know. She had an accident in engineering last spring, but I think she broke her foot."

"Her heart is racing—I think it's related to the hormonal surge I picked up with my tricorder."

"Wait!" Shavoh said suddenly.

"Is there something I need to know?" Julian asked.

"Check her palms, Doctor."

Tenmei lifted Tlaral's arm and turned over her hand. Her palms bore the faint imprint of a blue starburst.

Relieved, Shavoh sighed. "She's ready to go into the waters! It's her time to mate. This is her first time and I'm sure she didn't know what to expect. But she'll be fine. I'll fetch her consort. Minister M'Yeoh will be pleased." Shavoh sprang to his feet and ran out the door.

Julian dropped back on his heels as Tenmei eased Tlaral back into her tunic. "Learn something new all the time. Today it's Yrythny fertility."

After a few minutes, Tlaral's lids flickered back, her eyes darting anxiously around the room. "What happened—I was sitting and then it all went black."

"As your colleague Shavoh put it, you're ready to go into the waters. She's gone for your consort."

She pressed her hands to her temples. "Oh. That's unexpected. I didn't think it would be for another year," she said nervously.

"Breathe a little more slowly. You might hyperventilate." Julian rubbed her shoulder, hoping it would calm her down. "The scar on your back—it's directly behind your heart and your pulse is highly irregular. Did you have an injury?"

Slowly, she relaxed, taking a proffered blanket from Prynn, tucking it up around her chin. "As a child, Doctor. I was caught in a coral tunnel near my House. Nothing to worry about."

Shavoh appeared with Minister M'Yeoh in tow. He waddled across the room and squatted down by his consort. "Thank you, Doctor," he said, taking Tlaral's hand in his.

"Congratulations are in order. You're going to be parents, I think?"

M'Yeoh didn't have time to follow up with Bashir; an announcement boomed over the comsystem, announcing the *Avaril*'s approach to the Consortium.

When Vaughn arrived on the *Avaril*'s bridge, he saw what looked like a frozen spray of brilliant white gold exploding on the viewscreen. For a moment, he questioned whether they'd actually dropped out of warp, though the warp-engine pulse had been replaced with the static hum of impulse. He looked more closely. Geyserlike eruptions of a giant-size gas particle fountain spread slowly with spindly, chrysanthemum grace.

"Magnificent, isn't it?" Minister M'Yeoh gurgled, wiping his mouth on his sleeve.

Absorbing the spectacular vista, Vaughn simply nodded.

"Our scientists have postulated it's a ruptured singularity," M'Yeoh said.

"A white hole?" Vaughn ventured, wishing Shar were here.

"I'm afraid I'm not familiar with that term, Commander. Nevertheless, I think you'll agree it is a glory to behold by any name."

The navigational sensors were recalibrated. Chieftain J'Maah barked an order to raise shields and increase stabilizers in response to the ebb and flow of gravitational winds originating from the fountain, but not soon enough. Forceful gusts slamming into the starboard side sent the massive *Avaril* lurching and swaying. Yrythny crew and guests alike grabbed onto the closest fixed rail, chair or terminal to avoid being thrown to the floor.

"These straits before we reach the Consortium are the worst, storm-wise," J'Maah explained to Vaughn. "We'll be rocking for a few more minutes and then it's steady traveling until we dock."

The *Avaril* heaved with drunken equilibrium until she passed into a dome-shaped debris field created when matter spewing from the fountain coalesced and cooled, leaving hard, pitted asteroids behind. Nearer the fountain, hot particulate globs glowed white, gradually darkening to invisibility as the vacuum of space cooled them. It was for these nondescript space rocks that they had traveled so far, motivated by the hope of obtaining material resilient enough to manufacture femtobots.

Because the *Avaril* moved slowly, using her tractor beams to move the larger space rocks (some the size of starships) blown into the shipping lane,

Vaughn had time to watch the small mining pods flitting around the debris field closest to the particle fountain. He admired the ingeniousness of the mining pods utilizing small ram-scoops to gather in the cooling particle matter. As J'Maah had explained, the total matter collected by a pod on a single trip to the particle fountain was called a "load." Each Consortium member was entitled to a fixed percentage of loads. Once the member quotas were satisfied, loads became available on the open market. Tomorrow, Vaughn anticipated that one of those mining pods, now flitting about like pollinating insects, would be bringing back a load with *Defiant*'s name on it.

Full pods flew back to their launch bays in the heart of one of the larger asteroids. Rimmed with flashing lights, silver doors rose open and the pods skimmed along narrow octagonal tunnels drilled inside. Hints of the asteroid's internal structures emerged on the surface: glittering domes, needle towers, tunnelways, and massive, reinforced support struts linked to other inhabited asteroids.

One asteroid linked to another and another, and still others beyond Vaughn's sight, creating a massive, asymmetrical structure resembling a complex molecular model or the frame of a geodesic dome. Here, a surface glowed with radiant lights where architects had burrowed deep into rock; there, derrick-style living space perched on the surface of an asteroid. J'Maah had shown him a Consortium map more akin to a molecular model than any city-state Vaughn had familiarity with. He had counted more than eighty-five "suites" (as inhabited asteroids were called) before J'Maah clicked to the next screen.

The *Avaril,* because of her size, would dock at a publicly held platform. Such a location facilitated better access to the Core, host to the Consortium's primary business operations, the matter collecting operation, and public facilities.

Vaughn's task was straightforward. A small Starfleet contingent would go with Minister M'Yeoh to the Member Business Offices. The necessary permits would be acquired, a trade negotiated, and once the matter load was safely ensconced in the *Defiant*'s storage bay, the *Avaril* would return to Vanìmel. Vaughn expected to see Dax's away team six days from now, even anticipating a few bumps along the way. Rare was the plan that proceeded without some complication. Consequently, he decided to hold off contacting Dax until the deal had been settled. That way, she'd have a better idea of how much time she had to work with the Yrythny assemblies. Reassurance that a critical component of the *Defiant*'s upgraded defense system had been acquired would put her mind at ease. If luck smiled on them, they might be able to establish a sub-space link early enough in the evening that Julian and Ezri could exchange good nights before retiring for the day.

All in all, a workable plan, he thought, and left his observation post to set the gears in motion.

"File these," Lieutenant Dax ordered, offloading a shoulder bag and passing it to Shar as they walked down a winding streetway in one of Luthia's upscale residential districts.

Taking the bag, Shar studied his commanding officer quizzically. What exactly was it he was filing, where was he supposed to file it, and how was it, after four years at Starfleet Academy where he'd won a shelf full of awards, published several well-received articles and graduated with honors, he was filing at all? Mostly he was unsure how moving padds, tomes and isolinear chips from conference room to conference room would help resolve Yrythny civil unrest. "Yes, sir," he said neutrally. "Is there anything else you need?"

Lieutenant Dax seemed not to notice his uncertainty. She'd hardly looked at him this morning. Earlier, she'd walked past him to her desktop terminal, pulled up her daily meeting schedule, and brewed a hot seaweed tea before saying "hello." Not that her preoccupation wasn't understandable: the Yrythny committees she worked with had a tendency to change their minds almost hourly.

"Breaking down the historical precedents for establishing Wanderer rights—" she said, "—have you written the summaries yet?" Dax absently waved to an Assembly official Shar remembered meeting during yesterday's padd and data shuffling. Attended by servants and clerks, the official cocked his head in their direction, looked down at his hand, clearly wondering what Ezri meant by wiggling her hand in the air.

"They're in your database, filed under 'representation issues,'" Shar answered. "Delegate Keren signed off on them late last night. She will join us at the Aquaria."

"With Vice Chair Jeshoh following shortly after, I suppose?" Ezri said, rolling her eyes.

"Yes, sir." The morning argument between Jeshoh and Keren had become part of the daily routine. Keren would arrive with her agenda; Jeshoh would arrive with his and the two would quarrel until the next meeting. Whenever they entered the room, Shar's antennae tingled with the kinetic energy they exuded. He found them more stimulating than most of their colleagues.

Dax suddenly stopped. "Let's eat. Once the Assembly members start arriving, they'll keep us talking nonstop."

Chasing after her, Shar cut in front of a pushcart loaded with bushy, orange flora, past several apartment courtyards to a merchant window where a line of Yrythny waited for *shmshu* cheese and leaberry pastries. Ezri ordered one for each of them, using her Assembly meal card to pay the vendor. She took a few bites and crooked her finger at Shar, pointing them in the direction of a crescent-shaped bench. Between nibbles, Shar determined the time had arrived to present a suggestion to Dax.

"Lieutenant," Shar said, hoping he looked authoritative, but respectful; he strove to avoid the just-beneath-the-surface insolence that his *zhavey* accused him of when he was determined to make his point. Insincerity would not help his case with Dax. "I have a request."

Without interrupting her breakfast, she mumbled something about his continuing, put down her pastry, made a notation in her padd, and returned to her eating.

Maybe while she's distracted, she might agree without thinking too hard about it . . . "Sir, while I agree that an understanding of historical and social precedents provides context for your work with the committees, I think we're neglecting a critical area of research."

"Go on." She dabbed at the corners of her mouth.

"The Yrythny conflict is based on the supposition that the Wanderers are biologically inferior to the Houseborn." Shar struggled to keep the excitement out of his voice. "But what if the Houseborn supposition is wrong and we can prove it scientifically?"

"That the inequities between Houseborn and Wanderer biological programming are perceived, rather than actual? My guess is that it's mostly perception," Ezri agreed, throwing her legs out in front of her. "At least I haven't noticed much difference between the groups I've been working with. I think they've built a complex social culture of castes and customs based on suppositions and preconceptions, regardless of any basis in actual fact." Dax wadded up her paper refuse and held it in her fist. Looking at Shar, she smiled indulgently. "Perception is nine-tenths of reality, and in the perceptions of the Houseborn, the Wanderers are inferior. I doubt scientific proof would change that perception. Besides, sometimes even the most absurd traditions and customs evolve as a way to preserve a species or protect a planet."

Shar agreed with Ezri in principle, though he didn't say so. Over the years, he'd learned from Charivretha how the seemingly illogical customs of many worlds had legitimate roots. For example, many religious dietary codes emerged from pragmatic realities. How avoiding a forbidden food because it would make one "unholy" before the divinity sounded more meaningful than saying it was forbidden because it would make the follower hallucinate, foam at the mouth and die. Still, not all customs and codes were so well intended. Prejudice and fear still allowed for cultures to rationalize bad policy. From his own studies, Shar had discovered that the Wanderers had emerged as the artisans, architects, and scientists among the Yrythny. The Houseborn's insistence that the Wanderers "lacked proper instincts" wasn't logical in the face of such clear, measurable evidence of superior intellectual abilities. He was surprised Dax didn't raise the point herself. "In most circumstances, a species is better protected by developing a quantifiable strategy," Shar reasoned. "Such as resource management or environmental restoration."

"Since the Yrythny didn't evolve naturally, it's possible that whoever augmented Vanìmel's primordial soup intended these instincts to play out." She shrugged. "Maybe there are chromosomal mutations or weaknesses in the helices."

"Maybe there aren't," Shar argued.

"For example," Ezri went on, "what would happen if every Yrythny were allowed to reproduce? Could the planet sustain that kind of population explosion?"

"It may not," Shar conceded. "On the other hand, perhaps it can. I've seen no evidence that anyone has yet attempted to answer the question. But even if it can't, science might solve that problem, too."

Ezri sighed. "Maybe these social customs, as repulsive as they may seem to us, serve a purpose not immediately obvious to the outsider. That's why examining their history is crucial. Tracing the origins of this social order might help them course-correct. If you pull out a weed without killing the root, the weed will grow back."

"Yes, sir," Shar said. He set down his pastry, his appetite withering.

"You should know something of restrictive social customs and how they relate to physiological and biological realities from your own experiences."

Shar looked away uncomfortably. He knew that over the course of Dax's eight previous lives, knowledge about Andorians that was unknown to the majority of outsiders had entered into Dax's purview. How much knowledge and how explicit that knowledge was, he couldn't say. Shar hadn't yet probed Ezri's recollections or allowed her to probe his, but he did know Dax wasn't speaking carelessly. He considered what she had said for a moment longer before responding. "But it's my opinion, Lieutenant, after years of studying the interrelationship between sociology and physiology among my people, that it is the rigid structure of our customs that have, in part, landed my species in the predicament it now faces."

"You're saying that the Yrythny adherence to a rigid caste system might be leading them to a similar fate as the Andorians?" Lieutenant Dax said, skeptically.

"I am saying I believe we need to ask the scientific questions in addition to the historical and cultural questions." Shar knew he could prove it to her, given the chance.

Her face softened and she offered him a half-smile. "I don't disagree with you, Shar. But let's look at this realistically. To conduct a proper scientific inquiry, you'll need enough time and cooperative research subjects to create a viable statistical sampling. Otherwise, your conclusions might be specious to the Yrythny."

"Their universities must have databases—"

"We have finite time. Finagling access to those databases could be difficult, especially since the decision to admit me as a mediator was hardly unanimous. Not everyone likes—or trusts—us."

"Respectfully, sir, I am not questioning your decision to pursue the angles we've worked through so far. What I am asking is whether I can tackle some of the scientific questions. I'll complete everything you assign me and pursue those issues on my own time, if you'd rather."

She paused, resting her hand against her lips as she studied him. "All right then, Ensign. I can agree to that, but if I believe you're neglecting my assignments, I'll ask you to desist."

"Yes sir." *A fair enough compromise,* he thought.

"Any word from Commander Vaughn?"

"Not since yesterday. I know he said that he expected they would reach the Consortium today, but circumstances—"

"I know, Shar." She gazed up at Luthia's clear ceiling, starlight refracting through the panels, spraying faint rainbows on volcanic rock facades adorning the surrounding buildings.

Shar knew she worried, though Vaughn hadn't given her any specific reason to be concerned during his regular check-ins. Shar might not have a lover on *Defiant* as Ezri did, but after weeks of working closely with his shipmates, he'd grown accustomed to having them around. Not a day had passed without Shar turning to ask Nog for input on what tools might be more effective in his inquiry on Yrythny genetics. Each time he gazed out Luthia's windows, he wondered how long it would be before Ensign Tenmei persuaded Commander Vaughn to let her try surfing on Vanìmel. He'd also come to know Dr. Bashir on the trip. It had become a private game for Shar to see if he could beat Bashir at anything, be it darts or data recall. So far, Shar had lost every time. The sooner *Defiant* resumed its journey, the better. On this, Shar and Ezri agreed.

At last, Ezri said, "We should go. I'm sure they'll be waiting."

She predicted rightly.

The Aquaria's excellent acoustics allowed the hollow dissonance arising from the Assembly officers milling about to be heard several streetways down from the entrance. Shar and Ezri descended a flight of coral stairs to discover that not a single empty seat remained in the amphitheater. She climbed back up the stairs where she could view the gathering.

Shar waited for Dax to indicate where she wanted him to sit, but with a minimum of five officials dogging her, he assumed she'd appreciate his taking care of himself. On the landing across from her, he noticed an open spot beside a plant bed, swollen with speckle-throat roses and vines twisting over and under small trees. There, he could listen and observe Dax and stay out of the way. Gazing through the Aquaria's transparent floors at Vanìmel's whorled cloud cover, he watched shuttlecraft streak back and forth between the planetside Houses and Luthia's ports. He was intrigued by the illusion of being able to free-fall, through the floor, into the atmosphere. He enjoyed how the Yrythny incorporated awareness of their planet into their living spaces; Luthia felt like an extension of their world, not something separate.

"On the morning agenda—" Ezri began loudly.

Reluctantly, he tore his eyes away from Vanìmel and listened—or tried to listen—to Ezri. Officers continued their discussions, ignoring her.

She cleared her throat. "We're discussing civil rights issues." A pause. The chatter continued. She linked her hands behind her back and rolled back and forth on her shoes a few times before asking loudly, "Can we please focus on the issue at hand?"

Shar looked on helplessly, knowing nothing he could say or do would make them pay attention.

Skin pockets quivering, Rashoh ringed the room, forcing his associates into chairs. Other senior officials, including Jeshoh and Keren, followed suit. Shar was reminded of his *zhavey*'s favorite plant, a leafy tree that refused to accept pruning. Trim a branch, within hours a new shoot had sprouted.

Ezri climbed atop a stool, put a finger in each side of her mouth and whistled.

Pained by the shrill tone, Shar winced, his antennae curling.

But the chattering stopped.

"You and you," she pointed at Jeshoh and Keren. "Select small groups of trusted associates because from now on I'm dealing only with representatives of each Assembly. It's the only way we'll accomplish anything. And if you want to schedule a meeting, a discussion, or a visit, you will first clear it with my assistant, Ensign ch'Thane."

His initial gratitude at regaining control over their schedule dissipated slowly as the implications of his new assignment gradually dawned on him. The Yrythny officials stampeding toward him with their demands represented minutes, hours—possibly precious days—where research would be rendered impossible. *Dax knows what she's doing, focusing our time on her chosen issues,* Shar reasoned. *After all, hadn't she been Curzon Dax, one of the most renowned diplomats in recent Federation history?* Removing a padd from his pocket, he organized petitioners in a line and patiently took down their requests for appointments.

Since his night with Keren's underground, Shar had burned with a yearning to help these people. He simply had to believe, to trust, that Dax knew the best way.

8

"You might try *shusha* herb packs for the swollen ankles," Kira said, tipping back in her chair and resting her feet on the console in front of her. "Apparently the leaves contain some chemical that helps the tissues shed any water they're retaining. Julian doesn't like them because he can't prove in his lab that they work, but most Bajoran women swear by them." She took a sip of her *raktajino* and waited for a response from the viewscreen.

Kasidy Yates, sitting in a loose lotus position on a braided rug in front of her fireplace, wrinkled her nose. *"You think those will work for a human woman?"* She yanked strands of blue yarn out of a skein and was winding them into a ball in preparation for knitting . . . something. Baby footwear, Kira supposed.

Kira shrugged. "Humans and Bajorans have enough in common that what works for us usually works for you. Give it a try. Couldn't be worse than having to stay off your feet."

"True enough," she conceded. *"You look tired, Nerys. Still haven't taken any time off, have you?"*

Dropping her feet to the ground, Kira leaned forward, resting her elbows on the desk. "I'm fine." Shrugging off Kasidy's dubious expression, she reiterated her stance. "Really. With all the VIPs around, the tempo around here's a little more crazed than usual. But I'm staying on top of it all, though I'm still working on the fine art of balance. The captain had it mastered."

"True. Ben could throw a dinner party in the middle of a crisis—or take time to visit his land when he faced a serious decision," she said while focusing her gaze on the length of yarn she'd just pulled out. *"Sometimes he'd go out in the back where the porch is now, pull out the baseball bat, and whack some balls. Made him feel better."*

"Are you saying that taking up a hobby will better my leadership skills? Or are you guilting me into coming to Bajor?" Kira chuckled.

"You caught me." Kas smiled, allowing the yarn to roll off her lap. She looked up at Kira. *"I'd like the company. Someone who knows me for me and not merely as the Emissary's wife and mother of the Avatar. And don't forget the farmers are bringing in the katerpods over the next few weeks. You don't want to miss that!"*

Memories of dark, smoky autumn nights nudged their way into the present. Kira sighed, feeling pangs of longing for those few simple moments her people had stolen from the Occupation: walking winding farm lanes with lighted copper lanterns to ward off the inky darkness, and singing the harvest melodies, thanking the Prophets for another year of bounty, even though that bounty might be little more than a handful of katerpods.

"I know you want to visit," Kas said. *"I have your room all ready—it has a lovely view of the river. They're starting the sugaring in a few weeks. . . ."* Her voice trailed off, her tone teasing and tempting.

"All right, all right! You've convinced me." Kira held up a hand in good-natured protest. "I'll talk to my staff and see what works best into the station's schedule."

"If you're structuring your plans on the station's schedule, you'll be here about the time my child's grandchildren are born," Kasidy snorted.

. . . and that may be how long it takes for my fellow Bajorans to start speaking to me again, all things considered, Kira thought ruefully. "Work before play, Kas. You know the drill."

"Yeah, I do." Kasidy nodded. *"But that doesn't stop me from trying. We'll talk next week?"*

"Sooner if we have word from Jake. I promise."

Kasidy closed her eyes and inhaled deeply. *"And please let there be word from Jake,"* she said, invoking whatever powers the universe might use to bring him back home.

"Prophets willing, Kas," Kira said earnestly. She straightened up, slapped her thighs and smiled to lighten the mood; she wanted to end their conversation on a positive note for Kasidy's sake. "Besides, I'll want you to tell me how well the herb packs worked on those swollen ankles. Without having Julian around to tell you how it's all just a bunch of folk hokum, you don't have any excuse not to try them."

Kasidy smiled. *"Yates out."*

Before Kasidy's face winked out, Kira noted that it had started to exhibit that soft roundness characteristic of mid-pregnancy. Her hand dropped to her own belly and she ran her fingers over her flat stomach, remembering what it felt like to carry a life inside her. She wondered how Kirayoshi liked Earth, if her presence even shaded his memories.

Enough, Nerys, this is the part where you look at your endless to-do list and come up with meaningful reasons why you won't be tumbling back to your quarters until after midnight. She gave a cursory glance to a half dozen padds sitting on her desk. Ro's mostly informational report on the Ohalavaru trinkets left on her doorstep awaited her attention. In moments of morbid curiosity, she watched reports from the Bajoran news feeds, read the opinion pieces cropping up in the journals; the furor had yet to die down. She wanted desperately to believe that the late-night visit to her door was only a misguided gesture by some well-meaning individual. But in her heart she feared it was a portent of things to come . . . things she herself had set into motion by making the banned Ohalu text public.

Stop it, she told herself. *This is getting you nowhere.* Before diving into Ro's report, she decided to scroll through the list of music selections in her personal database: Charlie Parker, Dizzy Gillespie, Sarah Vaughn . . . *Hmmm. I have to remember to ask Elias if there's any relation.* She mulled over the list, figuring something among the unfamiliar titles would help her to relax. They were all Captain Sisko's choices: a gift to her some years ago on the occasion of a Terran holiday, she couldn't recall which one. The memory made her wish she'd made as much of an effort to share Benjamin's culture as he had always made to share hers.

"Computer," she said finally. "Play Sisko Jazz Compilation Number Nine, track seven: 'Yardbird.'"

A wailing alto saxophone pierced the stillness, its clear, passionate notes lulling her into passivity as she contemplated the vast canvas of stars outside her great eye of a window. *I could stand here and dream all night, except for that nagging sense of duty that never goes away. Even if I put off the reports, I still have one last bit of business that won't wait. But then what? Catch up on latest Starfleet regs. Call it a night, take a late supper in quarters.*

Or not.

She hadn't felt this restless for a long time, plagued by the feeling that she had a forgotten task. Unknown anxiety twisted her stomach. Not with anticipation so much as apprehension. *What's next? If I had a friend close by, I'd go for a walk.* A stroll along the Promenade balcony would be a perfect distraction. Maybe Kasidy was right: time for a hobby. A new sport like orbital skydiving. Plant sculpting or cultivating orchids. She could start knitting something for Kasidy's baby.

Or . . . I could figure out what the Cardassians are up to.

Now it was out there. She dared to think it. For the bulk of the day, Kira had ignored Macet's surprise visit except in the most superficial terms. Avoidance wasn't her usual method; tackling conflict head-on was more her style. Considering how she'd allocated her time these last months, Kira realized she'd spent little—if any—on Cardassian matters. Outside of keeping the supply line of humanitarian aid flowing to Cardassia as the ships came through the station, and the brief interaction she'd had with Macet during the Europani evac, Kira had pushed Cardassia far out of her train of thought. Let someone else worry about them for a change.

Hadn't she done her part, training Damar in "Resistance 101"? To her knowledge, she was the sole Bajoran hiking through Cardassia's bombed-out ruins after the Founders meted out their punishment. *What do they want from me? From us,* she amended quickly. *This wasn't personal. Whatever Macet and Lang had come for, it wasn't about Kira Nerys.* All that was required of her was to serve honorably as commander of Deep Space 9. Follow orders, make sure nothing blows up, protect the public trust, end of story. Her chapter in the Cardassian saga ended with her testimony to the Allied Tribunal negotiating the Dominion War Accords. Period.

Her stomach growled and Kira wondered if it might be time to replicate dinner. Aching muscles up and down her spine begged for attention. She ignored her discomforts. "Computer, search main library database for references to knitting with yarn."

"Two hundred ninety-two thousand, seven hundred sixty references. Narrow search parameters."

"Maybe I should just call Kas back," Kira muttered.

"Input not recognized," the computer intoned.

"Never mind. Cancel search," Kira said irritably. The computer issued a bleat of acknowledgment before falling silent. Her musings ended abruptly when, out of the corner of her eye, she saw the indicator light on her desk that signaled the arrival of a turbolift into ops. She checked the time; too early for her last appointment. Kira turned toward her office doors, looking through the windows and across ops to see who her visitor was. When she saw him, she found herself fighting down the instinct to go for her phaser.

He descended the stairs into the pit with slow, steady steps, past the situation table and toward the opposing stairs that led up to her office. She could see several of the ops crew reacting to the new arrival, looking to her for orders. In response, Kira steeled herself and touched the control on her desk that would open the office doors to admit her visitor. *No ghosts tonight. No ghosts.* She mouthed the words, intent on believing them.

He paused before stepping over the threshold. "Colonel Kira. I hope I'm not interrupting anything important."

Kira couldn't suppress the grim smile that came to her lips at the Prophets' sense of humor. "What can I do for you, Gul Macet?"

"... and while I recognize that postwar reconstruction tends to focus, by necessity, on basic needs like potable water, adequate food supply and medical care, don't you think that expending resources on life's little luxuries serves morale?" Quark waited for Natima to agree with him, but she'd half turned away from him, peering out into the crowds. "Yoo-hoo." He cleared his throat, waved a hand in front of her face, but she brushed it aside.

"Check out what's going on across the room," she admonished him.

What could be more interesting than me? he thought. Glancing over Natima's shoulder, he saw Ro run-walking toward the Andorians' table, reach up to touch her combadge. *Something's cooking. Glass shattering! What the hell—?*

From over the din of customers, he heard a plaintive exclamation, "You push and you push, but I'm not giving in this time!" and the sounds of scuffling. A chilling scream.

A hush descended on the bar. Curious onlookers left gambling and eating to get a better view, effectively blocking Quark's as they huddled around the table. Rising from his own chair, he caught the dabo boy scurrying to the bar and ducking behind the counter.

"Let her handle this, Quark," Natima warned. "She seems capable of managing far worse."

Yeah, but how many chairs and glasses will be broken in the process? Quark smiled. "I'll be right back. Don't give away my seat."

Racing across the bar, Quark pushed his way through the crowd to the front just in time to witness Ro spinning into a sidekick, her foot connecting with the Andorian's arm, sending a broken glass spinning through the air and vaporizing when it hit the floor. The Andorian retaliated, slamming her fist, full speed, into Ro's cheek. He took a few steps backward to avoid the falling bodies; the Andorian's momentum had toppled them both.

Ro planted her hands on her attacker's collarbone, shoving against her. She threw an elbow into Ro's stomach; Ro replied with a leg hooked around the Andorian's hip and a boot heel jammed into the small of her back. The Andorian jerked back with a wail and crumpled onto her knees, giving Ro a chance to untangle herself and scramble to her feet.

With split-second response, the very attractive (in Quark's opinion) Andorian sprang to her feet and lunged at Ro, who successfully sidestepped the Andorian's attack. The women circled each other.

"Stay out of what doesn't concern you!" she shouted.

"Back off!" Ro ordered. "Now!"

"Can I help anyone here? Drinks? Maybe take a few wagers, 3 to 1 odds in Lieutenant Ro's favor." Quark hastily pocketed latinum slips, hoping he remembered who bet what.

A pair of security officers arrived to assist Ro. Quark held them back until he could be assured that their involvement wouldn't compromise Ro's safety. The blood pooled on the floor beneath the table testified to Quark's fear.

The Andorian lunged and tackled Ro, pinning her flat to the floor. From her back, Ro had been unable to assume a proper offensive position, giving the Andorian time to pull back her arm for another punch. Ro swept her opponent's legs from beneath her and sent her sprawling. She had a sidearm out of her concealed holster and targeted on the Andorian before she could make a second pass.

"That's my girl," Quark said to the impressed onlookers.

"I dare you to fire," the Andorian hissed, her chest rising and falling rapidly. Crouched and tensed on her hands and knees, she resembled a Norpin falcon ready to spring on her prey.

"Don't tempt me," Ro countered. Keeping her weapon fixed on her assailant, Ro scrambled to her feet and turned to one of her deputies. "Sergeant Etana, I want this individual in restraints. If she resists, shoot her. Quark, can I get a glass of water?" She swiped the sweat off her forehead with her sleeve.

Quark dispatched a slack-jawed dabo girl to fill Ro's request. No way was he going to miss a moment of Laren in action.

"Eat. Drink. Gamble. Leave." Ro shooed away the crowds, encouraging a return to whatever form of debauchery they were indulging in. When they were satisfied she wasn't cheating them out of any action, they gradually dispersed. The dabo girl arrived with Ro's water; she downed it in one swallow. With the Andorian restrained, Ro took her by the arm and dragged her toward the door. "We're going to have a little chat in my office, Thriss."

Thriss complied, but before she left the premises, Ro turned to Quark with a wrinkled brow and opened her mouth as if she had something to say.

"Something the matter?" Quark asked.

"Only three to one in my favor?"

"I'll lay better odds next time," he promised, giving her a wicked grin. *What a woman!*

In each encounter, Macet's appearance rendered Kira momentarily dumbstruck: the resemblance was extraordinary.

His voice had the same rolling timbre, the rounded rising and falling tones and elongated diction as Dukat. Kira saw him in profile: the aquiline nose and square chin casting an exaggerated silhouette on her wall. She pushed away images of Dukat's hand curling around Meru's chin, his fingers stroking the surface of her mother's ugly facial scar. Of a blue velvet dress he had sent her to wear to a dinner party, as if she were a decorative accessory whose purpose was to bring him pleasure. Of him standing at the altar of the *pah-wraiths* on Empok Nor, seducing his followers into decadent, sensual worship. But Dukat was gone. Kasidy had confided what she'd learned from her vision of the Emissary, and Kira believed the story. She took comfort in it.

Especially now.

"I didn't anticipate meeting with you until tomorrow," she told Macet. "I'm sorry that I wasn't able to greet the *Trager* when it docked. First Minister Shakaar has given me several assignments, including overseeing the planning of the reception—" Kira gazed over at him, standing statue still. *No ghosts . . .*

"It's the reception I've come to speak with you about." Macet strolled languidly toward her desk. "Alon Ghemor has a gift he'd like presented to Bajor on behalf of the Cardassian people. We'd expected to give it to the first minister privately, but since Minister Shakaar elected to have our first official meeting at the reception, it seems appropriate to share it there." He stopped in front of Kira's desk, hands folded before him.

He has an almost noble carriage, she thought. *And his mouth has none of Dukat's cruel twist about it.* Nonetheless, her skin crawled. Kira pursed her lips. "Ensign Beyer—one of my staff—is doing the bulk of the planning. Feel free to contact her."

"Our request is simple," he said. "We would like the opportunity to say a few words. The presentation will take fifteen to twenty minutes."

Grateful for the excuse to look anywhere else, Kira turned to her console and pulled up Beyer's files on the reception. Playing music proved to be a fortuitous choice: the energetic jazz melodies filled a potentially uncomfortable silence nicely. "Based on what I see here, I think we could manage a half hour after dessert."

Macet acknowledged her offer with a smile. "I believe Ambassador Lang will be satisfied."

"I'll make sure it's arranged. Would it be too much to ask for some idea about what we might expect?" *Ladies and gentlemen, presenting Skrain Dukat! And for his first act, he'll invite a pah-wraith to possess the first minister.*

"Something that I believe will set the proper tone for our visit," Macet said earnestly. "I'd rather not say more until the reception."

Kira frowned. "Let me be frank, Macet: I hate surprises."

"You'll like this one."

Steady, Nerys. This is still the man who helped us pull off the Europani evac, when he certainly didn't have to. "In that case, I'll look forward to your—surprise. Thank you for stopping in."

Macet didn't move from where he stood, lingering expectantly for a long moment. Kira straightened up. She'd be damned if she'd cower in his presence. Even raised to her full height, she had to look up at the gul to meet his gaze.

His broad, thick shoulders enhanced his dominating stature. *So what.* She'd taken down opponents far more intimidating than Macet.

"There is a story going around," Macet said at length, "that you had a—how shall I put it?—a unique experience during the gateway affair. I'd be most interested in hearing about it."

Kira had to admit it took a certain amount of fearlessness to seek out, without support personnel or weapons, a former enemy in the enemy's territory. Wasn't that what the entire Cardassian delegation was doing? Still, Macet had yet to provide answers about the purpose of their mission. *Not too much trust on your part either, gul.*

"Actually, I have another appointment due to arrive at any moment," she said.

He nodded, his expression once again emotionless. "Another time, perhaps. Forgive my presumptuousness, Colonel. But please reserve a moment for me tomorrow at the reception, should duty permit." Not waiting for her to reject him again, he offered her a brusque nod of his head and promptly exited her office.

Kira watched him leave. It seemed to her as if it took forever for the turbolift to arrive. When it finally did, it was occupied.

Taran'atar stepped onto ops. From her vantage, Kira could see the cold set of his eyes. Symbolically adjusting his weapons belt, the Jem'Hadar's hand hovered over his sidearm as he strode past Macet without acknowledging him, a pointed gesture he clearly wanted the Cardassian to see. Because in seeing his hands ready to engage a weapon at the slightest provocation, the gul would know Taran'atar was prepared to fight. *He's laying the footings for a psychological war with Macet.*

Macet responded to the Jem'Hadar with a smirk before he entered the lift. "Habitat ring," he said, and as the lift descended, he turned his smile on Kira before disappearing from view.

"You wished to see me, Colonel?" Taran'atar said as he entered her office.

Kira was still looking thoughtfully at the turbolift doors when she got down to business. "I believe there was an incident recently involving your continued shrouding aboard the station that we need to straighten out . . ."

When she reached her office, Ro pushed Thriss into a chair and immediately contacted Dr. Tarses with a request that the new Starfleet counselor stop by for a consultation. Councillor zh'Thane would have concerns about privacy, but Ro didn't give a damn. Thriss had started a bar brawl and deserved to be treated like anyone else who might have started a fight, be she common drunk or royalty.

As she began to process Thriss—taking her personal belongings and performing a general scan to assure she wasn't carrying any hidden weapons—Ro couldn't help thinking how ironic it was that trouble hadn't come from where it had been expected. They'd taken massive precautions to assure that the station would be safe from the Cardassians and that the Cardassians would be safe from the station. That Ro's biggest headaches had come from the Andorians instead of Macet's crew was predictably unpredictable.

Thriss complied completely with Ro's orders. She didn't cry, offer protestations of innocence or petulant sarcasm; she stared off at nothing. Neither did she resist being led away to the holding cell and once she was there, she immediately lay down and fell asleep. Ro wrote her incident report, ignoring the semiregular pages from Councillor zh'Thane. She told the night shift corporal to take the names of anyone—meaning zh'Thane—who wanted to talk with her. Or let them make morning appointments and she would deal with their grievances then. From her monitor, she periodically checked in on the sleeping Thriss until she was satisfied this round was over. At least until Thriss woke up and then, with any luck, Ro would be back in her quarters and the counselor could manage any outbursts. Overall, Ro had guardedly optimistic expectations, though Councillor zh'Thane might still make her life a living hell in retribution for locking up Thriss.

When the therapist arrived, Ro put aside her usual distrust of counselors and shook Lieutenant Commander Phillipa Matthias's offered hand. The counselor met her eyes directly when they exchanged names, unapologetically bypassed the usual social niceties and went straight to business. *Impressive,* Ro thought. If Matthias didn't employ the usual touchy-feely, mind game hocuspocus techniques, she might look forward to involving the counselor in more of her investigations. Ro had developed a healthy dislike for mental health professionals during her incarceration. *"Could this be latent anger against your sense of childhood abandonment?"* had been Ro's favorite query. *Excuse me? A sense of abandonment? How about wholesale repression of your people as justification for being a little pissed off!*

When Matthias asked for background information, Ro launched into the story of the bar fight and the parameters of the odd meeting with Councillor zh'Thane. Matthias halted Ro before she could get into specifics.

"Councillor zh'Thane's perspective, while illuminating, is still her perspective. Thriss deserves an unbiased evaluation. Knowing that there's some precedent for Thriss's behavior is enough to get started. You have her in a holding cell. That would be . . . ?" She gestured, inquiring at the four doors in Ro's office that led deeper into the security station.

Before Ro could reply, a dark, bearded Bajoran man, hair threaded with gray, entered from the Promenade carrying a squirming toddler—a girl—and holding a young boy's hand. Ro didn't need to ask who the children belonged to: they had the same hazel-green eyes she'd been looking into for the past few minutes.

"Sibias . . . ?" Matthias said, clearly fishing for an explanation.

She nodded toward her guest. "Lieutenant Ro, station security."

"Chon Sibias, Commander Matthias's husband, and these are our children," he said, shifting his daughter's weight from one shoulder to the other. "Pleasure meeting you, Lieutenant."

Whenever Ro met a Bajoran, she peered at their earring to see if she could discern the individual's family or geographical origins. The unique characteristics of Chon's earring intrigued her, but before she could inquire further, the chubby-fisted girl wriggled out of her father's arms and threw her arms around her mother's legs, nearly tipping her backward.

"I couldn't sleep, Mommy!" she wailed.

"The children wanted to say good night, Phillipa," Sibias offered apologetically. His wife threw a hand against the wall to maintain her balance. The boy, about eight, shuttled behind his father, peeking out from behind his legs with shy seriousness. His rumpled pajamas and mussed hair indicated he might have been roused from bed to accompany his sister on this late-night visit.

"My room is scary. There are monsters in my closet," she pouted, petulantly extending her lip.

Brushing the child's tangled dark curls out of her face, Matthias dropped to one knee and refastened a crookedly done-up nightgown. "Mireh. Your father will make sure you have a wristlight so you can check under your bed as often as you like, but you need to go back to your bed. No dropping your tooth cleaner in the replicator and pretending you can't find it. No hiding Walter in Arios's closet. Your father will say no if you ask to sleep in our room," she said over the child's head, directly to her husband. "Right, Sibias?"

He rolled his eyes in mock protest. "You say that like she's the one in charge, Phillipa."

"Isn't she?" Matthias said, arching an eyebrow.

"My father used to play the *klavion* to keep me from being afraid," Ro interjected. She crouched down beside Matthias. "Maybe your dad has something special like that he can do for you."

"Hey, you have funny wrinkles like my dad and the kids in my class," Mireh said, pointing at Ro's nose. "And like me!" She touched her finger to her own nose and began giggling.

"Mireh has never been—I've never been—around a lot of Bajorans. It's still a novelty to her," Sibias explained.

Matthias stretched an arm toward her son. "I'd like to say good night before you leave, Arios." The boy twisted his head into his shoulder, blushing. Sibias lifted him by the collar and pushed him toward his mother. She caught Arios's elbow and pulled him into her arms, feathering his forehead with kisses.

Ro stood up, giving the mother and her children some room to be affectionate. Normally such scenes of domesticity pressed all the wrong buttons with Ro. Having been orphaned young and having grown up in the resettlement camps, Ro had known little of family life, the closest thing being the time she served on the *Enterprise* and she had more or less messed that relationship up. But this family, for some reason, didn't annoy her so much. *Maybe I'm mellowing in my old age.* She stood next to Sibias, who appeared content to let his wife have some one-on-one time with their children.

"You didn't grow up on Bajor?" she asked him.

"I was an orphan in the Karnoth resettlement camp, or so the records say," he said matter-of-factly. "Smuggled off when I was Arios's age. I grew up far away from here on a Federation colony. While Phillipa is stationed here, I'm hoping to find out exactly where my family comes from." He twirled the earring chain between his thumb and forefinger, as if this piece of his heritage was at once familiar and foreign.

Ro had heard far too many stories like Sibias's during her years away from Bajor. Thousands of misplaced children were spirited away from starvation and disease only to discover as adults that they lacked cultural bearings. "Start near the Tilar Peninsula in the Hedrickspool Province. These markings," she pointed to several ridges and runes, "they're unique to an area just outside the outback."

He touched her arm, his eyes full of questions she knew he couldn't ask. "Thank you."

"If I can help . . ."

"I know. I'll stop by sometime. I'd like to talk with you."

With a reluctant sigh, Commander Matthias sent both children scurrying back to their father. "I might be all night," she warned her husband.

Sibias nodded. "I plan on attending the first service in the morning. Will you be back by then?"

"I hope so, I—" With eyes watering, Matthias pinched her lips tightly together; she swallowed a yawn with a gulp. "So tomorrow night?"

"We'll try to go out again." He kissed her. "You know how much I hate sleeping without you." They exchanged smiles and she watched as her little family departed.

"Let's go see Thriss," Matthias said, letting Ro lead her out of the office. As they walked, Ro guessed the holding area wouldn't be the most pleasant spot to work from; it was designed to accommodate prisoners and guards, not host therapy sessions. "The visuals can be transmitted into the conference room if you'd rather work in comfort."

Matthias didn't seem concerned. "All I need is a place to sit—the floor is fine. I'd like to start off with in-person observations."

They wound through a hallway and passed through another door before arriving at the holding area. The Andorian hadn't moved since Ro had last checked her; prostrate on a hard bench without a pillow or blankets, she slept with her knees curled into her stomach, her hands balled into fists. She failed to stir when they entered. "She doesn't seem to be in a talking mood," Ro pointed out pragmatically.

"Exhaustion will do that to a person," Matthias said, walking up next to the force field where she could study Thriss at closer range. She tipped her head thoughtfully, brought a hand to her chin and gnawed on her index finger. "I'm satisfied to work from here. Thriss's posture, her muscular tension, the length of her REM cycles—all can yield significant data about her state of mind." She patted an equipment bag she had thrown over her shoulder. "Besides, I have a tricorder I've engineered to my own specs that can help out." Matthias paused, scrutinizing Ro after a fashion that made Ro wonder if her secret thoughts were translatable via the number of times her eyes blinked or how often she pushed back her bangs. Counselors, even reasonable ones, made her nervous.

"Your cheek," Matthias said, addressing Ro's quizzical expression. "You might want Dr. Girani to look it over."

"Good idea." *Still more than ready to assume the worst about people's intentions. Nice going, Laren.* Ro touched her face, feeling out the size of her bruise with her fingers; she had forgotten about her own injuries. A swipe with a dermal regenerator would likely fix the bruise on her face, but there was always the chance Thriss's assault had resulted in a fracture or sprain. "Okay. Since I'm done here, go ahead and make yourself at home. The replicator's over there. If you need additional help, page the corporal on duty. Don't hesitate to contact me if the situation blows all to hell."

"Oh believe me. If it goes to hell, you'll be beamed here in your sleep-wear."

Ro appreciated the new counselor's lack of faux sympathy; she hated how some counselors felt obligated to put on the "I-feel-your-pain" face. Matthias knew her job and went about doing it—without theatrics.

As Ro started for the exit, she heard Matthias move to the replicator and say, "Espresso, double and black," before she settled in to begin her observations of Thriss.

9

Down a dim tunnel, the rattling slidewalk chugged toward the Core, periodically stalling when the grinding gears jammed, only to resume with a jerk and continue forward. Vaughn hardly noticed: he might as well have been standing still. Seething sounds receded as his thoughts consumed his attention. The dregs of the Gamma Quadrant swirled around him, hefting their tankards, negotiating sales and sharing canisters of psychoactive vapors. So preoccupied was he, that when a Knesska miner's red horned lizard jumped off his master's shoulder and onto Vaughn's it took a moment to register. In the last few minutes, an inescapable sense of déjà vu had vaulted him back more years than he'd admit to.

During the summer between Vaughn's second and third years at the Academy, he and a group of friends had heard rumors of an exotic shrine on a tropical world in the Braslota system. Supposedly, drinking the water flowing through the shrine from the underground pools endowed the partaker with potent aphrodisiac powers. Lured by the promise of decadent delights, native men and women would sneak out of their homes at night and into the pilgrim camps where they would offer themselves up for seduction. While most thinking individuals would find such a legend highly suspect, Vaughn and his classmates, looking for diversion from the rigors of academia, decided a vacation was in order. They procured passage on a Rigelian shuttle, transferred to a freighter bound for Volchok Prime and met a merchant willing to drop them off.

After three days hiking through the jungle, they found the shrine, attended by a wizened humanoid of unknown extraction, drank the water, retired to their sleeping bags and awaited their prospective encounters.

Instead, Chloe came down with dysentery, Vaughn's tricorder was swiped from his backpack and everyone awoke with a profusion of deter-fly bites. The experience taught him the wisdom of the old adage: if it sounds too good to be true, it probably is.

This humiliating moment from his youth replayed in vivid detail as he listened to Minister M'Yeoh explain that for all their painstaking efforts during the last day, the desperately needed matter load eluded them. Everything M'Yeoh and Runir had said indicated that success was guaranteed; Vaughn hadn't even conceived a contingency plan. Yes, there was something to be said for enjoying the journey, as he'd learned from his encounter with the Inamuri, but with each passing day, he wondered how long the mission would be bogged down in this region. If there was quicksand in the Gamma Quadrant, they'd flown into it.

As he half listened to M'Yeoh's quasi-intelligible explanations about how and why the trade might have failed, Vaughn reviewed the day, from the beginning, and tried to figure out where he misstepped.

Early in the Consortium's thirty-hour day, Vaughn and Minister M'Yeoh obtained the proper permits for trading on the Exchange, the forum where loads were traded. M'Yeoh took Vaughn to meet the broker—a mild-mannered Legelian named Runir—who would represent them on the Exchange floor. Runir handled the Yrythny accounts. From the plush divans to marbled-glass light fixtures, he appeared to successfully manage the accounts of other clients as well. *Maybe this is where we fell down—all the documentation we signed off on had to be translated into Federation standard. If our translators missed cultural nuances . . .* He shook his head, knowing they had to solve this problem quickly.

"Can we resubmit our bid tomorrow?" Vaughn asked, loathing the prospect of wasting more days attempting to devise an alternative defense to the web weapons.

M'Yeoh pushed his hands up into caftan sleeves, pinching his mouth into a tight line. "I think not. We start over."

"Runir must earn profit by the word," Nog groused. "But the thing that doesn't make sense . . ." He twisted his lobe between his thumb and forefinger as his voice trailed off. When he realized Vaughn, Prynn and M'Yeoh waited for him to complete his sentence, he grinned broadly. "Never mind. It's nothing. I still say we should reuse the contract."

Vaughn recognized that look. Nog was on to something. Thankfully, his chief engineer knew when not to finish a sentence.

And Nog was right. It had been a perfectly decent contract. He had examined it with an eye to every possible deceitful angle and found nothing. Initially, Nog had been invited to join Vaughn and M'Yeoh to evaluate the metallurgical quality of available matter loads. His radiant face as he'd watched Vaughn and Runir wheeling and dealing proved that you can take a Ferengi out of commerce, but you can't take the commerce out of the Ferengi. The femtobot simulations back on the *Avaril* were all but forgotten as Nog had hung on Runir's explanations, constantly interrupting the trader with nitpicky questions: "What are the currency units?" "Who sets the exchange rates?" and the finer points of the Exchange's bartering protocols. Nog's willingness to do most of the talking had allowed Vaughn to keep his eye on M'Yeoh, look for any hint of impropriety. He hadn't forgotten the tactics employed by the Yrythny back on Luthia, or discounted the fact that the *Defiant* had been illicitly boarded within hours of the *Avaril*'s launch. Surrendering the acquisition issues to Nog served both of their causes. Even the needs of their other companion, Prynn, appeared to be met as she enjoyed every hour away from *Avaril*.

Cabin fever had started taking root when the relentless engineering repairs, disrupted routine, and being caged aboard the *Avaril* began to wear on the crew. Morale had steadily declined since leaving Luthia and he sympathized. As a goodwill gesture, Vaughn had offered the "break" as a poker bet in last night's game. Prynn rode a lucky streak to a win. *Who'd have guessed my own daughter would turn out to be a card sharp?* For the others, mini–shore leave would come after business was taken care of.

Except now it appears business won't be taken care of, he thought. Shoulder to shoulder, aliens blocked Vaughn from being able to see how much distance separated them from the Core's Central Business District. He leaned off to the side only to have his view obstructed by clouds of chemical coolants bursting from cracked conduits.

Behind him, M'Yeoh muttered a question that Vaughn couldn't hear over the racket. "Excuse me, Minister, but would you repeat that?"

"Runir," M'Yeoh sniffed, "believes that depressed interstellar commerce has reduced the demand for the starcharts and navigational data, even though the information you offered is unparalleled in this sector. Our explorations simply haven't taken us as far as yours have."

"What I can trade, I've offered. I've nothing else," Vaughn said firmly.

"There's always something," M'Yeoh said, "If the need is desperate enough."

The slidewalk ended. They walked with the anonymous masses into the sweltering Core quad. Stalls sandwiched between kiosks and storefronts hawked spangled jewelry and *objets d'art* interspersed with much less innocent contraband. Vaughn suspected the services of prostitutes and slaves were as easy to purchase as gaudy earrings. M'Yeoh led them to a booth out of the traffic flow, presumably to regroup.

Once seated, M'Yeoh twisted the sleeves of his government robe, his expression puckered; the Yrythny appeared to be legitimately miserable. Runir's failure cast aspersions on M'Yeoh's competency. Explaining to his superiors back home why the mission to the Consortium failed would be unpleasant. But Vaughn didn't give a damn whose fault it was—he just wanted it fixed.

The group scooted into the half-circle booth, the rubbery seat coverings sticking to their uniforms. A dingy globe rested in the table's center, providing minimal muddy light to see by. Nog hastily lifted his tricorder after discovering gummy residue on the table's surface. Prynn's hands stayed safely in her lap.

Vaughn shooed away a drink server; the time to unwind would come later. Time to reassert his authority—he'd followed M'Yeoh's lead long enough. "Prynn, Nog. Head back to the *Avaril*. Rerun those femtobot simulations and see if there's something we've overlooked—maybe an alternative deployment method that won't require the degree of structural integrity we're looking for. We may have to take our chances with whatever we have on hand."

Nog failed to veil a dubious expression, but accepted Vaughn's order with a nod.

His beady eyes darting from side to side, M'Yeoh hunched closer to Vaughn. "There are still some who might help you. No legal protection. Very dangerous, but you could see—"

"Belay that," Vaughn called to Nog and Prynn, then turned back to M'Yeoh. "Back up a step, Minister. Say that again." Vaughn interrupted, knowing if he didn't the minister might yammer on endlessly without reaching his intended point.

He gulped and whispered, "A shadow trader."

"You mean a freelancer. An unauthorized broker," Vaughn guessed. Minister M'Yeoh nodded.

Now that's interesting, Vaughn thought. "Tell me more."

"It's a dangerous undertaking," the minister stressed. "We could be duped if we link up with the wrong one." M'Yeoh nervously scanned the crowds, presumably for hostile elements. "But they don't trade what they don't have. Find the right one, you'll have your load." Sweat drizzled off his forehead; he dabbed at it with his sleeve, his gray-brown skin took on a decidedly paler hue.

Vaughn exchanged looks with his chief engineer. He was counting on Nog's acute listening skills to pick up nuances in the business discussions that Vaughn might miss. Nog looked intrigued, but suspicious.

Turning back to M'Yeoh, Vaughn said, "If such an option ensures results, why didn't we start with a shadow trader?" Why was it that at every turn in his dealings with the Yrythny, he found that they'd conveniently omitted information? Not enough to technically be considered a lie, but certainly less than all the facts.

"A shadow trader's demands may be costly or risky," M'Yeoh squeaked. "Outlawed technology. Slaves. Illegal goods. Weapons. You made it clear what you were willing to negotiate with. Your terms would be better accepted on the Exchange."

Or you were too afraid to deal with anything but the known entities, Vaughn thought. He needed to remove M'Yeoh from the equation if he wanted to make a quick deal.

Loud, laughing revelers stumbling toward a casino careened toward their booth, drinks held high. They jumped out of their seats, missing a frothy soaking by seconds. Prynn and M'Yeoh stumbled into a cloth barrier that delineated the workspace of an odd-looking creature, sitting staring at the wall. Tools crashed; bins toppled, drizzling milky syrup on the floor gratings.

Startled by the invasion of his workspace, the creature glared glassy-eyed at Prynn, while one of his five hands scraped brownish wax off strands of hair with his fingernails. Once he'd collected a thumbnail full, he dropped it on his black tongue, smacked his lips and repeated the process. Prynn slowly backed away, but the creature hissed at her. She stopped.

Vaughn, no stranger to unusual life-forms, had never seen anything like it. A cross between a squid and a mantis might explain whatever it was. He looked to his Yrythny host for information, but M'Yeoh tiptoed around the basins and back toward the main walkway.

"Excuse me," Prynn apologized, extracting her foot from a pan of goo. "I hope I didn't ruin—"

The creature scrambled off his chair, thrusting his face as close to Prynn's as he could without pressing their lips together. Vaughn's hand inched toward his phaser . . .

"You," the creature burbled rapturously.

"Huh?" Anxiously, Prynn's eyes darted first to Vaughn, who shrugged, and then to flustered M'Yeoh whose lips flapped soundlessly.

"The one I search for. To finish my commission." The creature clapped two of its hands together. "I sit day after day, hoping to find the one I need to finish my commission and I see nothing. I sense nothing. Until you." Spittle flecked the matted hair around its mouth.

Taking a step away from him, Prynn smiled weakly. "You've mistaken me for someone else. We're not from around here."

Vaughn assumed a position at Prynn's side. "We apologize for intruding on your space. If there's something—"

"No, no!" the creature protested. "I don't want apologies. I want—that one," it said, jabbing a finger at Prynn.

With surprising courage, Minister M'Yeoh lifted up the goo-pan and sniffed the contents before dabbing a finger inside and wiping the goo on an adjoining wall. Gradually, the goo turned blood red. Recognition registered on his face; M'Yeoh's breathing steadied. "Commander, I don't think you have reason to worry. I believe this is a sense artist."

"Yes! Yes! I have a commission," he said, throwing a canvas drape aside to reveal a three-meter-by-two-meter collage of multi-hued textures. "For the Cheka Master General. He is unhappy that I haven't finished, but you will make it complete."

"Sense artist?" Vaughn asked.

"This substance," M'Yeoh indicated the goo-bucket. "When it comes in contact with living tissue, it takes a sensory impression based on body temperature, metabolic rate, body chemistry . . ." He dipped in his hand until it was covered with goo and then removed it to dry in the air, fanning it carefully. The clear sticky substance slowly assumed a creamy lemon tone. "Once the polymer dries," M'Yeoh peeled from the wrist, carefully easing up the now rubbery impression of his hand until it slid off readily, "this is what results. Sense artists collect a multitude of impressions and then arrange them in sculpture, hanging mobiles, wall mountings—"

"My commission for the grand foyer of the Master General's suite," the creature said proudly. "I need the last element. I have waited for weeks. And now you are here!" His grin revealed a mouth of crooked, graying nubs Vaughn assumed were teeth.

Prynn combed her fingers through her spiked hair. "We're only visitors and won't be staying long."

"Oh please oh please oh please change your mind. Oh please oh please oh please!" He threw himself prostrate before Prynn. "Only you!"

Taking Prynn by the elbow, Vaughn extracted her from the creature's ardent attention to her feet. "Tell you what. If our business concludes and time allows it, we'll come back and you can take your impressions."

"Commander!" Prynn exclaimed, drawing back. Vaughn expected she might throw him a punch under different circumstances.

The creature knelt penitently and while its ratty hair failed to camouflage his despondent posture, Vaughn's words mitigated his sadness somewhat. "Fazzle. Ask anywhere in the Core for Fazzle and you will find me."

As they walked off, pushing their way through the thronging crowds clogging the Core's central district, Vaughn couldn't resist teasing his daughter, "Think of it as a new cultural odyssey: immortalizing yourself for posterity."

She smirked at him. "I'll stick to living fast, thanks."

Waiting for the lifts back to *Avaril*'s platform, Vaughn approached the minister. In a low voice, he asked about making contact with a shadow trader.

"Word of the needy spreads quickly. The Exchange is watched. When the shadow traders figure out what you have, they will find you."

"So we wait," Vaughn said.

M'Yeoh nodded.

Vaughn closed his eyes, wishing circumstances could be different. From the first moments after the *Defiant* had triggered the Cheka weapon until now, Vaughn had felt he'd been standing at the helm of a rudderless craft. At every turn, he'd been compelled to accept whatever course circumstance had selected, whether it was the not-so-subtle attempt of the Yrythny government to engage Dax as a mediator, having to turn over bartering to a broker or this latest pronouncement of M'Yeoh's. Vaughn didn't like it. He understood that part of the hunt was patiently waiting in the tall grass for your prey to stroll into your sights, but some part of him couldn't shake the feeling that he was the one doing the strolling, not the waiting.

"So how much fun are you having, Ensign ch'Thane?" Keren asked, taking a seat on the edge of Shar's desk. They were alone in the government office Lieutenant Dax's team had been provided.

"Work doesn't need to be entertaining," Shar said practically, dropping an unused data chip into a drawer.

"But your antennae . . . they're drooping. You could borrow my headpiece to cover them up and then no one would be the wiser."

"Oh." Andorian antennae often conveyed emotional states. Any hope he'd had of getting to his genetic research today had vanished when Ezri had given him his daily orders. His antennae must be betraying his down mood.

Keren examined a statue of a naked Yrythny riding a whale-size sea animal—a gift from a well-meaning Assembly member courting favor with Ezri—now residing on Shar's desk. Upon seeing this odd gift, Ensign Juarez had doubled over, convulsed with laughter. The Wanderer delegate appeared equally bemused. "Where's Lieutenant Dax?"

"I'm surprised you don't know. She went with Jeshoh and the Houseborn contingent for a planetside tour of one of the Houses." Juarez, Candlewood, and McCallum had gone with her. Shar had—meetings. Ezri apologized profusely for asking him to act in her stead, but she felt the mission needed to proceed on two fronts.

"Ah. Probably House Tin-Mal. One of Jeshoh's pet stories. I'll be interested in her conclusions."

"Tin-Mal?" Shar thought he knew the names of all the Yrythny Houses, but Tin-Mal wasn't familiar to him.

"My Houseborn brothers and sisters are excavating the bones from the House crypt in an effort to make a point. I'll have my office send over the Journals of Tin-Mal," she said. "I'm certain they aren't in the database you've been given."

"You're saying the historical and cultural data the Houseborn have been providing us is incomplete?"

Keren shrugged. "A politically sound tactic. Select the facts that prove your argument, suppress the rest."

The constant push and pull of politics had always seemed futile to Shar. It had been his observation that after the arguing and manipulation and propaganda, truth eventually won out. Dealing in postulates and suppositions and perceptions . . . what a muddle. He liked pursuing causes he could measure—and not in votes. "What do the Houseborn want Lieutenant Dax to see?"

"The ancient majesty of these castles rising out of the water, with the lava and coral walls, sea glass sparkling. It's quite seductive." Keren reached over Shar's shoulder, tapped in several access codes, bringing up a vid of an underwater seascape that played on his viewscreen. "But Tin-Mal happened because both sides made mistakes and I believe she'll see through the facade put up by Jeshoh's people. She has to."

But how would that help? Shar thought. For almost a week, Shar had stayed on Luthia. He had watched Houseborn and Wanderers live in segregated neighborhoods and walk on opposite bridges. Houseborn Yrythny congregated, usually by House affiliation, for dinner and social events. Wanderers, orphans all, used separate eating and recreational facilities. How Ezri Dax could find a working solution when the Yrythny were determined to live separately, Shar couldn't imagine. Behavior patterns had been ingrained for generations. And now, with the Cheka siege, when the planet would most benefit from putting internal disputes aside, the Houseborn and Wanderers seemed to be finding more reasons than ever to distrust each other. *If only I had more time for my study,* he thought. A realist, he knew that science couldn't solve everything, but it was a solid way to start.

Keren interrupted his thoughts. "You're certainly solemn about something."

Shar flushed. "I-I—" he sighed. "I have an idea about how to approach your internal issues, but I don't have enough time or resources to make it workable."

"Go on," Keren said, resting her elbows on the desk and watching him intently.

"I've studied your DNA and to say that it's a marvel of genetics is an understatement." He'd spent hours last night, watching the computer simulate Yrythny cellular mitosis, the DNA unzipping, spiraling in a dance of base pairs lacing together to create life. "I have a . . . a hypothesis that whoever aided your evolutionary process—call it the Other if it suits you—whoever could engineer your biochemistry to the extent I've observed so far, could have forecast problems with genetic drift or mutation. Like those recessive traits that make Wanderers, Wanderers."

"And you think the answer to our problem might be in the Turn Key?"

Shar nodded. "Maybe. But access to your labs is restricted—even to Ezri—and I can't organize a statistically significant sampling in the time we've been given."

"For fear of the Cheka stealing and exploiting our results, we haven't done significant genetic research in decades. What we *have* done is barricade what data we have behind layers and layers of security." She furrowed her brow thoughtfully. "You need a large body of DNA samples to make your generalizations and forecast possible conclusions, correct?"

"Yes," Shar answered. "And because one of my specialties is cytogenetics, I'm actually uniquely qualified to undertake genetic mapping. I could process the information quickly if I had it."

"Let me look into it," Keren said. "I may be able to help." She turned on her heel to go, but suddenly spun back around. "Oh. I almost forgot the reason I came to see you. The Cheka broke through the defense perimeter again."

"That's the third time since we've been here." Beetlelike strikers had penetrated Yrythny defenses, raided the mating grounds and attacked planetside villages. The assaults happened so quickly that the military could rarely be mustered in time.

"The Cheka are getting impatient. I know at least three of the systems under their domination are revolting. To maintain the military advantage—at least as far as the numbers go—they're going to need to augment their armies, especially if they plan to continue their expansion."

"Negotiating a treaty with the Cheka isn't possible?" Shar asked. "If their goal is to isolate the Turn Key in your DNA strands, why not just give them the computer models? Or cryogenically preserve cellular samples?"

"The Cheka are only satisfied with fertilized, viable eggs that they can experiment on as they develop. They do surgery. Augmentations. They monitor when certain genes are activated in the course of maturing so they can develop their own chromosomal map."

"Successful research sometimes requires unorthodox methodology," Shar conceded, guessing that while the Cheka approach might not be ethical by Federation standards, the moral codes governing Cheka society might view experimentation on sentients differently.

Filmy eyelids lifting abruptly, she gaped at him. "You're thinking reasonably. That's your first mistake. The Cheka aren't reasonable."

Shar believed the Yrythny perceived the Cheka as evil, but civil war was an evil of a different kind—a reality that loomed larger each time they violated the perimeter, for every ship that a web weapon destroyed. "Still. The Cheka blockade is exacerbating the discord among the Yrythny. Is there no compromise to be reached?"

"I have something to show you." Keren had crossed to the door before Shar could turn off and secure his terminal.

"I have a meeting," Shar protested, knowing every postponed item carved precious minutes from his research.

"On my authority, consider it canceled," she said.

"But—"

"Please, Thirishar," Keren said. "This is more important."

How the message arrived on Vaughn's workstation aboard the *Avaril,* the commander never learned. He had intended on sending a recorded greeting to Dax on subspace, updating her as to the latest stumbling block, when he noticed a blinking yellow light. Touching the button affiliated with the light had launched an audio-message. M'Yeoh had been right: a shadow trader had found them. The trader had designated a time and place for a meeting where they would discuss terms. Vaughn was to come alone.

So he stood, as instructed, in the hall outside the Cheka suite, wondering if he was supposed to knock.

On the other side of the door, the shadow trader, a Cheka named L'Gon, waited. If he had been truthful, he owned the load that would solve Vaughn's (and thus the *Defiant's*) problem. Vaughn's concern was that while he technically honored L'Gon's request and came alone, L'Gon was under no obligation to do the same. In fact, Vaughn believed that the Cheka Master General, several platoons of soldiers and whatever entourage a Master General traveled with would also be inside, but not a single operative representing his crew's interests. If there was any other way to get this job done. . . .

Two hours ago, he'd sat in the repair bay with Nog, Bashir and several of the engineering staff, watching computer simulations of Nog's proposed *Defiant* defense system. Every alloy Nog had synthesized failed. Most of the femtobots were destroyed as soon as they were deployed beneath the shield envelope. The femtobot defense would have to be scrapped unless a solution could be devised. Attempting to leave this region without protection against the Cheka weapon wasn't an acceptable risk as far as Vaughn was concerned. Yrythny intelligence had persuaded him that they would be facing additional Cheka weapon deployments indefinitely. *With time, we could find an alternative, but next to this raw material we need to make Nog's scheme work, time is the commodity we lack the most.* Vaughn had resigned himself to dealing with L'Gon.

The irony of transacting with the Cheka in order to combat their own weapon didn't escape him, and he took some satisfaction in the poetic justice of it, but another part of him resented having to pay the neighborhood bully for protection against the bully himself.

When M'Yeoh learned of the deal with L'Gon he'd offered a squadron of J'Maah's soldiers as backup, reminding Vaughn once again of the double-dealing ways of some shadow traders. The gesture had been appreciated, but Vaughn questioned the judgment of putting armed Yrythny within striking distance of the Cheka suite. Though the Consortium was politically neutral territory, legal declarations meant little in the face of heated emotions.

But Vaughn wasn't a fool. Knowing M'Yeoh's estimation of the danger was probably accurate—and having learned that Nog had succeeded in, among other things, restoring *Defiant*'s transporters—Vaughn put Bowers and Nog at his back. *Defiant*'s tactical officer would accompany him as far as the suite. (Certainly L'Gon wouldn't consider that a violation of their agreement.) His job was to stay in the corridor, prepared to contact Nog for an emergency beam-out, should Vaughn fail to emerge at the designated time. Bowers treated the task like something out of the old Western vids he loved so much: he would be the gun-toting deputy while Vaughn was the sheriff heading in to negotiate with the criminals. Vaughn appreciated Sam's enthusiasm, but cautioned him against scratching the proverbial "itchy trigger finger."

The door slid open at Vaughn's approach, and he stepped into the darkly lit lobby, clicking on the alarm on his tricorder's chrono. In half an hour, without word from him, Bowers would send the signal to Nog, and Vaughn would be transported back to the *Defiant*. *And how hot is it in here? If I'd known I was walking into a sauna . . .* He dabbed at his forehead with his sleeve. When his eyes adjusted to the lack of lighting, he realized a robot had arrived to serve as his escort.

"You are expected," the robot squawked. "Follow."

Vaughn complied, still not sure if he was walking toward *Defiant*'s salvation, or his own doom.

Funny how childhood memories color present expectations, Ezri thought, *literally.* She stood at the fore railing of the great hydrofoil, watching the rise and fall of teal waves garnished in white foam, still surprised that oceans could be any color but purple. She might have been raised around the mines on New Sydney, but extended family on Trill brought her regularly to the homeworld and its violet seas. The first time she'd walked across the Golden Gate Bridge during her Academy days, her eyes seldom lifted to the shimmering cables suspending the bridge above the bay, but focused instead on the dark gray-blue waters, all the while wondering why they were blue. On this world, blue waters would have been too staid; teal waters better suited this stirred-up planet.

The view of Vanìmel from Luthia's observation decks and windows captured a portrait of a warm, sleepy moss-green world, with white clouds sedately churning through the atmosphere. Descending through the clouds and close in on the surface, Ezri expected a dewy spring day and primeval forest; plants unfurling tender stalks and limbs to the sun's soft tickle, waters lapping at the seashores with a puppy's harmless eagerness.

Instead, hurricane-force winds forced a bumpy detour away from a storm-sieged landing pad, swerving in and out of the lava-belching volcanoes that dominated the northern continent until finally, the shuttle skidded onto the flat top of a dormant volcano. She questioned the dormant part, seeing as steam oozed out of the cracked ground, the rotten-egg stench of hydrogen sulfide permeated the air and she *swore* she'd felt the earth beneath them trembling. Ashen landscapes extended in every direction as far as the eye could see, the terrain devoid of flora and fauna. None of the Yrythny seemed worried.

Vanìmel was a geologically volatile world whose rapid plate tectonic shifts had more in common with a game of checkers than a reluctant, long-simmering buildup that resisted release. As a counselor, Ezri had known those who nursed grudges, simmering privately until some provocation unleashed suppressed torrents of anger, and those who lived daily from eruption to eruption. Vanìmel appeared to be the latter type.

A swift land shuttle delivered them to the port city of Malinal where they boarded the hydrofoil that took them out to sea. By her calculations, they had been traveling for several hours, past kilometer after kilometer of water farms and quaint aquaculture villages mounted on stilts. Village residents tended the plants and animals being cultivated in surrounding waters, or served as look-outs, protecting the spawning grounds nestled along the continental shore-lines. Once, the hydrofoil paused at the request of three marine patrol boats. Uniformed naval personnel talked in hushed tones with the hydrofoil cap-tain—Ezri gathered they had been traveling on the border of a military train-ing reservation and the officers wanted to examine the travel logs for security reasons. Later, one of the Yrythny representatives explained that a Cheka spy craft had been detected making several attempts at shoreline penetration; the military wanted to make certain their enemies weren't gaining access to secure areas with Yrythny assistance. Otherwise, the journey had been uneventful, al-most leisurely. Had the circumstances been less formal, Ezri would have been tempted to throw on some sunlenses and sunscreen, sprawl on a deck chair and make shore leave out of it. She had a feeling her hosts might not like that too much, though she wasn't sure exactly what it was they would have pre-ferred instead.

From the start, the Upper Assembly committee had been vague about what they wanted her to see, plying her with exquisitely prepared food, of-fering her comfortable seating, and breathtaking views from the hydrofoil's observation deck. *Schmoozing,* as the humans called it, was expected in this line of work. In the course of his years serving the Federation, Curzon had been offered latinum, liquor and the company of beautiful women (he'd taken them up on that offer); a little gourmet finery didn't faze Ezri. She liked the pampering. All the fuss hadn't totally distracted her—she hoped. Several times already she'd found her mind wandering through the last time she'd done this—right before Risa, when the Federation Council . . . *Scratch that. The last time Curzon had done this.* But did it really matter who did what? She was Dax. Curzon was part of Dax, and allowing some of his harmless vices to creep into her own behavior couldn't be all bad. Besides, she'd al-ready learned a lot during this trip, even if it hadn't been synthehol in that last carafe of wine. Dax had a good head for liquor, having drunk more than her fair share of unsavory types under the table . . . Had that been Curzon, too? Or had it been Jadzia? Ezri shook her head, hoping the cool sea spray might sharpen her senses and make her forget her argument with Julian over these very issues.

Unbidden, she remembered a similar conversation she'd had with Dr.

Renhol of the Symbiosis Commission during the Europani evacuation—how she'd confronted Ezri with her recent tendency to slip into her past-host personae, blurring the lines between present and past. And it wasn't like the weeks and months after joining either, where she'd wake up uncertain as to her sex. More like she didn't feel inclined to rein in Dax's various personalities. Maybe when she got back to the Alpha Quadrant, she'd return to Trill for her *zhian'tara*. She could only imagine what it would be like to meet these people she so enjoyed being. Ezri snorted. *Who am I now, standing here looking out over this ocean? One thing's certain, Lela would be more on task than I am.* She could hear Lela's firm, focused voice. *"Time to buckle down, Lieutenant. Start putting the pieces together so you can do the job you were left here to do."* Recommitting herself to the task at hand, Ezri considered what she'd learned.

What struck her most, as she considered the day's observations, was how lacking in arable land this planet was. It was astonishing that the population had proliferated as well as it had, considering. Yes, Vanìmel had five primary continental masses and hosts of island chains. Faults, toxic levels of minerals leaching into the watersheds from constantly shifting land plates, and geological instability (such as the volcanoes) made utilizing the planet tricky for sentients like the Yrythny, whose life cycles required both land and water. The degree to which they'd adapted the oceans for their use was a tribute to their cleverness. Yet at some point, Vanìmel's capacity to sustain life would be maximized.

Adding more modules to Luthia or farming more square kilometers of the oceans would work, but not indefinitely. During their first year, Yrythny hatchlings required thousands of kilometers of open seas. Confined spaces inhibited their maturing processes. Consuming ocean acreage to feed a growing population would only bring another level of complications.

Ezri had caught her first glimpse of "newborn" Yrythny about an hour before, when a school of hatchlings swimming close to the surface had been pointed out to her by Jeshoh. Longer tails and the undifferentiated limbs indicated these hatchlings had been in the water only for a short time. He'd explained that during the first year, hatchling respiratory systems gradually matured beyond utilizing gills to extract oxygen from the water, to lungs requiring gaseous oxygen. By the time they came ashore as younglings (as Yrythny in their first five years out of the water were called), the Yrythny were dependent on the atmosphere. Vanìmel's geography made it difficult. Even with the aquaculture villages, Luthia, and other communities built over the water, dry surfaces were difficult to come by. Maybe she'd been correct in her hypothesis, that indeed, caste customs, especially those related to reproduction, had arisen out of a fragile planet's needs.

When she noticed the hydrofoil slowing down, she turned to one of her Yrythny escorts for an explanation. He had said simply, "Force field ahead," and left it at that. Ezri guessed that they might be entering a section of the military reservation. McCallum, Candlewood and Juarez, her companions on this trip, emerged from the lower decks to see what had stopped the hydrofoil.

Together, they walked over to the port bow. From there, they had a clear view of multistory towers extending out of the water at kilometer intervals directly in front of them. Signal lights on the top of each tower flashed orange. The lights continued blinking for a moment longer, dimmed, and began flashing blue. The hydrofoil moved forward, between two of the towers, across the waters beyond.

A representative Ezri knew as Lesh approached the four Starfleet officers and indicated that she wanted them to follow her. Ezri found she needed to jog to keep up with Lesh's bowlegged amble. Thankfully, Lesh was impossible to lose in a crowd, her distinctive mottled brown-yellow striping running from her forehead, beneath her headpiece and down her neck, setting her apart from the others. Color and striping, she knew, unlike the distinctive ridges of the Klingon crest, were not necessarily indicative of an Yrythny's House affiliation. The real test of a returning hatchling's identity was the distinctive chemical taste of its skin. Hatchlings with the "wrong" taste were raised in the Houses they came to, but as servants.

A Wanderer, clearing dirty plates off deck tables, had coloring similar to Lesh's and Ezri wondered, not for the first time, how it would feel if you knew where you were supposed to belong, but were unable to do anything about it. *"Can't you simply send the lost younglings home? If a youngling from House Fnoral swims ashore to House Soid, why not send the lost one back to Fnoral?"* she'd asked.

Jeshoh had looked at her like she'd sprouted another head. *"Because if they can't find their way home in the first place, there's something wrong. Isn't it compassionate that the Houses take in one that's not their own instead of casting it back out to sea or killing it?"* he'd answered. *"A thousand years ago that's what the Houses used to do: club to death any hatchling that wasn't theirs. We've come quite a distance from those days, Lieutenant."*

As she watched the servant Yrythny scrape food scraps into the recycler, she wondered if the distance they'd come was as far as Jeshoh believed it to be.

Keren offered no explanations as to their destination. They passed the university, the health sciences center and the Aquaria before arriving in a nearly abandoned cluster of offices; none bore signage. Even the nondescript foyer—beige chairs, pale green carpets and white urns overflowing with flowers—provided little hint as to what the facilities' purpose might be. A flecked-skinned Yrythny female floated across the floor to greet them. Clasping Keren by the elbows, she said, "Come in, come in, Delegate. So pleased to see you. Your presence blesses us."

"Mresen." Keren nodded graciously, interlinking her arms with those of her hostess. She indicated Shar. "My companion, Ensign Thirishar ch'Thane."

Shar proffered the traditional greeting to Mresen. Her bejeweled skirt and the multicolored braids streaming to her waist marked Mresen as a high-ranking Houseborn. *Rarely do Houseborn—even Keren's colleagues—treat Wanderers so politely,* Shar thought, puzzled. A glance at Keren informed him that she expected his surprised reaction.

"A beverage perhaps? Take a seat where you're comfortable—" Mresen fluttered to an armoire, removed a serving tray from a cupboard. A click of her tongue brought a gaunt but more elaborately dressed Yrythny bearing baskets of braided seed crackers and pollen spread. Mresen poured coriander-scented water into the finger basins when Keren halted her.

"Ensign ch'Thane has come to visit our lost ones," Keren said, gnawing on a cracker.

Mresen clicked her tongue against her teeth, the skin drooping off her jaw jiggling apologetically. "Of course. You know where to take him." She reached for Keren's arm again. "Thank you, Delegate. For honoring us."

"The honor is mine," Keren replied, bowing.

When they'd left Mresen, Shar wasted no time in questioning Keren. "She's Houseborn."

"She is. House Soid, in fact. Her aide is House Yclen."

"And yet—"

"There are some aspects of Yrythny life even Houseborn and Wanderer agree on. Here we are—" A door hissed opened onto an arboretum, bordered on all sides by water gushing over fish ladders. They hiked up a carpeted ramp to where two rows of invalid chairs, suspended in the air before the floor-to-ceiling windows, provided their inhabitants an unobstructed view of Vanìmel. Where benches might be, Shar saw biobeds and in each, Shar discerned Yrythny patients. Medical attendants shuffled around efficiently, carrying trays with medication and nutritional supplements. Keren searched the residents' faces, honing in on one specifically.

"Witan!" she exclaimed, brushing her cheek against the ailing Yrythny's scaly scalp. Squatting down beside him, she checked out the view. "Are there storms in the archipelago today?"

The gnarled figure, prone in bed, twisted toward Keren's voice and garbled unintelligibly. The loose patient robes failed to hide the twisted vertebrae, the stump where an arm should have been. Witan's legs splayed limply on the mattress. Around the room, Shar saw Yrythny in similar physical states in every bed and chair. A few had smooth indentions where eyes should have been. Some lacked legs or arms. Others were attached to biobeds by sensors and life-support mechanisms. He understood that Yrythny technology hadn't yet attained Federation sophistication, but he was curious as to why little had been done to surgically correct the maladies these individuals faced. A VISOR transmitting sensory data to an optic nerve could provide sight. Biosynthetic prostheses could replace deformed bones. Even a vocal synthesizer properly implanted could allow a mute, bedridden patient to communicate. *Perhaps we might share some of our medical knowledge with these people, help them ease the suffering of their disabled,* Shar thought.

He followed Keren to the bedsides of several patients. The medical attendants—some Houseborn, some Wanderers—recognized Keren and offered her respectful greetings. Keren had personal words for every patient they encountered, all of whom suffered from different maladies. Whatever commonality brought the patients here was not readily evident in their symptoms. In Shar's Starfleet experience and in following Thriss around the medical wards on Betazed, he'd found that patients were usually organized by diagnosis. He suspected that Keren's agenda was the unifying thread here.

In a private moment, Shar asked at last, "What selected facts are you presenting me to prove your point, Delegate?"

"These are Yrythny rescued from Cheka research labs. All of them have undergone genetic tampering. The oldest residents were subjected to environmental research—like having limbs amputated or having their legs surgically fused together."

A wave of nausea squeezed his stomach; his antennae tensed. Although he'd been spared much frontline participation in the Dominion War, he'd seen enough of its horrors that he'd had to learn to cope with them: death, illness, destruction. Defending one's people or way of life, whether Federation, Klingon, Yrythny or Cheka, necessitated a degree of ugliness. But this . . .

Speaking softly, her voice coarse, Keren continued, "A few have been castoffs that we found by accident. That group over there"—she pointed to a number of patients suffering from orthopedic maladies—"was discovered left for dead in a damaged ship the Cheka had abandoned. Environmental systems had essentially collapsed. When we rescued them . . ." She inhaled deeply, sat silent for a long moment. She turned to Shar, her eyes glistening. "We can't negotiate," Keren said softly.

And finally, Shar thought he understood.

10

Lieutenant Commander Matthias rocked back and forth in her boots while she waited for the turbolift—in part, because her feet hurt. Never mind the progress of the last three hundred years, military bureaucracy was still incapable of designing comfortable footwear. Sore feet aside, falling asleep while standing was a real possibility considering how she'd worked through the night, managing only a few hours of sleep after she'd completed her chart notes around noon. Excited after a successful day at school, Arios had barged into her room and roused her from a satisfying dream of hiking across Vulcan's Forge. She'd hoped to rest a bit before the reception, but Lieutenant Ro paged her, requesting an in-person consultation before Thriss could be released from custody. Work waited for no one and mental health rarely conformed to a convenient schedule. Shathrissía zh'Cheen wasn't an easy case, though the patient wasn't necessarily the problem.

Ro's immovability in the face of family pressure impressed her. Councillor zh'Thane, after being told that her political standing had no sway in station security policy, had gone to Admiral Akaar. He, too, had contacted Ro and she repeated her assertion that Thriss would remain in custody until she was assured that there would be no further disruptive incidents. Nudging the process along, Akaar stopped by Phillipa's office with a request that she deliver her evaluation promptly, thus "assuring that the time of all involved parties be spent on the Federation's business and not on personal issues." Apparently, years of pushing her agendas through committee had forced zh'Thane to develop not only the interpersonal finesse to grease the political process, but mastery in the art of being an exquisite pain in the ass when circumstances required it. *I suppose becoming a Federation councillor involves learning how to get your own way,* she thought, hoping that she was never required to do more than brief zh'Thane.

To prep for the consult, she'd spent the last hour combing the Federation database for any information pertinent to Andorian psychology, going so far as to contact her mentor/professor back home on Centauri. The case wasn't as simple as pronouncing a diagnosis and offering appropriate treatment. Thriss had been schooled by her culture to repress her personal concerns in favor of the collective needs of her betrothed partners. Trying to weed out what issues were endemic to Thriss versus what issues belonged to Thriss by way of her bondmates proved challenging. The longer she worked, however, the clearer it became that she didn't have time to study for her meeting with Lieutenant Ro, feed the children, read them a chapter from *The Adventures of Lin Marna and the Grint Hound Challenge* and prepare to attend the evening's diplomatic reception for the Cardassians.

To placate her neglected spouse, she'd brought a formal dress, secure in the packet tucked beneath her arm (side-by-side with her dress whites), ostensibly to change into after her meeting. "Just ask them, Phil," he'd wheedled. "I'm sure this one time they won't object to you wearing a beautiful gown instead of that stodgy old dress uniform." Phillipa imagined that line of reasoning wouldn't work on Admiral Akaar. Nevertheless she carried both garments with her—the uniform for the reception; the dress for Sibias, *after* the reception.

Where's that damn turbolift? She continued to run through her mental checklist: the babysitter was supposedly on her way (once her botany final ended); Sibias, using a tricorder, had persuaded Mireh that nothing more serious than a hairbrush lurked beneath her bed; Arios had made a good start on his science project. On the frivolous front, she'd made an appointment with a stylist who had a booth on the Promenade, hoping he'd be inspired to do more with her hair than the ponytail she typically defaulted to. Tonight, she was slated to meet her new commanding officer and she wanted to make a good impression, though she doubted Colonel Kira was the type to care much about hairstyle.

Phillipa had met her share of fascinating people while warping around the quadrant studying xenoanthropology, but no luminaries in the colonel's league. News coming from DS9 usually had focused on Captain Sisko but it had been Kira's exploits that intrigued her. In the weeks immediately following the end of the war, she recalled watching the colonel's tribunal testimony over the newsfeeds, trying to fathom how one crossed the gulf between Bajoran resistance fighter and consultant to the Cardassian resistance. She studied Kira's body language, her vocal modulations, and her facial expressions, concluding only that if there were a more focused, intently devout person in the quadrant, Phillipa hadn't heard of them. *Now I'm about to serve under her command,* she remembered thinking. She'd wanted to get every detail right.

I just hope my dress uniform still fits, she thought, trying to remember if she'd worn it since Mireh was born. *Not much need for dress whites while doing post-traumatic stress counseling in a war zone. Maybe Ro will let me change in the security office* . . . Focused on planning for the hours ahead, she missed hearing the approaching footsteps.

"Lieutenant Commander Matthias?"

Phillipa spun on her heel to see that Colonel Kira, striking in her dress uniform, had joined her. *And me completely preoccupied and frazzled.* "Yes, sir." She snapped her ankles together and tried not to stare too obviously at the colonel. Even if she hadn't already known what Kira looked like, she would have recognized her from the absence of her earring. To her knowledge, Kira was the only Bajoran officer on the station who didn't wear one: even Ro wore hers, albeit on the "wrong" side.

"At ease," Kira said with a smile. "When I saw you waiting here, I thought I'd introduce myself more informally than tonight's reception may allow. I'm just sorry we haven't met sooner. As you probably know, circumstances have been a bit more chaotic than normal."

The turbolift finally arrived and both women stepped in, Phillipa requesting the Promenade; Kira said nothing, apparently headed for the same destination.

"I don't mind at all," Phillipa said. "I appreciate being able to stay busy. My patients so far have proven to be—challenging."

"From what I understand, Shathrissía zh'Cheen comes with her own set of issues," Kira said. "I'm sure you've had your hands full—though I was hoping for your sake that she'd sleep it off. Have we seen the end of her outbursts, or can we expect them for the duration of her stay?"

Ro's report must be pretty comprehensive, Phillipa thought, wondering when Kira would have had the time to concern herself with one visitor. Her confident tone in speaking of Thriss was also surprising considering she hadn't shared her notes with anyone, including Lieutenant Ro. Maybe Councillor zh'Thane had been hounding Kira with her own version of Thriss's problems. Or the colonel might be drawing conclusions based on Phillipa's appearance.

Staying focused, all night, through Thriss's flare-ups of temper and her long, stony silences required Phillipa to stay physically sharp for extended periods. She'd managed, but not without paying the price. Untreated bloodshot eyes hinted at sleeplessness and she'd acquired a stiff walk from six hours sitting in a standard-issue, hard-bottomed chair. Since Kira had shown up, Phillipa had periodically rolled her shoulders to loosen them; her neck muscles remained sore, even after Sibias's massage. Kira wasn't stupid—she knew physical exhaustion when she saw it and could logically conclude it was the result of a night spent battling Thriss. Still, Phillipa, feeling protective of Thriss, wouldn't share information with Kira without cause. It was an old trick: pretend you know something in the hopes that the person who really knows will talk.

"While I respect your interest, I'm not at liberty to discuss specific patients, Colonel," she said politely. "Patient confidentiality."

Kira threaded her arms across her chest and stepped closer to Phillipa. Her expression, were it not so serious, could be read as humoring. "Regulations permit me to supersede all confidentialities—clerical, medical and therapeutical. You know that I could request your chart notes and you'd be obligated to produce them. Instead, can we agree that you'll share what's relevant to station security?"

Without ever raising her voice or moving into Phillipa's personal space, Kira had deftly established her authority. *Excellently done, Colonel. I can be reasonable—but on my terms.* "Patient information relevant to station security will not be shared with family members, however well intentioned those relatives might be," Phillipa said, quickly adding, "Just so we're clear on that, sir."

Kira laughed. "I'm not spying for Thriss's family, though based on the number of people hassling you about it, I could see why you'd think I might be. You think this emergency exit permit Councillor zh'Thane asked for is justified?"

"Councillor zh'Thane has cause to be concerned. This is a trying time for Thriss. Going home to familiar surroundings could be critical to her well-being, especially if something unexpected happens to Ensign ch'Thane." While Thriss hadn't been willing to talk about why she launched herself at Ro, by dawn, Phillipa had learned Thirishar ch'Thane's history by heart.

"Does the station have a reason to be concerned?" Kira asked.

"Thriss isn't a threat to the station or anyone presently residing here."

"And to herself?"

Phillipa contemplated how to answer, mulling through the long night's events. At one point, she'd seriously considered calling in Dr. Tarses for a neuropsychiatric consult, wondering if psychoactive medication or neurological mapping techniques would benefit Thriss. *For some, depression meant too much sleep or blue moods. For others, it took a more violent turn. For Thriss, it's probably a bit of both.* "Thriss is impulsive, volatile and passionate. Those traits, individually, are problematic. Combined with depression, they can be deadly. Her bondmates can offer her a measure of emotional stability that might mitigate any motive she might have to hurt herself. She wants desperately to please them. In fact, one of her biggest worries last night was how what she'd done at Quark's would reflect on Anichent and Dizhei. With their support, I can help her."

Silently, Kira considered her. Meeting her gaze directly, Phillipa didn't shy away from the colonel—whatever it was that she was measuring. She had nothing to hide.

The turbolift stopped with a soft thud and the door admitting them to the Promenade opened. Not sure that she had been dismissed, Phillipa walked beside the colonel, who moved at a brisk clip through change-of-shift crowds milling about.

Finally, Kira stopped and smiled. "Ro was right about you. Keep me apprised of any developments with Thriss."

"Yes, sir." Phillipa waited for Kira to disappear beyond the curve of the Promenade before she headed for the security office. *So that's what a legend looks like,* she thought admiringly. *Your reputation hardly does you justice, Colonel.*

And that's saying something, she amended mentally.

"Have you ever been in love?"

Positioned within a meter of the force field, Ro blinked her eyes a few times, and mentally replayed Thriss's question. Thinking that perhaps she hadn't heard Thriss correctly, Ro asked that she repeat it.

"Have you been in love?" Thriss said, enunciating her words loudly, ensuring that Ro couldn't misunderstand her. As she strolled the length of the holding cell, she never broke eye contact with Ro.

Though the question's frankness startled Ro, she refused to be the one to lose the staring contest. "That's not relevant to the issue at hand."

Thriss tossed her hair. "If you knew exactly how relevant that question was, we wouldn't be having this conversation. I've answered your questions. Humor the crazy Andorian. Answer mine."

Combing her romantic history for anecdotes that might satisfy Thriss appealed to Ro about as much as eating an oversized bowl of gree worm consommé. She wasn't so obtuse that she didn't get the gist of Thriss's line of questioning. After all, the primary reason Ro was carrying on a pointless discussion with an uncooperative Andorian (instead of hiding out at a dark balcony table in Quark's, pretending she didn't have a party to go to) was that

Shar had left his lovesick bondmate for a mission into the Gamma Quadrant. Ro Laren was many things, clueless not being one of them.

"I've been involved in relationships. I understand how complex they can be."

She stopped pacing and studied Ro. "You never have been in love. I can see it in your face. No wonder. . . ." Her voice trailed off. "I'm sad for you."

"Don't be," Ro snorted derisively.

"You've never connected with another person out of more than primal urge, loneliness or social obligation. That's sad."

Ro gritted her teeth. "My choices, my life—have no bearing on whether you get out of here."

Thriss turned toward Ro, the smooth folds of her pale green tunic rippling as she walked. The cool cell lighting illuminated her white blond hair; the long wisps wreathed her face like a halo. "What you're missing is the interconnectedness between individuals that transcends biology or emotion. It's about redefining your life because another exists. You breathe because they do."

Thriss's voice, low and musical, had a mesmerizing quality that, when combined with her unabashedly romantic words, simultaneously enchanted and embarrassed Ro. All this ethereal sentimentality made her queasy. Commander Matthias better arrive pretty damn quick to rescue her or she would, she would—Ro didn't know what she would do, but it wouldn't make Councillor zh'Thane happy. Still, minus the dramatics, Ro understood Thriss's passion when framed in the context of what she'd been willing to sacrifice for the Bajorans.

Ro allowed an uncomfortably long silence to elapse before she addressed her prisoner; she wanted to control the tempo of their conversation and silence was an effective tool in accomplishing that. "I understand those emotions. I also know how incredibly dangerous they are." Her chest tightened at a flash of memory—Picard, seated across a barroom table, his hand on her cheek, his voice in her ear telling her in no uncertain terms that she would not betray Starfleet for the Maquis.

"I'm not a risk, Lieutenant." Thriss balled her fists and planted them on her hips. "You got caught in something that started between me and my bondmates before we even came to the bar. What happened at Quark's won't happen again."

"Damn straight it won't." Promises rarely persuaded Ro. "Because if it does, even Councillor zh'Thane wouldn't be able to prevent your deportation."

Thriss and Ro stood, face-to-face, separated by less than a meter. Ro searched for the rage she'd witnessed in the bar, but failed to find it. Yes, Thriss appeared to be penitent—for the moment—but what about later when zh'Thane said the wrong thing or loneliness got the better of her. What then?

"Will anything satisfy you?" she pleaded. "Can't you believe that the knowledge that I hurt Anichent has almost destroyed me? I won't hurt anyone again. I promise to control my temper—to behave myself in public. And if I break my promises, I'll surrender willingly to your custody and allow myself to be returned to Andor. Would that be enough?"

"If I thought that you kept your promises."

"Might I state, for the record, that I believe you're safe in releasing her, Lieutenant."

Two heads swiveled toward the new presence. How long Commander Matthias had been standing in the rear of the room listening to their conversation, neither could guess. *I must have been pretty focused to miss the door opening.* Ro, for her purposes, hoped the counselor had heard the unsettling conversation Thriss had initiated, believing it was proof plenty that Thriss was a bit unbalanced. But Matthias's perfectly neutral face failed to yield even the smallest clue of what she might or might not have learned. Matthias's opacity contrasted sharply with Thriss's transparency: when the counselor spoke, Thriss's shoulders relaxed and she inhaled like a swimmer rising to the surface to take a swallow of air. For the first time during this latest conversation, her antennae stopped twitching nervously.

"Go ahead. Disable the force field," Matthias said.

What? Ro failed to understand what it was Matthias was trying to accomplish by releasing Thriss. She looked questioningly at the counselor who nodded, as if to say all was well.

When the barrier fizzled off, the counselor stepped into the cell. Thriss remained fixed in the spot she'd been in when Matthias appeared. *So far, so good,* thought Ro.

Moving to Thriss's side, Matthias talked in hushed tones; Ro couldn't make out much that was said until the counselor informed Thriss that she could leave the holding cell. The Andorian left first, compliantly, following Ro to the main office with Matthias picking up the rear.

Matthias waited for all to be seated and comfortable, before addressing Ro. "Thriss understands that if there is any hint of a problem, if her bondmates or Councillor zh'Thane have concerns about her behavior or if situations arise that require security's attention, she will be returned to your custody. From tomorrow forward, she will have daily appointments with me until such time that I feel we've resolved the issues that prompted the outburst at Quark's. Are these terms agreeable to both of you?"

Thriss and Ro exchanged wary looks before Ro answered affirmatively; Thriss's eyes dropped to her lap and her antennae curled slightly down. But she, too, nodded in agreement.

"I took the liberty of contacting Dizhei, Lieutenant Ro. She should be here soon."

"How, how—" Thriss began haltingly "—is Anichent?"

Matthias touched Thriss's knee, saying gently, "Dr. Tarses released him to his quarters early this morning. He'll be fine. He'd be coming along with Dizhei, but he's still physically drained."

Silent tears dripped down Thriss's face. "I have to fix it—make it up to him somehow. I am horrible to have become that carried away . . ." Hunching over, she buried her face in her hands.

Ro looked out through the clear door and saw Dizhei entering the Promenade from the habitat ring bridge. Thriss twisted her dress fabric between her fingers and tapped her foot. "Can I have some juice?" She hiccuped.

While Ro went to the replicator, Matthias leaned forward, resting a hand on Thriss's chair. "I talked with them. They're fine and they love you," she said softly. "Thriss?"

"And I love them, but . . ."

Before she could finish, Dizhei entered, greeting them in polite tones, but her excellent manners failed to hide her tensed antennae and tight-lipped smile. Since the previous evening, her skin had paled markedly.

Ro handed the juice to Thriss who gulped it eagerly; she seemed relieved to have something new to do with her hands. "Thriss agreed to the terms we set forth for her release," Ro said to Dizhei. "She's free to leave with you, if she chooses. Or she can leave here when it suits her." Thriss deserved the right to decide whether she went with her bondmates; Ro wondered if some of Thriss's frustration stemmed from her relationships with them, though neither Thriss nor Matthias had mentioned problems within the bondgroup.

Thriss looked between Dizhei, who, given her longing gazes and quivering antennae, might gather Thriss into her arms any moment, and Commander Matthias, who offered encouraging smiles. Scooting back deeper into the chair, she took another swallow of juice.

"If you'd like to move into the anteroom, you could talk with a bit more privacy than you have here," Ro said. She touched her combadge. "Ro to Sergeant Etana. Please make the interrogation room available to the guests I'll be sending into your office within the next few minutes."

"Zh'yi?" Dizhei whispered.

Thriss turned abruptly, looked up at her bondmate and searched her face for answers to some unspoken question.

"Sh'za," Thriss said, rising from the bench. Dizhei was at her side, pulling her into a hug before she could take more than a step. A flurry of embraces, concerned glances and excited exchanges followed. Standing apart from Dizhei and Thriss's emotional displays, Matthias gently ushered them toward the adjoining room; the two touched constantly until the door closed behind them.

Grateful that they had left, Ro exhaled loudly. "I have a few questions, Counselor."

Matthias shrugged. "Ask away."

"How do we know Thriss won't be back here by tonight?"

"Typically, we're bound by expectation." Matthias placed her palms together contemplatively. "Since Thriss defines herself by others' expectations, I wanted to make sure she knew we believed she was capable of meeting ours. I wanted her to know she has our trust, that we believed she could succeed."

"Is she really going to be okay?" Ro asked, recalling Thriss's longing as she talked about love and emotion and her life.

"She's not going to hit you again, if that's what worries you."

. . . Have you ever been in love? That question defined Thriss for Ro. "No, what I mean is, can she make it until Shar comes home?"

The counselor sighed. "If I were laying odds at Quark's, I'd say better than even that two months from now, she'll be on her way to Andor, with Shar, for the *shelthreth*. Once it's taken care of, the worst of Thriss's obstacles will be overcome."

Whatever it takes. She deserves a reward for her fidelity. Though satisfied with Matthias's answers, Ro wanted to make certain Thriss was comfortable with how her situation had been resolved. "Could you stay around, you know, just in case Thriss has any concerns, or if her bondmates decide they'd rather not have her at home?"

"I expected that I would." She paused. "I have a favor to ask."

"Sure." Matthias had proved to have very few demands so Ro was willing to accommodate her in whatever way she could.

"Is there somewhere around here that I could change my clothes for the reception?" she said sheepishly.

Ro laughed, causing Matthias to blush. "You're going? I'd heard it wasn't mandatory for Starfleet personnel." Would that First Minister Shakaar was as flexible as Admiral Akaar on social matters. Shakaar wanted to be impressive, prove that Bajor wasn't the backward, orphan child of the Alpha Quadrant anymore, that she deserved to be included in the first worlds of the Federation.

"I don't *have* to go. I like to dance," she explained. "I take it if you had a choice—"

"I'd be at the gym. Or the Replimat. Or scrubbing plasma conduits. Anything but a party with dozens of dignitaries and high-ranking political figures." Ro shuddered, picturing herself monopolizing the quietest corner of the buffet table. "At least I'm on duty. Maybe I'll get lucky and voles will invade the duct system, giving me an excuse to leave."

Matthias laughed.

Ro gestured back toward the holding cells. "You're welcome to use the head next to the guards' station to change. I probably should be getting ready myself. Let me know—"

"—If there are any problems with Thriss. I will."

"Thank you, Commander."

"Thank you, Lieutenant. See you tonight?"

"I'll be the one eating the dip," Ro said, hoping that Quark would supply at least one dish that wasn't pus yellow, alive, or raw. The prospect of spending three hours in a large crowd was trying enough without having to go hungry.

Matthias pursed her lips thoughtfully, her expression entirely innocent. "I can ask Sibias to take you for a spin on the dance floor. He's very light on his feet—"

"Don't make me issue an order, Commander," Ro warned, mock seriously. "You need to treat your station security chief with a certain deference."

"Yes *sir,*" Phillipa said.

As she exited, Ro glimpsed Matthias's cheeky salute. *Maybe there's hope yet for me with Starfleet if this is the kind of officer they're growing these days.* An optimism she hadn't felt in a long time suffused her. *I might actually survive the reception,* she thought. *Or not. Wouldn't want to become too optimistic . . .*

Cynics who thought Alpha Quadrant sentients could never peacefully stand side by side on any matter had never seen the stirring sight that met Kira's eyes when she entered the formal reception room in the office station's Upper Core, a few levels below the Promenade. Sirsy and Ensign Beyer had outdone themselves.

Festooning one broad side of the great elliptical room were vividly colored flags and banners representing the Dominion War allies and non-Federation worlds like Ferenginar. The Bajoran flag had an honored position at the front of the room, standing a half meter taller than the other flags on the right side; the Cardassian flag stood exactly opposite the Bajoran flag on the left. The United Federation of Planets flag stood even with Bajor's and Cardassia's flags in the room's center. Vivid colors and symbols representing thousands of years all brought together in one place on this optimistic occasion—Kira thought she finally understood why Shakaar had been so adamant about having a celebration.

Quark's staff had already brought down the cold appetizers and set up the heating units for the hot dishes that Kira assumed would be arriving shortly. Platters of pulpy melons, *q'lavas,* Palamarian sea urchins and finger-size vegetables sat beside baskets overflowing with *mapa* bread and whole Tammeron grain rolls. The bar had been fully stocked with *languor* and *kanar* for the Cardassians; and a selection ranging from Bajoran springwine, *tranya,* Saurian brandy and tulaberry wine to Vulcan port and Terran Cognac had been provided for everyone else. A service turbolift hidden behind a curtain opened, admitting half a dozen servers carrying containers that billowed steam clouds. The smells of rich broths and spices permeated the air.

Everything appeared to be coming together as planned.

Kira walked along the tables, checking the place cards by the layout displayed on her padd. . . . *Ambassador Gandres, Andar Fal, Hiziki Gard . . . that takes care of the Trill delegation. Now to the Romulan attaché*—carefully situated far away from his Klingon counterpart on the other side of the room, Kira noted with relief—*the representatives from the Bajoran Commerce Ministry and the Vedek Assembly; Captain Mello and her executive, Commander Montenegro, from the U.S.S. Gryphon.* Thankfully, Beyer and Sirsy's collective attention to detail resulted in perfect execution of tasks such as this one. Though Kira knew it was too late to make dramatic changes in how the room was configured, she still second-guessed the decision to put all the VIPs in one place instead of dispersing them throughout the room. She didn't want to appear elitist, but a more egalitarian approach would have required stricter security measures and social protocols, neither of which she had time for.

Important guests would eat at long, rectangular banquet tables placed in two L-shapes mirroring each other; all tables faced the center of the room so every honored guest would be visible to every other honored guest. Additional invitees would be seated at smaller, more intimate circular tables behind the main tables. Seating decisions had been preassigned based on rank, delegation, and organizational and planetary affiliation. Since Kira had received the guest list, Beyer had learned of several old grudges still being nursed and a few badly ended romantic relationships that required a reassessment of some of those assignments, but for the most part, this was a group that knew how to behave themselves.

At Sirsy's insistence, Kira sat between Admiral Akaar and the Bajoran government's delegation. "A bridge between who we are and who we will be!" she'd enthused. Kira didn't buy the symbolism. As station commander, she held a highly visible position, but this night—this reception—wasn't about her. It was about Bajor's and Cardassia's tentative steps toward dealing with each other as equals. She didn't want to distract from the task at hand on any level and she accepted that, to many Bajorans, she was a distraction.

She already knew that Shakaar had tapped Second Minister Asarem to deal with any Cardassian business that might follow the reception, while he, as first minister, would remain focused on the Federation talks. Though they'd met before, Kira knew Asarem mostly by reputation: a sharp negotiator who had campaigned for her present job by taking a hard line on all things Cardassian. Her party's role in Shakaar's coalition had been to represent the views of older, Occupation-era Bajorans who still favored a hawkish stance; Kira had heard gossip that Asarem had privately protested Kira's role in helping Damar's resistance during the Dominion War. Asarem felt that, regardless of the strategic value of undermining the Dominion's stranglehold on the Cardassian military, a Bajoran national such as Kira shouldn't serve the Cardassians in an advisory role: should complications arise, it would be too easy to blame Bajor or make accusations that escalated the existing bad blood between the two worlds.

Kira hadn't seen Gul Macet since he'd visited ops. She assumed he'd been assisting Ambassador Lang. Since Macet had requested time on the program, Kira had contemplated—and worried about—what he or Lang might have planned. *It's probably nothing worse than a proclamation from Alon Ghemor or a plaque commemorating this "historic occasion."* But no matter how she tried to reassure herself, Kira remained uneasy. Cardassians irritated her.

No, she amended her last thought. *Macet especially irritates me.*

From out in the corridor, Kira heard the low buzz of chatter from the first group of guests to arrive. Shakaar's enthusiastic voice rose above the noise. Seeing that the first minister would be serving as the gathering's host, Kira was glad he had arrived before the others; she had no desire to play host, covering for his absence with small talk. Because Sirsy accompanied Shakaar's party and she knew how the evening was to go forward, Kira could disappear until her presence was required. The room might be ready, but she still had a few items on her list before she could say she was finished. She discreetly moved to a position by the curtained turbolift and touched her combadge. "Kira to Ensign Beyer."

"Go ahead, Colonel."

"Report to the reception hall, Ensign. Guests are arriving and I don't have a clue what to do with them," she whispered, hoping she could go unnoticed for a few minutes longer.

"On my way, sir. I was helping Quark solve a replicator problem—"

"Nerys! What are you doing hiding behind there?"

She startled and took a sideways step to peer beyond the curtain. Shakaar stood directly in front of her, arms outstretched, with an exuberant grin on his face. So much for going unnoticed.

"Get out here," Shakaar continued jovially. "I have people you need to meet. Come socialize! This is your night, too—this is Bajor's night!"

Propelling her toward the group, he steered her past Sirsy and in the direction of a handsome black woman that Kira recognized from the newsfeeds.

"Second Minister Asarem, you remember Colonel Kira, your Militia contact here on the station? I know you two have met, but this is the first time you've worked together. Kira also plays a mean game of springball should you be in the mood."

Minister Asarem nodded politely; Kira reciprocated.

Kira surveyed the guests, checking to see if there was anyone else she needed to greet, if any old friends had come calling. Behind Shakaar, a prylar she recognized as being a protégé of Yevir chatted amiably with one of the trade ministers. He must have sensed he was being observed because he looked up to see Kira and frowned; his eyes instantly shifted to a spot directly over Kira's shoulder before physically turning his back to her.

When Yevir had first passed down his judgment, Kira believed she would gradually desensitize to the Attainder's consequences. As one of the faithful, she understood her peers' behavior and couldn't fault them for following the edicts of their religious leaders. But each cold encounter still smarted and this last one had a sharper sting considering present circumstances.

Here in this room were former enemies, people representing repressive or violent cultures, those espousing primitive traditions and backward belief systems, and yet all worked to overlook what divided them and focus instead on their commonalities. And Bajor, pious, spiritual Bajor, couldn't let go of punitive measures against one of their own for one night. This was supposed to be a reception celebrating Bajoran progressivism!

To Yevir's credit, the Attainder was working. Being the conspicuous outcast in almost every room she walked into assured that she would never forget what she'd done, never stop atoning for her mistake, and wasn't that, in part, what it was supposed to accomplish?

At least Yevir himself isn't here to add insult to injury, she reflected. He'd been on the original guest list, much to her consternation, but had been forced to bow out, citing some "Assembly business" that apparently superseded an official state function. Kira found herself wondering if the "Assembly business" was related to schism rumors Kasidy had told her about.

She felt Shakaar's hand on her elbow again as he directed her toward the back of the room where the newest group of guests to join the reception stood: the half-dozen Cardassians.

"I haven't met Gul Macet or Ambassador Lang, yet, Nerys," Shakaar said cheerily. "I'd appreciate it if you introduced us."

And the evening just gets better and better, she thought, putting on her most polite expression as she prepared to face the evening ahead.

With the servers dispatched to clear the tables, Ro decided to take a break from her scintillating dinner companions (a doddering member of the Alonis delegation, and the governor of one of the Klingon-controlled Cardassian protectorates) and went in search of Quark. As she crossed the room, she spotted Kira chatting with Shakaar and the Cardassian delegation, the colonel somehow managing to look far more at ease within this gathering of luminaries than Ro imagined she would. Ro's eyes panned the room as she went on, pausing to note Hiziki Gard, seated a few tables away, looking in her direction. The Trill ambassador's aide—and her counterpart in Federation security—smiled pleasantly and raised his glass to her. Ro nodded back, accepting the compliment graciously: *Nice work,* he was saying.

She wound her way through clusters of servers milling around in the side rooms, diligently recycling used glasses and plates while replicating condiments and flatware in preparation for the next round. Quark's bellows were better than sensors or tricorders when it came to tracking him down. The employees grew progressively more anxious the closer she came to where he was working.

"Vulcan port is served by request only! It's too expensive! Push the Gamzian wine—we have that by the crate load. So help me, Frool, I'm deducting that port from your wages. Now get to work!"

The chastised waiter skulked by Ro, who had been waiting in the doorway. Quark finally noticed her. "Oh. Hello, Laren. How's it going out there? Everyone talking about how wonderful I am? The artful presentation and the balanced diversity of my menu? Who needs the bar—I'll have jobs lined up until the end of the century when this is over." He scanned the crates piled up around him, making notes on a padd about what he'd used from each before closing it up and shoving it off to the side. Later, he'd send employees up to take each container back to whichever cargo bay he was using these days to stash his legal goods.

"If you say so," she answered. "As long as it isn't field rations, I'm happy." Ro knew all Quark's black market and embargoed items had been stowed away in cargo bays 16, 43 and 51. She was saving that knowledge for the day when she needed to motivate Quark to help her on official business. In the meantime, she knew that everything he thought he'd hidden from her was more innocuous than dangerous. Well, *mostly* innocuous.

Quark removed a meter-high stack of plates from a shelf and placed them on a cart. "Broik! Take these to Shakaar's table." He continued his inventory as he resumed speaking to Ro. "You're staying for dessert, right? You *have* to stay for dessert—it's Spican flaming melon."

"You know, I meant to ask you about that. Are you using actual flame gems for the effect?"

"Just three in each dish," Quark said absently. "I assume everybody will know not to eat them. Except maybe the Klingons." He stopped his inventory abruptly and looked at her. "You aren't gonna tell me they're toxic, are you?"

"No, that isn't what I—"

"Because the last thing I need is some extended family member of Chancellor Martok winding up facedown in the melon."

"Relax, Quark. No one's going to die tonight from eating your food . . . strange as it is to hear myself saying that." Ro hurried on before Quark could retort. "To answer your original question, though, I'm stuck here for the duration." She hopped up to take a seat on the edge of a table. "The colonel's pretty uptight about whatever Lang and Macet have planned."

"I don't know why she's worried. Natima's about as honest as they come—I always liked her in spite of that."

"You have any clue what she might be up to?"

"You're asking me? I thought you two were best friends these days. Doing each other's hair and having sleepovers."

"Quark—"

"All I meant is that you have better access than I do under the present circumstances. What did you come out here for, anyway? You miss me?"

"Don't flatter yourself. I came by to tell you I decided what we're doing for our evening in the holosuite." She slid off the table and started back toward the reception hall.

"Oh? And what might that be?" he pursued her doggedly through the maze of tables and chairs.

"I think I'd rather surprise you."

"Surprise? Is this a 'you're under arrest for tapping the comlinks to the habitat ring' kind of surprise, or is it a 'I'm not wearing anything underneath this raincoat' kind of surprise?"

She turned around to face him, stopping his mouth with her index finger. "I swear, Quark, you say one more word and this little experiment is over. 2100 hours. In two days. Holosuite one. Assuming you aren't on my last nerve by then." Quark opened his mouth to speak. "Not a word," Ro said, cutting him off.

Quark's mouth snapped shut. He smiled genially and nodded to her before retreating into the side rooms.

Ro wondered not for the first time since she agreed to see Quark socially whether such an agreement was a monumental error in judgment. Regardless, she'd said she'd give it a try and she felt obligated to keep her word. And it wasn't like she wasn't getting anything out of the deal. Quark liked her for herself, taking her on face value. And he didn't have any expectations except to have a good time (she wanted that, too) and good company. Whether there was any potential for something more than friendship had yet to be seen— actually going on a date with him would go a long way in establishing whether they were hopelessly incompatible.

Empty plates were coming off the tables when Shakaar stood and moved to the front of the room, holding a full glass of springwine. He tapped the goblet, calling for his guests' attention.

Shakaar might have protested his unsuitability for politics when the idea of running for first minister was first suggested to him, but he'd certainly grown into his leadership role in the years since. With hundreds of eyes focused on him, he radiated a serene confidence that Kira admired. In that moment, she found it easy to forgive the ongoing strangeness between them because he was so good at what he did. She was grateful it was him, and not anyone else, who was navigating Bajor through these confusing times.

"Our visitors, the Cardassians, have requested a moment of our time tonight and we are honored to hear from them. It's my understanding that our visitors hope to invite us to embark on a journey with them. And while we Bajorans have traveled with the Cardassians before, we must have courage to explore new territory. I don't anticipate this will be an easy journey, but this time, we have another companion to offer us aid and support: the Federation." He placed his glass down on a buffet table, freeing up his hands to applaud. Everyone in the room followed suit. "So let us move forward bravely, always mindful of what brought us to where we are now but always hopeful of where we can someday be. I raise a toast to the hope of new friendship!"

Over two hundred voices joined to proclaim Shakaar's toast and Kira, her own glass raised, gazed out over the room, filled to capacity with peoples of every species and political stripe, unified. To her immediate left, she saw towering Admiral Akaar leaning down to speak with Ambassador Lang, a mere slip beside him, and beyond her, Macet, nodding his head in apparent agreement with whatever Akaar was saying. The Andorians—Dizhei, Thriss, and zh'Thane, the councillor a portrait of elegance with her upswept white hair—earnestly conversing with the Romulan attaché and Captain Mello. Across the room stood Minister Asarem beside Klingon Governor Krodu, listening intently to the very animated Trill Ambassador Gandres.

Only the Federation could have done this: brought together, in friendship, former enemies and associates of disparate political stripes. *What the Federation does best,* she thought with a wry smile, pleased that someday, Bajor would be part of facilitating this process.

A young Cardassian, presumably an aide, pushed a portable holoprojector into the center of the room. Kira was suddenly jarred back to anxious expectation. There was a lot of present that needed to be lived through before that idealistic future came into being.

Lang assumed the spot where Shakaar had stood only moments ago. The crowd hushed.

"Because I believe First Minister Shakaar articulated very eloquently the task at hand, I wish to offer, on behalf of Alon Ghemor and the people of Cardassia, a token to christen this journey. A symbol of hope that personifies not only the terrible beauty of where we have been, but a vision for the future." She nodded to her aide and the lights dimmed.

Kira directed her gaze to the center of the room and waited. The hologram flickered into focus.

Of the many possibilities she had imagined, what followed was not one of them.

11

Jeshoh treaded water while patiently waiting for Ezri to adjust her gear. Activating the lens datafeed proved challenging with her dexterity hampered by the gloves she wore, but she had it working properly after the third try. The goggle viewscreen was a neat feature. Instead of Jeshoh providing her with a running narrative, she had only to press a button on her wristlet to take a sensor reading. Within seconds, the data would be displayed on the lower quarter of her goggle lenses. At that point, she could request further clarification. She double-checked her suit temperature, made certain the rebreather's oxygen ratios were comfortable, and then indicated she was ready to explore the ocean. While most of the committee—and Dax's crew—went one way, Jeshoh pointed Ezri in the opposite direction.

No one had told her what they were visiting or why. Ezri assumed that she would learn as she swam. Dax stirred inside her not long into her dive. Since her joining, Ezri noticed she responded more intently to liquid environments, from the glub-glub of air bubbles rising to the surface and the feel of water caressing her body to the swish of sea grasses swaying with the currents. And that was odd. Ezri paused, studied the environment more intently and realized it was devoid of any plant life. She initiated several scans, discovering that outside their dive party, only microbial life existed within sensor range. Not even algae or barnacles grew on the empty shells scattered on the sea floor. An ocean not teeming with life didn't seem possible, especially on this world. Jeshoh noticed her falling behind and swam back to check on her.

"Is something wrong?" he said over the comlink.

Ezri shook her head visibly. "What's wrong here? Where are the fish? The seaweed?"

Jeshoh pressed a series of buttons on his own wristlet, pointed it in the direction of Ezri's and transmitted data to her.

Ezri read the chemical analysis scrolling across her goggle lens. "The levels of nitrogen in here are toxic. What—?"

Nudging his head in the direction of dark, shadowy mounds, Jeshoh swam off, with Ezri following behind. She kept expecting to tangle her feet in a kelp bed or encounter a school of fish; the eerie lifelessness made her nervous. The sound of her own breathing was foreign, and in the vast, empty plain rolling out as far as she could see, she felt vulnerable, exposed. Increasing the tempo of her kicks, she propelled nearer to Jeshoh.

Growing closer, Ezri recognized that the mounds weren't the coral or rock formations she'd supposed; as her eyes adjusted to the goggles, she discerned several carved archways, one partially collapsed, a lump became a fallen dome and so forth until she realized she saw the remains of a city. All the way out here? Corroded skeletons—hundreds of Yrythny—lay beneath fallen walls and wedged in window frames. Swimming from ruin to ruin, the sights varied only minimally. Such destruction characterized worlds less evolved than this, usually those fumbling toward warp in the fossil and nuclear fuel stages. What happened here? A nuclear blast? She activated her sensors, and while waiting for the results to appear, Ezri asked Jeshoh to explain what she was seeing.

"You're looking at the remains of House Tin-Mal, a social experiment of four hundred years ago," Jeshoh said. *"You see, Lieutenant, we're not the narrow-minded elitists you might think we are. In fact, in the case of Tin-Mal, my ancestors were very progressive."*

"This was a Wanderer city, wasn't it?"

Jeshoh retrieved a platter-size chunk of wall carved with Yrythny pictographs and passed it to Ezri. Brushing off the sand, Ezri traced the story with her gloved fingertip, imagining that by so doing the tale was being written in her mind.

"Your translator program will confirm this, but this segment explains how House Tin-Mal rose from the sea off the Fès reef, glorious in its spires and towers, a testament to how wrong the Houseborn were to repress our brethren. They grew in numbers. Built more platforms. Advanced aquaculture."

Among the litter on the sea floor, Ezri deciphered the rusted outlines of machine gears, tools, weapons and primitive energy chambers. Of course she couldn't be certain, but the design exhibited the same original flair she'd seen in Luthia. The Wanderers didn't seem content to make something work when it could work with panache. She had to admire their creativity, though she knew their boldness likely resulted in the disaster crumbling all around her. "They did this to themselves, didn't they?" she asked, more to affirm her suspicions than to learn something new.

"Carelessness. Arrogance. Stupidity. Pick one. For all their intellectual capacity, the Wanderers decided their energy system wasn't adequate so they began augmenting the existing infrastructure with incompatible technologies. There was an accident, an explosion and everything for a thousand kilometers was contaminated and destroyed. How many hatchlings died, the fish and plant life, the reef itself? None of it survived. Now, almost half a millennium later, the waters are still recovering."

His mournful tone touched Ezri and she wished she could offer him consolation. During the time she'd worked with Jeshoh, his love for his planet informed his every word and action. She knew he believed in pressing forward, taking Vanìmel into a new era. For all his efforts, however, the consequences of the past reverberated through generations. How well Dax understood that truism! Wisps of memories—especially Lenara and Worf—drifted back for a wistful moment. And Dax was reminded that by constantly revisiting the past, one could easily be shackled to it. Time passed, circumstances and technology changed. As horrific as the Tin-Mal experiment was, Vanìmel had moved on, as had the Yrythny. Maybe the time to rethink this chapter in the past had arrived.

Though she had no doubt that Jeshoh spoke from knowledge and conviction, she had lived far too many lives to accept only one perspective on any situation. Expect a child to do an adult's task, the task will be done as a child would do it, not as an adult. Ezri suspected the Wanderers had been set loose here with all the exuberance and idealism of youth, but with no practical experience. House Tin-Mal was doomed to fail before the first archway had been built. How to say this to Jeshoh? Audrid had always had a way of phrasing things just right. What words would she use? Ezri allowed Audrid's steady nurturing nature to suffuse her before speaking again. "While the outcome speaks for itself, I can't help but wonder if these Wanderers had been raised with the same opportunities and experiences as the Houseborn, would the outcome have been different? Couldn't they be taught how to be proper caretakers?"

"And in the course of teaching, how many more mistakes would they make? How many mistakes could Vanìmel's fragile ecology withstand?" he argued. "I accept that Houseborn history is not without its ugliness. Pollution, destruction, squandering resources. And how we treated the Wanderers? I am ashamed by my ancestors' ignorance. But now they have representation, education—everything they need to lead long, fulfilled lives. Is it so hard to understand why we don't permit them to breed and pass on their weaknesses?"

Thick silence fell between them as Ezri searched for the right words, the only sound, faint echoes from far above them, of water curling up into frail crests, crashing into weak whispers.

So far, so good.

L'Gon waited for Vaughn in a cramped vestibule located down the hall from the main door. The dark paneling and orange-tinted lighting made it hard for Vaughn to see much. Squinting, he saw the brushed fold of floor-to-ceiling velvet draping, a plate bearing food scraps—greasy bones and skins sitting in a pool of bloody juices—and in the rear was L'Gon, clinging to a silken web. Vaughn's misshapen face mirrored in the burnished surface of his eyes. The Cheka declined to rise, instead gesturing with one of his slender legs for Vaughn to take a seat on a backless stool sitting beside his couch. The robot offered beverages, brought a bowl of fried cartilage to snack on.

L'Gon didn't waste any time dancing around his payment demands. As soon as the robot delivered Vaughn's drink, the Cheka listed them.

Because the Cheka's vibrating metallic voice took some getting used to, Vaughn asked his host to repeat his request. *Doubt I heard L'Gon correctly, hundred-year-old ears and all,* he thought cynically.

"We want your cloaking technology." With pincers affixed to the end of a leg, he clipped a fine filament suspending an amorphous chrysalis from the ceiling. L'Gon squirted sticky brown liquid into the sac, waited a moment, and then slurped up the liquefied contents through a tubule. Carelessly, he chucked it aside, biomatter dripping off his fangs onto the fine hairs growing around his spinnerets.

Vaughn's face betrayed nothing. How the Cheka had come by his knowledge of *Defiant's* cloak didn't matter at the moment. What did matter was that Vaughn treat the revelation as nothing unexpected. "I'm afraid that's impossible."

"We don't require the device itself," L'Gon went on, "just the engineering specifications and any parts we might find difficult to reproduce. In return, the matter load you require can be delivered immediately."

Vaughn dropped his glass on a drink tray and stood up. "Thank you for your hospitality. I'll let myself out." He'd taken only a few steps when L'Gon stopped him with a question.

"You do understand how this process works? I have something you want, you have something I want. We negotiate."

"I've made clear what I was prepared to offer in exchange for the matter load. So by all means, please let me know if you change your mind." Vaughn turned back for one last look, though L'Gon's hard-shelled thorax made reading body language impossible.

With silk thread extending from his abdomen, L'Gon lassoed fried cartilage from the tray, dousing it in gooey enzymes before lifting it to his mouth.

For a moment, Vaughn waited, watching L'Gon for a sign that he was interested in further negotiations, but saw no indication the Cheka wanted anything but lunch. "I'll let myself out." He left without another word, even to the android chasing stiffly down the corridor after him.

When the Cheka suite doors locked behind him, Vaughn checked his chronometer. Less than ten minutes. He'd always been a man who knew what he wanted—why waste time tilting at windmills? Bowers looked disappointed when he saw the commander emerge unscathed, having looked forward to a showdown at the O.K. Corral. Vaughn slapped him on the back, assuring him that he was fairly certain the bad guys hadn't yet left town and that he still might get his chance.

Not wanting to risk an encounter with any of L'Gon's henchmen who might be lurking in the Core, Vaughn called Nog and requested a beam-out.

How the hell did he know about the cloaking device? The question ran round and round in Vaughn's mind. Few of *Defiant*'s crew had left the *Avaril* since they'd arrived at the Consortium and knowing them as he did, Vaughn believed all to be the soul of discretion. Once again his mind was pulled back to their first day on the journey here. *Someone is watching us. The question is, who?*

By his calculations, Shar and Keren had been hiking along the cliffs for almost an hour. Whether they'd made any progress was another issue entirely: every time the trail turned, Shar expected to look down and discover they'd reached the top. Instead, he faced trudging through yet another stretch of rocks and mud, sending pebbles skittering through the grasses with every step. Rainstorms had brought down weathered branches, gravel and debris from the above hillside onto the footpath. One way, Shar would have to scramble up a collapsing slope; the other required secure footing on water-slick lava rock. His muddy uniform testified to how much success he'd had the last time he'd gone off the path. How he wished they were traversing the wonderfully flat stretch of black beach below. He'd happily walk from here to where the beach vanished into the horizon if it meant he left the mud behind.

It hadn't looked this difficult when he'd agreed to hike in lieu of using transporters. He enjoyed hiking—having grown up in Andor's western hill country, he spent a good deal of his youth scrambling up and down the slopes around Threlfar Province. But the terrain hadn't been anywhere near as treacherous as this.

Before they left Luthia, Keren had shown Shar a regional map of the Hebshu Peninsula, one of Vanìmel's few land-based farming provinces. The two-dimensional version of the peninsula showed the trail as leading from the landing strip, cutting switchbacks across the steep mountain foothills, curving sharply near the summit, and dropping into the valley gap where they would make a swift descent into the peninsula's chief agricultural region. Simple enough. For a nimble-footed *tathrac,* perhaps.

"I have the remote transporters activated, Keren," Shar panted. "We could use them."

Keren spun around and walked backward, never making a misstep. "Consider this part of your research. Firsthand understanding of the environmental conditions." Laughing, she turned and skipped up the trail.

"And the farmers and herders have to bring their goods down this track to ship them?" Shar called. He couldn't fathom any vehicle successfully navigating these ruts.

Keren, deftly picking her way around mud puddles in the path, laughed. "Our transporters don't have the range yours do and weather conditions aren't always ideal—atmospheric interference and all that. When the volcanoes go off there's further interference—"

"And the most valuable resources you're transporting are dairy products and animal hair, correct?" Food made sense. The value of the hair puzzled him, but Thriss had always accused him of being obtuse about fashion.

"Excuse me, Thirishar ch'Thane, you of many locks, could it be that the quantity of hair on your head impairs your brain function? Why do you think hair is such a status symbol among my people? If it were easy to come by, why would it be so prized?" She tossed her long braids to make her point.

"I apologize. Questions of commerce are lost on me. My friend Nog has a much better grasp of such subtleties than I do." Drained, Shar paused and leaned back against a boulder. "I'm sorry, but I'm not used to this gravity—or the thin air at this elevation."

Keren backtracked and joined him. She closed her eyes, threw back her head and soaked in the sunlight. "It's always lovely after a storm. The skies are so brilliantly green they almost hurt to look at. And the smoke-wisps of clouds . . . I love it here."

Ocean breezes blew steadily, tossing his hair, chilling his antennae. He, too, turned his face toward the sun, seeking warmth. "So why not live planetside?"

"Choices for Wanderers are sorely limited. I could have learned aquaculture or raised livestock. I could have tried to work my way up the ranks of the serving staff in a House or tried to find a noble lady to be my patron. None of those things appealed to me. As soon as I came of age, I left the House where I was raised and went to school on Luthia."

"But you chose your life's work. You didn't have someone standing over you telling you what you could and could not do." Shar cringed inwardly, remembering the series of arguments he'd had with Charivretha about going to the Academy before the *shelthreth*. Dizhei and her put-out sighs, Thriss pretending that she hadn't been crying, Anichent spending longer hours in the observatory. Pleasing any one of them was difficult; pleasing all four was impossible.

"I want you to see something, Thirishar." Throwing her cloak to the side, she untied her blouse cord and pushed the fabric down her arm, revealing her bare shoulder. She turned her back to Shar so he could have a clear view. Above her protruding shoulder blade, her gray-brown skin was rough with three scars each outlined in black dye. "When I was five years out of the water, they strapped me, facedown, on a board and burned those markings into my back with a surgical laser. To make sure the meaning was clear, they injected black dye into the scars. Every Wanderer female is so branded. It's the Houseborn way of assuring that we are marked, set apart. That way, Houseborn males have no excuse. They can't take a fertile Wanderer female as a consort and be deceived." Keren pulled her blouse back over her shoulder and replaced her cloak.

"You see, Shar, my choices about what I can do with my life are limited. Could I ever do what you're doing? Explore the universe? Travel far from my homeworld and find a different life somewhere else? Unlikely. Even here, I can't take a consort. Not really, anyway." She pointed out a moss-covered monolith in the distance, rising out of the surf, residual morning fogs not yet fully burned off. "Close by those rock formations is an entrance to a series of grottos. They're only accessible by sea—and half the year, they're submerged when the glacial runoff from the Pyoyong River comes from the mountains, but for centuries, Wanderers have used those caverns as spawning grounds."

"I thought that—"

"Yes, Wanderer males are sterilized as younglings, but Wanderer females can't be sterilized without sustaining permanent physiological damage. Too many Houseborn females want us as servants to risk killing us off. We're *compassionately* force-fed hormones from our youth, supposedly preventing our reproductive systems from maturing. But the supplements don't always work, like in my case, and so we submit ourselves to injections once we reach adulthood. But there are those of my sisters who don't comply with the law and sneak away to mate with Houseborn males."

"That's not legal, either," Shar observed. "The taboos for crossing castes are as old as your recorded history."

"True. Houseborn males breaking the law are executed. Some pairs, however, are willing to take the risk. They can't have an official union so they take a chance and share the one thing they can."

Shar exhaled deeply. "This I understand."

"What do you mean?" Keren asked.

"The lengths your sisters take to be with the one they love. The one they choose to love. How trying it must be for you." He flashed to a memory of his own Time of Knowing, when he received the identities of his bondmates, how terrifying and exhilarating it was to find out who he would be bonded to.

What if it was someone he hated? Or someone dull-witted and stupid? In hindsight, his youthful fears seemed simplistic.

"Ah! Ensign ch'Thane has a consort waiting for him back in the Alpha Quadrant," Keren teased. "Tell me about it while we walk." She dragged him to his feet and they resumed walking up the hillside.

"It's a long story. Something we don't usually talk about outside our species."

"But you seem to come from such an open society," Keren said.

"True, but even my people are unique within the Federation. Our physiology, our rigid social customs dictate that we keep to ourselves those issues relating to family life."

"I've heard Ensign Juarez use the word 'family,' is that like a House?"

"A smaller unit—where adults nurture young who are usually related to them. Because most humanoids where I come from carry their offspring within them until they are ready to live semi-independently, the identities of the parents are rarely in question. Such children can't properly develop apart from their parents, unlike Yrythny."

"It would be as if I returned from my year in the water to live with the consorts who laid me," Keren clarified.

"Yes. Exactly," Shar said, thinking for a brief moment that being raised in a large group—like the Yrythny younglings were—might be easier than being tied to a parent. Pleasing his *zhavey* was complicated, but he couldn't imagine living his life without her.

"What about your family, Thirishar?" Keren prodded gently.

From his first night on Luthia, Keren had openly shared her life with him. The underground. Her career. Shar's sense of fair play dictated that he ought to reciprocate. After all, wasn't he prying into the most intimate threads holding their society together? He took a deep breath. "On my world, we don't have 'pairs,' we have quads. I have three bondmates."

"Three?" Keren looked surprised.

"Shathrissía, Thavanichent, and Vindizhei," he said, seeing their faces flash before him as he said their names. "You have two sex chromosomes. Andorians have four sex chromosomes—we have four genders. It's challenging for most two-sex species to delineate the physiological differences between us, so we accept being called 'he' and 'she' rather than try to explain why those pronouns are an oversimplification."

"What *are* you supposed to be called?"

Shar smiled and rapidly reeled off a series of Andorii words, enjoying the confused expression on Keren's face as he said them.

"Do you mind if I think of you as 'he'? Like Jeshoh is a 'he'?" Keren asked sincerely. "I don't mean any offense by it."

"I've spent so many years away from Andor that I rarely think about it anymore. Sometimes, I even think of myself as 'he.' "

"I don't know what's harder—not having any parents—as we Yrythny—or having four."

Shar agreed, but felt that was a discussion for another time. "Among my kind, producing offspring isn't as simple as a female laying eggs and a male fertilizing them, as it is with your people."

Keren considered him thoughtfully. "I can imagine. Tell me about it. We have a long way to go."

They had cleared another stretch of trail as they walked; Shar admitted to himself that talking had made the hike go faster. *Why not?* "In recent times, my people endured a horrific biological holocaust, resulting in wide-scale chromosomal mutations. More *zhaveys* miscarried; more offspring were born with trisomy or hexsomy complications. In short, reproduction became much more difficult, when it was learned that the window of an individual's fertility had narrowed to a scant five years.

"Our scientists initiated a comprehensive gene-mapping project. Every family's genetic history was decoded, recorded and added to a database. The scientists' intention was to track genetic drift, to note when mutations occurred and to repair what abnormalities they could."

"I see why the Other's Turn Key is so fascinating to you," she said.

Shar nodded. "It might be that the genetic engineering that allowed the Yrythny to successfully evolve might also be applied to shoring up Andorian chromosomal problems."

Keren latched onto this idea of gene mapping, peppering Shar with questions. The more he talked to Keren, the more he hoped that this trip would help him locate the information he needed to help the Yrythny. Intuitively, he knew he'd find their answers written into the elegant helices of deoxyribonucleic acid, though gene mapping hadn't readily yielded any solutions for his people. He explained this to Keren.

"In spite of science's efforts to prevent or correct genetic disorders," Shar went on, "our reproductive problems persisted; population numbers continued slipping.

"Another approach was taken: instead of trying to genetically engineer a way out of the problem, scientists used the database to match mates with the highest likelihood of success. When I was born, my genetic profile was matched with those of three compatible bondmates."

Incredulous, Keren clicked her tongue against her teeth. "You didn't choose your consorts?"

Shar shook his head. "And once the matches are made, our focus is on providing a stable homelife for a child, placing the child in a community where he can grow up naturally with his bondmates. Without knowing I was bound to them, I'd worked side by side with my bondmates in school—since I was two and three years old."

"For all the trouble your people went to, I hope it worked."

If only you knew how complicated that statement was, Shar thought, recalling years of classwork, all-night study sessions, papers and days on end of lab work, focused on just that question. But Keren didn't need to know how the answer to her question had shaped his life. This time was about her world—not his.

"Our population stabilized for a time, but in recent generations, new genetic ailments appeared. Weaknesses in certain chromosomal segments left us vulnerable to a host of maladies; these new mutations proved elusive to identify and fix. Bondmate matching has becoming merely a stopgap measure."

"And so . . ." the sober expression on Keren's face revealed that she expected what Shar would say next.

"Barring a permanent solution, we face extinction." *Why is it easier to say these things to Keren, a stranger, and not Nog or any of my other Starfleet colleagues?* It felt good to say the words aloud, especially since he usually checked every word he said, being careful to shield his people from outsider curiosity. Not once had Keren made a face or snickered; Shar couldn't say the same for several of his Academy roommates.

The unique dynamics of Andorian sexuality meant the most intimate parts of their lives could easily be misunderstood or exploited. In truth, Andorian familial structures demanded a far more conservative approach to sexuality than most humanoids employed. Shar had been amazed by the number of partners humanoids "tried on" before finding the right fit. Because his gender identity wasn't easily quantifiable to those enmeshed in cultures that defined reproductive relationships by twos, it had been easier to rebuff interest expressed by his peers, either as a potential romantic partner or in his unusual physiology, than try to explain himself. Modesty was a natural outgrowth of his culture. Keren seemed to understand that.

The telling of his story lasted the duration of the hike and they arrived at Valley Gap about the time he'd finished. Finding a relatively dry spot in a hollowed-out tree root, they broke for lunch; Shar ate another ration bar, Keren brought bread and fruit. Sunshine broke through the towering evergreen forest canopy, dappling the scrub brush and carpet of fallen leaves in light and shade. Occasional wind gusts rustled the highest boughs, sending dried needles and flaking bark scattering to the ground.

Keren turned to Shar, studying him. "Just so I understand what we've been talking about for the last hour, your life is oriented around creating a new life with your bondmates? Having offspring?"

"It's supposed to be. Every choice was made to better facilitate my contribution to creating a child."

"Supposed to be?"

"I have rather . . . radical ideas about how to help my people."

"Why doesn't that surprise me?" She offered a toothy grin. "But surely such sentiments aren't unique among your kind? Many must feel as you do."

"Feeling as I do and acting on those feelings are very different things. I want to be brave enough to ask every question." *"But the answers are at home, with the* shelthreth," *Zhavey* had said. And risk losing an unprecedented opportunity? He recalled a story about a pharmacologist seeking a treatment for the *nezti* flu. Months in the lab yielded nothing. To clear his head, he'd taken a vacation. And while on that vacation, he discovered a rare plant that made the difference in developing a cure. To Shar, life was about countless intuitive choices, and listening to his inner voice had guided him surely. Choosing between *Defiant*'s mission and the *shelthreth* was choosing between two correct choices. Shar had followed his intuition here, to Vanìmel. He now had to trust that in time he would find the answers.

"I can only imagine your claustrophobia," Keren said.

"When I was younger, the stories my *zhavey* told me were moralistic parables and fables, praising the virtues of living for the needs of the Whole over the needs of the individual," Shar said, walking beside Keren. "My life's purpose is to live for the Whole. And yet, I believe that as an individual I can still make a contribution to the Whole."

"In this area, Shar, we aren't that different," Keren said finally. "I've never known anything but a collective life. Now I want to know something else. I want to choose my own destiny. What I wonder, though, is why you haven't done what your people want? Go home, start a family—and then once those obligations are met, you're free."

"Because no matter where I might go, I'd still be bound. My child's life, my bondmates—the only way I can have the life that I choose"—*maybe a life with Thriss,* he amended mentally—"is if I help solve the problems facing my people."

"I see," Keren said. She pointed out the road ahead. "We're only a short way from the valley now."

From the gap, the whole valley panorama spread out like patchwork; neatly groomed fields, rows of vegetables, farm buildings in miniature, herds of *shmshu* grazing. A ribbon of water snaked through the land, reflecting silver in the noon sun.

"I think, Ensign ch'Thane, that the Other did bring you," Keren said, quirking a half-smile.

Shar didn't feel compelled to respond, though his antennae vibrated inexplicably with an excitement. *There are answers here,* he thought.

Through an archway of densely foliated tree branches overhanging the road, Shar and Keren began their descent.

One advantage in dealing with Ferengi was their sense of pragmatism. Whatever was needed to do the deal was accepted without question. Nog hadn't so much as creased his forehead when Vaughn had interrupted a trying diagnostic with a request for a private conference off the *Avaril*. He'd delegated the remaining tasks to Permenter and Leishman, and followed Vaughn down to the Core.

In a dark corner of the crowded casino, Vaughn waited for the server to fill his drink order before raising a finger to indicate that he wanted Nog to refrain from speaking. Taking out his tricorder, Vaughn surreptitiously ran a scan across the booth and table before relaxing. He pulled a chip-size device from a hidden fold in his jacket, pressed a button that started a light flashing and placed it between them on the bench.

"A signal-jamming device?" Nog guessed.

Vaughn nodded. "I couldn't find any indication that there are listening or visual sensors in here, but if you've got good tech—"

"You won't be able to detect them," Nog finished for him.

"Right. This is a little something Starfleet Intelligence uses sometimes to annoy the Tal Shiar." Vaughn accepted the drinks and a basket of snacks from the server, paid her with currency that M'Yeoh had provided them and turned back to Nog.

"Before I forget," Nog said, "I wanted to tell you I sent our report to Colonel Kira this morning. It's about three days late, but she'll understand why when she reads it."

"Good work. And Ensign ch'Thane's letter?"

"Piggybacked it on the transmission. Ops will be able to extract it, no problem."

"Nice to cross one thing off our list, considering how many items still remain." Vaughn sipped his drink.

"I take it your meeting with L'Gon didn't go well?"

Vaughn scanned the crowd—the dancers strutting down a catwalk, anonymous faces hunched over drinks and games of chance. Through the loud chatter of the cooling system gears and the music, he doubted their conversation could be eavesdropped on, but he still wanted to be cautious. "He wanted the cloaking device."

Nog's eyes widened. "He didn't! We've had *Defiant* under surveillance since the first day. No unauthorized personnel have been in or out of the bay without my sensors recording it."

"Then we need to start looking at the authorized personnel," Vaughn said, "because someone is leaking information to the Cheka and I want to know who. What about the Yrythny engineers?"

"Why would they deal with the Cheka?" Nog picked through the appetizer basket, arranging the geometric-shaped crackers in patterns on the table. "I thought something was up the day we went to the Exchange."

"How so?" Vaughn sipped off his wine spritzer.

"I listened very carefully to Runir's explanations. Even did some independent reading on the subject to cover the subtleties."

Vaughn laughed.

"I'm a Ferengi!" Nog reminded him unnecessarily. "It's my moral obligation to take any and all opportunities that further the advancement of commerce. I paid close attention to what happened on the Exchange and from what I could tell, our bid was successful."

Vaughn allowed the meaning of Nog's suspicions to sink in. "You think our load went to L'Gon just so he could deal with us for the cloaking device?"

"Probably. Maybe whoever wants the cloak was willing to share it with L'Gon and his fellow Cheka if L'Gon was willing to front the deal."

Vaughn considered Nog's hypothesis. "It fits. We have to stay one step in front of whoever it is. How long before the *Defiant* can fly?"

"Without the femtobot defense? Not more than a day or two."

"I'll let the Yrythny leadership know we'll be leaving the day after tomorrow."

"But sir, I have serious concerns about trying to leave this region without a defense against the web weapons."

"I'm sure you do. But we may have to take our chances."

Nog paused, pushed crackers around with his index finger, and pursed his lips together.

"Lieutenant?"

Dropping his eyes guiltily, Nog said, "Why not deal with L'Gon? If I can prove he has what he says he has, I say we get the load from him and be on our way."

"Out of the question." Vaughn frowned, willing Nog to meet his eyes.

"We're in a bad place, Commander."

Who am I seeing? he thought, studying the Ferengi for evidence of artifice. *The Starfleet officer striving to protect his crew or the Ferengi willing to deal no matter what?* Through the pulsing red neon, Vaughn watched a scuffle over a prostitute break out across the casino. Law enforcement rushed in through the back door, hauling off a group of inebriated miners in restraints. "You might say that, Lieutenant," he said, polishing off his drink. Throwing some of M'Yeoh's currency on the table for a tip, he waved Nog in the direction of the door.

Ezri pulled herself up the rungs of the ladder and heaved through the hatch onto the bottommost deck of the hydrofoil. She craved a hot steamy drink—maybe a Tarkellian tea because she was missing Julian—but first a shower. The wetsuit had been comfortable enough, but she still felt chilled from the water. She eagerly peeled the clammy thing off and went hunting for her boots when she noticed—

A pair of armed soldiers guarded each entrance to the room. All the Yrythny who had accompanied her on her underwater journey to Tin-Mal knelt silently, hands at their sides. Candlewood, Juarez, and McCallum, all pale and with wet hair dripping into their eyes, stood next to Jeshoh.

"What's going on?" Ezri said finally, since no one seemed eager to provide her with an explanation.

"There's been an attack on an aquaculture village," a soldier said gruffly. "Explosives were set off by a signal from this vessel—shortly after another transmission was sent here from your workstation on Luthia. Everyone on this vessel is to submit to questioning."

"Surely you don't think that I know anything about this. My people and I have been away from my office all day." Then it hit her. *Shar.* Ezri touched her combadge. "Dax to ch'Thane."

No answer.

"There's a logical explanation for this, I assure you," she said. She tapped her combadge again, repeating the call and still, nothing. *Dammit, Shar, where are you . . . ?*

12

Kira heard the gasps, the whispered questions and sensed waves of confusion spreading through the crowd, but the tears pooling in her eyes blurred her view. Her breath caught in her throat with each ragged intake. Closing her eyes, she allowed silent tears to wash down her cheeks, grateful for how the dimmed lighting obscured her face. Her intently focused seatmates gave no indication they noticed her struggle; her emotional shock could pass without comment, and for that she was grateful. She needed to feel this alone.

From the center of the room, the hologram, a deceptively lifelike child-woman, shifted in her chair, her gaze directed at the unseen person capturing her image in photons and force fields. She dipped her head and laughed shyly. "My name is Tora Ziyal and I'm an artist," she said, trying to sound confident. "Or I'd like to be. My teachers—they say I'm promising. That's why they asked me to make this introductory holovid so that they can have something to present to the art council when they petition to have me included in the upcoming new talent exhibit at the Cardassia Institute of Art." She paused, squeezed up her shoulders, unable to repress her excitement. "I still can't believe they think I'm good enough!"

Kira had held up the drawing, impressed by the combination of simple forms executed with confident, elegant lines; the composition was thoughtful and expressive. Peering at Ziyal over the drawing notebook, she saw a young woman, anxious to please, and smiled. "These are lovely! Such serenity. You can really see Vedek Topek's influence in the texture of the shading over here," she pointed out the variegated, monochromatic tones of the rocks, "and in the geometric choices over here."

Ziyal had clasped her hands together with childish glee. "I'm so happy you like them. Do you think my father will like them?" she had asked.

"I'm certain he's very proud of you." Kira had hoped Ziyal didn't notice her smile tightening or her eyes glassing over at the mention of Dukat. Whatever her feelings for Dukat, Kira felt nothing but genuine affection for Ziyal. That Dukat was Ziyal's father was a curse of luck and genetics. The ability to sire a child and be a father weren't always mutually inclusive. She wondered, not for the first time, how such a monster could have helped create so lovely a soul.

"I wish I could say that there's some deep meaning I was trying to impart from my work." The hologram Ziyal shrugged. "I don't know that I know what each piece means, but if I talk about what I was thinking and feeling when I created them, perhaps it might help the committee discover whatever it is in my art that pleases my teachers. I just draw what I feel and somehow, it just comes out as art."

Wide-eyed, Ziyal had gazed lovingly between Kira and Dukat, relishing being between the two people she adored most. "It's a chance to show that Bajorans and Cardassians look at the universe the same way," she had explained to them. "That's what I want to do with my work: bring people together." The passion imbued in her guileless words broke Kira's heart.

Dukat had stood by, playing the proud parent, having convinced himself that he deserved credit for Ziyal's sweet sincerity. Kira had quelled her disgust for Ziyal's sake. Her loathing for Dukat needed to be kept from his daughter. Insulated from his crimes, Ziyal could continue to see him as her heroic rescuer; she deserved to see her father that way because that was how daughters were supposed to see their fathers. Kira understood that in her naïve fashion Ziyal believed she could bring Cardassia and Bajor together in her own world by casting Kira in the maternal role opposite her father. How could she comprehend what she hoped for? She had stood there, with Ziyal as the apex of their triangle, and hated Dukat for encouraging Ziyal's misplaced optimism. He had gone along with his child, allegedly being supportive, but in reality he was exploiting Ziyal to perpetuate some sick fantasy.

Kira shuddered, remembering. In light of what she now knew about her mother and Dukat, she understood that after a fashion, in another lifetime or reality, she and Ziyal could have been sisters. *Damn you, Dukat.*

Out of the corner of her eye, she saw Gul Macet, eyes trained on her. She swiped at her tears with her fist and fixed her gaze forward, pretending she didn't feel Macet's eyes drilling into the back of her head. She didn't know how much of her history Macet was aware of, but she wasn't about to give him any reason to go nosing around.

Holo-Ziyal rested her chin in her hand. "I think some of the reason why I draw—or paint—is because I'm looking for ways to make sense of my life. See, I don't entirely belong to either part of my heritage," she said, her voice cracking. The hologram swallowed, bit her lower lip and sighed. As Ziyal smoothed her skirt, twitched nervously—whatever business she could distract her hands with while she struggled to push down her emotions—the guests sat in awkward silence, uncomfortable voyeurs of her pain.

Kira watched her friend's shoulders shake. Trembling, she fought the illogical impulse to rush to her side and cradle the girl in her arms.

Kira had threaded her fingers through Ziyal's cold ones, searching for any sign that the life force, the pagh *she cherished, lingered. No vedek attended the body and where was the family to remove the Tora earring that by rights, Ziyal should have worn? The only family she had, her father, was in no condition to mourn. He rocked back and forth in his prison cell, prattling on about buying her a new dress or taking her home to visit, seemingly unaware of her death. To Dukat, she remained alive and Kira knew, after a fashion, she was, but where? What happens to the* pagh *of a child that no one will claim?*

Holding Ziyal's hand, feeling the warmth dissipate from her fingers, Kira refused to accept the notion that whatever energy it was that made Ziyal the vibrant, creative person she was had died with her. That all had been lost and that none of her lived on.

And now Kira sat in this place, predominantly surrounded by strangers, and knew, of a certainty, she hadn't been wrong. Something of Ziyal yet lived.

"I remember looking up into her face and wanting to have my mother's smooth skin. It looked so clean!" Ziyal whispered. "When I was very little, I tried scrubbing my face with the harshest cleaner, believing that I could wash this gray, this tint, from my skin. My mother had to mend all these scratches I'd given myself. Then she cried."

Covertly, Kira glanced at those sitting in front of and beside her; eyes glistened and sober faces abounded, stonelike with melancholy. She felt some satisfaction. *Finally, the grieving! And who cares if these are strangers. Ziyal deserved this!*

"And the relief I felt when I saw people who looked more like me—like my father." She gnawed her lip absently, contemplating what she would say next. "But I don't think I looked enough like him to please his people either. In my art, it was all me. In my world—where I was every shade of gray—life made sense. I hope it can mean something to someone else, though who, I don't know."

The projection paused and the lights raised. Ambassador Lang, serene, assumed a place in the room's center, the flags of many worlds hovering above her. Shoulders squared, she turned her gaze over the room's perimeter; she spoke without notes. "In a less enlightened time, with the vision of Bajor's *kai* and the political wisdom of Vedek Bareil Antos, Bajor and Cardassia negotiated a peace treaty. Alas, we were unprepared to honor our promises," she said, her voice tinged with regret. "We have a new opportunity in this postwar era to prove that we can be an honorable people. It's for this purpose I've come to Deep Space 9—to seek a meaningful, lasting peace between our worlds."

Deafening stillness overtook the stunned crowd. Kira knew everyone in the room, save perhaps the Cardassians, questioned the veracity of their understanding of Lang's words. She blinked back her own surprise. *Lang wants to normalize relations with Bajor. She's here, asking that Bajor recognize Cardassia as a co-equal partner in this corner of the quadrant. Can it happen?*

Lang continued. "But we understand why both the Federation and the people of Bajor might be skeptical. The leader of our provisional government, Alon Ghemor, believes we needed to offer a token of goodwill, to make a gesture that would both symbolize our hopes, and set the tone of our new relationship."

A dozen Cardassians filed in from the side doors. Each carried a large, flat, draped object, all in various geometric shapes. They lined up behind Lang, and waited, perfectly still. Kira tingled expectantly, knowing better than anyone in the room what was about to be unveiled.

Lang walked down their line and one by one, removed the coverings, revealing framed and mounted drawings. Some exhibited abstract qualities offering no discernible subject but rather studies of color and line; others were monochromatic pencil and ink still-life drawings of native Bajoran flora. A notable exception was a cubist study, all in gray tints and shades that showed the discernible profiles of two faces, welded together at the picture's center. But even the "face" painting and the unique personalities of the other pieces were unified by a consistent tone.

In a gallery covered wall to wall with a hundred artists' work, Kira would have recognized these pieces. Was this, then, where Ziyal's *pagh* now resided?

Waiting for the buzz of comments to simmer down, Lang resumed speaking. "The final days of the war destroyed many of Cardassia's monuments and historical treasures. Thankfully, the underground archives of the Cardassia Institute of Art in the capital city survived the worst of the attacks. The head of our government devoted some resources to finding what could be salvaged from the Institute in the hopes that any surviving artwork might re-ignite a sense of Cardassian identity—that my people could heal not only their bodies, but their minds. Holocaust, by definition, goes far beyond physical parameters, something my people have now learned.

"During our search, we discovered an archive in which the work of Tora Ziyal, daughter of Tora Naprem, a Bajoran woman, and Skrain Dukat of the Cardassian military, had survived. You see its contents here—her introductory holovid, her art portfolio. Understandably, it struck a chord with those seeking a different sort of healing—those who feel that the gaping wounds between Bajor and Cardassia must be healed before either of our peoples can move forward, Bajor into the Federation and Cardassia into wholeness."

Shakaar leaped to his feet with applause. Less speedily, Minister Asarem joined him, with the entire Bajoran delegation following suit. Kira scanned their faces, noting some discomfort but recognizing their reluctance to appear to be questioning Shakaar's enthusiasm. Kira stood, though in her heart she stood for Ziyal. Gradually, other members of the audience continued the ovation, the Starfleet personnel being the first to stand behind Bajor's gesture, with the Federation diplomats following almost immediately.

Smiling, Lang raised both of her hands and brought palms downward, asking for her audience to be seated. She continued speaking. "Symbolically, Ziyal embodies both the horrors of the Cardassian Occupation of Bajor, how women were taken from their homes and made to serve the military as concubines, and the possible glories that can come from a true alliance of our peoples. Our worlds *can* come together and create something beautiful. We see this in Ziyal's art.

"As a token of goodwill and a symbol of hope for the future, the people of Cardassia are giving a collection of Tora Ziyal's artwork to the people of Bajor to serve as memorial honoring the past, but recognizing the potential future we might find if we can find a way to see past our differences."

Another round of applause erupted, even louder than before. By now, the back walls were lined with Quark's servers and on-duty Militia and Starfleet personnel, crammed into every corner not filled with chairs, banquet tables, or bodies. Cheers rang over the steady clatter of applause. Lang nodded humbly, threading a trembling arm through her aide's proffered elbow.

Admiral Akaar nudged Kira, urging her out of her chair. She staggered up, her energy spent on emotion; she leaned against the table for support. The towering admiral bent down and asked her to accompany him to see Ambassador Lang. Kira followed, barely able to keep up with the admiral's strides that were nearly twice the length of hers. Standing in the circle around Lang, Kira fervently hoped she blended in; she had no desire to detract from Shakaar's moment.

The first minister had taken the ambassador's hand between his and had engaged her in an earnest conversation while Second Minister Asarem stood by. Kira recognized the fire in Shakaar's face. *He's really excited about this.* Standing less than a meter behind the admiral, Kira listened to the hopeful words being exchanged. When the conversation returned to Ziyal, she strained to hear Lang's comments.

"Ziyal's art, which embodies the traditions of both sides of her heritage," she said, "is proof that we can be harmonious. We can find common ground. This dream she had—of belonging to both her people—can be realized by us."

"Inspiring, Ambassador," Admiral Akaar said, shaking her hand again. "I must confess to being quite moved by your presentation. I hope this does indeed set in motion a new era of understanding."

Lang nodded graciously, thanking Akaar. Then she turned her gaze on Kira. "Ah, Colonel. I was hoping we would speak after the presentation," she said. "Were you pleased?"

" 'Pleased' isn't the first word that comes to mind, Ambassador, but I'll echo the Admiral's sentiments: I was very moved," Kira replied. "May I say that you're the perfect choice for this job. Good luck."

"First Minister Shakaar and I were just discussing beginning formal negotiations as quickly as possible. He has designated Minister Asarem to be Bajor's representative. But I was hoping you also would sit in on some of the talks, Colonel. That would be acceptable by you, First Minister, wouldn't it? Assuming it doesn't interfere with the colonel's command duties?"

A look passed between Shakaar and Asarem, and for a fleeting moment, Kira sensed disapproval from the first minister. While she knew she wasn't on the current list of Shakaar's favorites, she couldn't understand what would bother him about having her present during the talks. None of the others in the group appeared cognizant that anything passed between Asarem and Shakaar. *Maybe I'm just imagining things . . .*

Shakaar wrapped an arm around Kira's shoulder. "First thing tomorrow, Colonel Kira will need to locate an appropriate spot to house the Ziyal exhibit. I'm anxious to make it available to the station population for viewing immediately." He smiled down at Kira, who wondered what the hell he was doing with an arm around her in public. Leaving aside the fact that they were once romantically involved, it wasn't professional—and showing public approval of Kira wouldn't help push through his political agenda.

A waiter carrying a tray full of springwine passed behind her, giving her an inconspicuous way to maneuver away from Shakaar. "We're going to display the artwork here?" Kira was a little surprised. It seemed more appropriate to exhibit it at the Chamber of Ministers or the Museum of Bajoran History and Art in Dahkur.

"For the time being, until we can package it in such a way that it can travel all over Bajor for all of our people to experience. I think there are enough individuals on the station who remember Ziyal that it's particularly appropriate that it start out here. I'm certain you'll do a wonderful job." Shakaar carried on, seemingly oblivious that Kira had extricated herself from his embrace.

"However I can be of service," Kira replied, taking a sip from her goblet. With Shakaar's enthusiasm directed at preparing for the exhibit, she hoped the time had arrived when she could slip away before he demanded that she moonlight as the curator. Maybe one of these days he'd recognize that being a starbase commander was a full-time job! The reception had gone well, but she wanted to go back to worrying about malfunctioning docking clamps and temperamental Cardassian computers. "If you all don't mind, I'd like to check in at ops. Duty calls and all that." She stepped back, deposited her wine glass on a table and moved to leave when Lang stopped her.

"When you're finished arranging for the exhibit, I look forward to your visiting the talks. I think you could offer them a unique perspective," she said.

Before Kira could respond, Asarem, who had remained on the periphery of the conversation, stepped forward. "May I ask why you feel that way, Ambassador? Why you see Colonel Kira as being different from the rest of us? She's Bajoran. A former resistance fighter even." Asarem hadn't exactly thrown down the gauntlet, but she had offered Lang her first direct challenge, the opening move in a game of strategy.

Kira had almost wormed her way out of the group when Shakaar grabbed her by the elbow and steered her back into the circle, presumably to hear Lang's answer and provide any necessary clarification. *Damn. So much for getting out of here in a timely fashion . . .*

"Because Colonel Kira is a living witness to atrocities inflicted on my people, as well as her own," Lang answered, countering Asarem's pawn by moving out her own.

The conspicuous position Kira had been avoiding all evening finally found her; Admiral Akaar, Minister Asarem and Shakaar watched her, waiting for her response. *Wait a minute, I'm not one of the players here—I'm not even the referee. What I think—what I feel—has absolutely no bearing on this situation.*

And while Lang technically spoke the truth, Kira sensed that the ambassador's perceptions of the facts contrasted strongly with the second minister's perceptions of the same facts. She couldn't read Asarem, however: the minister's relaxed countenance betrayed nothing but impartiality. "I think you're overstating my understanding of the circumstances, Ambassador Lang," Kira said. "I'm only one person with one opinion."

Admiral Akaar's solemn face broke into a genial smile. "Among humans there is a saying that 'No man is an island, entire of itself.' Rather, every individual is a piece of the whole. I take that to mean that we do not have the luxury of thinking that our opinions—our actions—as individuals do not matter."

"I understand what you're saying, sir, but I hardly think that it's fair to give my opinion that kind of weight, under the circumstances. I'm not—I *can't*—speak for Bajor. That task has been assigned to Second Minister Asarem." Kira deftly forfeited her turn in whatever game Asarem had instigated. She had no desire to launch a political career and she wasn't about to be maneuvered into starting one. "Now if you'll excuse me, Admiral, Minister Shakaar, Minister Asarem, Ambassador Lang, I have a station to run."

Bowing out of the circle, she walked briskly away, her steps slowing when she discovered that Macet stood, like a sentinel, beside the exit. He smiled at her approach, which only got under her skin. Macet's persistent, unwanted attention was like having an itchy rash you couldn't scratch; except that, in this case, she wanted to scratch it with her fists.

"Gul Macet," she said with a nod.

"Colonel. It appears another evening has passed without us finding a moment to talk."

"That does, indeed, appear to be the case. We'll have to address that situation very soon."

"I'll hold you to that, Colonel. I anticipate being on the station for some time."

"I expect you will be. Now if you don't mind—"

"Of course." He unfolded his arm in an "after you" gesture, directing Kira toward the door.

Once she was safely beyond the reception room, beyond Macet's eyeshot, she threw back her head and tensed her whole body. If it wasn't Shakaar and his endless list of menial tasks or Lang wanting to use Kira as a buffer between her and Asarem, it was Macet, looking for a new friend. "Arrghh!" she growled, throwing a punch into the air.

Quark poked his head out of the doorway where he had been working. "You seem a little stressed there, Colonel."

"What?" she snapped.

"You should let off some steam," he said congenially. "Couple of hours in a holosuite. *Buff Beach Boys of Risa.* You might feel better. I'll even give you a discount."

"You're being serious."

"As a citizen of the community, I'm looking out for our best interests. A happy commander makes for a happy station."

Kira narrowed her eyes. "And you signed up to be morale officer . . . when?"

"Well—"

"I should take advice from the used spaceship salesman who probably put personal profit before the well-being of his nephew's best friend?" Kira wrapped her fists in his lapels. "I don't think so."

"What? Colonel, you can't really think I'd ever do anything to hurt Jake," he stammered. "You saw Nog's report on the shuttle I sold him—"

"Yes, I saw it. And lucky you, everything he found cleared you of any culpability for Jake's disappearance. But I'm more interested in what he may *not* have found."

"Really, Colonel, I was only trying to help your mood just now—"

"Twisting your ears off would help my mood. Are you volunteering? No?

Then shut the hell up!" Shoving him out of her way, Kira stormed past him toward the turbolift, then stopped. "One more thing, Quark. If I ever find out that what happened to Jake was the result of your negligence, there won't be a hole deep enough or dark enough for you to hide in. Are we clear?"

Quark frowned. "Crystal, Colonel," he said quietly.

Following Thriss's release from station security, Dizhei was relieved to see her rhythms return to normal. She seemed to enjoy the reception, though she was moved to tears by the message left by the late artist. The following day she ate meals with Dizhei and Anichent, something she'd stopped doing in recent weeks. She sent out several applications for available medical residencies and she was sleeping regular hours—not too much or too little.

Always an early riser, Dizhei awoke the morning of the second day after the reception to find that Thriss, too, was up, eating breakfast before an appointment with Counselor Matthias. *Oh, please let us be through the worst of it,* Dizhei thought. For the first time since they'd left Andor, she felt buoyed by hope.

Her cheery mood must have hastened their pace because they arrived in the station's hub well before Thriss's appointment. Since she hadn't had a chance for quality time alone with Thriss since before the arrest, Dizhei guided her away from the flow of pedestrian traffic and into a mostly deserted corridor, used primarily for service access, with the hope that they could talk.

"Are you sure you're going to be okay?" Dizhei asked, squeezing Thriss's hands tightly. "I can postpone my observations until later. The classrooms aren't going anywhere."

Thriss shook her head. "I'll be fine. After my appointment with the counselor I'm going to do a little shopping. I saw a new variation of *kal-toh* on display that day we ate at the Replimat. I think Anichent would like it—he can play it solo since neither you nor I are very good at chess. And I want him to know how much I regret hurting him."

After looking both ways in the hallway to ensure that they were, indeed, alone, Dizhei sighed and leaned into her bondmate's shoulder. "He knows, *zh'yi.* Despite the strife between us since we left Andor, he loves you deeply. And I think I've helped him see that you love him as well."

"I do! I'm sorry you feel that you're always caught between us. You manage your worries about Thirishar far better than we do—it becomes easy to take out our frustrations on each other, especially when Anichent's always certain that he's right," Thriss said, with good humor. She leaned back against the wall. "Remember that day in sh'Dasath's class when Anichent insisted that he knew better than sh'Dasath how to prove that theorem? Never mind that sh'Dasath had published papers on it. Anichent gets these ideas in his head . . ."

"I'd say between Shar, you and Anichent, it's a miracle we find consensus on anything," Dizhei said, taking Thriss by the hand. The feel of Thriss's elegant fingers against her wrist soothed her worries more than words possibly could.

Suddenly Thriss turned to Dizhei, concern written on her face. "You do know that I don't love Anichent any differently than I love you."

"But you *do* love Shar differently."

Twisting a straying lock of hair between her fingers, Thriss blushed dark blue. *"Sh'za—"*

"It's fine that you do, Shathrissía. I understand," Dizhei reassured her. "Maybe it would be more truthful to say that I respect your feelings." Or she hoped she did. She didn't like what she perceived to be between Shar and Thriss because it existed outside the bond, but she tried to comprehend it because she couldn't combat something she didn't understand. Keeping the bond strong meant she had to work with what she'd been given, like it or not, because the bond was first. *Always.*

From the time she was little, Dizhei relished that she was the most rare of her species: all Andorian offspring originated from her gender. Her unique maternal role suited her own career inclinations toward taking care of and teaching children. The entire focus of who she was—of what she believed she should be—was this deeply felt longing she had to be a parent, to be a part of a bond and create a life. At an early age, she came to understand the significance of her gender identity; all her priorities, all her desires fell into line behind that role. If anything, she envied Thriss's role as the *zhavey*. Their child would begin with Dizhei, but it was Thriss who would carry their offspring and give birth. Dizhei was continually astounded at how casually Thriss treated the privilege of carrying their child. What could possibly be a greater honor! Certainly not medical school or reputation. So many of their classmates had admired Thriss's vibrant personality, her zeal for new experiences and how quick she was to question the dictates passed down by the Elders. Dizhei never found Thriss's nonconformity as romantic as their peers did.

Since the day Thriss had been bonded to her, Dizhei had watched her *zh'yi's* moods—her passions—dictate her life path. Not a commitment to principles. And for some years now, Thriss's passions had centered on Shar; everything else was secondary. Even having a child seemed to be a means for Thriss to bind Shar closer to her instead of her life purpose.

The more she witnessed the consequences of Thriss and Shar's decision to violate their bondgroup covenant, the more she recognized the Elders' wisdom in establishing the boundaries of the *shelthreth*. Intimate acts belonged in a group context. Dizhei felt the longings, but as Thriss proved, the consequences for yielding could be dire; she refused to take the risk. Without proper guidance, Thriss might forfeit her responsibilities as *zhavey* to follow Shar. Should that happen, Dizhei was prepared to do what she always had: fix whatever had broken.

Nuzzling Dizhei's neck, Thriss sighed, bringing Dizhei back into the moment. She drew Thriss into her arms and held her close. *I hope I'm wrong, zh'yi. I hope I'm wrong about many things.*

"There's nothing to understand, *sh'za*. I love you and Anichent the same as I love Shar," Thriss said finally.

Dizhei pulled back, curled her hand around her bondmate's cheek and considered the beloved and familiar face. Thriss's words belied Dizhei's own time-distant images of Shar, dappled in long shadows, pretending that everything was as it always was, though his darkened eyes said differently. She closed her eyes, relishing Thriss's warmth and drawing comfort from her embrace. But as much as she might long to indulge Thriss's romantic notions, Dizhei knew those notions threatened their greater purpose. She extracted herself from their embrace and took Thriss by both hands. "Don't lie to me, *zh'yi.*"

"I don't know what you're—" Thriss protested, halfheartedly.

"Don't. Lie. To. Me," Dizhei reiterated. "We're betrothed. I sense these things. I've always known. Anichent knows, too, though he doesn't want to admit it. We both know you and Shar shared *tezha.*"

Thriss flinched. "We didn't do anything wrong. We belong to each other. You and I—we could share the same." Thriss reached up to Dizhei's face.

Dizhei pushed Thriss's hand away. "It was a mistake. A serious one. But it's done." Even as Thriss confessed, envy twisted inside Dizhei, threatening to taint her with bitterness. She would not, she could not, allow herself to become the source of conflict. *I will not condone—I will not give you permission to believe that what you've done is acceptable when it could still destroy everything we've worked for.* Oh, how she wanted to shake the selfishness out of Thriss! To make her understand that she didn't have the luxury of destroying herself without destroying Dizhei, too.

Even now, all these years later, Dizhei vividly felt each moment of the first day Shar and Thriss had violated the bondgroup covenant. The panic of the night before, when Thriss and Shar had been missing, hadn't yet subsided. Shar claimed he'd been performing research for his environmental studies class; Thriss had gone off to find him and they had spent the night away from the compound after becoming lost. Both her bondmates claimed that nothing forbidden had passed between them and Dizhei believed them. Especially Shar, who had barely contained his frustration with Thriss.

For hours, Dizhei had waited for Shar to return from his disciplinary conference, but he never appeared. She had checked with Anichent, *Zhadi,* and the school before discovering Thriss was gone. How long had she stood in the corridor, waiting for Thriss to come with her to dinner—the wait felt endless. When Thriss finally showed up, she had been so overcome, both physically and emotionally, that she could hardly move. Collapsed on her bed, Thriss drifted between sleep and delirious consciousness while Dizhei, numbed with jealousy, worry and fear, sat beside her, uncertain what to do next. Tell Charivretha? Tell Thriss's *zhavey?* The Elders? She worried that if she did tell, it would ruin everything. That the Elders would punish Thriss and Shar, and perhaps put in jeopardy everything Dizhei lived for.

She kept Thriss's secret. But she had never fully trusted Thriss since.

"You must hate us for what we did . . ." Thriss's voice trailed off.

"I could never hate you," Dizhei said, she hoped convincingly. A maintenance worker emerged from a supply closet. He nodded a polite greeting. Dizhei waited until he'd passed before saying, "We can't talk here."

Guiding Thriss farther away from the corridor, Dizhei found a darkly lit nook offering them greater privacy. "You know I'm not my *zhavey's* only *shei,*" Dizhei continued in a husky whisper. "Having had two siblings go before me, I saw some of what goes on after the *shelthreth*. I think I understand better than Anichent. He sees things narrowly. He sees our obligations as being precise, exact—not negotiable. Anything that he perceives as undercutting our greater purpose pains him."

"Which is why he wasn't happy when Shar took this assignment so quickly after the war. Instead of coming back to Andor," Thriss observed.

Dizhei nodded. "And why he's never been happy with the risk you and Shar took."

"Has he always known? I mean, like you?"

"Anichent probably knew on some intuitive level, but he didn't know, in fact, until Shar left for the Gamma Quadrant and I told him."

"Is that why he's been more angry with me than usual?"

Dizhei nodded.

"I'm so sorry, *sh'za.*" Thriss leaned forward and brushed her lips on Dizhei's forehead. "Believe me when I tell you that I want what's best, too. I can't wait to become a *zhavey,* but I don't think I'll be very good unless I have lots of help from you."

Dizhei knew that Thriss meant well; she didn't want to hurt anyone. If Dizhei could believe Thriss, their lives would be considerably simpler. But Dizhei had spent too many years following behind her, mending whatever Thriss had carelessly broken, to accept her bondmate's word. She thought about pursuing the conversation further but after taking note of the time decided they needed to move on. A quick hug would have to suffice.

With a gentle, but firm hand on the small of Thriss's back, Dizhei steered her toward Matthias's office. Keeping Thriss focused on most pressing concerns had always been her role and Dizhei anticipated it would take her soft-glove discipline to ensure that they all ended up back on Andor as soon as possible.

Word of the proposed exhibit spread quickly through the station community. Daily, dozens of private petitions filled Kira's message queue before lunch, variations on requests that the art be placed as far away from/as close to, their quarters/place of business/place of worship as possible. As she considered the list of spaces available for the Ziyal exhibit, Kira concluded that no option would please everyone. A curator from the Bajoran Museum in Ashalla would be arriving tomorrow, but Kira, who had the final decision, planned to consult with the expert before making a public announcement. At least that way, she would share the blame.

As much buzz as was floating around the station regarding the exhibit, the peace talks figured even more prominently in conversation. Kira's curiosity was piqued—she hoped to find the time to drop by and see the delegations in action—but snarls in the implementation of yellow alert protocols often required her personal attention. On the surface, those who saw Deep Space 9 as a spaceport understood the importance of increased security, but the pragmatic reality of changing plans, rescheduling deliveries, changing course or having cargo inspected inconvenienced more than a few ship captains. People tended to be very accommodating—as long as they didn't need to do the accommodating. Until her day-to-day duties became less laborious, Kira had to be satisfied with ops gossip if she wanted to stay updated on the battle of wills between Lang and Asarem.

Because the talks weren't public, the only record of the goings-on came from individuals who had been in attendance. Eavesdropping on two Militia corporals, Kira learned that the first few days of talks had accomplished little. She hadn't expected that the gulf separating Cardassia and Bajor would be bridged overnight, but she thought that Asarem would at least take a step. Find consensus on something, like come to an agreement about when to come to an agreement! From what she could gather, Lang's methodically planned agenda outlined discussions on issues ranging from sharing medical technology to ensuring the rights of Bajoran nationals while on Cardassia. Asarem's approach had been to nitpick every detail and definition Lang raised.

The days allegedly played out thus: Lang would explain Cardassia's concerns, what their position was on the issue and where they wanted input from Bajor. She would then look to Minister Asarem to elucidate the Bajoran response. So far, the breadth of Asarem's commentary consisted of variations on: "That sounds reasonable. I'll take it under consideration. What else would you like to discuss?" That Asarem was listening was positive; that she wasn't engaged in dialogue was puzzling. During her days in the Chamber of Ministers, she'd had a reputation as a tenacious debater and orator. To sit in a chair, hands folded in front of her, watching impassively—didn't sound like Asarem. It was distinctly possible that the minister's approach wasn't being fairly represented.

This, Kira knew, having based her suppositions on snippets of secondhand accounts, was a situation she planned on remedying as soon as possible. Because she anticipated being busy with the curator in the morning, she planned on dropping in at the end of her shift. As seemed to be the case every day, a situation arose that prevented her doing as she'd planned. Irregular Core readings troubled the engineering staff and they requested she remain in ops, should an emergency decision be required. Since the Core transplant, the engineering crews had been especially vigilant, always on the lookout for the one item they might have overlooked; Kira appreciated their thoroughness. When the diagnostics concluded, the acting chief engineer was satisfied, allowing Kira to escape. Though the hour was late, it wouldn't be unprecedented for the delegations to still be working.

Rounding one of the last corners before the conference room, Kira encountered the retinal scanner and voice imprint unit Ro had felt so strongly about installing. Lang had repeatedly reassured them that such precautions weren't necessary; she felt as safe as she could under the circumstances. Though safety was a concern, Kira knew Ro's primary motive in installing a checkpoint wasn't to protect the diplomats. She reasoned that if someone wanted to assassinate a member of either delegation, they'd have easier access from a location other than the conference rooms. No, Ro intended to monitor who went in and out of the conference rooms at all hours, should questions arise. Those authorized to pass had been approved by Lang, Shakaar and Kira. No one else needed access. Unauthorized personnel attempting to maneuver past the checkpoint would be stopped and interrogated.

On her way down the hall, she passed by a cleaning team—a couple of Bajorans she recognized as having worked in the habitat ring public areas—but otherwise, the sector was utterly silent, save the sound of her footfalls.

The talks must be over for the day, she thought, disappointed. Kira resolved to return first thing in the morning, when an odd scent attracted her attention. Ozone. Burnt synthetic materials—not organic. Maybe one of the nearby labs had a waste disposal problem, sending the aroma wafting through the air ducts. She resisted the impulse to call for an environmental systems diagnostic, choosing to investigate the situation herself. Scorch permeated the air the closer she came to the conference room. Wondering if a replicator was malfunctioning inside, she deactivated the door lock, grateful when a billow of smoke didn't greet her.

Her eyes took a moment to adjust to the dimmed lighting. When they did, she scanned the room for evidence of anything amiss and saw that most everything seemed to be in place . . .

. . . Save the silver, green, and sand-colored Cardassian flag draped over one of the chairs, stripped from the pole behind it, scarred with angry, carbonized wounds. The gleaming edge of a knife blade glinted in the starlight, stabbed through the heart of the chair.

Cursing, she stepped back into the foyer, instinctively touching her combadge. "Kira to security. We have a situation on level 10, section 65, conference room 4. I want a team up here *now.*"

13

Shar tingled with anticipation. He had never believed in fate or luck, but if this day turned out the way he hoped, he might be persuaded to change his mind.

Two hours before, Shar and Keren had entered the farm country of the Hebshu Peninsula. Carved out by a glacier millions of years ago, the region suffered from none of the geological dangers afflicting most of the continental masses; the closest active volcano was hundreds of kilometers away and there hadn't been an earthquake recorded in centuries. The peninsula enjoyed mild winters, rich soil and a long growing season. It was also one of the rare spots on Vanìmel (or Luthia for that matter) where Wanderers and Houseborn lived side by side on their farms. Mingling herds and sharing farm equipment wasn't unheard of. Keren had explained that because most Yrythny didn't consider living off the land a natural inclination, the Yrythny who ended up choosing to live here were nonconformists. Farming and ranching attracted a quirky, independent breed that followed their own rules, refusing to adhere to any but the barest caste frameworks.

Since they'd met on his first day in Luthia, Shar learned that Keren rarely acted without an ulterior motive. The trip to Hebshu proved to be consistent with her pattern, though he suspected where she was taking him concerned his research. They'd wandered down the lanes, chatting with the locals as they encountered them.

They'd eaten a basket full of berries offered to them by a group of young-lings combing the forest for the tangy treasures, and Shar had his first real encounter with Yrythny children. Like most children, they were inquisitive, and spent a great deal of time studying Shar, touching his skin and hair, climbing him as they grew bolder, and laughing delightedly when he made his antennae move.

Not long after that, Shar encountered his first *shmshu,* the primary suppliers of the hairpieces most Yrythny wore to indicate rank and caste position. Different breeds of *shmshu* provided hair in varying qualities. Shar had stood by a fence, watching as Yrythny carefully combed out their coats, waving over the animals from head to toe with a handheld version of a sonic shower. As diverting as the domesticated animals had been, Shar was ready to move on. They'd been walking for more than an hour when Keren finally explained why she'd brought him here. And when she did, Shar concurred that it was well worth skipping the meetings he was supposed to have attended.

Hidden here in Hebshu were the most comprehensive records of Wanderer genetics on Vanìmel. For obvious reasons, genetic research was tightly controlled and kept secret. Hebshu's rural, out-of-the-way personality made it easy to conceal equipment and files without attracting government attention. Most of the research was performed during the winter months when the ground lay fallow and the *shmshu* grazed in the fields instead of in the hills. Repairing equipment, reading and indoor pursuits grew tiresome. Intellectually rigorous scientific inquiry kept minds sharp and hands busy. From generation to generation, the equipment and records were passed down, with Kremoroh being one of the newest custodians.

Kremoroh descended the cellar steps first. He activated the light panel, inviting Shar and Keren to join him.

Shar's initial disparaging thoughts quickly dissipated when he considered how much painstaking work it must have taken for these scientists to labor with antiquated equipment, limited time and few resources. Most of what he saw crammed into corners and spilling out of boxes would have been current in the Federation two hundred years ago. Still, he couldn't help smiling, imagining these tall, gawky farmers hunched over cellular scanners, squeezing into these small underground labs, customarily used for off-season vegetable storage.

Taking a seat by one of the filing cabinets, Shar pulled open a drawer where he discovered dozens of neatly labeled, clear-lidded containers filled with data chips. Another drawer revealed identical contents. "Your records?" he asked.

Kremoroh nodded. "Those go back hundreds of years. Every Wanderer who finds their way to Hebshu ends up being mapped."

"Mapped?" Shar asked, wanting to make sure he understood the usage.

"Gene maps."

A miniature, cruder version of what existed in the Andorian genome database. Shar couldn't help but be impressed. With very little training—and no assistance—they'd tackled a sophisticated area of study. Looking around him, he imagined how these scientists had made do with ill-fitting parts and poor tools with which to assemble them. Everything in the room had been designed and built using whatever technology was available. Shar admired their creativity.

"The original idea was that we were going to figure out how to identify what House the Wanderers were supposed to be from and prove to the high-thinking Houseborn that the Wanderers weren't really wandering," Kremoroh explained. "Storms, water temperature, predators—any number of things could set a hatchling off course."

A variation on what I said to Dax, just yesterday. When this thought occurred to Shar, he looked over at Keren, who sat smiling serenely. *She knew what she was doing bringing me here, this is all part of her plan. After years of watching the machinations of the Federation Council, you'd think I'd be a little less trusting.* Shar turned to Kremoroh. "Since you're still here and Keren is still in the Lower Assembly, I take it you haven't been able to draw any meaningful conclusions."

"First, we had to figure out what part of which chromosomes did what. Without Luthia's computer power or the right splicers and scanners, it's been hit and miss about what techniques work, and avoiding contamination. What I'd do for a decent computer!"

They need more than tools . . . The nucleus of an idea formed in Shar's mind, but he needed a bit more information to ensure it was feasible before he could propose it out loud. "And as a comparison group? The Houseborn?"

"The other major problem. Not many Houseborn want to be part of a Wanderer genetic study. We can compare our DNA with our own kind, but we don't have the same basis of comparison for the Houseborn. We have a smattering from those Houseborn who've lived here on the peninsula, but not enough to draw conclusions."

Surveying the room, Shar realized some of the filing cabinets stood two and three deep, with drawer after drawer filled with variations on data chip storage. These farmer/scientists appeared to have accumulated thousands of different samples. "This is your main storage facility, I take it?"

"No. We have labs like this scattered all around here. Makes it easier to go unnoticed."

"Have you put all these into an aggregate database?" Shar said, hoping.

"In fact, that was last winter's project."

Keren perked up. "Is it possible—"

"The *Sagan*. It has the computing power—"

"And the Houseborn samples?"

"Medical records? Or we could take some ourselves from their drinking glasses—"

"Tonight! At dinner!" She jumped off her chair, clapping her hands.

Kremoroh scratched his head. "Excuse me? But I think I've missed something."

"You'd better come up with a new project for next winter, because I have a feeling that what Thirishar accomplishes with your data could change things—for all of us!" Keren beamed.

The cumulative datafiles were stored several farms over—a quick stop as they set out to return to the *Sagan*. Keren carried the bulk of the chips in her pack. Shar wanted to make the best use of his time so he planned on working as they walked, relying on Keren to prevent him from stumbling into trees. He reached for his tricorder, planning on formulating a few basic equations as he tried to frame the parameters of the statistical sampling.

"Ensign ch'Thane!"

Shar turned, and saw Kremoroh moving toward them from the farm. He had a youngling with him. And not just any youngling, Shar saw, but one of the ones he'd encountered earlier, who had shared berries with him and Keren. "Is something wrong?" he asked as Kremoroh caught up with them.

Kremoroh nudged the youngling forward. "Do it," he said sternly.

The youngling looked unhappy, but at Kremoroh's urging stretched out his arm, holding up Shar's combadge.

Shar's eyes widened. He accepted the combadge with a sincere word of thanks. "Where did you find it?"

"Tell him," Kremoroh told the youngling.

"I took it while we were playing with you," the child admitted. "I'm sorry."

"I accept your apology," Shar said kindly. *Idiot!* he chastised himself. *How could you not realize it was missing?*

"My apologies as well, Ensign ch'Thane," Kremoroh said. "Oh, and I feel I should tell you: a voice was coming from the device earlier; that was how I became aware that Cosho here had it. Whoever it was sounded angry, but it's since stopped."

Oh, no . . . "Thank you, Kremoroh. I'm very grateful to you." Kremoroh and the youngling departed, and with Keren looking on in concern, Shar steeled himself and pressed his combadge. "Ch'Thane to Dax."

"Shar, where the hell are you? Why haven't you answered until now?"

"I apologize, Lieutenant. I had a bit of a mishap involving my combadge—"

"Where are you?" Dax repeated.

Shar swallowed, recalling that he hadn't explicitly asked for Lieutenant Dax's permission to come planetside. "I'm with Delegate Keren, sir," he said evasively.

"But where? Someone appropriated the computer terminal in our office and used it to send an illegal communication to the surface. That wouldn't happen to have been you?"

"No, sir. Actually, I'm here, planetside. On the Hebshu Peninsula. Part of my fact-finding, Lieutenant."

"I assume you have the Sagan *with you?"*

"Yes, sir."

"Get airborne immediately and lock onto my signal. I want you to fly over my position and be prepared to pick up the away team."

"Understood, sir. I'm on my way." Shar swore and established contact with *Sagan's* onboard computer. "Ch'Thane to *Sagan,* two to beam back on this signal. Energize."

"He's just not being reasonable!" Nog growled. Frustrated, he threw the padd down onto the floor. He fisted his hands and kicked the broken tablet aside.

Rahim, Gordimer and M'Nok, who were sharing ration packs from *Defiant,* stopped talking when the padd skidded across the floor and crashed into M'Nok's shoes. Huddled in the corner, Shavoh, Tlaral and Ensign Senkowski halted their review of conduit repair specs when Nog spoke. The three engineers exchanged concerned glances. One by one, every person in the room looked up from what they'd been doing to see what might have prompted Nog's uncharacteristic entrance.

Realizing he had the room's attention, Nog scooted off to sit on his sleeping bag, dropping down cross-legged, making a deliberate point of sitting with his back to the group.

Chief Chao's fork, loaded with pasta primavera, paused midway between mouth and pack. "Excuse me, sir?" she said. "Is everything all right?"

Though he felt Chao's placid gaze on him, Nog kept his back turned. "Commander Vaughn! He isn't taking the threat of the Cheka weapon seriously enough. He wants to leave without a working defense against the web weapon! And we just don't have the resources or the manpower to handle repairs like this again, especially if we're stranded in the middle of nowhere."

Mikaela Leishman, the shift commander in Nog's absence, went over to talk to Nog; the two Yrythny engineers joined her. She squatted down to his eye level. "Lieutenant, is there something we should know before we return to *Defiant?*"

Throwing his head back, Nog laughed, a bitter sound that startled everyone within hearing. "Something you should know? How about we're killing ourselves trying to put the *Defiant* back together but our ever-dutiful CO refuses to let me have the tools I need to ensure our safety."

"I don't think you should be talking that way—" Leishman paused when Nog glared at her. "Sir?"

"We didn't get the load, Mikaela," Nog spat. "No load, no metal. No metal, no femtobots. No femtobots, we're ripe to be picked off like a *targ* running from a Klingon blood hunt."

"Commander Vaughn isn't one to make a decision like that lightly," Chao reasoned, twirling her pasta with her fork. "He wouldn't leave us virtually defenseless if he didn't think it was the only way. He must have a plan."

"But there was a way to make this plan work, Chief," Nog said, scrambling to his feet and stalking over to Chao. "That's what's so pointless about all this! If he'd given the Cheka trader what he wanted, we'd be starting to manufacture the femtobots next shift."

"Do I dare ask what he wanted?" Senkowski said.

"The cloak. The Cheka wanted the cloaking device."

A few pairs of Starfleet eyebrows shot up, but Tlaral gasped. "You can't give it to them! We'd never be able to defend ourselves if they could cloak their ships!"

"Or worse, their weapons platforms," Shavoh added.

"Practically speaking, Lieutenant," Chao said, "the commander can't give technology like that away. It's not Federation property, just a loan from the Romulan Empire. Besides that, what about Prime Directive issues? Cloaking tech would radically impact the balance of power in this region. I'm with the commander on this one. Sorry."

"Me, too," Senkowski added, returning to study conduit repair specs.

Permenter rolled over on her stomach and looked up at Nog with sorrowful eyes. "I know I've been complaining as much as anyone, but I'd rather play by the rules. You want some candy? A little chocolate might make you feel better." She held out the bag to him.

Nog slapped it away, got up, and stormed out of the room, growling, "This attitude is gonna get us all killed."

The aquaculture village burned.

Collapsing into the ocean from their derricks, the flaming houses and outbuildings outshone the setting sun. Filtered through the acrid smoke, the last rays of light burned brilliant fuchsia and tangerine; descending darkness gradually defeated the day. Greasy, rainbow chemicals glazed the sea's surface as unrecycled wastes spilled into the water. Dead fish and other sea life bobbed along with rising and falling waves.

Ezri stood on the observation deck, Jeshoh beside her, gazing out over the waters, trying to avoid looking behind her where the Yrythny military had lined up all the Wanderer servants working on the hydrofoil and prepared to interrogate them. Despite their claim that her workstation had been utilized to carry out the terrorist act, the soldiers seemed less interested in talking to the *Defiant* people than in rounding up every Wanderer on board. She couldn't bear to watch. Even with her back turned to them, blocking out the soldiers' shouted accusations and servants' protestations of innocence proved difficult. Ezri understood the troops had a job to do, and she knew that maybe one among those servants might have a connection to the attacks, but certainly not all. Why did so many people have to suffer?

Squinting out over the heaving sea, she hoped the dark objects floating in the water were broken pieces from buildings and not bodies. Another explosion burst after flames greedily ate through the planking outside the fuel cell supply. She vaguely understood the village layout, noting that another fuel cell supply was at risk. Not a problem if the villagers had been evacuated, but she saw figures still leaping from dock to dock, carrying younglings in arms or in backpacks. *Where are their evacuation craft? Surely there must be flying transports or marine vessels on their way.* She slammed her fists into the deck railing, frustrated. *There has to be something I can do to help.*

"I need a magnification device, Jeshoh," Ezri snapped.

He clicked open a supply station, and produced a boxy monocular device.

Taking readings off Ezri's optical nerve, the lens sensors fed information to its computer, sending the mechanism humming and whirring into focus.

After first surveying the shoreline where the lights of House Minaral blinked, Ezri shifted her focus to the waters, subsequently taking in the entire 360-degree view around the hydrofoil. Nothing. She saw nothing resembling a watercraft heading in their direction. Turning her attention to the burning village, she studied the surface of each dock and platform, then dropped the lens. Ezri stopped counting at twenty, no, thirty—too many—Yrythny, clinging to the pylons, structures collapsing all around, desperately trying to avoid falling into the convulsing waters.

"Your people are out there!" Ezri cried, throwing aside the magnifier. "We have to help them—"

"Shhh," Jeshoh admonished her. "We need to keep to ourselves until the commandant gives us permission to—"

"If you think I'm going to stand here and watch innocents die while that commandant throws his weight around, you haven't learned much about me during the last week." Ezri shot off across the deck, igniting commotion among the soldiers.

"Hey you! Stop!" a patrol leader shouted, running after her.

Smiling politely, Ezri waved to acknowledge that she'd heard the soldier's order. She dropped over the side, taking the ladder to the lowest deck, having some vague recollection of seeing the lifeboats and emergency equipment being stashed near where they'd changed for their dive trip. Dax lived by her own ethical compass; she'd be damned before she dawdled around, watching the military blowhards feeding already overinflated egos while people were dying. These Yrythny wanted her; she didn't ask to be their savior and they needed to remember that involving her in their civil conflict was *their* idea. Dax was a package deal—take all or none—but nothing in between.

Just as she'd started to go below, Jeshoh charged across the deck after her. He skipped rungs down the ladder to help him catch up, but she still beat him by a minute. She kept the exterior door propped open, but as soon as Jeshoh's feet touched the deck Ezri pulled him inside, closed the portal behind him and locked it. The clamor of boots clattering down the ladder outside didn't bother her in the slightest.

"I don't think the commandant wants you to leave—" he panted, bent over, trying to catch his breath.

With only a door between her and a squad of angry Yrythny, Ezri yanked off the doorpad cover, removed two circuit chips and snapped them in half. Two other doors led out of the room and deeper into the ship, but she figured it would be a few minutes at least before the soldiers made it down that way.

"What are you doing?" he said, incredulous. "They're going to be furious. They'll blow the door open."

"This is still a ship of state. You think the Assembly Chair would appreciate his hand-picked mediator being hunted like a common criminal?"

"You looked guilty when you ran."

"Let's not kid ourselves, Jeshoh. Your troops have already decided the Wanderers are guilty—they're not focusing on me or my crew. Well, I'm not about to lounge around, sipping wood wine when your people need our help. It's not like we don't have the resources." She walked down the hallway, examining each and every locker she found. If she had to dive into the water and swim over to those villagers with the lifejackets, she would. Let them try to stop her.

"There's a criminal investigation under way here, Lieutenant," Jeshoh said. "You heard the commandant. To the best of the military's ability to trace, the explosives that destroyed the village weren't triggered on site, but remotely, from someone on this ship, right after another signal was sent here from your office. You're right: they don't actually suspect you or your people, Lieutenant, but they do believe you may be able to help them identify the real terrorists."

"Why? Because only Wanderers commit crimes?" Dax mocked. She scanned the pictographs identifying the contents of each locker. *Rations, rope, water purification, emergency communications . . . ah! Here it is.* She opened the cabinet identified as storing the life preservers and removed the packs inside. An adjoining cabinet had the same contents. She repeated the process, tossing the packs to Jeshoh, who dropped them on the floor in protest. Ezri promptly scooped them up, slung them over her other shoulder and moved on to the next locker. "Is this knee-jerk assumption of Wanderer guilt the reason we aren't running a rescue mission?"

"In part," Jeshoh said reluctantly.

"What the hell does that mean?"

"The aquaculture villages are staffed with Wanderers," he said bitterly. "I've seen it before. When terrorist attacks take out Wanderers, the military is slow to rescue or help the victims. Partly because high body count bolsters military propaganda. The Wanderers are evil, dangerous and so forth." Jeshoh hesitated.

Ezri refused to let him off. "And?"

"And because they believe they shouldn't save the terrorists from the consequences of their actions. Their attacks hurt fellow Wanderers, let them take the blame for the casualties."

"That's despicable!" she said.

"Would you believe me if I told you I agreed?"

Looking deeply into Jeshoh's eyes, Ezri probed his sincerity. Physically, he towered over her; she knew if he truly wanted to stop her, he could probably overpower her with little trouble. He made no such move. Instead he willingly subjected himself to her scrutiny.

"Help me then," she said softly.

Knocks became kicks and kicks produced dents as the soldiers continued pounding on the outer portal.

Jeshoh nodded and reached over to free the packs of life preservers from Ezri's shoulder. "There are four rescue boats on the next level up. The door on the left is a back way. If we hurry, the soldiers may not realize our goals before it's too late."

The other door opened and Ensign Juarez peeked out, followed by four Houseborn assembly members, with Candlewood and McCallum bringing up the rear. Juarez sighed with relief when he saw Jeshoh and Ezri.

Good timing, Ezri thought.

"Everything all right, Lieutenant?" Juarez queried, stepping out cautiously.

Ezri filled him in on the proposed rescue mission. "I don't think the troops will be happy about it, but I don't really care. Still have your medkit? Good, you're gonna need it. Grab those as well," Ezri said, indicating some Yrythny medical supplies near the nurse. Ezri stuffed emergency blankets into her pack and threw assorted items at McCallum and Candlewood. Whether the Yrythny adapted well to water or not, the sun was dropping, and so would the water temperature. Shock would make survivors more vulnerable to hypothermia.

Jeshoh, who had been huddling with the other Yrythny, said, "They are willing to pilot the other rescue craft. I can persuade any other committee members remaining below decks to hold off the commandant and his men until we get the lifeboats into the water."

Ezri nodded in approval. "Looks like we have ourselves a rescue team."

• • •

The whir of computer circuits, the thrum of impulse engines and the patterns of blinking lights had a tempo Shar found comforting. From time to time, when his head spun with worries and have-to's, Shar found refuge in working a spacecraft. Performing routine physical tasks helped him wrestle down the mounting anxieties that sometimes beset him. Most of the time, a spacecraft followed predictable patterns. Shar enjoyed the orderliness of it all, finding it comforting when the world around him refused to conform. His peace would dissipate shortly.

Though the Tin-Mal quarantine zone was in the opposite hemisphere, once Shar had locked in the navigational data and checked weather conditions (storms directly to the east of Ezri's location), the *Sagan's* ETA was only twenty minutes. A massive force field surrounding Tin-Mal combined with the curve of the planet made it impossible for Shar to transport Ezri to the *Sagan* from where they launched. Rather than track along the surface, Shar launched *Sagan* out of the atmosphere and into an arc that would take them to Dax in minutes instead of hours.

Few words passed between him and Keren; he was grateful for the quiet. He had a feeling he'd be in a siege of words from Lieutenant Dax soon enough.

A signal from his console alerted him that *Sagan* was approaching Ezri's location.

"*Sagan* to Lieutenant Dax. We are within transporter range."

The comm system crackled with static. "*Stand by, Sagan. Prepare to beam up wounded Yrythny.*" Shar blinked. *Sagan* was a decent-size shuttlecraft, but Dax had to know the ship couldn't handle too many casualties.

"Coming through the cloud deck a hundred kilometers out, sir. I'll have you on visual in five, four, three, two—on screen." The companel monitor on Shar's console lit up, but billowing smoke in the twilight obscured the view. "Computer, increase magnification and activate beacons." Shar swept the ocean with spotlights, finally finding small dark figures on a dock. He thought he could see Ezri waving. Several midsize marine shuttles loaded with Yrythny were skimming away from the disaster site. "Keren, inside the starboard passenger bench are emergency medical kits. Please retrieve them." *What had happened down there?*

Clouds of fine ash hung on the wind. Coughing, Ezri raised her uniform sleeve, dank with smoke and Yrythny blood, to her mouth. She pillowed the head of a wounded Yrythny on her lap; he'd stopped moving a few minutes ago and she hoped the *Sagan* hadn't come too late to save him. Ensign Juarez had done what he could to stabilize his vitals, but the chemical burns to his lungs might have irreparably compromised his respiratory system. Waves heaved against the pier; the rotted wood platform groaned in response, swaying ever so slightly. Ezri envisioned the whole structure giving way, collapsing into the sea like most of the aquaculture village.

Her entire body, stiff with cold, ached. Over the last hour, she'd drawn on physical strength she didn't know she had. At one point, Jeshoh had tied a line around her waist and sent her over the side to help a Yrythny with a broken arm into one of the rescue boats. Dangling in the air, she was tossed by the wind like a ball on a pendulum. She remembered digging injured people out from under collapsed cottages, putting out fires and helping Juarez transfuse Yrythny blood. Even with the lifeboats, Ezri knew many Yrythny that had survived the attack had perished in the water. She couldn't think about her losses right now. She needed to assume command of the *Sagan,* deliver casualties to the proper medical facilities and figure out how to prevent her diplomatic mission from collapsing under the weight of suspicion.

When the shuttle spotlights finally appeared, the wait between transports felt unending, though she knew only seconds transpired between the time Jeshoh, Juarez and the five remaining wounded were beamed aboard. Her turn came. She blinked—it seemed once—and saw familiar environs, the shuttle's interior; Jeshoh huddled with Keren, Shar had left the *Sagan* on autopilot while he helped Juarez.

"It's gonna be a tight fit, everyone, so hold on to whatever's bolted down. Ensign ch'Thane, with me." Soot-smudged and soaked, Ezri settled in front of the conn, ordering Shar into the co-pilot's seat.

He complied without comment.

He'd damn well better follow orders without question, she thought. "Prepare to return to Luthia," she said hoarsely and cleared her throat.

"Lieutenant, I'm sure I can manage if you want to go back and have a medical check."

"You've managed quite enough for one day, Ensign," Ezri snapped. *I need tea, a hot bath and,* with a sigh she thought, *Julian.*

"Tell Fazzle he's getting what he wanted," Prynn said, trying to stay pleasant. The brutish guard posted outside the Cheka suite had no response. She shuddered when she thought about Fazzle touching her. *I don't care how badly we need those codes, I am not sleeping with anyone to get them. Lieutenant Dax or Doctor Bashir should be doing this. They seem like the types who really get off on the "let's pretend" stuff.*

"Can you tell Fazzle I'm here?" she said, forcing a toothy grin. *This crew is going to owe me . . .*

The guard raised his wrist to his mouth and whispered something unintelligible into his comm unit. A moment later, the doors opened.

"I can go in?" Prynn said.

Before the guard could answer, a familiar howling echoed from within the suite. She peered around the guard to see inside. On two hands and knees, Fazzle ambled down the hall toward Prynn, squealing, "Oh yes oh yes oh yes oh yes," as he approached.

Prynn gulped. *How did I get into this?* When her father approached her about a "special assignment," Prynn thought maybe he would ask her to take the *Defiant* for a shakedown before setting a course back to Vanìmel. Subjecting herself to Fazzle's artistic whims? Not even on the list of possibilities. If that weird creature said or did anything untoward, Prynn would demand unlimited shore leave. It was only fair.

"Come, come," Fazzle said, waving her in with one of his free arms. "My masterpiece is this way."

She strolled down the hallway, subtly checking out whatever could be seen through the open doors. One of these rooms had to have a computer interface. She didn't need the main computer itself, just a computer terminal. Her instructions were simple: find an interface, not in use, attach the encryption decoder/transmitter, known in Starfleet parlance as "the worm," and get out. Not in a way that would make the Cheka suspicious, but swiftly enough that should her gadget be discovered, she might escape without having a link drawn between her and the transmitter. A hostage was the last thing her father needed right now. After passing more than a dozen doors and not glimpsing anything remotely resembling a computer, Prynn started to despair, worrying about what she might have to do in order to find a computer. Fazzle had stopped; she knew his workspace was close by—she was quickly running out of options.

"Hurry, hurry!" he squawked, patting the floor beside him. "Sit here. Quickly."

As she approached, she began formulating several backup plans and then— there. She grinned. Over there. Beneath his tarp. Right in the middle of his artwork. The crazy creature had built his entire piece around a computer terminal. She could see from the wiring and sensors integrated into the various "sense peelings" that he intended this sculpture to be animated with lights or movement.

Prynn dropped down on the floor beside Fazzle and looked at him, but not "at" him. Over his shoulder, she had an excellent view of the computer. "What do you need me to do?" she said sweetly.

Lucky, lucky me, she thought. The terminal was active, the viewscreen displaying a root menu offering options ranging from data retrieval to food replication. *I've got me a live one!*

"Off!" Fazzle said, cocking his head.

"Excuse me?"

"Off." Fazzle pawed at her uniform.

Ugh. It just gets better and better, she thought, stripping off her jacket and turtleneck. Thankfully, the Cheka kept the room temperatures high; sitting around shirtless wouldn't be unbearably cold. *Now how to get at that computer,* she mused. *I can pretend to trip and when I stumble forward, I'll just—* "Yikes!" she shrieked. "What *is* that!"

Fazzle brushed the sense-artist goo on her shoulders. "Hold out your arms," he ordered, demonstrating by holding two of his arms straight out to the sides. "Like this." Prynn complied warily, but cringed when he started in on her neck, down her back, down her front—and as it dried, it itched. Prynn started making her mental list of all the places she would inform her father she would vacation when she made it back to the Alpha Quadrant. *Ewwwwww, this is so disgusting!*

Shar stood at attention in front of Ezri's desk, eyes fixed on the wall behind her. In a way, Ezri was grateful that he avoided eye contact. She could say what she needed to without feeling like it was personal. The present situation was about authority—hers—and regulations. And while Shar didn't blatantly disobey the letter of her orders, he rationalized his way into believing that flouting the spirit of them was acceptable.

"While I understand your intentions were honorable, Ensign, your timing was poor. And you should have contacted me with Delegate Keren's proposal."

"Yes, sir."

"Lieutenant McCallum, working with the Yrythny authorities, has been unable to uncover who used this workstation to send the 'go' signal to the hydrofoil. Fortunately, no one on our team is under suspicion."

"I assure you, Lieutenant, I took all necessary precautions before I left."

"I believe you, but in hindsight, there were other precautions that ought to have been taken." Of all the problems caused by Shar leaving Luthia, this was the worst. Yes, he'd left the offices secure and the terminals locked down, but he hadn't made provisions for covering his station. There wasn't a Starfleet officer anywhere in Luthia at the time the offices had been broken into and the signal sent. Lieutenant Candlewood, their computer specialist, had performed every diagnostic he knew and had come up with nothing.

Shar stayed silent, standing stone-still, his face composed. Even his antennae remained curiously unexpressive.

His mind must be elsewhere, Ezri thought, leaning back in her chair. She sighed. "Was it worth it, Ensign?"

"Permission to speak freely, sir."

Ezri sat for a long moment, wondering if she was capable of responding fairly to anything that he said, whether her frustration with him had abated enough that she could listen without reacting. The day's events had taxed her energy. She'd been placating angry Yrythny officials for hours; her rescue mission to the aquaculture village hadn't exactly endeared her to the military. On the other hand, she was curious to know what incited a usually compliant officer to recklessness. Finally, she shrugged. "Of course."

"I brought enough data back from the peninsula to conduct a statistically significant study of Yrythny DNA."

"What?" Now this was news. She leaned forward to listen more closely.

"The farmers on the peninsula have been collecting and mapping Wanderer DNA for several centuries. They wanted to use it to match Wanderers with their proper Houses. That way, they wouldn't have to be Wanderers any longer."

Promising idea. "Go on," she urged.

"But I think we can use this data to model Yrythny chromosomal architecture," he said. "To see if there's any genetic basis for the caste system."

"Those models will only work if you have the Houseborn samples to compare them to."

"We don't have them, but we can get them," he said pragmatically.

"That's pretty optimistic of you, Shar. Do you honestly think the House-born will cooperate willingly with your study?"

"No," Shar conceded. "But we can obtain the samples surreptitiously through Wanderer domestic laborers. I realize I haven't mentioned this before, sir, but Delegate Keren took me to a meeting of the Wanderer underground, and through her connections there—"

"Hold it," Dax said, standing. "Keren is connected to the underground?" The terrorists. Those responsible for planting the explosives in the village. The ramifications of Keren being the head of the Wanderer Assembly and working in the underground were staggering. All the negotiations, all their strategies, plans and schedules—she could be feeding confidential proposals to the underground. The agitators could have gained access to her office through Keren, if she had the security clearance. Ezri swore under her breath. *Has Shar been lying to me? He had to know getting mixed up in this would come back to haunt him later. Please let me be able to trust you, Shar.*

He met her eyes. "Yes sir, she is."

"And why haven't you come forward with this until now?" she asked. Shar hesitated a second too long and Ezri shouted, *"I asked you a question, Ensign!"*

Shar flinched. "I should have, sir. I knew I was wrong to go, but my curiosity got the better of me. Afterward I convinced myself that if I pretended it never happened, it would never come up. I was foolish. I'm sorry, sir."

"Yes, I'm sure you are," Ezri said, watching him closely. "You're certainly full of surprises this evening, Ensign." *How the hell do I salvage this?* "Tell me, from your observations of the underground, can Delegate Keren represent the Wanderer side fairly if she has any ties to those terrorists?"

"Respectfully, sir, to call them terrorists is an overgeneralization," Shar protested. "They're ordinary people who have been pushed to the verge of breaking. Not everyone affiliated with the underground endorses violence. Most of the agitators are looking for peaceful solutions."

"The fact remains that you've consorted surreptitiously with a political leader who may have been involved in the destruction of the aquaculture village, and dozens of casualties. And you still haven't answered my question. What can you say to convince me that Keren can be trusted?"

"Nothing, I suspect. But are you convinced that the Houseborn didn't blow those villages simply to persuade you that the Wanderers can't be trusted? Has anyone given you evidence that proves unequivocally that the underground is to blame?"

Ezri tried to ignore his insinuation that the day's events had been staged to influence her opinion, and remained focused on Shar. "The planetside incident is, more or less, an internal matter. What isn't in contention is that you acted in bad faith with respect to your commanding officer. You betrayed my trust, Shar."

"If you want to discipline me for going with Delegate Keren to the agitator meeting, I won't protest," he said. "But we can't ignore the potential significance of this scientific research. What we discover could transform their lives—"

"That's enough, Ensign."

"Please don't punish the Yrythny for my error in judgment," he whispered.

Was that the real question, then? Ezri wasn't a fool: If the research Shar proposed bore fruit, it had the potential to redefine the Yrythny identity, to find out, once and for all, whether there was any biological basis for the caste system. On the other hand, the Assembly had requested that she help mediate a resolution to their internal conflict—to find a way to help these people live together in peace. They hadn't asked her to conduct scientific research that would change the paradigm they'd built their society on. But truth was truth. If new truths forced the changes required to live in peace, their mission would be successful.

She looked at Shar, frustrated by the fact that she knew his intentions had been honorable. During the war, she recalled, even Benjamin had been willing to forgive her theft and loss of a runabout—not to mention subsequent capture by the Dominion—because not only had she managed to rescue Worf, she'd also returned with the knowledge that Damar sought the Federation's help against the Dominion. That information became the turning point of the war.

Sometimes, she knew, the only difference between poor judgment and a calculated risk was the outcome. In Shar's case, the jury was still out. But she couldn't ignore what he'd learned through his actions.

"You can conduct your research," she said finally, "but you can't use the underground to collect Houseborn data. If the Houseborn in the Upper Assembly agree to provide you with DNA samples, I'll authorize you to proceed. On your own time."

Dubious, he furrowed his brow. "Sir, I thought we agreed that the Houseborn will never willingly provide—"

"You think that any research performed with secretly obtained samples can be taken seriously?" Dax shouted. She'd spent enough of her 358 years as a scientist that she knew the rules of that game. "You'll be accused of using doctored samples. If you want your results to be legitimate, you have to start conducting *yourself* legitimately." Ezri could see from Shar's reaction that she was finally getting through to him.

"May I ask for official cooperation during our meetings tomorrow?"

"Yes. I'll present your proposal. If it's rejected, that'll be the end of it. Understood, Ensign?"

"Yes, sir."

Before she let him return to his quarters, she wanted to address—and bring to an end—the ongoing situation where Shar picked what rules he wanted to keep. "And Shar, I am repeating and reinstating Commander Vaughn's original order: you're not to have unauthorized contact with the

Yrythny. In the course of your work, I know you'll deal with them, but you aren't to be sneaking out to underground meetings or taking trips planetside without first clearing it with me. And I want reports of any interaction you have with Delegate Keren. Until I feel more comfortable with her status, we need to assume she's hostile to our goals. Is that understood?"

Shar nodded. "I'm supposed to meet with her later so she can give me the datafiles on the Wanderer genome. In all the confusion of the rescue, she mistakenly kept them when we dropped her off."

"Fine. And Ensign? I don't need an answer to this question, but I think you'd be wise to think about it."

"Sir?"

"Having a desire to answer the Yrythny's request for help is, by itself, an honorable motive for what you're doing, but is it possible that there's a deeper reason?" she said gently. "Maybe a personal one? Because the risks you're taking are extraordinary. I think whatever you believe you stand to gain from taking these risks ought to be worth the price."

Ezri waited for him to raise his eyes from the floor and for a moment their gazes tangled. Shar rarely unveiled his emotions in any circumstance, but she caught a glimpse of a ferocious intensity that might have frightened her, had she been his enemy. "Dismissed," she said. And when he had vanished into the corridor, she collapsed into her chair, feeling grateful to be alone.

14

His uncanny knack for bringing out the absolute worst in Kira notwithstanding, Quark ought to have been rewarded for his triumph at the reception. His heroic efforts had impressed all the guests. Sentients of every stripe, rank and affiliation continued to rave about the exquisite presentation, the excellent food and the unparalleled service. He'd assumed that going out with Laren would be the sauce on the slugsteak. The capstone of this exceptional week.

Quark pulled the brightly printed blanket tighter around his shoulders, hoping to stave off the chilly night breezes. But being wet made warmth difficult to come by. It wasn't like he didn't understand wet; growing up on Ferenginar meant he understood every nuance and permutation of wet. Perpetual wetness had a consistency that one could reasonably acclimate to. When wet was juxtaposed with dry, an uncomfortable state known as "cold" followed.

Quark *hated* cold.

Would he ever feel his ears again, was the question. He had spent a late afternoon hurtling across the water from crest to crest, white foam spitting around his feet, clinging to a skimpy sail and balanced on a board even Nog would find small, only to lose sensation in his lobes. No female was worth this.

Never mind that, in the aftermath of that ordeal, staying warm necessitated wrapping himself in a blanket, because he'd stupidly refused Laren's offer to modify the program just to make him more comfortable. What kind of an idiot was his infatuation with her turning him into? He should have at least let her delete the targ-size salmon that kept smacking against the rudder of his windsurfing board. Vile creatures. What kind of animal willingly takes the path of most resistance and swims *upstream* to spawn? Clearly those monsters with fins had compromised survival instinct because any sensible creature would have hailed a hovercraft and called it good.

Like me with Laren. Always swimming upstream because I can't seem to help myself.

Crouched down beside the flickering pile of sticks Ro seemed to think qualified as a fire, she placed a spit loaded with bird carcasses over the coals. She dabbed sauce into the meat's crevices; dripping off the sides into the heat, it sizzled and smoked, sending up clouds of ash. "Dinner should be ready in a half hour or so. I added a little kick to the fire in the holoprogramming," she said by way of explanation. "Temperature's a little hotter than it would be in real life."

Sounded better than waiting for that primitive stick heap to make the replicated bird edible, Quark thought ruefully. "Can't wait. I'm sure it'll be delicious," he said aloud.

Leaving the birds to roast, Ro circled behind the logs surrounding the fire pit to her backpack, which was filled with all the things one allegedly needed to survive in the outdoors. She rifled around inside, removing a wristlight, what looked like a wicked permutation of a knife, another fire starter, several field ration bars, an ax, and two long sticks with handles at the ends. "Aha. Here we are." She pulled out a clear container filled with dark, roundish objects.

Hoping she'd answer "tube grubs," Quark asked, "And those would be . . . ?"

"Chestnuts," she answered, dumping them into a metal foil pouch and securing the opening. "Roasted like this, they're really good."

He sighed. If he was lucky, she'd thrown a couple of Slug-O-Colas in that backpack so he could wash down the charcoal-covered bird with something palatable.

"The windsurfing wasn't that bad," Ro said, tossing the foil pouch into the flames. She took a pair of tongs, fished coals from the graying embers and placed them on top of the chestnuts.

"No, not at all. . . . If plunging headfirst into water is your idea of fun. I'm thinking next time we ought to pull out Worf's old *Road to Kal'hyaH* program and really have a party," Quark groused. Even his wilderness sojourn with Sisko and the boys a few years back hadn't made him *this* uncomfortable, not even after they'd been captured by the Jem'Hadar. Of course, single-handedly dragging a wounded, belligerent Odo up the side of a mountain on the freezing surface of a class-L planet had proven, once and for all, that Ferengi were made of sterner stuff than most people gave them credit for, but that didn't mean he relished such experiences, unlike *some* people he could name . . .

Ro snorted indelicately. "Oh please. The Columbia rarely dips below 10 Celsius this time of year and you fell in because you kept letting go of the sail handle." She retrieved a log from a woodpile she'd gathered earlier. "Besides, you had a wetsuit on. You should have been warm enough. I thought Ferengi were used to water."

"Damp, swampy, steady warm drizzle? Yes. Ice bath? No. It's the difference between wet and drowned." Shivering, he pulled the blanket tighter around him. "Not that I'm complaining or anything," he added hastily.

"You? Of course not," Ro said, clearly fighting down a smile. Placing the log on a large, flat tree stump, Laren raised an ax over her head and brought it down with a *thwack*. She gathered up the smaller pieces and fed them into the fire. Greedy fingers of flames gratefully accepted her offering.

"So," she said, tipping back on her haunches. Scooting through the dirt, she settled against the weatherbeaten log, leaning back to rest her neck. She continued shifting and adjusting until she'd fitted the curve of her neck with the curve of the log. Her gaze went up at the moonless spring night. Pines jutted up all around them, their straight, prickle-covered branches aimed at the sky, threatening to puncture the smooth night canopy. Only intermittent wind gusts swayed the trees from their rigid posture.

"So . . ." he answered, knowing he'd surrender half ownership in the bar to Treir if she'd only page him with an emergency.

"Not like this matters, but I spent the last week before I started the Academy here. I've been to more exotic places since then, but I always feel awed when I come here. Millions of years of the land submitting to the relentless waters. And it's like the water knew that if all the dirt and rock exterior was swept away, the planet's soul would be exposed and all could see how majestic that soul was."

Quark blinked. "I never took you for a poet, Laren."

"All Bajorans are poets, Quark. Don't you know that by now? We were poets when your kind were leaving slime trails through the mud of Ferenginar," she teased.

"Sure you were, but was there any profit in your poetry?"

Ro threw a pinecone at him.

"So what's next?" he said, imagining what recreational torture she might have conceived for round two.

"Ah. Now that's a multilayered question."

"Because—"

"Because if you're asking what's next tonight, I'd answer dinner, coffee, and maybe a night hike. There's a watering hole not far from here frequented by the local wildlife—deer and raccoons. A family of beavers dammed up a water trickle and it became a pond," she explained, scratching lines in the peaty soil with a stick. "But if you're asking what's next after today, or after next week, or next month after Bajor joins the Federation? Honestly, I don't know."

Quark said nothing. He knew that he and Ro were feeling the same sense of uncertainty about the future, both believing they'd have no place in the coming new order. For Quark, the prospect of starting over in some other galactic backwater didn't have the same allure it once did during his youth. He suspected that was even more true for Laren.

"You know . . . after my second fall from Starfleet, I started to believe the reason I had so much trouble playing by its rules was that I kept finding causes that seemed more important than my career. First Garon II, then the Maquis . . ." She sighed, sprawling out so she could study the night sky. "I never meant to turn against Starfleet—a lot of who I am I owe to what I learned serving the Federation alongside good people. Both times, I eventually found myself faced with a choice. Both times, I followed my conscience. And both times, it ended in disaster."

"So what are you saying?" Quark asked. "You think you made the wrong choices? Maybe you did, maybe you didn't. But that isn't really the issue."

"It isn't?"

"No. The problem with Starfleet is, its fundamental principles are flawed."

Ro raised a sardonic eyebrow. "Oh, I can't wait to hear where *this* is going."

Quark sighed, realizing he was joining the salmon again. "While it's all well and good to want everyone to be happy, the reality is that making sure every world has food, medicine and education doesn't guarantee happiness. As much as the Federation tries to fix what ails the quadrant—and hell, sounds like they're starting to preach their good news to the Gamma and Delta quadrants, too—their way of doing things doesn't work for everyone. Because no matter how hard they try, or how honorable their intentions, equality is a bogus ideal and you can never make everyone be 'good' the way they define it."

Even in the dark, Quark could sense Ro's dubious expression. He refused to give up without at least attempting to prove his point, so he continued, "You're one to believe in scientific principles. What's the law of thermodynamics that says that for every action there's an equal and opposite reaction? Or what about the one that matter moves from a state of order to disorder? Either way, no matter where you look, nothing and nobody stays the same. You can't have the good guys without the bad ones, and as quickly as you transform the fortunes of one backwater world, another one will be blown to hell. The Federation forgets that as quickly as you fix one problem, another one crops up. Starfleet flits about in their pretty starships, trying to make everyone happy, and it's mostly an exercise in futility. Is that what you want from your life, Laren? Chasing a dream that can never be realized?"

Through dancing flames, Ro studied Quark pensively for a moment. Finally, she asked, "What's better in life than dreams?"

"Results," Quark spat. "You sail the Great River, you throw in your nets, you bring in your catch. I measure my successes by the latinum in my vault. Quantifiable, measurable results."

"Latinum can't love you."

"Latinum can't hurt you either," Quark retorted sharply.

Ro sought Quark's eyes, scrutinizing him closely. "You're bothered about something. What?"

Commander Matthias's words about Ferengi being easy to read came back to him. He pulled the blanket up over his ears. "I don't know what you're talking about."

Suddenly, Ro was sitting next to him, yanking the blanket back down. "Come on. You can tell me willingly or I can coerce it from you. Remember I interrogate people for a living."

For once, bondage fantasies didn't enter Quark's mind. Instead, he considered what good it would serve if he talked about his feelings. He supposed if he wanted Ro to trust him, this was the moment to prove it. "Okay. Fine. I'm a little preoccupied with the Jake situation."

"What about it?" She looked confused.

"Kira pretty much laid the whole thing at my feet the other night. And even though I know the ship I sold him was fine, I keep asking myself, 'Am I responsible?' " *There, I said it. I might have sent a trusting young man to his death by trying to make a profit off him. And not that much profit at that.* He braced himself for Ro's response.

She chuckled.

"Oh, that's sensitive of you, Laren."

"Quark, I've had some of Starfleet's best engineers review Nog's inspection. They all concur: there was nothing to suggest there was anything structurally or systemically wrong with the ship you sold Jake. And Kira knows that."

Quark shook his head. "You weren't there—"

"No," Ro agreed. "But I'd been watching her most of the evening, and even though she did a fine job of masking it, I could tell her emotions were coming to a boil. My guess is she lashed out at you for reasons that had nothing to do with Jake, or you."

"You mean she put me through that abuse for nothing?"

Ro smiled, shook her head and rested her arm next to his. "I suppose that depends on your point of view. Probably did her a world of good to blow off some steam. And as a direct result, I just got to see your conscience working. It's a sweet conscience, Quark. You should let it out more often."

"It would ruin me," Quark said weakly, suddenly realizing he was no longer cold.

"Yeah, it might," Ro agreed, a small smile playing on her lips. "But I think you could stand a little ruining."

"Devil woman."

"Troll."

"Kira to Lieutenant Ro."

Quark closed his eyes and buried his head in his hands. *There's just no justice . . .*

Ro shrugged apologetically and touched her combadge. "Go ahead, Colonel."

"I need you on level ten. Section 65, conference room four."

"The Cardassians." Instantly, Ro was on her feet, brushing dirt off her clothes. "I'll be right there. Ro out." She turned to Quark. "Sorry, but duty calls. Computer, end program."

Earth's Pacific Northwest forest dissolved instantly, leaving Quark sitting on the hard holosuite floor, still wrapped in a blanket. Ro hollered her regrets for the abbreviated evening as she exited the room. He waved back absently, but remained seated on the floor for some time, trying to recapture the moment that the colonel had thoughtlessly extinguished.

From the beginning, Ro knew that putting Cardassians and Bajorans together on Deep Space 9 would be akin to a Rakantha typhoon. It might start off slow, but once the air masses collided, the tidal waves would start. *The first tidal wave came ashore tonight,* she thought, hoping this would be a sprinkle as opposed to a downpour. She had expected the storm front before now, but who was she to complain about a few extra days of quiet?

Traversing back corridors, an engineering turbolift, and not bothering to strip off her wetsuit, Ro reached the conference room in a matter of minutes. Kira, to avoid contaminating the crime scene, waited in the anteroom with Sergeant Shul, who ran security's delta shift. Two corporals stood posted outside the conference room doors.

Being prepared for the worst, Ro was initially grateful she wasn't dealing with a murder. On another level, the careful staging of what she saw inside the conference room was almost as chilling. Whoever, whatever did this, might well be capable of murder. She suspected the sick mind she now contended with would be vain enough to show off a few more times before blood was shed, giving Ro time to smoke out the culprit.

Ro performed a cursory inventory, looking for obvious clues, but didn't observe anything incongruent; even in the dimmed lights, she could see the conference room had been divvied up by delegation and individual, with each spot at the table corresponding to an identifying nameplate, indicating who sat in what chair. The Bajoran team lined one side of the table, with Minister Asarem seated in the center of her group; the Cardassian team lined the other, Ambassador Lang being seated in the spot directly across from Minister Asarem. Nothing unusual rested on the table either: neat collections of padds, writing styluses, maps and several legal tomes, etched with Bajoran pictographs. All the items appeared to be consistent with the work under way.

Whoever defaced the flag had used a natural flame of some sort, Ro guessed; the singed fabric edges had too much fraying to have been caused by a precision laser instrument such as an engineering drill or a surgical scalpel. And a beam weapon would have set off an alarm. The lines burned over the crest of the Cardassian Union followed an artful pattern, likely an Old Bajoran rune, though Ro wasn't sure which one. She looked over at Kira, who appeared to be studying the same insignia.

"I think it means 'war.' From one of the religious texts, I believe," Kira said.

After a tricorder scan of the flag proved inconclusive, Ro ordered Shul to comb every centimeter, every wall, keypad and hallway for evidence. No one was to touch anything. She didn't even allow Kira to sit until she'd scanned the chair for hair and fiber samples. Taking a seat beside Kira, Ro had her recite the sequence of events leading up to the discovery of the violated conference room. Unfortunately, Kira's experiences didn't cast any light on who might be responsible for the vandalism. The cleaning personnel Kira had run into as she entered had already been found and questioned by Shul. They claimed not to have seen or heard anything unusual.

"Whoever did this is playing mind games with the Cardassians," Kira concluded. "Now that I think about it, even the rune has layered meaning. It comes out of the *Book of Victory* from the First Republic. A rallying symbol. A symbol of righteous indignation that warriors would paint on their foreheads in the blood of their fallen comrades. Whoever did this wanted the message to have the narrowest of interpretations."

"But it was done quietly, in a clandestine fashion where the public won't see or find out about it. Quite an effort for such a small audience," Ro observed. "No chance of a rally when the propaganda warfare is invisible."

"I've reviewed the checkpoint logs. No one has been in or out of this area that hasn't been cleared through channels," Kira said, puzzled. "Is it possible someone transported this flag in?"

"The flag, maybe, but the knife through the chair more or less indicates that our vandal was in the room. The stabbing angle, the irregular entry. Maybe the vandal transported in and out from one of the docked ships. I'll check our transporter logs and request the logs of every ship in the vicinity." Ro repeatedly ran her eyes over the chair, the flag, the knife, hoping that she'd find a new piece of information.

"Will you brief Ambassador Lang?"

Ro nodded. "I'll give her all the forensic analyses as well. There's always the outside possibility that someone within her group did this. Kind of a reverse psychology approach from a Cardassian who wants to prevent the talks from succeeding." She had witnessed firsthand the reluctance among Macet's men to turn in their weapons. If the lack of progress in the talks had frustrated any one of them, Ro could envision a Cardassian sending a symbolic warning. The rune could have been pulled out of the station database. Hardly classified material.

"I'll sit in on the talks tomorrow," Kira said finally. "Ambassador Lang needs to know that she has our official support. If the culprit is on either side, it might not hurt to observe the parties involved."

Letting whoever it was know that they were being watched might not be a bad idea either, Ro thought. "Recommend we place a gag order on all Militia and diplomatic personnel. This incident shouldn't be reported anywhere outside the highest-ranking officials and those it impacts directly. From now on, information is on a need-to-know basis. We don't want to encourage our terrorist by providing publicity."

Kira nodded her approval. "You classify the report and briefings. I'll notify Admiral Akaar and the first minister."

Imagining how ratcheting up the tension on the station with rumor would complicate security matters, Ro hoped that senior staff would understand this wasn't an order to be second-guessed. If she discovered any in her purview that violated her declared policy, strict disciplinary measures would be taken. She felt grateful she had a commanding officer that put the interests of the job first, one who wasn't jostling for political influence or courting popularity. She walked Kira to the door. The colonel paused, resting a hand on the door frame. Since they had dispensed with business, Ro guessed what Kira might still have on her mind.

"I take it you were in the holosuite when I paged you," she asked, with a bemused half-smile.

"Windsurfing," she affirmed. "With Quark."

"And he—"

"Hated it."

"Are you two—" Kira began, then cut herself off. "On second thought, belay that. I don't want to know." The colonel shook her head as she left the conference room.

Walking the room's perimeter, Ro mapped out an investigation strategy in her head and then sent her deputies back to the office to retrieve the equipment they'd need. While she waited, she sat down in a chair across the table from the vandalized one, rested her elbows on the table, threaded her fingers together, meditationlike, and reexamined the room.

The calculated neatness felt especially wrong. Passion crimes tended to be messy. Ro hypothesized that the criminal had gone to his or her quarters, desecrated the flag, returned here to drape the flag over Lang's chair and then, as an afterthought, driven the knife into the chair, making certain the vehemence of the sentiment was unquestioned. Pathological anger, anger so vivid and vicious that it motivated one to lash out, rarely exhibited this kind of control. Not a padd out of place. Chairs tucked neatly against the table. All was in order. Her eyes traced the inscription on the nameplate marking the chair where she sat: "Asarem Wadeen, Second Minister, Bajor" in standard script. In an instant, Ro realized that she sat on the cusp of an investigation that required she scrutinize the most powerful individuals currently in this sector: the list of those with access to this conference room read like a list of who's who in postwar politics. Any one of the people sitting at this table might have a motive.

She toyed with the nameplate. *Even you, second minister.*

Only two hours into alpha shift and Kira felt like she'd never gone off duty. Dealing with last night's attack on the conference room continued into morning. She might have slept for a few hours, but she couldn't remember if there had been a pillow involved. Making an executive decision on the exhibit, she left orders to have Ziyal's art moved into its new home where the curator could spend the day arranging and rearranging it. *Time to take Lang up on her offer—and take a welcome break from ops at that.*

Sliding into the second row of chairs behind Sirsy and a handful of Federation observers, Kira's seat placed her within eye-line of Lang and the Cardassian delegation. With every clattering stylus or chair scraping the floor, Lang jerked abruptly or lost her chain of thought. *Damn, I knew the attack impacted her more than she let on.* The ambassador had received Ro's report with consummate professionalism, but the knowledge that she had an enemy making overt threats against her had to be disquieting. As she watched the proceedings, Kira brainstormed for more secure, alternate locations, on or off Deep Space 9, where the talks could be held.

When she changed to a new set of notes, Lang's eyes registered Kira's arrival and her mouth curved into a barely perceptible smile. She continued, however, with a seamless reading of her text.

". . . and to continue humanitarian medical assistance until such time as Cardassia's medical infrastructure has been reestablished and is strong enough to manage the needs of its people. Furthermore—"

"Excuse me, Ambassdor Lang," Asarem interrupted, raising a hand. "But I'm not certain that aid on the scale you're proposing is agreeable to our side."

Lang sighed, bit her upper lip and paused, clearly trying to hold her tongue. "This isn't a new proposal. These are the levels agreed to in the postwar Accords by the Romulans, the Klingons—"

"I'm aware of who signed the Accords, Ambassador. But that doesn't change Bajor's position that maintaining such levels of aid, indefinitely, is undesirable." Asarem leaned back in her chair and rested her hands in her lap. Though Kira couldn't see her facial expressions, she sensed Asarem felt comfortable in the lay of the battlefield. How she eased into the chair back, loosely crossing her legs and relaxing her shoulders, said that she controlled the field. The burden was on Lang to flank her.

Kira recalled an experience with Shakaar when their cell awaited the arrival of a Cardassian weapons shipment they planned on stealing since their own supplies were running low. Though they had been outnumbered five to one, Shakaar remained in good humor. When asked why, he answered simply, "Because we hold the hills." Watching Asarem, Kira couldn't help but think that the second minister believed she held the hills. And why not? Her delegation hadn't been threatened. *At least Asarem won't be susceptible to any Cardassian double-talk.* She felt reassured that Bajor had an excellent steward. *So why am I having a hard time trusting her?*

Earlier, the task of briefing the Bajoran delegation had fallen to Kira. Asarem made sympathetic noises when she heard of the surreptitious threat against the Cardassians. Her immediate concern had been for Ambassador Lang's safety and she asked what measures she personally needed to take to circumvent any future attacks. Nothing in Asarem's manner suggested insincerity. Her untainted political record served as proof that she was an honorable public servant. *Maybe that's my problem,* Kira mused. *I don't believe in perfection—there's something in Asarem's manner that's so polished, it feels scripted. Still, if I agree with her positions, what's my problem here?* A marked increase in the volume in the room startled her back into paying attention.

"You want to maintain our high infant mortality rate?" Lang said, unable to blunt the shrill edge in her voice. "The numbers succumbing to the Calebrian plague? What we're receiving now barely addresses those needs!" Her aide, the one Kira recognized as a former student, placed a reassuring hand on her teacher's arm, but Lang shoved it off.

Asarem shrugged. "No need to raise your voice, Ambassador. I'm merely pointing out a previously overlooked complication in providing your people with virtually unlimited medical supplies. When taken individually, crates of biomimetic gels and isomiotic hypos have legitimate applications. In combination with other agents, Cardassia could conceivably manufacture biogenic weapons," she said, her tone mild.

What? Startled, Kira sat forward in her chair, waiting to hear what would be said next.

The phrase "biogenic weapons" triggered a low hum of hushed exchanges from spectators in every corner of the room. Asarem must feel very secure in her position to make such audacious suggestions. Given the same evidence, Kira wouldn't have drawn those conclusions. Even in these days of quantum torpedoes and orbital weapons platforms, an unseen enemy terrified populations more effectively than any particle beams or warships ever could. *Why is it that we default to the presumption that we're safe simply because we can't perceive, with our senses, any immediate danger?*

Clenching her hands around the arms of her chair, Lang's eyes narrowed to dark slits, incredulity etched on her face. Kira felt the room collectively holding its breath in anticipation of the Cardassian ambassador's response. She scrutinized Asarem for a long moment, allowing extraneous murmuring to die down. Uncomfortable silence swelled until Lang spoke. "I accept that you hold us in little esteem. But what kind of soulless ghoul would I be to come here, begging for help, if it were my intent to divert desperately needed medical supplies to manufacture weapons? What possible motive would we have?" Her soft-spoken tone belied her incisive words.

Heart pounding in her throat, Kira willed Asarem to show mercy, to rise above forcing Lang to flay herself in order to prove good faith. *If we fail to show compassion when compassion is called for, we succumb to the same cruelty exhibited by our oppressors during the Occupation.* She held her breath.

"Reestablishing military supremacy. Blackmailing Bajor. There are a host of logical reasons that aren't unprecedented," Asarem said, sounding like she could reel off another long list of potential Cardassian black deeds if asked to. "Besides, what reason would you have to elucidate your government's true intentions here and now when you know Bajor and the Federation would never agree to assist in any sort of rearmament?" She paused, waiting for the meaning of her words to sink in. "And it's possible the Ghemor government could be using you: why would they tell you what their true intentions are if feeding you sympathetic stories about children and helpless pregnant women helps them accomplish their long-term objectives?"

Kira felt sick. *This isn't negotiation: this is retribution.*

Inhaling deeply, Lang gritted her teeth. "To this point, Minister, Bajor has been extremely generous in helping us rebuild a social services infrastructure that provides pediatric hospital facilities, vaccinations and basic preventative health care."

"And we will continue to be generous," Asarem said reasonably. "But I believe imposing some restrictions or implementing time limits on the type and amount of aid we continue to provide is not unreasonable, given the probability that Cardassia, at some point, might divert that aid for militaristic purposes."

Kira noted, with concern, the panicked expressions on the Cardassians seated beside Lang. And it wasn't the fear of being caught engaged in treachery, it was the fear of those watching hope flicker and die. All eyes looked to their leader for guidance.

Shadows, new since her triumph at the reception, darkened Lang's lower eyelids; her shoulders hunched slightly with fatigue. She leaned over the table, putting her in closer physical proximity to Asarem. "With all due respect, Minister, a week before I left, I spent five days helping deliver supplies to our medical facilities," Lang began, "and I have to ask, when was the last time you held a child in your arms dying from the curable Fostassa virus?"

Lang's words scraped Kira raw; a flood of memories poured over her, stinging like saltwater.

In the hours following the final assault on Cardassia, she and Garak walked the decimated streets, picking their way around twisted metal from collapsed buildings, chunks of stone and broken glass. Acrid smoke hung like thick fog: the breath of destruction. Weak cries attracted Garak's attention, leading him to a dirty-faced little boy in shredded clothes, huddled against a toppled pillar. The child rocked back and forth, crooning a discordant song to a floppy-limbed doll he hugged against his chest. When the boy failed to acknowledge either Garak or Kira's approach, Garak waved a hand in front of the boy's eyes, quickly ascertaining the child had been blinded. He had instantly scooped the boy into his arms, the child clinging to him, wrapping his gaunt legs around Garak's waist. Garak passed the doll off to Kira. She reflexively hugged the cold thing against her, knowing the boy would want his toy back until, horrified, she discovered the true nature of what she held. Mustering all her self-control, she avoided recoiling and tossing the baby's corpse away; instead, she waited until she found a small indentation in the ground, probably a bomb crater, where she could show the dead proper reverence.

And now she wondered if Lang had been there, that black night on Cardassia.

The Cardassians had paid exorbitantly for their arrogance. Regardless of what had been done to her—to Bajor—at their hands, Kira failed to see how extracting further payment would be justified. *I wouldn't take up the lash if it were handed to me.* The realization stunned her. Kira sought Natima's eyes, hoping she would find comfort in the knowledge that a former enemy understood, but Asarem's chair suddenly shoved back. Kira steeled herself for the minister's response.

Asarem stood up with deliberate slowness, her body vibrating with sinewy tension. Squaring her shoulders, she faced Lang, still posed offensively. "The last time a child died from Fostassa virus in my presence?" she said, her voice glacial. "Eight years ago. Just as the Cardassian Occupation of Bajor ended."

Lang froze.

Brittle quiet chilled all present.

"Ambassador, Minister," came Gul Macet's quiet appeal. Seated at Lang's elbow, he had thrown a cautionary arm in front of his superior. "I believe this is an appropriate juncture to call a recess. Our delegation will review the numbers your staff has provided us and after we've eaten, we'll meet back here to see where we can reconcile our differences."

Now composed, Asarem said softly, "Based on the substance of the talks to date, it's my judgment that we take an indeterminate recess until such time as both delegations are better prepared to delineate definitive parameters on the items we've discussed." With a visible tremor in her hand, she passed off a padd to an aide and turned piercing eyes on Macet. "When we both know how flexible our respective governments can be in negotiating specific points, I believe we'll accomplish more."

"You mean, when Cardassia is willing to do whatever Bajor demands?" Lang said cynically.

"Natima," Macet cautioned without looking away from Asarem. "By indeterminate recess, do you mean the rest of the day?"

"I mean as long as it takes," she said. Asarem cleaned up her workspace without comment as her aides packed up any extraneous supplies. Support staff for both sides studiously avoided contact with the opposition.

Shaking, Lang collapsed into her chair until Macet coaxed her outside, ostensibly for lunch. Her aides, some looking glum, others angry, followed close behind.

The Cardassians and Bajorans exited through opposite doors. Kira waited until all but Minister Asarem had left before she rose from her chair. *I'll be complicit in this injustice if I don't speak up.*

"Minister, might I have a word?"

Asarem arched an eyebrow. "Colonel Kira. I presume you want to share your enlightened perspective."

"I don't know what you mean by enlightened, but any reasonable person would be concerned about what just happened here." Whatever she had done to alienate the second minister, Kira wished she understood so she could apologize.

"You think I'm being unfair to the Cardassians?" she asked sourly.

Be rational, Nerys. Don't lose your temper, Kira admonished herself. "Lang is asking for medical supplies, not quantum torpedoes. She's not even requesting raw materials that could more easily be diverted to develop weaponry." From her own experience, she knew that crude weapons spewing shrapnel or obliterating infrastructure were just as effective as the sophisticated weaponry Asarem seemed to believe the Cardassians were interested in building. "What's unreasonable about wanting plasma replicators and surgical equipment? How does taking a hard line, making it difficult to save Cardassian lives, benefit Bajor?"

"Your attitude surprises me, Colonel," Asarem said pointedly. "You of all people should appreciate the need to do whatever is necessary to ensure that Cardassia is never again in a position to harm Bajor, or anyone else." The minister turned back to packing her briefcase. "Perhaps the reports of your patriotism are exaggerated."

I don't have to take this! I'm not the enemy. Kira resisted the urge to snipe at Asarem. "Last time I checked, I was wearing the uniform of the Bajoran Militia, Minister. I do have some experience relevant to this situation." Kira tried smoothing her sharp tone, but knew her impatience seeped through.

Asarem paused, cast a glance at Kira's bare ear. "Last time I checked, faithful Bajorans follow the counsel of the Vedek Assembly."

Kira's eyes narrowed. Biting back a dozen thorny responses, she pushed forward on the critical issues. "Have you even been to Cardassia since the war?"

"No," Asarem said. "I haven't."

"Then how can you compare what you know of Bajor with what Cardassia is going through? What right do you have to dismiss Ambassador Lang the way you did just now?"

"The rights given me by the people of Bajor who elected me to serve them."

"And the people of Bajor elected you to be their avenging angel? To single-handedly make the Cardassians pay for fifty years of wrongdoing?"

Asarem slammed her case on the table. "I decided to hear you out because as the commander of Deep Space 9 you're owed a measure of input. But I'm done." Walking briskly, she left the conference room; Kira maintained her pursuit. She locked onto Asarem and refused to let her escape until she'd said her piece; her conscience wouldn't allow her to walk away.

Addressing Asarem's back, Kira persisted with her argument. "We may have been thrown out of our homes, seen horrible starvation and disease, but our shrines are still standing and after thinking the Celestial Temple was lost to us forever, the Prophets brought us the Emissary and we became stronger. The prophecies tell us that we will be stronger yet. For all the horrors inflicted on us by the Cardassians, half our population wasn't executed and millions of our children haven't died since with flesh melting off their bodies due to radiation sickness. We didn't emerge from the Occupation drowning in our own dead." Kira jumped directly into Minister Asarem's path, blocking her from moving any farther. "Where is your compassion, Minister?"

Cold fury burning, Asarem's voice shook. "With the generations of dead and brutalized Bajorans who committed no crime save being born Bajoran. The Cardassians allied with the Dominion. They brought destruction on themselves. Now get out of my way before I call First Minister Shakaar and inform him that we need to reconsider your position as commander of this station."

For a long moment, Kira stood rooted to the spot, staring defiantly at Asarem, daring her to make good on her threats before finally stepping aside and allowing her to pass. She watched Asarem disappear down the corridor. *I hope the air is pure enough for you there on the moral high ground, Minister.*

How dare Asarem talk to her like she had some vastly enlightened understanding of collaboration and innocent Bajorans dying that Kira didn't have! She knew. She had lived it; the Occupation had set the stage—had framed her decisions—for her entire life. But at some point, Kira had to stop defining her life by her losses and if that meant accepting friendship with Cardassia, then she damn well would! Breathing deeply, she closed her eyes, mouthing a prayer for peace, hoping consolation would come from faith. As much as duty pressed on her mind, Kira knew she had to sort out all the confusing threads unraveling in her mind.

Did I just leap to the defense of the Cardassians? Prophets help me, what am I doing?

First order of business upon retiring to her quarters was changing into civilian clothes, but the usually comfortable, well-worn fabric irritated her skin; the sleeves and neck felt tight and confining, like she'd accidentally put on another's clothes. She gave up on eating when her replicated hasperat tasted like spicy sawdust. Her mind dulled whenever she attempted any routine task; she found herself in a stupor, wondering what it was she had started but now couldn't recall. The staticlike quiet pressed on her.

Opening the cupboard that housed the few small remains of her religious life—a few candles, incense, an icon—she removed her earring from a shelf and draped it over her palm, feeling the cold metal links, the weight of the silver. She encapsulated the earring in her fist, gripping it until she felt its edges digging into her skin. One by one, as if in a trance, she lit the candles.

With hands outstretched and eyes closed, Kira prayed.

She interspersed recitations of every prayer she'd memorized since childhood with blunt, almost impatient pleas for the clarity that had thus far eluded her. Time drizzled away—maybe hours—and Kira remained standing. She would stand until she dropped or until her prayers were answered.

At last, her hands fell to her sides and she knew what was required. She considered her earring with longing one last time before she reverently replaced it on the shelf, blowing out the candles and locking the cabinet door.

Gul Macet scrolled through one of several intelligence files he'd brought with him from Cardassia. While he hadn't always approved of Central Command's tactics, he wasn't above sifting their refuse if it aided Cardassia's cause. A good strategist never discounted information on the basis of how it was collected or who had done the collecting.

Before him on the table, Kira Nerys's official Singha Internment Camp record lay open, accompanied by the annual ID holos taken until she left the camp to join the resistance. He thumbed through the screens, finding nothing new—nor did he expect to. *I thought we had her this afternoon,* he thought, recalling the conflict playing across her face. He knew she'd been in the capital city the night of the attacks. Something haunted in her eyes told Macet he shared that in common with the young Bajoran.

The door chimed. Expecting that Natima had returned to take him up on his offer of a late meal, he ordered the computer to admit his guest. *We'll have to make a plan for tomorrow—Asarem will make us fight for the privilege to return to the table.* "Natima, did you have any luck contacting Sirsy?" he asked without looking up from Kira's file.

Silence.

Usually, Natima's gown swished as she walked; he hadn't yet heard footsteps. *Perhaps young Vlar has brought me dinner.* He twisted away from his studies to see what awaited him.

"Gul Macet," Kira Nerys began, "I wondered if you might be interested in taking a walk?"

15

"She did it!" Bowers exclaimed. "The worm is transmitting. It'll only take me a minute to search their system and see if I can find the codes to claim that matter load."

"Timer set," Julian said. "We have three minutes before the Cheka system security starts their sweep of the computer. Ensign Tenmei's lock shows green." With a transporter lock on Prynn, Bashir tracked her location from the sciences station. She hadn't moved for ten minutes, but her vitals remained normal, other than indicating agitation.

"Status of Chief Chao?" Vaughn asked.

Bashir rechecked his display and reported, "Also in position."

Now comes the fun part, Vaughn thought. *Waiting.* He paced the *Defiant's* bridge slowly, keeping his head clear, focusing on the next step in their plan. "We can't get overconfident, Sam. Breaking into the Cheka system isn't enough. If we can't locate the codes, we'll be right back where we started without the materials Nog needs for the defense system." And there was the little matter of making sure Prynn had enough time to escape the suite before security linked the computer penetration with her presence. She had been insistent about avoiding a beam-out while she was with Fazzle, wanting to avoid drawing any unnecessary attention. Once she attached the "worm" to the terminal, she'd initiate her exit strategy.

Hunched over tactical, Sam attacked the incoming data with the determination of a grint hound on the tail of a razorback. He tapped through screen after screen, filtering data, running language decryption algorithms and using the *Defiant's* computing power to run a separate search, narrowing the amount of information he had to plow through.

"Two minutes," Julian announced. "So when's part 'b' of our plan supposed to play out?"

Vaughn checked the time. "Shortly. Where are we at, Sam?"

"The computer is searching the Cheka's trade records"—he paused, grinning—"hey, this is interesting. You think an up-to-date map of where the Cheka weapons are deployed in this sector would be helpful?"

"The codes wouldn't be as critical, then," Julian said. "Simplify our lives considerably."

"Only data for this sector, I'm afraid," Sam said. "We'd still need the femtobot defense, but it would buy us time to test and deploy it."

"Download it," Vaughn ordered. "And any other strategic or military information that might help us navigate our way out of here."

"Yes, sir." Sam continued hunting through the data.

Vaughn rested a hand on the back of Sam's chair and watched. He struggled to believe that such a politically powerful species could manage with such crudely constructed databases. *But that's what happens, I suppose, when you're too lazy to innovate or organize for yourself.*

"Gordimer to Commander Vaughn. We have a situation."

"Go ahead, Ensign."

"Yrythny security caught Lieutenant Nog making an unauthorized attempt to leave the Avaril. *He had classified Starfleet technology downloaded into his tricorder. Specs for* Defiant's *cloaking device."*

Stunned, everyone on the bridge turned to look at Vaughn. "Stay focused, people," he said sternly. "Ensign Gordimer, keep Lieutenant Nog in protective custody until I get there, and secure the tricorder. Vaughn out."

"One minute," Bashir announced.

"Okay, sweetheart, talk to me," Sam coaxed his console. "Wait . . . here we are. I'm gonna grab it all and we'll sort through it later."

"Just do it," Vaughn urged. "Doctor, go ahead and signal Prynn that we're clear." Before she left, Bashir had fitted her auditory canal with a tiny receiver that allowed her to hear signals, but not send them. Concerned about activating any sensors in the Cheka suite's security net, Vaughn insisted on radio silence until the computer break-in succeeded or failed.

"Done, sir," Julian said. "No indication that she's left Fazzle's work area. Thirty seconds."

"Almost got it—" Sam said.

Based on the percentage of information that Sam had captured, Vaughn could see that the data transfer would take more time than was safely left. Prynn needed to leave. Soon. Worry sent his heart racing. "Status of Ensign Tenmei, Doctor?"

"Still no movement, sir. Fifteen seconds."

"Prepare for emergency beam-out," Vaughn ordered.

"I'd advise against that, sir. She's in the heart of the Cheka suite. A sudden beam-out would—wait. She's moving."

Vaughn sighed, watching the blinking dot on Bashir's screen progress down the hall.

"Ten seconds."

Come on, Prynn, get out of there. Keep moving . . .

"Five." With only a few meters to go, the blinking dot paused.

"Time's up," Bashir announced.

Sam turned toward Vaughn. "I'll have the end of this file shortly, but an internal computer sweep is underway. Depending on their sweep sequence, it might be two seconds or twenty minutes before they find us."

"I want her out of there, Julian," Vaughn demanded.

"I'll grab her as soon as she makes it out of the main entrance."

"Cheka sensors nabbed us, sir," Sam said. "But the data transfer is complete. I'm shutting down the link . . . now. Link severed."

The blinking dot on Bashir's screen moved quickly, streaking down the hallway and out the front door.

"Initiating transport," Bashir said. Then he added with a smile, "She should be downstairs, Commander."

Vaughn exhaled with relief. *Thankfully, L.J. isn't around with his fifty reasons why having your daughter under your command is a bad idea.*

"I've isolated the codes, sir," Bowers announced. "Transmitting to Chief Chao . . ."

Moments later, the bridge doors opened, admitting Prynn. She marched onto the bridge, wearing her regulation tank top, but with her uniform jacket tied around her waist. Bashir's eyes widened when he saw the scaly purple blotches covering most of her exposed skin.

"Someone better produce some damn rash spray in the next twenty seconds or I'm resigning my commission!" she announced, jamming her fists into her waist.

Bashir and Vaughn exchanged glances before bursting into relieved laughter.

"What?" Prynn demanded.

"Nothing, Ensign," Vaughn said. And, throwing protocol out the airlock, he walked over to her and placed a soft kiss on her forehead. "Good work. The doctor will take care of you while I take care of Lieutenant Nog. Sam, advise me when Chao is back aboard."

Shar exited Ezri's office, only to discover Keren waiting in the outside corridor. Hundreds of Yrythny coming from the day shift or going to the night shift streamed past, making it easy for Shar to pretend he didn't see her. Without any acknowledgment, he headed in the direction of the guest quarters, knowing she'd be chasing after him anyway.

"Thirishar!"

"If I talk to you, I have to report it to Lieutenant Dax, so don't say anything you don't want repeated," he said as he walked rapidly away.

"They've sent armed squads into the Old Quarter, Thirishar," she said, her voice tinged in fear.

"What?" He paused, waiting for her to catch up.

"The Assembly. Looking for those responsible for the attacks. They've gone into the Old Quarter with weapons," she said breathlessly.

Keren was panicked, and Shar sympathized, but hadn't her own kind landed themselves in this mess? "Can you blame them for wanting to prevent further attacks?"

"I don't know that the underground is responsible for them," she confessed, averting her eyes.

"What do you mean?" Shar demanded.

Grabbing Shar by the sleeve, she pulled him into a dark, deserted side corridor. She peered down the hallway in each direction, before leaning in close, speaking directly in Shar's ear. "A schism has formed in the underground leadership. Some believe that the only way we're ever going to help our people is by force. Waging a war of fear might pressure the government into conceding. The rest of us, me included, believe that we should take up arms only if negotiations don't work."

"Keren, what do you want from me?" he hissed. "It isn't as if I have troops that can defend the Old Quarter. Even if I rounded up all my colleagues, it wouldn't be appropriate for us to play a role in an internal stand-off."

"I'm not asking you to, but your research has become more urgent. You have to press forward as quickly as possible."

"And I plan to go to work as soon as I can."

"That's the problem. The data files, they're hidden in my apartment. If I go back there, I won't be able to leave again—perhaps indefinitely."

"Keren, you're not listening!" Shar pleaded. "I've been ordered not to spend unauthorized time with you. If the lieutenant finds out that I've disobeyed her orders, I'll spend the rest of this mission in the brig. You need to send them by messenger."

"You have to believe me. The casualties in the village will be minuscule compared to what will happen if the Old Quarter is provoked into riots."

More deaths. More delays. More shadowy choices. *Damn it, I've been given a direct order and if Ezri checked up on me and found me missing. . . .* Maybe he could talk to Lieutenant Dax and see if she had any ideas. But there was always the chance she'd refuse to involve Starfleet. Should that happen, Shar wouldn't have a choice of whether to retrieve his data. He needed a little more time. "I can't come immediately."

"In a little while, then. I'll come to your quarters with clothing like I did the first time." She clutched each of his arms in her hands.

"Give me half an hour. I'll meet you in the courtyard. But this has to be the end of it." He had serious reservations about going through with this, but in the end, his personal commitment to the pursuit of scientific truth won out. That . . . and his wish not to have Keren come to harm.

Without a word, Keren turned on her heel and left, Shar watching as she walked away. *This whole situation is about to ignite,* he thought. *Both sides are so busy taking revenge that the truth is slipping between the cracks. This has to end.* Marching back to his quarters, he wondered whether he'd have time for his project before civil war erupted. *I'm going to make this work,* he vowed. And maybe there was a better way to help Keren . . .

Upon entering his quarters, Shar went immediately to the computer terminal, calling up the Luthia root menu. *The military here doesn't do anything without making a big show of it . . . there has to be an announcement or a policy statement about the troops going into the Old Quarter.* There. Shar tapped in the commands, captured the page and saved it to his personal files. Then, he browsed until he found a public mail outlet on Luthia's main system and forwarded it to the terminal in Dax's quarters:

LUTHIA: *Pending a conclusion to the criminal investigation into the attacks on the Coral Sea Bay aquaculture village, the Old Quarter will be under martial law. All residents will be required to submit to police searches, on demand and without resistance, or risk arrest. Force will be used as necessary. Any informa-*

tion leading to the arrest or capture of those responsible for the attacks will be rewarded.

Hopefully Ezri would read between the lines and take action. Shar sent the message, clicked off his terminal and waited for Keren to arrive.

"I apologize for any inconvenience caused by Lieutenant Nog's action. Thank you for detaining him for us. I'll have Ensign Gordimer escort him to our brig," Vaughn said to Chieftain J'Maah and the other Yrythny staffers standing around, horrified by this latest development. The Yrythny had offered to meet Vaughn aboard *Defiant,* but not wanting to burden his hosts, he told them he would come to the *Avaril* to take Nog from their custody.

Vaughn nodded his head at Gordimer, who stood beside Nog. Gordimer grasped Nog's arm, but Nog jerked away, sending a sour expression in Vaughn's direction. Gordimer gripped Nog's arm harder this time, refusing to be dislodged by the Ferengi's thrashing about.

"Sir? The item Lieutenant Nog was carrying?" Gordimer said, tipping his head toward the chair where Nog's tricorder sat.

"I'll take care of it. Make sure Lieutenant Nog is safely ensconced on the *Defiant* until his disciplinary hearing."

Nog glared at Vaughn as Gordimer nudged him forward. The whole pathetic display was embarrassing. Placing Nog under arrest was bad enough, but having it play out in public was humiliating, especially when it had been Nog's Yrythny technologist friends who turned him in. When he'd arrived on the *Avaril's* bridge, he discovered the entire senior staff and Minister M'Yeoh were in attendance. *The more the merrier,* Vaughn thought.

Shoving Nog into the in-ship transport car, Gordimer ordered the door closed and the car shot off, winding its way down the dozens of decks to the bay housing the *Defiant.* After the junior officers had left, J'Maah turned to Vaughn. "When you told me the *Defiant* was repaired and ready to return to Vanìmel, I'd so hoped we'd have enough time for proper good-byes. I'm sorry our last day together had to end on such a tragic note, Commander."

"As am I, Chieftain. But the sooner I can reunite my crew and resume our mission, the better for all of us," Vaughn replied. "As you can see from Lieutenant Nog, the stress has taken a toll. I'll now retrieve the rest of my crew from their accommodations, and we'll prepare to depart."

J'Maah clasped Vaughn by the elbows. "Farewell, Commander."

"Farewell to you, Chieftain." Holding the tricorder tightly in one hand, he started back toward the bay, relieved to have finished playing this act of the drama.

Within minutes, he'd arrived back at his crew's makeshift quarters. Off-duty personnel pounced on him the minute he walked in the door, asking questions, expressing worries and concerns about how to proceed. Vaughn held up his hands to quiet them.

"One thing at a time. First, the Yrythny caught Lieutenant Nog attempting to abscond with the specs for *Defiant's* cloaking device." Gasps went up; a hum of curious murmurs emitted from each segment of the group. Vaughn shushed them again. When they were quiet, he continued, "Apparently, he believed he could negotiate a deal with the shadow trader for the matter load behind my back. He has been relieved of duty and will remain in custody until we've returned to Vanìmel."

Brow furrowed with worry, Ensign Permenter called out, "Sir, who will be overseeing engineering?"

"The *Defiant* hasn't had a shakedown yet, there might be problems," echoed Leishman, Nog's designated shift chief.

"Ensigns Senkowski and Leishman will co-manage the *Defiant's* engineering department until other arrangements are made," Vaughn said. "The *Defiant* will leave for Vanìmel at 2130 hours. Please prep your gear and wait for any further instructions from Lieutenant Bowers. Once we've cleared Consortium space, a staff meeting in the mess hall is planned for 2200. Attendance is mandatory. Ensigns Leishman and Senkowski, you're with me. That'll be all."

Confusion and concern persisted among the crew; Vaughn wished he could alleviate their fears, but he knew they would have answers soon enough. Leishman and Senkowski followed him out. He would take them to the *Defiant,* pass over the material load, and put them to work on the final phase of the femtobot defense. Until a short while ago, Vaughn had worried that they'd end up launching without the defense system. But as he was leaving *Defiant* to deal with the Nog situation, Bowers had contacted him to confirm that Chao successfully procured the materials from the mining office, using the codes taken from the Cheka. Vaughn had finally relaxed. If Leishman and Senkowski asked where the load came from, Vaughn would tell them, honestly, that they discovered that a matter load belonging to them had been illegally transferred to another buyer. Nog's assumption had been correct: Runir's negotiations on the Exchange had been successful but their codes had been routed to the Cheka. Prynn's covert operation was merely to reclaim what was rightfully Starfleet's. No point in saying "stolen," an inflammatory word indicating criminal behavior, when the phrase "returned to its rightful owner" better fit the situation.

One concern still nagged at Vaughn. All their detective work had failed to yield the identity of who might be undercutting their efforts at the Consortium. If their luck held, the bait he'd left behind might yet be taken and Vaughn would have his first solid night's sleep since encountering the Yrythny.

Ezri almost missed the blinking light on her console.

She had returned to her quarters, immediately undressed and showered, but still feeling wound up, decided to sit and read by the courtyard fountain, hoping the distraction would help her unwind. As she unlocked her courtyard door, the reflection of the blinking light on the glass caught her eyes. *Maybe it's a message from Vaughn.* By her calculations, the *Defiant* should be starting home within the day. Opening the message file, she puzzled for a moment over the contents.

The sender, anonymous—though Ezri suspected one close to the talks had been responsible—felt the matter urgent enough to request her attention tonight. Her first perusal of the contents didn't yield the implied meaning immediately; before completing the second pass through, she'd roused Assembly Chair Rashoh from sleep, and demanded that he meet her in her office; or, she would be at his apartment within the hour. What the hell did these fools think they were doing reacting with military force? Any kind of consensus she'd built—or could build—would be shattered if the patrols went into the Old Quarter to implement a crackdown.

The fools! Never pick a fight with a wounded animal. And like it or not, hundreds of Wanderer dead numbered among the day's casualties. Who was responsible for those deaths didn't matter one iota right now. *My guess is the Wanderers believe the attack was a setup to give the military an excuse to search their properties and make arrests. The Houseborn are poised to give the underground a pantheon of martyrs if they don't keep their tempers in check.* The more she considered what the night might bring, the more worried—and angry—she became.

Flattened against the wall, Shar watched, waiting for the "all clear" signal from Keren. His hand rested on his phaser, but so far, he hadn't drawn it once.

Word of the imminent crackdown had spread quickly. All public places in the Old Quarter had been abandoned in favor of private dwellings. The desolate plazas hosted empty merchandise carts and litter, but not much else. Even the halls, normally jammed body to body with Yrythny, were bare as far as the eye could see. The swift evacuation made Shar and Keren's task difficult. Lacking crowds to hide in, they crept along walls, using shadows for camouflage. They avoided main thoroughfares, choosing alleys and the backdoors of businesses instead.

Keren waved him across the alley. Avoiding patches of moonlight, Shar chose an irregular path, pausing behind a bin, dropping to his knees and crawling beneath a fence before dashing across a slip of open space. Upon reaching her, Shar followed Keren closely up a narrow set of stairs. At the top, where the stairs ended, she soundlessly pulled herself up and over a balcony railing. Shar joined her a minute later and they sat, catching their breath for a long moment.

"We need to be careful entering my apartment. There's a chance that enforcers have been sent ahead to take me into custody," she whispered.

"Why would they do that? What have you done?" At this point, Shar wasn't even sure she'd tell him the full truth if he asked. There was so much subterfuge surrounding Keren's life, Shar wondered how she kept track of what was real.

"Because it's an easy way for them to make a statement, and because I don't keep my politics a secret. If they want to harass civilians, they'll want me far away where no one can hear me."

"I'll go in first," Shar volunteered. He unholstered his phaser, double-checked that it was set to stun, and eased up to his knees. Looking out over the edge of the balcony, he saw that the alleyway behind remained empty. He climbed all the way to his feet and moved toward Keren's quarters a step at a time. As he drew closer, he noticed her window was open, curtains fluttering. He twisted back to check with Keren, whispering, "Is it supposed to be open?"

Keren shook her head.

Replacing his phaser on his hip, Shar took out his tricorder. A quick scan revealed at least one Yrythny inside, hiding in the dark. He put his tricorder away, pausing to focus his senses on any discernible energy. *Curious,* he thought, his antennae twitching. *The energy is charged—intense—but not angry, not so much fearful either. More like . . . worried?*

Shar braced himself on the window ledge and pushed off to get the leverage he needed to throw his leg over. Straddling the frame, Shar shifted to a sitting position and soundlessly dropped to the floor. Gradually, his eyes adjusted to the dark; surveying the cramped quarters, Shar saw no evidence of a break-in. He considered taking another tricorder reading, but he froze where he stood when he heard the intruder shuffle around in the next room.

In a flash, a hooded figure streaked toward the apartment door. Shar lunged to block his escape. A plant-filled urn tripped him, sending him careening over the top of the couch.

The hooded figure unlatched the door, throwing it open, admitting the bright lights of the inner compound. Shar winced, squinting enough to see Keren's intruder pause, also blinded. Untangling himself from the clutter, Shar lurched for the door, grabbing onto a wrist. He pulled back, dragging the intruder back into the apartment. The intruder brought his forearm and elbow down, the hard blow breaking Shar's grip. Clutching at the knobby Yrythny fingers proved futile; the intruder eluded him, escaping into the hall. Shar staggered outside, realizing whoever it was had vanished.

Keren came in from the balcony and turned on the lights. She immediately went to a floor tile in one corner of the room and pried it open, revealing a secret compartment. "The datachips are still here," she said with relief. "Are you all right?"

Shar sat down on the couch. "Whoever it was seemed more interested in escaping than in hurting me," he said, dropping his head into his hands and rubbing his eyes.

"Did you get a good look at him?"

Shar shook his head. "But I did notice something. There was a mark on his hand. I don't think I've seen it before."

Eyes wide, Keren sat down beside Shar, draping her arm over the top of the couch and tucking her legs up beneath her. "Describe it."

"A blue starburst pattern over the palm. A tattoo?"

Keren considered Shar soberly, her lips pressed tightly. She had something to say, he waited—and then the moment passed.

"Let me check the alert status before you leave," she said. "I'm surprised we haven't heard anything by now." She left Shar sitting on the couch, nursing his bruised arm, while she checked her terminal. "This is odd. The alert has been changed. Martial law is still in effect, but patrols—unarmed—won't be coming in until morning. Questioning is voluntary. That's unprecedented."

My turn for secrets. Thank you, Ezri. "The danger seems to have passed. I should be heading back to my quarters."

"Thank you," Keren said simply.

Accepting the proferred datachips finished the business between them. They took reluctant leave of each other, Shar knowing that Keren, too, understood that their unusual relationship would end here.

Careful to avoid being seen, he moved swiftly through the Old Quarter. He encountered few Yrythny until he reached the outer neighborhood. As the modules transitioned from the antiquated crude technology to the newer, modern systems, crowds increased. Where he could, Shar looked at the palms of those walking by. Once, he thought he might have seen the mark and he followed the Yrythny for almost a kilometer past his own turnoff before losing him in the crowd. *Maybe I'm imagining things,* he thought. *Darkness can deceive the eye.* Becoming conscious of his own exhaustion, he made his way back to his quarters.

He didn't drift immediately off to sleep. Lying on his back, Shar held his hands in front of him. With a finger, he traced the shape of the mark on his own palm, over and over.

With a satisfied grin, Bowers looked up from his station. *"U.S.S. Defiant* ready to go, sir."

Vaughn turned in his chair to face forward. "Conn, prepare for launch."

"Gladly, sir," Tenmei answered, hands dancing over her console. *"Avaril,* this is the Federation Starship *Defiant* requesting departure clearance."

"Defiant, *this is* Avaril. *Bay doors opening. You are cleared to depart. Safe travels."*

Like great teeth-lined jaws, the doors groaned open, and Prynn eased the starship through, into open space. "We've cleared the *Avaril,* Captain."

Cheers exploded from every station; Vaughn savored the moment. "Follow Consortium shipping lane to grid number 8-5-1 delta, Ensign Tenmei."

"Yes, sir."

Until the femtobot defense was on-line, Vaughn anticipated taking advantage of the nonaggression treaty that protected the Consortium shipping lane. The Cheka wouldn't touch them through those sectors unless they wanted to forfeit all their matter rights.

"Leishman to bridge. We're good to go in engineering."

"Good work, engineering. Ensign Tenmei, when we've cleared the particle fountain perimeter, lay in a course for Vanìmel, warp five." Vaughn breathed deeply. Tonight, he would sleep. First, he would read—maybe that Klingon romance novel he'd won in the poker game. He would drink a steaming mug of mulled cider and then he would sleep.

"Gordimer to Commander Vaughn. Lieutenant Nog is missing!"

Vaughn smiled. He'd discreetly released Nog to his quarters 45 minutes ago. The chief engineer had been quite convincing in his traitor role. A career in holoacting surely awaited him should he ever find Starfleet not to his liking. Once underway to Vanìmel, Vaughn had intended to explain the ruse to the entire crew. "Nothing to worry about, Ensign. Lieutenant Nog has been released to quarters."

"Begging your pardon, sir, but I checked the brig logs and I already know you used your codes to release Nog. I assumed you'd decided he'd be safe confined to quarters, so I didn't question it. But on my last pass through the ship, I stopped by Nog's quarters to see how he was doing and the lieutenant wasn't there."

"Computer, locate Lieutenant Nog," Vaughn ordered.

"Lieutenant Nog is not aboard the Defiant."

Once again, every eye on the bridge focused on Vaughn.

"Well, *that* wasn't part of the plan," he said through his teeth. Taking a deep breath, Vaughn clasped his hands together and raised them to his lips. So much for sleeping. "Ensign Tenmei, when we reach the end of the shipping lane, find an asteroid and park the *Defiant* behind it. Ensign Cassini, sweep the Consortium for any Starfleet homing beacons."

He had an answer within seconds. "I'm picking up a low-frequency homing device coming from Consortium grid 4-7-5. It's the *Avaril,* sir."

Not surprising. Not surprising in the least. "Address intership."

"Intership open," Bowers acknowledged.

"Attention all hands, this is Commander Vaughn. Lieutenant Nog has been abducted and is being held on the Yrythny ship *Avaril.* Our return to Vanìmel will be postponed until he is safely returned to us. Strategy and possible solutions will be discussed at the crew meeting scheduled at 2200 in the mess hall. Vaughn out."

"Sir," Cassini said, "why would Chieftain J'Maah take Lieutenant Nog?"

"I don't think it's Chieftain J'Maah, Ensign. In fact, I'd bet Chieftain J'Maah doesn't know Nog's aboard the *Avaril* and that whoever has taken him has him well hidden."

"Any clues as to who it is?" Bowers asked.

"We'll probably find that out about the same time J'Maah does." He wasn't sure who exactly was responsible, but he hoped the bogus cloak specs he'd deliberately left aboard *Avaril* would unmask the perpetrator. Apparently Vaughn and Nog's sleight of hand had been too convincing—or not convincing enough—because Nog was snatched along with the tech, possibly because giving the Cheka an engineer familiar with the technology would sweeten whatever deal was being made.

Time to dip into my bag of tricks and see what we can come up with. Getting Nog off the *Avaril* before the Yrythny ship pulled a disappearing act of its own might require more than magic.

Any doubts the Assembly might have had about Ezri's fitness to be a mediator vanished after her swift, decisive intervention averted violence in the Old Quarter. During their midnight meeting, she persuaded Rashoh to see the folly of offensive action when the Wanderer population was already inflamed. The Assembly leadership's astonishment at her prescient understanding endowed her with a certain degree of clout. All she'd done was spell out logical consequences, where both Houseborn and Wanderer leadership lacked the emotional or intellectual distance to find reason themselves.

She wasn't about to admit that had it not been for the anonymous message, she would have gone to bed without a second thought. No need to needlessly confuse the outcome. In the following days, a grateful Assembly Chair Rashoh readily agreed, on behalf of the Upper Assembly, to provide DNA samples to Shar for his genetic experiments. Rashoh's reasoning had been that Shar would put to rest, once and for all, any doubt of the Houseborn's superiority. Whether Shar would finish his research in a timely fashion was debatable, but he could always transmit the results to Vanìmel when and if he drew any substantive conclusions.

In Ezri's eyes, her diplomatic victory vindicated her methodology. There had been a few moments along the way when she doubted her own competence, worrying that the Yrythny conflict would only be settled through war. Even Shar's insistence that a scientific solution should supersede diplomatic initiatives caused her to waver in her commitment to see the talks through. In hindsight, thanks to Dax's cumuluative wisdom, she'd instinctively known the best course from the start.

With Shar analyzing Yrythny DNA and word from Vaughn indicating that the *Defiant* was three days out from Vanìmel, Ezri recognized she'd reached a place where she needed to pull all her fact-finding, interviews and analyses together. The Assembly expected, and deserved, a proposal and they would have one.

She didn't have the luxury of waiting for Shar, who might or might not have concrete results before Vaughn returned. The underground might launch another attack. Yrythny life didn't stand to change much before Dax left.

Returning to her quarters, Ezri stood on her head to think. She considered her knowns. The most reasonable among the Houseborn, Jeshoh for example, still had legitimate, significant doubts about the Wanderers' capacity for self-regulation, and House Tin-Mal was proof enough to him. From her own experience on Vanìmel, Ezri wasn't convinced the planet could sustain unlimited Yrythny proliferation. If the Wanderers were allowed to reproduce, both sides would have to impose limitations on reproduction unless the sustainability questions could be suitably resolved. The Wanderers, justifiably, wanted to be held as equals, to escape servile lives, to take consorts and mate as other Yrythny did—and they were prepared to use violence to secure those rights if the Houseborn didn't agree to their demands.

Ezri didn't need blood rushing to her head to conclude that she didn't see a way that these two castes could continue to coexist on the planet unless one side or the other was willing to divvy up the ring city, the oceans and the arable land. Partition it all. Nothing in Vanìmel's history or her knowledge of either side led her to believe that the Yrythny would accept this as a solution.

Dropping her feet back to the floor, Ezri slowly stood up, trying to avoid the lightheadedness that often followed a headstand. Padds and datachips covered her couch. She picked through the pile, searching for inspiration, passing over histories, legislative calendars until her hand hovered over starcharts for the surrounding sectors. Hadn't Vaughn's last message said that they'd figured out how to make Nog's femtobot defense work? Once the Yrythny had that technology and could use it to defend themselves, her solution would be much more hopeful than it currently seemed. It wasn't a glamorous solution or an original one, but it had the benefit of successful precedents.

She touched her combadge. "Dax to Candlewood."

"Go ahead."

"Bring me anything in the *Sagan*'s database on Earth's 16th through 18th century colonial movements."

"Will do. Anything else?"

Ezri plopped into a chair and threw her feet out in front of her. The triannual Yrythny Homecoming was scheduled to begin the day after tomorrow. Three times a year, Houseborn Yrythny returned to their House of origin to go into the waters with their consort and lay eggs. A good time to announce her proposed treaty. "Yes. Please set up a meeting with Assembly Chair Rashoh. Tell him I think I've got something he'll want to hear."

Sitting down at the terminal, Ezri forced herself to work on the draft proposal. Her hands hung in the air; mentally, she drew a blank as she tried to coax out the language. *At least I have something to offer. Throw in a few Dax flourishes and they'll be pleased. I'm sure of it. Of course they will. Why wouldn't they? It's not like they have any ideas of their own and this is a solid solution.*

Her hands remained suspended over the terminal keys.

Nothing else has been proposed. What are you waiting for, Dax? Go for it.

Drawing from the initial draft of the Khitomer Accords, Dax composed the opening of the Yrythny Compromise, all the while unable to ignore the nagging feeling that she ought to wait. But didn't she know everything she needed to know by now? She'd lived longer than all of them put together.

Under cloak, *Defiant* shadowed *Avaril.*

The Yrythny ship hadn't strayed too far from the Consortium shipping lanes to Vanìmel. Once Nog had been rescued the *Defiant* wouldn't have far to go to reunite with the away team, though Vaughn hadn't been able to contact Ezri and update her as to their latest dilemma. To avoid detection by the *Avaril,* the *Defiant* had remained under cloak and maintained communications silence.

Having left Bowers, Prynn, and Senkowski manning the bridge, Vaughn went to the mess hall to meet with the rest of the crew for the strategy session. The bridge team would attend via the ship's comm system. Part of Vaughn's agenda for the meeting was to buoy morale. Nog's kidnapping had been a blow. Every crewman wanted to help, but no one knew how. By bringing everyone together, Vaughn hoped to make his team feel like they could make contributions to solving the problem.

By the time Vaughn arrived, five minutes early, the crew had already assembled. *Eager to go to work. Excellent.* "Let's start with what we know. Ensign Leishman, your report," Vaughn said.

"Wherever Nog is being held, there's some kind of transport-inhibiting field in place. We can't beam him off. If he's moved, we might be able to grab him, unless the inhibitor is something on his person. But in order even to make the attempt we'd be risking exposure."

"The *Avaril*'s offensive weaponry and maneuverability are limited," Gordimer interjected. "If we decloak and fix phasers or torpedoes on them, they might give up Lieutenant Nog without a fight."

Shaking his head, Julian countered, "We could be in an indefinite standoff, waiting for one side or the other to blink. If Nog's kidnapping has been done without J'Maah's knowledge, who's to say the kidnapper won't escape with Nog while we're arguing with J'Maah. Or worse, kill him."

"J'Maah might not be involved at all. This could be a conspiracy in his ranks," Vaughn said. "With members of his crew going against orders, the *Avaril* and her 1,800 crewmembers could be in serious danger."

Bowers's voice suddenly rang out. *"Captain. We've picked up something new on long-range sensors. You're going to want to see this."*

"What is it, Sam?"

"Judging from the biosignatures I'm picking up . . . I think it's a Cheka warship, sir," Bowers said.

"Show me," Vaughn ordered.

On the viewer of the mess hall companel, a blade-winged starship appeared. Not as large as the *Avaril,* but definitely more powerful, if its energy output readings were any indication. In a fight, the *Defiant* might be the underdog.

"Sensors show the Cheka vessel is following a trajectory that'll have it intercepting the Avaril *five hours out from Vanìmel at current speed."*

So is she planning on poaching the Avaril? *Or is she meeting up with them?* Vaughn mulled over both possibilities, looking for clues as to which one was most likely. He kept returning to the fact that whoever had sabotaged the deal on the Exchange had used the Cheka as a go-between. The Yrythny cut a deal with the Cheka. *What the Cheka want is clear—the cloaking device. But what the Yrythny want—that they'd be desperate enough to deal with the devil on . . .*

An idea struck him. "Sam, keep track of the Cheka's progress. Let me know if it changes course. See if you can listen in on their communications. If they're in contact with anyone, I want to know who. And I want details about that ship. Life-forms, energy sources, propulsion, tactical systems, everything."

"I'm on it," Bowers replied.

Vaughn turned back to his crew. With all eyes fixed on him, Vaughn clasped his hands behind his back and announced, "I think I've figured out how to get Nog back."

16

Oh, to see the look on Vedek Yevir's face when he learns I went walking with Gul Macet! Kira thought, amused by the shocked expression on Prylar Kanton's face as they passed him. Kira knew that being seen publicly with Macet would have only minimal impact on her reputation. Those who knew her well would see her as being fair-minded; those who were wary of her would have another item to add to their arsenal of reasons why she wasn't trustworthy. A public walk also assured that she could honestly answer any who might express concerns about a potential conflict of interest: if she had something to hide, she wouldn't be talking about it in public.

And Kira wasn't fool enough to believe this impacted only her. There were those in Macet's company who would have reservations about the gul talking with a Bajoran. They both needed protection from accusations that might arise from either camp.

Hoping to minimize civilian contact, Kira elected to take a route that took them over the habitat ring bridges and up to the Promenade balcony. At this hour, minimal foot traffic meant fewer encounters with curious onlookers, but the constant security presence in the area assured reliable witnesses to whatever passed between them.

At first they walked in silence, searching for a comfortable rhythm, neither of them certain where one began a conversation like the one they needed to have. About the time they approached the Promenade balcony, Kira finally decided she felt safe to begin.

"I realize I haven't been very hospitable since you arrived. I apologize," she began, clasping her hands together behind her back.

Gul Macet smiled, his face softened by amusement. "It's not all that surprising, Colonel, that you find my presence disturbing, as do your fellow Bajorans. I'm not troubled by it."

"Good," she said, nodding her head with relief. "I'm glad that you don't hold our prejudices against us." They rounded the final corner before moving into the main walkway. Only a handful of people milled around the balcony at this hour: lovers cuddled on a bench, dismissing the awe-inspiring expanse of space out the windows for the wonders in each other's eyes; intoxicated revelers stumbling out of Quark's, lighter in pocket and spirit; and Ro's security people, watching it all.

"My likeness to Dukat isn't exactly positive for either of our peoples," Macet acknowledged. "For everyone who celebrated him as a hero, there were many of us who saw his egocentricity as an obstacle that prevented him from serving Cardassia's best interests. He didn't want power for the good he could do, he wanted power for the good it would do him. There's a distinction there that I think you Bajorans saw before my people did. Our loss."

"Indeed." Kira nodded an acknowledgment to a security officer keeping watch at the top of the spiral staircase. If Kira's companion startled him, his alert gaze offered no evidence of it.

As she and Macet strolled along the Promenade balcony, the exquisite irony of the situation didn't escape Kira. Had it been only days ago when she sat alone in her office, wishing for a friend to walk with? She had envisioned that she and her companion would walk this very stretch she presently stood on. And here she was, standing beside someone she could hardly call a friend, knowing that she was exactly where she was supposed to be, with the person she was supposed to be with.

Her thoughts were broken when Macet said abruptly, "And now that we've reestablished why you feel awkward in my presence . . ."

Kira wondered if she wore her ambivalence on her face. "Gul Macet—" she began, feeling compelled to explain.

". . . I think we can move on to more pressing matters. The talks."

Out of the corner of her eye, Kira noticed the not-so-subtle pointing and gawking that had begun below as worshipers from evening services flooded the Promenade. An idea occurred to her. "I think we'll accomplish more if we find a quiet place to sit down."

"Your office?" he suggested.

"I have another idea."

Within minutes, Kira had admitted herself and Macet to the Ziyal exhibit, on display within the walls of Garak's old tailor shop. And indeed, the tailor shop, vacant and dark since the end of the war, had been transformed into a gallery.

The curator from the Bajoran Ministry of Art, one who had known Ziyal, designed the exhibit. Recessed lighting had already been installed, canvases stretched, and several holoprojectors installed to display representations of works lost in the war. The curator had used blue- and red-tinted spotlights to bring added drama to Ziyal's stark, jagged charcoal lines, to illuminate the multilayered oil paint dabs, roughened by bold brush strokes. She had drawn from both sides of her heritage to create thematically challenging pieces: some of her paintings dripped with the violent blood-reds and slate gray tones of war, while others conveyed the serenity of spirituality through water and nature. Kira wondered how Garak, with whom Ziyal had somehow forged a special connection during her time on the station, would feel when he learned to what purpose his old space was now being put. She thought he would approve.

After a fashion, Ziyal symbolized a trying time for those station residents who lived through the Dominion War Occupation, reminding some of Dukat, others of Vedek Yassim's suicide. For others, Ziyal recalled a darker era, an era when Bajoran women were slaves to Cardassian soldiers. Because Kira loved Ziyal, she didn't want her memory dishonored in any fashion. On Bajor, where fewer individuals had personal associations with her, people would be more inclined to find hope and insight from her story than to resent it.

Public access to the exhibit wouldn't begin for a couple of days; if casual talk between staff working in ops represented a cross sampling of the station's opinions, the admission lines would be long. All those who had been privileged to see Lang's presentation at the reception had openly conveyed their enthusiasm for the Ziyal project.

With the ever-vigilant presence of Militia security hovering outside, Kira and Macet strolled around the various artworks, making simplistic comments about the personalities of the pieces and saying little else until they gravitated to the center of the gallery, where the curator had placed a bench. Macet sat down, facing a floor-to-ceiling canvas—an abstract cubist-style oil painting entitled *Gallitep*—and threw his legs out in front of him. In counterpoint, Kira sat beside, but apart from Macet, facing the opposite wall where a more modest, pencil drawing—warm chalks on black paper—called *Mother* hung. Pale blue lights, the room's sole illumination, shrouded Ziyal's artwork—as well as its two viewers.

"Have the talks always been as contentious as they were today?" Kira asked, still dismayed by the stubborn posturing she'd observed.

"Minister Asarem has always been eloquent," Macet answered, "but her pleasant manners fail to mask the rigid, almost provocative positions she's taken."

Kira shook her head, allowing her eyes to meander over the pale colors puddled on the canvas in front of her. "I had no idea how stuck both of the delegations were," she said. "I sincerely believed that our people could find at least a place to start, but it doesn't appear that either side can agree on even that. If you can't find consensus on humanitarian issues, I don't know how much hope we can hold out for normalized relations."

"This, I believe, is where you come in, Colonel," Macet said gently. "You need to be our intermediary."

"Me?" Kira said. Keeping her back to Macet, she walked over to a painting that hadn't been hung yet. Crouching down, she tried losing herself in an analysis of the geometric forms, but Macet's absurd suggestion intruded on her thoughts. Asarem had hardly been subtle in hiding her dislike for Kira; Shakaar didn't mind using her as a social liaison with the Cardassians, but had reservations about her assuming a larger role, if she'd correctly read his behavior at the reception. Admiral Akaar didn't have a say, yet—this was still a matter between the Bajoran and Cardassian governments, not the Federation. Macet must be delusional. "What exactly do you see me doing?"

"You are the one to put the talks on a successful path," Macet explained. "Even with your own people, you've handled more difficult scenarios."

"I don't know who you've been talking to, Gul Macet, but obviously you have outdated notions about how much my opinion matters around here. Maybe once upon a time . . . Right now, I serve in a quasi-military but primarily administrative capacity. The replicator in your quarters isn't working? Call me. I have an in with the acting engineering chief. Anything requiring politicking, influence peddling or persuasion? I'm more or less useless."

He chuckled. "I'm beginning to see why, at least on some level, you and

Gul Dukat were fated to hate each other. As much as he saw the universe circumnavigating him, you're just the opposite."

Kira stiffened. "Don't make the mistake of thinking I didn't have better reasons to hate him, Macet."

"My apologies, Colonel. I only meant that you seem unexpectedly—humble—for someone of your accomplishments. I noticed this at the reception. How can you not appreciate your own magnitude, even among the formidable figures assembled on Deep Space 9 right now?"

"I don't think you understand what an Attainder means among my people."

"Actually I do. Quite well. I spent this afternoon reading up on it. After Vedek Nolan told me what to look for," Macet said. "I accept that your present status imposes a separation of sorts between you and your people, but that doesn't negate who you are."

Kira stood up and turned to face him, arms folded, only to find that Macet was no longer studying the oil painting, but watching Kira intently. "What exactly do *you* know about who I am?"

"Of all the people on the station, you have the unique position as one who has earned the respect of Bajorans, Cardassians, the Federation, even the Romulans and the Klingons," Macet explained patiently. "You've worn the uniforms of both the Bajoran Militia and Starfleet. And you've succeeded Captain Sisko as commander of one of the most critical outposts in the Alpha Quadrant. Now a Starfleet officer serves as *your* second in command. To my knowledge, it's unprecedented."

Kira studied Macet, looking for proof that he might be lulling her into letting her guard down. "All these things are true, but you're neglecting to mention that each one of these items predated my Attainder." Kira had her own version of the truth to offer. "I retain command of this station because Shakaar can't risk looking provincial while he's trying to win the favor of Councillor zh'Thane and Admiral Akaar. Dismiss me and he has to explain to the Federation why a perfectly qualified officer is dismissed on religious grounds unrelated to command duties. Those who I count as my friends in Starfleet are either in the Gamma Quadrant, on Earth, or with the Prophets. And I'm fairly certain that Minister Asarem would like nothing more than to shove me out the nearest airlock."

Macet tossed his head back and laughed heartily. "You sound not unlike the precocious, brilliant student whose cleverness has left him working off demerits after school, never mind that you're graduating first in your class."

"You're overstating my influence in the circles of power," Kira said.

"And you are obviously not the best judge of your capabilities. I'm sure most would see you as a true daughter of the Prophets," Macet pronounced solemnly.

"You have a helluva lot of nerve talking about what makes a true daughter of the Prophets," she said sharply, refusing to be bought off by Macet's lofty rhetoric. "If anyone thinks that the resemblances between you and Dukat end at appearance, make sure they're informed otherwise. Flattery won't negate the reality of my situation."

Macet met her gaze. "It isn't flattery, it's truth. And it's why Ambassador Lang, and I, speaking on her behalf, are asking you to use your influence to help us broker peace."

"I thought we'd established my lack of influence." Kira rubbed her forehead, wondering how awful her headache would be by the time she and Macet stopped arguing in circles.

"You are the only one who truly understands all sides in this, as your remarks to Minister Asarem proved today."

"You overheard?"

"You weren't exactly keeping your voices down, Colonel."

Damn. If Macet heard, who else might have eavesdropped on her conversation with Asarem? For a moment, Kira worried about the vandal who had targeted the Cardassian delegation, hoping her outburst eluded that pair of ears. Her words might be interpreted as being too supportive of the Cardassians, and she didn't want to further stoke the anger that had defaced the flag. She knew then that she needed to do what she could to hasten this process along. "What exactly is it that you expect me to do?" she said at last.

"Appeal to First Minister Shakaar. Ask him to intercede."

Kira shook her head. "You don't know what you're asking."

Macet suddenly stood up. "You've seen for yourself what's happening. Minister Asarem isn't interested in negotiating peace. She wants revenge."

"But how do I know that what happened today is typical of the talks?" Kira argued, remembering what passed between all the involved parties.

"Review the transcripts. Interview me, Lang, any member of our delegation. And I'm sure if you asked, you could talk to the Bajoran delegation as well. Weigh the evidence," Macet urged. "If you review the proceedings and find that all parties acted reasonably or that our party acted in bad faith, then I'd invite you to act on your conscience or walk away. But if you find that the facts support my contentions, will you go to First Minister Shakaar and plead our case?"

Kira rolled Macet's request around in her mind, looking for any possible loopholes or places that might ultimately damage the precarious situation between Bajor and Cardassia further; she found none. "I'll see what I think after I review the information."

"Isn't it accurate to say that true followers of the Prophets believe that all things may be done through their instrumentality?" he asked.

"If it's right for Bajor."

"And if brokering peace between our peoples is right for Bajor, do you not have faith that the Prophets will light your path?"

Kira met his direct gaze, seeing integrity in his eyes that Dukat had never feigned successfully. "If you know me as well as you claim to, you know the answer to that question."

"I'm counting on it," Macet said quietly.

That the security post inside the exhibit had been vacated without her being informed struck Kira as odd. She understood that the exhibit was to be guarded around the clock. The deserted Promenade pulsed with taut stillness, a tension that squeezed out all the sound. Without thought to Macet, she walked as if in a dream toward the front door, when the silence ruptured—an angry cacophony of screams and crashes, of breaking bodies and shattering glass.

A tangle of humanoid bodies was spilling out of Quark's, many clutching random objects from the bar as makeshift weapons. She saw a group of Cardassians wielding table legs like clubs at charging Bajorans brandishing bottles and chairs. An abandoned cart loaded with incense, crystals, and candles toppled over, spilling wares onto the floor; a pair of combatants skidded to a halt, falling flat on their backs before their fists could make contact. Bar stools sailed through the air. Scents of spilled liquors and hoppy Terran ale permeated the air.

Kira touched her combadge. "Kira to Ro."

"I know, Colonel. Quark contacted me. I'm on my way." Ro sounded breathless; she must be running from her quarters. *"I'm closing the Promenade to everyone except security and medical personnel, and yourself, until we get the situation under control. All my off-duty people have been summoned and I've alerted the infirmary— but even so, this sounds pretty bad."*

"Actually, it's worse. I suggest you hurry, Lieutenant. Kira out." With her phaser drawn, Kira charged onto the west platform. She estimated the number of brawlers higher than sixty. She turned to Macet to ask for his assistance in putting down the tumult, but realized, too late, he'd already raced into the crowd and was prying his men off whoever their opponents might be. She quickly lost track of him in the sea of constantly heaving bodies. Hoping that any security officers present might help defuse the fray, she saw, to her anger, the unmistakable colors of the Militia swirling in the mix of Cardassian gray. *Our own people are part of this. . . !*

Kira scanned the room with her eyes, seeking a position from which to disrupt the melee in the quickest, surest way possible. She saw arms, bloody uniforms, limbs twisted at grotesque angles, and was wondering where the hell the medics were when she spotted Dr. Tarses. Simon had begun treating an injured Cardassian when he was suddenly accosted by an enraged Bajoran. The man started beating Simon until Sergeant Shul appeared from somewhere, yanked him off the doctor, and put him in restraints. For his part, Tarses went back to caring for his patient, ignoring the bruises that were already darkening his face.

Crouched down, out of sight between the gym and the jeweler's, she waited for the strategic moment, phaser pointed at the ceiling, finger on the trigger. . . .

Shielding himself with a tray, Quark bellowed demands for order, utterly ignored by anyone who heard him. Kira watched as he pushed anyone still inside the bar—anyone who even looked dangerous—out onto the Promenade. When he appeared satisfied that only his staff remained (and Morn, peering out at the chaos from behind the dubious safety of the bar), Quark activated a force field to prevent the brawlers from returning to further damage his establishment.

Macet was having mixed success in stopping his men; he'd break up one quarrel only to be drawn into another. Suddenly Kira saw an enraged Klingon, wielding a *d'k tahg,* charging Macet after the gul had forced the Cardassian that the Klingon had been fighting to retire.

Kira pivoted out, spraying a round of warning shots at the walls behind the Klingon. Startled, the Klingon turned to face his new assailant, only to be tackled by Macet. Keeping a knee wedged between the Klingon's shoulder blades, Macet waved appreciatively to Kira.

Several brawlers had paused and ducked when the metallic sound of phaser fire rang out; some dove to the floor, but one particularly determined pair continued trying to kill each other until Kira stunned them both. They dropped, grunting. Kira kicked them out of her way.

"This is Colonel Kira!" she shouted. "Any and all Bajoran nationals are to stand down immediately or face criminal charges!" Several Bajorans paused, midpunch, to look toward Kira's voice, but many ignored her demands.

Another round of phaser fire whizzed from the balcony above and everyone looked to see Ro standing over them all, phaser held out in front of her, and flanked by a dozen armed security officers. "The next person to flinch gets more than a warning shot!" Ro shouted.

As if daring Ro to make good on her threat, a man Kira recognized as an off-duty Militia engineer charged a Cardassian who had just allowed a badly beaten Bajoran to fall to the deck, unconscious. Another well-targeted shot from Kira's phaser brought the engineer down instantly. A wave of compliance flowed through the crowd as fists fell, neck holds were released and all matter of objects being used to pummel clattered to the ground.

Ro nodded appreciatively at her commanding officer, then began deploying her people into the crowd below, keeping her weapon trained. "Everyone remains where they are," she cautioned. "No one moves until you're given permission to move." The security chief found the man Kira had wounded and, hauling him up by his good arm, led him off to sit in front of the shrine as medics swarmed from the infirmary.

Macet appeared at Kira's side. "Colonel. I apologize for the behavior of my crew."

Kira shook her head. "We don't know who started this."

"It doesn't matter who started this," Macet said sharply. "My men were wrong to have been fighting. They will be appropriately punished, I assure you, and will submit to any interrogations Lieutenant Ro might require."

"Interrogation is a very strong word," Kira said, picking her way through collapsed, bruised and beaten revelers toward the west platform.

Macet walked alongside Kira, paralyzing with a cold glare whoever among his men dared look at him. "If interrogation is required to ensure my people's compliance you have my blessing to do whatever you need to do."

"Thank you. I'm sure Lieutenant Ro will appreciate your cooperation."

As she walked, Kira began making mental calculations about how much damage had been done, what the cost would be, who would pay, and whether they would even be able to reopen the Promenade before morning. Irritated by the pointlessness of such wanton destruction, she gritted her teeth. *When will we ever learn?*

Out of the corner of her eye, Kira saw Dr. Girani and four nurses rushing out of a turbolift to join their colleagues already tending the wounded. Several of the medics appeared to have been roused from their beds: Lieutenant Chagall, usually a stickler for regulation, wore shorts and his Academy T-shirt; and Ensign Mancuso had thrown on a flowered bathrobe. Kira allowed herself to relax a bit: at least the wounded could be attended to properly.

"Considering the numbers involved, I hope that you don't have any objections to my securing Cardassian prisoners in the brig on my ship," Macet said. "Lieutenant Ro can post her own squad of security guards, of course, but I suspect your facilities will be overtaxed if she has to detain my men as well."

Kira paused to look over at Macet. *He's trying as hard as the rest of us.* "I'll inform Lieutenant Ro. Let's get to work."

After Ro delegated the investigatory assignments, she went to interview Quark. Kira made herself useful helping out both the security and medical teams. Amazing how a threatening glare from the CO helped induce a belligerent Militia member to cooperate, or how an extra pair of hands, regardless of rank, were appreciated. Case in point: a massive, but unconscious Cardassian had collapsed on top of his groaning crewmate. With Kira taking the shoulders and a security officer taking the legs, they heaved him off, leaving the formerly pinned crewmate available for Macet to take into custody.

How could this have happened? Kira wondered, nauseated by the smells of sweat and blood. A hand touched her shoulder and she turned to see Counselor Matthias and Thriss standing behind her.

Matthias, like Ro and some of the others, looked like she'd tumbled out of bed. Unlike Lieutenant Ro, who had been striding around barefoot, Phillipa had managed to slide her feet into a pair of fuzzy pink slippers. Gratefully, Thriss wore sensible, nondescript civilian clothes.

"Ummm, Colonel," Matthias started in a gravelly voice before interrupting herself with a yawn. "I only have Starfleet's field medicine certification, but when I heard the emergency call go out over the com, I knew you'd need extra hands. I'm here to help."

"Thank you, Commander. And Thriss has joined you because . . . ?"

Commander Matthias rubbed her eyes with the heels of her hands. "Thriss trained as a medic through level three. Preparing for med school, in fact." Phillipa yawned again. "She worked with the civilian population on Betazed after the emancipation. Situations like these are all in a day's work for her."

"I spent two months working in hospitals in the capital city," Thriss said, thrusting out her medkit for Kira to inspect. She appeared to have the right tools, but Kira had reservations.

At Kira's skeptical look, Matthias added, "I'm confident that Thriss can handle anything Dr. Girani would assign her. Allowing her to help out could be mutually beneficial."

"Report to Dr. Girani, then," Kira instructed them both. "And thank you."

Matthias lingered behind for a moment, waiting for Thriss to be out of earshot. "Colonel, I'll stay close by. If I sense that she needs to leave, I'll escort her back to her quarters."

"Thriss does seem more—alert—maybe cheerful?" Kira observed.

"She expects to hear from Ensign ch'Thane when the next batch of communiqués comes from the *Defiant*. She loves him—misses him. Hearing from him reassures her," Matthias explained. She yawned again and trailed off after Thriss.

Kira appreciated Matthias's efforts: the only way they'd survive the current craziness was to be vigilant in looking out for each other. *No matter the planet of origin, parentage, past misdeeds or present challenges—we have to assume that our successes or failures come by every individual's choice.* She considered the work being done before her, the cooperation of diverse organizations and species in helping these stupid fools who probably deserved their misery.

A Cardassian sporting a bruise on his forehead the size of a *jumja* fruit moaned somewhere to her left. She dropped to a knee, clicked the tricorder off her utility belt and scanned his skull, looking for evidence of a concussion. Jerking away from her, the soldier stared up at her, fear and distrust in his eyes, his body rigid.

"You're going to be fine," Kira said, reassuringly. "I'll find you something that will take care of the pain."

Ro made her way around the debris until she reached the keypad access port to Quark's bar. An alphanumeric combination overrode Quark's lock and the door obediently opened. Nonchalantly, she strolled into the bar, nodding a hello to Morn, who sat nursing a mug.

What a mess.

Shattered goblets and snifters, malodorous cheeses and seafood sauces smeared into the upholstery, wadded-up napkins, overturned *tongo* wheels, and more than a dozen broken wine bottles drizzling fermented fruit juice onto the floor. Navigating this in bare feet was akin to picking her way through a minefield. There had to be something . . . an idea occurred to her.

"Hey, Treir! You around here somewhere?" Ro called, craning her neck, trying to catch a glimpse of what other surprises might yet await her.

Quark popped up from behind the bar. "Not even a 'Hello, Quark, I was worried about you'? We had a regular Core breach in here tonight and you're not the slightest bit concerned." He clicked his tongue. "You and Treir don't have something going on that I don't know about, do you?" he said, a shade too casually.

"Shut up, Quark. I need shoes."

"Now that you mention it, your wardrobe is on the skimpy side tonight. I'm sure I've got something in the storeroom. Back in a flash." Disappearing into the rear, he materialized a moment later, a pair of spangly, sparkly-blue high heels dangling from his ring and pinky fingers.

Ro resisted her impulse to force him to contort his feet into those podiatric nightmares. "Be serious," she snorted.

"You have such pedestrian taste, Laren." He pulled a pair of flat sandals from behind his back and plopped them onto the counter. "Better?"

Taking a seat on a bar stool, Ro hoisted one foot onto her knee and into a shoe and then repeated the process with the other foot. "You wanna tell me what happened here tonight?" she said, sweeping aside ground-up matza-stick crumbs with her elbow. She needed a space to work.

"Ask five different people who started it, you'll get five different answers," Quark said solemnly. He took a bar towel and brushed refuse into a dustpan, whose contents promptly went into the replicator. "All I know for certain is that it was Bajorans and Cardassians failing to work and play well with each other. Like it takes a quantum physicist to understand that the bad blood between your people and the Cardassians is destined to lead to disaster."

Ro placed a padd on the cleared spot on the bar and began to take notes. "Other than your astute, upbeat analysis of Bajoran/Cardassian relations, any specific things you might remember—you know, clues that might help us toss some hotheads in the brig—assign some accountability?"

"Not offhand, no. But speaking of accountability, who's going to pay for this disaster? Because there's no way that this is my fault." Quark threw open his arms, indicating the expanse of his establishment. "And the lost revenues! We're not going to be cleaned up in time for alpha shift. This is an outrage. I demand to speak to Colonel Kira and Gul Macet!" Continuing to prattle on, Quark walked from one end of the room to the other, interspersing diatribes with his cleanup efforts. He tried to impress upon Ro the gravity of every scratched chair and crumb-covered table.

Ro massaged her ridges with the tips of her fingers. *High noise, low signal,* she thought, hoping he might deign to throw in a few useful facts between his explanation of thread counts and his assertion that he'd never known a Cardassian to complain about *kanar* just past the "use by" date. Not surprisingly, he unequivocally denied any culpability for Cardassians put in sour moods after partaking of bad liquor.

A couple of hours later, Kira believed they were on the downside of arrests, medical treatments and cleanup. The Promenade wouldn't be ready by the start of the business day, and morning Temple services would also be canceled. Still awaiting her was the unpleasant task of rousing Shakaar with the update of the night's goings-on. He wouldn't be pleased.

Starting toward ops, she glimpsed Macet on the opposite platform, herding the last of his shackled men toward a turbolift. She stopped to watch him, presuming that he likely felt the same exhaustion she did. He must have sensed her because he stopped to meet her gaze. Their eyes linked only long enough for a mutual understanding to pass between them. Turning away, he barked orders to those assisting him and disappeared from her sight.

When she was satisfied he was gone, Kira said quietly, "You can deshroud now."

Taran'atar shimmered into visibility beside her. "Colonel?"

"Maintaining surveillance on Gul Macet will no longer be necessary," Kira said, still staring after the departed Cardassian.

"I concur," the Jem'Hadar said. "Will there be anything else?"

Kira considered the question. "What do you think of him?" she asked finally.

Taran'atar hesitated. "He isn't what I expected."

Kira nodded. "I know exactly what you mean."

17

Water-light reflected in lazy loops on the rust sandstone walls, disrupted by stones skimming the surface. Rippling rings emerged as the rock fell to the streambed with a hollow plop, a prelude to the storm rumbling in the distance. The air crackled, anticipating release.

Crouched low to the ground, Shar scooped up a handful of gravel and rocks, sifting it through his fingers, fishing out the smooth flat stones, tossing aside the dross. He skipped one across the stream and another, losing himself in the rhythm of the mindless task.

"The rules of conduct are not negotiable," the headmaster had explained patiently in a tone he'd use for an idiot. "You are not an exception."

He skipped another stone.

Her antennae rigid with barely contained fury, zhavey had bellowed, "Tezha is reserved for the shelthreth! Don't tempt fate, Thirishar!" He'd protested his innocence, but she refused his explanations.

He scratched through the damp sand for another stone, willing away their chastisements. Gradually, the voices of zhavey and the headmaster twisted and twined into the low moans of the growing wind. A gust shaved dry needles off spindly conifers, flipped dry leaves onto their backs. Shar pulled his tunic closer to him to stave off the chill. He shivered.

And then he sensed her.

Without hearing her bare feet sending pebbles skittering up the path or seeing the sheen of perspiration damp on her arms and face, he knew she stood behind him, watching. She always watched him and he hated her for it. He could be standing across the hallway or tucked in a window seat reading and her eyes would always find him. When he felt her closeness, his throat tightened as the air became unbearably dry.

"What are you doing here?" he said disdainfully, willing his thudding heart to steady. He refused to look at her. Attention would only encourage her. She'd been impossible yesterday, following him out into the hills, an act that had led to them both ending up in the headmaster's office to receive official notations on their records.

"That's a fine hello, Thirishar," she sniffed, tossing her hair.

That hair of hers, *Shar thought, annoyed.* That ridiculous fine, straight hair, soft like spun silk thread when she brushed against him . . . *"If I'd wanted you here, I would have invited you. Of course, that didn't stop you yesterday when you invited yourself along on my research trip. I neglected to thank you for that, by the way. I've been given a failing grade on the project."*

"Rules say you aren't supposed to go alone." She circled closer.

He picked through the dirt. "Rules say you're not supposed to go alone with a bondmate."

"You would have ended up half-frozen if I hadn't been there."

"If you hadn't been there, I might not have gotten lost!"

"And to think I came up here to apologize!"

Shar snorted. "Your apologies won't help me pass environmental studies." Reluctantly, he tore his eyes from the ground and looked at her, radiant in the bruised, colored half-light, gauzy skirt flapping in the wind. She granted him only a momentary glance of her gray eyes.

"Fine then." Thriss threaded her arms across her chest and jumped up onto a boulder sitting beside the spring. She began crossing to the opposite side, jumping sprightly from rock to rock with balletic grace. Her shimmering hair, blown by the wind, strayed across her face and she threw back her head, gazing up at the darkening sky. She closed her eyes, slightly arching her back, and threw open her arms, embracing the imminent storm.

Shar watched the gentle rise and fall of her breathing. He swallowed hard and looked away.

A shadow crossed over. A violent clap of thunder announced the storm. Raindrops pelted the earth, sending up clouds of pink dust from the pathway. The stony metallic scent of rain on hot canyon rock drenched the air.

Thriss laughed, cupping her palms to capture the rain.

"Get down from there!" Shar ordered.

"Why should I?"

"Because you'll be soaked, that's why, and I refuse to accept the blame when you come down with a raging case of zhem!" Sloshing across the stream, he tamped down the impulse to yell. A loss of control would only exacerbate this situation. He refused to yield the upper hand to petulant Thriss because that was precisely what she wanted. Reaching for her wrists, he encircled them with his thumb and forefinger. He tugged gently; she might be equal to him in height, but he was stronger than she.

Refusing to budge, she said, "You come up here." Her eyes danced playfully.

"Thriss—!" he warned loudly, his voice muted by the rain's plip-plop chatter.

"I think you'll find the view is quite lovely from here."

He followed her gaze to the billowing dark clouds, backlit by flashes of lightning. A stray bolt leapt out, igniting dry scrub growing in canyon rock crevices. Flames greedily devoured the parched wood, leaving behind steaming, charred carcasses.

The flash sent the nerves of his antennae tingling almost painfully. Exasperated, Shar yanked her down. Thriss lost her footing on the algae-covered rock and she slipped forward, sending them both tumbling into the water.

Bracing herself over him, Thriss sputtered, pushing sodden tendrils out of her face. She narrowed her eyes. "You always have to have your way."

"We wouldn't be here—I wouldn't be here—if you knew how to stay out of my life!"

"Your life?" Throwing back her head, she laughed grimly. "Fine. I'll go." She struggled to her feet, trying to untangle her limbs from her sopping clothes as she walked. A misplaced foot caught on her hem and she tripped, landing facedown in the shallow spring. Weakly, she pushed up on her elbows.

"Thriss!" Shar scrambled over to her side. Ignoring her halfhearted protests, he hooked her by the arm and eased her to her feet. She stiffened at his touch, jerking away as soon as they reached the bank. Shar's fears for her well-being persisted until he was satisfied that she sustained only scratches and bruises from her fall. He exhaled raggedly.

Assuming she would resist his help, Shar threw an immovable arm around her *waist, guiding her inside the cavern where he'd left his pack. Thriss perched on a rock while he searched for a survival blanket or dry clothing. Teeth chattering, she crossed her arms over her chest, hunched her shoulders and shivered for warmth. Shar dropped down beside her and tended her wounds.*

"You shouldn't have come up here," he said at last.

"I'm sorry," she whispered.

As he mended her scrapes, her shivering evolved into trembling. A sob escaped her throat; Shar knew that she wept often. "Come here," he said, drawing her onto his lap, wrapping her in his arms and pulling her tight against him. He rested his cheek in her hair and rubbed her back. Murmured words from an unknown place inside him settled her. Gradually, her ragged sobs ceased; she hiccupped a few times and then rested her face against his chest with a sigh. Her antennae brushed a ticklish spot beneath his chin.

He didn't feel like laughing.

He became sensitized to her hands resting on the small of his back, the way she curved into him, molding her body against his. Taking her chin in his hand, he tipped her face up. For as long as he had memories, she was in them. Difficult, childish, lanky . . . sweet-smelling like challorn *flowers, hair gossamer soft and her eyes—her stormy eyes swallowed him. Exploring the velvet hollows of her throat with his fingertips, he felt her pulse quicken as he traced the edge of her collarbone with his thumb. He stared.*

Thriss held Shar's look, loosened the tie on her blouse, pushed back the wet, clinging fabric, pulling it down to puddle around her waist. He reached for her and hesitated, knowing her apparition would dissolve with his touch as it always did in his dreams. Until she placed his hand on her chest and he felt the warmth of her skin against his palm. Startled by her realness, he pulled away, wincing upon losing his connection with her.

I need her. *He received this revelation with the same faith that allowed him to understand the revolution of planets and the nature of light.* I need her.

He fumbled with his tunic. With shaking fingers, Thriss, too, clutched at his clothing, but her clumsiness matched his own. Pressing foreheads together they shared an awkward laugh. Hands linked, they yanked his tunic over his head and tossed it on the ground.

They pressed close, antennae touching, stroking, until trembling cascaded over them. He nestled her back against his chest, embedding each delicate vertebra into his skin; his hands settled on the slope of her hips, caressed the curve, and stroked the small of her back. She reached her arms behind her, drawing his face into her neck, knotting her fingers in his locks. All that he had been taught and warned about dissolved into languid twilight. She had been given to him, and he to her. And he accepted at last what elemental thing had been between them since their memories began.

A chime started Shar awake. His eyes opened and he found himself sitting in front of the main console of the *Sagan*. At last check, it had been close to dawn; now, it was four hours later. The vaguest sense that he was forgetting something lingered in the back of his mind.

"Model complete," the ship's computer intoned. *"Image available upon request."*

"Display," Shar ordered. Maybe seeing the model would help jar his memory about which of the three or four data files he'd been working on before he fell asleep. Sleeping was counterproductive, especially when his vivid dreams left him wondering what reality he was in.

I wonder if the others ever suspected. It isn't like I wear a visible mark, he thought. Recollections of intimacies shared with Thriss often dredged up guilt. Though he'd never regretted the choice to initiate *tezha,* he knew Anichent and Dizhei would be hurt by their choice to go outside the bond. Not only because it was forbidden but also because their choice implied infidelity to the bond as a whole. Over the last six years, Shar had gradually recognized that he would eventually face consequences for breaking the covenant. Anichent would feel betrayed. Dizhei would fear for the stability of the bond. But Shar was confident they could surmount these obstacles. *I've maintained strong, healthy relationships with all my bondmates,* Shar reasoned. *I love them all and I anticipate sharing my life with them for many years to come.*

He considered this latest holographic model of Yrythny DNA. Since his trip to the peninsula, Shar had worked, day and night, processing the data by utilizing the Andorian gene-mapping strategies he was familiar with to develop models. Thankfully, he had enough Wanderer data to track the subtle nuances of their genetic drift. Houseborn information was spottier. The samples from the Assembly and those the Hebshu farmers had managed to collect from their Houseborn colleagues provided Shar enough reference points from the past with which to compare current data.

Identifying primary gene functions had been his first priority. Once the chromosomal architecture had been adequately mapped, Shar began tracking mutations and the consequences of those mutations. The computer had spent the night comparing Wanderer samples, synthesizing generalizations about where mutations occurred and what consequences resulted. If there proved to be a pattern, Shar would project future drift and see what conclusions could be drawn.

"Computer, display results from Yrythny data analysis ch'Thane Beta four."

So far, the results hadn't yielded many surprises. In the genes governing intelligence, both Wanderer and Houseborn Yrythny had equal potential. Similar results cropped up in areas of physical strength and health. More distinctions existed on the Houseborn side between Houses. *What am I not seeing?* Shar thought, frustrated. *There's something right here in front of me and I'm not seeing it.*

"Shar?" Lieutenant Dax said, climbing through the entry hatch.

His nagging sense of forgetting vanished when he remembered the imminent trip planetside for Homecoming. "Yes, Lieutenant. I'm here."

"We missed you at breakfast," Dax said, clicking open a locker and tossing a shoulder bag inside.

"We?"

"We, Ensign." Keren entered behind Dax, with Vice Chair Jeshoh bringing up the rear.

"Oh. I didn't realize we'd have company, Lieutenant."

"Keren and Jeshoh did chair the committees I worked with. It's only fitting that they come as co-presenters. Besides, Jeshoh is House Perian's favorite son. We're VIPs when we travel with him." Dax slid into the seat beside Shar. "How's the research coming?"

Shar hesitated. He didn't want to reveal any strategy Ezri might be still trying to protect.

"Speak freely, Ensign," Dax said, evidently surmising his reservations. "I doubt your study will change much at this point."

Unfortunately, she's right, Shar thought regretfully. "On the face of things, the data indicate that the Yrythny, generally, don't have a lot to differentiate them. Statistically significant variations exist within the body of Houseborn data and the body of Wanderer data, but not between Houseborn and Wanderer."

"See, Jeshoh, I told you that I was your equal," Keren teased.

"You can say it, but I don't believe it," Jeshoh retorted.

"What's next?" Ezri asked, thumbing through Shar's results on her own viewscreen.

"Projecting the long-term genetic drift. Mapping the likely mutations and the probable outcome of those mutations. I expect to complete the analysis by tonight."

"Excellent. Keep me posted." Dax leaned close enough to Shar that only he could hear her. "I know you had a lot invested in this project, and you've done superior work. Don't beat yourself up about not finishing in time. The Assembly is happy with the compromise I proposed. I think we've succeeded in helping the Yrythny."

Eyes straight ahead, Shar said politely, "As you say, sir."

Dax turned to the passengers in the aft seats. "Strapped in?"

Keren and Jeshoh answered affirmatively.

"All right, then. Ensign, prepare for launch."

"Yes, sir," Shar acknowledged. "Luthia launch control, this is shuttle *Sagan* requesting clearance for takeoff."

"Shuttle Sagan, *you are clear for launch."*

For Shar, knowing he was going to Vanìmel for the last time felt bittersweet. Vaughn and the *Defiant* would return tomorrow, prepared to resume their explorations. Dax's assurances aside, he berated himself for failing to accomplish his personal goals. He ought to be satisfied with the away team's work; they'd all played a role in Ezri's diplomatic efforts. Her proposed compromise was logical, if not particularly original. If the committees' response indicated how the Yrythny, as a whole, would respond, her ideas would be well received. But he could have done more. *I should have done more,* Shar thought. *After all we've been through, this can't be all.*

In the days since they left the Consortium, all crewmen had worked on their designated pieces of Vaughn's plan and now, they waited. Experience had taught Vaughn not to be impatient. All hell would break loose soon enough. In the last hour, the finer points of the femtobot defense had been finalized. Though engineering wasn't his forte, he found Leishman's report fascinating, including the successful synthesis of a particle fountain metal with a Federation alloy.

Excitedly, Rahim called from his station, "I've got them, Captain."

Vaughn looked up from the padd he'd been studying. "Let's hear it."

The bridge officer hurriedly tapped in a few commands. "Compensating for radiant interference, audio feed—"

"—*when the shuttle with our payment leaves the* Avaril, *it will also carry the alien's chief technologist, Nog. You'll need him to translate the specifications into a working device.*"

"This is from the *Avaril?*" Vaughn asked.

Rahim nodded.

Vaughn knew from time with J'Maah that the subspace channel hosting the transmission wasn't a usual Yrythny frequency. *So we are dealing with a conspirator. J'Maah will be a sitting duck.*

"*What are we supposed to do with him?*" a metallic Cheka voice reverberated through the bridge.

"*Once he's built the cloak, you can do with him as you please. It's of no consequence to us.*"

"Can we identify the vocal patterns?" Vaughn asked. If he could figure out who the traitor was, he might be able to send a covert communiqué to J'Maah before the deal went down.

Rahim apologized. "No, sir. I've already had to modify the audio to work with our decryption algorithms."

A small price to pay for confirmation, he thought.

The channel clicked off, but Vaughn had gained a clear visual of how the pieces would move across the chessboard. He touched his combadge. "Vaughn to Permenter."

"*Go ahead.*"

"Have you ever heard of a noisemaker, Ensign? The tactical variety?"

He could hear her hesitation.

"I'll be right down. I have another project for you. Vaughn out. Sam, you have the bridge."

Bowers looked up from his console. "Noisemaker, sir?"

Vaughn paused at the door. "If this plays out the way I think it will, the *Avaril* will be completely vulnerable when the Yrythny conspirators initiate the trade with the Cheka. We have to make it as hard as possible for them to attack the *Avaril*—or at least improve the odds. I've had quite enough of playing by their rules." Vaughn knew he spoke for every member of the crew. *Time to blow the lid off this con game.*

Sidestepping a group of servants carrying large bins overloaded with fish, Shar ducked beneath an awning and waited for them to pass. He fingered the padd in his pocket, longing for a minute to sit down and review his research data.

He'd downloaded the rudiments of his study to carry with him, anticipating that the evening's official schedule would allow him plenty of work time. Besides Ezri, most of the major government players were slated to speak; if they resembled most officials, they would have lengthy, repetitive and self-aggrandizing rhetoric to propagate. Considering he more or less knew what would be said, he felt no guilt about using the time more effectively.

As he approached the end of the walkway, Shar realized he was lost. He had taken a left turn at the Fountain Triad, passed by the servants' quarters and circled back along the north boardwalk to the plaza. Keren had instructed him to meet her near the entrance to the Colonnade, the facility hosting the evening festivities. Instead, Shar arrived at the end of his walk facing a black sea wall marking the narrow alleyway running behind the residents' wing. From what he'd seen of House Perian, little if any logic had gone into the design. The original House had been built three thousand years ago—the plaza had been at the center. Three millennia had allowed time for the natives to add on the accoutrements of modern life from a marina to a shuttleport to aquaculture outbuildings. Over the course of the afternoon, Shar had seen most of Perian but had yet to retrace his steps. He turned around, looked up to see if Keren might be descending one of the outer staircases or if he could recognize any landmarks. A cluster of Yrythny emerged from the alleyway; Shar approached them. "Excuse me, but I'm looking for the Colonnade."

The tallest in the group, an Yrythny who reminded Shar of Jeshoh, laughed heartily. "You're all turned about, stranger. We're headed there ourselves. You're welcome to walk with us."

"Thank you," Shar said, hoping this group was headed directly for the Colonnade and not eventually to the Colonnade by way of the café, the apartments or the docks. He followed alongside, seeking to regain his bearings. After walking a short distance, Shar recognized a familiar landmark and relaxed. "I'm Thirishar, by the way," he introduced himself. "But most call me Shar."

"I'm Nensoh, these are my friends Dernah and Spetsoh. I assumed from the look of you that you're part of the alien delegation from Luthia. Your hair is astonishing."

Shar had discovered his hair inordinately fascinated the Yrythny. "Do you live here?" Shar racked his brain for other questions one asked when making polite conversation. He doubted the finer points of chromosomal architecture would interest this trio.

"Only during the summer. To help with the farming. During the winter, I serve on a starship," Nensoh explained. "I'm home because my consort and I will go into the water. Here we are."

The group emerged onto the open square, crowded with Yrythny waiting for admission to the Colonnade. Shar split off from his Yrythny escorts, knowing if he followed them into the throng, he'd never find Keren. "Thank you, Nensoh!" Shar yelled over the cacophonous crowd. He waved farewell.

Puckering his face strangely, Nensoh raised his hand, mimicking the unfamiliar gesture.

And then Shar saw it. The starburst mark.

"Wait!" he called, running after Nensoh.

Nensoh paused when he saw Shar coming toward them. "Shar?"

"The mark on your hand. I've seen it before."

Nensoh shrugged. "It's not unusual. It appears on the palm of a fertile Yrythny as they enter their reproductive period. My guess is, were you to check the palms of all of these Yrythny, most would bear the mark."

Shar nodded absently, his mind racing through questions. The night in Keren's apartment haunted him. In subsequent discussions with Keren, he'd asked about the mark, but she shrugged off his concerns, believing Shar had scared off the invader and thus any potential threat. At least the mark's commonness made it less likely that Keren was protecting a specific individual. Still . . .

"Thirishar! Over here!"

Seeking Keren's faint voice, he narrowed her location to the fringes of the plaza. He squinted, discerning that she had climbed up onto a bench, enabling him to see her over the tall Yrythny. Fixing his bearings on her location, he wormed his way in and out of the tight, packed-in crowds, relieved to emerge from the claustrophobic gathering. Before he could greet her, she jumped down and said, "We can't stay. There's an emergency."

"What is it?" He followed her away from the plaza, jogging toward the seaside path.

"Jeshoh contacted me. The Perian authorities believe the mating grounds are being raided. They'll be launching the patrols as soon as they can, but all the visitors have blocked the harbor with their watercraft."

Damn. Without hesitation, Shar tapped his combadge. "Ch'Thane to Dax. We have an emergency."

With the first moon hidden behind clouds and the second still rising over the mountains, there was little natural illumination as the *Sagan,* once again carrying Shar, Dax, Keren and Jeshoh, came within visual range of their targets.

"Increase resolution," Ezri ordered.

Shar tapped in a few commands, sharpening the visual sensors' acuity by compensating for the diminished light.

Within the small screen on Shar's console, three hovercraft skimmed in and out of the reed patches of the mating grounds while another paused in the very thick of the sea grasses. Shar zoomed in on a cloaked figure leaning over the railing, plunging a long pole, with a net attached at the end, into the water. Beside him, another cloaked figure thrust the nose of a long tube into the reeds, pumping a handle mounted on the end.

"Clever," Jeshoh muttered. "I'll wager they're spraying the reeds with tetracoxiclan to melt the adhesive seal between the reeds and the egg sacs."

"Second one follows behind with the net and scoops them out of the water," Keren said, finishing his thought. "But who among us would steal fertilized eggs?" She frowned, disgusted.

"Computer, identify life-forms in Vanìmel sector zero-four-seven," Ezri said.

"Eighteen Yrythny life-forms in grid zero-four-seven."

Imagining the anguish his own people endured while trying to procreate successfully, Shar was struck by how having an abundance of offspring shifted one's paradigm. Wondering about the reasons behind such a choice, he asked, "Why would Yrythny want to strip eggs from the mating ground?"

"Why would Yrythny blow up an aquaculture village?" Keren countered. "It's a mind game. With House Perian hosting the Compromise announcement, the eyes of Luthia and Vanìmel are focused on this hemisphere tonight. Stage it well and they'll have the attention of every Yrythny."

"Not if I have anything to say about it," Dax said firmly. She turned to Shar. "Options, Ensign?"

He'd been mulling over how to immobilize the raiders since they'd arrived. "It seems simple enough. The Perian authorities will be arriving here within the hour. In the meantime, we immobilize the hovercraft, secure the eggs in our custody and hold the criminals for the proper authorities."

Ezri nodded her approval. "Disable their engines with phasers. Make it impossible for them to move anywhere. They're far enough from shore that they can't swim to land. We'll beam-out the eggs. Proceed, Ensign."

"Aye, sir," Shar said. "Targeting phasers."

The cloaked figures on the first hovercraft scrambled for cover from the phaser fire, waving their arms to clear away the smoke churning out of the rear of the craft. Sensors indicated phasers had destroyed the engine and caused a minor water leak. But the authorities would arrive before the hovercraft sank.

Shar repeated the process, disabling both remaining hovercraft within minutes of each other. The fourth one, trying to avoid its companions' fate, led them on a brief chase; the hovercraft was no match for a Starfleet shuttle.

Circling the area in the *Sagan,* Shar double-checked sensors to make certain that no other raider craft had entered the area. Save the official vessel coming from Perian, the seas were clear.

"What about the eggs?" Jeshoh asked finally.

"We'll beam them out now," Ezri said.

Shar's scans revealed that only one vessel had successfully stripped eggs out of the mating grounds. Ezri beamed out the small storage crates and went with Keren to the rear of the shuttle to secure and properly store their cargo. Allowing viable eggs to be damaged now would be unconscionable.

Programming an elliptical trajectory around the mating grounds, Shar switched the navigating systems to auto and focused on keeping track of the criminals trapped on the hovercraft. Making a meaningful contribution to the final leg of their away mission satisfied him deeply. He hadn't wanted to admit it to Lieutenant Dax, but he did feel like his research efforts had been for naught. While rescuing fertilized Yrythny eggs from unscrupulous raiders didn't equate with making a scientific discovery that might have changed the planet's destiny, he would savor his small victory.

From around a peninsula jutting into the bay, a Perian hovership churned into the mating ground. Shar dispatched a directional flare, pointing the authorities to where the disabled hovercraft bobbed in the water.

"Shuttlecraft *Sagan* to the Perian authorities. There are four unauthorized hovercraft in the area. Transmitting locations of craft to you now. We have secured the harvested eggs and will be returning them to House Perian."

"Acknowledged, Sagan. *We have received your transmission. See you back home."*

Shar tapped Perian's coordinates into the navigation panel when Jeshoh touched his arm. "What can I do—" his voice trailed off at the sight of an Yrythny sidearm trained on his head. Jeshoh held the weapon flush against his chest, obscuring it from Dax and Keren's view. From the rear of the shuttle, Shar heard the women rearranging equipment to accommodate the eggs. They talked quietly between themselves.

"These crates belong to an acquaintance of mine," Jeshoh whispered. "We're going to deliver them. I'll provide you with coordinates. Once we clear Vanìmel's gravity well, you will set course as I direct and go to warp. We're running late, so please don't pull any tricks to provoke me into shooting you or Lieutenant Dax."

Locking out his adrenaline surge, Shar nodded. *Where does Jeshoh fit into the puzzle? I've never sensed hostility from him. He's Houseborn, what could he possibly want? Unless . . .* He wanted one answer before surrendering to Jeshoh's control. "Show me your hand."

Jeshoh smiled, raised his left arm to the square, palm forward.

The blue starburst.

"It was you in Keren's apartment that night," Shar whispered. "That's why she wasn't concerned afterward. Why would you be there . . . unless . . ." Wide-eyed, Shar stared at Jeshoh, his antennae tense with understanding.

"I went there to protect her, as I always have," he said wistfully. "We've chosen each other as consorts. Didn't she tell you that we were raised together? She swam ashore at House Perian."

"I assumed you met at the Assembly." Shar recalled the many hours he'd worked side by side with Keren and Jeshoh over the past week, their easy familiarity, their gentle ribbing. All of it fit together now.

"We can work together and no one looks askance if we're alone. But even that has become risky." Jeshoh sighed. "Our last hope was your people."

"My work's not done yet," Shar tried persuading him. "We still might have a chance. I can go back to Perian, work through the night—"

"We're out of chances. Time to leave," he said, resolutely.

Ezri called from the back, "Why are we gaining altitude? The ceremony starts in twenty minutes and I'm not sure how long these eggs can remain viable out of the water."

Uncertain as to what action Jeshoh would take, Shar said nothing as he entered the coordinates the Vice Chair whispered to him.

"Is there a problem, Ensign?" Ezri said at last.

Jeshoh and Shar exchanged looks. Shar kept silent.

The locks on the crate lids clicked from the rear of the shuttle. Shar heard Keren's light footsteps as she walked back to her seat. Ezri followed after. He sensed Keren pause and he willed her to take her seat. But she waited and Shar felt her studying him from behind.

"That worried, Ensign?" she said, her gruff voice laden with emotion.

Involuntarily, Shar raised a hand to his crown, realizing his antennae had become taut. She approached, her footfalls slow.

"Shar, what's going on?"

Shar sensed Ezri's irritation; heard her press past Keren, felt her step between him and Jeshoh. Her hands dropped to her sides. The lieutenant took a deep, steadying breath and she stood rigid.

Keren's hand curled over the top of Jeshoh's chair, her fingers trembling. "You have a weapon, Jeshoh."

Jeshoh said nothing.

"I've never known you to carry a weapon, and yet you have that sidearm pointed at Shar."

"I'm defending something, Keren. I'm defending our right to have a life together."

She became visibly pale, shaking as she tried to maintain her control, even as her words became choked with sobs. "You were at the meeting—you agreed with me that the radicals' plan could destroy everything we've worked for. Please tell me you didn't join them, Jeshoh!"

Jeshoh turned his sidearm on Ezri; her eyes darted between Shar and Jeshoh. "You," he pointed at Ezri, "you take my seat."

She complied.

"If you do this, Jeshoh, we could lose it all. Nothing has to change. We can continue our struggle honorably," Keren pleaded.

"That's where you're wrong, my love. Without change, we have no future."

"Where are you taking us?" Ezri asked.

The shuttle had cleared the atmosphere. Cold starry space awaited outside the viewport.

"You'll find out soon enough," was Jeshoh's reply, and once again he turned his weapon on Shar. "Prepare to go to warp."

As Vaughn anticipated, the Cheka warship maintained a direct intercept course with the *Avaril*, a fact that satisfied him; he enjoyed a predictable adversary. True to Bowers's original estimate, the Cheka warship would intercept *Avaril's* meeting tonight, five hours out from Vanìmel. *"Meeting" is probably the wrong word*, Vaughn thought. *More like an "ambush."* The *Defiant* would level the playing field. He conceded there was a slim chance that the Yrythny leadership had masterminded Nog's kidnapping, but his gut told him Chieftain J'Maah would be caught unawares when the Cheka finally showed up. Bowers continued to monitor communications from both the *Avaril* and the Cheka warship, hoping that additional information would be revealed.

Meanwhile, the crew of the *Defiant* worked; no one had any desire to leave much to chance.

For the full shift before the showdown, every crewmember perfected his or her roles. Vaughn had walked about, first observing Chief Chao's transporter simulations, moving along to Prynn who studied the lay of the sector the *Defiant* would be flying through. Together, they visited the database for ideas to make evasive maneuvers more effective. On the bridge, Bowers analyzed every snippet of data the sensors revealed about the Cheka warship to devise their strategy. Lankford, one of their conn officers, upgraded the *Defiant*'s navigational database with the starcharts purloined from the Cheka with, among other things, web weapon locations. Vaughn admired the crew's single-minded intensity.

Foremost among the single-minded was engineering. Nog's team had been assigned the most critical tasks. Ensigns Permenter, Senkowski and Leishman had hid out in a lab, working with surprising focus considering their long hours over the past twelve days. Or maybe their dedication wasn't surprising: they worked on behalf of their beloved chief.

Permenter had quickly taken to the idea of a noisemaker, once Vaughn had explained the twentieth- and twenty-first-century tactic.

"So when an aircraft or a submarine was targeted with a missile, a noisemaker was released, tricking the missile into fixing on the noisemaker instead of the intended target?" she had reasoned.

"Exactly," Vaughn had answered, pleased that she'd readily caught on to the idea.

"In this case, we want the *Avaril*'s shuttle to be the noisemaker." She had chewed her fingernails absently. "Trying to trick the Cheka into thinking that they're seeing two *Avarils*. Mess with their sensors. Possibly project a false visual."

"Again correct. Can you do it?"

She had nodded. "Yes . . . But you realize the real *Avaril* could still be attacked."

"In a situation like this, I'll take fifty-fifty odds over a hundred percent any day."

"Good point, sir," Permenter had agreed. "I'll get right on it."

Vaughn had smiled as he left engineering. *Whether we rescue Nog—whether the* Avaril *survives—may come down to how good they are at their jobs. They'll want to make him proud.*

Vaughn continued surveying the ship, stem to stern; he wasn't looking for anything specific, more like feeling his way around, renewing his acquaintance with an old friend. When the battle began, he needed to know who he was in the trenches with, to trust her without hesitation. Should the Cheka ship suddenly attack or if the *Avaril* proved to be a foe, Vaughn was prepared to go on the offensive. *Defiant* needed to be prepared for whatever she faced, for good or ill.

Quiet pervaded; all crewmembers soberly focused. If Vaughn was right, they had one chance at rescuing Nog. One chance. No one wanted to be the reason they lost another friend. Roness's loss over the Vahni homeworld was still fresh in their hearts and minds.

Having finished his review of the lower decks, Vaughn circled by transporter bay 1 where Chao rechecked the system, and then on to the bridge. He replicated a cup of *raktajino,* took his place in the captain's chair, and waited with the rest of them.

Because Shar had programmed the coordinates into the flight controls, Jeshoh rotated Ezri and Shar between piloting duties, anticipating that frazzled nerves might "accidentally" send them off course. Ezri had lost track of the number of hours they'd been flying, but she knew that dawn on Vanìmel was imminent.

When Ezri exchanged places with Shar, he immediately buried his attention in his padds. She couldn't fathom what he'd be working on at a time like this—or how he could focus. *If only I had access to weapons! I'm an excellent shot and could take Jeshoh down in nothing flat.* At the outset, she'd agreed to travel and work unarmed. Personal phasers were locked up in one of the shuttle's aft storage lockers. With little else to do, she eavesdropped on the interplay between the two Yrythny. Ezri wondered why she hadn't pegged them as lovers. Maybe her sense about such things was backfiring on her. She kept her eyes on her console, listening as Jeshoh tried, once more, to lure Keren into a conversation.

"Sending the Wanderers away to colonies won't solve our problem," he argued. "We still can't be together. Isn't that why we joined the underground? To find a way we can be together?"

"Orchestrating terrorist attacks on aquaculture villages won't solve our problems either," she hissed. "Nor will trading eggs to the Cheka for weapons to use against the Houseborn. When the Cheka steal our offspring, you're outraged. But now you sacrifice our young to our enemies?"

"We've sought to change our world since we were younglings. We vowed to do whatever was necessary, to make whatever sacrifice was required. This is the required sacrifice, Keren. These eggs aren't ours. They belong to those who deny us our chance to have offspring. We owe them nothing."

"This trade offers no hope for my people. Or for us," Keren said.

Ezri listened as the argument volleyed back and forth, until Keren refused to respond to Jeshoh's pleas. If only she'd anticipated this, she might have been able to work something into the treaty about the Houseborn-Wanderer taboos. *Dangerous relationships were a Dax specialty,* she thought wryly. Hadn't she been willing to accept the consequence of reassociation to be with Lenara? The torrid, consuming kind of love—that kind of passion—prompted the most irrational behavior.

"Lieutenant," Shar whispered. "I think I've got it."

Dax turned and saw Shar's antennae trembling with excitement. *The boy will never be a poker player.* "You've got what, Shar?"

"A preliminary genetic answer. But it will only help these two if Jeshoh can be convinced to forgo the trade."

"Pass it over," she ordered, taking the padd from Shar. Only a little of Jadzia's scientific training had been in genetics, but she knew enough to interpret Shar's data. He was absolutely correct: these findings were nothing short of astonishing.

Extrapolating the future path of genetic drift for both the Wanderers and the Houseborn, Shar's models predicted that selective mutations in Wanderer DNA indicated that they, not the Houseborn, were the next step in Yrythny evolution. The creativity and cleverness that made them innovative artists and engineers coupled with their ability to adapt to the environment ensured long-term survival.

On the other side, lacking the resilience of the Wanderers (and because of heavy interbreeding), Houseborn DNA would weaken over time, bringing on problems not unlike those now facing the Andorians. Over the generations, the Houseborn would become vulnerable to chromosomal maladies that would spell their end as a species.

The solution, ironically, was that intermating among Houseborn and Wanderers would create the genetic diversity the Yrythny species needed to survive. If present taboos and traditions continued—Wanderer sterilization, the Houseborn narrowing of the gene pool, Wanderer females not being allowed to reproduce—the Yrythny would spiral toward extinction. In fact, a reasonable conclusion was that the "Wanderer traits" were appearing precisely in order to ensure the Yrythny's survival as a species.

"This is incredible, Shar," Ezri whispered.

Shar nodded his head, appearing very pleased.

A sensor went off on Ezri's board. *Sagan* was rapidly approaching two much larger vessels. One seemed to be the *Avaril*. The other—

"The Cheka," Keren moaned.

"You have to tell them," Shar whispered to Ezri.

"Tell us what?" Jeshoh said.

"Shar's research," Ezri said, holding up the padd. "This is the answer you've been looking for." *Please let this be enough to put a stop to this insanity.*

"Not offworld colonization, Lieutenant?" Jeshoh said, cynically, walking toward Ezri. "What about the magnificent compromise you negotiated with such skill among my fellow Assemblymen? Peace at last for Vanìmel! All the Wanderers have to do is leave."

"It's colonization, not exile!" Ezri insisted. "There are many cultures in my part of the galaxy where those unhappy with the status quo start over again somewhere else. Earth, Vulcan—" She stopped herself, knowing the names would be meaningless to Jeshoh. "The point is that colonization has often been the most viable solution to the kind of dilemma facing the Yrythny, and it's *always* been a better option than genocide."

"Are you trying to convince me or yourself, Lieutenant?" Jeshoh asked. "If the former, then how is it that you now believe the answers we've been looking for are on that little device?"

Ezri sighed and shut her eyes. "Because even though colonization is a better option than genocide, *this* is a better option than colonization." Keying the padd to display the text in Yrythny, Ezri passed the padd to Jeshoh.

He perused the results, paging through each section of Shar's research until he reached the end. Tossing the padd on the deck, he laughed. "You expect me to believe this? Days of discussions and analyses come up empty. But in our darkest hour, you hand me research that purports to offer me the very thing Keren and I have been fighting for? It's a hoax. It has to be."

Ezri bit her lip. "The lateness of the research is partially my fault. I wasn't as supportive as I should have been in helping Ensign ch'Thane pursue his study."

"So you say now, Lieutenant," Jeshoh said.

"Persuade him, Ezri," Shar urged.

"I appreciate your efforts, Shar," Jeshoh said with a sigh. "Your heart is well aligned, but the Cheka are going to get their eggs, the blockade will end, the underground will receive arms, and the fight between the Houseborn and the Wanderers will finally be a fair one. Proceed to the rendezvous point." He walked back to his seat, still tightly gripping the sidearm.

As the senior officer, Ezri knew devising a plan fell to her. She considered Shar and Jeshoh, who embodied the extremes of reason and emotion, and puzzled over this impasse. In lieu of a phaser, she could pull out a few Klingon martial arts moves that had worked on a belligerent drunk. Startle Jeshoh. Throw him off his game. But that was Jadzia. Tobin had done that thing with the transporter to defeat a Romulan. Clever enough, but Jeshoh would be dead. She had no desire to kill anyone unless she had no other choice. Torias would do some daredevil flying to throw off his enemy, but then Shar or Keren might be hurt. And . . . Emony . . .

Stop it.

Her head hurt. She massaged her neck against the headrest, wishing away the voices in her mind. Clamoring for attention, the voices talked over one another; she couldn't think straight through the noise.

"Ezri, you're a counselor," Shar whispered anxiously. "Talk him out of it."

She stared at Shar.

Through many lives, Dax had averted crises with clever talk, brilliant (occasionally crazy) technological twists, raw nerve, unhesitating bravery and a few well-placed punches. Of these tools, none were Ezri's, save maybe the bravery. Ezri alone had studied the workings of the mind and it was Ezri who needed to fix this. *Not Curzon. Not Lela. Not Jadzia. Ezri.*

Licking her lips, she took a deep, controlled breath, willing her respirations to steady her. Ezri rolled her head back and forth, stretching her muscles. A class she'd taken on crisis negotiations—what was the procedure? Build a rapport between perpetrator and negotiator. Focus on the perpetrator's needs. The time she'd spent with Jeshoh gave her a powerful advantage. *Responsibility, loyalty and integrity motivated him. Appeal to those traits.* She rose from her seat, resting one hand on each chair.

"Jeshoh, I know you're concerned about reaching the rendezvous on time, but maybe we should take a moment, settle down. Eat? We missed dinner at Perian. The hour is late. I know I'm sleepy. Aren't you a little hungry?"

He turned to Keren. "Are you hungry? Lieutenant Dax could bring you food."

"Thirsty," she conceded. "Something to drink."

He's more concerned about her needs than his own. That's where I have leverage. "Keren, water? Fruit juice?"

"Water is fine," she said.

"Shar, take conn, would you?" Ezri said, and went to replicate Keren's drink. Handing it to her, she said, "You look tired, Keren. Take the copilot's chair." She paused. "If that's all right with you, Jeshoh."

He nodded. A tenderness suffused Jeshoh's face as he watched Keren move to the front.

Assuming Keren's seat, Ezri asked Jeshoh, "Are you sure I can't get you anything?"

"Just make sure Ensign ch'Thane takes us to the rendezvous." He refused her attempts to engage him.

Ezri leaned over, speaking so only Jeshoh could hear her. "Keren's exhausted. This day has taken a toll on her."

"We'll be done soon enough."

Now to induce doubt about the viability of his choice. "I wouldn't count on that. You and I have both been in negotiation situations. They can drag on and on." Ezri shrugged, stole a glance at Jeshoh who seemed to be listening. She continued, "Your contact could back out at the last minute—the Cheka could change their minds about the deal and demand higher payment. And then there's the question of how to get back to Vanìmel without the defense forces on Luthia coming after you. We could be on the run for a while."

"We can handle it," he said stubbornly. Distracted, he twirled the weapon around his fingers.

"But if you're on the run, you won't be able to bring the Cheka weapons back to the underground."

Jeshoh hesitated. "We'll find a way."

"And Keren? She doesn't deserve to never be able to return to Vanìmel."

"We would be free. Together."

"Until when? Until my commander and the *Defiant* catches up with you? Until the *Sagan* flies into a Cheka web weapon and you're cooked? And then there's the Yrythny military who will hunt you down."

"When we're done, I'll leave you and Shar somewhere. Your commander can find you."

Ezri watched Keren, flaccid and pale, in the front seat, her chin propped on her hands, her shoulders slumped. *He had to see what his actions were costing her.* Believing she'd found a wedge to pry open Jeshoh's defenses, Ezri resolved to persist. "Oh, I know I'll be fine. And so will Shar, but what about Keren? Look what this situation is doing to her. It's a lot of stress. Especially since I know she's coming into her fertile cycle soon."

"There will be other seasons. If all goes according to plan, next year Keren and I will be able to go into the water together, without hiding."

"If you live that long," Ezri muttered.

"What?"

"Nothing." She considered the flight controls, trying to figure out how much time she had to devise an alternative plan. If she couldn't convince him to give up his scheme willingly, she would use force. At their present course and speed, she guessed they had 10 minutes before circumstances required she act decisively.

"Say it," Jeshoh persisted.

He's listening, at least. I need to keep talking. "The odds are against Keren surviving this adventure you're taking her on. The *Sagan* can't travel indefinitely without refueling. And without energy, life support will dwindle, and the replicators won't work. Then there's the problem of living on the run. The fugitive lifestyle is hard and for you to choose it for her. . . . But I'm certain you'll find a way to make it work." She shrugged and offered him a wan smile.

He fixed his attention on Ezri for a long moment. She remained composed under his scrutiny, saying nothing further.

Without a response, he vacated his seat and approached Shar, though he kept his weapon trained on Ezri. "Shar, a shuttle will launch from the *Avaril*. When the shuttle crosses over from the *Avaril* to the Cheka warship, my contact will instruct us where to transport the eggs."

He's still planning on carrying out the trade, but he doesn't sound quite as confident as he did at the start. Ezri still needed to know how the exchange was supposed to happen. If needs be, at the last minute, she would risk changing courses. "I'm curious—are you going aboard the Cheka ship, Jeshoh?" she said smoothly. "Or are you supposed to transport the eggs to them and they in turn will transport the weapons to you? Or is there another ship that's taking the weapons?"

Jeshoh appeared legitimately startled by Ezri's question. "I—I—I don't know. I was supposed to receive my instructions when I arrived."

"I'm not trying to tell you what to do, but open-ended deals usually end badly. Too much room for a double-cross."

"That won't happen."

"Yeah. But you don't know for sure. Think about Keren, Jeshoh. We should transport her to the *Avaril*. At least she'd have a better chance of getting out of this alive."

Twisting to consider his lover, Jeshoh's weapon hand bobbled. Ezri thought she might be able to wrest it from him, but if she failed, he wouldn't listen to anything else she said. She elected to be patient; the *Sagan*'s cause was better served if she hung back, waited, and watched.

"Shuttlebay doors on *Avaril* are opening," Shar announced.

But not for long. Either Jeshoh would choose or she would.

18

Other than the few naps that interspersed her reading, Kira worked through dawn and into the morning hours, both watching the Promenade cleanup efforts proceed from monitors in ops and reading the negotiation transcripts. Considering the edginess suffusing the station, she was thankful she had an office where she could sequester herself with a desk full of work. The Promenade merchants had contacted her every half hour, wanting updates, complaining about broken merchandise or malfunctioning equipment. Several vedeks had protested in person, resenting the cancellation of shrine services. Parents, spouses, children and lovers affiliated with anyone involved in the fight worried about the well-being of their loved ones. Kira could say, conclusively, that the only people unquestionably happy today were Thriss, whose capable assistance had prompted Dr. Girani to ask if she'd accept regular shift assignments in the infirmary for the duration of her stay, and the children, for whom school had been canceled.

Reports to Akaar and the first minister had gone as well as she could have hoped. While Akaar had focused on the long-term, probable outcomes following such an outpouring of hostility, Shakaar saw the night's disturbance more like a field commander would see any turn of luck that went against his forces, be it bad weather, inaccurate intelligence or unforeseen cunning on the part of the enemy. He went into counterattack mode, immediately strategizing as to how Bajor would hurdle this latest obstacle. His predictable unhappiness increased when he heard the number of Militia personnel involved in the fight. A Militia Internal Affairs officer was ordered to report to Deep Space 9 to review the individual cases. The officer would mete out whatever disciplinary actions were called for, saving Kira from the detestable task. Now that it was approaching noon, she was due to brief Shakaar, in person.

While waiting in the antechamber to his office, Kira made distracting small talk with Sirsy. She had spent the last hour trying to formulate the best way to present what she'd concluded from her night's reading—that Macet's concerns were founded in fact, not supposition. Almost from the start, Asarem's approach had been to block rather than negotiate; she refused to budge on any point, even those already conceded in the postwar Accords.

As soon as Minister Kren exited, Kira ventured in to see Shakaar. With his usual energy, he bounded about his office, loading up a travel bag that lay open on his desk. Monitors running newsfeeds from Bajor and adjoining systems flashed breaking reports on screens lining the walls. From appearances, Shakaar kept continual tabs on many situations.

"Nerys!" he said with a smile. "Come in, come in."

"You're leaving the station?" Kira wondered if the Promenade brawl, combined with the vandalized conference room, had led his advisers to recommend that he return to Bajor until the station situation stabilized. An attack on Shakaar's staff or offices—even worse, an assassination attempt—would send any peace efforts spiraling into a quagmire, possibly even derailing the transition into the Federation. *He would hate having to run from a fight,* Kira thought, remembering how eagerly he plunged into the unknown, dealing with whatever challenges lurked ahead without fear for his own well-being.

"Yes and no. The Federation meetings are in recess, and I've decided to use the opportunity to accept Captain Mello's invitation to tour the *Gryphon* during one of its patrols of the system." He removed several items from his desk—a book, a plain metal case, several isolinear rods—and placed them neatly into his travel bag before he started searching the office for something else. "I expect to return to the station the day after tomorrow."

"Sounds like fun," Kira said, wondering what it was he couldn't find and whether she should help him look. She perused the items scattered over his desk, trying to imagine what a commander-in-chief took along for a visit to inspect the troops, but saw nothing she considered important.

"Anything new from Lieutenant Ro's investigation?" he asked, his voice muffled as he ducked under his desk.

Opening and closing desk drawers, throwing opening cabinets and shuffling through padds, Shakaar never stopped moving. Kira felt dizzy watching him. "It appears the toxic combination of gambling, liquor and rivalry exploded at Quark's. We haven't been able to ascertain who threw the first punch, but it seems that after the initial taunts, it was only a matter of friends coming to the aid of friends. Everything escalated from there. No fatalities, thankfully, but at least two dozen serious injuries." She held out to him the padd she'd brought with her. "You'll find Ro and Dr. Girani's complete reports here. We're keeping all pertinent information out of the main data core until both sides can agree what details are relevant to the station population. Everyone is anxious, sir, as you might imagine."

Shakaar accepted the padd, but didn't look at it. "Understandably. And without any sign of tensions abating soon. You know, Nerys, I was thinking . . ."

"Sir?"

"We've both been working hard. We could use a break. How about joining me at the holosuites for a round of hang gliding off the Cliffs of Bole when I get back from the *Gryphon?*"

Kira snorted indelicately. "I think you've forgotten how much I dislike holosuite adventures, First Minister. I'll have to pass, but thanks for the invitation."

"Nerys, please. We're alone in my office—it's just us. You can call me Edon." He held up the padd Kira had given him and quickly scrolled through the contents. "So Quark agreed to the settlement proposed by Gul Macet and my office?"

"He groused about the *yamok* sauce he lost, but Ro knew he'd been stashing it in a cargo bay for the last six months, so he can't claim it as one of last night's losses." She owed Ro for acting as the intermediary between Quark and her office. If she'd had to deal with Quark's whining on top of everything else today, she might have been here informing Shakaar of another homicide on the station.

Shakaar tossed the padd into his travel bag. "Sounds like you have everything under control, then."

"I hope so, sir," Kira said. She remained standing, fixed in front of his desk, uncertain as to how to transition into the next topic, especially since Shakaar appeared to be done with her. For all her desire to remain uninvolved in the politics surrounding her, she knew the time had come for her, as commander of the station, to voice her concerns about a process that impacted them all. "Minister?" she said at last.

"Yes?" he said, his tone and expression obscure.

Once upon a time, she would have been able to read him. How she lamented the gradual erosion of trust between them! In the past, she could have—would have—come to Shakaar with anything, spoken plainly and known that she wouldn't have been misunderstood. Now, she had no idea what to expect from him. Kira took a deep breath. "While I was waiting for reports to come in over the last eight hours, I took the liberty of reading the transcripts of the negotiations between Ambassador Lang and Minister Asarem."

He didn't appear surprised or concerned. "Haven't yet had the chance myself. How's it going?"

At last, an opening! "I'm glad you asked that, sir."

"Edon, Nerys," he said with a smile.

"Edon," Kira repeated. "To be blunt, I think Minister Asarem's approach is unreasonable."

He looked at her blankly. "You have a basis for that conclusion?"

"I've reviewed the transcripts of the meetings, and it seems very clear to me that the second minister is obstructing the initiatives you began when the war ended, to have Bajor spearhead and coordinate the Cardassian relief efforts."

"How so?"

"Those initiatives were designed to be progressive," Kira reminded him. "We're supposed to be helping Cardassia not just survive the next five years, but get back to being a self-sufficient civilization under its new democratic regime. But everything Asarem is doing seems designed to keep Cardassia crippled and dependent on outside aid indefinitely. I think she's made this personal."

Shakaar's eyebrows went up. "That's a strong accusation, Colonel. What made you look into this?"

The time of reckoning is here, Nerys. Kira made sure Shakaar was looking directly into her eyes before she answered. She needed him to see that she told the truth, that she had no hidden agenda. "Gul Macet asked me to review the transcripts."

"Nerys—"

"I wouldn't be here if I didn't think his concerns had merit."

"To do this right, you shouldn't go around—"

"Old grudges are getting in the way of our delegation's doing its job. The Federation, with cause, could delay our petition again if they think we're not prepared to be forthright in our dealings."

Shakaar frowned. "You haven't taken this to Akaar—"

"Of course not!" she said, indignant at his suggestion.

"Because if you had, Colonel, I'd be questioning your loyalty."

Kira took a deep, steadying breath before answering. "I came to *you* because I've been implementing your initiatives toward Cardassia for the last six months—initiatives I believe in—and I'm seeing the original intent of those initiatives being compromised." She locked eyes with Shakaar. "And more to the point, I came out of my own sense of right and wrong. And what Asarem is doing is *wrong.*"

They lingered in uncomfortable silence until Shakaar at last said, "You're right and I apologize for overreacting. It's just that knowing who your friends and enemies are these days is harder than ever."

No one knows that better than me, Kira thought. *So which are you, Edon?*

Shakaar, however, seemed to feel that they'd resolved their disagreement; he smiled pleasantly. "Send the meeting transcripts to Sirsy for my database. I'll look into the matter personally."

Relief washed over Kira. "Thank you, sir."

"No need for that. I realize what you must think of Minister Asarem, but you have to know she's an absolute patriot. Her love for Bajor is as deep as yours. While she may seem harsh and inflexible, she stands on equal footing with you in terms of her loyalty. Separating her personal views on the Cardassian question from the need for political expediency has always been a struggle for her. I think you two are more alike than you know."

Kira winced involuntarily at the comparison, thinking of the rigid, inflexible politician she had observed, what was it, only yesterday? It felt like an eternity ago. *Maybe once I was like Asarem. Maybe it's true if you still think of me as I once was. Now, I don't think you know me.* Edon would never see the subtle distinctions. "I'll go, then. If there's nothing else . . . ?"

Shakaar waved her out the door, and as he had said, Minister Asarem had arrived for her meeting. An unspoken greeting passed between the women. Kira hoped that in the future, likely after the talks had wrapped up, she could get to know Asarem as the well-intentioned woman Kira knew she must be. Until then, politeness would have to suffice.

Later in the day, when word came from Macet that Minister Asarem's office had proposed resuming talks the following morning, Kira exulted. To celebrate, she left ops early, planning on rewarding herself with an hour at the spa for a mineral soak. It pleased her to walk through the Promenade, now bustling with normal activity. Particularly gratifying was seeing the long lines waiting for admission to the grand opening of the Ziyal exhibit. For the first time since the Cardassians' arrival, Kira felt hopeful.

Once she arrived back in her quarters, she opened up her next day's schedule and cleared out a block of time where she could sit in on the talks. Not so she could gloat, or take credit for helping to break through a seemingly insurmountable barrier. Kira wanted to be there so she could one day tell her grandchildren about how she witnessed the day when Cardassia and Bajor began forging a fragile peace.

As a man of action, waiting was never Quark's strength. Under circumstances such as these, he failed to understand why he, Chairman of the Promenade Merchants' Association, wouldn't be given due deference, VIP admission, a priority position. One of the downfalls of Federation philosophy that Bajor was so hot on embracing was the misguided notion that social status should, for the most part, be irrelevant. Otherwise, he'd be at the front of the line instead of waiting with all the other plebeians to see the exhibit.

And who decided *not* to charge admission? Talk about a missed opportunity. Maybe he could come up with a promotional tie-in for the bar. *Hmmmmm . . .*

On the plus side, the longer he waited, the more time he had to spend with Laren. She wasn't in a terribly talkative mood tonight, not like he could blame her after breaking up a midnight riot and subsequently having little or no sleep. She seemed content to watch the people in line instead of gazing at him. He needed to fix that.

"Um, Laren?"

"Yeah, Quark?"

"Thanks again for getting everything paid for. There was no way I was going to ask Rom to float me a loan while I argued with the colonel." Gratitude, real or feigned, tended to grease the conversational wheels.

"It didn't take much convincing. I think part of her regrets the way she treated you that night at the reception. But paying the repair bills for the fracas is as close to an apology as you're likely to get."

Quark held up his hands. "I'm not complaining. As nonapologies go, I could do worse."

"Expecting coverage for the *yamok* sauce was pushing it, though."

"A Ferengi can try. The 10th Rule of Acquisition: *Greed is eternal.* I wouldn't be me without it." He grinned amiably. "So you got me the latinum. You have any pull with making this line move?"

"You complain about waiting again, I'm going home."

"Right, right," Quark said quickly. No need to make his tired and cranky companion more tired and cranky.

The line trudged forward a few steps, brushing against the line ropes as another group was admitted to the exhibit. A pile of program cards outlining the exhibit's contents sat in a stack. Ro removed one and began reading while they walked.

When they stopped again, Ro turned to Quark and studied him thoughtfully. "You knew Ziyal, didn't you? Who was she?"

In his mind, Quark conjured up a picture of the wide-eyed child-woman. He wasn't one to be sentimental about much—life and death happened in the course of business—but Ziyal had a genuine sweetness that couldn't help but touch you. "She was a good kid. Really. Good isn't generally a word I use to describe Cardassians—ruthless, cold, predatory, devious—all qualities I can appreciate, to be sure—but good? Except Natima, and you already know she's amazing.

But, Ziyal. She was special. Never could figure out how a bastard like Dukat popped off a kid like her." Quark *tsked* as he thought of the former prefect.

"What do you remember most?" Ro asked.

"She called me 'Sir' or 'Quark,' instead of 'Hey you, Ferengi,' like most Cardassians. She'd sit on her stool, talking with Jake or the colonel—even drink root beer with him—and they'd yammer on about holovids and games and such." Had it only been a few years since she died? It felt like another lifetime when all of them had been together on the station . . . Jadzia, Odo, Rom, Leeta, O'Brien, Captain Sisko, Jake, and . . . Quark stopped. No, Ziyal had her weakness. "The only thing she did that didn't make much sense was falling for Garak. If Ziyal was good, Garak was just wrong. You could never really trust him, except to be himself, and that was the problem, because no one ever really figured him out."

Ro nodded. "I've learned a lot about Garak since coming to the station."

Quark grunted. *I can only imagine. Odo must have kept quite a file on Garak. But Garak never got to Ziyal. No, I think she got to him.* Ro continued looking at him expectantly, probably waiting for him to expound further on Garak. He shrugged. "I think Ziyal's death changed Garak. Who knows? Maybe that's what finally snapped whatever loyalties he still had to the old Cardassia. You just never knew with him."

Their group reached the entrance. A security officer scanned their retinas and then waved a tricorder over them, searching for weapons. Satisfied with the results, he waved them in.

The guests wound past a wall screen scrolling through an official welcome from the Bajoran government. Whatever chatter had been underway when guests entered dissolved promptly when they were presented with the first painting. A deferential hush filled the room, more like at a place of worship than an art exhibit. Even Quark, who prided himself on being a connoisseur of any and all valuable art commodities from the famous and infamous, found himself lacking any words to describe what he felt.

Suspended from the ceiling was an oil painting on matte black canvas. Monochromatic tints and shades in juxtaposed violent and graceful brush strokes carved the two-dimensional surface as surely as a sculptor's chisel would stone. A straight-on perspective of a face dominated the center, with two sharply geometric side profiles adjoining the central face at unwieldy angles. Surrounded with tempestuous swirls of gray and white, shiny black triangles, presumably hair, sprayed out in wakes behind the heads.

Ro had immersed herself in reading the biographical texts scrolling across the monitors lining the walls, but Quark remained fixed in front of the painting, pondering. He grabbed Ro by the elbow.

"What?" she said, puzzled.

"Look." He nudged his head toward the painting.

"I did."

"No, *look*. That's the answer to your question. Who is Ziyal. Look."

Standing shoulder to shoulder with Quark while the other guests milled about, Ro contemplated the painting. Quark watched her eyes following the eruptions of color, the soothing organic forms mingled with the stark triangles and squares. Nodding her head almost imperceptibly, she leaned closer into Quark and gave his hand a tight squeeze.

They stood together until another guest, hoping to obtain a better view, asked them to move along.

Her step buoyant, Kira passed through the security checkpoint, headed down a hallway and turned a corner . . . *Wait a minute,* she thought, puzzled. Ambassador Lang, Gul Macet and several of Lang's aides huddled tightly together. The schedule indicated that the lunch break wasn't due for another hour. Why would they be . . . unless . . . Tense with uncertainty, Kira strode toward the Cardassians. They parted when they recognized who was approaching.

"Colonel, please join us," Ambassador Lang said, opening her arms.

Kira took a spot beside Lang. "What's going on? I thought you all would be in the conference room. I'd heard opening statements were scheduled to begin an hour ago and—"

Macet interrupted her. "Minister Asarem announced that Bajor would be withdrawing from any diplomatic proceedings until after completing its probationary period for joining the Federation."

A mountaintop avalanche inundating her path might have shocked Kira as much as Macet's revelation. Maybe she was still asleep. Maybe this was some stress-induced bad dream . . . "What? That's not how things were supposed to go. At least, Minister Shakaar never said anything about postponing the talks. I thought Minister Asarem would take a more open approach, not shut things down altogether." Her head spun with the implications of Macet's words.

"Apparently, Minister Asarem believes that binding Bajor to a path independent of the one Bajor is forging with the Federation is a waste of time," Lang explained patiently, whatever shock she might have felt gradually giving way to the sadness brimming in her eyes. "Existing treaties between the Federation and Cardassia will apply equally with Bajor—there's no need to negotiate something separately."

This is ludicrous! Kira refused to accept this turn of events. "You've talked to First Minister Shakaar, Ambassador? He can't have signed off on this." She scanned the lobby, peered down the hall, hoping to see evidence of a Bajoran presence, but found none. *Cowards turned tail and ran.*

Sullen-faced, Lang said, "I'm told Minister Shakaar is currently unavailable."

Kira took a deep breath and started pacing. "All right. Let's say, just for the sake of argument, that Asarem's position really is what's best for Bajor. Why *not* wait until after the transition to settle this—why now? Why push it?"

"Ironically, our situation isn't unlike Bajor's was seven years ago," Lang replied. "The allies govern our territories while Cardassia Prime struggles to rebuild and redefine itself. A single epidemic and what remains of our civilization could be brought to its knees.

"We can't rebuild without outside help, we can't secure outside help unless we prove we can be trusted. If we fail to obtain the assistance we need, our world will revert to the same principles that led to our downfall. We are fated to repeat history unless we can prove we can move beyond the place where Cardassia began to go terribly wrong—and that's with the Bajoran Occupation. If we can start again with new Cardassia forging ties with new Bajor, my people stand a chance."

And the only way my people stand a chance, for all the same reasons. "I'll do what I can," Kira said, intending to go straight to the minister's office and demand to be seen or block Asarem's doorway until she agreed to see her. Kira tolerated the vagaries of politics because she understood that government's rigidly defined rules and protocols had to be navigated somehow, but this kind of game playing didn't serve anyone. She shot off down the hallway, back toward the security checkpoint.

"Colonel, we don't expect you—" Lang began, walking after her.

Kira stopped. "No, I know you don't expect it, I expect it of myself. Asking another generation to fix this is wrong—for both sides." In her gut, Kira knew she spoke truth. Her mind was clear, she believed the Prophets guided her. "This ends here. This thing between us will end *now.*"

After a brunch stop, Phillipa had come into her office to find that Dr. Girani had left a list of individuals he was recommending for anger management counseling. She'd encountered a few of the more surly characters during her time helping out the previous night so she had expected some referrals, but this many? If she followed standard Starfleet protocol for anger management therapy, she'd have half her daily appointment schedule filled with Girani's recommendations alone. But because there were disciplinary and incarceration issues pending, Phillipa recognized how vital her services were. What she wouldn't give for the odd, criminally insane schizophrenic or even marriage counseling to provide a little diversity. She sighed and ordered the computer to search the database for all the latest research on anger control issues. Maybe there was something new and exciting she could use to throw a new spin on her therapy sessions. She'd just reached the good part of "Guided Imagery and Brain Chemistry," about the effectiveness of role playing in holographic scenarios, when a chime notified her that she had visitors. Knowing that she didn't have any appointments scheduled until after alpha shift, she ordered the door open, hoping yet another crisis hadn't erupted.

Hand in hand with Dizhei, Thriss entered. Phillipa smiled reflexively. Thriss had progressed from small, subtle steps like remembering her appointments without reminders and choosing to eat breakfast with her bondmates to more noticeable moves forward such as pride in her physical appearance. No longer dull and listless, her straight white hair, interspersed with small braids, shimmered. She chose elegant, attractive clothing instead of rumpled, careworn caftans and smocks. When she walked, she took long, purposeful strides instead of allowing Dizhei or Anichent to pull her along. Her antennae relaxed, responding to pleasure, not just anger. *Some excellent progress with this patient and we started after she instigated a fight at Quark's. I can only hope I have such good luck with the other night's rioters,* she thought.

"I know I don't have an appointment," Thriss began apologetically.

Dizhei maintained a placid demeanor, smiling indulgently at her bondmate's earnestness. Phillipa had discovered that while Thriss tended to be emotionally obvious, Dizhei was the opposite. Yes, she was sweet-natured, always talkative, eagerly discussing her bondmates, but more reticent about herself. But from time to time when Thriss began rhapsodizing about Shar, Phillipa observed that Dizhei's smile tightened noticeably. *There's obviously subtext here . . . I need to get her in for a session. She has the too-bright smile on now. Interesting.*

"Don't worry about it. Have a seat." Phillipa gestured for her Andorian guests to make themselves comfortable in the visitors' chairs or the therapist's couch facing her. Thriss hadn't been sitting a minute before she started wiggling her foot, twisting it around the chair leg. *Whatever it is, she certainly is anxious today.*

"This isn't really about therapy either," Thriss said. "I probably shouldn't be here, but I didn't know who else to ask and—"

Phillipa shushed her. "Ask."

Thriss exchanged looks with Dizhei and took a deep breath. "I heard a rumor that ops downloaded communications from the *Defiant* today, but with all the problems last night, no one has the time or inclination to check. Councellor zh'Thane is away with Admiral Akaar on Bajor so she can't ask."

"You want Shar's letter." Phillipa grinned. "No problem." She tapped a few commands into the computer, entered her authorization codes and was able to ascertain from the communications logs that indeed, a Gamma Quadrant transmission had been received an hour before. "It's here, but it's above my clearance level. Colonel Kira has to review and disperse the information, but I could check and see when that might happen."

"Would you?" Thriss scooted to the edge of her chair expectantly, placing her hands, palm down, on the desk and drumming her fingers. "I don't want to cause problems."

"Relax. It'll be fine." Phillipa touched her combadge. "Counselor Matthias to ops."

"This is Ling. Go ahead."

"I have Shathrissía zh'Cheen, Ensign ch'Thane's bondmate, in my office. I was wondering when the communiqués from the *Defiant* would be distributed?"

"Colonel Kira reviewed them some time ago, and to my knowledge, all the personal messages went out to individual databases."

Thriss's incessant finger drumming suddenly stopped; she eased back into the chair, molding her shoulders to the curved backrest. In contrast, Dizhei remained poised, her antennae soft and flexible.

Phillipa reached across the desk and rested her hand over Thriss's. "Is it possible to check with the colonel to see if there was any word from Ensign ch'Thane?" she said to Ensign Ling.

"*The colonel has asked not to be disturbed except in an emergency, but I'll relay your inquiry at the earliest opportunity.*"

"Thanks. Matthias out." Thriss shrunk before Phillipa's eyes. She tucked her legs beneath her and dropped her head on the armrest. Were it not for her shallow, ragged breaths, Phillipa might have worried that she'd stopped breathing.

Phillipa tightened her grip on Thriss's hand. "Don't jump to conclusions, Thriss. There might be something embedded or included in Commander Vaughn's datablock. Be patient. Colonel Kira has a lot to deal with right now."

The two bondmates exchanged a rush of whispered Andorii; Dizhei did most of the talking, finally resting a possessive hand on Thriss's knee. "Thriss has a shift with Dr. Girani. If you want to contact her, she'll be there until late this afternoon. Shall we go, *zh'yi?*"

"Wait." Phillipa looked between both Andorians, but directed her words at Dizhei since she believed Dizhei would need persuading. "Why doesn't Thriss stay here for a few minutes? We can talk a bit, and then I'll take her down to the infirmary."

But Dizhei had left her chair and was guiding Thriss along with a hand placed in the small of her back before Phillipa had finished speaking. The decision had been made, though how much input Thriss had was questionable. Once more, Phillipa reiterated her offer for on-the-spot counseling, but Thriss shook her head weakly and waved a good-bye.

Absently twirling a lock of hair between her fingers, Phillipa sat in her chair staring at the words filling her desktop screen like white noise. She filtered the last fifteen minutes through years of academic and field training, plus a healthy dose of intuition.

Not one logical interpretation of the scene she'd witnessed reassured her; every extrapolation she worked through had negative connotations. So she resolved to sit there and spin every potentiality until she came up with a positive outcome. She turned off her desk screen. There had to be a positive outcome somewhere. There had to be. For Thriss's sake. For all four of them.

Kira had no intention of calling ahead to warn Minister Asarem that she was on her way. She'd followed protocols and niceties until her mouth ached from trying to smile away her frustration. No more. The minister's office door slid open obediently on her order. Sitting behind her desk studying a tome of Bajoran law, Asarem appeared legitimately shocked to see her. Kira relished the advantage of surprise for only a second before walking right up to the side of her chair. She didn't want anything between them when she had this conversation.

"I don't recall that we had a meeting, Colonel," Asarem said, turning her chair toward Kira and offering a serene smile.

Good recovery.

"We didn't. I let myself in."

"So I noticed," she said dryly.

"One of the few fringe benefits of being in command around here: there's no place on this station where I can't find you." After her conversation outside the conference room, she'd had the computer track Asarem's every move on the station.

Asarem tipped back in her chair, throwing her legs out in front of her as if she were stretching post-nap. "Manners and civil liberties never figure into your games of hide and seek?"

"Don't be clever with me, Asarem," Kira snipped. "We're both old hands at this. We can trade barbs and witticisms until we're hoarse, or we can have an honest discussion."

"I have nothing to discuss with you," she said dismissively. She snapped a law book closed and shoved it back on a shelf behind her desk where other old-fashioned volumes were stored. Thumbing a switch, Asarem made a show of pulling up her schedule. "I have state business to attend to, Colonel."

"Oh, I don't believe you do." Kira reached across Asarem's desk and turned off the desk screen. "Just what the hell were you thinking when you shut down the talks today? What's all this about waiting for Bajor to adopt the Federation's treaties with Cardassia?"

"It's a logical move," Asarem said, shoving Kira's arm off her desk. "Transitioning an entire planetary system into a completely new governmental form involves a lot more than making sure there aren't hurt feelings between neighbors."

Kira clenched her fists. She so wanted to punch something, but her hot-head days were behind her. *Keep a steady course . . .* "This thing between us and Cardassia—this is our issue to resolve, not the Federation's. Passing it off for them to handle is cowardly."

"I resent that characterization." Asarem left her desk and exited down a private corridor.

Kira followed. She wished she could tie Asarem to a chair and force her to see reason, a tactic that worked effectively in the Resistance, but might earn her a court martial if she employed it here. No, she had to play by the minister's rules.

Asarem spoke to Kira as she walked. "Waiting to take on something of the magnitude of normalizing Bajoran/Cardassian relations until after the Federation is pragmatic. Why make promises we might not be able to keep once the Federation is in charge? Why duplicate efforts? We need to use our time to help Bajor." She turned into a side room, likely a records office. Pulling a stool out from beneath a desk, Asarem climbed atop it and started browsing the countless rows of padds, books, and scrolls.

Kira hopped up on the counter closest to where Asarem stood. "Bajor will never heal until we deal with the mistrust festering between us and Cardassia. We'll come into the Federation weak. We'll be hiding behind our mother's skirts."

"You're free to assume what you want, Colonel, but the decision is made." She removed a scroll and jumped off the stool. "It's not negotiable."

How could Asarem treat Bajor/Cardassia relations with the same indifferent concern that one might reserve for street signage? Kira grabbed Asarem by the shoulder. "This is wrong!"

With a swift elbow shove, the minister dislodged Kira's grip. She spun around, eyes blazing. "How *dare* you! You have no idea what this is about."

"I don't? Because it's pretty damn obvious what's happening here!" Kira shouted.

"You think you know it all," Asarem said through gritted teeth. She stepped closer to Kira. "You've always been that way. So self-righteous. Well, this time, you're not even close." Turning on her heel, she half walked, half ran from the records room. Shoulder to shoulder, the women raced down the hall, surprised aides ducking out of the way right and left.

"If you do, as you claim, have Bajor's best interests at heart," Kira said, "then you and I want the same things. But from where I'm standing you and I couldn't be on more opposite sides."

"That's where you're wrong, Kira." She laughed bitterly. "The irony of all this is that you and I are on exactly the same side down to the last detail."

Kira halted in her tracks, wondering if in her anger she'd missed something Asarem had said previously, because she believed she'd just heard Asarem say that they were on the same side. *How could that be? None of this makes sense.* She knew what she'd seen during the talks, what she'd read in the transcripts.

Seeing the puzzled expression on Kira's face, Asarem laughed again. "You should see yourself, Kira. It's almost worth putting up with your attitude to see how confused you look right now." Asarem grabbed Kira by the elbow and dragged her into the closest vacant room. When she was assured they were alone, she explained, "Yes, Colonel. It's true. I want peace with Cardassia. I came to these talks prepared to negotiate—to give probably more than Ambassador Lang would ask for. And you know why I didn't? Because I was ordered not to."

Still convinced Asarem had an angle, Kira said suspiciously, "Ordered?"

"Shakaar instructed me to take a hard-line position," Asarem explained. "He told me to make it, in his exact words, 'as difficult as possible' to find reconciliation."

"Shakaar wouldn't do that."

Shaking her head, Asarem plopped down in a chair and sighed resignedly. "I knew you wouldn't believe me. Considering your history with him."

Forcing herself to consider that Asaraem was being truthful with her, Kira tried to visualize the talks from the minister's perspective. How aggravating it must be to have to sit, day after day, representing an agenda not of your own making. Kira imagined that spinning fabrications, deliberately blocking legitimate dialogue, would take a toll on a person of integrity; an alibi existed for Asarem's seeming unreasonableness. *But what was Shakaar trying to do?* "If that's true—" She looked directly at Asarem.

The minister met Kira's eyes. "Then he lied to you." She let her words linger between them before offering further explanation.

A tightening in her chest made the air in the room feel too thin to breathe; the implications of Asarem's accusations were staggering. Kira rubbed her temples with the heels of her hands. Asarem waited while Kira struggled to formulate a response. Finding that quick explanations for the inexplicable proved futile, Kira said nothing. She didn't know what to say.

"If you don't believe it, go to him," Asarem said, not unkindly. "He comes back tomorrow sometime. Ask him. See if he's brave enough to be honest with you." Soundlessly, she left Kira alone in the half light to struggle through what she'd do next.

She was sitting there still when Ro's urgent page found her.

19

Talk about your circadian rhythms being off.

Not long after being snatched off the *Defiant,* day and night blended together for Nog. Constantly wearing a hood would do that to a person. He vaguely recalled being woken several times. After the gag was yanked out of his mouth, someone held up water for him to drink and shoved stale kelp cakes into his mouth. Given a choice, Nog would have passed on the kelp cakes.

While he couldn't see, his already superior auditory abilities were significantly heightened. He heard every opening door, could count the number of Yrythny passing by and understand most of the conversations. If what he picked up from eavesdropping was true, the *Avaril*'s general population wasn't aware he'd been stowed away in a storage closet near engineering. He knew he was close by engineering from the tone of the plasma coursing through the conduits, the rhythmic percussion of the warp core. The engines' presence comforted him.

Whoever his captor or captors were, they went to significant lengths to avoid being identified, utilizing different clothing, shoes, scents and never speaking when he might overhear. Consequently, he had no idea what his ultimate destination might be. Whether he was fated to be held hostage for ransom, killed, or sold to be the cabin boy for some Cheka general, Nog wasn't sure. If killed, he hoped his kidnappers would have the decency to send his body to Commander Vaughn. His father, at least, ought to have an opportunity to profit from Nog's misfortunes. The desiccated remains of the first Ferengi in Starfleet had to be worth *something.* Sobering thoughts for a young Ferengi.

While he might not know what time of day it was, Nog heard feet shuffling in the corridor at every shift change. *Vanìmel is a day away, give or take six hours, accounting for the time I was knocked unconscious. With any luck, my present circumstances are a misunderstanding and my gracious hosts will put me in touch with Commander Vaughn as soon as we touch down.*

The pitch of the warp engines vibrating through the deckplates suddenly dropped to nothing; Nog heard the impulse engine attempt, unsuccessfully, to engage. Given the backup systems on *Avaril,* impulse should be available soon, but not for another fifteen minutes or so. The *Avaril* was adrift. The expected panicked footsteps rushed up and down the corridor. Still no engine. Nog guessed at least ten minutes had passed since the warp core failed.

The storage closet door swished open. Hands grabbed at Nog, hefting him into the air. A Yrythny threw him over a shoulder, the gag stopped his protestations; his bound hands and feet prevented him from fighting his way free. The hood stayed in place, but Nog discerned the general direction his captors took him: a quick transport car downward. The air on the lowest decks had a dank, dusty quality. Hazarding a guess, he was being hauled to the *Avaril*'s shuttlebay and taken ... he had no idea. There were two Yrythny in his party;

neither of them spoke. Doors opened and shut until the distinctively hollow sound of footsteps on metal gratings confirmed Nog's suspicions. A pause while the group waited for a shuttle's doors to open. Nog was thrown, like baggage, into the rear of the craft. He listened as switches flipped, engines activated; a preflight diagnostic ran. He had no clue how long they would idle in the shuttlebay or where he was being taken, but he suspected it had to do with the tricorder holding the cloaking specs (actually a homing beacon—very clever). Nog put his faith in the Great River, hoping that once again it would provide in his hour of need.

With *Defiant* maintaining its cloak, Vaughn sat on the bridge, watching the pieces of the chessboard move into place. He would make his move when he was ready and not a moment before.

All eyes watched as the *Avaril* continued plodding toward Vanìmel while the Cheka ship maintained a parallel course beside her. The main viewscreen displayed a computer-generated graphic of an uninhabited planetary system where Bowers had projected the Cheka would intercept the Yrythny.

The first piece fell into place when the *Avaril*, a green ellipse on the screen, tumbled out of warp, and stalled. The *Defiant*'s scans indicated internal engineering problems—not even impulse engines could be activated. She was stranded.

"The *Avaril* is transmitting a request for emergency assistance to Luthia control. They suspect internal sabotage to their engines," Bowers reported.

"Continue to monitor communications, Lieutenant," Vaughn ordered. At least initial appearances indicated that J'Maah hadn't sold them out.

The *Avaril* had only minutes to cope with their misfortune before the Cheka warship *Ston'yan,* a diamond-shaped graphic in red, rumbled into position off the *Avaril*'s port side.

"*Ston'yan* dropping out of warp and powering weapons. *Avaril* unable to activate defensive shielding," Bowers announced. He looked up at Vaughn. "Showdown at the O.K. Corral."

Vaughn laughed grimly, wishing this could be settled with the sheriff and the black hat dueling with Colts at high noon. *Here we go,* he thought, rising from his chair. "Sound red alert. All crew to battle stations. Ensign Tenmei, ahead full, course one-nine-seven mark two." It was a trajectory that would place them dead center between the *Avaril* and the *Ston'yan.*

"*Avaril,* twenty-six million kilometers," Prynn announced.

"Steady as she goes, Ensign. Any sign of attack from the Cheka, Mr. Bowers?"

"No, sir. The *Ston'yan* remains on alert."

On the outside, Vaughn remained composed. No need to add to the anxiety of his crew; on the inside, he held his breath. Within minutes, they would know whether they had a chance at rescuing Nog.

"*Avaril* one million kilometers," Prynn announced.

"Take us out of warp," Vaughn ordered. "Maintain cloak."

Rahim looked up from sciences. *"Avaril* shuttlebay doors have been activated. Sensors detect the launch of one Yrythny shuttle."

A third spacecraft graphic, a smaller version of the *Avaril*'s green circle, appeared.

"Scan the shuttle, Ensign." *This is it,* Vaughn thought.

"Two Yrythny life-forms—" Rahim paused to smile. "—and one Ferengi."

Vaughn turned to Leishman at engineering. "Transporter lock?"

Leishman studied her panel and shook her head. "Not possible. We should be able to knock out their shields, but whatever inhibitor field they were using before is now encompassing all three shuttle occupants. Looks like it's plan B, sir."

Vaughn turned to conn. "Ensign Tenmei, follow course two-one-zero mark zero and bring the *Defiant* within ten thousand kilometers of the Yrythny shuttle. Lieutenant Bowers, power phasers and prepare to drop cloak on my mark. Ensign Leishman, report to transporter bay one."

The tall engineer vacated her post and started for the exit.

"Good luck, Mikaela," Vaughn said as she crossed close to his chair.

"Yes, sir," she said with a wink. "I'll give 'em hell."

On the viewscreen, Vaughn saw the shuttle, just a little bigger than its Starfleet analog, cross the expanse between the two ships, dwarfed by the massive *Avaril* and the equally formidable Cheka warship. At the requisite distance, Prynn adjusted the *Defiant*'s course, bringing her parallel with the shuttle.

"Chao to the bridge. Ensign Leishman is ready to transport to the Yrythny shuttle."

Vaughn didn't hesitate. "Drop cloak, Lieutenant Bowers. Target the shuttle's shield generators and fire phasers."

"Phasers firing, sir," Bowers said.

Green circles rippled and winked out around the Yrythny shuttle, indicating a direct hit. "Shuttle's shields are down, sir," Bowers reported.

"Energize, Chief!"

"Ensign Leishman is away, sir," Chao replied over the comm.

Vaughn sat back down. *Now that we've crashed the party, let's see who tries to throw us out first.*

Sensors told Ezri that the *Avaril* was having technical trouble and that the Cheka warship had powered weapons. *Looks like an ambush,* she thought helplessly. The *Sagan*'s weapons might divert the warship's attention for a minute, but ultimately, she could do nothing to help the stranded Yrythny vessel.

"What now, Jeshoh?" Ezri said.

"We wait." He sat stiffly in the chair beside her.

"Fine. All stop, Shar."

As the *Sagan* held position, Keren left her seat, dropping down to crouch beside Jeshoh. She rested a hand on his leg and tried gazing up into his face, but he twisted away from her. "My whole life's work has been about helping all of my people. Not myself. Please don't keep me from helping them," she pleaded.

"Sit down, Keren. We'll talk when this is over," he said gruffly.

"Jeshoh, we can stop this now. Let's dock on the *Avaril*. Turn in the terrorists. They'll reduce our punishment."

"Yrythny shuttle launching from *Avaril*," Shar reported. "It's moving toward the Cheka vessel."

"Please, Jeshoh—" Keren whispered.

"Wait for a signal from the shuttle," Jeshoh ordered.

"I'm monitoring communications channels," Ezri said. A cursory survey revealed the Yrythny shuttle wasn't transmitting, but jamming the *Sagan*'s inquiry. *Something's not right here.*

"We should be receiving instructions by now," Jeshoh said, jumping from his chair and pacing. "I wonder—"

"Lieutenant, look," Shar said excitedly. "The *Defiant!*"

Keren scrambled to her feet, crowding next to Jeshoh so she could see the console screen. Keen in her focus, Ezri gasped when *Defiant*'s phasers took out the shuttle's shields.

Jeshoh slumped forward. "It can't be . . ."

"Were I to hazard a guess," Ezri said, "I'd say your deal is off."

"No!" Jeshoh slammed the console. "No!"

Anticipating the Cheka's displeasure with *Defiant*'s appearance, Vaughn made a preemptive move. "Tactical, raise shields and ready phasers," he said. "Ensign Rahim, monitor all transmissions between the three ships. Audio feed over the comm system."

"*—a direct hit to our shield generators. You have to help us!*" the panicked Yrythny voice said. "*We have the cloaking specs and an engineer who can install and replicate the technology.*"

"What about the eggs?" came the vibrating Cheka voice.

"*—the* Defiant *off starboard—*" static disrupted the transmission.

Vaughn searched his memory to place the Yrythny voice; he knew he'd heard it before.

Ensign Permenter suddenly looked up from the engineering station, where she'd replaced Leishman, recognition written on her face. "That was—"

Tlaral, thought Nog, wondering why he hadn't pegged her before. For his money, he thought it would be Minister M'Yeoh. No one in a position like his was that incompetent unless it was for show. But he hadn't had any latinum riding on the deal so he'd live with the disappointment.

I'm being traded to the Cheka. In exchange for what? What do the Cheka have that the Yrythny want? Uncle Quark always says the four hungers are food, sex, power and money, not necessarily in that order. But because money can buy food, sex, and power, money trumps them all. If I'm the money, the Yrythny are trading me for . . .

Wait. Not all Yrythny are in need, Nog amended his thought. *Only the Wanderers because—*

They want weapons. To push Vanìmel into a civil war. If they can't wrangle their rights legally, they'll take them by force.

The shuttle's control panel beeped like crazy. Before he could guess what might be happening, the shuttle rocked a second time, tipping from side to side, and acrid smoke filled the cockpit.

"We've lost our shield generators. Grab hold of—"

Suddenly he heard the whine of a Starfleet transporter beam.

"We've been boarded!" Tlaral shouted. *"Get—!"*

Feet hit the deck, followed by scuffling, rustling, clattering and a thud. Nog hitched along the floor toward the rear of the shuttle to avoid being dragged into the fray. Having heard the Yrythny use the word "defiant" he hoped it meant Vaughn was close by. For now, however, as much as he wanted to believe he had friends aboard, he couldn't be sure. Braced against a metal corner, he pushed his wristbands against the edge.

"Lock onto the Yrythny. Two to transport," he heard someone say. *Mikaela.*

The sound of the transporter beam filled the cabin again. Then hands pulled the hood off his head and yanked the gag out of his mouth. "You okay?" Leishman asked, performing a cursory check.

"Could be worse," Nog answered, managing a smile. "You couldn't have just beamed me off first?"

" 'Fraid not," she said, holding up two ripped armbands with little devices attached. Transporter scramblers, Nog guessed. She reached for the one on Nog's arm and snapped it off as well. "You ready?" Nog nodded, and Mikaela tapped her combadge again. "Leishman to Chao. Lock onto Lieutenant Nog and beam him out."

He didn't even get to say good-bye before he rematerialized in the transporter bay. Chief Chao informed the bridge that he was back aboard. Maybe he was imagining things, but Nog thought he might have heard applause.

Suddenly Dr. Bashir was there, hauling him off the transporter pad and sitting beside him. He unfastened Nog's restraints and checked him over to make sure he wasn't bleeding, broken, or too badly bruised.

"You had us worried," Bashir said, examining his wrists and ankles. "Welcome home, Lieutenant. I wish I could let you retire to your quarters, but we're a little shorthanded in engineering, and we still have to get out of here."

"What about Mikaela?" Nog cried.

Ensign Leishman dropped into the pilot's chair and made a cursory inspection of the controls before activating the shuttle's sensors and computer systems. The hours she'd spent with the *Avaril*'s engineering staff finally paid off. *Okay, little David, we're going to make the bad guys think you're Goliath.* She took out the makeshift device Permenter had given her and plugged it into a port on the shuttle's main console. True to Bryanne's promise, it fit perfectly into the Yrythny system, and instantly initiated an information upload. As the "noisemaker" programming poured into the shuttle's computer, Leishman reconfigured the navigational system, integrating a datachip that allowed the shuttle to be remote piloted from the *Defiant*. The download completed, she reinitialized the computer matrix. Then she thumbed the switch on the transmitter, hailing the *Avaril*. "Shuttle to *Avaril*. This is Ensign Mikaela Leishman of the *U.S.S. Defiant*. Do you read?"

After a pause that was likely only seconds—but felt like minutes—the *Avaril* answered. *"We read you."*

"Power down primary systems, *Avaril*. Repeat, power down primary systems."

"Ensign, if you'd clarify—"

"Scan the shuttle, *Avaril*. Tell me what you see."

Another long pause. *"Powering down primary power. Thank you, Ensign."*

She touched her combadge. *"Defiant*, what do you read?"

"Nice work, Mikaela," said Bowers. *"If I didn't know better, I'd think there were two* Avarils *out there."*

The Cheka ought to be seriously confused by the decoy, providing the real *Avaril* a chance to restore their defensive capabilities. If *Ston'yan* decided to attack, at least the odds of the *Avaril* surviving had improved, though she doubted Vaughn would let it get that far. He'd draw the *Ston'yan's* fire before he allowed innocents to die.

"Leishman to Chao. Beam me out." She closed her eyes . . .

. . . and opened them when she was back home. Leishman stepped off the transporter pad, nodding to Chao, who reported Leishman's safe return to the bridge.

She once again heard Bowers's cool, steady voice. "Ston'yan *targeting weapons.*"

"Ensign Tenmei, prepare to engage Ston'yan. *Evasive maneuvers,"* Vaughn barked.

"Sir!" Bowers said. *"It's the* Sagan!"

"Shall I open a channel to *Defiant*—?" Shar said.

"No!" Jeshoh touched the emitter tip of his weapon to Shar's neck. "Proceed toward the Cheka vessel."

"Jeshoh, don't do this!" Keren begged.

"That's odd," Shar said, assessing the sensor data. "I'm picking up two *Avarils*."

"Why would there be two—?" Recognition dawned on Ezri. "Oh, that's clever—Vaughn's created a noisemaker." She smiled, admiring the commander's tactics.

"Sir?" Shar said.

"Trick the enemy's sensors into believing that there are two ships out there. The enemy has to guess which one to hit first. The confusion buys time."

"Giving the *Avaril* time to escape," Shar reasoned.

Ezri nodded.

"Approach the Cheka ship, Lieutenant," Jeshoh ordered.

Looking over her shoulder, Ezri recognized panic spreading over Jeshoh's face. *Should I say something . . . no. All his options need to be gone before he'll budge.* She nodded to Shar, who tapped in the commands to ease the *Sagan* toward the Cheka warship.

"Hail them," Vaughn ordered. *What the hell does Dax think she's doing out here?*

"They're not answering our hails, sir," Bowers reported.

"Who's on board?" Vaughn asked. He stood behind Rahim, assimilating the data as it came up on screen.

"One Trill, one Andorian, and two Yrythny."

"Are all their systems operational?"

"Yes, sir," Bowers said. "Full shields, weapons, communications, and life support. They've set a course for the *Ston'yan.*"

What could Dax be up to? Without knowing why the *Sagan* was joining them, and because the *Sagan* wasn't answering their hails, he had to assume that this might not be a friendly visit. But he had to trust his senior officers to wrangle with the problem.

"Ensign Tenmei, proceed on course zero-nine-zero mark three," Vaughn said. "Sam, get ready to throw a punch at the *Ston'yan.* Just hard enough to get their attention."

"Aye, sir." Sam grinned. "Preparing full spread of quantum torpedoes."

Rahim said, "The Cheka have fired polaron cannons on one of the *Avarils,* sir."

"They took the bait." Vaughn expected they would. Having failed to receive their cargo from the Yrythny, they would attack. He was certain the Cheka had planned on taking out the *Avaril* from the onset. Many who double-cross find themselves double-crossed at the end of the road. "On screen."

Yellow and blue light erupted as an engine core breached. The brilliant flare dissipated, providing a full frontal view of the *Ston'yan.*

"Attack pattern beta, Ensign Tenmei!"

"The Cheka have destroyed an *Avaril,*" Shar announced, his listeners all watching him as they awaited the verdict: "The false one."

Ezri wondered how much longer they could hover on the perimeter of the standoff. To this point, the *Sagan* didn't pose a threat to any of the parties and was easy to ignore. With one of the pieces off the board, Ezri bet that the Cheka would come after them next—either tractor them in or blow them up. Neither option pleased her.

"Jeshoh, what's to say the Cheka won't turn on you?" Keren said, reaching for him.

He jerked away. "Because I have something they want."

"And Keren? If the Cheka turn on you, they turn on her," Ezri said calmly. "You don't want that, Jeshoh. You know you don't. Let me open a channel to the *Defiant*. You and Keren can take asylum with the crew until we can negotiate with your govern—"

"The way you negotiated the colonizing compromise?" Jeshoh snorted.

Ezri winced inwardly. *I've failed the Yrythny spectacularly. All the more reason I have to figure out how to make it right.*

She pressed on toward the *Ston'yan*.

On approach to the warship, Ensign Prynn Tenmei decided she didn't like the look of it. Not because she found the Cheka to be foul creatures (though she did), or because the *Ston'yan* appeared terribly menacing. No, Prynn felt the Cheka starship lacked panache.

During the Dominion War, she had flown against (and admired) Jem'Hadar attack ships, *Galor*-class Cardassian cruisers; she'd flown in formation with Romulan warbirds and gone into battle alongside Klingon Birds-of-Prey. She might not like the Cardassians' way of doing business—or the Romulans' and Klingons' for that matter—but at least their empires had developed spacecraft worthy of engagement. The *Ston'yan,* by contrast, was a clumsy predator, more like a blind shark battering its prey with its head before moving in for the kill. No style whatsoever.

"*Ston'yan* twenty-five thousand kilometers and closing," she said.

"Acknowledged, Ensign. Maintain course," Vaughn said.

Prynn hit the touchpad for navigational reference and considered the territory ahead. A wild-goose chase through one of this system's asteroid belts might be fun. Close to the sun, maybe, or toward that gas giant . . . *Hello?* She broke into a smile when she saw the last piece of navigational data. *Now that's a nice surprise,* she thought. *Oh to be on the* Ston'yan'*s bridge when I sock this one to them.* She tapped her combadge. "Conn to engineering. What's the status on the femtobots?"

"*Untested, but ready to go,*" Nog said. "*We need a 30-second window to activate the system and tactical will have to power down weapons.*"

"Captain, I have an idea—but it's risky," Prynn said, wanting to give her father and Bowers a heads-up as to what she had in mind. "Transmitting navigational data and proposed target to your stations now. I'll easily outfly the *Ston'yan,* but can we survive without weapons for half a minute?"

"I'm game," Bowers piped up.

Vaughn looked up from reviewing her data. "Proceed, Ensign."

"Thank you, sir," Prynn said, speedily tapping the commands into the flight control panel. "*Ston'yan* within firing range."

"Fire when ready, Lieutenant," Vaughn said.

When Bowers let fly his spread of torpedoes, Prynn initiated evasive maneuvers. She'd covered twenty thousand kilometers before the *Ston'yan* caught up with the *Defiant*. Steady rounds firing from Cheka polaron cannons forced Prynn into a pendulumlike flight pattern.

"*Avaril* has regained impulse engines," Rahim said.

"Good. What about the *Sagan?*" Vaughn asked.

The entire crew—including Prynn—hung on Rahim's answer. The shuttle still hadn't responded to their hails.

"The *Sagan* is behind the *Ston'yan*. Not quite sure who they're trying to catch up with, though, us or them."

This may be a case of the inmates running the asylum, Ezri thought, plotting the *Sagan*'s course behind the Cheka. Far in the lead, the *Defiant* led the *Ston'yan* on a merry chase at dizzying speeds. *Prynn must be in her glory.*

Incredulous, Keren asked, "What are we doing?"

"We need to keep up with the Cheka. We still have what they want. And they have what we want."

"Listen to yourself, Jeshoh!" Keren protested.

He turned away, unmoved by her pleas.

To Ezri's side, Shar blanched pale blue. "The Cheka are releasing a wake of mines. Boosting shields."

"Taking evasive maneuvers," Ezri barked. *Sagan* veered to port, avoiding a mine aimed for starboard only to fly straight toward another. An explosion rocked the shuttle.

Ezri heard the dull crunch of flesh against metal; Keren cried out.

"Jeshoh!" Ezri shouted. "Help her, dammit!" She fought the instinct to abandon the conn and rush back to tend to the wounded Yrythny.

"Shields at seventy percent," Shar said, his antennae rigid with tension. "The *Defiant* appears to be going in close to this system's star. *Sagan* isn't designed to withstand—"

Out of the corner of her eye, Ezri saw Keren slumped on the floor; she groaned, twisting her head from side to side as delirium overtook her.

"Shar, check on Keren."

"But the shields—"

"That's an order, Ensign."

Shar jumped up from his station, went for a medical kit, and started passing a tricorder over Keren. Jeshoh, still clutching his weapon, stood statue still, shell-shocked and pale.

"Change your mind, Jeshoh," Ezri said calmly. *Don't let him see your fear.* "It's not too late."

"No!" he despaired. His eyes dropped to the floor where Keren had fallen into unconsciousness.

"Ensign Tenmei, move into the final phase," Vaughn ordered.

"Yes, sir." For her plan to work, Prynn needed to keep the *Ston'yan* off its guard long enough that they wouldn't have time to back out of her trap. Considering what she had to work with, she decided on playing chicken with the Cheka around the star. *Let's see what your ship is made of,* Prynn thought.

"*Ston'yan* closing," Rahim said.

Plunging toward the sun's corona, she faked to port, before peeling out abruptly to starboard. In following the *Defiant*'s port-side fake, the *Ston'yan* cooked its underbelly. Prynn eluded their fire for a few more minutes, buying her the time she needed to set up the last leg of the chase.

"*Ston'yan* still in pursuit with weapons off-line," Bowers said. "Correction, *Ston'yan* weapons are back on-line and attempting to lock onto us."

"Target destination in fifty seconds," Permenter said. "Twenty seconds until femtobot shield augmentation activated."

The *Defiant* shuddered.

"Direct hit. Shields at sixty-five percent," Bowers reported.

Permenter looked at Tenmei. "The femtobot augmentation can be activated all the way down to fifty percent, but I strongly suggest we try not to put that to the test."

"Course locked in," Prynn said. "Here we go."

Though still hot on the Cheka's tail, Ezri eavesdropped on Shar's medical explanations to Jeshoh, discovering she had a new problem.

"According to my scans," Shar said, "she has a subdural hematoma. A blood bruise on the brain. I could attempt to treat her, but my paramedic training is limited, and I fear I don't know enough about Yrythny blood chemistry." His tone wasn't hopeful.

His calm evaporating, Jeshoh slammed a fist into a compartment.

"We can help her, Jeshoh," Ezri said. "Dr. Bashir on the *Defiant* is one of the finest medical practitioners you could ask for, and he has a fully equipped medical bay. He'll stabilize her until we can get her to your people."

"No!" he shouted, breathing ragged. "We'll never be together if we go back now."

Ezri said simply, "If we don't go back, she'll die."

"You don't know that! Shar, treat her now," Jeshoh snapped, pacing the small compartment like a caged animal.

This has gone on as long as I can allow, Ezri thought.

"*Help Keren,*" she whispered gruffly. Her body was perilously close to caving in to stress; her shoulders ached from sitting, tightly wound, for so long. Fatigue and hunger would soon blur her ability to focus and if her calculations were right, in less than a minute, all the rules of this fight would change again. She dared to glance away from the flight controls to meet Jeshoh's eyes. "Please," she begged. "Do this for her. I've watched you stand against your leaders, your culture—all because you believed in doing the right thing. You know what you have to do, Jeshoh. *Do it now.*"

"Thirty seconds. Activating shield augmentation," Permenter said.

"*Ston'yan* one thousand kilometers and closing," Bowers reported. "Weapons charging."

Trusting that her crewmates would back her up, Prynn drifted into a mental place where the conn became an extension of her fingers, responding instantaneously to her thoughts. *Just a little closer.* . . . The bridge crew snapped reports back and forth. Prynn ignored them. *Almost there . . . we should be crossing the threshold. . . . NOW.*

A blinding, brilliant flash consumed the darkness. Prynn pulled all the power she could from the engines, determined to fly through the descending web weapon's net. The tactical readout confirmed that the *Ston'yan* had been caught in the weapon's perimeter. For one terrifying moment, she wondered if the Cheka had friend-or-foe technology that would allow them to escape, but she had to hope that overconfidence would be their downfall.

"It's working," Bowers said. "The femtobots are preventing the nanobots from penetrating the ship!"

"We aren't out of the woods, yet," Vaughn cautioned. "Keep it together, Ensign Tenmei."

Because the *Ston'yan* remained tight on the *Defiant*'s heels, Prynn wasn't sure the web weapon had caught their pursuer. In one last evasive tactic, Prynn piloted the *Defiant* into a sharp seventy-five-degree pull-up, banking in front of the Cheka ship, flipping over and flying back the direction they'd come, over the top of the *Ston'yan*.

"The web got them!" Bowers shouted. "*Ston'yan* is no longer in pursuit."

"Status of the femtobots?" Vaughn asked.

"It worked," Permenter confirmed. "Nanobots were all neutralized."

Prynn's elation enhanced the adrenaline coursing through her veins. *What a rush.*

"Sir," said Bowers, "the *Sagan* is hailing us. Audio only."

"Put them through."

"*Defiant, this is Lieutenant Dax. Permission to bring in the* Sagan."

"By all means, Lieutenant. Bring her home."

Julian raced into the shuttlebay, eager to be the first to greet the *Sagan*. Impatience wasn't his usual style, but he needed to know that Ezri was all right.

The shuttle doors hissed open with Shar jumping out first, standing aside while two Yrythny exited; the tall, handsomely dressed male cradled an unconscious female in his arms. All three passengers trudged toward him as if heavily burdened.

"Doctor," Shar called. "We have a medical emergency."

Thoughts of Ezri temporarily forgotten, Julian pulled out his medical tricorder and scanned the wounded Yrythny. "We'll need to operate. It may take me a few minutes to synthesize her blood, but she should be fine," he said to the Yrythny he now recognized as Jeshoh. "Shar, take our guests to sickbay. I'll be right behind you." Tapping his combadge he said, "Bashir to Richter. Prep for surgery. We have a Yrythny with a subdural hematoma. I'll be there presently."

With the distraction of a new patient, Julian hadn't heard Ezri exit the shuttle. He stopped when he suddenly heard:

"Hey. Can I walk with you?"

He paused, smiled broadly and reached for her proffered hand. All of him relaxed at her touch. For a moment they said nothing. Her appearance worried him, dark circles around her eyes, porcelain skin paler than normal, her shoulders hunched with fatigue.

"What exactly happened in there?" Julian asked, concerned.

She smiled weakly. "Ask me later. I just . . . I just want you to know I love you."

"I love you, too," he said simply, deciding it would be best not to press her for explanations now. They were back together. For now, that was enough. Julian draped an arm around her waist, and together they headed for the medical bay.

20

"Computer, lights at full illumination," Shakaar ordered. He dropped his travel bag on his desk and began rooting around inside.

Kira waited for him to toss out some clothes and his other personal belongings before deciding to interrupt him. "I hope all is well on the *Gryphon*."

Startled, he spun around. "How did you—?"

"You may be First Minister of Bajor, but this is still my station, Edon."

"This couldn't wait until morning?" he asked.

"No," Kira said simply. She walked over beside him, braced herself against his desk and watched him sort through his travel bag.

Shakaar thumbed on his desk screen, perused a memo or two and replicated a glass of *pooncheenee*. Kira watched sedately, following his every move with her eyes. Finally, he motioned for her to take a seat; he dropped into his own chair, a rare occurrence since he preferred standing.

Electing to perch on the edge of his desk, she peered down at him. "Yesterday, Lieutenant Ro discovered that the Ziyal exhibit had been brutally vandalized." Brutal understated the degree of calculated destruction. Twisted, maybe. Depraved, better.

His eyebrow shot up. "Have the culprits been identified?"

"No. But the damage was extensive." Acids melting paints off canvases, water smudging delicate charcoals, knives slashing obscenities . . . as if Ziyal, through her work, had been tortured incrementally, murdered anew.

"Can the artwork be repaired?" Shakaar asked, putting away personal items from his bag.

"The curator can restore some of the pieces—it could take weeks." *Assuming she can be persuaded to stop crying at some point,* Kira thought ruefully. "But there are a few that are beyond repair. Those pieces might be holographically reproduced, but the originals are irreparable."

"Tragic," Shakaar muttered, thoughtfully rubbing his chin with his thumb. He took another sip of his juice, pausing to peer over the glass at Kira, who remained fixed where she sat. "You didn't have to make this report in person."

"I didn't," Kira admitted. "But I felt like what happened tonight at the exhibit can be attributed, in part, to a station environment hostile toward Cardassians. And I think you're feeding that hatred, Minister."

Mustering indignation, Shakaar spouted off a biting retort, but Kira dismissed it. "You know what I'm talking about, Shakaar. Don't play coy with me."

Lips pursed, he glared at her. Kira had known him long enough to recognize his shift into tactical mode as he tried to ascertain whether she was friend or foe. She sat, unflinching, while he appraised her. Finally, he said, "Go ahead. Get it off your chest. You'll feel better."

"You told Asarem to back out of the talks," she said, modulating her anger by infusing her voice with syrup.

"Straight to the point, Nerys." He smiled grudgingly. "I always liked that about you."

"You don't deny it, then?"

"You've never asked me for my position on the talks, you've only complained about Minister Asarem's behavior and asked me to use my influence on her," he rationalized.

"Don't mince words with me, Shakaar," Kira growled. "You knew what I was asking."

"You wanted Minister Asarem to be nice to your Cardassian friends. I told Asarem to be less confrontational. I did what I said I would."

"You have a chance to help Bajor and you run away like a deserter."

"Part of being a leader is choosing between equally good options. Forging peace with Cardassia, as a Bajoran nation, is a good choice. But a simpler path—one that recognizes that our relationship with Cardassia will be normalized when we join the Federation—is also a good choice. Why choose the more complicated option?"

"Because we aren't whole, as a people, without closure. As Bajor, sovereign and independent," she argued. "You've always fought your own battles and now you're turning the biggest one of all—the one that wins the war—over to someone else?"

Shakaar continued his oratory as if Kira weren't even in the room. "Consider their gift, even. How like them, to remind us of our humiliation."

"What?"

"All those pretty pictures, Nerys, they came from Dukat's bastard. Because Dukat took a married woman from her home and children and raped her, a great artist was born. I'm not one who believes the end justifies the means."

"What does Ziyal have to do with peace negotiations?"

"The Cardassians don't really want peace. They came here, with their *gift*," he spat the word, "to remind us exactly who we are to each other. They're the masters and we're the slaves. Not while I'm First Minister of Bajor. Never again."

"Ziyal was Bajoran, too!" she protested.

He laughed, dismissing her with the indulgent mien of a wise teacher amused by his student's naïve assertions. Sipping his juice, he studied his desk screen and continued to putter about his office, blithely indifferent.

He's misdirecting you. He wants to provoke you, make you lose your temper so he can discredit your accusations. Kira called on memory for strength. *Holding the soft, cool hand of her dying friend against her cheek . . . Cackling voices from her childhood hissing that Cardassians were without* pagh *. . . The smell of her mother's hair as she said good-bye. . . .*

Lies. *Shakaar lied.* Trembling, Kira dug her fingernails into the palms of her hands and rushed through a silent prayer. "Lending your support to the talks—giving Minister Asarem the go-ahead to negotiate—will help you let go of the past, Edon," she pleaded softly. "Let it go."

His face softening, Shakaar tenderly took her by the wrists and one hand at a time, pried her fingers off her palms, feather-tracing the remaining angry red indentations with his index finger.

A searing wave of bile scalded her throat. *Who are you?*

Jerking her hands away from Shakaar, she clenched them into fists and thrust them at her sides, sending his travel bag and the metal box he had just unpacked clattering onto the floor. The box opened, but nothing spilled out.

Utterly unruffled, he dropped to the floor to retrieve the empty box, gather up the bag and a few clothes, and return them to the desk. Smiling kindly, he said, "You need to relax, Nerys. I'm worried about how stressed you are. You should take some time off. Go away. Clear your head."

She stared at him, still clinging to the one idea that made sense to her. "You don't know—you couldn't have—there's no way—" she stammered.

"Yes?"

"The vandalism. The veiled threats at the Cardassian delegation. You didn't have anything to do—?"

"Come now, Nerys—this is me you're talking to." He placed his hands on his chest. "Listen to how ridiculous you sound! I'm the First Minister of Bajor. I don't deal in criminal conspiracies. Besides, I wasn't even here tonight. You *know* me, Nerys. Almost better than anyone."

Kira shook her head in disbelief. "You know, logically, you're right. And I am under a lot of stress. But I *don't* know you anymore," she confessed. And it hurt to say it. Who she was resulted from, in no small part, the time she had spent with Shakaar. To have arrived at a place where she could even fathom making an accusation against him. . . . Her convulsing world left her unbalanced, disoriented. "But if Ro's investigation uncovers even the smallest link to you, Minister, nothing will protect you from me."

"I'll submit myself to your lash if I'm found guilty of skulking around Deep Space 9 and terrorizing its residents," he said sarcastically.

The door chimed; Sirsy announced Vedek Nolan, who became distinctly uncomfortable upon seeing Kira as he entered the office. His beady eyes darted between her and the minister. "Late night shrine services, Minister. You asked for an escort?" he questioned.

"Yes, I wanted an update about how the station's religious community was faring in these troubled times," Shakaar explained to the confused vedek who clearly was wondering what Kira was doing here when business hours had ended earlier. "I think we're done here, aren't we, Colonel?" he asked Kira mildly.

Their word battles had been punctuated with dueling glares; this last round proved not to be an exception. This time, Shakaar looked away first.

Kira knew he could afford to lose because circumstances provided him the perfect snub. *He's going to services. He's actually going to services and I can't! And he enjoys that.* "Yes, we're done."

Shakaar nodded and launched into animated dialogue with the vedek as he swept past Kira and out of the room.

"For now," she said softly.

• • •

They still hadn't answered her calls, even though she'd started signaling at their door five minutes ago. And that was after three failed attempts to contact Thriss from her office, once Dr. Girani had told Phillipa about the latest incident. Phillipa believed herself to be a patient person—except in an emergency. Present circumstances certainly qualified.

Over the course of their sessions, Phillipa had pieced together Shar and Thriss's history. By calling in a few favors, she'd been able to gain access to an Andorian database that explained in academic terms the physiological processes Thriss had described. Shar and Thriss had initiated *tezha,* a facet of sexual intimacy, but not in the conventional sense that most humanoids understood. *Tezha* literally created a tangible, biochemical attachment between bondmates; bodies became tuned to each other, with brain chemistry and endocrine balances responding to the unique combination of sensory markers that identified the bondmates. It wasn't unlike imprinting between young and their parents. When bondmates ventured into intimate associations before the *shelthreth,* the overall cohesion of the bond wasn't assured. Bonds between segments surpassed bonds within the whole group. Because Thriss's attachment to Shar surpassed what she shared with the others, Phillipa worried that Anichent and Dizhei wouldn't be adequately attuned to Thriss to provide her the emotional support she needed to weather this crisis.

Phillipa rolled back on her heels outside Shar's quarters, wondering if Thriss would answer a direct call if she used her combadge. Before her hand reached her chest, the door hissed open, revealing Anichent.

"Good day, Counselor. Have you anything new to report from Colonel Kira? Perhaps a letter from Shar?" he said, his tightly tensed antennae betraying more about his frame of mind than the lackadaisical way he leaned against the door frame. *As if he's trying desperately to appear casual in order to mask his emotional state. Nice try, Anichent.*

"Dr. Girani told me what happened. I'm here to see Thriss." She took a step toward the threshold, but Anichent made no move to get out of her way. *Not being one for words, he resorts to physical intimidation,* she reasoned. *If worst comes to worst, I've mastered the Vulcan neck pinch. I could have him on the floor in a second. And Dizhei? I could take her, no problem.* Phillipa only pondered violent impulses—she never seriously considered instigating a fight. But she took comfort knowing she was equally matched with most who might threaten her. *Nobody ever expects the counselor to kick ass.*

"Thriss is resting now. You can see her in the morning," Anichent said, folding his arms. "I understand why you're here. We appreciate your concern. But this is a family matter and Dizhei and I will handle it."

"She almost assaulted a patient, Anichent," Phillipa said. "A child. That's completely uncharacteristic of her. Adults? Yes. Children? Never. Her disappointment at not receiving a letter from Shar could be triggering a serious relapse." She hadn't had time to read the whole report, but she'd read enough to worry her.

A primary schoolchild with a fracture received during exercise period had come in to have the bone mended. A routine procedure Thriss had performed many times. Busy with an OB exam, Girani had asked Thriss to assist Ensign Mancuso, the nurse. While Mancuso prepped the fracture repair kit, Thriss had grown frustrated with the child's persistent tears and had screamed at her, thrown a tray of medical tools across the room and scared the wits out of the child.

"We're all saddened by not hearing from Shar, but there's always next time. We're here for Thriss. We'll help her cope with this." Anichent wouldn't budge. "We're waiting to confirm our decision with Councillor zh'Thane, but I believe we'll be leaving for Andor tomorrow. It's what's best for us."

Phillipa shifted her weight to one hip. "This persistent focus on 'we,' while admirable in its loyalty, fails to acknowledge Thriss's needs as an individual. She might not be as well-equipped to deal with this as you are, Anichent." When Thriss had become Phillipa's patient, she had spent hours scouring the database for any helpful information. A portrait of a species intent on protecting the needs of the whole over the one had emerged. Not an easy obstacle for a therapist to hurdle when one of the parts of the whole was broken. "You're making a mistake," Phillipa reiterated, hoping Anichent would relent.

"You come from a species that has the luxury of considering the needs of the individual first. We do not," Anichent said quietly. "Our social customs are complex, Counselor. I think we're the best first line of defense for Thriss. Out of deference to you, we'll bring her to your office first thing tomorrow, before we leave for good."

Perceiving Anichent as immovable, Phillipa backed away from the threshold of ch'Thane's quarters and watched the door close in her face.

As much as she wanted to help Thriss immediately, believing that one could bleed to death as easily from a slow hemorrhage as from a severed artery, she would compromise rather than cause conflict among the bondmates. Their relationship had the deceptive fragility of crystal: smooth and hard to the touch, but quick to be crushed with any measure of applied force. Phillipa refused to push, lest she be the one to finally shatter Thriss.

With deliberate concentration, Thriss lifted her head from the pillow. "Is Counselor Matthias out there? I thought I heard her voice." The room heaved and swayed; she tried merging the two Dizheis rushing toward her with her eyes but her bondmate moved too quickly and the effort made her dizzy. Collapsing into the covers she willed her weighty limbs to float, to dissolve into boneless liquid. Her joints ached; their burning tightness cinched tighter like a thousand pinches in her hands and knees and hips and feet.

Dizhei smoothed her hair with a dry, cool hand. "It's all right. Don't push yourself. I know it's been a hard day."

She rolled her face down into her pillow and sought the anesthetic of memory. Shar came to her unbidden, and she eagerly allowed the room to recede from her senses as she willed her mind to recall the soft brush of his lips mapping her face. The tone of his voice that he reserved for quiet, dark moments when she molded herself to his back, absorbing with her own body the heat he radiated. Nestling her nose in his chest, inhaling the myriad of scents that were Shar. Breathing came easier as she drifted into dreams. She could almost hear him whispering the silly endearments that they'd invented as aliases, to prevent their clandestine meetings and notes from being discovered.

She missed him. Every part of her was meant to fit with him and without him, she felt adrift. Somewhere among the lights of a billion worlds he wandered where her net couldn't draw him in. Frozen darkness, like the void of space, extinguished any warmth she could cull from her dreams.

He was lost. He had forgotten her. Since he was far away, she had passed from his memory. He wasn't coming home. He'd never come home. Not truly. Not to her.

In the haze of sound and light, she imagined she heard Anichent and Dizhei's voices, elongated and garbled. *Home, we need to return home,* she heard one of them say. She tried to explain that Shar wasn't home so it didn't matter, but it took more strength than she could muster. And *Zhadi* was here? That couldn't be. Thriss squinted at the wall and thought she saw *Zhadi.* Only *Zhadi* wore such bright, gaudy colors, colors that Shar thought were ridiculous. But it couldn't be *Zhadi:* she was away and wouldn't be back for days. Unlike Shar, who would never be back.

She wanted sleep. She wanted the dark numbness of sleep so she pushed past the disappointment and the pain and the useless aching prison that was her body . . . her body that would never carry Shar's child . . . and willed it all to fade away into nothingness.

Kira picked her way past the crime scene barriers and into the nearly desolate gallery. A few of Ro's people and the curator's staff sorted through the disarray, searching for evidence, and gently handling the remains of Ziyal's artwork. No one smiled.

Had it been only a few days since she'd walked here with Macet as they both sought to find a workable solution for both their peoples? In spite of the brawl and in spite of Minister Asarem closing down the talks, Kira had remained hopeful until her encounter with Shakaar. Try as she might, she couldn't understand his untenable machinations. Yes, postponing the normalization of relations until after Bajor joined the Federation made pragmatic sense, but ethical sense? Though they'd had their disagreements—and Kira had found herself increasingly on opposing sides with him—she had always believed Shakaar to be a man of honor, a man who saw his role not only as a policy leader, but as a protector of the people's integrity. Kira couldn't see where the integrity was in his present course of action.

She shuffled past hateful words carved into the walls and paintings, over puddles of red paint still drizzling off benches and walls. Beneath the sadistic violence lacerating the room, Kira sensed Ziyal's spirit—it was weaker, but it lingered. Kira's eyes watered. Her friend's *pagh* had been given a chance to live anew; after a lifetime as a fugitive, she had found a place to rest, where she could be safe from the cruelties of bigotry. *And we couldn't even shield her here,* Kira thought sadly.

She wandered from space to space, lost in her thoughts, so when she stumbled upon a civilian she was slow to fix on her identity. *This is a closed area. Authorized personnel only,* she prepared to say until she recognized she stood face-to-face with Minister Asarem.

They considered each other awkwardly, neither knowing what to say or how to begin. That Asarem had chosen to come here now, to witness this tragedy, spoke well of her to Kira's way of thinking.

The dullness in Kira's chest receded, replaced by warmth. Maybe there was a reason why her feet brought her here instead of instinctively guiding her back to her quarters. After that distasteful meeting with Shakaar, she longed to shower, wash her hands of him, but instead she'd ended up taking a different turbolift and walking across the Promenade and now, Asarem Wadeen stood before her, hands laced behind her back, waiting, watching.

Kira didn't believe in coincidences.

They exchanged civil greetings, words about the shocking nature of the crime, and then, again, lapsed into awkward silence. Neither woman moved to leave.

"Minister, do you mind if I take a minute of your time?"

"Do you have another lecture for me?"

"No, more like an apology. I talked to Shakaar."

"Ah," she said, understanding.

"The situation is just as you said," Kira admitted. "But you have to know that in all the years I've known Shakaar, to choose such a course isn't like him."

Asarem nodded. "We don't always come down on the same side of things, the first minister and I. He tends to be more progressive while I feel safest with a more conservative, traditional approach. But even knowing our stylistic differences, the way he chose to handle this situation with Ambassador Lang surprised even me."

Moved by Asarem's gracious frankness, Kira felt ashamed by her own hasty judgment. "I'm sorry. For what I've said. For how I've behaved."

"If I were in your place, I would likely have done as you did," Asarem said graciously.

"Shakaar did say he thought we'd find we had a lot in common if we had a chance to get to know each other."

"I believe that as well."

They continued walking, avoiding looking at each other until Kira stopped. "I know as things presently stand, talks won't resume. You can't call Ambassador Lang and start things up again without going against Shakaar's orders."

"True," Asarem conceded.

"But if you knew, in your heart, that Shakaar was wrong and that he was walking contrary to the path the Prophets have set for Bajor, would you go against him?"

"What are you asking?"

"Please. Can we sit?"

They found a small, mostly unsoiled section of carpet in front of a maintenance closet. Pushing aside a broken piece of bench and other dusty refuse, the women dropped down cross-legged to the floor. Kira fumbled around for the words, seeing her own confusion reflected on Asarem's face until she fell back on the oldest convention of storytelling: start from the beginning. Haltingly, she asked, "Have you ever heard of the *Ravinok?*"

And from there, Ziyal's story, as Kira recalled it, tumbled out. She related her own conflicted emotions upon finding Dukat's illegitimate daughter in the Dozarian system, Dukat's willingness to murder Ziyal, in cold blood, rather than risk her existence being discovered by his family or the Cardassian government, and Kira's forcing him to accept responsibility for the unwanted child. Details that faded from her recollections due to the passage of time flooded back to her and Kira found herself explaining Ziyal's uncomfortable initiation into Bajor's art community, the prylars who grew to treasure her, and her tentative exploration of a relationship with the Prophets. How Ziyal had come to love Garak, much to the dismay of her friends on the station. Of her final days, when Sisko and Starfleet prepared to retake the station and Dukat was forced to flee or be taken prisoner, how Damar ultimately completed the murder Dukat had originally intended and how it felt to see her lifeless body. And as she spoke, Kira knew her cheeks were wet with tears and that she'd shared thoughts and impressions she'd never before voiced aloud to a virtual stranger, but she felt compelled to continue. When the last words left her lips, Kira felt she'd finally arrived at the place the Prophets intended her to, and the restlessness that had haunted her since Macet's arrival finally abated.

Asarem said little in response and Kira understood why. What else could be said? Knowing she had done as she should, Kira decided to leave. She had decisions to make and now she might be able to make them with a peaceful heart. Wishing her good night, Kira started toward the exit when Asarem called after her.

"So what will you do next?"

Kira shrugged. "I don't know. Keep pummeling Shakaar until he relents. Help Ro. Go to Bajor. I'm not sure." She hovered between exhaustion and collapse—a change of scenery could allow her to refuel, gear up for the next challenge. But Ro had two critical open investigations—the Promenade riot and the still unsolved vandalism; responsibility effectively tethered her to the station.

"Walk with the Prophets, Colonel," Asarem said.

"So she finally fell asleep," Phillipa announced, flopping backward onto her bed. She ordered the lights dimmed and sighed. Punching and pulling her pillow succeeded in reconfiguring lumps, but not much else; her neck muscles felt like knotted cords. She rolled over onto her stomach, dangling her feet over the side of the bed, and watched her husband undress.

"Rubbing her back works every time. Mireh drops off like that—" Sibias snapped his fingers.

"And how did you figure that out?"

"Works with you."

"You're just a little too sure of yourself, smart man. I don't think a little pressure between the shoulder blades is going to work for me tonight."

"That a challenge?"

"Maybe."

"Tough day?"

"Oh yeah," she groaned. After she'd returned to her quarters, she tried contacting Thriss several more times before her family's needs pressed her into temporarily forgoing her professional concerns. She and Sibias helped the children with homework, played Kadis-Kot and wrapped up the evening with a chapter from Arios's latest favorite, *The Adventures of Lin Marna and the Mystery of Singularity Sam*. Sibias defused Mireh's stalling tactics while she took a sonic shower and now, with the children taken care of, she allowed herself to resume worrying about her patient.

Kicking off his slippers, Sibias sat down beside her. His thumbs massaged the hollows of her shoulder blades. "Can you talk about it?"

Relaxing proved challenging for Phillipa, though Sibias kneading away her muscular stress didn't hurt. She willingly yielded to the pressure, enjoying the sensations his hands produced. "Is this how it works with Mireh? You keep her talking while your hands work out every kink in her back?"

"More or less. But there aren't many kinks in her back, being two and all," he said, working down her rib cage. "Mireh isn't as concerned about saving the universe as you are—yet."

Closing her eyes, she blanked her mind, focused on his touch until . . . "I'm sorry," she said, pulling herself up on her elbows, "I can't stop thinking about my patient. I'll just find something to read. Maybe one of your architectural history journals can bore me to sleep. That research on jevonite looks fascinating."

Carefully, Sibias eased her over onto her back. "You can't make it better for everyone, Phil. You can't force people to make good choices. Sometimes, they mess up and you have to be okay with that." He toyed with a lock of her hair, mapped the outline of her cheekbone with his finger.

"I know, I know. . . ." She inhaled sharply. "But I have this feeling that if I could just see her, talk to her, I might be able to make a difference." She covered her face with her forearms. It was just so damn frustrating when you had the tools to fix something and you couldn't. She had to confess, however, that the way Sibias grazed her bare arms might fix her problem with settling down to sleep . . .

He nestled his face in the crook of her neck. "You say that every time, my wife."

"Your beard is ticklish," she laughed.

"Think of it as a variation on massage therapy," he murmured into the hollow of her throat.

Phillipa loved how he smelled—in her imagination he was musty archeology texts and crisp autumn days and smoky tallow candles. She dropped her arms to her sides, tipped her head toward his and rested her hair against his face. He reached for the top of her pajamas and in one smooth motion, undid the first button, and then the second.

"So I'm thinking if the backrub isn't going to work . . ." he began.

"Damn straight." Twisting onto her side, she wriggled her leg between his and pulled him into her. As they kissed, a blurry thought of Thriss sleeping without the one she loved tightened her throat, until a warm fog of sensation gradually diluted her coherence, leaving her worries to be rediscovered in the morning.

Dizhei stretched awake, wondering when she'd fallen asleep on the couch. A vague recollection of a middle-of-the-night communication from Charivretha explained why she would be in the living room, but not why Anichent had left her there, instead of rousing her to return to watch over Thriss.

This latest bout of moodiness seemed to be following her usual pattern. An angry outburst followed by a verbal tirade, directed most of the time at Anichent until guilt supplanted anger and she dissolved into a quivering mass of tears. Last night, Thriss had cried herself into a migraine before sleep overtook her. Both Dizhei and Anichent had been grateful for the reprieve.

Without question, Thriss's anguish would be better dealt with on Andor. Those of their own kind could counsel with her, provide her with the emotional support she needed to survive the remainder of Shar's absence. If needs be, she or Anichent could return to Deep Space 9 closer to the time the *Defiant* was scheduled to come home. They would insist that Shar take immediate leave for the *shelthreth*. The anxiety plaguing all of them would end. Decisions about who would stay with whom and where could be made later.

Stumbling to her feet, she stretched again. Perhaps she should check in on Thriss. See how she was feeling this morning. If they were fortunate, her mood might have lifted, allowing them to enjoy their final hours on the station. Dizhei didn't hear Anichent stirring. He'd likely gone to the gymnasium for an early workout. She hoped she could interest him in breakfast at Quark's, anything but replicated—

The door slid open. Dizhei paused. Blinked. And shook her head hoping she might be victim to a sleepy hallucination. But her quivering knees, her racing heartbeat, and the scream that leapt to her throat meant her body understood what her mind refused to accept.

21

Vaughn waited at the bottom of the stairs for Dax. He'd finished his testimony in Tlaral's hearing a little more than an hour ago. Though he hadn't had any direct interaction with the Yrythny technologist, the judicial panel had requested that he explain the situation and circumstances surrounding the Consortium trade. Over the course of the day, Lieutenant Nog and Prynn had also offered their testimonies. His sense was that Tlaral faced an unpleasant fate.

The least of her crimes had been hiding her Wanderer identity and becoming a consort to a Houseborn male. Violating those laws meant, at minimum, a life in prison. Add conspiracy charges stemming from the attempted weapon/Cheka trade and Vaughn was certain the judicial panel would have few options in determining her punishment. She had helped her case by offering to share intelligence on the underground's radical wing. Should her information prove valuable, the panel might be able to exhibit leniency, though some might argue a swift death was less painful than a lifetime haunted by bad choices. Vaughn wasn't sure they would know Tlaral's fate before they left in the morning. He almost hoped the panel would deliberate slowly, avoid succumbing to public pressure for a swift, dramatic verdict. Rash decisions were rarely the correct ones.

At last, the tall, curved doors opened. Ezri slipped through, her attempt to make a soundless getaway failing miserably when the metal handle clanged against the door panels. She swiftly sprang down the stairs, skipping every other step.

"Ready to go, Commander?" she said with a heavy sigh. She had been testifying for more than two hours.

"In every possible way," Vaughn said.

Together, they strolled silently through the long, echoing halls of the Assembly Center, where only two weeks before Ezri had been brought to speak before a joint meeting of both assemblies. Vaughn wished he could have been there to hear her triumphal oratory—at least that's how Shar referred to it. Ezri had been more circumspect in her replies to Vaughn's inquiries. Maybe once they were back on the *Defiant* she would share her account of her experiences among the Yrythny. Sensing that a more complex story lurked beneath the surface, Vaughn was willing to bide his time. "How is it going for Jeshoh in there?"

"Even though Keren's facing charges of her own, her testimony was persuasive," Ezri said. "I believe the panel accepted her explanation of her relationship with Jeshoh, that for most of their lives they'd been friends and they intended to follow the law as best they could. She came off sounding like she'd made the only possible choices in an impossible situation."

That she'd done well pleased him; Vaughn had liked her since their first day on Luthia. If he'd had his druthers, she would have come to the Consortium in Minister M'Yeoh's place. He had to pity the science minister, however.

Within a day, he'd lost his consort and likely his political future. The Assembly had demanded the details regarding his union with Tlaral, assuming that he'd either conspired with her or was too easily deceived. When faced with similar circumstances, Keren had chosen the better path. Vaughn concluded, "Keren strikes me as an honorable individual."

"Who broke the law. Who's lost the position she's worked for since she was 10 years out of the water. Who may lose the one she loves. And Jeshoh, because he aligned himself with the terrorists, is facing far worse charges," Ezri noted pragmatically.

"At least you and Shar were able to persuade the panel to drop any charges relating to hijacking the *Sagan.*"

"It may not be enough." She shook her head. "The panel hearing Tlaral's case and Jeshoh's will compare notes. If Tlaral shoulders primary responsibility for orchestrating the plan, Jeshoh's punishment should be reduced."

"Is he worried about the potential outcomes?"

"As always, he's more worried about Keren." She pursed her lips, wrinkled her brow thoughtfully. "For himself, I'm not sure. Losing his position as Vice Chair of the Upper Assembly didn't seem to upset him, though the leaders of House Perian were devastated that their favorite son put illicit love above duty to home and world."

"In all the wisdom and experience of the ages, no philosopher has yet found the magical formula for balancing love and duty," Vaughn noted. *God knows I've looked for it.*

They exited through the Assembly Center's main doors and into the Great Plaza. Every corner bustled with activity: vendors, government workers coming and going from their jobs, military officers and Vanìmel dwellers armed with petitions, lined up to enter the Assembly members' offices. Vaughn had been surprised how well Luthia had absorbed the events of the past day. The population appeared quite calm, considering a top Houseborn official had been brought up on treason, the Wanderer underground had attempted to instigate a civil war and news of a major scientific breakthrough had broken within the last few hours. *The business of daily life always propels us forward,* he thought.

"Commander," Ezri said, stopping in her tracks. "Before you go, you ought to try this delicacy from the Black Archipelago region. House Soid harvests massive *darro,* fillets the meat into thin strips and marinates it for a year." She tipped her head in the direction of a vending cart where a long line of Yrythny waited.

Having had little time to experience Yrythny culture, Vaughn readily assented. Any regrets he had about leaving involved not having had time to be immersed in the wondrous strangeness of this remarkable world.

They procured their lunch and resumed their walk back to quarters.

"You seem to have enjoyed your time here," Vaughn said, chewing the dried fish off a skewer.

" 'Enjoyed' is how I refer to vacation," Ezri said. "I prefer to think I made the most of my time here. I learned a lot, not just about the Yrythny, but about myself."

"Over my lifetime, I've found that often the most important thing we take from exploration is a better understanding of the world within than the worlds outside."

Dax looked at him quizzically. "What are you suggesting? That the final frontier is less about exploring space than it is about exploring ourselves?"

Vaughn smiled. "Isn't it?"

"You can follow along with the model on your desk screen," Shar said to a filled auditorium of scientists, sitting in semicircle rows around the rostrum where he stood. More Yrythny sat in the aisles and squeezed in around the rear doors. The spotlight trained on him made it difficult to discern exactly how many had gathered to hear his presentation, but he sensed he had a full house. Nog was somewhere in the room, though that didn't make him feel much better. He was still outnumbered about two thousand to one. Not seeing Yrythny faces made it easier to pretend he was back on Andor, presenting his senior thesis prior to his first year at the Academy.

Shar indicated the holographic projection of the Yrythny chromosome. "Here, on the nineteenth chromosome is where the most critical deletions and mutations are occurring." He highlighted the segment in question. "The genes in this segment are responsible for frontal lobe development—upper brain functions. In this segment over here . . ." Shar continued speaking from the text he'd memorized earlier. Having reviewed his results dozens of times with Vaughn and his own staff, Minister M'Yeoh and his committee, and the senior Assembly staff, he could recite this presentation in his sleep.

No one had slept much in the two days since the Defiant returned from the Consortium. The whole crew had been enjoying reunions among friends, staying up late swapping stories, and those who could finally took long-overdue shore leave. The Defiant hadn't been back an hour before Prynn was grilling Juarez and Candlewood about any and all knowledge they might have about Vanimel's oceans. Earlier today she had caught the first shuttle to the Coral Sea, leaving word that she would be back to Luthia in time for tomorrow's launch, but not to call her back to the Defiant unless the Cheka, the Borg and the Romulans decided to drop by. After hearing Nog's version of the Consortium trip, Shar couldn't say he blamed her.

Shar had spent his time working on his research, promising himself that as soon as he finished he would start analyzing the Yrythny chromosome with an eye to helping his own people. He still believed the "Turn Key" segments might provide clues as to how he might fix weaknesses in Andorian chromosomes. He would focus on his own projects later, after he'd finished reporting to this surprisingly large group of Yrythny.

"Over time, the Yrythny have selected their consorts from a narrow pool of genotypes, enabling recessive mutations to be passed down with increasing frequency," Shar continued. The holoprojection of the chromosome was replaced by a simplified graphic of a Mendelian-style flow chart, showing five generations of Yrythny genotypes. He kept expecting to be interrupted with questions; if he were at home, he'd have been answering questions every minute or so. But he suspected his audience was still reeling from the revelations in his research. It wasn't every day an alien presented a planet with information that had the potential to alter thousands of years of rigidly held social and cultural traditions. He couldn't fathom what would happen, long term, with the Yrythny. The leadership might try to dismiss Shar's work, continuing with the status quo. Already the Assembly had imposed strict controls on who had access to the data, but word traveled rapidly in Luthia and many uninvited guests had shown up for Shar's presentations. Over time, Shar was confident his discovery would have impact. The farmer-scientists on the Hebshu Peninsula would ensure that.

Shar deactivated the hologram and the room lighting came up. "That concludes my presentation. If anyone desires further clarification, I've uploaded my data to the Luthia Scientific Archives and the Assembly network. Thank you for coming." He turned to collect the few items he'd brought with him, loading them into his briefcase. When he turned back around, he discovered no one had left. Before he could ask what his Yrythny colleagues were waiting for, every scientist, engineer, and ordinary citizen who had attended his lecture rose to their feet, all eyes focused on him. His antennae tingled, overwhelmed by the deeply felt emotions in the room. Scanning their faces, looking into their eyes, Shar saw mixtures of amazement, gratitude and shock greeting him. He fumbled for the right words, but Nog rescued him, springing to his feet and launching into hearty applause. The Yrythny stared, watching Nog smack his palms together, but gradually, they followed suit, until the entire room thundered.

Shar blinked back incredulity. *I am at the beginning of a path I've been searching for my whole life. I've found my mission.* He looked over at Nog, who hadn't relented, and back at his Yrythny colleagues. Lacking the wherewithal to share what this moment meant to him, Shar accepted their adulation.

Thriss will be proud.

Time to relax, Ezri thought. She splashed on her wrists some perfume that had been among the dozens of gifts she'd received, baskets and packages stacked atop the table in her Luthian quarters. Simply standing in one place, squeezing the plush rug between her toes, had an unexpected charm. Doing nothing was a nice change. She'd hardly had a chance to enjoy Julian. Studying for and delivering testimony before the judicial panel had consumed a good deal of her time, as did preparing to return to their mission and wrapping up loose ends with the Yrythny. Since it was their last night in Luthia, Ezri felt like she deserved to be idle.

Emerging from the bathroom, she yanked her crimson robe tight and plopped down on the couch beside Julian, tucking her bare feet behind her. "Have I told you how wonderful it feels to have this back?" She fingered the robe's lapels. "I should have taken it from our quarters before you all left for the Consortium, but now I have the fun of rediscovering something I missed."

"I hope you missed me as much as the bathrobe," Julian said dryly. Scooting closer to her, Julian reached around her shoulders and pulled her close. Ezri snuggled into him, draped over his lap and nestled her head in the crook of his arm. He ran his fingers through her hair, smoothing and tucking it behind her ears.

"Your hair is longer," he observed.

"It's been two weeks, not two months," she laughed.

"Yes, but did you know that a Trill's hair is capable of growing half a centimeter a week?"

Leave it to Julian to prove his point, no matter what the circumstances. "We could continue discussing my amazing follicles, or you could find other equally intriguing aspects of my anatomy to study." She walked her fingers up his neck and ruffled the hair on the back of his head.

"As much as that suggestion appeals to me, I think I want to talk to you before we further my studies of Trill anatomy." Julian linked their fingers together. Bringing her hand up to his lips, he placed a kiss on each knuckle.

"Isn't the woman supposed to be the one who likes to talk?" Ezri pouted.

"No, seriously. We haven't talked much about what happened while we were apart. You clearly have something on your mind," Julian said. "When you aren't being frivolous, you're quite pensive. I'd like you to share it with me."

Rising from Julian's lap, Ezri curled into the couch, resting her cheek on the cushions. She studied her lap while she struggled to find the right words.

"You were right," she said finally, meeting his eyes. "I still haven't found my equilibrium."

He waited patiently for her to elaborate at her own pace.

"I was so sure of myself, Julian. So sure I could do it all. And you were right. I'd started to believe no challenge was beyond me. That I had no limits. But this experience taught me otherwise. My time here wasn't what I thought it would be. It was, in short, kind of humiliating."

"That's hardly what I've heard. The Yrythny were wowed by your diplomatic savvy. The compromise you negotiated before Shar made his discovery is still going to be ratified, except now some of the inter-caste taboos will be lifted for colonists. You blazed the trail."

"See, that's the thing. I didn't blaze the trail." She rolled her eyes, embarrassed. "Technically, Curzon, Lela, Audrid, and Jadzia did. They did most of the work. Even the speech I gave at the Assembly that first day? I stole it from Lela."

"What's the benefit of having a symbiont if you don't learn from past lives?"

"I'm not supposed to *live* my past lives and that's what I've been doing. By the time I started working on the compromise, it was Curzon doing the work, not Ezri." Ezri brought her knees up into her chest. "Being joined isn't supposed to work like that. I'm supposed to augment the symbiont's experiences with my own, but sometimes it feels like Dax has already done it all."

"Ezri, I think you're being hard on yourself—" Julian tried to hug her, but Ezri backed away.

"I'm not asking for pity, Julian," she said earnestly. "Honest. Dax's past hosts made incredible contributions to the Federation. Books could be written about Curzon and Jadzia alone! But then the superlative Jadzia is followed up with Ezri Tigan, who didn't want to be joined in the first place. I'm kind of the place-holding host until some brilliant initiate can receive Dax after I die."

Julian took Ezri's hand and squeezed it, willing her to look him in the eye. "Listen to me. Right now, you're giving Dax experiences none of the other hosts could. None of them ever ventured on an exploratory mission like this one. The things you've seen—and will see in the years to come—will be different from anything the others experienced."

Grateful for his sweet words, Ezri kissed Julian's palm. She knew, however, that she needed to own up to her mistakes. "I had no idea what was being asked of me when I agreed to help the Yrythny. Part of me thought that I needed to prove to Commander Vaughn, and to the crew, that I was good enough to be his first officer, to be a leader. That choosing the command track was the right decision at this point in my personal evolution." She sighed. "But then when I started working with all these committees . . . I'm not an ambassador or an anthropologist. It became easier to know what to do when I allowed Lela or Curzon to take the lead instead of myself."

"In the end, though, it was Ezri who triumphed," Julian pointed out. "Nothing Dax had done could have helped you. When you trusted *your* experiences and training, you succeeded brilliantly."

She quirked a half-smile. "I know. That part I feel good about. When I think back to the previous two weeks . . . not so much. I was a fool. Poor Shar, I think he knew it and he was very, very patient with me."

"All's well that ends well?"

"Yeah. I suppose."

A beep sounded from the wall console. Ezri looked over and saw the message light blinking. "I'd better check that. With us leaving in the morning, you never know what might be coming up at the last minute."

She crossed the room to pull up the message, quickly scanning the contents. "It's from the judiciary panel. They'll have a ruling on Jeshoh's case tomorrow morning. Is it a good sign that they've come back with a decision so quickly?" Part of Ezri worried, hoping her testimony had helped his case. What happened on the *Sagan* was an aberration from the Jeshoh she'd grown to like and admire in her time on Vanìmel.

"If you think about it, there wasn't that much to decide. His guilt wasn't in question, more what the consequences would be."

"I'm glad we'll know soon."

"And yet another triumph for Ezri. Without you, Jeshoh might have gone through with Tlaral's plan. You might have saved him—and Keren—a lot of heartache."

Shoving her hands in her pockets, Ezri said, "Are you hungry? I'm hungry."

Julian laughed. "Not so much hungry, but thirsty. How about—"

"—a Tarkelian tea. You're so predictable," she said affectionately. "Sorry, you'll have to wait until we're back on *Defiant* to indulge that particular vice. Tell you what, though, try this." She tossed him a self-heating bulb from among her gifts. "Local brew. You might like it." For herself, she selected a slice of a fruit torte she'd grown to like during the official dinner parties she'd attended. Someone who'd apparently noticed sent her a dozen.

"Not bad," Julian said after an appreciative sip. "We should save one for the replicators to analyze."

"That's a good idea. In fact, I should do the same with all the—*OW!*" Ezri dropped her plate on the table and hopped up on one foot while massaging the bruised toes of the other. Bending over, she reached for the offending item. "Your dufflebag belongs in the middle of the rug?" she said with mock annoyance.

"I was so eager to see you I didn't bother to put it away in the sleep-room."

"Yes, well explain that to my toes," she said, hefting the bag onto an empty chair. "Hey . . . what's this—" Ezri removed a padd from inside. Clicking it on, she thumbed through the contents. She read aloud, " 'Lughor pulled her close and bit her cheek, snarling, "You will be my mate, my Ngara—" Umm, Julian, what are you doing with *Burning Hearts of Qo'noS?*"

"Oh, that." He tapped his foot absently. "Commander Vaughn was finished with it, so he handed it off to me."

"Did he say if he liked it?"

"I asked him. He just rolled his eyes."

Ezri continued perusing the padd, thumbing through a few more screens. "You know, Jadzia wouldn't consider this fiction, she'd see it as an instruction manual." She raised a teasing eyebrow.

"And Ezri?" Julian said, rising from the couch.

"You want to find out?"

"Did you even sleep last night?" Nog asked, rubbing his eyes and yawning.

Shar looked up from his computer terminal. After dinner, he'd come straight back to his Luthian quarters to work on his chromosomal studies. Once the *Defiant* resumed its mission his time would, by necessity, belong to Vaughn and the needs of the mission. Returning to Deep Space 9 having made meaningful progress on his goals would go a long way to silencing those who had cast aspersions on his choices (most notably, his *zhavey*). "It's morning?"

"Morning usually is when the sun comes out. Unless this world is backward and they call it morning when it's dark outside." Nog padded over to the replicator, ordered up a root beer and collapsed on a chair.

"Adrenaline must have kept me up," Shar said. He closed the file he'd been working on and uploaded it to the *Defiant*. "Yesterday was a rather unique day for me."

"Don't let it go to your head, Ensign. Even if you solve the universe's problems, I still outrank you." Nog winked and took a swig of root beer.

"Noted, sir," Shar said, suppressing a smile. "Do you want to grab breakfast here or wait until we return to *Defiant?*"

"What exactly *is* a Yrythny breakfast?"

"Fish, *shmshu* cheese on kelp cakes, sea melons—"

Nog's face puckered. "I'll eat on the *Defiant,* thanks. Grubcakes in slug sauce. That's a meal."

The door chime sounded. Since Nog still sleepily nursed his soda, Shar figured he'd better see who their visitor was.

"Keren—" he said. Her rumpled clothes and grayed complexion bespoke the stress she'd been through since they'd landed at Luthia. He hadn't talked privately with her since they'd left for House Perian to hunt the raiders.

"Try not to be so surprised, Ensign ch'Thane," Keren said lightly. "Your feelings are showing."

"What? Oh, of course. My antennae."

"I wanted to tell you about the ruling before you heard it officially." She peeked into Shar's quarters and noticing Nog, said, "Can we go someplace to talk?"

"The courtyard?"

She nodded.

As she sat down, Keren dropped a small backpack on the ground beside the bench. Both shifted uncomfortably, neither knowing how to broach the events of the previous days. Finally Keren said, "The panel issued their findings for Jeshoh and me. They let me off easy. When the first colonists leave Vanìmel I will be with them. They've decided exile is better than prison. I think they're worried that I might be a martyr to whatever is left of the underground."

"You would have tried to go off-world anyway, wouldn't you?" Shar asked. "Now that your people have a working defense against the web weapons—"

"Yes. But I have to admit that being sent away and never being allowed to return is a sobering thought. Whether the colonies are successful or not, I will live out my life elsewhere." Keren reached over, stroking the velvety petals of a trumpet flower. "This is still my home and I love it."

I wonder how I would feel if I could never return to Andor. The thought struck him as ironic, considering he'd been avoiding going back for over four years. *The time has come. I'm ready for the* shelthreth. And until the thought crossed his mind, Shar hadn't known that he would choose the *shelthreth* when his current mission was over. In a few days, he'd sit down with Commander Vaughn and negotiate the terms of his leave. The more he imagined making a life commitment to Anichent, Dizhei and Thriss, the more excited he became.

"Understandably, Jeshoh's sentence isn't quite as lenient as mine," Keren continued. "He will serve a prison sentence. The number of years will be decided after Tlaral's hearing wraps up."

"After prison, isn't he free? There aren't any more restrictions imposed on him."

"Yes. At that point, he will join me wherever I am . . ." She gripped the edge of the bench, her shoulders tense.

A sense of dread filled Shar. "What is it, Keren?"

"With his position, with his involvement in the underground, the panel decided that they couldn't excuse his relationship with me." Closing her eyes, she whispered, "He'll never be able to go into the waters."

Her bravery, her resolve in the face of these consequences, humbled Shar. After spending her life working for the right to take a consort and have offspring, she wouldn't have the chance unless she chose someone other than Jeshoh. Having witnessed their devotion to each other, Shar couldn't fathom that she would abandon Jeshoh now.

"Of course I'll wait for him, Shar," Keren said. Seeing his puzzled expression, she clarified, "You're wearing your feelings again."

"I'm sorry. I wish there was a way . . ."

"We knew the risks." With a distant look in her eyes, she said, "Jeshoh and I will have a home together someday. I know we will." She patted his leg. "I have another reason for visiting. To say good-bye, yes, but I have a gift."

"But—"

"No protests." Reaching into her backpack, Keren removed a sealed container about the size of a dinner plate. "The eggs stripped from House Perian couldn't all be saved. Most of them had been out of the water for too long under variable temperatures and became nonviable. The government destroyed them, but before they did I persuaded them to let me give you an egg pouch in thanks for your research." Reaching out to take his hand, she turned it palm up and placed the container into it, smiling gently. "I know what you're trying to do for your people, Shar. This way, you have proper samples to work with and not just computer models."

Emotion tightened Shar's throat. He swallowed, opened his mouth, but nothing emerged. Continuing to stare at her, he reached for her hands and squeezed them.

"It's a small thing, Shar. You've more than paid for the right to take these." Standing up, she lay her cheek in his hair for a moment and walked away. When he shook off his astonishment, he searched the courtyard for her, but she had vanished, leaving his life very much the way she had come into it.

The doors to his quarters opened and Nog poked his head out. "Hey, Shar. I've decided to head back to the ship. The commander called a minute ago. He said an encrypted message came through marked 'eyes only,' but apparently it was for you and not Vaughn. He's having it rerouted here."

"Thank you, Nog," Shar said, gazing at the egg container. "I'll be along soon. But I want to sit here for a few minutes longer."

"Okay. I'll see you shipboard then?"

Shar nodded.

He ran his fingers over Keren's gift, imagining that the answers he'd sought his entire life might lie within. Bowing his head, he covered his eyes, offering gratitude to whatever power in the universe had brought him to this place at this time. He would never regret the choices that brought him here; he would never be the same person after today. For a moment he meditated, savoring the gentle trickle of water spilling over the fountain, the occasional rustle of leaves. When he opened his eyes, he was ready to return to duty. Holding the gift protectively against him, he entered his quarters.

Sleeping late was a rare indulgence, but it felt nice to flout the routine one last time before starting up the rigors of co-commanding a Starfleet mission. Soon enough, Ezri would be stumbling into the mess, muttering her request to the replicator and feeling her way to a table. Choosing to loll about, half dressed, eating a breakfast of succulent fresh fruits and licking the juice off your fingers wasn't something she anticipated being able to do before she returned to Deep Space 9. Never mind that she had the guest quarters to herself. To provide him with adequate time to restock the medical bay, Julian had reported to duty two hours ago. Ezri stayed behind, wrapped up in her covers, relishing the warmth streaming through the courtyard windows. A check of the chronometer indicated she still had another hour before she met with Vaughn to allocate duty shifts. *A walk. A walk sounds nice.* She pulled on an old favorite pair of Academy sweats and ambled out to the balcony.

Spending these weeks on Luthia made her wonder if more nature could be incorporated into the station's auspices. Outside the arboretum and a few botany labs, assuaging a craving for trees and flowers required time in a holo-suite, or a trip to Bajor. Leisurely, Ezri walked down the stairs, bending over to examine the fragrant ground cover. She took a seat on a bench, throwing her legs out in front of her, throwing back her head and closing her eyes, soaking up the light for a last few precious minutes.

"... I wish there was something we could have done. Dr. Girani had no idea the infirmary was missing anything and ..."

Ezri sat up straight. *I swear I heard voices.*

"—until you come home. I don't know what else to tell you. The others are too distraught to speak right now."

She twisted around, trying to see who might still be in quarters because if she had to guess, she'd just heard Charivretha zh'Thane. *Maybe I drank too much wine last night or those chocolate pastries didn't sit well with my stomach.* Shar's courtyard door was open, the curtains blowing. Cautiously, Ezri approached the open door. The closer she came, the more clear the voice and as she listened, the context became clear. Standing outside, Ezri braced herself on the doorway, willing her thudding heart to stop. *What can I do?* She considered walking away. Invading his privacy right now could be exactly the wrong thing—or it could be exactly what he needed. She pushed aside the curtain and stepped inside.

With his back to the courtyard door, he sat on the floor in front of the console. She had been right—the speaker was zh'Thane. The Federation

Councillor sat in a chair in what looked like VIP quarters on DS9, the pain etched on her face expressing more than her words could.

"Her death was painless. I know you wouldn't have wanted her to suffer. None of us understand why she did it. She seemed—better. I am sorry, my chei."

The screen turned to static and then the message replayed.

"Thirishar, I wish I could be sending this message under happier circumstances, but a great tragedy has befallen us—"

Ezri knelt down, touched Shar's shoulder. He turned with a start, his limbs trembling uncontrollably. Wide-eyed, he stared at Ezri, his pain unfathomable. Helplessness swelled inside her and she ached for him. She opened and closed her mouth several times, searching for words. *I shouldn't be here.* Zh'Thane's heartbreaking message continued to play in the background. *What can I give him? I'm not equipped for this—I can't make it better!* From deep inside her, an answer, of a kind, came. Not so much an answer as a knowing, a knowing from Dax.

You. He needs you, Ezri.

Tears welled in her eyes. "I'm so sorry . . ." She gathered him into her arms and he yielded to her touch.

They wept together.

Epilogue

"I'm not an invalid!" protested Kasidy.

"No, you're not," Kira said patiently, clearing the dessert plates off the coffee table and heading off to the kitchen, "but you've spent the last half hour rubbing your arches. Your feet must be killing you after our walk today. Let me remind you that visiting every last stall at the market was your idea."

"If my feet get any bigger, I'm going to have to attach warnings to my shoes saying, 'Watch out—wide berth.'" Wincing, she threw her body forward, hoping the momentum would help her off the couch. The baby, however, had different ideas, choosing that moment to thrust its head squarely into her diaphragm. She grunted as it suddenly became hard to breathe. "I'll think I'll just stay here for a bit," she said, settling back into the cushions. From across the room, Kasidy saw Kira grin.

"Having a laugh at my expense, Colonel?" Kasidy teased, grateful that Kira had gradually unwound over the past few days; initially, her smiles had been infrequent.

Upon arrival, Kira had been so pale (Kasidy swore she'd lost weight as well), Kasidy thought she might be coming down with something serious. A more logical explanation for her condition quickly became apparent: she hadn't been on Bajor an hour before the station contacted her, with the next message arriving fifteen minutes after the first. Kasidy had quickly instituted a daily pattern of long walks—asking Kira to leave her combadge back at the house.

Kira scraped chocolate frosting off the plates into the recycler and deposited the plates in the sink to be washed later. "I was just remembering this time . . . a month before Kirayoshi was born. Sitting in Quark's with Jadzia, I'd probably had a liter of juice. The little guy decided it'd be a good time to play hoverball with my bladder."

It was Kasidy's turn to laugh, relating all too well to Kira's anecdote. Throwing her legs up so she sat sideways, Kas rested her chin on the back of the couch and watched Kira continue cleaning up. Though the meal had been simple, salads made with fresh greens and vegetables from her garden and squash soup, old-fashioned cooking tended to make a mess no matter how many shortcuts technology might provide.

"I vote we replicate breakfast," Kira said, pouring the last of the soup into a storage container. Clearing off the counters, she shuttled clean goblets into the cupboard and tossed a handful of *katterpods* into the produce basket. Wiping her hands on a towel, she crossed back to the sitting room and resumed her perch on Kasidy's favorite overstuffed chair.

"Cooking can be bothersome," Kasidy conceded, "but there's nothing quite as satisfying as getting your hands dirty *doing* something and then enjoying the fruits of your labors."

"You know . . . you sound like Benjamin when you talk like that," Kira said wistfully.

"I think that's one of the reasons I cook: it helps me keep him close."

"Do you—" Kira began, but hesitated.

"Get lonely?" she said, completing the question. "Miss him?" Since Kira arrived, they both had kept their conversations light. Kas assumed Kira needed the respite from her worries about the station as much as Kas needed to stop dwelling on Jake.

"I wasn't trying to be nosy," Kira apologized.

Kasidy held up a hand to stop her. "Everyone wonders and my honest answer is, of course. After the station—after being a ship's captain—the quiet around here took some getting used to. Now I actually like it." She said it and she meant it. At first, Kasidy followed through with the "dream house" project because she felt like she owed it to Ben. Gradually, she became caught up in the details, grateful to be staying busy. She was surprised how much time she spent selecting the stones for the fireplace, talking with the carpenter who carved the mantel, and finding just the right hand-thrown pottery plates that would sit on her kitchen table. Attributing her preoccupation with rugs and end tables to a maternal nesting instinct felt plausible to her. Then one day, standing in this very room she sat in now, she was savoring the warm sun streaming through the windows when she realized that she loved it here. This was *her* home. Her lullabies would whisper through its rafters. Fresh asters and Bajoran lilacs from the garden she planted would fill vases in every room. Jake—and Ben—would return here. Until then, she would make it ready to welcome them. "I have my fears," she said at last. "And I'd sleep easier knowing Jake was safe, but I'm happy."

"I'm glad you're happy, Kas. You've had more than your share of heartache since the war ended," Kira said, turning her gaze to watch the evening's first moonrise.

"We all have," Kasidy replied. "I hardly have a monopoly on suffering. I consider myself very blessed. You've shouldered your share of struggles."

"Mine are relatively small," she said lightly. Since her arrival, Kira had avoided talking about any work-related problems she might be having, focusing instead on Kasidy's baby, her search for dependable farm help, Jake, and the general political situation. Kas assumed that Kira didn't want to "needlessly worry the pregnant lady," a sentiment she'd become intimately familiar with. As the days passed, however, Kasidy began suspecting Kira's reticence wasn't solely motivated by benevolence. Perhaps, being immersed in DS9 and Bajor's needs had acclimated Kira to ignoring her own. *And that's not good,* she thought. "It's my turn to ask an impertinent question, Nerys."

"Fire away."

"Are you happy?"

Kira snorted. "Kas—"

"I'm not budging from this spot until you tell me what's on your mind," Kasidy said.

Kira inhaled deeply. She toyed with the macramé vest she wore, threading her fingers through the holes. "There's not a simple answer. I wouldn't necessarily change my life—" she lifted heavy-lidded eyes to Kasidy "—except the Attainder. That I could do without." The weak smile she offered Kas failed to offset her worry wrinkles.

Kira carries her burdens in her eyes. Shades of Benjamin, Kasidy thought, imagining she could see the mantle of command bestowed upon her friend by her husband. "Talk to me. I've been told I'm a good listener—and I know how to keep a secret."

Considering Kasidy for a long moment, Kira's brow furrowed. "Where to start? Double-dealing Shakaar, the peace talks mess, the daughter-in-law of the Federation councillor's suicide—and that's the appetizer. Believe me, Kas, you don't want to hear about this."

"Yes I do," Kasidy insisted. "You've done a great job catching me up on all the station gossip, though I'm still not sure what to make of Lieutenant Ro, um, socializing with Quark. Now I want the rest of it."

Kira rose from her chair and walked over to turn on the fireplace. Resting her arm against the river rocks, she stared into the flames. "You know I even tried knitting? And I found it incredibly frustrating. I followed the instructions from the database to the letter and no matter how meticulously I worked, I managed to drop stitches or purl when I was supposed to knit. When the yarn became all tangled up and knotted, I figured, the hell with this! And that's how I feel things are at the station right now—just like my knitting." She ran her hand along the mantel's smoothly carved curves and curlicues, pausing to pick up the amber-gold figurine given to Kasidy by Prylar Eivos. "I do the best that I know how to do and where has that gotten us? Promenade fights, vandalism, threats against the Cardassian delegation. I hate saying it, but I almost miss the war. At least then we knew who we were fighting and what we were fighting for."

"Nerys, I'm no expert on commanding a—" The door chime rang. *Oh, who could that be?* Kasidy thought irritably. In her early days here, well-meaning Bajorans seeking to "help" the Emissary's wife stopped by, uninvited, as if she were building a shrine, not a house. Gradually, as all parties came to an understanding she'd stopped being a curiosity to the locals. Now her neighbors vigorously protected her privacy, refusing to dole out the smallest tidbit to strangers seeking her, even those on religious pilgrimages. *I hope there's not an emergency. Wouldn't they call first?* Kasidy scooted to the edge of the couch, psyching herself up for whoever might be visiting.

"I'll get it," Kira said. She set the figurine down on the coffee table and vanished into the foyer.

"I'm not an invalid," Kasidy muttered, pushing up onto her feet and following after Kira. The baby snuggled into her ribs; she paused to push gently on the head, trying to dislodge it. No luck. She heard the beeps of Kira tapping in the lock release.

"You?" came her visitor's shocked exclamation.

"Not who you were expecting, Vedek Yevir?" Kira said.

Inwardly, Kasidy groaned, wishing she could become invisible; Yevir was about as welcome as a malfunctioning phaser in the middle of a firefight. While she found most Bajoran clerics to be pleasant (being the Emissary's wife meant they were on their best behavior around her), Yevir was the exception. Kasidy couldn't stomach his sanctimoniousness, how he wrapped his unapologetic quest to be kai in a cloak of piety. He'd shown his true character when he slapped the Attainder on Kira; Kasidy wasn't prepared to forgive him for what she believed to be a vindictive, politically motivated punishment. That Bajor would be better off with Yevir as kai than they were with Winn was doubtful to Kasidy's way of thinking. For a moment, Kasidy considered turning back around and hiding in the sitting room. Kira would get rid of him.

...But how fair was that to Kira?

Kasidy turned the corner and saw Kira had blocked the doorway, arms linked across her chest. From her posture, Kasidy surmised it would take a Klingon with a *bat'leth* to pass into the vestibule.

"With all due respect, Vedek, why not go back to town and call back in the morning? Make an *appointment* with Captain Yates," Kira said coldly.

Peering at the vedek from behind Kira, Kasidy said, "So you were in the neighborhood and thought you'd stop by for a visit?"

Her tone provoked a deep pink flush in Yevir's cheeks. His eyes fixed on Kasidy. "I know I've come without an invitation, Captain Yates, but my business is urgent. I've come to believe Bajor's spiritual health is at stake."

Kira was impressed. To Kasidy, she said, "I'll take care of this." And to Yevir, "Take it up with the Vedek Assembly."

Kasidy stopped her. "I'm not the Emissary, Vedek. Even though it seems I keep having to remind people—"

"Please," Yevir said. "Captain, I need—I assure you the situation is quite dire." Yevir took a step toward Kasidy. Kira glared at him and he promptly stepped back.

Still the master of overstatement, Kas thought, *and still unable to take a hint.* "I'm sorry, but we were in the middle of something and—"

"A moment of your time—that's all I ask. I beg of you." The look in his eyes was imploring.

Suspecting he might be prostrate on the porch at any moment, Kasidy wondered what to do next. If she shut the door on him he'd probably still be around at dawn. Kasidy sighed. *I can't put Nerys through that.* To Kira she said, "Why don't you start walking without me? I'll catch up with you after the Vedek leaves." *Please, Nerys, take the hint,* she wished fervently.

Puzzled, Kira looked over her shoulder at Kasidy, raising a questioning eyebrow. Kasidy shrugged as if to say, *Let's just get this over with.*

Kira stepped aside, gesturing for Yevir to enter.

When he made a visible point of squeezing through the door frame rather than touch Kira, Kasidy began to wonder if she'd regret her invitation. She indicated she wanted Yevir to follow her to the sitting room where she and Kira had been only minutes before. Kasidy felt Kira's eyes trained on their backs as she waited for Yevir to misstep.

If Kira's scrutiny bothered Yevir, he didn't show it. Walking behind Kasidy, Yevir's apologies continued until they were both seated. Once Kasidy heard the door close—with Kira on the outside—she felt reassured that her friend would be spared any further indignities.

Dealing with Yevir should be easy in comparison to some of the tight spots she'd had to negotiate her way out of over the years. She recalled arguing with a Nausicaan who insisted Kasidy had picked up the wrong cargo. *He* was difficult; Yevir was merely bothersome.

Since Yevir had been the one to request speaking with her, Kasidy expected him to initiate the discussion. She would nod her head politely in response, tell him there was nothing she could do and send him on his way. Folding her hands in her lap, Kasidy waited.

Yevir sat perched on the edge of the chair, blinking nervously, saying nothing, unwilling or unable to meet her eyes. Uncomfortable silence followed.

At last Kasidy said, "Please get on with your business, Vedek."

He cleared his throat, shifting a few times, and licked his lips. "The present state of affairs troubles me," Yevir stammered. "I believe recent events bode ill for Bajor."

"I'm not in a position to do anything about the state of Bajor, Vedek," Kasidy said pragmatically.

"But *I* should be!" He stood up, pacing back and forth in front of the fireplace, his robes swishing as he walked. "I was chosen by the Emissary to be a spiritual leader among my people. As such, I should know how best to guide them. But for the first time since Captain Sisko set me on my present course, the way is dark to me."

Kasidy shook her head. *This was a mistake . . .* "If you're truly concerned for Bajor, Vedek, you need to have this conversation with someone else. Somebody in the Vedek Assembly, the Chamber of Ministers . . ."

"I'm not sure I know what to say to any of them. What I do know is my people have reached a crossroad on the path of the Prophets, with no arrow to point us toward the true way. They're in danger of becoming lost, and I must learn what I need to do to help make things right."

"If you want to make things right, start by rescinding Kira's Attainder," Kasidy said tightly.

Yevir frowned and looked away. "The Colonel's standing within our faith is unrelated to this issue."

"If you want to have this conversation with me, in my house, it's not."

Yevir was silent a moment. "I'm sorry," he said finally. "I know you have a close relationship with the Colonel. And in a way, Kira's situation is part of the crisis in which my people now find themselves."

Concerned by where Yevir might be headed with this, Kasidy said, "Go on." *Give me one more reason, Yevir, and I'm tossing you out on your ass. See how good that looks on your application for kai.*

"As I said, from the start, I've tried to follow the way your husband laid out for me. Or, more accurately, what I believed that way to be. I sought to destroy Ohalu's book because I truly believed that was best for Bajor. But now . . . now I'm not so sure . . ." He fell back into his chair, folding his hands tightly before him as he concentrated on what he needed to say. "The greatest moment of clarity in my life came when I spoke with the Emissary. I knew in that timeless instant he was setting me on the path I was always destined to walk, and that it would lead me to become kai."

"You sound almost as if you don't believe that anymore."

"I don't know what to believe," Yevir said softly, in tones that convinced Kasidy the admission was painful for him to make. "Nothing is unfolding in a manner I understand. The Ohalu text, the sundering of the faithful, the failure of the peace talks with Cardassia. . . . So much is happening that threatens Bajor's spiritual well-being, I no longer feel I understand the role the Emissary chose me for.

"I came here tonight—to you—hoping that whatever illumination filled him might have touched you and that you might . . ." His voice trailed off into silence. Finally he shrugged and said quietly, "I felt compelled to come."

Kasidy probed his face, searching for insincerity, and found confusion; Yevir appeared truly flummoxed. Not for the first time, Kasidy wished being the wife of the Emissary came with a handbook. "I wish I knew what Ben would have told you if he were here."

Closing his eyes tight, Yevir slowly shook his head. "I understand. I apologize for disturbing you. Forgive me." In a paternal gesture, he lifted her hand off the armrest and pressed it between his own. "Thank you for your time, Captain Yates. I'll let myself out." He backed away, bowing—and froze, eyes fixed.

Kasidy scanned herself, the floor, the furniture, for a clue as to what had transfixed Yevir. "What is it?" she said, worried.

Still staring, he appeared not to hear her.

She followed his eyes to the figurine Kira had placed on the coffee table before answering the door. Amber and gold, the flecks inside caught the firelight and shimmered with otherworldly radiance.

"What *is* that?" he whispered.

"It's from B'hala. Unearthed during the excavation," Kasidy explained. *Jevonite,* Eivos had said it was made of. *Have I missed something?*

Hesitantly, Yevir reached toward the figurine, his trembling hand hovering. He looked at Kasidy. "May I?"

"Go ahead."

Yevir scooped up the figurine, holding it in his palm, slowly turning it over and over. "I don't have the right to ask, but—" He raised his eyes, wide with childlike wonder.

"Take it. Please," Kasidy said. "If it has some significance to you, then by all means, it's yours."

He clutched the figurine tightly in his hand. "Thank you." His head dipped in a respectful nod. "Thank you truly, Captain."

"I didn't do anything," Kasidy protested, rising.

"I believe the Prophets led me here for a reason. I don't know exactly what it is yet, but this—" He held up the hand closed around the figurine. "—I think this may be the arrow I've been searching for."

Puzzling over his effusiveness, Kasidy walked him to the door. *He believes he found what he came for,* she thought as she waved good-bye. *And knowing where you're supposed to go can make all the difference.* She watched Yevir until he disappeared around a bend in the road. *I hope that soon the same can be said for Kira.*

Kira slammed her heels into the dirt with each brisk step, grimacing at the thought of that—that—of Kas having to deal with that man! Yevir wasn't Kas's problem, he was hers. Disgusted, she spat. *I know how to take a hint from the universe.*

Yevir showing up as she was attempting to untangle her snarled life had to be a sign that she wasn't meant to understand "why." Why Thriss took her life only two days before Shar's message arrived from the Gamma Quadrant. Or why some bastard felt the need to make an example out of Ziyal—yet again. And her favorite "what-the-hell-is-he-thinking" question mark, Shakaar. Sure, she had her quarrels with him on an interpersonal level. He might use their past together as leverage over her politically, but she had trusted his leadership skills. So what happened to cause Shakaar to suddenly come down with a case of blindness equal to or surpassing Yevir's? Bajor was being led on both the secular and religious fronts by blind men. And who was she to even presume she was better than them? Nothing she was doing seemed to be working out either. To expect guidance or answers when her whole world might be walking into darkness was pretty selfish of her. She needed to let go and trust that the Prophets had a plan. Surely they wouldn't let Bajor fail because of the stupidity of her servants. *Damn!* She kicked at the dirt, sending rocks skittering. Following the gentle slope down to the riverbank, her walk gathered speed, gradually becoming a full run.

Jeraddo had risen into the sky. The moon's wan face rippled silver on the water's surface, its pale illumination providing enough light to see by. A chilly breeze blew off the river, rattling the dry leaves clinging to the trees and numbing Kira's ears. Breathing deeply burned her lungs but she pressed on, picking her way around the clumps of river grass. She relished pushing her body until her sides ached, being driven by instinct instead of rational thought.

How long had it been since she let go? Keeping a tight rein on her emotions was part of her duty. When everyone around her completely unspooled, Kira remained in control. Take away her beloved captain. Take away her love.

Take away her right to publicly practice her religion. Throw disillusionment, confusion and frustration at her and she'd bat them away, one, two, three. Nothing to it, because that's who she was. But now the rules of the game were changing yet again, and she began to doubt her ability to keep up.

Kira followed the path away from the river into the forest where gnarled, knotted trees cloaked her in shadow. She continued running. With each step, she gagged on the pungent smoke-tinged wind blowing over from the adjoining farm. She pushed through anyway.

I'll keep going as long as my body has breath, if that's what the Prophets want from me, she vowed. If she had to pinpoint what intimidated her most about the road ahead, it was the sense that she was headed straight for a cliff with only the hope that there was some good to be achieved by her jumping.

Leaping over roots, she followed the twisting path, her view of the trail ahead obscured by tree trunks and waist-high bushes, bobbing and swaying. Her blood hammered in her throat and in her ears as her feet pounded the ground, until her boot hit something hard and she slammed into the path, knees first, then her chest, knocking the wind out of her. The stinging scrapes shocked her and she rolled over, tasting peaty dirt mingling with blood, leaves clinging to her clothes. A cry welled up in her throat but refused release.

Flat on her back, Kira looked up through knobby, stripped branches at the starless sky, feeling sharp waves of pain stabbing through her knees. She clenched her teeth, focused intently on controlling her breathing.

She lay on her back, listening to the murmuring wind, the occasional crack of a breaking branch, the swish of bird wings. Staring at the sky, she pretended the wormhole was fixed above her position, promising herself that if she could see the flash of it opening . . .

She waited. She waited until damp numbness overtook her limbs and still, nothing. *I don't know what I was expecting. I should just go back. Kas will be worried.* She sighed. Kira might have witnessed her share of miracles—and had exquisite spiritual experiences in her lifetime—but she wasn't foolish enough to believe that the Prophets gave you a sign simply because you asked for one.

Grunting, she eased herself up so she was sitting with her legs stretched out in front of her. Luckily, it didn't feel like she'd sprained or broken anything, though she could feel small rocks embedded in the skin of her kneecaps.

She brushed herself off and then, placing the heels of her hands behind her, she pushed off, succeeding only in dislodging a stone she'd braced herself against. *Let's see if I can do this without cracking my tailbone, too,* she thought ruefully. But then her fingers brushed against the stone again, piquing her curiosity. *This isn't a rock.* Yanking it free from where it was wedged under an exposed root, Kira held it out in front of her, hoping a beam of light breaking through the forest's canopy would help her better see what she held.

She thought her eyes must be playing tricks on her.

Her hands began furiously brushing off the dirt encrusting the object. Muddy, frayed, and lost here among the trees of Captain Sisko's land since when, she couldn't say. But there was no denying what she held in her hand.

A baseball.

Stitching unraveling, leather stained and pocked, and so waterlogged it was unusable—but none of it changed the fact that Kira held one of the Emissary's baseballs. Her mind raced. Kas had told her he used to bat them out here to clear his head, but—

Slowly, Kira smiled. Then the laughter came, softly at first, but gathering strength until it engulfed her.

Knowing Kasidy would be waiting, Kira returned to the path and pointed herself toward home.

About the Authors

David R. George III has written seven *Star Trek* novels and a *Trek* novella, as well as the story for a *Voyager* episode. His novels have appeared on both *The New York Times* and *USA Today* bestseller lists, and his television story, "Prime Factors," was nominated for a *Sci-Fi Universe* award in the category "Best Writing in a Genre Television Show or Telefilm." His most recent trio of novels—*Provenance of Shadows, The Fire and the Rose,* and *The Star to Every Wandering*—compose the *Crucible* trilogy, a set of books penned and published to help celebrate the fortieth anniversary of the original series. Three other novels—*The 34th Rule, Twilight,* and *Olympus Descending* (the last of which appears in *Worlds of Deep Space Nine, Volume Three*)—take place in the DS9 milieu. Another novel—*Serpents Among the Ruins*—and a novella—*Iron and Sacrifice* (which is contained in the anthology *Tales from the Captain's Table*)— are so-called *Lost Era* stories, set in the years between the original *Star Trek* and *The Next Generation.*

A native of New York City, David presently makes his home in southern California, where he lives with his delectable wife, Karen. They are both aficionados of the arts—books, theater, museums, film, music, dance—and they can often be found partaking in one or another of them. They also love to travel, and are particularly fond of France, Italy, and Australia abroad, and of Hawai'i, the American northeast, and the Pacific Northwest in the United States. They also enjoy sailing on cruises and following their beloved—though often heartbreaking—New York Mets.

Heather Jarman has made several critically acclaimed contributions to the *Star Trek* universe, including *Worlds of Deep Space Nine, Volume Two: Paradigm* and *Balance of Nature* for *Star Trek: Corps of Engineers.* At present she is applying her writing energies to her long-neglected university education, but finds academia to be a bit less thrilling than starships and aliens. Still, the expatriate life in Moscow, Russia, where Heather lives with her family, has provided her with rich new material for future literary efforts. Perhaps one day ideas inspired by her travels may find their way into a *Star Trek* novel.